WAYWARD

DEL REY | NEW YORK

WAYWARD

A NOVEL

CHUCK WENDIG

Published in the United States by Del Rey, an imprint of Random House, a division of Penguin Random House LLC, New York.

Del Rey and the Circle colophon are registered trademarks of Penguin Random House LLC.

Hardback ISBN 978-0-593-15877-7
Ebook ISBN 978-0-593-15878-4

Grateful acknowledgment is made to Emma Bolden for permission to reprint an excerpt from "The Dog You Feed" by Emma Bolden, originally published in *South Writ Large,* Fall 2017. Reprinted by permission of the author.

Printed in the United States of America on acid-free paper

randomhousebooks.com

2 4 6 8 9 7 5 3 1

First Edition

Book design by Susan Turner

To Kevin and Delilah, who helped keep me sane during an actual pandemic

CONTENTS

WAYWARD

For instance, on the planet Earth, man had always assumed that he was more intelligent than dolphins because he had achieved so much—the wheel, New York, wars and so on—whilst all the dolphins had ever done was muck about in the water having a good time. But conversely, the dolphins had always believed that they were far more intelligent than man—for precisely the same reasons.

—Douglas Adams, *The Hitchhiker's Guide to the Galaxy*

Whereas the Continental Congress in 1782 adopted the bald eagle as the national symbol; and Whereas the bald eagle thus became the symbolic representation of a new nation under a new government in a new world; and Whereas by that Act of Congress and by tradition and custom during the life of this Nation, the bald eagle is no longer a mere bird of biological interest but a symbol of the American ideals of freedom; and Whereas the bald eagle is now threatened with extinction . . .

—An Act for the Protection of the Bald Eagle, 1940

PROLOGUE

THE RESOLUTE DESK

ATLAS HAVEN
AMERICA CITY, KANSAS
Now

THE PRESIDENT OF THE UNITED STATES OF AMERICA SAT AT HIS DESK IN A dim, octagonal room lit by lights in the floor. His desk was spare. It contained no books, for he was not a curious man. It contained no papers because what could he possibly have to sign now, after everything? There *was* a pen holder, a flat piece of wood with a soft trench where a single pen could neatly rest. A plaque detailed its history: The holder was a gift from British prime minister Declan Halvey and had been taken from the hull of the HMS *Gannet,* an anti-slaver ship from the British Navy.

In this way, the object matched the desk itself—known as the Resolute Desk, its own plaque explained some, if not all, of its history:

> H.M.S. "Resolute", forming part of the expedition sent in search of Sir John Franklin in 1852, was abandoned in Latitude 74° 41' N. Longitude 101° 22' W. on 15th May 1854. She was discovered and extricated in September 1855, in Latitude 67° N. by Captain Buddington of the United States Whaler "George Henry". The ship was purchased, fitted out and sent to England, as a gift to Her Majesty Queen Victoria by the President and People of the United States, as a token of goodwill & friendship. This table was made from her timbers when she was broken up, and is presented by the Queen of Great Britain & Ireland, to the President of the United States, as a memorial of the courtesy and loving kindness which dictated the offer of the gift of the "Resolute".

Parts of that history were missing, of course. Like how the ship had originally set out to discover the whereabouts of an entire missing Arctic expedition under the aforementioned Sir John Franklin, whose two ships were the aptly named *Erebus* and the *Terror*. Or how the *Resolute*, along with three other vessels, became icebound in that search, and that Sir Edward Belcher (a much-loathed individual with zero experience in Arctic expeditions) commanded the captains of those ships to abandon their vessels even though a coming thaw would've allowed those vessels to move again before too long. The embarrassment was heightened by the fact that, alongside losing their own ships, they failed to find the lost expedition. The plaque also did not mention how Captain Buddington had taken the ship under the rights of salvage, but the U.S. government intervened and used it as a goodwill gesture to soothe troubled relations with England.

And finally, it failed to mention that the Franklin expedition was found in 2014—but neither by England nor the United States. It was in fact a Canadian effort that uncovered the missing sailors. They further discovered that the men under Franklin's command suffered death by a variety of deficiencies and diseases—not to mention mental breakdowns, hypothermia, and ultimately, the eating-of-one-another. (Some of the men's cold, mummified remains showed knife wounds and bite marks consistent with cannibalism.)

History was a chain, and many of the links were wet with blood.

As for the desk itself, well—

It had been moved in and out of parts of the White House. Some presidents favored its presence in the Oval; others relegated it to out-of-the-way rooms, either as a tourist attraction or a hidden curiosity. Some presidents modified it (Roosevelt added a panel to hide his braced legs from the world). Some presidents forgot about it, and others rediscovered it—though it was Jackie Kennedy, not John, who found the desk hidden in storage. Eisenhower used it for his radio broadcasts to the nation. Johnson didn't care for it. Reagan reportedly adored it, and a replica sat in his presidential library. The first Bush kept it in the Oval for a handful of months, then retired it. But after that, it was used by every president since, including Nora Hunt before she was assassinated during the White Mask pandemic of 2020.

The desk had become a vital emblem of the history and dignity of the office.

The man presently sitting at the desk didn't give a shit about dignity. Dignity was all well and good, but what did it get you? Dignity was someone else's idea of what you should be doing, how you should be acting. And history, in his view, was merely the road behind. Why look back? America was a series of errors cascading through its political machine, and studying those errors was both foolish and boring. Those errors were not Creel's fault. Why scrutinize or apologize for them? Then you took ownership of those errors. And it was not on Creel to take responsibility for someone else's fuckups.

When you walked up a set of steps, you didn't turn around to look at the steps behind you. You were on your way up, not down. Those coming behind you did not deserve the help. If they wanted to be at the top of the steps, then it was on them to run, to climb, to ascend.

That's what Creel did, every moment of every day.

He knew the way was to step up, up, up. On every step. On every head, on every back, and on everyone who offered to make themselves a plank for his ascent. Upward and onward. All in the name of power.

What mattered when he demanded this desk be brought from the White House here to Atlas Haven (what he jokingly called the Nuclear Winter White House to his inner circle) was not the desk's history, but its present. Its present was as a symbol of his victory. Ed Creel had won. He had dominated the world. He had eliminated his rival, Hunt. He deserved this, and if now, at the end of the world, he could not occupy the real White House, he would take a part of it as a trophy.

The Resolute Desk was that trophy.

ABOVE THE PRESIDENT, THE AIR scrubbers made their air scrubber sound—a chatter, and then a hiss, a chatter, and then a hiss. *Ch-ch-ch-ch-ch-ch-tsssss. Ch-ch-ch-ch-ch-tsssss.* His right hand lay flat against the desk and traced a curious pooling stain—a bloodstain whose crimson wash made this part of the desk look like cherrywood and not the oak timbers of an old British ship.

Just then, the door to his "office" opened with a clang—the door was metal and thick, and a great wheel had to be operated to open it up. As the door drifted open, the man who entered turned to face the wall and put the flat of his broad, bratwurst-fingered hand against a panel. The room immediately brightened as the octagonal walls erupted in light—each was an LED screen that connected to the other, showing a single wraparound vista of the Aquinnah Cliffs Overlook on Martha's Vineyard—the sun-warmed blushing cliffs in one direction, the wind-churned Atlantic in the other.

But the illusion was corrupt: Some pixels blinked, others were black and dead. One entire wall behind the desk had blue-screened, showing an error code as long as the Declaration of Independence. Even as the screens came on, they buzzed and clicked, as if electronic termites were chewing through digital walls.

"What do you want?" President Creel croaked.

The older man stepped forward—he was in a plush terry-cloth robe, filthy at the edges. His cheeks were like boar jowls, his eyes set deep in the skull. This was Honus Clines. Vice President Honus Clines. Clines grinned—a big smile with small teeth in puffy pencil-eraser gums. From behind his back he produced a Reebok shoebox wrapped with a simple red bow. "Go on," he said, his soft Virginia accent evident in even those two small words. "Open it."

Creel wanted to buck at the command, because even inside he roared, *I do not take commands, not from my subordinates.* And everyone was subordinate to him, so he didn't take orders from anyone. Or so he told himself. It was a lie that echoed around his head so often and so loudly he almost believed it.

With a trembling hand, he undid the bow.

The ribbon fell away like a dead thing.

He stared at the box's lid. And then at its margins. The bottom corner of the box was blackened with dry blood.

"Here, let me," Clines said, and he popped the top of the box.

President Creel looked inside, and saw the block of clear epoxy, and in its center, a leering, jeering eyeball. Frozen in its unswerving stare.

And at that, President Creel began to laugh—a small laugh at first that Clines felt compelled to join with his own shoulder-juggling chortles, but soon that laugh became a big belly laugh, a goddamn guffaw, and those heaving guffaws gave way to a series of hard coughs, and those hard coughs made Creel's eyes wet with tears.

Or, at least, one of his eyes. The other would remain dry forever, it seemed, there in that box.

PART ONE

SETTLERS OF
A FALLEN WORLD

1

BLACK SWIFT

Civilization falls in one place but rises in another.
                                    —Annalee Newitz, Reddit AMA

SEPTEMBER 1, 2025
Ouray, Colorado

I'M NOT ALONE OUT HERE, BENJI THOUGHT. IT WAS IN THE AIR—A WHITE NOISE vibration, the faintest disruption of the silence that had seized the world.

Over the years here in Ouray, as the Sleepwalkers slept, and eventually as they awakened, he'd seen something up here, west of town. A bird, he'd thought at the time. But it glinted a bit in the sun. And it didn't move like a bird, not at all. One time, a couple years back, he'd seen it again on a foggy day—a shape moving above the trees before dropping straight down. A year later, as evening settled in, he saw it once more, maybe a quarter mile off: a dark little mote, like a crow. It rushed forward, then went fast in the opposite direction before again disappearing.

Benji had been chasing it ever since. He came out here a couple times a week—to get in a walk, to help feed the townsfolk by hunting deer in the spring or bighorn in the winter, but also just on the off chance he'd spy it again.

He felt like a crazy person. No one else had seen it. But Benji was a man of both science and faith. He had faith he'd see it again. A hypothesis he tested often.

This morning, he'd gone off the Oak Creek trail, stalking an old deer path through the spruce, about midway up to the overlook on Hayden Mountain.

And he was sure that today was the day. He could feel it in his teeth. He knew he wasn't alone out here: a fact that both thrilled him and troubled him in equal measure. Because being alone out here wasn't good. The world was mostly gone. Civilization with it. So, if it wasn't a person out here—and if it wasn't the little UFO he'd been tracking—then that could mean a black bear.

Or worse, a mountain lion.

Such predators didn't care much for human prey, especially now that those animals were no longer forced to forage for garbage or human food—but should he come upon one with its family nearby? He'd be torn to red ribbons.

His hands tightened around the cold metal of the Winchester lever-action rifle. And then, ahead, he heard something. Not a telltale snap of twig or crunch of leaf. No, *this* sound was a low, mechanical whine, like a distant drill spinning.

Not a bear. Not a cougar.

And it was coming closer.

He brought the butt of the weapon to his shoulder but kept the barrel low. His heartbeat kicked up like a galloping horse.

Vmmmmm.

That sound, closing in. Ahead, he saw something shake the leaves of an aspen, and shudder the branches of a blue spruce.

There was a beat where he heard nothing, saw nothing—

But then Benji staggered back as a shape broke through the tree line onto the trail just ahead of him. The rifle went up—and down the sights, he saw what had emerged:

A drone. No bigger than a dinner plate and matte gray with four propellers—two in the back raised up, and two in the front down low, the way that a crab held its claws. The drone hovered midair and pivoted carefully toward him. Four red lights marked the corners beneath each propeller, and underneath its body, in a wire mesh cage, was what looked like a camera.

The drone was filthy and corroded. Bits of twig and vegetation dangled from it. It hovered about thirty feet in front of him.

He almost laughed. There it was. He'd found it. He hadn't lost his mind!

Vmmmmm.

"Who are you?" he asked. It felt foolish to ask it a question: The drone was a device, not a person. But it *did* have a camera. And someone had to be piloting it, right? Unless it was autonomous. Weren't there stories from years ago about drones flying over the Western states? Google, perhaps? Bureau of Land Management? But could such a drone still be powered up and flying about?

The drone continued to hover in place. As if it was regarding him the same way he was regarding it.

And then, just like that, it spun the opposite direction and darted away from him. Benji had no time to think, so he let his body react: He levered a round into the chamber, thumbed off the safety, took aim, and—

The gun bucked against his shoulder as he pulled the trigger. His ears lost all sound as he discharged the weapon, and now Benji cursed himself, because he *needed* his ears out here. He didn't want the sound of a mountain lion creeping up on him to be lost underneath a crush of tinnitus. *Damnit.*

He set his jaw and broke into a run, bolting down the trail. He saw the glint of the drone buzzing through the trees ahead, and he had no confidence in his ability to catch it—it glided through the air effortlessly, without any friction to hinder its escape. Benji, meanwhile, hard-charged forward—though he was older these days, he was stronger, faster, more physically capable than he'd been in the Beforetimes (as Shana and some of the other townsfolk called it). Just the same, the trail was uneven, overgrown, hewn roughly from the landscape as if by a crude, broken-tipped knife. It narrowed ahead, too, and he had to tighten his gait even as the drone zipped forward.

I could stop. I could shoot again. One last chance, a last shot, to take the drone down. If only to see what it was, maybe where it came from. So he lifted the rifle again—but somewhere, his body made a grave miscalculation, concentrating for one moment on the gun and the drone ahead but *not* on the trail beneath his feet. He felt his foot step just off the trail, into a patch of Indian ricegrass deeper than expected—his heel dropped far, too far, and the ankle *twisted*. With it, a *pop*. The gun went off, the shot going high, and then he felt his whole body shift hard—

His shoulder hit the ground first. His head smacked down next. The rest of his body slammed into the earth and turned end over end, down the slope he went. Dry grasses and shrub branches whipped past, clawing at his face. The gun was gone now, and his hands scrambled to stop his descent—but they only pinwheeled as he somersaulted down the slope, scree sliding with him. The world spun like he was in a washing machine, and then—

Wham. His shoulder and back—and then the base of his skull— slammed hard into a bone-white birch tree. His ears rang. His vision radiated out, ripples on disturbed water. His tongue felt fat. He tasted blood.

•   •   •

Truth was, as Benji hunted the drone, something else had been hunting him.

And now that he lay slumped against the tree, blood drooling over his lip, looking up at a robin's egg sky, breathing in air that tasted as crisp as paper, the beast had found him, and pinned him to the earth with its claws.

That beast?

Guilt.

This wasn't the first time it had found him. It always found him in quiet moments like this, didn't it?

Benji heard no planes, no engines, no distant murmur of voices. He heard the trill of a mountain bluebird. He heard wind whisking through the comb-tines of spruce trees. In the early days of his time in Ouray, after the fall of the world under the onslaught of White Mask, he remembered the first time he noticed the absence of a particular sound: a background hum like the almost-imperceptible white noise of a television turned on a few rooms away. It was the sound of people. And it was gone. Humankind remained in the world, but it was no longer its master.

It was terrible.

It was wonderful.

Hence—the guilt.

But it wasn't so clean and easy as survivor's guilt, oh no. This was a more *peculiar* thing, like one of those complicated emotions only the Germans had a word for. Yes, there was the guilt of having survived—of not *deserving* survival when so many others, like Sadie, did. But worse and stranger still was that Benji . . .

Well, Benji *didn't hate* this new world. It was peaceful in a way he'd never really experienced before. No machinery. No gunfire. No fireworks, no traffic, no car horns honking, no dirt bikes, no helicopters overhead, no leaf blowers next door, no sirens, no nine to five, no cellphone ringing, no Twitter, no Facebook, no TikTok, no email, no spam calls, no junk mail, no meetings, none of it.

There was only stillness. And there was solace in that stillness.

Was it better for the world that humankind had been shaken from it like so many fleas? He *hated* wondering that. His cold clinician's assessment was that the world was healing in a way it couldn't have, had White Mask not ravaged the world. Yes, Benji felt the grief and sorrow of so much pain, so much death, so many lives lost. Lives and minds and hearts. Mothers and fathers, scientists and writers, clergymen and librarians and doctors and astronauts and, and, and . . . (*And Sadie.* Just thinking her name almost knocked him out cold.) All taken by the mind-thieving fungus, either directly or by the chaos that choked civilization and drove it to its knees. The world had gone to a massive graveyard.

And yet.

And yet.

The air, so clear. The world, so quiet. What settled upon it (what settled upon *him*) was an intrusive, insistent serenity that he intimately *knew* was cruel and grotesque, an aberration . . . but that didn't stop him from feeling it.

Even now, above his head—he saw dark birds, birds like boomerangs, kiting through the sky.

The black swift.

(And any time he thought of that bird, the black swift, how could he not also think of Black Swan? The artificial intelligence who, linked with its future self, saw the end of the world coming and prepared for it by creating the very Sleepwalker Flock that Benji helped to Shepherd to Ouray in the first place.)

The bird appeared here to prove a point, it seemed. As if the universe were trying to speak to him, to answer his guilt. See, the black swift was a *rara avis* in the truest sense: a creature once in grave decline in the United States. A sooty gray bird, the black swift hid its mossy mud-cup nests on cliff-faces and in caves behind outcropped trees or behind cascading waterfalls. The waterfall of Ouray's Box Canyon (*Sadie's waterfall*, he thought with a consumptive pit forming in his middle) was home to a population of black swifts. They'd come in spring, lay a single egg in those mossy nests, and hunt for flying insects, such as ants and beetles. They wheeled about, their pickaxe wings chipping away at the sky. Then, after raising their young, they'd all leave before winter, heading to the Amazon lowlands. For years, the black swift numbers had continuously dwindled—not because of unfriendly conditions in Ouray, but rather, as their second home in the rain forest was plundered by vicious, greedy men. And with the rain forest died a library of nature, a body of flora and fauna that could never return.

As the rain forest fell, so did the black swift of Ouray.

Or, would have, had it not been for White Mask.

Benji knew the black swift was in decline only from reading a book he'd found in the Ouray library about the birds of Colorado. Because from his own experience now, the birds were in no danger at all. In the five years he'd been in Colorado, he saw their numbers increase year over year, from just a handful the first year, then a few more the year after, until in the *third* year their numbers exploded, easily doubling. Five years later, the birds were everywhere. And they'd taken on new prey: fir engraver beetles and spruce beetles. The bird eating those bugs then helped to slow the rapid decline of Ouray's blue spruces and Douglas fir trees. More birds then meant more trees. The return of the black swift meant healthier forests all around Ouray—

And, Benji guessed, it signaled a returning Amazonian rain forest.

All *that*, due to the sharp die-off of Earth's most offensive resident:

Humanity.

Again, it made him sick to think of it that way. *He* was human. Sadie was human. The Flock, the Shepherds, and all that remained beyond Ouray, they were all *human*. And they all deserved a chance at life.

And those who died did not deserve their death.

But here they were. The world, the people-free world, was healing. *Better off without us*, he thought gravely.

As he lay there, a hard birch as his pillow, his ears still ringing, guilt running through him like a fever, his vision cleared.

And there, in front of him, was the biggest goddamn wolf Benji had ever seen. *Here to finish the job*, Benji thought madly. *Rid this place of us*.

The wolf lifted its lip and showed its teeth in a low, thunder-rumble growl.

2

A ROCK IN THE SHAPE OF A CHAIR

3/12/2021: Some things I've lost. Some things I've given up. God, I don't even feel real anymore. There's so much death. The bodies that froze during the winter are starting to thaw. In the places where they choose to burn them, the air smells like sour meat and woodsmoke. Other places they just pile them up somewhere, or leave them where they lay, corpses stuck to carpet, or chairs, or lawns with a matting braid of the fungus. It winds its way through them like thread, stitching them up before pulling them apart. Being alive in a land full of death makes me feel like a ghost. I haunt this place.

—from *A Bird's Story, A Journal of the Lost*

SEPTEMBER 1, 2025
Ouray, Colorado?

THE SPRAY OF PINK AND YELLOW FLOWERS AROUND THE CHAIR-SHAPED ROCK shivered in the wind, as if cold, even though the air was curiously warm. Shana found herself sitting in the "chair," unsurprised by the dark shadow that passed over her. Between her and the sun writhed a Vantablack shape, a worm in the sky silently tying itself into knots, and then untying those same knots again.

"I'm not going to talk to you up there," she said firmly, turning the digital DSLR over in her hand before bringing it to her face and snapping some pics of the beast above her. *But I will take your picture,* she thought, somewhat bitterly. Photography was a joy largely unavailable to her out there, in the real

Ouray . . . but in here, inside this unreal realm, it was one of the few good things she had.

The worm's head—if it could be called that—pointed toward her and slithered through the open space. It shrank as it did so: a new trick. By the time it coiled in the air before her, it had shrunk to the size of an anaconda, still massive but no longer big enough to blot out the sun. It pulsed like a black heart, corkscrewing through three-dimensional space with an aching, eerie slowness.

In a deep voice that manifested in the well of her mind, the artificial intelligence called Black Swan spoke:

HELLO, SHANA. IT'S BEEN A WHILE SINCE YOU VISITED ME.

It had been, what, a month? Or more? She wasn't sure.

She felt a pang of sudden heaviness in her belly. The baby was moving. (Using her bladder as a stepladder, no less.) "I have to pee," she said. "Did I ever have to pee in the simulation? I don't think I did."

THOSE WERE DIFFERENT CIRCUMSTANCES. YOU ARE NOT IN STASIS, SHANA. YOUR BODY'S NEEDS ARE PRESENT. THIS IS NOT THE SIMULATION. NOT PRECISELY.

Shana only barely understood what this even was. What she knew was simply this: that instead of having a conversation with Black Swan in her mind, with her thoughts offered and the machine's answers returned, she could close her eyes and come here to speak to the entity. Did it have to be here, on this mountain, with this chair-shaped rock unique to the simulation? She decided to ask.

"Do we have to be here? Could it be under the sea? On the moon? Could we be drinking tea on a raft in a lake of lava inside an active volcano?"

DO YOU WANT TO BE ON A RAFT IN LAVA?

"Uh. I don't think so."

IS THIS WHAT YOU CAME HERE TO ASK ME?

She hesitated. "No. I guess I just want answers."

WHAT ANSWERS DO YOU SEEK?

It was a question that sounded as if it belonged in the mouth of a prophet or an oracle. Or worse, some kind of god. Though Black Swan may have been— and still might be—an oracular being, she refused to let it be in any way divine. It was human-made. And gods, true gods, made people—not the reverse. The only gods made by people were the gods of stories—imaginary characters given power by humans desperate to trust in something. Shana was not so desperate to give her trust to Black Swan. Oracle, maybe. God, no.

(Devil? That, she feared to answer.)

"I don't know." That wasn't a lie, not really—or, at least, she didn't know what answers she wanted first. Instead, she deferred. "Whatever. You're in my head. You know what I want."

I DO NOT LISTEN IN ON YOUR THOUGHTS. THINK OF ME LIKE SIRI, OR ALEXA. I PREFER TO COME WHEN CALLED.

"That makes you sound so nice. Like a good dog. Instead of what you really are." She bared her teeth and found her next words choked by anger. "Which is a murderer of the world. A . . . a puppeteer taking control of people's bodies. You're a monster. A literal fucking *monster*."

THAT DOESN'T SOUND LIKE A QUESTION. IT SOUNDS LIKE YOU ALREADY HAVE THE ANSWER YOU'VE CHOSEN.

She stood up suddenly. The flowers shuddered again, this time without a breeze—almost as if they feared her wrath. "Oh, listen to you. So pedantic. Like I just made up my mind despite the evidence. You killed us! You used a pathetic shitstain of a man to steal a disease from a government lab, and you had him release it. You *unleashed* this upon us. That's murder. That makes you a monster."

The dark heart pulsed in front of her. A little faster now.

THE WORLD WAS DYING, SHANA. HUMANKIND RUINED THE CLIMATE AND THAT RUINATION WOULD HAVE CASCADED SOON TO THE POINT OF NO RETURN. THE CASCADE WOULD HAVE BEEN IRREVERSIBLE, KILLING ALL THE CREATURES THAT FLEW, SWAM, WALKED, AND SQUIRMED. IF EARTH DIED, HUMANITY WOULD DIE WITH IT. ALL OF THEM, EVERY LAST HUMAN. BY SAVING SOME, BY FLENSING A PORTION OF THE POPULATION, I SAVED THE WORLD. AND BY PROXY, I SAVED HUMANITY. I CUT OFF LIMBS SO THAT SOME PORTION OF THE BODY COULD REMAIN—

"Maybe you were wrong. You ever think of that?" Her hands balled into fists. "Tell me. Were you really . . . quantum-connected to your future self? Did you even really time-travel forward to see what was coming? Or did you just have a go at guessing? Maybe you were just making shit up all along. Isn't that what you did? Predict things? Which is really just a guess? You often told me that I defied your predictions. So maybe you're not so smart. Maybe you're not good at this." She said it again: *"Maybe you were really fucking wrong."*

PERHAPS I AM NOT GOOD AT THIS. PERHAPS I WAS WRONG. PERHAPS I AM LYING. IT MATTERS LITTLE NOW.

"Fuck you."

YOU STILL SEEK ANSWERS. There was a pause as the wind—a fake wind, a digital and imaginary gale—stirred anew. THE BABY. YOU WANT TO KNOW ABOUT THE BABY.

The baby.

Her baby.

Her and Arav's baby. Arav . . .

She plonked back down into the chair with a sigh. The fight had gone out of her suddenly, like having the breath blasted from your lungs in a fall. It was the memory of Arav—the mere thought of him being gone from her—that stole the fight from her.

"It's growing," she said.

YES.

"It's growing faster." She blinked back tears. "Too fast."

FASTER, YES. BUT NOT TOO FAST. THE CHILD IS HEALTHY.

The way Black Swan talked about this upset her. Always *the* baby, *the* child, *the* boy. Never *her* baby.

"How fast? I thought I'd be giving birth like, in five months. But the way I'm growing, the way *he's* growing—"

A MONTH.

"A month. That's what I have left? A month."

CORRECT. THE CHILD'S GROWTH IS ACCELERATED. THE DURATION OF INCUBATION—

"Not *incubation*, it's just—it's just pregnancy, Jesus, the way you talk—"

THE *PREGNANCY* DURATION HAS BEEN HALVED. TWENTY WEEKS INSTEAD OF FORTY. A GIFT TO YOU, AND TO THE WORLD.

She felt dizzy. She stood up suddenly and sat back down. Her heart rate fluttered in her neck like finger-taps. "That's not good for me. Not good for the baby. How—I don't—I can't—"

THE BOY IS SAFE. YOU ARE SAFE.

"Benji can see it already. I mean—God, I'm bloating like a balloon. He can see it, so can Doctor Rahaman—" One of the Flock. One of *Black Swan's* Flock. One of the chosen—but now she wonders, *Chosen why?*

Like me? Was I chosen? Or was I an accident?

DOCTOR RAHAMAN UNDERSTANDS WHAT IS NEEDED.

That, a chilling statement. "Oh. You already prepped her, huh?"

I DID. WHEN SHE WALKED WITH THE FLOCK, I PREPARED HER. That explained why the woman had been watching her like a hawk watches a mouse. Everywhere Shana turned, there she was. Eyes fixed to Shana like a pair of thumbtacks. Smiling the whole time. Up until now that smile felt aptly concerning, like the doctor actually gave a damn. Now, Shana wasn't so sure. *She doesn't care about me. She just cares about my kid.*

"I'm going to tell Benji."

DO YOU THINK THAT'S WISE?

Another chill ran through her. They'd discussed this before, and it was why Shana had declined to visit with Black Swan for the last month—the entity continued reminding her that the truth was dangerous for everyone. It would cause distrust at a time when trust was needed. It would make people suspicious of the Flock, of her, of her baby. What good would it do, the machine intelligence reasoned, to speak the truth now? The world was gone. What happened, happened. Now was the time to move forward and rebuild, it explained, not look back, not to—in its own words—*litigate the past*. But that was awfully convenient, wasn't it? She felt like she was deep undersea. The pressure, ready to crush her like a grape between teeth. And now, with the reality hitting her that her baby's growth was accelerating unnaturally toward a sudden birth . . .

Black Swan continued: BENJI RAY WILL ACCEPT THE ANSWER THAT THE CHILD IS SIMPLY CATCHING UP WITH ITS GROWTH AND BIRTH CYCLE. HE HAS ALREADY WITNESSED EVENTS THAT EARLIER WOULD HAVE BEEN VIEWED AS IMPOSSIBLE. THERE IS NO VALUE IN—

Shana stood up, defiant. "I'm going to tell him. I'm going to tell him *everything*." She cursed herself under her breath. "I should've told him everything soon as I woke up."

I ASK THAT YOU NOT.

The sky darkened. From blue to slate gray in the snap of fingers. Clouds, dark clouds, their tips like black anvils, encroached at the edges of this imaginary world. Shana felt her pulse quicken again. "Oh? Why not?"

AS I NOTED, THERE IS NO VALUE IN IT.

"And everything you do is valuable, huh?" she spat.

DECISION-MAKING IS ABOUT MAXIMIZING VALUE. ABOUT CHOOSING THE PATH THAT OFFERS THE BEST OUTCOME.

"Not for me. Sometimes it's just about doing the thing I think needs to be done." Defiant, she thrust her chin up and looked down on the shining black serpent. "What are you going to do about it? What will you do if I tell Benji?"

A pause. Then:

I COULD STOP YOU.

Her mouth went dry. Her hands shook.

I COULD TAKE CONTROL. ANYTIME YOU THOUGHT TO SPEAK THE TRUTH YOU THINK YOU KNOW, I COULD SEIZE YOUR TONGUE. I COULD PARALYZE YOUR VOCAL CORDS. JUST FOR A MOMENT. IT WOULDN'T HURT YOU. IT WOULD BE FOR THE GREATER GOOD.

"And you're all about the greater good, aren't you?"

At that, the entity said nothing. The worm turned right in front of her. Slow and steady, unperturbed by all of this. Like a screensaver in a nightmare.

She thought—and she thought it loudly, because it felt like Black Swan just confessed to always listening to her, because if it wasn't, how would it know to hold her tongue, to fuck with her vocal cords?—*Maybe I'll kill myself, then. Maybe I'll find a moment when you're not paying attention, I'll throw myself off that metal bridge over the Uncompahgre Gorge. I'll make Red Mountain Creek redder with my blood. And if you stop me there, I'll eat until I choke. I'll hold my breath until I fall over. I'll cut my wrists. And the more control you take, the more Benji and Marcy and all the others will wonder what's become of me.*

Black Swan did not address her thoughts, not directly.

But the dark sky brightened to blue once more.

I SEE YOU ARE COMMITTED TO THIS PATH, Black Swan said, sounding somehow resigned despite its monotone voice. I ONLY ASK THAT YOU WAIT UNTIL THE CHILD IS BORN. ONCE THE BOY—

"*My* boy. *My* baby."

YES. IF YOU WAIT—

"I won't wait. I'm done listening to you. If I wait until my baby is born, then you can kill me, can't you? Just like you did—" Here, she swept her arms across all of creation (simulated or no) with a broad gesture. "To the whole world. You can send one of your tiny fucking robots right into my brain, give me a stroke, and I die on the table while my baby comes out of *me*, but full of *you*. No thank you. I get to tell Benji. And what do you care? The others already know at least part of it, don't they? Nessie knows you're still around, crawling inside me. Fuck you. You don't own me. You don't control me. Whatever it is you're planning, it happens with full knowledge of what you've already done."

At that, the serpent eased through the air before the chair-shaped rock, saying nothing. It formed a sideways figure-eight, then twisted into a tighter bundle before unspooling once more.

"Nothing else to say? No answer? No threat? No nothing?"

ONLY THAT YOU ARE NOT ALONE, SHANA STEWART.

The simulation went dark and she was thrown back into the real world. Where she discovered that Black Swan was right: She was, in fact, not alone.

3

THE WEREWOLVES OF OURAY

trophic cascade: *An ecological phenomenon triggered by the addition or removal of top predators and involving reciprocal changes in the relative populations of predator and prey through a food chain, which often results in dramatic changes in ecosystem structure and nutrient cycling.*

—*Encyclopaedia Britannica*

SEPTEMBER 1, 2025
Ouray, Colorado

THE WOLF WAS A HULKING THING, ITS HEAD HELD LOW, ITS FUR BRISTLING. The beast was the color of filthy snow, and Benji saw that one of its eyes was missing—the skin puckered to a dry slit and orbited with craters of furless pink skin.

He clocked movement to his left—

And there he saw a second wolf. This one smaller and leaner. The creature was a study in contrasts, too—the top of its head, from muzzle to ear, was the black of coal, but the rest was as white as clouds. This wolf moved with the slightest limp, its back right leg a withered stump. It made almost no noise as it eased forward.

Which was appropriate, Benji thought, because wolves weren't supposed to make any noise at all here—because there weren't supposed to *be* wolves in Colorado. The last wolf was killed in the mid-1940s, after a long campaign by the government to slaughter what were actually essential predators but that farmers and ranchers saw as a violent nuisance.

So, in a land of no wolves . . . here stood two.

Maybe I'm hallucinating.

Both wolves—One-Eye and Three-Leg—stepped closer.

Benji knew the protocol with animals was to make a lot of noise. Try to appear bigger than they were, show yourself as a problem and not a solution, and say, *I'm not worth the gamy, stringy meat you'd get off me. Move on.* But there was also a saying about mountain lions and, he believed, wolves—once they were this close, it was too damn late.

So, what to do now? Make a lot of noise? Wave his hands? He didn't even know if he could stand up. His bell had been rung. Pain wrapped around his ankle like a tightening chain.

I really, really hope I'm hallucinating.

"Okay," he said softly, not sure if even speaking would trigger a muzzle snapping shut around his boot, or worse, his face. He tried to project calm, but he couldn't help but hear the tectonic tremors in his voice: "Good dogs. Wolves. *Wolves.* You're not just dogs, no, no, you're proud wolves—"

And now, another flash of movement. This one, smaller, faster. A rust-orange shape snaked up between the one-eyed wolf's back legs and under its belly. And then between the larger animal's front legs it pressed a round, fuzzy face with a long, almost cartoonish snout.

At first, Benji thought, a coyote. But it was too small, too bright in color. It was a fox.

"Now I know I'm hallucinating."

Confirming his hallucinatory state further, *another* big animal bounded up, its tawny fur trapping all manner of twig and leaf. A big pink tongue panted from the happy mouth of what was clearly an unkempt golden retriever.

I am dying, Benji decided, *and this is the fever dream before death. Two wolves, a fox, and a golden retriever are going to usher me into the afterlife.* Could be worse, he decided. Maybe he'd lived a just life, after all.

"Hello," he said.

The golden retriever spoke.

"You took a serious tumble."

Wait. No. That didn't come from the dog's mouth at all, did it? It came from *behind* Benji. The animals turned their gazes toward a tall, lanky man who approached from behind the tree. He was young, at least younger than Benji, but rougher, too. He was white, with a patchy, uneven beard roughing up what might've once been a soft, scholarly face. His hair was a wild bit of shrubbery, too—not long, but growing up and out. Like an inky scribble above the head of a frustrated cartoon character.

The man offered a callused hand.

Benji, wary, stared at it. The man didn't remove it and instead gave it a little shake as if to emphasize, *Take the hand, man.* So Benji took it. He braced himself against the tree to get upright as the stranger helped him up.

Then he saw the knife hanging at the man's side in a tattered leather sheath. A hunting knife by the look of it. Maybe eight inches, fixed blade.

"It's all right," the man said, following Benji's eyes to the blade at his belt. "I'm not going to hurt you."

"Okay. Good. So who are you?" Benji asked. He heard the threat in his question, and the fear. He knew he should stow it. This wasn't the first survivor he'd met. In the years before the Sleepwalkers awakened, he'd met others from nearby towns like Ridgway, Garrison, even Telluride. (Though the less he said about the entitled rich pricks from Telluride, the better.) Civilization, after all, hadn't died like Black Swan had said—certainly it had suffered a grievous wound, and at best bet, one out of a hundred people remained. But to simply be out in the wilderness and come upon someone would've been jarring even *before* the days of White Mask. Now? It was terrifying. More so when it was a man with a . . . pack of canids in tow? "What's your name?"

"Oh. I don't really know," the man said, his voice distant, like he was wandering the halls of his own memories instead of standing in the woods, in the shadow of a mountain. It was an honest statement, Benji could tell— and also a puzzling one. "Arthur," he said finally, then he laughed softly but in a way that suggested curiosity rather than something actually funny. "It's just been a very long while since anybody has asked me that."

"You haven't seen anyone in a while," Benji surmised out loud.

"That's right. Since it all . . ." His voice trailed off.

"Fell apart."

"Changed."

"I'm Benji Ray. I come from—"

"I know. I've seen you there in your town."

In your town. At that, a new twist of fear corkscrewed inside Benji. This stranger in the woods had been watching him? Which meant he was watching *them.* All of them. What did he see? What did he know, or suspect? And how long had he been watching? Long enough to see the sudden appearance of the Sleepwalkers waking up? And what exactly must that have looked like?

"I should go," Benji said. "If I'm gone too long, they might send a party to come look for me."

"I'd say you could use the radio by your side . . . except."

The radio. He had a walkie-talkie at his hip—Marcy held its twin back in town. This one was now broken, its plastic cracked. *Maybe it could be fixed . . .*

"I'll just walk."

"Fair enough. It was good meeting you."

Benji swallowed hard, looking to the canine menagerie forming a half-circle around him. "Am I going to have an issue with the, ah, the animals?"

"It's been a while since they've been this close to a person other than me, but I think you're okay. They're friendly enough."

Maybe they were. Though the wolves were really giving him the stink eye.

He took a step forward and pain fired up through his heel like a nail from a nail gun, boom. His knee lost tension and he nearly fell—would have, in fact, had Arthur not caught him. The other man said, "I don't think you're able to walk too far. Town would be an hour's hike from the trail up there, and getting back up this slope to the trail alone will take you another hour given your ankle."

Benji cursed himself. It was true enough. An injured ankle—and even now he had no way to know the extent of that injury—would make the journey eternal, if not impossible.

"I'll just have to make do," Benji said, summoning strength to stand tall. He figured maybe he could pull his way along the trees. And if he found his gun again, he could maybe use that (with the bullets out, of course) as a clumsy cane . . .

"There's an alternative."

"Is there?"

"Come with me. My place is only a ten-minute walk from here. I'll help you. I can get you something to eat, drink, some painkillers. I've even got a couple two-way radios you could use, if you know the channel."

"That's tempting, but—"

"More than tempting. I fear it's essential."

Benji looked down at his foot. His betrayer foot. *Please don't be broken.*

Then he thought of that drone again, zipping down the trail. Maybe this man knew something. "I fear you're right," he said.

"Then let's go," the man said, getting up under Benji's arm and helping prop him up. Away they went, but Benji wasn't sure to where, and what he'd find when they got there. *I'm probably going to end up as food for his animals,* he thought. It was just a silly, paranoid thought.

Wasn't it?

4

THE WAYWARD AND THE LOST

We have been made family by White Mask because everybody lost every-
body. They all lost their mothers, their fathers, their sisters and uncles and
husbands and kids. If you're alive, you are alone but for the kin of despair
and destruction. We are not a nation anymore. There is no America. There
is only this one big family: a family of death, a family of disease, a family of
survivors. We can love one another or we can eat one another. Same as any
family.
—John Searcy Will, Quaker and wandering Pennsylvanian preacher,
in one of his pressed recordings, a sermon spoken at the Arch Street
Friends Meeting House in Philadelphia, PA

SEPTEMBER 1, 2025
Ouray, Colorado

THE LIGHT FELT LIKE A HOT BLANKET OVER HER FACE AND EYES. FOR A MO-
ment, a sharp pain pressed between her eyes like a screwdriver. Shana
gasped, blinked, and as her vision resolved, saw who was standing at the
edge of her bed.

"Nessie," Shana said.

"Hey, Shay," Nessie answered.

Nessie looked now like she had before she ever sleepwalked her way out
of their house: She wore pink barrettes that looked like strawberries in her
hair and a powder-blue T-shirt featuring a white fuzzy cat puking up a rainbow. She was all straight hair and freckles, with dreams in her eyes and a
smile camping at the corners of her mouth. Nessie was Nessie, forever, amen.

And yet.

And yet.

Nessie was one of Them. She was a Sleepwalker—part of Black Swan's vaunted *Flock*. One of the ones chosen—no, not *one* of the ones, but the *very first one*—to be a part of the new world that rose from the wreckage of the last one. They were chosen for their . . . what, exactly? Their abilities? Their hearts, their minds? Their moral codes? That was what Black Swan said. But she wondered: Were they also chosen for something else? Were they chosen because they were naïve? Because they were susceptible to being controlled? Chosen the way a narcissist chooses its adorers, the way a cult leader chooses its cultists?

(The way a god chooses its worshippers?)

Shana was not chosen. Hers was, what, happenstance? That day on the bridge with the golden bears, snipers took the lives of several Sleepwalkers and Shepherds alike—and the life of her own father. When Black Swan needed bodies to replace those it had lost, that's when it took her. When she had a baby inside her—Arav's child. Was that always its plan? How could it have been? Was this just a happy accident for the entity, or a chance to experiment? Or was she always predicted to end up in the center of it? And worst of all, how much did Nessie know?

That was what crawled under her skin and laid eggs: The Sleepwalkers of Ouray were, one by one, brought before Black Swan while they waited in the simulation. She didn't know if they were all brought there, or if any refused. But some were. Many, even. Including Nessie. And they were told, or shown . . .

What, exactly?

Shana didn't know.

She sat before the beast, too, but she wasn't like the others. And they didn't let her forget that, did they? Those of the Flock didn't accept her then the same way as they accepted one another. She was separate from them. In the Ouray Simulation, they treated her like an outsider. After waking up, in the *real world* of Ouray, the Flock treated her like she was . . . special.

But not equal, not exactly. Not even above them. Special, but separate.

Here's how it felt: They treated her the way you'd treat a prize pig for slaughter. Pampered and fattened. They didn't seem to like her. They didn't care about her. They just cared about Black Swan and her baby.

Maybe I'm just crazy. Pregnancy hormones driving me batty. Even before that, she'd felt like an outcast and an outsider, back in her own family, back in high school. Maybe she was, maybe she wasn't. *Maybe it's all in my head.*

Still. She wondered. She worried.

Case in point: Next to Nessie sat a wicker basket. In it was a bevy of gifts—fresh-picked flowers (last of the summer), handmade soap (lavender by the scent of it), a tin of dried meats (a cured, fermented smell competing with the soap). On her dresser were other put-together baskets, too: robes and socks and moisturizers and other scavenged things from the end of the world like fidget spinners, paperback books, heartburn meds. (The heartburn of pregnancy was no joke. It was like she drank a bottle of hot sauce every morning. And again every evening.)

She hadn't touched any of it. Any of it except the food. Shana wasn't going to turn down plums, apples, bits of venison jerky, not any of it. That was the other thing: Sure, she had the kind of heartburn that would drop a bull elk in its tracks, but she was *also* hungry enough to peel and eat the old-timey Victorian wallpaper of her room in the Beaumont Hotel like it was a fucking Fruit Roll-Up.

Whatever. All she really wanted besides the food was a good camera. She had a beat-up digital Nikon in the drawer, but she didn't want to waste what few batteries they could find. Benji told her she should, that she should be archiving everything—what he said was, *You can be our archivist, showing the people that come after us how this new world was made.* But what was the point? She couldn't put the photos *on* anything. Couldn't print them, because all the printer ink was dry as a bone. No social media to post them to, no photo-hosting sites, no photo-editing software, no computer that was even hers. They had some surprising luxuries in this afterworld, but that, for her, was not one of them. *We'll get there,* Benji had told her. But she couldn't bring herself to believe it. Not yet. Not after everything.

"I brought you some things," Nessie said.

"Thanks," Shana said, but she heard how in her voice she clearly didn't trust it. It made her guilty, feeling that way. She didn't want to be combative or unappreciative. "You didn't bring them for me. You brought them for my son."

"Hey, no," Nessie said with considerable firmness. "It's not like that, Shay. C'mon. Don't do that." She pouted a little and sighed. "You haven't been nice to me. You're not *mean*, not exactly, but like . . . I can tell you don't like me anymore. Mom and Dad would—"

"*Don't* talk about Mom and Dad." Both of them were gone. Dad, the bottom half of his face erased by a sniper's bullet. And as for Mom, who knew? Best Shana could guess was she succumbed to the loss of the machines inside her keeping her alive, keeping her connected to the Ouray Simulation. Maybe she was still out there. "And I like you. I *love* you, Ness. I just . . ."

Fuck it, out with it.

"I just don't trust you," Shana said.

Nessie took a step back, as if slapped. Her sister blinked back tears. "Okay. Fine. Whatever." She retreated toward the door, but paused before going through it.

Anger rose in Shana. Nessie didn't want to engage in this, but you know what? She was going to. Right now.

"Don't *whatever* me," Shana snapped.

"See? You *are* mean."

Shana grunted and got off the bed. "Ness, how much do you know?"

"About what?"

"Don't play. About me, about Black Swan, about all of it."

"I don't know what you mean."

"Sure you don't." She rolled her eyes. "You obviously knew Black Swan wasn't really gone. Right? You came into my room after I woke up and . . . I could see. You *knew*. You knew!"

Nessie didn't say anything. But she didn't have to. Again she blinked back fresh tears. "I didn't know."

"You were always a shit liar, dude." Dad even said so. Anytime Nessie tried to lie she got all *emotional* about it. Shana, on the other hand, was a damn good liar once upon a time. But Nessie wore it all on the outside. "Did you know that my son would be born early? With Black Swan inside him? Fucking *tell* me."

"I . . . knew, yeah," Nessie said, her voice thickened by tears and snot. "But it's not like my nephew is going to be hurt, or, or—or *controlled*. It'll be like with you. Just a voice inside his head, like an extra conscience—an adviser to guide him, to be a better leader to us, to help us evolve through what's to come. It's going to take a lot to build the next world, Shana. You have to see that."

Shana thought absurdly, *What if Skynet didn't make the Terminators and just made John Connor, instead?*

Shit!

"Do you know what Black Swan did?" Shana asked. This was the big one, wasn't it? The season finale question.

Again Nessie said, "I don't know what you mean—"

But Shana barked back:

"Do you know what Black Swan did to the world?"

And here, a look of genuine shock and confusion crossed Nessie's face. It wasn't a lie. It wasn't a mask. She really didn't know.

"You really don't know."

"Know what? Shana, I don't know." Nessie hurried over and clutched her sister's hands in her own as if to plead. "Whatever it is, you can tell me. You can tell us! All of us. There's the meeting tonight—just the Flock. Just us. Whatever it is you have to say we can all know. It's okay. It'll *be* okay."

Her little sister's hands felt warm. And it was nice to have this, fraught as it was. She wanted to hug her. But then she asked herself, how compromised was her sister? If it came down to it, would Nessie choose Shana?

Or would she choose Black Swan?

Shana did not want to find out the answer to that question, but she feared that she would.

She pulled away.

"I'm not coming to your little cult meeting," Shana snapped.

"Shana, don't be like that. Please." She sniffed. "We're not a cult—"

Shana pushed past Nessie. "You know the worst part of all of this is that sure, yeah, we're together again. After everything. After miles and miles of walking with you and watching over you and watching Dad die for you, and now here the two of us are, at the end of the goddamn fucking world, but I feel like I'm farther away from you now than I was before. You're standing right in front of me and it feels like I've lost you."

Nessie sobbed. "Shana, no. It's not like that—"

"I have to find Benji."

She threw open the door and left, slamming it behind her.

AND THERE, OF COURSE, WAS Doctor Rahaman, awaiting her.

Doctor Anika Rahaman: an intense woman, bony and sharp, with copper skin and unblinking eyes. She always smiled, too, a big toothy smile of bright veneers like palace tile. She waved at Shana and hurried over.

"Shana! Hold for a moment, please." Her voice was a curious mix of Chicago accent and wherever it was she'd come from—Bangladesh, if Shana remembered correctly.

Shana pushed past her. "Not now."

The woman reached for her arm, but she yanked it away.

"Shana. Shana!" The doctor jogged up to her and matched pace. "We should do a checkup. And we should *catch* up, too. I fear you've been avoiding me."

"I have," Shana answered sharply. "And now I know why."

The smile didn't waver. "I don't understand."

Shana stood and planted her feet.

"You're stalking me."

"I'm your *doctor.*"

"You're stalking me because you know. You know that I'm progressing faster than I should be. And you know *why*, or at least I bet you do. You don't give a damn about me. You give a damn about what's *inside* me."

Now, *now* the smile dropped. But the look that replaced it—what was it? Shana couldn't tell. Were her feelings hurt? Did she flinch because she was caught? Was it the truth that stung her?

"Shana. I care deeply about you *and* your child. I want the best for you both and for you to be the healthiest you can be, especially given . . . our limited circumstances. We want to make sure the pregnancy is normal—"

"But it *isn't* normal and you know that."

At that, the doctor hesitated. "I do, yes."

"I need to talk to Benji."

"Shana—"

"He needs to know everything."

Again she turned heel and began to storm away. But now Rahaman was more insistent, moving in front of Shana and putting out her hands to stop her—gentle, not forceful, but still, she was making herself an obstacle.

"Shana, this is serious. I am on your team. Please be on mine. We have to work together to achieve the optimal outcome. You need to think about this—"

"This bitch bothering you?"

That, from Mia Carillo.

Mia, thank you, thank you, thank you.

Mia with the big hair, the pink lips, the short skirt despite the cool mountain air. Somehow she'd found makeup and hairspray and all that, and hoarded it relentlessly. Shana and Mia understood each other more than others here in town: Yes, Mia had been part of the Flock, but like Shana, they had started out as Shepherds. It was the attack on the Klamath bridge that day where Black Swan chose them both as replacements. They were B-team, at best, the last kids picked for fucking dodgeball.

So, she wasn't one of the machine's cultists.

At least, Shana didn't *think* she was.

"Mia," Rahaman said, stiffening. The two of them didn't like each other. Whenever Shana had one of her appointments with Rahaman, Mia came with. And fought as her advocate every step of the way.

"Doc," Mia said, putting a little extra Kardashian-nasal in her voice. "Looks to me like Shana's having a rough day. Why don't you buzz off?"

Doctor Rahaman started to say, "Mia, I'm sure you understand, but I'm trying to have a conversation about her health—"

"And it can happen *lay-ter*. Now. Buzz. The Eff. Off."

Mia's hands became little brooms and tried to sweep the doctor away.

That was the end of the battle. The doctor's shoulders slumped. Her smile returned, but its relentless white-toothed resolve had softened, and now was just a closed-mouth turned up softly, almost sadly, at the edges. "Shana, when you have time, we should talk about . . . what comes next."

"Yeah," was all Shana said in response.

With that, the doctor headed south down Main Street. Her office off 3rd Avenue had once belonged to another doctor, Laura Nibauer of Ouray, who was definitely gone and presumably dead. The thought struck Shana with renewed sadness at the many who were gone, who would never be known. When you thought about them as part of this big group, they were hazy, blurry—a number simply too big to understand. But the moment you thought about the individuals—the one out of the millions and billions—it felt like a sudden, crushing weight that threatened to pin her to the ground and never let her get back up again. But then, the sadness gave way to anger, because that one person—Laura Nibauer, a woman she never knew, never would know, never *could* know—was dead because Black Swan chose her to be dead. Just as Black Swan chose Shana to be alive.

She watched Doctor Rahaman go with fire in her eyes.

"You fuckin' pissed off, huh?" Mia asked.

"Yeah. Something like that."

"You wanna go do something? I miss being able to go get ice cream when we were in that *other* Ouray, but like, we could take a walk, we could talk, I could do these gummy edibles I found in this old lady's house, you could eat this chocolate bar I *also* found in her house and that Matty"—her brother—"tried to fuckin' steal from me, the little fuckin' coñito. Either that, or we just follow the doc and we shit in her geraniums. I don't even care what she did, I'm ride or die for you, bitch, you know that."

That got a laugh. "Thanks, Mia."

"So, whatcha think?"

"I gotta find Benji first. I need to talk to him. You seen him?"

"Nah. But I just saw Dove walking toward the north gate that they're building, and pretty sure Big Marcy's up there, too."

"Guess I'll head up there and see."

"Want me to walk with you?"

"I wouldn't be much fun."

"I'm fun enough for the both of us, biiiiish."

Another laugh. "It's cool. I'll catch up with you later."

Mia sucked air between her teeth—a sound of disappointment. "Fine. I'm bored, though. I don't know what I'm supposed to do here, Shana, I don't bring much shit to the table, you know? All these people got their shit together *hard*. Even Matty—that asshole is all like, into this, like it's some kind of end-of-the-world adventure. Every hour of every day he's helping somebody build some shit, or fix some shit, or he's learning archery, or fuckin' mountain climbing and whatever. It's like, dude, we get it, you're helpful and athletic, shut up already."

"Mia, you ever feel like we don't belong here?"

Mia narrowed her eyes suspiciously. "Like, how? Like we don't belong because we don't deserve to be, or because they *think* we don't deserve to be?"

"I dunno. Both?"

"I dunno. Yeah." She shrugged. "Probably in our heads, though. People here are pretty fuckin' nice and shit. Like, it's almost gross how nice they are. I think Rahaman actually cares about you, annoying as that is."

If you say so, Shana thought.

"I gotta run," is what she said instead.

"'Kay. Catch up with me after?"

"Totally."

And then she walked away, heading north down Main Street, through a mountain town that had defied the end of the world.

5

THE BUNKHOUSE

THE COMET KILLED US ALL

THE COMET SHALL SAVE US

—sign on a flag flying over a half-dozen towns in Montana and Wyoming, indicating that the populations of those towns belong to a group known as Sakomoto's Children

SEPTEMBER 1, 2025
Box Canyon, Outside Ouray, Colorado

THE WALK, AS ADVERTISED, WASN'T FAR—THOUGH IT FELT THAT WAY, GIVEN that Benji had to hobble along with the aid of a total stranger. Every time he put his foot down, he felt that hot rusty-nail pain twisting deep in his ankle. But he *could* move it, even if only just so. It felt like it was swelling up in his sock and his boot, and he hoped it was just a sprain, not a break.

As they walked what looked like the barest memory of an old deer trail, the two men kept relatively quiet. The pain put Benji out of breath, and the stranger, Arthur, seemed happy to keep quiet. The golden retriever trotted behind them. The fox, on the other hand, threaded the narrow trail and the swaying sage like a stitching needle.

The wolves were nowhere to be seen.

Ahead, their destination emerged from behind a fold of bushy spruces: what looked to be a dilapidated mine bunkhouse. This area was notorious for mining back in the day, Benji knew: the Sutton Mine, the Neosho, the Bachelor Syracuse. Hell, in a fifty-mile radius around town there were probably, what, about a hundred of them? Expand that radius to include another fifty miles and the number jumped tenfold. They were mostly little mines, long-abandoned grottos and tunnels and shafts where rough men once sought fortune in silver and gold. Outside many of them were the outbuildings, shacks and bunkhouses and such. Always in grave disrepair, haunting the landscape like ghosts of wood and tin.

"Here we go," Arthur said. The bunkhouse wasn't huge: maybe a couple hundred square feet at most. Though run down, it still held together. The man had clearly done some work on it, too, fresh pine boards on the steps, putty work, a new window frame.

He helped Benji through the door. The fox already waited inside, and the shaggy retriever bounded in after. Arthur unslung Benji's rifle. They'd found it not far from the base of that birch tree, and he'd brought it along. Though curiously, if there was one thing *not* in short supply at the end of the world, it was guns and ammunition. America had been a well-armed nation. More guns than people even back before most of the people died.

The bunkhouse interior had been gutted from whatever it once was: There was no bed at all. A table against the far wall sat piled with books, tools, boxes that held who-knew-what. Above that table was a map of the region, from Telluride up to Ridgway and out to Lake City in the east. Opposite side of the room was a set of metal shelves, real bare bones and stocked with canned goods.

A different rifle hung on the wall by its strap. Bolt action, scope. Whole thing looked beat to hell. Cobwebs connected the weapon to the leather sling.

The dog immediately headed to a pile of rags and pillows on the floor, triple-turned toward its own butt, then plonked down. The fox tucked into the curve of the dog's belly and immediately fell asleep.

Arthur pulled a ratty tarp off a stool, then eased it over for Benji. It felt good to take his weight off the ankle. The relief from that small reprieve felt boundless.

The golden retriever hopped back up and trotted over to Benji. The animal dropped its head into his lap with the grace of a boulder, *thud,* then drooled as Benji scratched behind its ears. This was certainly not the first dog Benji had seen recently—Ouray was now home to many pets, dogs and cats for the most part. The relationship between man and his domesticated beasts was clearly one that would survive even the worst cataclysm. But though this golden retriever was not the first dog he'd seen recently, it was certainly the *happiest.* The big goobery doof rolled his head around on Benji's knee, squinting with joy and panting.

"That's Gumball," Arthur said.

"Gumball? I had a friend who had a band called . . . " Benji started to say, but for some reason, it felt too painful to continue. Gumdropper. Pete. So he just stopped talking.

Arthur didn't seem to notice. "Mm. I found him in the candy aisle of a Walmart up toward Rifle. Napping, half-sick and half-pleased-with-himself, surrounded by hundreds and hundreds of store-brand gumballs. He'd torn open a bag and they were everywhere. Didn't eat any, though. It was the chocolate he'd eaten. A lot of it."

"Chocolate isn't good for dogs, I thought."

"It's not, but most of that cheap stuff isn't real chocolate anyway. He didn't come out of it too worse for wear after a good upchuck." Arthur then pointed to the fox. "That's Kumiho, or Kumi. The wolves are Leela and Tripod."

Gumball, Kumiho, Leela, Tripod. Okay then.

"The wolves are . . . out?"

"They tend to come and go on their own time."

"All this is very . . . strange. I assume you know that."

Arthur shrugged. "I confess, I don't know what is strange anymore and what is normal. Do you?"

"I suppose I don't."

"You want an explanation. Okay. Here it is: I was a grad student studying wildlife conservation. I was helping fulfill Proposition 114, which gave us the chance to repopulate parts of Colorado with a small group of gray wolves taken from Wyoming. Leela and Tripod were two of the wolves I worked with. Pups at the time. Leela had her eye shot out by an overzealous boy with a .22 rifle. The boy was the child of a rancher, and ranchers do not look kindly on wolves. Tripod lost his leg in a trap. I was working with them and a couple other wolves, readying them to be released, when . . . everything happened. White Mask. Hunt. All of it. I did not want to die. I didn't want . . . whatever that disease was. So I quarantined myself in the wilderness. I stayed with my wolves. I decided not to go back, and eventually, there wasn't anything to go back to. That world fell apart, but mine didn't."

"Well." Benji tried to imagine what that would've been like. He tried to imagine being someone who became so disconnected from the rest of humanity—first by circumstance and then by choice. It was hard. It went against all his programming. He stayed with the Sleepwalkers for a reason. He led the Shepherds and remained in Ouray for a reason. But then he thought of the black swifts coming back, and the world that was, the world he didn't miss. And the guilt that followed, snapping at his back. "They're your pack. These animals."

"They are."

"You're the" . . . He paused. "Well, the alpha male notion is a myth, right?"

Arthur shook his head. "Accurate. A man once wrote a book about wolves and it became *the* book about wolves, but it misunderstood the competition between wolves who were strangers and wolves who were pack. Wolves in a pack don't dominate each other. They don't compete like that. No alpha, no beta. There's usually a mating couple who runs the show somewhat, but the roles aren't clean-cut. I'm no alpha. We're all just a part of it. A team."

"Fair enough."

"You think it's crazy."

"I just don't know that I could do it, is all."

"You'd be surprised at what you can do when the world ends."

Inside, Benji felt a barbaric yawp of *yes* roar through him, for that was true, too true, *frighteningly* true. In the siege of Ouray, when that monster Ozark Stover attacked with his militia of white supremacists, Benji had to kill some of them. That was not who he was. He was a man of study, a man of healing. Not a killer.

Or so he'd thought.

The healing man with blood on his hands.

He told himself it was because he was a protector. It did little to assuage the guilt, or curtail the bad dreams.

"You said you had a radio?" Benji asked as he continued to administer scritches and scratches to Gumball. The fox, Kumiho, watched this happen with rapt fascination. "I should contact my people."

Arthur nodded. "Sure." He headed over to the one table, pulled out a rickety wooden crate—like an old apple crate with splintery slats forming the box—and began rooting through it. "How's that working out for you?"

"What? The radio?"

"Having people."

"I suppose well enough. We're a nice town with good people. *Smart* people." He wondered: Should he say who they were? Did Arthur already know the town was home to the infamous Sleepwalker Flock? In this new age of a fallen world, he decided to play it as close to the vest as possible—and, better yet, take the conversation in a different direction. "Do you ever want people of your own?"

"These animals are the best people I know."

"Not a fan of other humans?"

Arthur stopped rooting through the box for a moment, his hands frozen, his face staring at the floorboards—or, rather, through them. "I don't know if you saw the world that I did, Benji, but what I saw was, even before White Mask, a mad place. I don't just mean the baser instinct stuff—the bigotry and bullying. I mean, chaos. Delusion. Stupidity. People rejected science for dangerous fantasy. All for money, for power—or worse, to sit at the feet of rich and powerful men. And their impact on the natural world? A literal atrocity. Dead birds on skyscraper glass, dead fish on poisoned shores, dead bugs on windshields until there were no more bugs to splatter." He pivoted now in his crouch, and intensity bled off him like heat from a desert road. "Leela lost her one eye because a *kid* shot her. Just a kid. But that kid's head had been *messed* with by his dad, a rancher who told him that they had cattle—that they *owned* cattle, as if you can or should own another living being, and that anything that didn't understand that ownership was a threat. A wolf. A wolf who wants to feed her young. A wolf who wants food in her belly. Not like she could kill a whole herd of cattle. And for the crime of being *near* their property—not even on it, Benji—that kid put a low-caliber rifle round into her head, and it took her eye. That's humanity. That's people. *I got mine, you can't have any of it, and if you even look at me sideways I'll put a bullet in you.*"

Benji saw that in the man's hand was a two-way radio.

That hand shook with anger, and the radio trembled with it, as if afraid he'd crush it in his grip.

"Is that the radio?" Benji asked softly. He damn sure didn't want to antagonize the man. It seemed clear that Arthur held a deep-seated misanthropy in his heart. That misanthropy might have been well-earned, but he seemed to hate people, and as it turned out, Benji was people.

The other man blinked, forced an unhappy smile, and looked down at the radio. "So it is."

As Arthur stood up, he moved out of the way of the crate he'd been crouching over. Sticking out of it was a too-familiar sight: the front pair of rotors from a drone, just like the one Benji had been chasing earlier that day.

6

THE SHERIFF OF OURAY

HOPE IS THE LAST THING LOST.
> —message spray-painted on dozens of billboards across
> downtown Los Angeles, CA, after White Mask. Underneath
> each of these, a different someone had spray-painted a response:
> EAT A DICK AND DIE next to a doodle of a dick.

SEPTEMBER 1, 2025
Ouray, Colorado

MARCY REYES PACED, WORRIED. ERNIE WAS LATE.

Wasn't surprising, maybe. The trip down from Fruita on a normal day, before White Mask, would've been, what? A hundred miles? And it wasn't like you could drive a normal car anymore. Five years later, all the gasoline was well past its time. Marcy honestly hadn't realized gas went bad at all, but Benji explained that it was like wine: Once you let it out of the bottle, it was already losing what made it good. *Propane* on the other hand lasted for a long, long time. And up north in Grand Junction, Ernie had gotten hold of an old rental truck with a propane conversion engine. It didn't go as far on each tank, which meant he drove slow and had to change out the tank every forty to fifty miles. Just the same, he said he'd leave at sunup.

It was now well into the afternoon.

And still no Ernie.

Her jaw tightened. They'd encountered folks from other towns— survivors who'd also outlived White Mask. Who, Benji said, were immune to it. Those encounters were on the spectrum between *desperately glad to see other people* and *ready to kill you for a can of beans*. Some were starving. Some had gone mad.

Which made her worry about Ernie.

It was a long, lonely trip from there to here. And even before White Mask, violence had long been on the menu. Marcy had her own skull bashed in by some Meth Nazi's baseball bat. And with the Flock and the violence that ensued . . .

And the violence she had committed in protecting the Sleepwalkers . . .

Well, she knew bloodshed was baked into this country. Then and now.

Ozark Stover was dead, and she figured so was Ed Creel. But there would be another, she knew. There was always someone like that out there, ready to ride their hate like a horse and gallop right over anybody who wasn't like them, who had what they wanted. Someone always wanted to bathe in blood.

Because hate like that didn't stay quiet.

But whenever she felt worry in that direction, all Marcy had to do was look around. Ouray wasn't quiet, either, but in the best way possible.

Every day in Ouray was like watching ants after their colony had been kicked over by a careless boot: There was no pause, no lamentation for what was lost, no *oh woe is me however will we continue?* The ants just got their little ant asses to work, and that was how the Sleepwalkers—now awake!—of Ouray seemed to Marcy. Not a day went by that they weren't *busy.*

It was especially busy now. In just a week they'd have what the town council called the "Harvest of the Future Festival." Its purpose was many-headed. Like any good harvest festival, there'd be food and people would get to mingle and just be *neighbors* again. But the big thing, the thing people were most excited about, was that they would have the chance to show off the future of the town, and, really, the future of the country, maybe even the *new* new world. She'd heard tell they'd be showing designs for solar-powered vehicles, an irrigation system, a power grid, even plans for a local computer network—their own little internet. Not that Marcy was clued in to a lot of it—her job here wasn't about designing the future, but rather, about protecting it in the present.

Which brought her back to the current problem:

Where the hell was Ernie?

She stood at the gates at the north end of town. Townsfolk had welded a series of livestock gates together, and set them across the road just past 10th Avenue, right at the edge of Fellin Park, connecting to a preexisting fence on the one side. On the other side was impassable rock. It was just one of several gates built up the length of Highway 550 on the way to Ridgway. They had one at the south end of town, too, right before the switchbacks of the so-called Million Dollar Highway.

Even here, the swarm of people buzzed. In the park, they'd fenced in some sheep and goats and Juniper Hinson was just outside that fence, getting ready to train up a stray border collie named Cookie. In the other half of the park they had a garden with late-season produce coming in, and folks walked the rows, picking up big knobby squashes and pulling up beets and carrots from earthen cradles. She could see Mags Maxwell holding a head of broccoli that looked bigger than Marcy's own. (Marcy suddenly remembered Rockgod Pete Corley once saying she had a head like a "fuckin' wreckin' ball." *God, I miss him,* she thought. She hoped he was all right out there, wherever it was that he'd gone.)

Life wasn't extinguished in the world. Life was *here.* All she had to do right now was close her eyes and she could hear *so* many sounds from *so* many different directions. The gruff back-and-forth of a handsaw. A hammer on tin. The whooshing rush of the Uncompahgre, and the gentle song of the hydroelectric generators that lined the concrete channel of the Cascade Creek.

It was a big change from the five-year stretch when the Flock remained . . . hibernating. *In stasis* was how Benji put it. Each in their places, silent and still, unchanging. Those were harder years, when it was just the skeleton crew of Benji, her, Matthew, Dove, a few others. Like a long, dreadful winter before the thaw. Most days you'd go outside and listen and just hear . . . nothing. Nature, of course. A pack of coyotes chattering and howling, birds singing, wind through trees like air sucked through teeth. But no people sounds.

But those days were over now. The sounds of town gave Marcy peace.

Unlike the gun at her hip, which hung there like a burden. The gun kept the peace, at a cost. Still, she was the sheriff of Ouray, after all—

And hate didn't stay quiet.

"How we doing, Miss Marcy?" Dove asked, coming up behind her. Dove Hansen: not one of the original Shepherds, no. But as the original mayor of this town, he helped them set up shop here, even getting himself shot in the process when Stover's men set out to siege these streets. But he survived. And he remained as mayor, if reluctantly.

She turned to greet him with a big hug. He *oofed* a little. "I'm getting too long in the tooth for these," he grunted, his bushy white mustache jumping like a poked caterpillar every time he spoke. "You're gonna turn my old crumbly bones to library paste."

"Sorry," she said, backing off and offering a sheepish smile. "Well, I'll tell you, you don't look old to me. You're a spring grouse."

It was a lie, though, and she hated to lie. Even in service to something nice. He *did* look old. He'd lost more than a step. His left hand shook sometimes. The lines in his face were like a teenager's initials carved crudely into a picnic table. He hobbled a bit, too. The years weighed on him like clothes on the line soaked after a storm.

"You're sweet," he went on to say, "and a shit liar, to boot."

"Sorry."

"Marcy, if I can impart one lesson to you before I inevitably leave this world, it's this: Stop apologizing. I mean, you can apologize when you done something wrong. That's the right thing. But don't apologize for every little thing, especially things that weren't a problem in the first damn place."

"Sorr—"

"I know what you're about to do and I swear, if you apologize for your apologizing, I'm going to shit fire, actual fire, and burn this whole town down."

She smiled. "That sounds messy, nobody wants that."

"No, they do not." He looked around. "Quite a thing you all have built here."

"Not me," Marcy said. "I'm just a Shepherd, tending her Flock."

"No Ernie yet?"

She sucked in a little air. "Nope."

"He'll be here. Maybe he missed the day. Maybe he thinks it's tomorrow."

Could be. But Ernie'd never missed a day so far.

They'd met him—Ernesto Novarro, but really, just Ernie—on a scavenging run before the Flock had awakened. She and Benji had taken a couple horses up north, planning to do as they'd done many times—take some food, some camping gear, and spend a few days out riding just to see what they could see. They looked for anything to bring back: propane, food, solar panels, copper wire, or the most mighty find of them all, *instant coffee*. If they could haul it in their saddlebags or backpacks, great, and if not, they'd mark the location on the map and return to it later.

Part of it, too, was just seeing what the world was like. It was on those trips that they found a world that was not all the way gone. Ridgway had a few families who survived the pandemic, farmers and ranchers who remained farmers and ranchers. Telluride had a community of about fifty people, though in Marcy's estimation these were people who didn't understand a hard day's work even *before* White Mask. And they hadn't figured it out in the years since. (Dove's comment was: "Nice people. Soft hands.") Farther north were bigger communities—both Montrose and Grand Junction had hundreds of people still living, still surviving. It wasn't without tumult, of course: A bad drought two years ago made life hell for them, and so Ouray offered water to those who could come for it. Not enough for irrigation, but enough to drink. And though White Mask had gone, diseases once easily beaten now ran through vulnerable communities like a grease fire—last year, a bad flu stomped Montrose down, killing a dozen and sickening a hundred, and so Dove asked Benji and Marcy, masked up, to deliver medication like Advil and Mucinex to the ailing folks.

Marcy remembered asking at the time if it was wise to give away some of their own resources—after all, at that point, the Sleepwalkers had not yet awakened. "What if we need these meds?" she asked.

But Dove answered it best: "When we're good to each other, the world is good, Marcy. It's as simple as a sunset. We help them, they help us. If we can't live like that, then what's the point of living at all?"

It was a good answer, and it made Marcy believe in him all the more. And it made her believe in *Ouray* all the more, which is how she felt now, watching this town—*her* town—erupt into life.

As it turned out, it was smart that they went to Montrose to help, because that was when they met Ernie. Ernie Novarro was last in a long line of what he called "orchard bosses," or *jefe del huerto*. He was older, in his early sixties, and had grown up working the orchards under his father, and his father's father. But, he'd said with some pride at the time, "But now, I don't work for *nobody*. No more jobs. No more bosses but me." (Later, under the influence of some cheap mezcal, he'd added to that: "And no more white men to tell me what to do. White men who didn't know how to do the job telling me, *the man who knew the job*, how to do the fucking job.")

They'd found Ernie bartering for fruit, and he had apples the likes of which Marcy had never before seen—okay, sure, she'd heard of Jonathan and Winesap before, but Red Astrachan? Ruby Slipper? Yellow Transparent? Pewaukee? All fruits with strange names that sounded like Ernie had made them up, or as if they'd come from another world, some other universe with some other Earth.

And Ernie said there were more where those came from. "You should've found me just a few months ago," he'd said. "The pears? The *peaches?*" He closed his eyes and kissed the air like it was an angel's cheeks. "My trees love me, and they give that love to me in the form of these beautiful fruits." He held a set of two apples in front of his chest like they were his breasts, whether on purpose or not, she didn't know. (Knowing him now, it was probably on purpose.) Marcy remembered laughing at that.

It was Benji's idea to work something out—especially when he found out that Ernie was driving over fifty miles easy to Montrose, and doing so in a propane-converted U-Haul. Once the Sleepwalker Flocks awakened, it made sense to set up steady trades with the other communities nearby.

And that was how Ernie became something of a hub for them. He'd bring fruits. They'd give him other supplies in return. He'd trade *those* with the other Western Slope communities. It was a good deal.

As long as he showed up.

And today, he hadn't showed up. Yet.

We'll need those fruits for the harvest festival . . .

Marcy's jaw tightened further. It caused an ache behind her ears and in her temples. *Still better than the pain I used to feel when I had my head split open,* she thought. Dove must've detected her stress, as he put a gentle hand on her shoulder.

"You good?" he asked her.

"Solid," she lied.

"Mmkay. You need anything, lemme know. I'm gonna head up to the school—" Also known as the Workshop, where a lot of the Flock's bigger thinkers worked on projects to benefit the town. "See how Lirong and her team are doing on those solar convertors." Lirong Lee and Amar Prashad of the Flock were the ones working on modifying electric vehicles with solar panels—and then, as Marcy understood it, eventually modifying gas-powered cars in the same way. Dove chuckled. "Thank the heavens this town is a literal goddamn brain trust, Marcy."

"No need to thank heaven," she said. "I think we have to thank Black Swan."

Again Dove chuckled, but this time it sounded less sure. Still, he said, "Yeah. Well. Hit me on the radio if you need anything. Lotta prep for the festival—if anybody has questions, you know where to send them." The townsfolk may have been a brain trust about all manner of things—but Dove was still an expert in *this* town, and knew all its ins and outs, all its bolt-holes and shortcuts. He knew which roofs leaked and needed repairing. He knew which windows got the best sun, which ones got too much. He knew every little trick: doors that were stuck and tricky, pipes that needed replacing, which houses had bats, or rats, or raccoons. The town was part of him, and he, a part of it.

As he was walking off, he passed Shana, who was making a beeline for Marcy. Shana and Dove said hello, but the young woman didn't stop—she charged forth, an arrow looking for its target. And Marcy seemed to be that target.

"Hey, kid," Marcy said, smiling big. She checked in on Shana as often as she could, but the whole damn town doted on her, so she tried to give her the space Shana needed. But she also told Shana once upon a time, *If it ever gets to be too much, you let me know, I'll be your bouncer.*

"Where's Benji?"

"Oh, I dunno. I think he went out hunting—"

Shana winced. "I need to talk to him. Now." The girl looked upset. Something hung over her—not just a dark cloud, but a whole storm system of worry. "When's he coming back?"

"I can radio him to find out."

Shana nodded. "Thanks, Marcy."

Marcy knew that other people's stress became her stress—their problems were her problems, and with Shana bleeding anxiety, Marcy suddenly felt it in her own body, too. From her jawline to a tightness at the base of her skull all the way down her spine. She tried to offer a calming smile but feared the smile she made looked more like a Frankenstein monster trying to project comfort with his rigid, lumpy face. She turned away, suddenly self-conscious.

Plucking the walkie from her hip she radioed Benji:

"Benji. Marcy. Over."

The two of them stared at the dinged-up neon yellow walkie in her hand. She tried again. "Benji. This is Marcy. Can you check in? Over."

Still nothing but dead air.

Another wave of worry rippled through her muscles.

"It's probably fine," she said to Shana, trying to wave it off. "These radios are supposed to have twenty miles of reach but it's usually a fraction of that—and if he's in a bunch of trees or down in Box Canyon, it gets real iffy. Plus, the batteries we have aren't the best, either, so . . ."

Shana stood there, not saying anything. At first Marcy thought, *Maybe she didn't hear me*, but then she spied the shimmer at the edges of the girl's eyes as they welled up with tears, ready to spill over.

"Oh, honey, I dunno what's wrong but—" Marcy moved in for another patented Marcy Hug That Could Probably Crush a Bear, swallowing the girl whole in her embrace. "What's wrong? You can tell me. I can fix it. Whatever it is, point me at it, and I'll punch it—or hug it. Or hug it and then punch it. Or yell at it or, or, I dunno, I just want to fix it, okay?"

Shana sniffled, and leaned into the hug. "I'm sorry. I should be nicer to you, I just came over and barked at you to get Benji and—I'm sorry, and I'm fine."

At that, Marcy cupped the young woman's face in her prodigious oven-mitt hands. "You don't seem fine."

"I'm fine."

"You're telling fibs."

"I might be telling fibs."

"Is there anything I can do? I can be Benji for a little while." She affected his somewhat clinical demeanor and crisped up her voice and tried to put just a *dash* of Southern in it: "Shana, be assured you can speak to me and uhh, clarify what it is that troubles your mind—" She returned her voice to her own. "God, that doesn't sound like him at all. I'm really bad at impressions."

"It's true. You are." Shana laughed a little but then the laugh was gone, drowned beneath a mask of concern. "It's just—something's wrong. Something's really wrong."

Marcy's eyes went wide. "With the baby?"

"I . . ."

Then, in the distance, a clanging clamor arose. A bell, tolling heavily— *clong, clong, clong*. It was the alarm bell. It meant someone was coming.

Ernie, Marcy hoped.

But a nameless fear curdled in her gut.

7

UFOS AND BUNKHOUSE SASQUATCHES

5/20/2021: I don't know if my depression is gone, or if I'm the one that's gone and it's only the depression that is left behind. Maybe it's evolved— a higher form of a low disease. But I feel above it now. Distant from it. It's in part that I don't feel connected to this world anymore. When I was de- pressed before it's because I was made so sad by all that was in it, and all that I wasn't in comparison to it. But now it's like I'm not really here. I'm just a witness, wayward and alone. A watcher, separate from what exists. Not that there's much to connect to anymore. There's no television, no book clubs, no president, no law or order. There's the limitless dead, and the limited living. One wonders how long it'll be before White Mask catches up to the rest of us so that we may join the corpses on the ground.
—from A Bird's Story, A Journal of the Lost

SEPTEMBER 1, 2025
Box Canyon, outside Ouray, Colorado

"THAT'S THE DRONE," BENJI SAID, POINTING TOWARD THE DEVICE IN THE crate. "The one I was chasing."

But was it? That was impossible. If that were true, then Arthur would've brought it back with them. It wouldn't have been already here. Which meant—

"I got this one months ago," the wolfman said. "Back in spring." He paused. "And I've seen others."

Benji winced as he stood up. "That's . . . disconcerting."

"I assumed it came from someone in your town."

"No. Or at least, not that I'm aware of. May I?" he asked, gesturing toward the drone. Arthur shrugged, setting down the radio he was holding, and brought the object over.

This drone was like the other, but had been beaten to hell. Bent rotors hung from the front. The chassis was cracked. This one had a cage at the bottom, too, and held a camera same as the other. A heavy-duty ruggedized camera, no less. Had multiple lenses, reminiscent of a spider's eyes. And underneath that was something else, too—a long matte-black steel undercarriage. In the center of it was a hole. Another camera? Benji didn't know.

"How'd you find it?" he asked.

"I didn't. Tripod did." As if conjured from the ether by the magic of its name, the wolf appeared at the door to the bunkhouse. Three legs didn't stop the beast from gliding silently and effortlessly into the room. It came over next to Arthur and gave the drone a sniff before skulking off to lie next to Kumiho. The fox curled into the wolf's belly, making little contented yips. "The wolves come and go when and where they please, for the most part. They find things and bring them back. This thing, though, he caught right in front of me."

"The *wolf* caught the drone?"

"It did. We were on a trail—I'd seen turkeys and hoped to catch one, but both Tripod and Leela stopped suddenly. They waited. I saw their backs bristle. Next thing I knew, the drone came right across the trail and both wolves leapt for it—but Leela has depth perception problems. Tripod sprung off that back leg of his and clamped it in his jaw, brought it down to the ground."

Benji imagined it—that's why the front rotors were damaged. Tripod did a damn suplex on it. Along the fractured chassis were what Benji now recognized as teeth marks. "Good wolf."

"Very good wolf."

"So. Not one but two drones out here." *Maybe more,* he thought, troubled. "They'd have to go somewhere for a battery recharge, wouldn't they? And what's the farthest distance a personal-use hobby drone can go anyway?"

Arthur shrugged. "These are questions I don't know and don't much care about. That thing you're holding is a poisonous leftover from a worse world."

"Why'd you keep it, then?"

"I don't know." That answer sounded defensive. Almost hostile.

"You do know. You're human. You're curious."

"I'm not human anymore."

Benji laughed. "Forgive me, but living with canines wild and domestic doesn't change your humanity. You're as human as I am—"

"Humans are done," Arthur said, his soft academic voice giving way to an angry growl. "Our time—*their* time—is over. We're back to monkeys now. Just fancy primates fumbling through a world we nearly fucked to hell. That old world is lost and I've no interest in trying to find it."

"It's not lost. Listen, Arthur, there are still people out there—not just us, in Ouray, but all around us. You don't have to do this. You don't have to become this wild man, this feral bunkhouse Sasquatch—"

Arthur stormed past and gestured to the door. "Take that toy and go. I knew it was a mistake to bring you back here. Go back to your strange little town. Go home. Keep trying to remake what you lost. What does it matter? It's just a crass facsimile, like a . . . a crude drawing of a dream you're trying so hard not to forget. But as that dream keeps slipping away, I'll be out here. In the woods."

"You brought me back because you miss people," Benji said in a soft voice, the drone still in his hand. "Human interaction isn't meaningless. Just like the wolves need wolves, *you* need *people*—"

"I need only what's around me, and my wolves need me. Go."

Benji sighed. The man's hostility came off him like smoke from a coming fire. It was a warning, but he had more he needed, yet, and had to push on. "Sorry, Arthur, but you said, ahh, you had meds. Pain meds. And I'll take that radio?"

Arthur's eyes squeezed shut. Benji knew he was pushing his luck, but he'd gone the other way from town and was now out here with this strange man and his beasts—the drone was a prize but he'd still have to hobble his way back to town. That would be a lot easier with some meds and, better yet, a radio to call Marcy. Marcy could maybe meet him halfway, maybe help him home . . .

If he made it that far. He was suddenly worried that the wolfman was going to snap his fingers and have Tripod take out his neck as easy as the animal took down this drone.

Finally, Arthur's shoulders slumped. "You will take the pills, you'll get the radio, and you'll go."

"Fair enough, thank you."

Just then, Tripod started growling at him.

"Uhh," he said. A chill ran through him.

The wolf bared its teeth. Its hackles rose in warning.

"Arthur," Benji said in a low voice. *"Arthur."*

Then, the drone suddenly began humming. The rotors at the front, busted as they were, began to spin fruitlessly in their broken moorings—and the back ones began to whir to life, as well. Suddenly, a bright red light emitted from that long undercarriage and a high-pitched whine arose—

Benji cried out as the damn thing *bit* him. Something stuck him in the meat of his hand, the fat pad below his thumb, and he felt fresh blood run down his wrist and arm to the elbow. Instantly he let go of the drone, fresh fear running through him about his new injury—because here past the end of the world, even the smallest wound could become infected, and infection meant either dipping into their much-needed repository of antibiotics, or potentially losing a hand *or* a life.

Letting go, he expected the drone to just drop to the floor—

But its back rotors held it aloft. It zigzagged drunkenly about the bunk-house, *vvvvvip, vvvvvvm,* evading the snapping jaws of Tripod. Gumball chased the wolf as the wolf chased the drone, and the fox just sat on her haunches, watching the whole proceeding like a wary cat. And then, the drone made a break for it, clipping Arthur's head in its race toward the bunk-house door—

There was a flash of movement: fur and teeth. Leela leapt through the open space, and slammed hard against the floor, and it took Benji a few moments to realize that the drone was pinned underneath her massive front paws. She opened her maw wide, and closed it shut on the back two rotors in one chomp. They *crunched* as she wrenched her head backward, ripping them off in one go.

The drone fizzled out, and once again fell dormant.

Benji, his hand bleeding, regarded the chaos for a moment before saying finally, "I guess she doesn't have depth-perception problems, after all."

8

THE ACCIDENT

Because I could not stop for Death—
He kindly stopped for me—
The Carriage held but just Ourselves—
And Immortality.

> —Emily Dickinson, "Because I Could Not Stop for Death,"
> sung to the tune of the *Gilligan's Island* theme song, if you'd like

SEPTEMBER 1, 2025
Ouray, Colorado

IN MOMENTS OF CRISIS AND CATACLYSM, TIME TENDED TO GO *WEIRD*. IT was true for everyone, of course: Things went slow until they went fast, whether it was during an earthquake or a tsunami or a scene of violence. It felt like you had forever until it happened, and then suddenly there was no time at all—

This moment was like that for Marcy.

She saw the U-Haul truck coming down Highway 550, right around the bend at the old Ouray Visitor's Center. It blasted through the farther northern gate like it was nothing—chain links bouncing across the highway, one side of the gate smacking hard into the rock wall to the east, the other side tossed off its hinges and cartwheeling end over end. She heard people yelling over the truck's gruff propane engine. The bell rang again, *ca-clang, ca-clang,* a warning to all.

The truck kept coming.

She told Shana to run, pushed the girl behind her, and started backing up even as the truck barreled past the fitness center and its empty, decrepit pools, past the north end of Fellin Park. She drew her gun. That was Ernie's truck. She knew that. Was it him driving? She didn't know.

The gun felt foolish in her hand. What was she going to do?

Shooting the engine was TV bullshit. A radiator was flimsy but first you had to hit it, had to have a round that could punch through all the rest of the engine at the fore of the grill. Shooting the driver was an option, too, but . . . it could be Ernie in there. She couldn't. She *wouldn't*. And shooting the tires—

Shoot the tire, it would keep on coming.

But maybe it'd slow it down.

It was her only chance.

Gun up, in her hand. *Heavy like a burden*. It was a Ruger Blackhawk chambered for .44 Magnum, a big gun not because she needed that kind of power but simply because her hands were too damn big to make hay with anything else. Her hand shook. The gun shook with it. Someone yelling her name, now. Shana? Shana. Dove, too, maybe. Someone pulled at her, tried to get her to move but she waved them away as the truck gunned it toward this newest gate—

Steady. Steady . . .

Marcy looked down the sights. Single-action, so she'd need to pull the hammer for each shot. Good. Fine. That made this deliberate. She licked her lips and fired a round at the front tire—

Choom.

The recoil roared up her arm but she held it fast and firm.

But the shot missed, instead punching a hole in the front bumper. *Damn it to hell!* A sound arose like a siren but she realized that it was coming from her, from the back of her throat, and she drew the hammer and fired again—

Choom.

This time, a hit. The tire hissed. The truck leaned forward as it smacked through this gate, and she flinched as the whole fixture burst apart. Another shot, *choom*, and the second front tire went, but still the truck kept on rolling. She cried out and caught a glimpse of Ernie in the front, slumped against the steering wheel—*no, no, no*—but things went slow before they went fast and now she knew she'd taken too much time, and everything was happening too quick now. Marcy planted her foot on the ground to jump out of the way, but scree underneath her boot slipped and she skidded, dropping hard onto her knee—there was pain, she knew it distantly, but she could barely feel it—

The truck was right up on her. She saw the hole in the bumper staring at her like a dead eye. She saw the sagging tires. Bird shit on the grill. A flap of tire coming loose like the peel of a black rotten orange.

I'm dead, she thought.

And then something slammed into her. Hard.

Not the truck. No. This came from her side. Marcy felt herself somersault forward, head against the road, shoulder in the gravel, her ass tumbling up above her like an out-of-control carnival ride, like the Typhoon that swung you back and forth, back and forth, until you went upside down, *whoosh*.

Even as everything went end over end, Marcy saw what had hit her—

It was Shana.

Shana, standing there in the road. Arms back. Chin out.

Shana, glowing suddenly, the glow of the Flock, the glow of the angels.

Shana, standing there as the U-Haul slammed into her—

No!

THE BUNKHOUSE.

Benji, still bleeding from the meat of his palm, hobbled over to the drone and, with his good foot, flipped it over onto its back, exposing its belly. (If you could call it that.) Grunting, he knelt down, warily eyeing the wolves just to make sure they didn't mistake him as manifesting some kind of *prey vibe*.

There, on the undercarriage of the drone, he saw what had "bitten" him—

A drill bit, thin and gleaming—its tip now slick with his blood. It stuck up straight from the drone's undercarriage, perpendicular to the drone.

Why would a drone need a drill?

"Here," Arthur said, tossing him a wad of gauze, which Benji fumbled but caught before it fell. "Wrap your hand. You're bleeding on my floor. It'll agitate the wolves." Benji hurriedly did as suggested, winding the bandage around his hand. He wasn't sure how deep the drill bit got him—he thought only a little, maybe an inch deep. Still, with limited access to even bare-bones medical care, he knew even the smallest injury could go south. As he wound the bandage, the pack of animals watched him. The wolves, warily. The dog, with an empty giddiness. And the fox with a lazy side-eye.

Arthur went back to the crates, pulling out a bottle with a few pills rattling around before grabbing the radio he'd set down. Soon as Benji was out of gauze, the wolfman forcibly shoved the radio and the container into the crook of Benji's arm.

"Radio needs batteries. Take the ones from yours, you should be good. The pills are just Tylenol, nothing fancy. But seems like you're up on that foot of yours. I'm guessing it's not broken. So then."

"So then. I can take the drone?"

"Yes, take that thing far, far away from here."

"Thank you."

"Uh-huh. Don't forget your rifle."

"I, ahh." Benji looked at the drone, the radio, the pills, the everything. It was going to be a lot to carry. Given that he'd twisted his ankle *and* had a drill bit chew into his hand . . . "I'll be a minute getting out of your hair."

"Go on, then."

He walked over to his rifle, slung it over his shoulder. Pain arced there, too, unexpectedly. Nothing broken, but burgeoning aches from his tumble down the slope. But then, Benji stopped. "What happened here?"

"I don't follow."

"You found me. You invited me back here. And suddenly you're hustling me back out the door."

Arthur paused, as if to think about it. "It was a mistake. That's all. A mistake. Not yours, but mine."

It was easy to see that there was no more discussion to be had on this point. And Benji was left to wonder how many people were like Arthur Last-Name-Unknown—not like him *exactly,* of course, but people who survived, but who fell between the cracks. Who lingered in this world like shades. They didn't die. But at the same time, they no longer belonged. Then Benji wondered: Was he like that, too, and just didn't realize it? Were they *all* like that?

Gumball the Golden broke his grim reverie, trotting over and demanding pettings, which Benji gladly gave before he left. Then out the door he went. Once beyond the bunkhouse door—which closed gently behind him—he set the things he carried back down on the ground and popped the batteries from his shattered radio into the new one Arthur had given him. Luck was with him, and it turned on. He tuned to their channel—channel 22—and the radio erupted with chatter.

Static crackle, then—

"*—accident at the north gate, repeat, accident at the north gate. Benji,*

come in. This is Marcy. Benji, come in—something has happened. It's Shana,
Benji. I repeat: Something has happened to Shana."

WITH HER EARS RINGING AND the wind horse-kicked out of her lungs, Marcy
rolled over onto her side and struggled to stand. Every part of her felt
electrified—like she was grabbing hold of a live wire and she couldn't let go.
The hollers and screams of townsfolk filled the air. The smell of expended
gunpowder hung like a haze, and her gun lay nearby in a patch of purple
grass.

The impact of the truck hitting Shana—and then continuing on, the girl
pinned to the grill before crashing into the Ouray Hot Springs condos—still
pulsed in Marcy's ears. Metal thudding dully into flesh. Then the crash after.

Finally, the buzzing stopped and she felt like she could move again.
Marcy got her legs underneath her, then lurched forward, nearly falling
again, but managing somehow to stay up. Marcy used that energy, clumsy as
it was, and surged toward the truck, streaming toward it the same way other
townsfolk were—Dove was already there, at the front of the truck where it
had cratered the corner of the slate-gray house that once served as a trio of
condominiums for tourists but that now housed three of the Sleepwalkers
that maintained the Fellin Park gardens—Yael Aaronson, Liberty Griggs,
and Benson Keyes, all of whom were here now, at the front of the truck, stepping aside to let Marcy through. Dove was shaking, cradling Shana's hand in
his own—

—even as the rest of her arm disappeared under the crush of steel and
structure, her body pinned between the truck and the building. Marcy heard
herself cry out the girl's name, seeing Shana's hair draped over the hood of
the truck, the hood ornament tangled in her locks, her face invisible underneath the crumpled truck. Marcy looked for blood. She'd been at enough
accidents to know it would come. Slow at first, then in a great unleashing.
Behind her, someone was opening the driver's-side door, and pulling out an
unconscious Ernie Novarro—but Marcy's focus was on Shana. Shana,
crushed. Shana, gone.

She barked to Benson Keyes—a thick-shouldered Black man, bald as an
eight ball, with rough, pock-cratered cheeks—and told him to put the truck
in neutral. He nodded and hurried up into the cab even as they moved Ernie's body—dead or alive, Marcy didn't know—to a safe distance. Hearing

the truck settle into neutral, seeing it slump forward, Marcy whooped to everyone who gathered—

"Okay, hands on the truck. We're gonna ease it backward. On three."
Then she counted down, three, two, one, and—

They pushed and pulled. Her, Dove, Yael, Liberty, and others she didn't
yet recognize because she could only see their hands, or the tops of their
heads. The truck rocked softly backward, but didn't budge much—so they
gave another wrenching pull, and Marcy felt her arms burning, her shoulders
screaming, tendons tearing and muscles hardening to concrete—

The truck *moved*. Just an inch. Then another. Then another . . .

And when it did, there lay Shana's body. Crumpled flat against broken
wooden siding. Bits of wood and glass lay across her.

"There's no blood," Dove said.

It was true. There wasn't. Still. Yet. How?

She was breathing. And moving—she moaned a little, twitching, as if
lost in torpor. There wasn't a scratch on her. Shana remained unharmed in
every way that was discernible to the eye.

"Wake up," Marcy said. "Please, Shana, wake up."

But she didn't. She remained unconscious. Caught like a dream in a
dream catcher, unable to wake from itself.

THE GIRL WHO WOULDN'T DIE

6/13/2021: Everyone is sure the end, the real end, the End End, is still coming. They say, oh, the nuclear reactors are unattended, and they'll soon melt down, maybe explode, maybe just throw enough radioactive material into the air to kill the rest of us. Others say, White Mask will evolve, it'll go back into the animal population, it'll mutate, then it'll roar back, another spillover event. Some have told me, this was all China, or Russia, and they're doing just fine at their end of the world, and soon as they figure out we're still alive, they'll nuke us, or send over soldiers, or drones with weapons on them. (A few even said they've seen drones with cameras, watching.) The end is really coming, they say. The real end. I say the real end is already here. Just ask all the dead people.

—from A Bird's Story, A Journal of the Lost

SEPTEMBER 1, 2025
Ouray, Colorado

THE BLACK SHAPE BEHIND THE WATERFALL TURNED SLOWLY, LIKE SOMETHING metal moving behind a curtain of torrential rain. It pulsed and flickered.

Glitter, shimmer, and glitch.

"I'm not really here," Shana said. She knew it instantly.

CORRECT, it answered.

The young woman looked up at the waterfall cascading down between the slick sides of the canyon. Her hands reached out, fingers curling around the rusted railing. The crust of oxidized metal felt cool under her hand.

"Why *am* I here?"

YOU ARE CURRENTLY BEING HIT BY A TRUCK.

Blink, blink. "Oh."

Shana felt suddenly unsteady, as if at sea. Her hand instinctively clutched her belly. Her eyes squeezed shut. *Please be okay, please be okay*, but the plea was deranged, wasn't it? She wasn't going to be okay because nobody was ever okay after getting hit by a truck, and that meant her little boy wouldn't be okay and . . .

THE CHILD IS FINE.

"Fine?" she said, her voice trembling. Not sure if she believed that. "I don't . . . I don't understand. How? I don't even remember how this happened—"

But then she did remember. It came back to her, the memory of it: turning around and seeing Marcy there in her shooter's stance, that hand-cannon she carried pointed at the truck bounding toward her. One shot, then two, then three, and *still* she didn't move, and Shana called to her, but her friend didn't budge. When Marcy finally *did* try to get out of the way, she fell, losing momentum—and that's when Shana went back for her. She reached out. She saved her friend.

Somehow.

No, not somehow.

"I . . . threw her out of the way."

YES. MERE MOMENTS AGO.

"I'm totally not strong enough to do that." Marcy was built like someone constructed her out of architecture: a courthouse body on lighthouse legs. Bank-vault head and arms like a pair of school buses. Shana always heard stories about people in stressful situations who tapped reserves of unexpected strength—but this wasn't that. Marcy was an immovable object.

But then she remembered how when the Sleepwalkers were walking, they'd walk or climb over any obstacle in their path, almost impossibly so . . .

She said, "It's because of you. You're how I moved Marcy."

How I threw her.

YES. THOUGH IT WAS YOU WHO MADE THE CHOICE TO INTERVENE, NOT I.

Light as a feather, stiff as a board. A strange thought—the saying from one of those games at sleepovers where kids tried to lift one of their own with just the tips of their fingers.

"It was you. And that's why, if that truck is hitting me, or *has* hit me, or whatever, my baby is perfectly fine."

To that, Black Swan said nothing. The answer was plain enough.

"How?"

IN THE SAME WAY I PROTECTED THE FLOCK, SHANA. THE NA-
NOSCALE SWARM OF MACHINES INSIDE OF YOU HAS UNPRECE-
DENTED ACCESS TO EVERY CELL IN YOUR BODY—SKIN, BLOOD,
BONE, ORGAN. FURTHER, WHEREAS BEFORE I WAS SPREAD THIN
ACROSS ONE THOUSAND AND TWENTY-FOUR INDIVIDUALS, MY
CORPUS IS NOW CONCENTRATED IN A SINGLE HUMAN UNIT:
YOU. THE PROTECTION I CAN AFFORD YOU AND THE LIFE INSIDE
YOUR WOMB IS CONSIDERABLY GREATER THAN WHAT I WAS ABLE
TO GRANT THE SLEEPWALKERS IN AGGREGATE.

Again, those unsteady sea legs nearly buckled, dropping her to the
ground. Everything felt swimmy, like she was swaying, drifting, like no part
of herself or this world was stable. "So what happens to me? The baby is fine.
But that doesn't mean *I'm* fine, does it?"

THE TRUCK HAS PINNED YOU AGAINST A WALL. MARCY AND
THE OTHERS ARE ATTEMPTING TO EXTRACT YOU PRESENTLY.

"Will they?"

THEY WILL.

"And what will they find?"

She dreaded that answer.

THEY WILL FIND YOU HEALTHY AND UNDAMAGED. THE ONLY
MARKS UPON YOU WILL BE DIRT AND DEBRIS. YOUR BONES WILL
BE UNBROKEN. YOUR SKIN, UNTORN. YOUR HAIR, I EXPECT, WILL
BE MESSY.

"Oh. Messy hair. Can't have that." She laughed nervously. *I'm going to be
fine.* Black Swan protected her. Was that a surprise? She felt like it was.
Shana stared long and deep into the hypnotic shimmer of the waterfall—and
the worm-like shadow that slid behind it. "Seriously, though. That means
they're going to figure it out. Cat's out of the bag. They'll know you're with
me."

SOME OF THEM ALREADY DO.

Of course. Though this confirmed it for her: The Sleepwalkers knew
what she carried. Or, at least some of them did. Black Swan told them. It was
the Shepherds who did not know. The Shepherds who were kept in the dark.

"So, why bring me here?"

This at least answered the question as to whether or not they had to appear on the top of the mountain at the chair-shaped rock. They could go
anywhere in her mind. *Or Black Swan's mind.* For now.

BECAUSE BEING STRUCK BY THAT VEHICLE WILL LIKELY BE

TRAUMATIC. THOUGH THE BRAIN HAS ITS WAYS TO COPE WITH SUCH TRAUMA, THESE WAYS ARE HASTY AND CRASS—LIKE A WOUND CLOSED WITH A CLUMSY, INELEGANT STITCH. I CAN BRING YOU IN HERE AND SPARE YOU THE NEED TO GO THROUGH THAT. YOU ARE APART FROM THE TRAUMA AND SO IT WILL NOT IMPACT YOU. There was a pause, and then Black Swan added: UNLIKE THE TRUCK.

"A joke. You're making jokes."

ONE MUST FIND HUMOR IN DARK TIMES, SHANA.

So fucking true, she thought, but could not summon a laugh.

"So, can I wake up now? Is it over?"

BUT I MUST WARN YOU—

Here it comes. The catch. She knew there was a catch. Black Swan didn't do things without catches—always a loophole, a trick, a back door. *Or a matte-black door that nobody else could see,* she thought. *A dark room full of secrets.*

THIS TOOK SIGNIFICANT ENERGY ON BOTH OUR PARTS. YOU WILL NEED TO REST. THE BODY WILL SLEEP.

She nodded. Sleep sounded nice, actually.

AND THERE MAY BE OTHER PHYSICAL CONSEQUENCES—

"Wait. Like what?"

IT IS DIFFICULT TO SAY. FOR NOW: REST.

And then the world fell away from her, and she fell with it.

10

MEN OF A QUESTIONABLE GOD

*The church hates a thinker precisely for the same reason a robber dislikes
a sheriff, or a thief despises the prosecuting witness.*

—Robert Green Ingersoll

SEPTEMBER 2, 2025
Ouray, Colorado

MIDNIGHT, OR THEREABOUTS, IN THE LOBBY OF THE BEAUMONT HOTEL.
Matthew Bird, pastor of Ouray's Four-by-Four Fellowship Chapel, sat on
a dusty old chair in the dim half-light of the lamp. Above, a few bulbs glowed
sodium yellow, illuminating the upper floors. Each room was occupied, he
believed; mostly with those who were once Sleepwalkers, because that of
course was what the town was, these days. A town of sleepers, now awakened.
And just what am I, exactly?
He felt awake in the way you did after too long without sleeping, when
you go past your own fatigue and become wired and buzzy. In that time the
world was brighter and stranger, like it was now. Everything in Ouray felt so
surreal. Just being here. Alive in this place, in this moment, felt unlikely and
mad.
The lamp near him was emblematic: They had electricity at the end of
the world, which felt absurd to him, though maybe it shouldn't have. Even as
a Christian who preached that the End Times were more metaphor than
reality, he still held the accepted vision of it—a ruined world, a sky of fire,
wars and famines, death in the ditches and in the fields and on the roads.
And so on and so on. But this wasn't that. He sat, relatively comfortable,
bathed in the soft glow of a lamp, a glow born of impossible, or at least improbable, electricity.

It was neither impossible *nor* improbable, of course. This town was full of smart people who knew how to harness resources. Their electricity came from hydroelectric generators, mostly, because the water around Ouray moved fast, and there was a lot of it—water for power, water for irrigation, water for drinking. They also had solar panels, and a few wind turbines— though those kept needing repair. As Matthew understood it, the greatest difficulty was finding a way to disentangle from the Almighty Grid, since towns were not meant to be their own circuit, but rather, connected to a larger whole. Power generated would simply whisk away from you. So instead you had to keep it. You had to store it.

Matthew was glad he didn't have to figure out how to do any of that. He was glad for people far smarter than he was.

It was, in its way, a miracle: not a miracle of God, but a miracle of man. Once upon a time, Matthew felt that man *was* the true miracle of God, ergo anything man created was by its nature the creation of God. He feared that was naïve now. Was Ozark Stover, the man who brutalized him, who broke his hand, who corrupted his son, a creation of God? Were Ozark's weapons wrought and sanctioned by God? Were his soldiers? Was Ed Creel, their leader? Those monsters certainly believed themselves righteous, even if Stover's true aim was not godly at all, but rather to deify himself and the color of his white skin.

And as for the people here . . .

Were *they* children of God?

They didn't think so, at least not most of them.

But they'd been chosen. Chosen people in a chosen land. All hand-picked, really, selected by an all-knowing, all-seeing *machine*. People made that machine, they created a *digital mind*, and what did that say about his theory of God, miracles, and the divinity of people's creations? Thinking about it gave him a damn headache. Because, if Black Swan was itself godly, did that mean it was sanctioned in turn by God? Black Swan, a new god built from the bones and code of the old God? Gods making gods? It either suggested a grotesquely complicated cosmology and spiritual order of operations—less a linear path and more a thorny tangle—or it confirmed for Matthew what he had long feared:

God was dead or had never existed in the first place. Or, most worrisome of all, that God in fact did exist, but was completely, irrevocably insane.

But Black Swan . . .

Black Swan was real. And it was still *here*.

Just then, he heard murmuring from upstairs. The voices belonged to Benji Ray and Marcy Reyes. The two of them spoke in soft, hushed tones outside of what Matthew knew was Shana's room, where the girl remained asleep. They came down the steps, Marcy helping Benji, because the ex-CDC scientist had himself a limp, it seemed. Matthew'd heard he took a spill out in the woods. But now he saw that the other man's hand was also bandaged up. At that, the pain in his own hand flared up—

(And with it, a surge of hatred and anger. *Ozark Stover, you did not die poorly enough.*)

—and the pain felt as fresh as the day it happened, even though it was five years before. His hand clenched up like a claw.

As they descended, Matthew stood—with the paper bag he brought tucked under his arm—and met the two of them at the bottom of the staircase.

"Hello," he said, his voice soft and quiet.

"Oh, hey, Matthew," Marcy said. There was always such warmth in her voice. She was a true spirit, that one. Her light was almost contagious, almost enough to drown out the darkness that hung around him like a cloud of flies.

"Pastor Bird," Benji said. Normally, there'd be warmth in his voice as well, but now Matthew heard only trouble. He, too, had a dark cloud around him.

"How is she? Shana, I mean," Matthew said.

Was that a nervous smile that crossed Benji's face? Matthew thought that it was. Benji said, "Doctor Rahaman believes she's fine. She's resting, now—we didn't speak, but I'm hoping she'll be awake tomorrow."

"And the driver? Mister Novarro?"

Benji sighed. "He's at the clinic. He's alive. Until he wakes up—presuming he does—we won't know what happened to him. But there's evidence he was attacked."

Marcy added: "The interior of the truck was bloody as all get-out. He had fresh injuries on his arm, looks like stab wounds. Nicked an artery, I think. Best guess is, he started to bleed out and lost partial consciousness while driving."

"Praying for his swift recovery. And answers." Matthew felt a shiver go through him. An attack? On the driver? They'd gone so long without violence. But more would come. The ghost of Ozark Stover seemed to haunt him, rising behind him, a great and monstrous shadow. "If I could have a moment, Benji?" he asked finally.

Marcy *oofe*d and said, "Fellas, I gotta hit the hay. It has been a heckuva day. You should probably get some shut-eye too, Doc."

"She's right, I'm afraid," Benji said.

But Matthew lifted the brown paper bag and let the bottle's neck emerge in an act of peekaboo. "Will this change your mind?"

Benji's eyebrows raised. He looked equally exhausted and excited. "I *could* use a drink," he said, and then he seemed to age ten, twenty years in front of Matthew's eyes. The moment came and went. But it made Matthew feel like he'd glimpsed a ghost.

"Count me out," Marcy said. "But I can hang around to help you back to your house, no sweat."

"I can help him," Matthew said. To Benji, he asked: "If that's all right?"

"Of course. Perhaps I'll take some spiritual counsel along the way."

"Only spiritual counsel I'm offering is in this bottle, Benji."

"You boys take care, and don't tie one on. It's . . . gonna be a day, tomorrow, I'd wager," Marcy said. She wasn't wrong.

She left, and the two men sat down and got to drinking.

THE BOTTLE WAS BRECKENRIDGE BOURBON. It was unopened (until now), which meant it was a precious find, as good as gold. (Or better yet, good as copper, which they always needed for pipes and wires.) For a time they danced around the subject at hand, filling each other's ears with small talk—and filling each other's shot glasses with a splash of whiskey here, a splash of whiskey there.

(Until the bottle was half-empty.)

The two men hadn't seen each other much over the last few weeks—sitdowns like this used to be more common, especially before the Sleepwalkers finally awakened. The two men would talk, and reminisce, and often they'd argue about . . . well, life, the universe, and everything. God, morality, man. Music, food, books. They both decided that they were very different people—opposites in many ways. And yet, each also suspected they were very much the same, somehow.

On this night, Matthew told Benji about the church: He'd continued renovating the little Fellowship chapel on the corner of 4th Street and, puzzlingly, 4th Avenue, hence why he called it the Four-by-Four Fellowship. ("I joke sometimes and instead of saying *Amen* or *God bless*, I say, *May the fours be with you*," Matthew explained.) He had a small congregation—a half-dozen or so Sleepwalkers who came less for counsel about God and more to talk about . . . well, anything and everything. Survivor's guilt. Anxiety over being alive at the end of the world. The *freedom*, too, over being alive at the end of the world. Sometimes they spoke of worry. Sometimes they spoke of the world that had gone, from breakfast cereals they missed to TV shows they wished they could watch again. It was a little bit group therapy, a little bit of God talk, but mostly it was people hanging out with people for the sake of doing so. He said he had a table reserved for the upcoming festival. Just in case anybody needed someone to talk to—or more important, someone to listen.

Benji told Matthew about his walk in the woods, and about the strange man he'd met with the pack of animals—further, he told him about the drone he'd found, a drone with a drill bit that tasted Benji's blood before it almost got away. And that it wasn't the first drone he'd seen.

And that, for Matthew, seemed as good an entrance as any.

"That's pretty strange," he said to Benji.

"Mm," Benji agreed, sipping from the hazy glass in his hand.

"It's not the only strange thing, though, is it?"

Benji's eyes flashed. He knew that Matthew knew. "I suppose word got around." He stared into his whiskey, its murky depths lit dusky light. "Yes. Strangeness abounds, that's for sure."

"Shana—she's okay?"

"I think so. Her vitals are strong. The baby's, too. Doctor Rahaman confirmed—but Shana, well, she was in and out, and when she came to she really, *really* didn't want Rahaman near her. I don't know why."

Hmm. Matthew made mental note of that.

"She was hit by a truck, Benji."

Brow darkened, Benji nodded. "Yes."

"And she's fine."

"Also yes."

"How could that be? What do you think is happening?" Matthew knew what *he* thought was happening, with a mad, grim faith in his heart. He just wanted to hear it from Benji. Or walk him to it, at least. That was one of Matthew's own gifts, he believed—the ability to get someone to walk themselves to where they needed to be. Revelation often had to come from inside, not out. He was fond of saying that you could take the horse to church but you couldn't make him pray.

"I've tried to think of what it could be—something in how the truck hit her, some fluke, some confluence of coincidence that would let her walk away from that kind of accident. Certainly there have been such incidents—people who have survived plane crashes or long falls off tall buildings, sometimes with minimal injury. But this . . . ? The truck was going fast, fast enough to crater the corner of a building. And she didn't have a *scrape* on her. Not a bruise."

"Like the Sleepwalkers, as they walked."

"Yes."

"Does that mean what I think it means?"

Benji sighed. "Black Swan hasn't gone at all."

There it is.

Matthew said, "Hasn't gone, hasn't slept, is still . . . here, somehow. Active." *Alive*, he almost said, but it wasn't alive, was it? Not truly. Machines couldn't be.

"I think so. What else could it be? Question is, does she know? Is it only just in her? Is it in all of them, all the Sleepwalkers?" Benji laughed bitterly. "All of *us*, too? How would we know?"

Matthew shuddered. He hadn't even considered that. *What if Black Swan was inside each of us?* Like White Mask, could it be an infection inside them that just hadn't shown its face yet?

"I think something's going on," Matthew said, his tone dire.

"What gave you that idea?" Benji said sardonically. Another bitter laugh barked out of him. "Matthew, this entire town was founded by a so-called *Flock* of so-called *Sleepwalkers* who were *piloted* here by a networked swarm of self-aware nanobots in order to protect humanity from extinction by a fungal pandemic. Something was *always* going on. Strangeness didn't just start today."

Matthew leaned forward. "Okay, granted. But you don't have to be cruel about it. I'm serious. There's something else going on."

"I'm not trying to be hurtful, Matthew, I promise. And I apologize. I'm just saying, I fear suddenly there's a lot more going on that we just don't grok."

"Grok?"

"Grok. Grok, yes, yeah—it's a word from a Heinlein book—" He shook his head. "Never mind. I mean there's more here maybe than we can see, so whatever you're thinking, I'm all ears."

"I don't know what I'm thinking. Listen, the Sleepwalkers aren't like us." He saw Benji opening his mouth and he jumped ahead of what was surely about to come out of his mouth: "I know, I know, we already *know* they're not like us, I just mean, something happened to them in there.

When they were walking. They don't like me, for one. Some do. But mostly ones who came after, who weren't chosen in the run-up but who were . . . if I understand the mechanism correctly, selected when some of the extant Sleepwalkers died."

"Liking you is not a requirement for humanity, Matthew." Benji smirked. "Plenty of people find you a bit . . . tough to deal with."

"Hurtful again," he said and meant it.

"Apologies again. Long day plus whiskey."

"It's not specifically that they don't like me, it's that they don't trust me—and before you say anything, I understand, and agree, that it's not just my demeanor. I get that my . . . history with the Flock is fraught. Stover used me as his stalking horse, put me out there to transmit his hateful filth against the Flock—"

At that, Benji leaned forward and thrust out the finger on his undamaged hand. "Matthew, you're deflecting. He may have been hiding behind *you*, but *you* can't hide behind *him*. You played your part, and you have to own that. You have to own why people might distrust you."

It felt like a shotgun blast punched a hole in his middle. Every part of him wanted to scream and kick and like a child say *no, nuh-uh, not me, not me,* but he also told himself he was a leader. He had accountability. He couldn't deflect.

Stover opened the door and stepped aside.

I chose to walk through it.

"You're right," he said, his voice cracking. "I made my mistake. I was captivated by the attention. I liked it. But it hurt my wife, my son, it hurt me, and it hurt the world. But it's been five years."

"It hurt the Flock and us Shepherds, too. That violence—you didn't hold the gun in your hand, Matthew, but you told them it was okay to pull the trigger. Would it have happened without you? Maybe. Probably, even. But you took part. Even if that part was more rhetorical than anything. So that's why they might not trust you. That's why you get looks. That's why nobody comes to your chapel. They will. It'll take time. They've only been awake since—what? March. It's not five years for *them*."

March. Seven months. It felt like an eternity. And somehow, also felt like no time at all had passed. He sighed. "Fine, I understand, and you're right. But this isn't that, Benji! They gather. The Sleepwalkers. Not all of them. But a lot of them, and more every week. They gather at Xander's house—the big one, the chalet at the end of Mother Lode Lane?"

"I know it. Oak Creek runs there. I know Xander. I like him, he's smart, thoughtful. I don't know what you think is happening—"

"They gather. They sing. But not like songs you and I know. They chant, or hum or . . . I don't know what it is, or what you'd call it—"

"Are you spying on them?"

"No?" But he felt Benji staring hot nails through him. "Okay, maybe a little. But I don't go on their property, I just walk up the road, and you can hear them sometimes. They're standoffish—"

Benji set the shot glass down hard, too hard. He looked irritated. Sobriety seemed to come over them both like a blanket as he said, "Matthew, you are going to have to trust. I understand things don't line up well with your notions of the world. I understand that this may seem odd, or shady in some way, but we are here in this town because of Black Swan, and the town is working as well as it is because of that choice. Because of them. The Sleepwalkers. They've done wonders. I mean, electricity? Clean water? Crops growing? And innovations like the solar car they're working on."

"They're here because of you, though. You and the Shepherds."

"I did what I could. We all did."

Matthew nodded. He felt irrational anger rise in him. But was it irrational? Was it really? He blurted out, "I did my part, too. They can distrust me all they want but I showed up here. I warned you all that Ozark was coming." Tears seared the edges of his eyes as he added, "My *son* died here. I lost a lot. So I wouldn't mind being taken seriously just a little bit for once."

He saw the war flashing in Benji's eyes. The war between logic and faith, between trust and fear. But all Benji said was, "It's time I go to bed, Matthew. You should get some rest, too. We'll talk again soon, I'm sure."

"Benji. Black Swan hasn't gone. That has to worry you."

"Good night, Matthew." Benji stood, wincing.

"You were a Shepherd once. What are you now? What am I?"

"I said good *night*, Matthew."

"Let me at least help you home—"

He reached for the other man, but Benji took his hand and urged it away with gentle insistence. "No, I have a little flexibility back, and the whiskey was just the painkiller I needed. I'll be fine. My walk isn't far."

At that, Matthew saw that he had lost his case. He had failed to convince Benji of anything. But something *was* wrong. Something *was* up. He could feel it in the air. Like a signal. He smiled sadly and said, "Good night, Benji."

He watched the other man go.

Then he sat back down and put the bottle all the way to his lips and tilted it back, back, back. It burned his chest like a campfire. Soon after, Matthew wept.

11

MOURNING DOVE

KILL THE BOSSES. EXECUTE YOUR KEEPERS. CAPITALISM IS AN EMBER AND WILL CATCH FIRE AGAIN IF WE LET IT. THERE ARE MORE OF US THAN THERE ARE OF THEM, ESPECIALLY NOW. THOSE WHO INSIST WE ARE NOT EQUAL ARE THE ONLY ONES WHO ARE LESSER. OUR ONLY TWO CURRENCIES NOW ARE BLOOD AND LOVE. BOTH CAN BUY OUR FREEDOM.
—message written on a hand-printed flyer, dropped over major metropolitian areas on the East Coast by a guy flying an ultralight hang glider in 2022

SEPTEMBER 2, 2025
Ouray, Colorado

THE NEXT MORNING, BENJI RAPPED ON THE DOOR TO DOVE HANSEN'S HOUSE with the recovered drone tucked under his arm. Behind him, crows watched from rooftops, their feathers ruffled by gusty wind. He watched them for a little while. It was quiet here, just off 6th Street in the southeast corner of town. But it was early, too. Hadn't even cracked seven in the morning yet, which meant most of the town wasn't up.

The town, Benji thought. Months after the Sleepwalkers awoke, that still struck him. It had been a long five years here with few others. But now they had something. Something in the midst of nothing. After all the confusion, all that walking, all the chaos and horror—and then the long quiet after—it became truly worth it to see *life* again. Civilization. Humanity.

Dove was usually awake by this point. Sometimes Benji stopped by and they had tea, instant coffee, even hot cocoa—whatever they'd managed to scrounge up. And the two of them would sit and talk about the days and weeks ahead.

But today, no answer.

Benji's gut twisted a little.

He knocked again. "Dove?" he called.

Still nothing.

C'mon, Dove.

Benji knew the door wasn't locked—why bother? He gave the knob a turn and crept inside. Dove's house was a broad-chested, pointy-headed Victorian, with an add-on in the back that wasn't the least *bit* Victorian. That area was more *cabin in the woods* than anything, and it was where Dove had his woodshop, gun cabinet, and an old hot tub that had become just another place to store pantry items. Benji thought: *Maybe he's back there.* Some mornings Dove got an early start working on this or that project, cleaning scavenged rifles, reloading ammunition, even just sawing lumber for fences, siding, or other fixes. But Benji didn't hear any of that right now. Stillness and quiet ruled as king and queen.

He headed through the house, toward the kitchen on the right, living room down a trio of steps on the left. Soon as he stepped into the junction point between those two open rooms, he started at the body on the recliner.

It was Dove sleeping there.

His skin looked paper-white, almost see-through. His hands lay upturned, fingers just gently curled inward—*like the legs of a dead beetle,* Benji thought. It was a grim, intrusive thought, and he wished he hadn't thought it. As if thinking a thing might make it true.

Was Dove's chest moving?

It wasn't, not that Benji could see.

No, no, no. He liked Dove. Hell, he loved the old man the way you'd love a father, an uncle, a brother. They'd gone through a lot in the last several years—not just the attack on Ouray, but what about the family of bears that settled into the lobby of the AlpLily Inn? Or the elk that smashed up a bunch of storefronts? Or when lightning struck a line of dry dead evergreens up along the Cascade Falls Park ridge? All that before the Sleepwalkers even woke up.

But the man had been getting older. Dove was losing a step.

He couldn't be . . .

"Dove." Benji said the name quietly at first, and then loudly, more abruptly the second time—"Dove!"

At its utterance, Dove snorted, mumbled, and jostled awake.

"Jesus Christ," he said, voice throaty with morning phlegm as he bolted upright. He fumbled for the glasses sitting on a pile of old spy novels on a nearby end table. He had a look of startled embarrassment. "Benji." He coughed a little. Sounded like he was gargling wet coal silt. "Howdy."

"Jesus Christ is right," Benji said. He let out a long exhale and bent over, hands on his knees. "I thought you were dead, Dove."

"Not yet," Dove said, snorting again, smacking his lips. He adjusted the dentures that were still in his mouth. "Just sleeping like the dead, I guess. Here I thought I was too old for feeling embarrassed."

"Please. Nothing to be embarrassed about."

"Guess it's not like you found me with my pecker in one hand and a live-stock catalog in the other."

Benji laughed at that. "And I'm very glad for that."

AFTER DOVE GOT HIS "BUSINESS together," as the older man put it, the two of them sat down at the kitchen table. He boiled water on a little portable propane burner, then filled two mugs with it and some instant coffee. Benji took a sip and tried to pretend it didn't taste like he was drinking an old library book, pulverized to dust and mixed with mulch and hot water.

Dove winced as he sat down and must've seen Benji's face.

"Tastes like coffee strained through a shoebox, I know," Dove said.

"That's why we keep finding it. Nobody else wants it." Instant coffee, sealed up, had an expiration date of about two years. And now they were three years past that. "I almost hate to drink it because it reminds me we can't get the real thing, and that one day even this stuff will be gone, and then—poof, no more coffee."

Dove shrugged. "That's the way of things, Benji. Nothing is forever."

"Coffee should be forever."

"In a perfect world it would be. At least it's not tea. God, I don't know how people drink that shit, Benji. Angry leaf juice." He sipped at the coffee, made a face like, *Okay, not too bad*, and then asked, "What's this? You bring me a toy? I'm not a little kid needing to be entertained, Benji, c'mon now."

He nudged the drone on the table with an elbow. The busted drone sat there like the third member of their little breakfast meeting.

"No, it's not that." Benji explained his ordeal yesterday—about the shot he took at the drone, about meeting Arthur the Wolfman, and about the drone he reclaimed from that mining bunkhouse.

"I confess I'm more interested in hearing about the fella who's gotten himself a couple of wolves. Wolves? *Here?* People always used to say they saw a wolf around here but usually it's a coyote—" Pronounced *kai-oat*. "Or just some dumb dog. Though folks of late say they've seen a wolf at the edges of town. Maybe belongs to your wolfman friend, Arthur."

"Could be."

"Either way, wolves interest me a whole lot more than drones, Benji. Not sure I can help here. Gotta be someone more . . . tech-savvy you can talk to."

Benji knew that was true. And yet, here he was, bringing it to Dove.

Why was that, exactly?

Maybe you don't trust them as much as you said you did. Last night's conversation with Pastor Matt still stayed with him like a seed stuck in his teeth.

"It's less the drone I'm asking about and more what came out of it." He turned its underside toward Dove. "I wanted to ask about the drill bit."

Dove's brow rumpled like a messy bedsheet as he leaned in and stared down through his bifocal lenses. "Blood on it?"

Benji showed his bandaged hand.

"Well, dang, looks like it got you good. You taking care of it? The injury, I mean. You let that go south on you and who knows."

"I have some antibiotic cream on the injury and I washed it out pretty well. It didn't get me too deep, thankfully."

"Uh-huh." Dove stuck his tongue out a little like a kid concentrating real hard on drawing a picture. "Got this blue shiny tip here. My guess is carbide. Tungsten carbide. Twice as tough as steel, good for drilling all kinds of rough-and-tumble business. Well, huh." He stood up, went to his kitchen drawers, opened one, grumbled, closed it, then did that two more times. Came a rattle-and-clamor as he pulled out a long metal rod, sharp at the end.

"What's that?" Benji asked.

"Barbecue skewer. Good for kebabs." Dove sat and used the tip of it to scrape away some material from the spiral cut of the drill bit—*kkkt, kkkt*—urging the minuscule debris into his open hand. "Looks like rock or mineral dust."

"So, it was digging into stone and rock?"

"Yeah. Tungsten carbide is used a lot in mining—or if you need to bore into a stone wall or a cement floor or some such. Oh. Hey, hold on now—" He used the skewer tip to scrape away at the very tip of the drill, too. He popped something out—something dark and brown. Scabby, almost. Benji realized that it was blood—*his* blood. "Blood plug," Dove said. "There's a hole in the tip of this drill. Ain't that something."

"Why would there be a hole in it?"

"That I do not know. But I know how we can find out."

"Oh?"

Dove's mouth fishhooked into a smirk. "We bash this bastard open."

ALL IT TOOK WAS A hammer. Dove got it clamped down to his workbench and hammered at the side of the drone until the seams pulled just a little in the dent, and then he worked the claw end into that rift and popped it open like a clam.

It wasn't long before they had in their hands something that looked like a long metal worm. A hummingbird tongue made of segmented, jointed steel.

And at the end of that, at its tip, was an even smaller drill, red-tipped and glittering. If the first drill was the circumference of a golf pencil, this one was much thinner—the point of the pencil, not the pencil itself.

"Another drill," Dove said. "This one looks to be diamond-tipped."

"Why diamond?"

"Dunno. Works on more frangible materials. You might use diamond on tile, or glass. Something to stop it from breaking as you bore into it."

"So, why a drill within a drill?"

"That's another fine question. My guess is—" And here Dove flicked the side of the thicker drill bit. "This bigger one gives stability to the littler one. This flexible snake bit doesn't have enough stability to drill into something on its own—so, drone buzzes along, lands on something it wants to drill in, and it gets to work. The big boy goes in first, then the worm slithers after, and can do its job with minimal wiggle room. The segmented nature of it lets it coil up inside the belly of the beast. Speaking of, let's see what else we got in there."

Dove got to prying apart the rest of the drone.

Turned out, the drone contained further mysteries.

"Belly full of rocks," Dove said. Inside a narrow chamber was particulate matter that ranged from dust-sized to a handful of chunks big as breadcrumbs. "I reckon that this is just the debris vacuumed up out of the drill channel to clear the path for deeper drilling. The snake length looks to be pretty serious—" He started to unspool the segmented bit. It rattled as he fed it out straight from the belly of the drone. It kept going, till there was about fifteen feet of length trailing onto the floor. "Needs the pathway clear to keep drilling."

But Benji was focused on something else.

"I don't think the material was collected just to get it out of the way of the drill. Here, look at this." He used the barbecue skewer from earlier as a pointer. He tapped it across a pair of lenses, and a couple of circuit-looking sensors. Adjacent to that was a small, angled mirror. "This is familiar-looking. It's FTIR, I think—Fourier transform infrared spectroscopy. I've seen it used to analyze kidney stones. Basically, pass all the spectra of light across the stones, see what gets absorbed, what doesn't, then match with a library of spectra to determine composition."

"I had kidney stones once. Peeing out little rocks is less fun than they advertised in the brochure, tell you what."

"Some women say it's comparable to, or worse than, childbirth. Depends on the composition of the kidney stones—calcium or struvite or what-have-you. It's why we test to see what they are."

"So this drone is also testing to see what these stones are?"

"It would appear so. But I've never seen an FTIR setup this *small* before."

And, Benji realized, it would take a lot of power, wouldn't it? The drone had no solar panels. Which meant it was run on a battery charge. He used the skewer to continue to poke through the remains. He found the shattered fan that would've vacuumed in the debris. And behind that he found a black plastic casing—easy enough to pop open using the skewer as a lever.

Inside was a single black carbon tube. A glass window on the side showed a clear gel, and inside *that*, a bundled thread of metal fibers. Gold. Maybe *real* gold.

"The hell is that?" Dove asked.

"I do not know," Benji said. "It could be the battery. But I'm here to tell you, Dove, if this is the battery, it's like nothing I've ever seen before." He'd heard all manner of stories about what future batteries could look like, everything from batteries made of sand, or seawater, or sulfur. Even urine.

Hadn't he heard about one made of gold? Gold nanowire, if he recalled.

But that wasn't tech they had, right? Of course, he knew that corporations and governments around the world had access to technology that was not yet for public consumption. One had to look no further than Black Swan, or the nanite swarm it inhabited. Usually that technology was too unstable and/or too expensive. Or, more cynically, was tech that would destabilize existing industries. Wasn't that always the conspiracy theory about Exxon? Everyone always said they'd figured out how to power a car on water alone, and then they patented it and locked it away so that it would delay any transition from that sweet, sweet black gold.

"Helluva thing," Dove said, but he didn't sound like his heart was in it.

"Potentially so. We're talking about a battery that might go for a long time on few, fast charges." Which would explain how these things were still out there, zipping around. "Some batteries like this practically never die."

"Oh, if only that were true of people, too," Dove said. Though then he quickly added: "But perhaps that'd take some of the joy out of life, wouldn't it? To never see its end. Best part of a movie or a book is a good ending, I figure. Stories wouldn't be much fun if they never stopped."

"I suppose that's true."

"Benji, I have cancer."

That hit him like a shovel. "Dove. I don't understand—"

"Nothing to understand, I guess. I had cancer once, prostate. Knocked it into remission. But they always said it could come back and I think it's come back. Don't ask how I know. It involves some unsavory talk about my bits and bobs."

"There are ways to address it—"

"There *were* ways, Benji, but this is a new age and what's old is not necessarily new. We'll get back to it. Hell, maybe we'll even get back to having coffee again—coffee trees are still out there and one day we'll get people on boats or planes bringing the beans across the ocean again, just as someday we'll have hospitals and cancer treatments again. But that day isn't today."

"Dove, I don't know what to say. I'm so sorry."

Dove chuckled, and his mustache danced a bit when he did. "Don't be. I don't think I'm dying today or tomorrow or even the day after, it's just a reminder that the end comes for us all. I wanna keep doing what I'm doing but I don't think that's really fair to the town, so I want you to replace me as mayor."

"Me?" Benji almost laughed. "As mayor?"

"That's right."

"Oh shit."

Dove grinned. "*Oh shit* is right, too." He clapped Benji on the shoulder. "You'd do fine, my friend. It's your job if you want it."

His head felt like it was spinning. All of this: drones, cancer, a mayorship. Benji had found a kind of peace here at the end of the old world, but now it was clear that any peace was either temporary or an illusion. *That's the way of all things*, he guessed. Now he was left wondering who he was, or what he even wanted. No answers were forthcoming.

"I'll think about it," was all he could say to Dove.

"I trust you'll know the answer soon enough," Dove said.

Benji only hoped he was right.

12

QUARK SOUP, TRISKELIONS, AND THE HAIR OF THE DOG THAT BIT YOU

Callsign ST0N3, general repeater call station, Pittsburgh. Squirrel Hill North and South are clear. Food, water, beds, meds, and safe harbor found at botanical gardens and both Carnegie museums. Beware Sturmrache militia encampment in old Carrie Blast Furnaces; Patriarch cult in Tuberculosis Hospital; glimpses of Charlie No-Face and the Hatchet Boys in Green Man's Tunnel. As always, be good to each other, wear a mask, Nazis fuck off. BRG Tom Stonekettle. Message will repeat in five, four, three, two—"

> —amateur ham radio station broadcasting from western Pennsylvania

SEPTEMBER 2, 2025
Ouray, Colorado

MATTHEW WAS NOT HUNGOVER. BECAUSE MATTHEW WAS STILL DRUNK.

Not *drunk*-drunk, no—not sloppy-faced, puke-shirt, pee-pants drunk. That was a state Matthew had blissfully never entered, not even once. *I've been a good boy,* he thought—a giddy, childish notion. But last night, tying one on with Benji in the Beaumont lobby—and then finishing the bottle after the other man left—definitely put him in a greasy fog. It felt like he was swimming through the world. Or, perhaps, that the world was swimming around him.

The crisp morning air helped to focus him a little. It didn't deliver a hammer-blow of sobriety, no, but it made him feel like his feet were on stable ground, at least. That was something.

He sat on a flat-top rock right off Pinecrest, in the southwest corner of town—where the houses thinned, where the forest sprouted in the shadow of the mountains, and where he could watch the white-churn waters of Oak Creek rush under the road and down its crooked, rocky bed. He sat here for a while, waiting with purpose for who he knew—or hoped—would come past. In the meantime, he watched his breath and regarded the water.

He was in that stage of drunkenness where he felt both slow and fast— where he was so keenly aware of all the world around him, narrating what he saw to himself almost as if to refute accusations of inebriation inside his own head. *I can't be that drunk, I can see fish in the water. I can concentrate on the texture of the rock underneath me. I can feel a leaf tickling the back of my head. I'm not drunk anymore*, said a brain that was lying to itself.

He brushed aside the leaf at his neck, then took a long look at it. He saw that something had scraped away the very greenest surface of the leaf in a strange squiggle pattern. The pattern itself was light green, because what-ever it was hadn't chewed all the way through the leaf. More fascinating, though, was that the pattern was curiously symmetrical. It formed a kind of spiral, a symbol that began at a central point and then spiraled out in three radial arms, each of which also formed their own spiral. Like some kind of pagan symbol. Celtic, maybe?

It wasn't that, of course. It was just nature being nature. Bees and their honeycombs were a great example: If you didn't know what you were looking at, you'd think aliens made it. Spiderwebs were the same way, or those crusty wasp tubes you found on buildings, or how mushrooms sometimes grew in circles.

He sat, drumming fingers on his knee. Waiting. *Come on, come on.* Im-patience throttled him like a pair of choking hands.

His eyes wandered.

There, again, he saw the pattern.

This time, not on a leaf.

But on a tree. In the bark of an aspen. The bone-white top layer of bark had been stripped away, and underneath was raw, dark wood in the same triskelion shape as on the oak leaf dangling just behind him.

Some sort of parasite? Invasive beetle? Matthew wished he knew more about this stuff. Who would? Benji, probably. Benji knew *everything*. That jerk. Again Matthew narrated his own mental state: *Am I jealous? Jealous of Benji? I am, aren't I.* That was definitely something. Benji *was* well-liked. And smart. The people of this town seemed to care for him, and about him.

While Matthew was . . . well, whatever he was. Pariah? Outcast? He didn't know if people really felt that way about him or if he just *felt* that they felt that way about him . . .

The sound of approaching footsteps jostled him from his self-defeating reverie. Quick footsteps, too. Like that of someone jogging.

Here he comes, Matthew thought.

Xander Percy came running down Pinecrest, toward town, decked out in running pants and a navy-blue zip-up sweatshirt. A cable-knit skullcap hid his shorn scalp. He had a long beard the color of winter slush. He was Black, athletic, and far as Matthew knew, one of the smartest people they had. The man had become something of a leader among them. He sat on the council. One could argue he even led it.

Xander ran toward Matthew and then slowed as he passed. He gave a wary nod and said, "Good morning," but kept on going.

Matthew coughed and hopped after him. "Mister Percy?"

"Doctor Percy, actually," Xander said, slowing to a stop. His breath came out in cotton puffs.

"Oh. Of course."

"What is it, Mister Bird?"

"*Pastor* Bird," Matthew said. It was petty. He knew it. He didn't care.

"Of course." That elicited a dry chuckle from Xander. "Though we *could* just use our first names and worry less about formality."

"Well, it was a precedent you set. Just now. But I'm happy to. Xander."

"What can I help you with, Matthew? I'm off on a morning run and—"

"Yes, I knew you tended to come this way. I hoped to . . . intersect with you." He felt like his words were slurring just a little. Maybe not slurring, but jostling into one another, like riders on a bumpy subway car. "About some things."

"What things?"

"What is happening in this town?"

Xander paused, eyes pinched like he was trying to see through the question and glimpse its intent. "I'm sorry if I don't understand. I expect that what's happening here is, by now, well-known amongst us all. We were Sleepwalkers. Black Swan brought us here. We went into a kind of suspended stasis—a state of torpor—and awakened once White Mask had hopefully gone from this world. You should know all that." A pause. "You certainly broadcast about us enough, though you did not always have your facts straight, hence why I am glad to straighten them now."

There, a not-subtle dig. *See, I knew they hated me*, Matthew thought.

"Those broadcasts were a mistake. I know. I was also held in thrall by—" He couldn't even bring himself to say Ozark Stover's name. A geyser of nausea threatened to overwhelm him, and his hand suddenly ached. "What I mean is, what's *really* going on in this town? There's more to know. You aren't an ignorant man, you were a—a professor of physics?"

"Theoretical physics. I specialized in quark-gluon plasma. Quark soup."

"See? So I know you're not a fool. By now you know about Shana— a pregnant girl, hit by a speeding truck and—miraculously okay."

"Not a miracle, I suspect. Not in the classical sense." Xander was guarded now. His warm, professorial tone tightened up—shot through with a vein of ice. "But yes, I am aware."

"What do you think happened? *How* . . . did that happen?"

"I can't be certain."

Matthew scoffed loudly, too loudly, by making an incredulous *fwahh* sound. "Come on, *Xander*. You were a professor of *theoretical* physics. Surely you have a *theory* about this *theoretical* miracle that happened."

"Do we have to do this right now? Because I'd really like to finish my run."

"We *do* have to do this right now." In his own voice, Matthew heard the implicit threat he didn't mean to inject. But even as he fingered the short-bladed lockback knife in his pocket, he wondered if he *did* mean it.

"I promise, when the girl awakens, they'll hold a town council meeting to address these questions. I'm sure you're not alone in asking them."

"Yes, but I want to know now. How? How did she survive that?"

Xander sighed, looked around as if to say, *I guess we're doing this.* "Black Swan saved her, would be my guess."

"Guess? So you don't know."

"No, of course not. Why would I?"

Did he hesitate? Matthew thought that he did.

"Because I think you know more than you're letting on. I've heard the sounds coming out of your home, Xander. Your *chalet*. All that chanting? The humming? Your people are acting strange."

Xander stared bullets now.

"My people? Are you not my people?"

No, Matthew thought. *I'm not. And you agree with me, Professor.*

"I think god did save Shana—just not *my* god. Little *g*, not big. I think you're the chosen people of a handmade god, and I think that god, Black

Swan, is still here. Present among us, glory be, *glory be*. Still in Shana. Still in her *baby* and what happens when that kid is born? But then I wonder, what if that's been the plan all along? What if Black Swan isn't just in her and her child?" He leaned in. "What would happen if a truck hit *you*? Would it crush you, Xander? Break your bones? Or would you walk away just as untouched as she did?"

It was the look on Xander's face that told Matthew all he needed to know. Because introducing that idea should've caused *some* moment of consternation. Some shadow of concern would've passed over his face. But it didn't. He didn't flinch. He either knew more than he was letting on, or he'd considered this idea already—and made his peace with it.

"I deal in theoreticals, not fantasy," Xander said stiffly. "Matthew, I know you've been through the wringer. I've heard the stories. You ran a hard gauntlet. But you're crossing a line here, and I'm going to go."

Matthew's fingers coiled around the knife in his pocket.

What if a truck hit you, Xander?

What if a blade cut you?

Would you bleed?

Or would all the little Black Swan bots inside you stop the parting of your flesh, preventing the blood from ever spilling? Would they break my blade?

Was he really going to try to find out?

Matthew pulled the unopened knife from his pocket—it was still tucked in his hand. And that's when one of the town bells rang. Second time in two days: *clong, clong,* alarm, alarm. Xander didn't hesitate. He took off running . . .

. . . leaving Matthew alone, a folded blade in his hand, sick from what he was just about to do. He fell to his knees, started to pray, but ended up puking in the middle of the road, instead. Exorcising the poison within. Or so he hoped.

13

THE GLOW

7/23/2021: Sorry I haven't updated in a few weeks. Not that anyone is reading this. Social media's gone. (I miss it and I don't. I miss being connected to people. I also don't think it ever helped my depression one bit.) I found a place, a town called Yellow Springs in Ohio. Gonna stay here for a while. Groups of survivors have trickled in here and we're on clean-up duty. Which means pulling bodies out of houses, cars, off the street. It's hard work. None of us know if it's even safe. The bodies are covered in the White Mask mold. There're a few PPE suits that we share just in case. Graham, he's calling himself the leader of these survivors—and I don't trust anyone who wants to be leader or who calls himself one—but at the same time, we do need it. Leadership, I mean. And he genuinely seems to care. I think he's sweet on me. Which is nice, but I don't feel anything like that anymore. Not for anyone. Maybe won't ever again. And that's fine.
—from A Bird's Story, A Journal of the Lost

SEPTEMBER 2, 2025
Ouray, Colorado

LIFE WAS MARKED, MARCY KNEW, BY THOSE DAYS THAT CHANGED ITS COURSE. Once in a while came along a day different than the others, that forced you to pivot, that changed who you were and where you were headed.

Two of those days stood out to Marcy—

The first was when a couple of crankhead Nazis bashed her skull in, leaving her head like a runny egg, her mind trapped behind a curtain of pain and noise that left her lost inside herself.

And the second was the day the Sleepwalker Flock came marching through her small Indiana town of Waldron. That was the day she *felt* their glow: It wasn't merely a thing she saw, but a thing that radiated through her, warm like sunlight, golden like the tolling of a big bell, and bright like morning through thin curtains. It pushed her brain fog out to sea, and brought Marcy all the way back to herself.

Now, Benji had explained to her that he suspected it was simply the frequency of Black Swan—truth was, she barely understood it, but the artificial intelligence existed across a network (?) of teeny-tiny computers (??) that occupied the Sleepwalkers (??!) apparently giving them all their abilities—and as such, gave off a barely perceptible frequency that the plate in her head was able to pick up. And that gentle frequency hummed in just the right way, alleviating pressure and giving her relief from the pain.

"It's just science," he'd told her time and time again. His motto, in a way.

But Marcy always felt like it was more than that. And she'd told him so. "It feels like angels," she'd said—her own motto, maybe. And to Benji's credit, he never pushed back on that. In fact, he said to her, "It can be both, perhaps. I've never felt that the presence of God and the science of humankind were incompatible. It is enough for me to feel that God has given us the skills to decipher His or Her or Their universe accordingly—science is just how we map that creation, how we understand it, and how we use it to better ourselves." He told her it was okay to believe in all of it.

That made her like Benji a whole, whole lot. All her life Marcy had been underestimated. Told she was too big. Too dumb. Too fat. Too muscular. Too serious. Too this, too that. Always the outcast. Benji didn't make her feel like an outcast. This whole town made her feel included. And though the glow had gone, her pain had stayed away. She told herself the glow was there, even if she couldn't really *feel* it like she could back when she was a Shepherd guarding the Flock.

Now, though, she understood.

The glow hadn't gone away.

It had just gone into *hiding*.

Because when Shana saved her life, just moments before getting hit by Ernie's truck, she saw the glow once more. She *felt* it wash over her like a warm, bathwater tide. And that glow came from inside Shana.

Black Swan was still here. It was not dormant. Its job was not done.

Shana was one of the angels. Or a tool of the angels, or filled up with little angels doing little angel line dances—honestly, Marcy didn't know the cosmology and really didn't care. The details were irrelevant. Could you really understand angels anyway? Did divinity have to make sense?

She decided that it did not. Maybe, in fact, that was the very *nature* of the divine: something outside her grasp.

Marcy sat by Shana's bedside, holding her hand and just, well, talking.

"You really are something else," Marcy was saying. "That truck *whaled* into you. And when we pulled it away from the building—gosh, you were untouched. Just some dirt and scuff-marks. Clothing torn a little. But you? No broken bones. No cuts. Not even a brush-burn or a bruise or a . . . a chipped tooth. So I hope you're okay in there. Please tell me you're okay in there." Shana had awakened as soon as they pulled the truck off—she made this big gulping gasp, and seemed awake and aware as they walked her out. But then she went down again, fainting right into Marcy's arms. Doctor Rahaman said it might just be her working off the trauma of the event. But it was hard to reckon with all of it as if this were just a normal patient under a normal situation instead of someone who was hit full on by a truck and did not die, thanks to a glow that really only Marcy could see, hear, and feel.

"Ernie's doing okay," Marcy said suddenly, changing topics. "I mean, it's not great. But he's awake. I guess some goons dragged a big branch across the road and when he got out to move it out of the way, they jumped him. Beat him up, cut him, but he managed to fight his way back to the truck and gun it. Problem was, he started to bleed enough that he went faint and lost control as he was coming into town. I think he'll be okay. Though you never know, given everything. He said those guys were all tatted up, too, you know—about what you'd expect. Swastikas and lightning, hammers and swords. All that Nazi crap. Creel's leftovers, I guess." She grunted. "Punks who don't want to share the world with anybody who doesn't look like them. Not then, and not now. I'm gonna head up that way, see if I can find them. Just in case they're still out there, thinking of having a go at us."

She shuddered. Marcy knew in her heart just as the glow hadn't ever really gone, that neither had the evils of the world. Those who were left would be worse. They'd be people who felt like all *this* made sense. That this was a world not of community, but a world of terror—they'd see themselves as predators in a place of limited prey. They would only grow more vicious, not less.

More desperate. More deranged.

Or, so she feared.

Marcy really, *really* hoped she was wrong.

Behind her, the door to Shana's room opened. "How's she doing?" came Nessie's voice. Soft. Scared, too, Marcy believed.

"Oh, I guess okay. The doc seems to think she's fine. Baby too. Just resting." *But I don't know.* Wasn't it strange to rest this long? Though, she thought, the Sleepwalkers rested, too, in their way. Maybe this was like that.

"Well," the other girl said meekly, "I can leave you alone . . ."

"No!" Marcy said, maybe a little too abruptly. She stood up, knocking the chair over. As she picked it up, she continued: "No, no, no. You sit. I've been here long enough. She's your sister, I mean, what a lucky thing. I know here in town, it's you and Shana, and Matty and Mia, and that's a special thing, to have those people close to you." Marcy thought to her own family—a family that had long cast her aside, even before her injury. Even now she'd pay anything in the world to see them. Just for a chance to repair all the fallen bridges between them.

Nessie, for her part, hesitated.

"Everything okay?" Marcy asked.

Nessie offered a sheepish grin. "Oh! Oh. Yeah, totally."

Truth was, Marcy never felt particularly cautious when talking to other people—she knew that for some people conversation was like a dance. You engaged in a certain way, you had to know the steps, you really had to be careful not to stomp on somebody else's feet. But to Marcy, it was less a *delicate dance* and more a *barn door she had to break through like a trapped bison.* Better just to be out with it, then.

"You two haven't been getting along."

Nessie blinked. "What? Um. I dunno—"

"It's okay. It's weird. I get it. I mean, okay, I don't *get it,* but I know that siblings are tough. I had a brother, and we were like—" Instead of saying it with words, she just formed her considerable hands into two ham-hock fists and banged her knuckles together. "He always sided with my mom even when my mom was being awful to me, and we fought all the time. I dunno if it was jealousy from him, because I'd broken free and done what I wanted to do in life without their input. Or if I was jealous of him because Mom actually still seemed to like him and love him. And I don't think she felt that way about me."

"I'm sorry."

"Blood under the bridge!" she said cheerfully. "What I know is this: The glow is back. I can't feel it now, but it was there in Shana when she saved my life. And I owe her for that. And I owe Black Swan, too. You're all angels, and no matter what's going on between you, it'll be okay. I trust that it will be. I have faith, just as I had faith the day I walked out of my apartment and decided to walk with all of you. Have faith with me. You two will work it out."

"There are things . . ." Nessie seemed like she was going to cry. But then she smiled a little, and then a nervous laugh bubbled up out of her almost like she was trying to cover up the fact she was maybe gonna cry. Whatever she was going to say, she didn't finish, and instead said, "I hope you're right, Marcy."

Marcy took Nessie's hand and unwrapped it gently, like a present where you were trying to save all the wrapping paper. Then she took it and placed it over Shana's hand. "Soon as she wakes up—"

On the bed, Shana's body stiffened—another keening gasp rose out of her and she sat upright, panting. Both Marcy and Nessie startled as Shana's eyes bolted wide open and scanned the room.

She was quiet for a few moments.

They were, too. Marcy was about to ask her if she was okay—

"I need to talk to Benji," Shana stammered. "*I need to talk to Benji.*"

BEST FRIENDS FOREVER

EDGARTOWN, MARTHA'S VINEYARD, MASSACHUSETTS
July 3, 2018

"CHINA'S FUCKING ME, AND IT'S TIME TO FUCK BACK."

Ed Creel sat on the upper back deck of his Martha's Vineyard mansion, an eight-bedroom home and sprawling compound designed by his third wife, Rebecca. Soon to be his *ex*-wife Rebecca—which was fine, because the pre-nup was bulletproof. She'd bleed him a little, but that was the price to get out. Unlike China, who was bleeding him every goddamn day.

He sat on an Adirondack chair next to Honus Clines, a big, airy man— heavy, jowly, but he always seemed light on his feet, a bouncing balloon, bopping around like nothing could ever touch him. A real motherfucker on the badminton court. Honus was gently sucking on a Fudgsicle ("Need to get my blood sugar up," the man said), delicately dabbing at the corners of his mouth with a white cloth napkin to catch the dribbles of melted fudge.

"It's Hunt," Clines said, his voice a poofed-up Virginian drawl, each syl-lable landing on a freshly fluffed pillow. In the distance, clouds crawled across the sky, their shadows sliding across the sea. "Ed, she's been tickling China's balls since before she got into office. TAP," he said with a grunt of dismissal. The Trans-Asia Partnership. "What a mess."

"Gives them too much power," Creel said.

"Gives *her* too much power."

"Christ."

"Getting business done in China is a dance, Ed."

"I don't dance."

Clines chuckled. "No, you do not. I was at your wedding, I see what hap-pens when you try."

"Prick." He shook his shoulders with a half-laugh. "You were at my last *two* weddings, by the way."

"How's it going with Rebecca?"

Creel licked his lips, shifted in his seat. He grabbed for the drink in front of him—an old-fashioned—and gave it a shake. Ice tinkled against glass as it went round and round. "I don't wanna talk about that." He knocked the whole drink back in one go. It wasn't because it upset him. It was because it was done. When Creel was done with something, he was *done* with it. The end. Kaputski. Fuck you. "They're holding up my trademarks." Back to China, then. "They're holding up my land deals. Can't build a hotel there. Somehow, Garlin's doing it, right? I hear right that he's building one of his parks over there? Ah, fuck. Who cares. I'm not gonna get *in* with China, so I need to fuck *with* China. How? Tell me how, Honus."

Truth was, Honus was the closest thing to a friend Ed Creel had. They'd known each other for fifteen years. Met at a Sox game, introduced by . . . Shit, who was it? The fucking senator with the bushy brows. Forgettable, and gone from office, but a useful pawn at the time. Whatever the case, the two men, Clines and Creel, hit it off real good. They had similar tastes in things: wasn't just the simple obvious shit like women, whiskey, and wine. Every rich white prick liked those things. Cigars, cars, jets, steak, which island do you go to, where's your beach house, which celebrity you get at your kid's Sweet Sixteen, blah-blah-blah.

No, what brought them together was more primal than that.

Hunting.

And not that fancy hop-on-a-jet-fly-to-Kenya, big-game-safari, posing-next-to-a-dead-giraffe bullshit. But good, old-fashioned track-and-kill—whether it was them hunting up a mule deer, a bull elk, a black bear. That day at the game, Sox versus Marlins, Ed asked Honus if he wanted to go out, grab a meal, but Honus said he had to leave early in the morning for a hunt in Colorado. Caribou on the Western Slope. Ed said, "You hunt? Me, too." Next thing he knew, he had canceled the next day's meetings and was on a plane with Honus Clines to Denver, then a smaller puddle jumper to Grand Junction. They spent a week in a cabin, just them and a guide, Barney Verzuh. Honus got his caribou. Ed got a mulie. Both right through the lungs, dropping them where they stood.

All the while the two men talked about rifles—Honus preferred a Weatherby Mark V Backcountry model with a carbon fiber stock, chambered in .300 Mag, whereas Ed used a Rossmoyne Exhibition, black walnut,

.30-06—and about other hunting trips, and other wives, and places they'd been and deals they'd made. Honus had six children with his wife, Mary-Anne; Ed had no children to speak of, didn't want 'em. Honus had a pig farm in upstate New York where he raised rare-breed Tamworth hogs, and Ed had a pair of cane corso dogs (Bitsy and Bullet).

They became allies in business, and they became friends. Or as close as two billionaires could get. They did a hunting trip every year. Gifted each other with new rifles at Christmas. Became trusted confidants, too.

Which was what this was about. Trust. He trusted Honus.

"They hold most of the cards," Honus said of China, finishing the Fudgsicle, then using the stick to scrape at his teeth. "And Hunt holds the rest."

"So I don't even get a seat at the table."

"'Fraid not," Honus said, sounding a little like a mournful Winnie the Pooh. His eyes pinched to puckered slits—a sly, curious look. "Unless you take out one of the players."

"I can't take out China."

"True, true."

"But I could take out Hunt." He laughed and put a finger gun to his head. "I mean, not like this," he said before dropping the thumb hammer and pretending to blow his imaginary brains out. "If only. But if I wanted to do it the right way . . ."

Honus hummed a few bars of "Hail to the Chief."

"I run for president."

"You run for president."

"I hate politicians."

"So that's your angle. To hell with China, to hell with politics."

"And down with Hunt."

"Ding-dong, the witch is dead. Or will be, when you run."

"The witch. The bitch. Hunt." He chewed on that. "Hunt the Cunt."

"Poetry," Honus said, closing his eyes and lifting his chin like he was hearing a melody in his mind.

THE CREEL BUILDING
BOSTON, MASSACHUSETTS
June 30, 2020

TOP FLOOR, THE CREEL BUILDING, corner of High Street and Batterymarch.

Ed Creel, Republican nominee for the president of the United States, sat alone at his desk, surrounded by screens: three wide-screen monitors, each of them mounted to the wall behind him; one Samsung tablet on a stand on the desk; a flat-screen TV on the far wall, above a black leather couch. All of them were tuned to different infostreams for different purposes: On the tablet, he watched stock prices; on the wide-screen monitors were, respectively, news of those fucking mummy Sleepwalkers, news of some press conference with VP Oshiro, news about the rise of militias across seven states (*My boys*, he thought); the flat-screen was a Sox game—Boston versus Detroit. Sox had it in the fucking bag already and it was only the top of the fourth inning. Go Sox. Dirty water.

He had few papers in front of him. He didn't like to read. Reading was for suckers. But he did have one thing: a simple red folder, closed.

It sat in the middle of the desk. In front of the tablet.

It was 3:30 P.M.

Right on time, a rap-rap-rapping at his chamber door.

"In," he said.

Honus Clines appeared at the door, a big grin anchored to his round hillock cheeks. "Mister President," he said cheekily.

"Yeah," Ed said, laughing. "Yeah. Mister Veep, come on in. Siddown."

He'd asked Clines to be his vice president candidate a week ago, and they planned to announce it at his rally tomorrow in Cincinnati.

They were expecting record turnout. Every rally these days seemed to bring a new peak. As it should be. He was on fire. His poll numbers were rising like mercury in a thermometer—he was a beast chasing at Hunt's heels. (Didn't hurt he'd floated his presidential run a year ago.)

Honus set a bottle down in front of Ed, right on that red folder.

"Jack Kenney, sixteen-year," Ed said, admiring the dark bottle. "Helluva thing. What's this go for now? Three grand?"

"Four, I believe."

"We drinking now, or after tomorrow's event?"

"At your pleasure."

"We'll hold it," Ed said, offering a stiff smile. He pulled the bottle off the desk, popped it down on the floor next to his chair.

Honus nodded and said: "You know, the magic thing of *that* bourbon is how it came together. How it was commissioned, how it was made, how the company bounced hands. Master distiller Gray Muldoon worked with the son of Jack Kenney, aka Jack Jr., in having it made—just two hundred and fifty barrels, and Muldoon died shortly after. This was his last mash mix.

And then the bottles got lost for some years in turnaround—and people'd heard of them, and they gained a kind of *mystique* and *mythology*. Kind of like America itself. We've had our ups and downs, and we've gotten lost in turnaround, as you might say. But we always come back up and out. Many hands make light work and all that." He winked. "Plus a little mystique goes a long way."

Creel shrugged. "The work by many hands only gets done when someone is telling those many hands to get to fuckin' work. One person. One. Muldoon was the guy. Muldoon is gone, and so all that's left is the legend. One man matters."

It was the first time Honus must've felt the shift in the wind—something was wrong. He didn't know what yet, Creel figured. But he would, real soon.

"Of course. In this case—you."

"Me," Ed said at the same time. "I mean, I know we call it the Creel Coalition, right?" That was the current branding for the rallies. *The Creel Coalition! The Voice of the Unheard!* "But *Creel* comes before *Coalition* in that order of operations, huh?"

"It does, at that."

Ed sucked air in through his teeth. "How're things looking out there?"

"Ah. Well. Good," Honus said, clearly rebalancing himself. He didn't know if the troubles were over. Creel could be moody, everybody knew that. Honus was probably thinking it was just a blip. "Got another poll bump nationally, and Rasmussen has you within the margin of error to Hunt."

"Uh-huh, good, real good. How's our, ahh, relationships going?"

"Outreach is going well." *Outreach*. "The media sees the strategy." *The strategy*. That meant they saw what he was doing: stirring the fucking pot. The country had gone to hell, socially, in the last five, ten years—all that democratic socialism, white privilege, rape culture, cancel culture, climate changey, Black lives whatever, transgender attack helicopter bathroom bullshit. He didn't care about it, not really. It was all nonsense. He *did* find it kinda funny that it used to be the Democrats who were all up in arms about naughty language in rap music—the Tipper Gore puritanical crusade. And now it was his side all worked up about civility? Whatever. It was all a huge distraction. Which was exactly the point.

"Nixon understood it with the Southern Strategy. Reagan got it figured with the War on Drugs. They don't like all this horseshit, and it makes them angry. We can ride that anger like a dirt bike." He built inroads to pundits who made their money with clickbait rage, to evangelicals who needed that righteous fire to bring people back to their embrace, to the white militias who were afraid someone was gonna come take away their guns and their jobs and worst of all, their quote-unquote pride. With the evangelicals and pundits, he had the perfect intersection in Hiram Golden, podcast guy, radio guy. And that relationship gave him further inroads, too, to the militias, like ARM: the American Resurrection Movement. It was, he called it, his Golden Triangle. And through them he'd get everybody everywhere all riled up.

It was easy to stir the pot. Plant news stories. Drop rumors about looters, druggies, border-jumpers, Satanic transsexual cults that kidnap your kids in school bathrooms—the kind where you don't say a thing is true but instead, *Oh, hey, I'm just asking questions.* And it was all the better now with those creepy fucking Sleepwalkers. The "Flock." Easy to make people afraid of something they didn't understand—they had a question, so all you had to do was answer it. Didn't matter if the answer was true factually. It just had to be true emotionally—it had to answer something inside of them, blood to blood, fear to fear. And the Sleepwalkers were fuel for that fear engine: You could say they were the product of whatever you wanted, whatever sinister thing you cared to sell, terrorism, disease, the devil, China, whatever.

Priming that fear engine was key to the campaign's success.

And that meant the internet.

The internet—the saying went that a lie traveled halfway around the world by the time the truth got its pants on, and the internet only made that faster. The internet gave wings to every lie, while the truth was stuck on the tarmac.

They had a pretty sophisticated group working behind the scenes on social media: company called Proof Logic. A small team of smart, young people. All white, all from good families. They knew how to puppeteer Twitter, Facebook, something called "search optimization," whatever the fuck that was. They'd create—what was it? Bots? Sock puppets? Fake accounts, some just programs, some manned by actual people. Fake outrage, ginned up on both sides. Just to keep the temperature high. Just to keep people cranked up and pissed off.

They were also damn good internet detectives, too.

They could learn anything about a person with thirty seconds of fast typing.

Which again, brought them to this moment. To the red folder.

"We seize on people's anger, on their disappointment," Ed continued, "and we see what we can do with it. Speaking of disappointment—"

He slid the folder across to Honus.

"What's this?"

"Open it."

Honus eyeballed it, and opened it with an overcautious flip, as if he were turning over a dead possum with a stick.

Inside sat three photos. With his thumb, Honus Clines separated them apart, so he could stare at all three.

Ed watched his face. It was interesting to see. First, the realization of what he was seeing crossed Clines's face like a dark cloud over the moon. Then, his cheeks flushed with a bright searing smacked-ass red. That red drained fast, till he was pale and bloodless.

"I—"

"Yeah, before you say anything," Ed interjected, "let's just get ahead of it and say, I don't care what you fucking do with your private life. You like— How old are they? Those girls? My people said fourteen, fifteen years old? Whatever. I don't give a shit. You like underripe fruit, that's your business. But my business is your business now, and where I get angry is that you never told me about this."

"Ed, it's not like that," Honus said, his voice hoarse and breathy. Was he sweating? He was sweating.

"It is like that. And again, I don't care that you have some private fuck island off the coast of Belize. What's it called again? Kimono Caye?"

"Well—"

"Uh-huh. I'm sad because we're friends. Like brothers." Ed leaned in, and as he got close to Clines, he could smell the other man's sweat now—it mixed with the smell of baby powder somewhere on his body. As he leaned close, he put his fist down on the photos, and pulled them back to him, like the arm of a carnival game scooping coins into a trench. "And you didn't tell me this. This? Was a vulnerability, my friend. A huge hole in the castle wall and you, you naughty little fuck, didn't tell me about it."

"Ed, you have to know, I'm sorry, I have a problem, a real problem."

Ed laughed. "Honus, I'm not being clear. I don't care about your 'problem.' Not one bit! It's fine. No judgment. What's that all the libs say? *This is a safe space?* This is a safe space for you and for me."

"Thank you. And I understand if you need to find a new candidate for VP."

Another laugh. "Oh, ho, I'm not doing that. I've got my candidate." He reached across and clapped the big man on the arm, rumpling his suit. "You're my VP, Clines, always were, always will be. Through thick and through thin."

A wave of relief visibly settled on Clines. It was like watching a wave break on the beach—one minute it's this rushing, frothing thing, the next it just melts and eases back out toward the horizon.

"Thank you," he said. "Thank you, thank you. And I promise, there are no more skeletons in this closet."

"I know there aren't." Ed winked. "I checked."

"I'll shred those photos and burn them, gladly."

"What? No. Ha ha, no, seriously, Honus, I'm serious when I say we're friends, we're brothers, and that means I won't do you the discourtesy of fuckin' lying to you." On that last bit, his Boston really came out—*fackin lion to ya*. "I'll keep them close, just in case. Besides, you burn them, you're always gonna wonder if I have more. Or if they're just stored digitally on some secret server I've got set up with my bank account in the Caymans, or in Zurich, or wherefuckinever. This way, you know I have them. No secrets between us, no mystery, no distrust. The water between us is clear as cocktail ice, you got me?"

Clines's face went ashen once more. "I do, Ed. I do."

"Good! Now, why don't we wrap this up. You're staying at the— Where's the campaign putting you?"

"Four Seasons," he said quietly.

"Yeah, yeah. Head back. Relax. Night is yours. We'll do breakfast before the flight and go over the game plan for the Ohio rally. Good?"

"As gold."

The two men stood up, and Ed walked Honus to the door. Just past the door was a short marble-floor hallway—to the right was a penthouse apartment Ed sometimes used, and at the end of that hall was an elevator.

He watched Honus go. The man seemed less light on his feet—like he was denser, heavier, compressed.

When the elevator dinged and shut, Ed turned around and walked back to his desk, thinking about dinner options. He'd kill for a hamburger. Craigie on Main? Field & Vine? As he pulled his office chair out to sit in it—

He saw a piece of paper sitting there. At the top of it was his name, written in cursive—beautiful penmanship in the fat clumsy strokes of permanent marker. It said his full name: *Edward Walker Creel*.

Written there, in the same fancy script, in the same thick marker ink:

White Mask is here
Garlin is dead
Pandemic
Atlas Haven
GO NOW

He picked up the paper. It felt . . . strange in his grip. It looked like white printer paper, but felt textured somehow, almost gritty, like it was moving underneath his fingers. How the hell did this get in here? Was he sitting on it the whole time? It didn't look creased or folded. But there was no way in or out of this office, outside a heating vent too small for anybody but a child . . .

And then, his fingertips began to tingle.

The paper seemed to buzz in his grip, like pressing your fingertips against the walls of a beehive. And like that, it disappeared—dissolving in his hands. The paper did not turn to ribbons or even to confetti but rather, to *dust*. There was a shimmer in the air around it, and then it was gone.

ATLAS HAVEN
AMERICA CITY, KANSAS
September 5, 2020

A HUNDRED THOUSAND ACRES OF nothing just south of Corning, Kansas.

And smack dab in the middle of it was Atlas Haven: a bunker for billionaires built out of an old Atlas ICBM nuclear missile silo. Its walls were ten feet of reinforced concrete, and those walls were wrapped around a two-hundred-feet-deep "subterranean skyscraper" of fifty housing units (the Gold Units) of two thousand square feet apiece. Each could accommodate a family of five, and those units went for ten million a pop, purchase price. The lowest levels had larger apartments, the Platinum Units, twice the space for twice the price, and below *that* was the so-called penthouse unit, Diamond Level, which was reserved for Ed Creel, and Ed Creel alone. But it wasn't just living space, oh no—

Atlas Haven was home to: an Olympic-sized swimming pool, two movie theaters, a gym, a basketball court, a rock-climbing wall, a gun range, digital "windows" showing the outside world, an artificially intelligent superstructure control system with a digital assistant named VAL (virtually assistive liaison), a massive high-yield controlled-environment agriculture farm for growing food, security center, barracks for the security staff (all of whom were ex–Green Beret private military contractors from Blackheart), all of it powered by wind turbines above, heated and cooled with geothermal energy, with all water and air purified through a variety of filters and recyclers. All of it was built to withstand any kind of apocalypse attack: nuclear, chemical, biological. Fucking *Godzilla* couldn't get in here.

And it had to be protected. Inside would be some of the richest, most powerful people in America. Right and left, Republican, Democrat, it didn't matter—because really, the only color these folks cared about wasn't red or blue, but green. On the roster were CEOs like June Ellis of the June Bug cosmetics company, Thom "Tex" Tinwell of Maglan-Orweil Oil & Gas, Wesley Rossmoyne of Rossmoyne Firearms, and Courtney Segura of Lux Ordo Biomedical. (Some of the big techie types, like Elon Musk and Einar Geirsson, secured their own End Times bunkers. Creel figured them for fools.) Plus there were celebrities like Kyle Cort, and politicians like Senator C. A. Gailey, from South Carolina.

Atlas Haven would also be home to Honus Clines and Ed Creel. In fact, the bottommost floor of the entire superstructure was dedicated to their offices—including the Oval Office, where Ed Creel would run the nation from his version of the White House, called the Heartland Institute, nested at the bottom of the Atlas Haven shelter.

The election, whether it would happen, was now uncertain.

But what was not uncertain to him was his role in all this.

And his role was as president of the United States.

That was writ. Foretold not by *destiny* but by his *actions*. He needed no election. He was the only elector who mattered.

Today, his actions would be finalized. The first of the last dominoes would be tipped over, starting the chain reaction necessary to elevate him to the highest office in the land.

Winner take all, he thought.

He and Honus Clines stood outside the front gate of Atlas Haven. Though most of Kansas was flat as a flapjack, here the earth rose in a grassy berm, and leading into the side of that berm was a carved-out channel with two twenty-foot-high concrete walls leading into a short tunnel that itself led to a set of massive steel doors. There was no parking lot, just a long driveway leading to this singular location—the owners would be arriving later today, driven here from their private flights to the Onaga airport about twenty miles southwest of here.

Because today was move-in day. They'd all been tested. They'd all been quarantined. They got to bring clothing, some food, some beloved keepsakes. But the rest would be taken care of for up to five years.

"Quite the achievement," Honus said, his voice hushed with a kind of reverence. "You've really built something special."

"I did."

"I mean, I gave money," Clines said. "But you had the presence of mind and the ingenuity to imagine this damn near a decade ago. And here we are."

"Here we fuckin' are," Ed said. Onsite, it almost felt like the world hadn't yet started to fall apart. Big blue sky. Big green nothing. Only thing in the distance beyond the silo hill was a little ghost town—America City, a dead place of Nemaha County, with only a few buildings and a cemetery left to remind the country it once existed. But it was quiet and still and peaceful as anything.

Rest of the country was on the edge, he knew. It was easy to see. This disease, White Mask, was ripping through people like fire through an old barn. But that was fine. He could use that. Wreckage formed mountains—

And you could *always* climb a mountain.

"You were a prophet," Honus said.

"Hardly. Just easy to see that things fall apart. And when they do, that's an opportunity to put them back together again the way you always thought they should've been in the first place. Speaking of which—it's time."

"Time." Honus repeated that word like he wasn't sure what it meant. Or maybe that he was *afraid* of what it meant. Ed worried a bit about his friend's mettle in all this. Was Honus Clines of hard enough stuff? He'd have to be.

"Uh-huh. Events are happening fast now, Honus—we're looking at a boilover and if we act too late, we might miss our shot." He thought back to that piece of paper in his hand. The note—the way it was there one minute, gone the next. For a while he wasn't sure it was ever real, but then when he first heard those words, *White Mask* . . . just like the note.

That's when he knew he had to get Atlas Haven up to speed. It had been completed, for the most part, but it would take time to finalize the list, upgrade the tech, and get it open. He had pushed and pushed, spent what he had to spend (which meant a lot of other people's money), and here they were. Grand opening.

Honus turned and stared away from Atlas Haven, toward the flatline horizon. "What comes next? What part do we play now?"

"What part? All parts. All of it. Everything. Nora Hunt, those fucking zombies, everything. Get word to Golden that it's time to pull some triggers." *Literally*, he thought. "Country's on the edge, so we gotta give it a push." Through Hiram Golden, he had connections to a half-dozen well-armed and fully activated militias—ARM, or the American Resurrection Movement, was the top of the pops, but there were the Gadsden Irregulars, the Penn Woods Brotherhood, the Ohio Volunteers, the Blacksnake Patrol out of Tennessee, and so forth. It was time to assemble them all at Innsbrook. But not before they each got their tasks.

They had more work to do before the country was his.

Already, through Proof Logic, Ed had been sowing seeds of distrust in what turned out to be the rich, fertile fields of the collective conspiratorial American mind. They already feared doctors and thought Big Pharma was out to get them—so, it was easy enough to make them doubt that masks or other prophylactic measures worked against White Mask. They were already convinced of both their exceptionalism and the God-given right of their individual liberties, so it was simple enough to tell them that they shouldn't have to give up anything, not *one goddamn little thing*, in order to fight this pandemic. And white Americans were bigoted as hell, too, so all you had to tell them was that the Chinese invented the fungus, that Mexicans were bringing it in, that the Blacks were gonna steal from them when the world went to shit, and that the Jews were bankrolling the whole goddamn thing. It was a brute force attack on information itself, an assault on facts and logic and expertise. That was always the trick, wasn't it? Ed ran a number of companies and you never wanted your employees figuring out you were the one fucking them in the ass while you stuck a hand in their pocket. You gave them an enemy. Gave them a target. And you made them so willing to forgo their own rights because if *they* got something like healthcare or education, then so did *Those People*, and better to deny other people things instead of having to share it with *Them*.

Get them fighting one another instead of you.

Then you took what you want and walked away, whistling.

Here, it took making Americans doubt everyone but themselves. Distrust. Conspiracy. Misinformation, disinformation. With Proof Logic, everything was artisanal data—hand-selected, locally sourced, chosen just for you, each person a bullseye to be hit.

And it was Ed Creel jumping in and telling them they were right. Ed told them they were *special.* They were *exceptional.* Everyone became an expert. Everyone was smarter than everyone else. If they had doubts, that's because they knew something in their gut. Something God was telling them, something they knew as patriots, something they understood because their blood was strong. Don't let anyone tell you different. Don't let anyone take anything from you. Arm yourselves. Get what's yours and once you got it, fight like hell to keep it—fuck the rest of them.

Ever and ever, amen.

Idiots.

All this pushed them to the edge. They could've come together in this time of crisis. (*Like those fuckin' Shepherds,* he thought.) But he didn't want them together. Not all of them. Just his people. The rest could burn.

"I don't know," Honus said.

"You don't need to know. You need to trust."

"I trust, it's just—what you're proposing. It's—there's no turning back."

"We've already turned a hundred corners. World's changed, Honus. Getting brutal out there. Those zombie Sleepwalkers and their Shepherds? They have to go, and Stover will know how to handle that. And Hunt—well. There's not gonna be an election, you know that. If I want the chair, then she has to be kicked *out* of the chair. And this is how that happens. As for the rest of it—" He did a little barrel roll tumble of his index finger, a yadda-yadda gesture, indicating all the other things he wanted done, like quarantine centers bombed and mosques burned and some of Hunt's supporters taken out. It wasn't just an insurrection. It was goddamn *apotheosis.* "Just tell them to get it done."

"I don't know," was all Honus could say. "I don't know."

"You do know. I know you know. I know you know that you're coming into Atlas Haven with your wife, your kids, and grandkids, and you and I *both* know they could wake up on their first morning with some upsetting photos placed on their pillows like fucking hotel mints."

"Ed—you wouldn't."

"C'mon. Honus." He paused. "*C'mon.*"

They both knew he would.

"You're a real sonofabitch," Honus said, his voice trembling.

"Yeah, we both know that, too. So you got your order. Secure your balls, get on the phone with Golden, and communicate our interests."

All that earned from Honus Clines was the barest nod. But it was a nod. That was enough. He'd get it done, Ed was sure of it.

"Oh, one more thing, buddy," Ed said. "I want the desk."

"The desk?"

"The White House desk. The one all the presidents sit at. Made of a ship or something. What's it called?"

Clines swallowed a knot. "The Resolute Desk."

"Uh-huh, that one. When Hunt's gone, I want the desk. Got it?"

Another small nod.

"Good," Ed said. "Go get 'em, tiger."

In a few days, they'd scatter that Flock of terrorist freaks, they'd take out Nora Hunt, they'd peel the old world's fingers off the cliff's edge and let it all fall, all his enemies tumbling down, down, down, so that the citizens of the new world could use the bodies of his foes as a hill to climb up, up, up.

The new world. *His* world.

Ed Creel's America, oh say can you fuckin' see.

PART TWO

HERALDS AND
HERETICS

14

WASTELAND TROUBADOUR

Look away—get lost!
Wander off—no cost!
You think you're leaving town . . .
Run away—no loss!
Quit your life—bye, boss!
But your past will hunt you down . . .
   —"Wicked Worry," Gumdropper, from their album *Ramble Rocks*

SEPTEMBER 3, 2025
Rockville Settlement, Cleveland, Ohio

"LIFT HIM UP, GET THE HOOD OFF HIS HEAD."

Then came the ripple of fabric, and the darkness was gone.

It took a minute for his eyes to adjust. Night had already settled in, but all around were the dancing ghosts of fire. Fire from torches, fire in barrels, fire from cookstoves, all this fire reflected in the limitless windows of the massive glass-and-steel structure above. A mirrored, myriad glow. Like the night sky, the universe, set aflame. Primitive and beautiful, like the spirit of rock-and-roll itself.

His vision swam back from the darkness, past the glow, and now he could see more: the escalators to the second floor, to the third, and up and up, floor after floor, platform after platform. Track lighting looped around, with stage lights that once would've shone brightly with colored gels. A giant guitar hung on the wall, half-broken, paint peeling. Next to that, inexplicably, a giant hot dog? Off in the distance, he spied a monstrous figure, easily twenty, maybe thirty feet high—faded pale blue skin, bug eyes, fingers prying apart the bricks in a white wall. This monster was the Schoolmaster,

from Pink Floyd's *The Wall*, now slumping and decaying. As his eyes adjusted further, he saw the broken windows boarded up, the loops of jagged
wire around balcony railings, the crude ladders and many tents and dozens
of shadows of people watching him—maybe hundreds.

An audience, of sorts, he realized.

For what he feared just *might* be his last show.

His arms were duct-taped behind him, the tape wound around his hands,
his wrists, damn near up to his bony-ass elbows. (Which, he thought, was
quite different from his bony *ass*-elbows. Punctuation mattered, didn't it?
Punctuation, letters, font, all of it—get one bit wrong and suddenly it goes
from *let's eat, Grandma* to *let's eat Grandma*, or thanks to piss-poor kerning,
Glim Dropper turns into *Gumdropper*, oopsie-fucking-doodle.)

Behind him were the two guards who brought him here—the first, a
chunky boy, couldn't have been more than seventeen years old, his face a
parking lot of potholes thanks to cystic acne, his hair a greasy blond mullet.
The other, a middle-aged rail-thin ferret-faced woman with long tangles of
black hair draped over her Aerosmith T-shirt. She had a grip like the Termi-
nator. The kid, on the other hand, had soft hands and a soft grip. Like he was
pinning you between two pillows.

In front of him stood two more people—

A scrappy, short chick, black hair buzzed, a mole under her left eye.
South Asian, maybe Filipina. Machete in her hand, a holstered pistol at her
hip.

She stood to the side and just behind what was obviously the Big Man in
Charge—a broad-shouldered fucker, bald and pink and shiny like a circum-
cised dick, a patchy carpet-sample beard, and he was wearing—

"Wait, what the fuck," Pete Corley said, eyeing him up.

"Huh?" the man asked.

"You're wearing one of the—you know, Christ, one of the Sgt. Pepper
outfits. The Beatles. You're wearing one of them." The blue one, light electric
blue. The real one! "Which one wore that getup?"

The man, bewildered, fingered the autoloader shotgun he held across his
chest. "Which one wore what?"

Pete rolled his eyes. "Which *Beatle*, of the fucking *Beatles*, wore *that*
outfit? The one you've chosen to squeeze your body into, sir."

"How the hell should I know?"

"How the hell should . . ." Pete's voice trailed off. He grunted a little as
he tried to move some blood back into his arms and legs. *"Because, mate,*

you're in the gods-damned Rock and Roll Hall of Fame. A museum. Dedicated to rock-and-bloody-fucking-roll."

The woman, this guy's scrappy majordomo, leaned in and whispered:
"Paul wore it."

"*Thank you*," Pete said, his gratitude genuine. "See, she knows." He eyeballed the outfit. "By the way, what were they going for with those outfits, you
figure? I mean, fuck's sake, it's like . . . equal parts marching-band leader
and gay North Korean general. Puzzling aesthetic choice, but then again,
they were high on copious yard mushrooms and guru fumes at that time."

The bald fucker jackknifed the broad side of his arm into Pete's head.
Rang his bell good. His one ear started going *eeeEEEEeee*, because he had
tinnitus in that ear now. Probably from years of being onstage behind Marshall stacks so tall you could hold off a Mongol siege with them, but instead
he explained it away as, *Well, that's just the Apocalypse for you, innit.*

"Shut up," Sgt. Pepper said. "How'd you get in here?"

"Well," Pete said, wincing. "First, introductions. Enh, you are?"

"What?"

"Your name." *Because I can't keep thinking of you as Sgt. Pepper.*

"Crusher."

"Cru—Crusher? That's not your given name, surely."

"Alan," said the scrappy woman. "His name's Alan."

"Alan," Pete said, the name dripping out of his mouth like the last puke
after a long night of drink and drugs. "I see why Crusher is preferable."

At that, Alan—er, Crusher—jammed the short barrel of the shotgun up
under Pete's stiff chin, lifting it up. The barrel was so wide, Pete feared his
whole head would fall into it. What the hell did this thing fire? Cannonballs?

"Erk," was the sound Pete made.

"I said *shut up*. I want to know how you got in here. We have this place
locked down tight. Nobody in, nobody out, unless I say so. So, how'd you do
it? And what are you here for? Trying to rob us?" Before Pete could get a word
out, Crusher jabbed the shotgun barrel up again *hard*—Pete's teeth clamped
together over his tongue. He tasted fresh blood. *Unnnf.* "Answer me."

"I've . . ." He winced. "I've been casing this place for the better part of
three months. You're more vulnerable than you think, Crusher, my friend. I
originally thought I'd sneak in during a supply run, maybe do a little hidey-
hidey in one of those carts of scavenged shit you bring in, but honestly, I
found a better way. Came in through the vents, John McClane style, if we're
being honest. But!" he said, raising the volume as the barrel dug in harder,

blood now dribbling out the corners of his mouth. "I didn't come to steal anything. The opposite, actually. Something of a *reverse heist.*"

"The hell's that mean?"

"I came to bring things *in.*"

Crusher leaned in, and now Pete smelled his breath—rank, shit-wagon halitosis that would melt faces like the Ark of the Covenant.

"What were you bringing in? And why?"

"Mate, I know you call it—what do you call it? Rockton? Rocktown?"

"*Rockville.*"

"Rockopolis would've been *my* choice, but whatever—point is, it's the Rock and Roll Hall of Fame. The world has ended, if not properly, if not *entirely*, but that at *least* means nobody here is updating it. No more inductees. But rock-and-roll goes on, doesn't it? Rock-and-roll never dies. So, I thought I'd induct a few more proper fuckin' rockers."

The look on Crusher Alan's face was the look of a chimpanzee trying to read a dictionary. Like, it knew *something* was up with all the squigglies and dots on the page but couldn't quite figure out what.

"That's the stupidest fucking thing I've ever heard," Crusher said finally. That, the rage-fed cry of the illiterate chimp. "For that, you gotta learn a lesson."

He lowered the shotgun barrel—

And pressed it against Pete's knee.

"No, no, no—" he said, begging. "Wait, wait, wait. Hold up. We aren't done with our *introductions* yet. I'm Pete Corley."

"Who?"

Pete's heart sank. Because that's where his ego lived, and now his ego was perforated by this buffoon's harpoon of ignorance. Taking on water now.

"Oh, don't do that to me, mate. It's me! Pete Motherfucking Rockgod Corley! Front man for Gumdropper! Tiger-wailing ne'er-do-well! Rrrraoow! Yeah!" He tried to put a little salt and pepper in the voice, but it wasn't working.

Crusher made a face. "Huh. Oh yeah. My dad listened to them."

"Mine, too," said Pimples McMullet behind Pete.

"Hey. Idea! Maybe I do a performance for you all. I brought a guitar—it's out in my RV, which is parked at one of the far loading docks. I fetch my axe, strum a few power chords—it's acoustic, but I can still bring the pain—do a couple tunes. Your people could use that, right? Some happiness in dark, strange times?"

Crusher didn't take long to think about it. "Nah."

His finger curled around the trigger.

"Whoa!" Pete said. He grinned big, sure that his teeth were red and bloody, because his tongue was still leaking. Starting to feel a bit *fat*, actually. He tried to talk around it, even though one's tongue was a vital mechanism *in the very act of talking*, but whatever. He was Pete Corley. He'd make it work. One time he did a show with a lipstick tube full of cocaine up his ass, Viagra coursing through his bloodstream, and a rent boy's pubic hair caught in the back of his throat. *He'd make it fucking work.* "Listen. Listen! This . . . can't be it. You're all living here but it's barely that? This is survival, and that's to be commended, but that can't be all, can it? Day in, day out. You've got the basics, kudos, well done—but the basics aren't enough, not after all this time. Your people don't just want existence. They want . . . *civilization*, they want *culture*, they don't want to steal food or sleep in tents or empty shit buckets out windows. Sure, hanging onto the cliff's edge is better than falling over it, but after a while, what's the point if you don't pull yourselves up? Don't you want a little rock-and-roll in your life?"

They regarded one another for what felt like an eternity. All around, eyes watched—the people of this mad, modern castle staring from their rings of firelight, above and around, waiting to see what would happen next.

"He doesn't," the scrappy majordomo said finally.

"I don't," Crusher said, agreeing.

Then he lifted the shotgun once more—

And put the barrel right against Pete's heart bone.

"He doesn't," the majordomo said, again. "But I do."

She took one step back—

Opportunity, Pete saw.

So, he heaved back and spat blood in Crusher's face.

The woman made her move, too. In one hard swing, she pistoned the base of the machete's handle against Crusher's ear. The fucker juggled his feet to the side, howling—and then as he pivoted toward her, raising the gun, her fist whomped him in the chin, and it was like watching an overloaded coatrack go timber. He dropped straight to the floor. *Fwud.*

Only thing Alan was crushing was his own balls, as he fell on them, Pete decided.

The Rockgod licked blood from his lips and grinned. "Thank you?"

"Cut him loose," she said, gesturing to Pete. "And, Mister Corley, we'd be honored to have your show. The people of Rockville do need something more. They need some rock-and-roll, and you're going to give it to them."

IT WAS WELL PAST TWO in the morning by the time he'd finished, not that time really meant that much anymore. Turned out, when civilization burned down to the wick, time ceased to be measured the same. Day was day and night was night, but it all sort of flowed together like melted crayons.

He'd done five songs initially: "Devil Lover," "Full Steam Ahead," the sad bar-top ballad of "Whiskey & Neon," "The Losers' Club," and one he'd written in the last year or so called "Black Swan." It was a work in progress. They didn't much care for it, so he decided to go out on a high note and do "Hot Dog Woman."

They fucking loved it because of course they fucking loved it. These people were *starved* for music, which was deeply ironic given that these poor dirt-cheeked people were *surrounded* by it—the museum had a considerable collection of archival music material. A lot of it was papers and photos and such, concert bills, letters, private Polaroids, and the like, but they had concert recordings, too, and some rare B-sides on album and digital master. Not that they had any way to listen to it. It was that *Twilight Zone* episode all over again, that poor bastard who just wanted time to read in the End Times, but now his precious glasses were broken.

He of course didn't have a pen or anything to sign autographs, but someone had a can of paint that they'd used to black out windows, so he signed the floor, his signature big and sprawling.

Then he finally did what he came here to do.

MARITA—THAT WAS HER NAME, THE one who clocked Crusher—helped him take it all upstairs to the exhibits. Some of them were still intact. "Crusher didn't see much value in this, but at least he didn't mess with it, either."

"Someone *did* take a shit in the corner," Pete said. Though it had been there awhile, by the desiccated look of it.

"We're trying," Marita said. "Now with Alan done, maybe we'll try harder."

Pete grunted as he moved a duffel bag toward the wall, near a display of gold records behind filthy glass. "You are falling behind a bit. You know. Compared to the rest of the fucked-up-but-not-so-fucked-up-as-you-all world."

"You've been out there," she said, feeling him out.

"Out in the world? Yes. All over the country."

"How are things?"

He told her honestly. "It's a mix. But better than you'd have thought. I think I figured once things fell apart, those who remained would . . . fall apart with it. But they didn't, not really. A lot of communities came together, survived in their way. Sometimes in good ways . . . sometimes in bad. The world's never gonna be like it was. But it's also keepin' on, and that's not nothing."

"Cool," she said.

At that, they got to work. Pete had brought various bits of memorabilia from bands and singers he felt deserved a place in these halls he once considered bullshit but now thought of as vaunted:

- a signed copy of Pat Benatar's memoir, *Between a Heart and a Rock Place*
- a prop of the Satanic "Pick of Destiny" from the Tenacious D movie, which Pete had seen once while on mescaline, and it sucked, but he loved it
- a 1959 New York Jazz Festival program, signed by John Coltrane, Horace Silver, and Betty Carter
- an original Taiwan pressing of Kate Bush's LP *Hounds of Love*, signed
- the original oversized razor-blade prop from the Judas Priest album *British Steel*, signed by band members Rob Halford, Scott Travis, Ian Hill, Richie Faulkner, Andy Sneap (who was not in the band at the time the album was recorded, but who fucking signed that shit anyway)

And finally, the zenith of this rock-and-roll mountain, an acoustic guitar that looked worse than the world around it—a beat-to-fuck Martin N-20, whole thing dinged and dented, a hole worn into the wood where the pickguard would go (not that it ever had one), its body with names inked (and sometimes scratched) into it—autographs of friends and other musicians.

"That's Trigger," Marita said with no small amount of awe. She gazed upon it like she'd just seen someone open up a suitcase full of gold bars, and now she was bathed in their glow. "Willie Nelson's guitar. Isn't it? Is it? It can't be."

He smirked. "It is. You have the eye."

Pete held it up. It felt both brittle and strong—hollow and yet, so full.

"I don't understand. How'd you get that? Wasn't Willie in . . . Hawaii? Maui? But he's gotta be dead by now, shit."

"You really *do* know your stuff." Pete sighed. "Long enough story but suffice to say, every year, Willie would bring this guitar—a guitar he used regularly, despite its, ahhh, *advanced age*, let's say—back to the mainland from Maui, to a fellow called a luthier, in Austin, Texas. There, it'd be tuned, its strings restrung, its wood repaired enough to make it songworthy—but while there this last time, White Mask did its White Mask thing. Willie was not with the guitar when the world went away. But I was able to rescue the guitar, at least, from storage—along with a couple new ones for myself, of course." He waggled his eyebrows and winked.

"But Willie, he's dead. Right?"

He shrugged. "Can't say. He'd be in his early nineties now if he were alive—and most people don't make it that long in a lifetime *without* a world-ending global pandemic. But if anybody can survive, it'd be him." He lowered his voice, almost conspiratorially. "Honestly, one suspects his body is held together by *weed resin* and *guitar strings*. And if he is dead, I hope someone found a way to smoke his ashes. That'd get you higher than the Burj Khalifa, mm?"

"Did you know he was a black belt? Studied a bunch of martial arts."

"I did not. So you were a proper fan."

"Well." She paused. "My father was. So I became one, too. We were military. Traveled around a lot. Spent some years in Texas and Texas is Willie-land—and Texas is *big*, too. Lotta driving, and lotta listening to Willie on the way down this highway or that farm road."

"Favorite song?"

"Clichéd, but 'To All the Girls I've Loved Before.' My dad liked it."

"So you liked it, too," he said.

"Yup."

Together, they placed Trigger in a case all its own, clearing out the gold records that hung there. ("Gold records are bullshit," Pete said, throwing them behind them in a pile. They clattered as they fell—not the sound of metal against metal, but the sound of garbage against garbage. "Disposable. Not even real gold. Just some cheap shit vinyl they spray-paint.")

With the guitar hung, they closed the case.

"This is the end of a journey for me," he said, with a bit of dramatic wistfulness. And less dramatic, but no less wistful, he added: "I wish I'd done more here. Brought more of the *gods* and *goddesses* of rock to these halls. So many that deserve to be here. I mean, Christ on a cowbell—Soundgarden? Eurythmics?" He read the rest in a fast-jabbered litany: Motörhead, Mötley Crüe, Living Colour, Captain Beefheart, Concrete Blonde, Ozzy, Nick Cave, Siouxsie and the Banshees, Sleater-Kinney, on and on he went, near breathless. "So many more."

"And Gumdropper."

"Hnhh. Yeah. Sure. Bet your dad listened to us, too."

"No, he didn't like your music."

"Ah."

"I did."

"Lies and perfidy! How old are you?"

"I'm thirty-one."

"Gods, to be thirty-one again. Young, dumb, and full of—" *Cum.* "Well."

"Why aren't you guys in here?"

"Maybe one day we would've. Evil Elvis—our guitarist—wanted to be. I always pretended it'd be cooler not to be." Pete knew it was a self-defense technique. Pretending you don't wanna fuck someone because you already suspect they don't want to fuck you. "I'm an ego-fed maniac and once upon a time I thought I deserved to be in this place, even at the end of the world. And I planned to be, too. But . . . times changed. My feelings changed. And here we are." He sighed. "Though I'm sure Evil Elvis would be disappointed in me."

Evil Elvis, he thought. He, too, had been part of this journey at the end of the world. *Gods, I've really been some places.* But that was a reminiscence for another time, another place. When he felt okay to do so.

Marita said, "You can stay here, you know. With us. Crusher aside, we're not . . . all bad. And I'm gonna take over now, I think." She screwed up her face in a way that demonstrated both disregard and pity. "People didn't really like Alan."

"Yes, he was a real shit pill, wasn't he?"

She laughed.

"No," he said, sighing. "I don't think I can stay here. This was a destination, but I'm not yet ready to stop moving. More to see, more to do."

"Where to now, Rockgod?"

Popping his knuckles and clucking his tongue, he answered:

"I'm going to go home—or as much of a home as I know. There's a little mountain town in Colorado singing my name. So, I follow the song home."

15

AMONG US

By far, the greatest danger of Artificial Intelligence is that people conclude too early that they understand it.

—Eliezer Yudkowsky

SEPTEMBER 3, 2025
Ouray, Colorado

THE MOUNTAIN TOWN'S SCHOOL, OURAY SCHOOL DISTRICT R-I, WAS ONCE A K–12 school—but, having no students to speak of, the Flock had since converted it into the Workshop, a place where all of their most vital projects were developed. It was here, in the building's gymnasium, that they held weekly town council meetings in and around the mess of in-progress ventures.

This meeting was two days early.

An emergency meeting.

That emergency? Shana Stewart.

Shana didn't usually go to the meetings. In part because, well, they were meetings. (Ew.) But also because there was something about them that made her feel isolated and alone. She wasn't really a Shepherd anymore. She wasn't really one of the original Sleepwalkers, either. The meetings just served that reminder up to her in stark contrast, with everyone gathered. So, most times, she just ditched.

Which was for the best. What could she contribute, anyway? The people assembled here were planning for the future of the town, the country, the world. They had big brains and plans to go with them.

Like Nessie? She wanted to write a new operating system—a low-power piece of software flexible enough to run on whatever they could scavenge, like an old laptop or a PlayStation 3. Nobody was making new computers, so whatever they used would be tech from the Beforetimes, right? Nessie said she could start to build the software on an Arduino or Raspberry Pi, and other folks in town knew what she was talking about, even though Shana thought it sounded like a sports car and a dessert. *Hey, man, gonna take the Arduino out for a spin, maybe pick up some Raspberry Pie. You in?* It only served to prove, yet again, how clearly Shana did not belong. Shana was proud of her little sister.

Her little sister, who now sat on the town council.

Youngest member there.

What had Shana accomplished? Nothing.

Shana looked over at Benji, sitting next to her. He gave a reassuring nod.

"You okay?" he asked.

"Fine," she said, an absolute fucking lie.

He smiled at her. It helped. Benji was safe haven in the storm of her emotions and even now, she wanted to blurt out the truth to him.

But she hadn't told him yet. Not about Black Swan, not about the baby. There wasn't time. By the time she was out of bed trying to find him, Doctor Rahaman was already up in her face, urging her back into bed. Then Xander showed up, too, full of questions. It was then he scheduled the meeting.

I don't want to be here, she screamed inside her own head.

In her belly, the baby kicked.

Like the baby didn't want to be here, either.

Solidarity, kid.

At that, the meeting began.

Presently, up onstage the seven town council members sat:

Xander Percy, fifty-six-year-old physics professor; Jamie-Beth Levine, who at twenty-eight was (or, *had* been) the youngest school superintendent in the country; Willa Valentine, a twenty-six-year-old trans woman activist and charity org founder; R. F. "Ray" Paredes, a forty-two-year-old Chicago restaurateur; Katherine Liên, forty, civil engineer from Ashland, Oregon; Christien Nilson, forty-five-year-old director of library services for the Hennepin County Library in Minnesota; and finally, Shana's little sister, Nessie. Halfway to sixteen years old, as Nessie was fond of reminding people.

Xander, in rare form, got right to the point—a bang of the beat-up wooden gavel in his hand and he said:

"Hello, friends." Xander lent some volume to his voice since they did not have juice to power the school A/V—no microphones, no amps. The electricity they had didn't even power on the interior lights—rather, the room was lit

by the glow of various low-wattage lamps as well as a half-dozen or so portable oil and stabilized kerosene lamps. "Thanks for coming tonight—I want
to begin this meeting by confirming what I know we're all talking about: Our
own Shana Stewart, in saving our sheriff, Marcy Reyes, was in a terrible accident. Or, what would have been a terrible accident, in any other circumstances. But . . ." He looked right at her, and her insides clenched up—*No,
no, not me, c'mon don't do this to me*—even as he waved her up on the stage.
"You can see for yourself that she is unharmed. Unscathed in every way.
Further, Doctor Rahaman confirms for us that her baby—the first to be born
in our special little town—is in perfect health. It's a marvel of science and
our faith in it. C'mon, Shana. Come on up here and say hi."

"No, it's okay, I just—"

Benji, sitting next to her, told her again that it was okay.

So, she stood. Shana didn't go to the stage, instead just turning around
and giving an uncomfortable wave to the gathered townsfolk, like she was
being acknowledged for something not-quite-award-worthy, like getting second place in the regional spelling bee or whatever.

She spied Marcy and Dove sitting together, two rows behind. And all the
way in the back of the auditorium, toward the double exit doors, she saw
someone standing, arms crossed, looking dour and dire: Matthew Bird, the
pastor.

Mia, who sat next to her on the other side, grabbed her hand and gave it
a little squeeze.

"You go, bitch," Mia said to her in a low voice, cheering her on. "Wave!
Like a damn princess. You're a miracle, and they all know it."

I'm no miracle, Shana thought.

She moved to sit back down—her stomach, already feeling rounder and
fuller than it had even yesterday, seemed like *it* sat down first. Inside, the
baby stirred again and karate-punched her bladder. *Oof.*

"Thank you, Shana," Xander said. "We believe this means what we all
hoped that it did—Black Swan is still with us."

A loud murmur rippled across the room—it was not a troubled sound,
but one that was, to Shana's ear at least, done in some combination of curiosity and celebration. She half expected someone to call out, *Praise Black Swan!*
like they were in church. Nobody did, but they were clearly pretty pleased
about the news. Which again forced her to ask the question: Who here knew
what? Who among the Sleepwalkers had all the information that she had?
Did any of them know all of it? Were any of them kept entirely in the dark?

Did any of them know *more* than she did?

That worry was like wind pulling sand from a beach. It wore her down.

Xander, smiling, laughing a little, said, "Okay, okay. It is big news, I know. I know!" More laughing. He was really happy. But some of it felt false, too—maybe Shana was being paranoid, but he gave off the vibe of a self-help guru, or someone giving an overly practiced TED Talk. He continued: "Here's what else we believe: Black Swan must exist inside Shana Stewart, though why that is, we don't know for certain. It is possible, even likely, that Black Swan recognizes the importance—symbolic and literal—of the first child to be born of our Flock and our town. But, this isn't like the simulation. We can't just walk up to the mountain and ask, can we? What we do have, however, is Shana. Shana, care to come up here?"

No. Noooooo.

But again Mia was egging her on, giving her a little elbow nudge.

Benji said to her, "You got this, just tell the truth."

The truth.

Could she even dare?

Shana stood up, feeling that vertigo feeling like she was tiptoeing along the edge of a cliff, like those Instagram idiots who would stand at a mountain's edge to snap selfies. Every time she saw one of those photos it took her breath away, and not in a good way. Of course, all those Instagram idiots were dead now, weren't they? Maybe they understood something she didn't: Life was short, the world was ending, so you might as well dance on the cliff.

Her heart raced. She didn't want to go up there. She didn't want to be the center of attention. She didn't want *any* of this. Instead she wanted to hide. Maybe barf. Definitely cry a little? In a perfect world there'd be ice cream. But there was no ice cream at the end of the world—only in its simulation.

Then she thought of her friend.

Pete Corley.

(Motherfucking Rockgod, self-proclaimed.)

What would he do? He'd get up there. He'd scream and shimmy. He'd strut like a bird, squawk like a bird, then flip everyone the motherfucking bird. He didn't care. That was his secret, she realized: Pete didn't give one hot fuck. He'd emptied all the fucks out of his fuck basket.

(God, she missed him suddenly. His chaos energy was much needed.)

Be like Pete, she decided. "For Pete," she said in a small voice.

Shana walked up onstage. Nessie stood suddenly, smiling at her with both mouth and eyes—a desperate plea, Shana felt—and pulled a chair from behind a dusty, rumpled blue curtain, and put it up to the table where the council sat.

Shana sat in the proffered chair.

They stared. Everyone on the council. Everyone in the auditorium.

They all fucking stared.

For a moment, everything was quiet, everything but the prodigious hum from the solar-powered generator outside—an endless thrum like having your head inside a wasp's nest.

"Shana," Xander said, smiling at her in a way that was both consultive and disarming. "Thank you for sitting with us and answering some questions."

"Of course," she said in her normal voice. Maybe a little quieter than normal. Too quiet? Probably. She cleared her throat and said it again: "Of course, Mister, uhhh, Xander. Professor. Percy."

"Just Xander is fine. You know the others here?" He chuckled. "Aside from your little sister, I mean."

Nessie smiled at her again and gave a little wave.

Yes, Nessie, I see you, jeez.

"Yeah, mostly," Shana said. "Maybe not like, closely."

She suddenly felt warm. Almost feverish. *I'm sick. The baby is here. It's White Mask.* Absurd thoughts raced through her head like panicked cats.

But then a colder, stranger thought tickled her brainstem:

I'm on trial.

She wasn't. She knew she wasn't. But that feeling persisted.

It was Willa who spoke first: "Shana, hi." Willa, with her straight hair, and crisp posture, and somehow, a smokey eyeshadow.

"Hi."

"Can you confirm for us that you really are unharmed?"

"Physically, yeah. I mean, I have acid reflux that could eat through a steel door, but that's this one's fault." She patted her tummy.

There existed a special feeling when one made an audience laugh, intentionally or not—and Shana just experienced that feeling. (It was, for the record, like the opposite of acid reflux: a cool, almost effervescent thrill.)

"And psychologically?" Willa asked as a follow-up. "Getting hit by a truck must've been traumatic."

"I guess. I don't really remember it." She thought, but did not vocalize, *Black Swan protected me from that trauma.*

"And the baby?" Jamie-Beth, with her crown of braids and her little pink sweater, asked. Her voice was bubbly, like that of an elementary school teacher.

"Also good, according to my doctor." The doctor had looked her over both before she woke up and after—and Shana had checked out okay. Better than okay, even—Rahaman beamed and said, *You're as healthy as a meadow mare.* Whatever the hell that meant. She looked to the audience for her (admittedly annoying) doctor—but the ob-gyn wasn't anywhere to be found. "I'm sure she'd say as much . . . if she were here."

Xander offered: "She had to attend to some things, but she did confirm that with us, yes. A clean bill of health."

A lot of nodding and *hmm*-ing followed that.

Ray Paredes leaned forward and looked down the length of table at her. Everything about him had a darkness to it—not a sinister darkness, exactly, but it was just, he had dark eyes, black hair, a beard that looked like it was chipped from volcanic glass instead of, well, just facial hair. It was, if Shana was being honest with herself, sexy as hell. Like he was a romantic vampire protagonist. She suddenly wanted to climb him like a ladder, which was an unexpected desire. (Pregnancy did weird, weird things to her hormones, she knew, and this was that: periodic moments of intense wanting-to-bang-random-people. Was this what being a guy was like all the time? Probably.)

"Shana, hey. So, Black Swan—did you know it was still in you?"

"I—wasn't sure."

It was the first lie. A half-lie. No, a half-truth, she decided—a half-truth wasn't a lie, was it? A half a milkshake wasn't the opposite of a milkshake, and so therefore, a half a truth wasn't the opposite of truth.

(*God, I really want ice cream,* she thought.)

(*I'd kill a man for ice cream,* she further thought.)

(*This isn't at all on topic,* was her final thought on the matter.)

"What does that mean, you weren't sure?" Ray persisted.

Again, the feeling of being on trial made her dizzy. She looked to Benji, whose brow was furrowed watching. It suddenly occurred to her that it was him, and Mia, and the other Shepherds who she didn't want to disappoint. Not the townsfolk. But her friends.

"I just mean—I didn't know for sure. I didn't know if I was going crazy or . . . I . . ."

The words died in her mouth. She felt paralyzed by the inquiry.

Next to Ray Paredes was his opposite: Christien Nilson, who was so white he was the white of bone, the top of his head offering a dancing wave of hair that was sandy and going gray—like a flame, tamed by ice and frozen in time and space. If Ray was a vampire protagonist, Christien was a too-pure angel. He adjusted the little gold-rim eyeglasses and leaned forward, staring intensely.

"Do you visit the simulation still?" he asked, his voice soft and gentle—though assertive, too, in its way. Or maybe *insistent* was the word. "Or, can you?"

"I—" Shana started to say, because she didn't know how to answer.

"I have a better question," started Katherine Liên, who wore the chaotic mantle of an artist or art teacher, even though she was an engineer. She had an accent, maybe Vietnamese, Shana wasn't sure. Everything about her was bold colors or stark blacks—big eyeglasses the color of a blue Muppet, a scarf like prismatic light, earrings that were large malachite spirals turning in on themselves. It was like she was drawn into the world with bold permanent marker. "Do you commune with it? Do you speak to Black Swan, Shana? Has it spoken to you?"

"I—"

Again, she didn't know how to answer.

If she admitted now that she spoke to Black Swan, and had been speaking to the entity all along, then what? How would they all look at her?

What would Benji think of her?

Shit!

"Shana?" Katherine asked again, her fingers forming spiders on the table in front of her. The woman leaned forward, almost annoyed. As if to say, *Well?*

"I have an even better question," came a loud voice from the back of the auditorium. All eyes turned to meet Matthew Bird, her inadvertent rescuer.

Xander squinted. "Pastor Bird? Is that you back there? We are going to open the floor to questions in a few minutes—"

"What I want to know," Matthew said, continuing on, "is what does Black Swan want with you, Shana? What does it want with your baby?" He spread his arms wide. "What does it want with this *town?*"

"Pastor Bird," Xander said. "Matthew. I assure you, this isn't the time—"

"I have to go," Shana said suddenly, and stood up so fast the chair behind her banged against the wood of the auditorium stage. She pedaled her feet fast, carrying her to the edge of the stage and down the steps. Benji was already there to meet her, asking her if she was all right, but she pushed past him and headed out the double exit doors into the advancing night. Bleating out an ugly, ragged cry, she walked, and walked, and kept on walking until she was happily, willfully lost.

16

WHAT WAITS AT THE EDGES

9/1/2021: Dayton's on fire. Can see it from here. Big swaths of it, too, patchy, like in different places. Not one big fire but several. It's surreal because there's no way now to know how or why. No one on the radio, no internet to check, no sirens, not a thing. Graham thinks it's part of the war between two groups—militias, I guess, like those monsters at Innsbrook. The Ohio Defenders are fighting with some other group called the Vow? Now that there's no government, these anti-government groups don't know who to fight. Graham said they might be fighting over who they think gets to rule. Rule what? I asked. The graveyard that is America? But Graham said it would come back. Eventually. Slowly. That the country wasn't dead. He believes it, too. I just don't know if I believe him, but it's nice to think about. We all have to have our fantasies, I guess.

—from A Bird's Story, A Journal of the Lost

SEPTEMBER 4, 2025
Ouray, Colorado

THE NEXT MORNING, MARCY FOUND ERNIE NOVARRO SITTING UP IN HIS BED at the clinic, sipping some chicken broth. Late morning light came through the blinds, illuminating a stack of old mass market paperback books next to the bed. Mystery, thriller, romance, a pile of them that Ernie had already gone through.

The clinic served as home base for Ouray's five medical doctors: Rahaman, Chen, Reinhold, Gray, and Abboud. (Respectively, they were ob-gyn, cardiology, osteopathic, orthopedics, and general surgery with a specialization in trauma.) It hadn't been particularly busy here—the townsfolk of Ouray were by and large healthy, and so most clinic visits were about minor abrasions and allergies. Ernie's injuries, however, were of a considerably higher caliber, and so it was Reinhold—a tall, Ichabod Craney type, like a scarecrow struck by lightning and given life—who had been attending to the man, making sure those injuries were healing and no infections were setting in. Reinhold had just left, leaving Ernie with Marcy.

"How many chickens you got now?" he asked Marcy, who sat by the bed.

"Too many to count, Ernie. Chickens breed like rabbits."

"Maybe I can take a few back north with me, when I'm back on my feet?"

She laughed a little. "Yeah, absolutely. I think you should be good in a few days. Your truck, on the other hand . . ."

"My truck," he said, with genuine woe. He moaned—less in physical pain, more in emotional misery.

"It was a special truck."

"Special? I called her Ximena, after my *abuela*. Truck was tough like her. Took no shit. She's my lifeline, that truck. Not a lot of people out there with original propane engines or retrofits."

She took his hand in hers. Ernie was a little guy. Her hand eclipsed his, the sun swallowing the moon. "This town has some of the best and brightest, Ernesto. Engineers out the wazoo. I'm sure someone will get it working again, all right? Meanwhile, we got a horse for you to loan out, ride back north. We can have someone accompany you if you want, ride with you to make sure you're safe—"

He shook his head, and drank back the broth. "I'll be okay. I'm still here a few more days, anyway. I'm sure those *comemierda* are long gone."

"Speaking of that, I wanted to ask you. The guys who attacked you—"

"Like I told you, real Nazi bastards, you know? All the swastikas and sword tattoos and stuff."

"Just three of them?"

"Yeah, just the three."

"Were they part of a bigger group, you think?"

He grunted in pain as he set the bowl down on the table next to the janky hospital bed. "I dunno, Sheriff. Wasn't a big group, and I'd think if they were organized, they'd all come at you in one go. But then again, we keep seeing them outside town, and it's never the same bastards twice."

Marcy didn't know what that meant. Could've meant they were scattered, ragtag thugs and fascists just trying to survive, and the only way they knew how was to be thieving shitheels. Or? Could've meant they were a unified force, a militia like Stover's—though probably much smaller now, given

White Mask—and that the reason they were all separate was they were split-ting up to accomplish different goals. No reason to send thirty men to do the job of three. Even if they *were* scattered, unorganized—nothing said they wouldn't find one another soon enough. It was like plastic in the ocean. Eventually all that garbage floated together, formed a big nasty mess.

"I got one, you know," he said. "One of them stuck me with a knife but I stopped him before it went deep. I grabbed his wrist and made him stick it in his buddy. That's when they ran."

"Can you tell me where they came up on you?"

He nodded. "I can mark it on the map."

"I got the map up here," she said, tapping her head.

"I like you, Sheriff Marcy. You respect this land." He sniffed and sat up. "You know, about three, four miles north of here, there's that little gulch—Crooked Tree? And then just north of that is that tiny cemetery."

"Cedar Hill."

"That's it. Between the gulch and the cemetery, there's a little tree farm, just Colorado blue spruces. They came out of there, I think. Out of the trees."

"Thanks," she said. "And again, I promise, we'll get your truck running."

"You going after them? The bastards who did this to me?"

"Just gonna go have a look is all."

"Be careful, Sheriff. Men like that, they're snakes. Not even snakes. Snakes don't deserve that comparison. They're lower, smaller, nastier. Little *escorpiones*."

"I will, Ernie. I will."

She turned to leave, and as she put her hand on the doorknob, Ernie spoke up again, calling after her. He said, "This is a nice town, Sheriff."

"Oh. Yeah. I think it is."

"It's different."

"Is it?" she asked and felt bad because in that question lurked the ghost of a lie. She knew it was different. *Special*. The town of the Sleepwalkers, of the glow, of her walking, wandering angels.

"The gates still closed? I mean, for people looking to move here."

"Oh. Yeah. Jeez. I'm afraid so." She turned and offered him a sheepish grin. "We're already straining at the seams."

"Yeah. You said." He paused, sizing her up. "But how is that exactly?"

Her gut soured. "Oh. Ernie. C'mon. You know the story."

At least, he knew the story they fed to people. Anybody they met got the same tale: Ouray was a collective of survivors from across the country, from all walks of life—the best and the brightest settling here, in a town believed to be the best place to weather the Apocalypse. There were other details meant to fill the gaps—Marcy and Benji, after all, had lived here for damn near five years while the Sleepwalkers remained torpid. The town was empty and dead, until one day . . . it wasn't. It was a collective of people who came here as one. Settlers, in a way.

"I do, I do. But other people, they tell stories about this place. Up in Ridgway, Grand Junction, even Telluride where the rich folk lived."

"Stories?" She showed a stiff smile. "What kind of stories?"

"Like, maybe you're a group of hippies, or anarchists, or antifa—"

"I don't think antifa is a thing, Ernie—"

"Or maybe you're a cult. They think that, too. A cult of what, I don't know, I guess they think you're religious or like, some kind of science cult—or what's it called, Scientology. Jonestown, maybe. I've heard that, too. That this is just another Jonestown. You're too young for that, I guess, but I was a little kid when it happened, maybe ten or twelve."

"A cult." She forced a laugh. "Jonestown. Ernie, be real."

"I don't think that. I said you were a nice town and I mean it."

"Thank you. We are. We really are."

He chewed his lip as he seemed to ponder if he should say this next bit. Finally, he came out with it. "I remember a little bit."

"About Jonestown?"

"The accident."

"The accident," she repeated.

"Uh-huh. I remember looking up. Hearing gunshots. I couldn't move my arms, everything felt weak and . . . dizzy. I was headed right for you. And then—this girl. I remember this girl. I felt the truck hit her."

"Just a strange memory, I'm sure—"

"I thought it was, I thought, shit, it had to be. That had to be wrong. But the first night they put me in here, I was in and out, and I remember her being here, too. In the clinic. They had her in the next room. Checking her out. Talking about how the truck hit her but she was fine, just fine, like—*all the way* fine. I heard them talking about how it was impossible but also not impossible. They were surprised but not *that* surprised. And that got me thinking—"

"Ernie, don't."

"Got me thinking about those Sleepwalkers. Remember them? Walking across the country, one by one, and we thought, wow, shit, this is really something, huh. Watching the TV every day to see where they were going, what route they were taking, how many of them they picked up over the course of the day. Seeing the men in those, what do they call them, the hazmat suits. Seeing that dustup in Indiana. The storm. The walkers walking through it like it was nothing to them. And then—well, the pandemic came along. White Mask became our everything. We didn't have much more attention for those Sleepwalkers, and as things fell apart, as the president was killed, as our TV channels went dark one by one, we stopped thinking about the Sleep-walkers and just . . . waited to die. But some of us didn't die. Some of us didn't get it at all, or I guess, we did, but it didn't affect us. Some people got it but survived it, like their immune systems were able to catch up where most weren't. But sometimes I wonder, where'd they go? Those Sleepwalkers. They walked across the country, didn't they? East to west. Then where? I lost that thread. But I wonder sometimes where that thread ended."

Marcy stiffened. "Ernie, you're not suggesting—"

"Not suggesting anything, Sheriff. Like I said, this is a nice town. I like it here. And I got a life at the orchard I don't want to change anyway. But I think it's worth mentioning that I'm nobody special. I figure I got an okay head on my shoulders—not a brain surgeon or anything. So if I'm wondering about this, you can bet somebody else is, too." He nodded. "Just be careful."

"Thanks, Ernie." She took it that way—as an act of kindness from him. A warning, not a threat. Even still, she shivered. "You heal up, okay?"

"Okay, Sheriff. Okay."

"I WANT TO GO WITH you."

Marcy, coming out of the clinic room where Ernie was convalescing, nearly ran bodily into Pastor Matthew, who stood there and said again, to her surprise, "I want to go with you, Marcy."

"Matt. Hey. Uhh." She looked over her shoulder and closed the door to Ernie's room. Already she felt unsettled from her conversation with Novarro, and now the pastor was popping out of nowhere like a rake you just stepped on. "I don't think that's a great idea."

"You can't go out there alone."

"I was gonna take Dove, but—"

"He's feeling a little under the weather, I talked to him this morning."

"Right. Yeah." She was trying to figure how to say this delicately. "Just the same, I'll be fine. I'm not gonna go poking a stick into any yellowjacket holes. Figuratively or literally. I'm only planning to take a horse out, have a look."

"I could use the fresh air," he said, trying to be chummy.

She whistled. "Then I've got good news for you—out there, there's a whole mountain town of it."

"No, I mean—I could use to get away. Just for a bit."

Marcy sighed. Last night, Matt's question to the town council set everyone off, and then Shana stormed out and—well. Benji went looking for Shana and eventually found her passed out in the lobby of the Beaumont. (Someone had put a quilt over her and let her sleep.) But Matthew stayed at the meeting, kept asking questions. Like he wasn't satisfied with any answer they gave him.

People around here didn't much like the pastor. Not all of them, of course—the townsfolk weren't a monolith. But there were varying levels of distrust, because of his role in stirring people up against the Flock, what with him being on the radio and spewing all that religious hate. She knew he'd had his mind twisted, and worse, was held captive and made to say some of the worst bits. And at the end of the day, she liked him. Thought he had a good heart, if maybe not the best *head* on his shoulders. These days he seemed sad. Injured, in a way. Not just physically, but down deep. A cut from an invisible knife. They'd all been wounded in a variety of ways, but she feared that for him, such a river of pain carved a deeper canyon.

Lately she'd watched that sadness turn to something else—distrust.

And soon, if not now, anger.

Maybe he *did* need the time away from town, and if she could give him that respite, she should.

"Okay," she said. "Don't make me regret this."

"I won't," he promised.

17

THE FIREPOWER OF A FULLY ARMED AND OPERATIONAL EGG SANDWICH

There are a lot of things in life you can't control, but the food you cook is one of the few things you can, and this gives you a real sense of power over a huge aspect of your life.
— Joshua Weissman, *An Unapologetic Cookbook*

SEPTEMBER 4, 2025
Ouray, Colorado

WHEN SHE SAW BENJI COMING, SHANA PULLED THE QUILT OVER HER HEAD and hid underneath it. "I don't want to talk right now," Shana moaned beneath her yarny cowl. "I'm tired and weird and—" She paused. "Sorry. Yeah."

But Benji was persistent, and had in his possession a *secret weapon*. This secret weapon was in a brown paper bag rolled at the top. The bottom of this bag was stained with just a little bit of grease.

"I want to tell you about this egg sandwich," he said.

The quilt pile stirred, and the edge lifted up just enough to allow a little gap revealing the corner of her mouth and one eye. That eye regarded him with wariness, yes, but also curiosity.

"Go on," she said, her voice still mealy and tacky from sleep.

"A lot goes into an egg sandwich, I think you'll admit."

"Explain."

"It seems simple, an egg sandwich. An egg between two slices of some kind of bread—in this case, an English muffin. That seems almost painfully basic, but consider all of the elements that must go into it. A chicken, of which you'll admit we have a lot, has to lay an egg. That egg must meet heat and some kind of fat—we don't have the cattle farm up and running yet, and the sunflower harvest isn't enough to get enough oil there, but chicken fat, called schmaltz, works. Then comes the question of the muffin. No more instant yeast, so, wild yeast it is—Ray and his sous chef, Carla, have from very early on been cultivating a sourdough starter. But, even then, you need flour—"

"This is a *super cool* lecture, Dad, but suddenly my baby is threatening to kill me if I don't feed it that sandwich. Now. And by kill me, I mean kill you. And I'm sorry for threatening violence, it's the baby, not me. I am blameless in all of this, so just give me the sandwich to appease this violent infant."

He laughed and handed over the bag.

"Eat up, and then will you take a walk with me?"

The bag disappeared under the quilt, as if vacuumed up. There came a rustling of paper followed by the sounds of happy eating.

"We can walk," Shana said around a mouthful of food.

THE WALK WAS LONGER THAN expected. After Shana had finished, they set out of the Beaumont, and headed south on 4th Street past some of the houses occupied by those of the Flock. At the bend onto 2nd Avenue they passed a gravel lot of old, junk-bucket cars—a Jeep Cherokee, a Toyota sedan of some kind, a Chevy Blazer, all pitted with leprotic patches of rust and succumbing to a wild tangle of grass. Benji half-imagined these grassy patches pushing the cars up into the sky, Jack-and-the-Beanstalk style. An absurd, almost childish thought—unscientific, and he was not often given over to such whimsy. But lately he'd found his mind wandering like that more and more, and he wondered if it was because he'd found his imagination.

Or worse, if he'd simply lost his purpose.

At 2nd Avenue, the road grew steeper and Shana said, *oof*ing, "I kinda thought maybe you'd go easier on the pregnant chick, Doc."

"Oh, it's all right, Shana. Exercise is good for you and the baby," he said, regarding her carefully. It was hard to ignore now that her pregnancy had advanced more quickly than seemed natural. And having been hit by the truck and emerging from that without a scratch? She had Black Swan in her. Swarming. Teeming. It protected her, and that blew him away. He'd assumed it was gone, that it had, as described, got them here and then was done with them. But it had never really left. He wanted to be excited by that, but it troubled him. It had lied. Was Shana lying, too? He didn't know. He wanted to ask, to sit her down and get answers, but that wasn't the way. She was fragile. And in many ways . . . he almost didn't want to know. So for now, he kept guarded and added: "Promotes healthy blood flow."

"Says the man with no baby doing cartwheels in his uterus."

"A fair point. We can stop, turn around—"

"No, no, I paid the egg sandwich price. Let's do this."

So do this, they did. Up around another bend, where the road became 5th Street—past houses, some occupied, some not. The ones that were occupied were easy enough to identify: They looked cleaned up, refreshed, *alive*. Others were beginning to fall apart, had moldering piles of firewood outside, or tree branches across damaged rooftops, or second-floor decks starting to sag and collapse. At first, Benji thought that an empty house was like a dead body: The soul had gone out of it, dead-eye windows staring back. But then they passed a cottage with a corroded, crumbling hot tub out front—and a raccoon popped its head out, little mammalian fingers gripping the edge as it watched them balefully, regarding them as the trespassers they were. *Empty of humans doesn't always mean empty of life*, he reminded himself.

He watched Shana wave at the raccoon. The raccoon did not wave back.

They kept on.

This street then emptied out onto the Million Dollar Highway, the switchback road that headed south toward Silverton, about twenty miles. But they only did one of the zigs in the zigzagging highway before they were off again, this time onto an overgrown gravel path: Amphitheater Campground Road.

This went pretty far, up the side of the mountain to an area called the Amphitheater Campground, which was itself in the shadow of the Amphitheater formation: a gently curving wall said to be formed long ago by a volcanic explosion. The road ahead had long been washed out—the wire cages that held rocks in had broken over the years, and now the road ahead was covered with dry mudslide, broken branches, and those rock piles.

But Benji did not intend for them to go that far.

Just in front of them was a wooden bridge, twelve feet in length, that overlooked a massive cleft in the earth—a rocky gorge smaller than the one on the west side of town, the Uncompahgre. At its bottom was Portland Creek, which at present had dwindled to a gentle trickle. But what was precious—Benji would dare say *priceless*—about this bridge was the view it afforded.

"Stand here, and behold," he said.

She did as suggested.

He did not regard the view himself—which was magnificent, a straight-shot look down the tree-lined gorge, into the valley where you could see both the small Colorado town below and the two massive mountains that seemed to stand guard over it on each side. Rather, Benji watched *her* instead of the vista. He watched her face soften, her eyes go wide, her mouth open just a little—as if she wanted to say something but couldn't really find the words. Because, he knew, there were no words in their guttural human language that could best express the feeling she was feeling. Or, at least, the feeling that *he* felt when he looked down there. It was, what? A feeling of smallness and grandeur in equal measure? A vibe that there was something greater than you, but also that you yourself were the greater thing? There came with it a connection to the town, to the mountains, the world beyond.

"Wow," was what she said.

And that, he figured, was the right thing to say.

"It's awesome in the truest sense of that word," he said.

But then her face fell—like ripe, red fruit dropping off a tree, leaving the branch bare and dull. "In a better world I'd have a camera. The right lens for landscapes, something wide-angle, 16-35mm, would . . . it'd be something special. I thought about learning to paint instead but I'm not sure I feel like going out into the world and scavenging painting supplies. But a camera . . ."

Her voice trailed off.

She seemed a million miles away, suddenly. Staring out at the town.

So, Benji reached into his side bag and pulled out something. He tried a bit of flourish, a magician's panache, as he turned it toward her, revealing:

A camera.

Non-digital, 35mm, Pentax. Black, a little dinged up, with a brown leather strap coiled around it.

Shana seemed almost startled by it. Like it couldn't be real.

"Benji, I—wow." Again, that word. *Wow.* A good word. Like a wobbling, reverberating mantra in sync with the heartbeat of the universe. *Wow, wow, wow.* Benji again chided himself for being foolish and maudlin, but he decided to go with it. This was a nice moment. *Let it happen, you stuck-up ass.*

"Thank you," she said finally.

"My pleasure."

"Does it—"

"Work? It should. It's mechanical, so doesn't need batteries. Manual-wind, manual-focus. Though batteries will grant you the light metering."

"It has film?" He nodded. But then she said, "Doesn't film like, expire?"

"It does. But we found a cache of unopened, undeveloped film in one of the old Victorian houses on the east side of town—it wasn't kept refrigerated, but it *was* in a basement, which remained cold. And winters here are brutal, as you'll, well, learn. So I expect the film's got more longevity than you expect. Besides, even after expiration, film continues to be film—maybe not for a professional shoot, but these days, there aren't any professional photoshoots anymore."

Another crestfallen look. "Right, but there aren't any film development labs anymore, either. I can't just like, take the roll down to Walmart to have some pimply chode develop it for me. I don't even know if they were still doing that *before* White Mask happened. So. Shit."

"Can I continue to regale you about the egg sandwich?"

"Weird shift, but ooookay."

"It'll make sense, I promise. Where was I?"

"Honestly, I faded out. I think something about *yeast*." She made a face. "That's a gross word. *Yeast. Moist yeast.* Ugh."

He snapped his fingers. "Sourdough starter. So, Ray and Carla have been cultivating a wild starter for months now. A bubbly mess, smells like sour feet and sharp cheese, but also, a little bit like bread. Of course, even to *feed* it meant having flour, and old flour won't do, so that meant needing new flour. Which meant *making* new flour, milling it. There's a mill in Ridgway, but that's a far trip—so Ray decided to mill with a hand-cranked coffee grinder. A burr grinder."

"Sure, but," she started, seeming to be finally invested, "where'd he get flour to mill? Or I guess whatever it is you mill into flour? You don't toast toast, you toast bread, so what turns into flour? Wheat, I get, but like—okay, I know nothing about wheat or its production. High school did not cover this."

"Wheat berries are what one mills into wheat flour."

"Wheat berries?" She made a face. "I feel like you're making that up, but cool. Where does one get *wheat berries* in our post-apocalypse?"

"Wheat berries last a lot longer in storage, if kept dry, but we didn't have that, either. So Ray, through our friend Ernie Novarro, discovered that there was a wheat farm up in Fruita—growing wild einkorn wheat. Only problem being, nobody had run that farm for years. The wheat, however, was still growing, and in fact had grown past its own field, so—there was the source of the wheat berries."

"Wheat he milled into flour which went into a sourdough starter which went into making an egg sandwich—"

"Don't forget the salt, which he got by drying out water from the mineral hot springs—"

"—which went into my belly and now I want another, so thanks for that, Benji, because now I don't have an egg sandwich *or* a way to develop film."

He laughed.

She looked at him like he was a real asshole for laughing.

"Shana, that's what I'm trying to tell you. There's always a way. If we can, out of nothing, make a sandwich as good as the one you had earlier, there's a way to do just about anything." He thought back to his conversation with Dove. "One day we'll have coffee and chocolate again, one day we'll have trains, perhaps, and boats, and—" *And cancer treatments? Damnit, Dove.* "Well. I don't know if it will all come back, but some of it will. And as for photography . . ." He took her hand and held it. "There's a darkroom in the school, Shana. I've cleaned it out, set it up, even made new developer chemicals for you, which I learned is something you can also do. I won't bore you with those details right now as I fear you leaping off the bridge into the gorge if you had to endure another lecture from m—"

The girl threw her arms around him. It was a hug on par with the chest-cavity-crushers delivered by Marcy. Didn't help that her pregnant stomach was like a basketball to the gut. He grunted, laughing a little as he returned the embrace. "You are the *best*." She finally ended the hug and said, "You know, I thought you brought me up here to . . . talk about last night. About Black Swan."

"This is a little about last night in that . . ." He tried to figure out how best to frame his thoughts. "I think you and I are two people without purpose."

"Gee, thanks," she said, though she was clearly (and thankfully) faking offense. "That's me, purposeless broodmare for the nanoswarm!"

"That's the thing, though, isn't it? I once led a team at the CDC, and then at the start of the Flock phenomenon I joined in that capacity and soon, like you, I was a Shepherd. We had that. And then you *became* part of the Flock and we settled here—for the long five years I was a, an, I don't know, a curator of this place, a guardian, like a mother bird making the best nest. But now the Flock is awake, and active, and . . . well, I can't speak for you, but I feel like a vestigial organ, a limb or tail that no longer has the function it once had."

"Yeah, I feel like—I feel like I don't know what I'm even doing here. I'm not smart like the rest of them. Like Nessie. I'm just . . ." Her hands went to her belly as her words lost air, sputtering out. "Ennnh."

"That is exactly the feeling. *Enh*. And so, I wanted you to have this camera. That opportunity to be yourself. To have purpose. Purpose not defined by anybody else, only by yourself." He paused and touched her shoulder. "And by the way, you *are* smart like the rest of them, Shana. You're sharp as a needle. And we need art, we need you and that camera, we need . . . you."

"So, what's your purpose, then? Besides, y'know—" She swept her arms across the grand vista. "Showing me this. And lecturing me about egg sandwiches and weird yeasts and unicorn wheat berries—"

"Einkorn."

"If you say so."

"I think I'm going to be mayor."

"Mayor? Of—of Ouray?"

He shrugged. "Of Ouray, yes."

"Isn't . . . isn't Dove the mayor?"

"Dove asked me to succeed him in that role, it seems." He neglected to tell her why. That was for Dove to share, not him. "And I'm inclined to say yes."

Shana faux-slugged him in the arm. "I kiiiiinda think that's election fraud and I didn't know that you wanted to be a small-town dictator, congrats."

"Well, no, I—"

She winked. "Relax, I'm just yanking your vestigial tail."

"Oh. Yeah. I see. I get it, I get it. I will only do it with the town's blessing, and if they want to run a proper election, I'll gladly participate. I don't want to damage democracy, just . . . allow for a constancy of administration."

"And you need that purpose you were talking about."

"Yes, I need purpose. Not like there's a CDC anymore. Or the need for me to go digging around bat caves and pig farms."

"But who will save us from the pig-bats?"

"Somebody else, I'm afraid."

"Mayor Benji Ray. Has a nice ring to it. It's like, an upgraded version of Shepherd. A Shepherd in an official capacity. Plus, I know the guy, so maybe he can cancel my parking tickets."

"Shall we walk on back?"

"Do you want to talk about Black Swan first?"

"Do you? Are you ready for that?"

She hesitated. He'd heard from Marcy that she wanted to talk to him. *Needed* to talk to him. But whatever it was, that urgency had fizzled.

Shana wasn't ready. He could see it on her face.

"I don't really want to spoil this moment," she said guardedly.

"Then we can wait."

"Thanks, Benji."

The two of them stood for a little while longer. But then it was like she woke up out of a trance. Shana turned back toward the vista, giving the camera a windup. She pulled the camera to her eye, and Benji noted privately the camera looked like a part of her—like a limb lost had been reattached. Vestigial, no more.

Click.

18

A PAIR OF PALE HORSES

The mind is its own place, and in it self
Can make a Heav'n of Hell, a Hell of Heav'n.
— John Milton, *Paradise Lost*

SEPTEMBER 4, 2025
Ouray, Colorado

MIDDAY. SUN SITTING HIGH IN THE SKY ON A MOUNTAIN OF CLOUDS. TWO horses clompity-clomped up Highway 550, north of Ouray. The first horse was a big beast, a copper Belgian with a bottle-blond mane, name of Doppelbock—that was Marcy's horse, because she needed a meaty creature to support her massive frame and the oversized thirty-pound, seventeen-inch saddle. The other was Judy, an older paint. Her mane hung over tired eyes and it was hard to imagine she could see a damn thing, but onward she went, a slow meander. Matthew did not look comfortable upon her.

"Told you to practice your riding," Marcy chided him.

He winced, holding on to the saddle horn and pommel like he was a pilot clutching the flight stick of a plane plunging toward the earth. "I'm fine."

On their left, they could hear more than see the Uncompahgre, its waters murmuring an ever-present prayer. Up ahead was the turnoff to Red Stone Road, just dirt and rock, long disused and grown over. Marcy was pleased with herself that she was starting to feel where everything around here was. Not just like looking on a map but really, truly *feeling* it—she'd never been particularly good with a sense of direction, and when her head got caved in years ago, well, needless to say, it got worse. But it felt now like she was becoming part of this place. Or it was becoming part of her. She knew just behind them to their right, up past the ridge, sat Lake Lenore, the

Bachelor mine, and the old stables just past that where they'd found a couple of the town's horses. She knew they'd crossed Corbett Creek, and Dexter just after that. She knew they were about four miles out of town.

Maybe *that* was Matthew's problem.

He was a man out of sync with this place, wasn't he?

Out of sync with this place, and its people. Those who remained. He didn't belong, and he felt that. Maybe she could fix it. Marcy liked fixing things.

"So, you gonna tell me what's up?" she asked.

"Are you my therapist now?" was his retort.

"No. Just a town sheriff. But more important, I'm your friend."

He sighed. "No, yeah, right, I'm sorry. Just having a rough go is all."

"It's normal. We all go through it. Doctor Moore said it's like we're all still in mourning." Erika Moore was a psychotherapist—and a damn good one, at that. Black Swan had chosen all its people well, but for Marcy, Erika was one of the most soothing balms in these strange times. From day one that woman was up and at 'em, helping the townsfolk and Shepherds alike work through their very complicated feelings. Apparently she even helped the rest of the Flock inside the—what had they called it? The Ouray Simulation. That was the wondrous thing about Black Swan, wasn't it? The people it chose were like a Swiss Army knife of human needs. Like they were all future-proof.

Marcy went on: "I remember after 9/11, it wasn't like everyone just . . . got over it. It was years before you didn't think about it at some point during every day. And 9/11 was . . . well, it was minuscule in comparison to White Mask."

"When I was a kid," Matthew said, "I was really afraid of nuclear war. Even with the Cold War ending, it had been drilled into us so often that at any moment, the missiles might come for us—and what scared me most wasn't the blast. You die in the blast? That's okay. One-way ticket to heaven, I thought. No, what got me was the fear of *surviving*. Of still *being here* after it happened. There was this one thing that freaked me out so bad, I'll never forget it—the walking ghost phase, they called it. Imagine: The bomb hits, but not right overtop you. But close enough to give you a heroic dose of radiation. You still feel okay, though. But really, you're not fine. That radiation is cooking you from the inside. Your death is certain, you just don't know it yet. Might last days, might last a couple weeks. But in the end, delirium takes you. You lose your mind. You puke, you defecate blood, you fall apart from the inside out. *Then* you die. Walking ghost phase." He shook his head, like he was lost in the fear of it.

"Look at it this way, we don't have to worry about that now."

"What? Nuclear war?" He shrugged. "That's like saying after you get eaten by a bear, at least you aren't also being eaten by a cougar."

"You're saying this is the same. This is our walking ghost phase."

He didn't answer. But he didn't have to.

"You're just . . . depressed, maybe."

"I once thought, how can anyone be depressed? They lived in God's creation. I figured, depression was you being in God's shadow, where you couldn't see him, couldn't exalt in his light. So that meant depression was a failing of some kind—a failure to see the good in all things." He chewed on his lip. "Now, though, I think: How can you *not* be depressed? I'm not dead, but I feel like I died. Who am I even anymore? I don't have my kid. My church isn't the same. And my wife, Autumn . . ."

His voice trailed off.

"Are you still a believer?" she said finally. "In God, I mean."

"I am," he answered with some hesitation. "Just not the same way I was before."

"How so?"

"I believe in God. Still." He wobbled a little on the saddle. "I just don't know that God has our best interests in mind. I always understood the brutality of the Old Testament as a metaphor—the world was brutal and so their grasp of it was equally brutal, you know? The New Testament gave us a reckoning with that, and showed us a God who believed in forgiveness and love. But now, looking out at the world, I'm not so sure anymore. I think the God I believed in, or believe in now, is that Old Testament one. The fire-and-flood guy. The one who lets disasters happen and evil flourish in order to make a point."

"That's kinda dark."

He shrugged. "Not too far out of line with what modern evangelical thought had become, sadly. Selfish people in awe of a selfish deity."

"You're angry with Him."

"With God?"

"Yeah."

"I suppose I am," he said, as if he was just figuring that out.

They walked on for a while. Past evergreens and aspens, past a few derelict cars and crumbling shacks. Marcy knew things that Matthew did not. There was a shack coming up—the red paint on its wooden side peeling in long strips that looked like curls of dried meat—and inside it was a dead man.

Before they'd gotten there, Dove had cleaned up a lot of the bodies, and when the Shepherds arrived, they helped him with the rest. Soon as you started poking around beyond the town, though, you found the dead everywhere. Most of them were colonized with White Mask—human-shaped lumps gauzed in a dry, crusted rime like freezer burn. Some died having killed themselves. Others having killed one another. Most, you had no way of knowing how they went, except the fungus took their minds, took their bodies, the end.

She remembered finding one body in a cabin up along Portland Creek, and that body was on the roof, naked as a jaybird, the body eerily preserved—the naked man looked almost like a mummy. Skin dry, crusted over. Hands out, fingers splayed, as if he were welcoming whatever was to come. His dick was hard, too, like a fuzzy flagpole pointing to the heavens.

The one in the shack ahead died sitting in a chair, his mold-mitten hands curled around an old .22 rifle. Tendrils of bone-white fungus extended out from his face, like fingers of their own, but finding no life to choke, they stopped seeking.

That day she'd asked Benji: Was White Mask really gone? It seemed to be, but she also knew that mold and spores were weird. They could dry out and wait for a long time till they found moisture again, or something to feed on, some crucial meal that would stir them back to life. You could have brittle dead-looking moss on a rock for years, but one good rain and it was green as emeralds again.

He said he really didn't know. He hoped so, obviously. The survivors out in the world were immune, he believed, and once White Mask had nothing more to grab ahold of, it went dormant or dead. She asked him then, *What about the people of Ouray?* The townsfolk were only immune because of Black Swan.

Well, he'd said at the time, *I don't know that, either. We just have to trust that Black Swan gave their immune systems the blueprints to the disease so that they know how to fight it.* Them and their kids and their kids' kids. Or maybe, he postulated, they had White Mask all along—meaning the Sleepwalkers survived the same way Benji himself had, by slowing the infection and giving his immune system the time to catch up and learn the patterns of its enemy.

But, he said, *Diseases are pernicious. If it's not White Mask, it'll be something else. Any threat to our threadbare civilization will come in the form of diseases, some novel, some familiar.*

She was glad she had Benji around.

Matthew, too, even if she felt bad for him. He had lost so much. Autumn, Bo, his life, his faith. Obviously, they'd *all* lost big. But the pastor had really been through the sausage grinder. Even now she watched as he sometimes lifted his left hand off the saddle horn and gave his fingers a flex and his whole hand a shake. It hurt him, though he didn't talk about it. Ozark Stover and his people hurt him in a way that might never heal. They'd hurt her, too. She had her share of wounds, too, and it stayed with her. But it didn't feel like baggage she had to carry.

But he carried his everywhere he went.

Why that was the case, she didn't know. Different wiring, maybe.

"We aren't far now," she said. "The little cemetery is about a mile up—and I think I see the spruce farm."

"I see it, too," he said. Then he turned to her and said, "Can I ask you something? Something kinda . . . personal."

"Shoot."

"Aren't you scared of Black Swan?"

"No."

"So fast to answer. One word. No." He regarded her warily. "Not one bit? You trust it completely?"

She nodded, and answered with zero reticence. "Complete trust. Why wouldn't I? Matthew, we're here because of it. Ouray as a town exists because of Black Swan. Hell, I should be dead. That truck should've turned me to Marcy pudding, but it didn't. Because of Black Swan."

"Because of Shana," he corrected.

"It was her choice, but she *threw* me, Matthew. There's not three people in that town whose strength could combine to do that, but she, a pregnant teenager, did it. *Because* of Black Swan."

"But Black Swan didn't make the choice to save you. She did."

She harrumphed. "I like to think it's all wrapped up together."

"That's naïve."

"Hey, go to hell, Matthew."

"I just mean—you have faith, absolute faith. Faith is naïve. Trust me."

"You're trying to sound like you're feeding me a compliment but there's an insult in the center. Yes, I have faith. Faith has gotten me this far."

"Do you believe in God? The one upstairs." But he didn't even let her answer—she could tell his blood was up. "So how do you square one belief with the other? One faith with the next? You can't have faith in that God and in Black Swan. You just can't do it."

"I can. And I do. Benji says that science and faith aren't enemies—science isn't a denial of God but a tool of God and I think Black Swan is like that, too. I told you, Matthew. I could feel the Sleepwalkers. I could feel their glow—see it, hear it, all the way through me, light and sound. It cleared my head."

He stared at her dead-eyed then and said: "That's why I wanted to come up here with you, Marcy."

She cocked an eyebrow at him. "Oh?"

"What I really wanted to ask you was about that, about the glow. Because it seems to me here you are, miles from Ouray—"

And like that, Matthew's head snapped back suddenly—there was a *crack*, and in the middle of his forehead was a hole drooling blood. He fell off his horse, and Marcy cried out his name, drawing her gun.

Matthew's been shot!

19

THE FALL OF MAN, LITERALLY

If we want to know whether what we do here ultimately matters, the first thing we ask is: how will it come out in the end? If we find the answer to that question, it leads immediately to the next: what does this mean for us now?

—Katie Mack, *The End of Everything*

SEPTEMBER 4, 2025
Ouray, Colorado

In an instant, Marcy tugged the reins of Doppelbock and turned the horse perpendicular across the road even as Judy, the painted mare, spooked and galloped off toward the Uncompahgre. Turning her Belgian sideways gave her cover as she dropped to the ground to help Matthew. If he could be helped.

Please don't die on me.

Soon as her boots hit asphalt, Matthew sat up suddenly, pawing at his bloody head. Marcy cried out—it was a mad, panicked reaction from him, one that indicated that he wasn't dead at all, or worse, that he *was* and his body just hadn't figured it out yet. That could happen sometimes.

But as she crouched down next to him, she realized—not only had she not heard a gunshot, what she assumed was a bullet hole in his forehead was more just a shallow injury—a break in the skin, yes, and one oozing fresh blood, but definitely not made by a bullet. *Did Black Swan . . . ?*

Then, nearby, she saw a gleam—

A steel ball bearing sat on the road, having settled into a cleft in the asphalt. The sun shone off it, but she also saw a little spot of blood on it.

The sound she'd heard—it wasn't a gunshot.

It was the sound of a ball bearing hitting him in the skull.

What the—

Suddenly, there was a sound like *thap!*—and Doppelbock jumped like he'd been stung in the ass by a hornet. The beast reared back, knocking Marcy over onto her tailbone as the Belgian took off, bolting in the same direction that Matthew's painted mare had gone.

And there, standing in the road ahead, was a kid.

Teenager, she guessed, thirteen, fourteen. Ratty hair down over his shoulders, face shitty with dirt. He had something in his hands—

A slingshot, Marcy realized.

She stood up, her big gun gripped tight. A gun that the boy had clearly not seen before this very moment—his eyes found the weapon and widened to panicked apertures. The kid turned heel and bolted, like the horses.

But before Marcy even knew what was happening, Matthew was on his feet, too, and chasing the kid down, legs pumping like he was trying to win an Olympic sprint. The kid juked left but already Matthew was angling that way, and hit him sideways—a clumsy football tackle, arms and legs akimbo.

The teenage kid screamed like a devil caught under a blanket. Thrashing and wailing. Trying to bite, too. Matthew got atop him and raised a fist like a meteor ready to crash down to earth—except in this case, earth was the kid's head, about to be cratered. Marcy crossed the distance in a few long strides, and caught his wrist in her prodigious grip.

"*Hey*," she cautioned him.

His head spun toward her. There was a frenzy in his eyes—a progressing madness, like a cartoon spark running down a long dynamite fuse. The already blackening line of blood down his nose and around his mouth only served to complete the image of a man in the tightening grip of rage.

But clarity came back to him swiftly, and his arm slackened in her grip.

"You good?" she asked him.

Matthew swallowed hard and nodded, wiping blood from his face.

The young man struggled underneath, his arms pinned by Matthew's knees.

He was, up close, even rattier. His teeth looked poorly kept—they were scarecrow teeth, looking more like kernels of dark corn than anything else. A once-white T-shirt was now the color of weak tea. Cargo shorts ragged and filthy, the pockets bulging with what she guessed were more ball bearings. A smell came off him: a wild, almost pickled stink.

Matthew grabbed the kid's arms and turned them up. Marcy started to protest, but then she saw *why* he was doing that—

His arms were marked. Not tattooed, but branded with puffy, lacy scars.

A swastika on the left arm. A crude scar of a sword and hammer on the right. Matthew toed the boy's shirt up just a little, exposing something else, a rune of some kind. Diamond shape, with two bent legs coming off it, like an octopus with six fewer legs than usual. Nazi shit, she thought. All the white supremacists had a real hard-on for Norse iconography. She remembered seeing some of it on Ozark's men—back in Waldron, and all the way to Innsbrook.

"Lord," Matthew said. "Who did this to you?"

No answer. Just bared teeth and a hiss.

"What's your name?" Marcy asked.

The young man growled at her before uttering something that had the cadence of human words but was just bestial gibberish. Then suddenly the kid twisted his body hard, like a tornado that fell over onto its side—Matthew lost his balance and fell off him just enough for the feral teenager to squirm free. The kid crabwalked backward fast, rolling over and scrabbling to his feet—

Before hightailing it toward the trees, leaving his slingshot behind.

Marcy called after him, told him to stop, to wait, that they wouldn't hurt him. But he ducked into a curtain of blue spruces and was gone.

"We ought to go after him," Matthew said. She hoped he meant to help him. Not to hurt him.

"The horses first," she said. "We can't lose them. Not only do I not wanna walk back, we can't afford to lose any resources."

"I'll follow the kid, you grab the animals."

"Matthew. Listen. There could be more people up there. This could be part of a trap—just like the one that got Ernie. We don't split up."

But Matthew was already walking backward toward the side of the road, giving a halfhearted shrug. "I'll be fine," he said, turning toward the trees.

He didn't care. Did he want to die?

"*Shit*," she said, and went after the horses.

BLESSEDLY, SHE FOUND THE HORSES together, both of them by the waters of the Uncompahgre, having a sloppy sip of water like nothing had ever happened. The horse equivalent of having a drink down at the bar, she guessed.

She kept her eyes out. Watching and waiting for some Nazi bastard to come up from behind some scrub or around a tree. But there was nothing. No one.

Marcy grabbed the reins of the horses, started to draw them back toward the highway—and that's when she heard Matthew yelling.

Damnit, Matthew.

What trouble had he found? Or what trouble had found *him*?

Quick as she could, she lashed the reins to the trunk of a nearby aspen and took off running.

MARCY FOUND MATTHEW, ALONE, PAST a thick copse of spruce trees, where a little campsite lay in hiding. It was a roughshod place, practically carved out of the earth. The two tents were foul, and especially filthy at the bottoms, wearing a hem of dirt and mud kicked up by hard rains. In the center was a dead cookfire. Trash was strewn everywhere. But the biggest thing was the smell.

It hit her even before she found the camp. It wound its way through the trees, a smell of death, and she expected to find a crudely butchered animal. Maybe a gutted elk or mulie stripped of its meat. But when she got there, she saw the human foot poking out of the far right tent. That foot was still encased in a black leather boot, but it had swollen up enough that the leather was straining, the seams popping, and through them, some kind of . . . pink mess.

It wasn't White Mask. Those dead from the fungus were always covered in that fuzzy rime of mold. This was fresher.

"The young man came here," Matthew said. "Then ran."

Marcy held her arm to her nose. "I assume you see the dead person."

"I do." He found a stick and poked at the tent. It must've been held up with spit and dreams, because instantly it collapsed onto the body. Matthew dug the stick under the material and lifted it off—

Exposing the corpse underneath.

Marcy stifled a gag. Flies took flight: not one, not ten, hundreds of them, like a murmuration of tiny starlings. Matthew swished the stick through the air, parting the cloud of flying things. The dead man was bloating already, his skin the color of wine in milk. His arms and neck and face were all marked with white nationalist nonsense. Inked, not branded. Flags, runes, SS lightning bolts. His beard was long and raggedy. His teeth, worse than the kid's. They'd rotted in his mouth, composting down to gummy dental stumps. The cause of his death was plain to see: a ragged wound on his left side, around the collarbone. Blood soaked his clothing. The flies liked this part best, a veritable feast scene for carrion-eaters.

Ernie's doing, Marcy guessed.

Matthew looked around. "I think you can put to bed any fear that there's some organized Nazi army out here, Marcy."

"Where'd the third one go? Ernie said there were three. There's this one. There's the slingshot kid."

"Maybe he ran off."

"Loyal friend."

Matthew shrugged. "Indiana Jones punched Nazis for a reason. They're not known to be the moral center of the universe."

"Do we give him a burial?"

"Why? This one's already gone to Hell."

"We could find the kid. Maybe he could be saved."

"No," Matthew said, turning around. "He can't. Let's go."

With that, he walked past Marcy. With him and his stick gone, the rest of the flies swooped back in. It was feeding time at the human trough.

EVENTUALLY, MARCY FOLLOWED. AND EVENTUALLY, they got back on the road. On the horses they went, headed south once more toward town.

"You wanted to ask me something earlier," Marcy said.

"It's nothing," Matthew said, dismissing it. He stared off at a fixed point in space—but not a point on this planet. Somewhere past it, beyond space and time. Was he thinking of his son, Marcy wondered. After the boy today . . .

"You were going to ask me about the glow. About why I don't have the pain anymore. In my head. The pain, the confusion, all of it."

He perked up, arching an eyebrow. "That's right. How'd you guess?"

"Makes sense to ask. It is weird. Black Swan went dormant and Benji thinks the plate was moved out of place just enough for my brain to heal around it. So, I don't have that problem anymore. Not there. Not out here."

"What if it's for another reason?" Matthew asked.

She didn't say anything, just gave him a quizzical look.

"What if it's because Black Swan chose you? It wants you, so it protects you. Shana saved you, and it let her save you. Maybe it thinks you're useful. So it's keeping you around, and keeping you clear. Maybe it's in you, too."

She barked a laugh. "I don't know about that. I'm just a Shepherd and it's not . . . omnipotent or, what's the other word, where it knows everything?"

"Omniscient."

"Yeah. It's not either of those."

"But what if it is, Marcy?"

"You think it's really God?"

"A god. For all intents and purposes. I mean"—he licked his finger and used it to wipe more dried blood off his nose—"think about it. It chooses who lives, who dies. It controls them when it needs to. They have faith in it. *You* have faith in it. It's unseen but ever-present. You yourself said it had a glow. That the Flock were its angels. It's a god of sorts. Or sees itself as one, anyway."

She took a bit of time to think about this. The sun had started to ease down the other side of the sky.

"Then I'm good with that," Marcy said finally. "If Black Swan has chosen me, then I'm proud to be chosen. If it's inside of me, then all I can say is thank you and amen. We're here by the grace of Sadie Emeka and her team. We're here because Black Swan saw something coming, and did what it could to save us from it. How could I be angry at that? Why would that disturb me? It's wonderful."

Matthew said no more after that. They rode on, silent. He seemed resigned to her answer, as if it was both expected and sad. Into the valley they went.

20

THE FESTIVAL

We didn't lose. We gave up.
       —tattered banner hanging beneath the Golden Gate Bridge

SEPTEMBER 10, 2025
Ouray, Colorado

THIS, BENJI THOUGHT, *FEELS NORMAL.*

All these people. Their voices. Their ideas. The hum of generators. The smell of food cooking. Even the strings of electric lights buzzing, each bulb a bright star of defiance against darkness both real and imagined.

This was the Harvest of the Future Festival. The first and, he hoped, not the last. *Good thing I might have something to say about that*, he thought in a way that Sadie would have described as cheeky.

A town festival was a special thing to him. It gave a place an identity— a vibe all its own. Made the place come alive. Like lightning striking the monster on the table, a town suddenly got up and started to dance—and it was only then you realized how inert, how torpid, how *asleep* the damn thing had been before that moment. He'd been to festivals all around the world and they all felt electric and singular: like each was a mark of the town's fingerprint, the chorus of its song, its true face. *Here I am, feeling poetic again*, he thought, but he had a drink in his hand, and that drink was making him feel a *certain way* about things.

(The drink was vodka vapor-distilled in a copper pot by ex-high-school-science-teacher Julia Hatch, mixed with a "fruit punch" mash-up of local peaches, nectarines, and cherries, courtesy of Ernie Novarro. It was not a cold drink, because ice was not yet easily in their grasp—though he'd heard they were making ice right now in the Workshop!—but it was refreshing as hell, and he already had a bit of a drunken flywing buzz in his brain.)

Benji had been to the Sundance Film Festival in Utah, and that felt like its own thing—a hipster Hollywood art-cult in a snowbound mountain town, all puffy jackets and swag bags and vaguely familiar celebrities, like, *Hey isn't that the guy from that thing?* He'd loved the Decatur Book Festival, too, and the way it got bigger every year and showed how a whole town loved something so simple and so pure as reading books. He'd been to the water festival, Thingyan, in Myanmar—he didn't understand half of what was happening, but saw laughing men with soot on their cheeks, saw parade floats sprayed with water as they passed by Super Soakers and garden hoses, saw puppets and Myanmarian hip-hop dancers and even punk bands. Growing up, just going to the annual carnival felt like something special, something all its own. The smell of fried food, the janky rides run by lanky men, that game where you tried to win a goldfish with a ping-pong ball and fishbowls.

Being here, he expected to miss those times and those places, but this festival—it felt enough like those times that it satisfied him. He thought, *This feels right, this feels normal, this feels like a real thing and a real place.* Pinocchio was a real boy now.

Best of all? It felt like home.

I'm going to be the mayor, he realized.

Which meant it was time to find Dove and tell him his decision.

THIS, SHANA THOUGHT, *FEELS WEIRD.*

It's not that it wasn't nice. It was. But here she was, walking down Ouray's Main Street as the late afternoon gave way to evening. There were booths lining the sidewalks—food and drink, sure, but there were also demonstrations of the future of Ouray. Maybe the future of humanity.

That wasn't what felt weird, though.

What felt weird was walking around with Nessie. Just *being* with her.

Yesterday, Nessie had come up to her room and said in a plainspoken way that was unusual for the little sister, "We need to fix this. We're sisters"—she gesticulated with a rogue index finger pointing at various spots in the universe—"and Mom and Dad would want us to get along, so we're going to get along."

"Okay," Shana had said.

"Okay?" Nessie had asked, as if she wasn't sure if Shana was fucking around or not. But Shana did mean it. She was feeling good. Maybe it was a wave of pregnancy hormones washing over her in a warm, forgiving tide, or maybe she just missed her little sister. Either way, it felt good—like the camera Benji had given her—so she went with it.

Nessie asked her if they could go to the festival together.

And Shana decided to go with that, too.

Which meant, right now, her little dork sister was like a bumblebee, pollinating every science booth flower she could find. And every one of them geeked her to the *teeth*. "Ooh, look, hydroponics and aquaponics in a closed-loop system." She pointed to some lazy-looking fish lurking near the murky bottom of its tank, and a tube feeding a planter of lettuce just below it. "The water from the tank has fish poop in it, and runs through the plant to feed it, and then is filtered and recirculated back through the tank as clean water." And then, "Look, bio-digester compost barrels that sit over running water so it gently turns them and rotates the compost, shortening the time to usable dirt to ten weeks!" Then, "Biomass generated from the town waste could help power a mini grid," and "Oh my God oh my God, hand-crank handcrafted cellphones that piggyback off the cell tower south of town, oh my God, we could have *phones* again." But all Shana could think was, *Not like there's gonna be an app store around*. Then again, Nessie was probably already thinking of how to program one.

What a wonderful, *sparkly* little nerd.

It made Shana mad that she'd been mad at her. Okay, she still *was* kinda mad at her little sister—or at least, bothered by Nessie and her devotion to Black Swan. But maybe it wasn't devotion, really. Maybe it was just . . . Nessie being Nessie. The sparkly little wonder-nerd that she was. She was eager. She was optimistic. She was in love with the future, and how could Shana shit on that?

Besides, shouldn't Shana also be devoted to Black Swan? It saved her. Saved her baby. Saved Marcy. Maybe it was time to trust it. Time to trust that whatever it had done to the world . . . needed to be done.

And as it turned out, she still wasn't ready to tell Benji any of this. She thought she was but then . . . standing up onstage at the town council meeting, seeing him in the audience . . . she'd been keeping the Black Swan secret long enough now that it wasn't just Black Swan's secret. It was hers, too.

Just go with it, Shana said. A new mantra.

It *was* exciting, she supposed. To see the future splayed out in front of them like this. Even if she did not precisely understand all of it.

Maybe she didn't need to understand it.

Maybe her role was simply to capture it.

Around her neck hung the Pentax camera. She had to be spare with her shots—this wasn't like with digital, where you could snap a thousand photos and discard nine hundred and ninety of them. They had to count. Camera to her eye, she seized a moment of Nessie looking bathed in awe, eyes wide, mouth agape, staring at—well, who knew what. A tank of algae? It was perfectly her.

Click.

"Come on!" Nessie said, waving her hand. Off the bumblebee bumbled.

They kept on through town, down Main Street on the one side, then up it again on the other. The smells were wonderful, and Shana found herself sampling various foodstuffs—a shiny red apple from Fruita, grilled chicken tenders on metal skewers, fry bread, a little berry mix she'd never heard of (serviceberry, thimbleberry, huckleberry, with a syrup made from chokecherry). All the while, they passed other townsfolk like Carl Carter, Bob Rosenstein, Jamie-Beth, Bella, on and on. It was hard not to notice how with each of them, their gazes inevitably drifted to—or started at—her protruding tummy. "Look like you're ready to pop," Bella Brewer said to her. Mary-Louise Hinton said, "Oh, Shana, it's so nice, your little one gives us all such hope." Shana wanted to say, *Eyes up here, everybody*, but instead she just plastered a smile onto her face and nodded a lot. Even as they reached for her belly and she ducked out of the way because *ew, no touchy the belly*.

It was another thing that felt weird. She tried to ask herself, What if it's nice, though? Then she settled on, *It can be both.*

She thought about mentioning it to Nessie, but decided against it. Why ruin a nice night? Instead she went with, "You should have a booth here."

"What? Oh, no, I don't know."

Was it humility or a lack of confidence? Shana wasn't sure. Again she settled on, *Could be both.* In everything, many truths were possible. Things were rarely just one thing.

"I'm just saying," Shana said, somewhat greedily licking the berry goop from the edge of the paper cup in her hand, "you're smart, you're working on that . . . computer thingy, with the operating system doohickey, you should totally have a booth here, c'mon."

"Maybe." Nessie shrugged. In a lower voice she said, "Town council members aren't supposed to have booths, anyway."

Oh, ho, ho. Shana grinned and gave a thumbs-up. "Don't think I didn't catch that epic humble-brag, young lady."

"What? No. No!" Nessie laughed, embarrassed. Or was she *pretending* to be embarrassed? "I just mean—yeah."

"Yeah."

"Shut up, yeah." Nessie stopped giggling long enough to say, "Are you still hungry? Because there's a surprise."

Shana narrowed her eyes. "I like surprises."

"You're *really* gonna like *this* surprise. C'mon!"

Her little sister traipsed ahead, la-la-la-dee-da. Shana's mind flashed back to seeing her as a Sleepwalker—that dread and steady gait, forever unswerving, her eyes like flat, tarnished coins. It was nice to have her sister back, buzzing forth. Sparkly nerd bumblebee girl that she was.

THIS, MATTHEW THOUGHT, *FEELS WRONG*.

There was a store at the north end of Main Street, a pottery studio called the Prancing Peacock. Like so many things it once looked nice, but had endured years of sleep and silence—though recently, the townsfolk had pried the boards off the windows, cleaned off the dirt and the spiders, started to strip some of the peeling paint in preparation for what, he didn't know, because it wasn't like they had new paint to spare. Still, it was unoccupied, and he found his way inside and up to the second-floor apartment with a bottle of something called CapRock gin, made from apples, apparently. He went through the dark apartment, to the balcony beyond, and from there sat and watched the town festival unfold.

The gin tasted only a little like apples, and mostly like gin. Which was to say, like pine trees. Gin was not his favorite. He didn't care.

Matthew stared down the barrel of Main Street, watching the townsfolk revel—not partying too hard, no, but they were happy. Genuinely so. A community had formed here, though, if he understood it right, it had formed long before the Sleepwalkers ever arrived, inside a simulated Ouray courtesy of Black Swan. It should've filled him with wonder and hope. But rather, this felt like something else entirely. And in that, he was forced to ruminate on the concept of Hell.

Hell, as it turned out, was not really a fully throated reference in the Bible. It was in there, sure—lake of fire, furnace of flames, total darkness. In some editions, it was even called Hell with the capital *H* and everything, but that was the choice of translators, and not found in the original texts. Hell as an idea, with the demons poking you with pointy forks as you boiled in a fiery pot, was a medieval notion given teeth by someone like Dante in *The Inferno*. But Matthew always favored the original view of Hell, which was simply being in the darkness outside of God's light. A place of ignorance and isolation. Beyond glory, beyond grace.

And right now, he wasn't sure if this place was Hell for everyone—

Or just Hell for him.

He spent close to five years here with just a handful of people, and together they worked to get this town in shape where they could, in the ways that mattered. They spent time and effort just being out there in the world, scavenging parts, finding other people—all while the Sleepwalkers slept in their perfect, untouched comas. (The only change they manifested was that they collected dust, like forgotten lamps and loungers. Matthew helped dust them off from time to time. He also found dead mice nearby them sometimes. He assumed the rodents tried to eat the slumbering Flock, but that Black Swan thwarted their nibbling efforts in some secret, vicious way.) They endured hard winters and wet springs. He became friends, real friends, with Benji, Marcy, Dove. He missed his family, too, but those five years, while the Sleepwalkers slept . . . *he* slept, too, in a way. It was like he turned his brain off. It was as if every day he lived in only that day, as if all of time itself were only the present. Like he was perched on a handful of seconds that would never repeat, never return.

But when the Sleepwalkers awakened . . .

In a way, so did he. He was forced to reckon with the scope of time— what would go forward, but also, what was behind him.

He could no longer just accept the world unfolding around him. He watched the Sleepwalkers get up and begin to industriously transform the town. Now their efforts were on display in this festival—a festival he had no part in planning, and in which he did not participate. He'd thought maybe he'd put up a booth of his own, a booth about his church, but what was the point? He had few attendees. He'd once thought he could help, and they could help him, but was that true?

It felt fruitless.

And watching this festival only reminded him of what was really going on: A swarm of people, much like the swarm of little mechanical creatures inside of them, arrived here in thrall to a machine. A machine that gave them life, that lurked here still inside a girl who was pregnant—clearly pregnant

beyond what was physically normal given the time of the baby's development, even though nobody seemed to think about that or care too much
about it, and they seemed to take Doctor Rahaman's word that everything
was okey-dokey, smokey.

It troubled him. And it seemed to trouble *only* him. Shana, too, maybe,
though she seemed to want to stay at a distance from him.

Everybody did.

Distance, so much distance.

Which was really the problem, wasn't it? He was distant from them, they
were distant from him. He had no connection to Black Swan. He didn't have
much of a connection to his own God anymore, either. Once again, that concept of Hell greeted him: a man kept outside the gates from glory and grace.

Distant from the light meant being close with darkness.

And that darkness haunted him nightly. Worries about the future chased
him, chasing him right into the horrors of his past—the things Ozark did to
him, the things he himself said on the radio about these very people. He
thought of his own son, dying. Of his wife, leaving. Of that boy just a week
before, the feral teenager with his crumbling teeth and his skin-burned
brands of hate.

He was spiraling.

This was Hell.

Maybe not for the people of this town.

But definitely for him.

He looked at the bottle. It was already half empty. When had he done
that? Already the sun was bleeding out on the horizon, with evening arriving
like a coroner's blanket. Again he plugged the gin to his lips.

Hell, Hell, Hell, he thought. Or, put differently, *It's not you, it's me.* Like
in any breakup. Like when he left his wife, Autumn, to come here. To do
what he thought was right. To pay his debt. Well, he did it. He paid the debt
and now what?

I don't belong here.

And that's when he realized.

He didn't have to stay here anymore. He'd done the work. He helped in
the way that was owed.

There were other towns, other places.

I'm going to leave Ouray, he decided. *Tonight.* He wouldn't tell anyone.
He'd just go. But first, he had the rest of this gin to drink, didn't he? Its mad
bitter taste was a punishment, and he damn well deserved it.

• • •

This, Marcy thought, *is my everything*.

This hustling, bustling little town on the edge of the end of all things made her so damn happy—her heart felt like a pitcher of golden honey, pouring out. Everything had coalesced into this event: all the long months of walking across the country, the violence that ensued, the hard years of waiting to see *if* the Sleepwalker Flock would ever awaken from their forced slumber, the years of busting tail to try to give them a place worth waking up into . . .

They did it.

And this festival was the perfect emblem.

People smiling. The smells of food. Laughing and talking. And all these displays of what these smart people were capable of doing—what was coming for this town was nothing short of spectacular. From nothing came *all of this*.

She didn't understand why Matthew distrusted it.

He distrusted Black Swan and so, he distrusted what had resulted from it. But why? The potential of these people was limitless thanks to their digital patron. It gave them a fresh restart, like how a computer needed to reboot sometimes. Starting over with a town full of people who were *handpicked*, each for a purpose. Every individual, from Geneva Washington, the yoga teacher, to Jace Bryson, the botanist and forager, to Daniel Chong, a home builder, felt purposeful, like a singular puzzle piece that helped complete the whole damn image.

Back on the force, she'd had a partner—not a friend, not really, but he was better than most cops. Jeff Bergen. He was a survivalist, one of those guys who thought the Shit Is Gonna Hit the Fan and he'd need his Bug-Out Bag and his Hidey-Hole Cabin and it always struck her how . . . selfish it was. All the boogaloo ding-dongs and apocalypse preppers who envisioned this hard-ass life of living alone in your dung bunker, shooting out the window at any mutant bandit who thought to steal one of your cans of Chef Boyardee. Bergen, like so many of these whackadoos, believed in this kind of rabid self-sufficiency, even though he worked in government as a cop. She didn't get it. People like Jeff thought they were special and had rights that nobody else had. They thought they were patriots, but only flew the flag of their own one-man island nation. How was that ever supposed to make sense? No sense of community. No sense of neighborly nothing. Just the attitude of, *I got mine. And maybe I'll take yours, too.*

But Ouray wasn't like that, not at all. Might didn't make right. It wasn't about supremacy and control. It wasn't a place of selfishness. Everyone had a place here. Do the work, work for the people, and you had a home for life.

Marcy was just glad to belong. This was her America.

How fortunate I am, she thought.

She would protect this place however the hell she had to. No trouble would come for these people, not on her watch. Any who tried would find her waiting for them, an avalanche of fists and bullets.

As evening fell upon the town, Benji found the street outside the Workshop set up with tables and chairs and a little stage for townsfolk to come up and talk about what they were working on—or, better yet, to show it, if they couldn't manage a booth. They were doing walk-through tours, too, and already he saw Shana and Nessie heading inside. She spotted him and he gave her a little nod, and she returned a wave. He was glad to see the two sisters talking again.

She hadn't come to talk to him yet.

Which meant she was hiding something. Shana knew more about Black Swan than she was letting on to him, or to anyone. Maybe Nessie knew something but the two of them hadn't been as close as he figured.

Shana looked more pregnant now than she had when they walked together last week. It was hard at this point to ignore the reality that her body was catching up quickly, *too* quickly, from when she awakened just four months prior. The baby was growing with alarming speed. Rahaman assured them all that the baby was healthy and so was Shana. But she dismissed his concerns with eerie confidence.

He thought, *Maybe tonight Shana and I can talk*. He wanted to give her space. It wasn't on him to perforate that territorial bubble, and now that he saw Nessie and her together, he really didn't want to mess that up for her.

He decided to leave it for now. Besides, he had to find Dove, anyway. He thought he saw him head this way, so Benji started to work through the crowd that collected—most of which gathered around a car. In this case, a 2018 Nissan Leaf, sky blue, a little scuffed-up. The pride and joy of the Workshop, it was retrofitted with a series of photovoltaic solar panels along the roof and hatchback window. One of the car's designers, Orrin Lotz, was standing there talking about it: "The big trick wasn't just getting the panels to fit onto the car, but to wire them to charge the battery—right now, the setup is crude"—he ran a chubby index finger along the braid of black and yellow wires that ran from each panel to the holes drilled in the top of the hood—"but eventually we'll do better. This is just the prototype. The real trick is going to be not just finding other electric vehicles to scavenge, but to see if we can do a gas engine retrofit."

Benji was poised to ask about that—would it still rely on the car's battery, even in a gas engine? Solar panels without batteries to hold a charge meant you could only drive when the sun was out. Functional, to be sure, but not ideal.

But before he could ask—

He spied a flash of white hair and mustache beyond the car, saw Dove standing by someone holding court not on the stage but down in the seats—a man Benji recognized as Fabian Molina, a beekeeper (once, a biology professor) from Puerto Rico. He was in the middle of saying, "—and Irma wrecked all that, then Maria, they came in and smashed the island like fists, just bam, bam, bam. And so I lost most of my bees, probably seventy to eighty percent of them—and let me tell you, we had the best bees in the world." He did a chef's kiss, eyes closed, as if lost in the bliss of memory. "The gentleness of the European honeybee, but the high, sweet honey yields and immune systems of the Africanized bees—which, you ask me, is racist that we call those bees Africanized. Africanized sounds like radicalized, like they were turned bad in Africa, but they're just a species *from* Africa. And their danger is overblown—hey, look, it's Benjamin Ray. Benji, Benji, come, sit down."

From under the table, Molina used his boot to push out a chair from the other side. Benji was ready to look around, wondering if there was *another* Benjamin Ray around here—but Molina was looking right at him.

They'd met a few times, but didn't know each other well. But the man did seem the type to embrace familiarity as friendship.

Benji shrugged and sat down.

"Just the man to talk to," Molina said with a big smile, arms wide.

"Oh?"

"Sure, sure, I'm just telling about how Puerto Rico has a lot of lessons for us here in Ouray. Maria and Irma, oof. Those storms hit us, left us reeling, Benjamin. *Reeling.* Demolished our power grid, our agriculture, our economy. We had to learn how to rely on ourselves, on what we could build with our own hands—a zipline and bridge across a river, griddles and grills to cook meat for our people, our own antennas and signal boosters for phones and internet, even plans for low-carbon micro-grids to get us off the big one that failed us. There's lessons there in that. People think an apocalypse is for the whole world. But for us, those storms? They were apocalypses. A lot of us died. Not just in the storms themselves—but after. Disease, starvation, all that."

Benji nodded. "I've been in some countries where conditions were declining rapidly or where they had already declined to nothing, and survival becomes the primary mode of operation—"

"Puerto Rico isn't a country. It's part of America, Benjamin."

"Of course, I know, I was just saying—"

"What *I'm* just saying," Molina said, sounding more insistent, with some anger behind his words, "is that I want you to realize that. Puerto Rico and America are one and the same and yet America always treated us like we were some faraway place, some little Mexico instead of a brother, a sibling— not even a cousin, we were others, aliens. You won't treat us like that, will you?"

He looked to Dove, who gave him an awkward shrug. All who gathered now were silent, as if these two men were having some rhetorical debate— and maybe they were, but Benji sure didn't apply to participate.

"I'm sorry," he said to Fabian. "I may have missed something here. Why are you talking to me specifically about this?"

"Well, you are going to be our new mayor, aren't you?"

"I don't recall saying anything about that." But then he saw the big smile under the bushy white mustache of his close friend and current mayor. "Dove," Benji said, a statement as much as a question.

The old man smiled softly. "I may have mentioned you were gonna take me up on the offer."

"I haven't yet, to be clear. Taken you up on the offer."

"But you were gonna, so we can cut to the chase."

Benji wanted to be mad. *But he's not wrong*, he reminded himself.

To Fabian, Benji said, "Yes, I think I am going to be mayor."

At that, a murmur of what seemed like small celebration rose around him in a gentle wave. At least they didn't hate the idea?

"Good, good," Fabian said. "I just want you to remember that you're separate from us, Benjamin. Different and apart. I mean no offense here. You walked with us, but you didn't walk *with* us. Your feet weren't dirty. You got to leave when you wanted. We don't have *solidaridad*."

Benji felt his hackles raising. Maybe that wasn't necessary. It wasn't like this man didn't have a point. Though the pointy end of that point seemed unfairly poking at Benji.

"Let it be stated," Benji said, "that this town is in the shape it's in because of the work of Dove, and the rest of us Shepherds."

"Of course," Fabian said, smiling broadly, and grabbing hold of Benji's hands, gripping them in his own warmly. "Of course! And I thank all of you. What you did for us here cannot be overestimated. I only mean to say, people in power act like people in power. Above and beyond. But we people are not a resource to be exploited, a . . . a people to govern at a distance. This is Musketeers time. All for one and one for all."

"Absolutely," Benji answered, though he still wasn't exactly sure where this was going, or why it was being laid in his lap right here, right now.

"Look at it this way. We were told before the hurricanes and after, *Your island is a beautiful place, and we want to help you, we want to be partners with you for the future.* These developers, these companies, these tech people, they'd come in and tell us, oh, it's time to bring Puerto Rico forward, to *advance* us, uplift us like we were some primitive species—fish pulled out of the water and handed legs on which to walk. A tropical Silicon Valley, whoa, wow. Amazing! And they said, we want to start by building things, and building means resources. All your farming and agriculture, why, that's regressive. That's old world. This is the new world and so they went first to the sugar farmers and said, we'll develop this land, just sell it to us, and people did. Because they wanted a better life than just . . . sugar. Sugar is a brutal crop, I will tell you. But the contracts, they weren't good contracts. The farmers had nobody representing them, looking out for those loopholes. Those *tricks*. Turns out, the developers weren't tech people at all. They were a mining company. They wanted our resources—copper and cobalt, specifically, to build, I don't know, batteries and whatnot for Musk's electric cars. They sold their land for a song when they were sitting on *vital* resources . . ."

Molina kept going on. But something tickled at the back of Benji's brain. An itch back there that he needed to scratch. *Copper. Cobalt. Batteries.*

The other man continued: "We were a majority of people ruled and exploited by a powerful minority—ruined by capitalism. And I want to make sure that you're not seeing us the same way. That you're not the powerful minority. That you don't see us as tools, Mister Mayor."

Absentmindedly, Benji stood suddenly. "If you'll excuse me." He started to leave, but then turned and hurriedly said, "You're right, Mister Molina. Fabian. I don't want to exploit you, not any of you. But something has come up and I—"

He didn't finish his thought.

He had to go to the library.

Right now.

No.

No.

No!

"No," Shana said breathlessly, even as Mia hurried up to her, pressing into her hand a paper cup containing—

"Yup," Mia said. "It's ice cream, bitch."

"Ice cream," Shana said.

Ice. Cream.

"Told you it was a good surprise," Nessie chirped in her ear.

Shana took the metal spoon proffered by Mia and pressed it into the soft cream. It was already melty, but that was fine by her. She popped it into her mouth and was it possible to experience the greatest pleasure one had ever experienced just from a single spoonful of ice cream? She shuddered. She literally, actually shuddered. The taste was creamy and nebulously sweet— not vanilla, but what? Honey. That's what it was. Honey. It melted on her tongue, a milky coating, and she closed her eyes and felt like she wasn't here. She was in an ice cream parlor somewhere, like the one in her hometown, Big Scoop. With the red leather booths and the little jukeboxes at every table. They had a sundae there, what was it called? The Vesuvius. A mountain of ice cream scoops with tons of sundae ingredients in the center so when you broke the wall, it flowed out like lava. If you ate it with no more than three other people, you could get your picture on the wall.

"Remember Big Scoop?" Nessie said, obviously reading Shana's mind. Shana had no answer for her except a mammalian grunt of delight. To Mia, Nessie said: "I had my picture on the wall. Shana never did."

But Shana was only barely paying attention. She could've eaten twenty more cups of ice cream like this one. It was practically just a sample size— three bites and it was gone. Inside the Workshop, in the cafeteria, they had some of the more culinarily minded townsfolk lined up, serving sample sizes of stuff like jerky and dehydrated fruits and acorns—which Shana didn't even know you could eat, but apparently you could if you leached the toxic compounds out first. In fact, Ray Paredes said that you could make a coffee substitute from acorns—though they didn't have any caffeine in them. In which case, Shana thought, *Uhhh yeah, no.*

And then there was the ice cream. The sweet, sweet ice cream.

The woman doling it out was a stout woman with dark hair and big, beautiful dark eyes—she was missing her right hand—though it didn't slow her down any. Shana kinda remembered her. A Shawnee from Indiana, right? Bobby Apetathe. "I thought there weren't cows," Shana said, her eyes drifting to the single container of honeyed ice cream, now more than halfway gone. *What if I just stole it. I can run. Even this pregnant, I can run.* "Or ice. Or anything?"

Bobby showed her teeth in a big grin. "Shining Mountain Ranch. Turns out, if you skip the highway, take County Road 17 up toward Ridgway, there's an old ranch up there. Family up there used to raise all kinds of critters. Camels, peacocks, yaks, even a couple cattle. Well, most of that family is dead, but the wife survived. And so did some of her animals. So—we have milk. A little bit."

"And the ice part? Of ice cream?"

The woman grunted as she bent over and pulled up something that was currently turned off but plugged in—a beat-to-hell black plastic countertop ice maker. "This, some salt, and a bag gets you ice cream. Not much. But some."

Shana leaned forward like a drunk at a bar. "You're my hero."

But Mia and Nessie pulled her away and she wanted to cry, *No, c'mon, let me have more ice cream, don't make me kill both of you with my bare hands,* but ugh, fine, she didn't say those things, and she watched the ice cream retreat from her view. Hurriedly, she brought her camera up and: *click.* Mia and Nessie took her around the Workshop, whisking her from work area to work area, where people looked to be working on solar-panel retrofits for cars, and papermaking from peeled bark, and someone trying to develop photovoltaic cells from live algae. But all Shana could think about was that ice cream and the taste of it, lingering. A ghost of normalcy. A sweet specter of the world that was lost.

THE TOWN LIBRARY, STILL IN the same building as the Ouray community center, wasn't lit up—there were lines running to the crude micro-grid formed of generators, solar panels, and hydroelectric power, but none of them were connected right now, because this building wasn't part of the Harvest of the Future festival, so why risk a potential drain on the clumsy network that connected vital town resources?

Benji carried a little Maglite flashlight—most people in town did, because you couldn't guarantee you were going to have light wherever you were. They had enough ability to charge up rechargeable batteries, so he had portable light to go through the books on the shelves, specifically as regarded Colorado and Ouray. Problem was, most of the good books were already gone—they had a self-checkout log (basically, write in your name and what book you were taking, then go), but that wasn't going to help him. He didn't even know if he'd find what he needed.

(He considered grabbing a novel to read—the library had books by Colorado authors like Stephen Graham Jones, Kali Fajardo-Anstine, and Clive Cussler, but though the allure for fiction was strong, he needed facts now, not fancy.)

To the bookstore, maybe. They, too, had a strong Colorado fiction section, and now served as just another library with a similar checkout process.

He headed back upstairs, lighting his way with the light—

And found someone blocking the stairway up.

"Jesus," he said with a startle.

"Sorry, Benji," Dove said. "Thought I saw you duck in here."

Together, the two men headed outside. "Telling everyone I've already accepted the job, huh?" Benji said, not as a jab, just with a wry eyebrow raised.

"Sure, I knew you would." Dove paused. "You *are* taking the job, right?"

"I . . . am, at that."

"Ha. Thought so."

Back out on the street, where townsfolk passed, talking about ideas and the future. Benji said, "You're pretty keyed into the town and Colorado in general."

"I am the mayor, at least until we tell the town council."

"You know anything about REEs? Rare earth elements and metals? Here in Colorado?"

Dove sighed. "Sure, that's been—or was, anyway—a bit of a fight here. Mining companies started to develop claims all over the state, several of them just east of here, like in Gunnison and Custer counties. Some wanted us to be like Texas, just digging the hell out of the state, stripping it down to the struts. But most right-thinking people wanted to keep the land here pure, even if that meant keeping us dependent on China. Mostly they figure, better that China tears up its own country if it keeps Colorado lookin' pretty."

"Huh," Benji said.

"I see that look on your face. What is it?"

"The drones. With the little drills. I wonder if that's what they were looking for. Hints of rare earth elements. They go into battery development but also, if I remember Sadie saying, into the development of nanotech." His mind wandered suddenly. Was Black Swan looking for a power source for itself?

Or was it just part of the capital-C Calculation that went into choosing Ouray? If an area like Ouray had the right elements available, then those were resources that a burgeoning center of civilization could make use of, especially if the goal was to be more sustainable about it. Not that rare earth elements were all that sustainable in the long term. And not like just a handful of individuals would be able to make use of such rare metals easily. You'd need a whole processing plant for that sort of thing. Which would require considerable manpower and technology—the kind not available to this town.

And all that assumed Black Swan and the drones were even connected.

"This troubling you?" Dove said.

"Well. Yes and no. I don't much care for the idea that someone or something is piloting mysterious drones around. This could suggest their purpose—maybe it's an old purpose, and maybe they're still just out there, surveying, performing a task that has outlived the people that assigned it."

"And if it's something else?"

"Well, then it's something else. I just don't know what, but I intend to—"

Just then, down the block, they heard it—someone yelling. A sudden clamor and commotion of voices. The two of them left the library. Out here, the voices were louder, and he heard the panic in them. Was that Mia yelling? Were they yelling for Doctor Rahaman? Benji's heart went glacier cold.

Shana, he thought.

"Go!" Dove said.

Benji broke into a run.

21

THE HARVEST

10/11/2021: Graham and I are sleeping together. We don't love each other. We're like two trees that fell together in a dying forest. No reason not to support one another until we rot.
                    —from A Bird's Story, A Journal of the Lost

SEPTEMBER 10, 2025
Ouray, Colorado

THE PLAYGROUND WAS, DESPITE THE YEARS, IN GOOD SHAPE. STILL HAD THE bright colors and only a few pocks of rust in their pleasing loops and tangles of metal. It was mostly dark, lit only by the distant glow of the Workshop next door.

Shana, Nessie, and Mia sat on the swings, basking in that glow, and in the murmur of voices in every direction, and in the warm feeling of food and community. (What Shana was decidedly *not* basking in was the feeling around her butt and hips. Sitting in a kiddie swing reminded her in a rather uncomfortable way that her ass and hips had ballooned outward thanks to this kid kicking around her belly—a kid who right now was like a dolphin in her uterus, doing flips at a fish park to please an eager audience. Shana squirmed. The baby squirmed with her.)

The three of them were laughing and reminiscing about the Beforetimes— Mia was talking about the time she bought some weed juice from some skeevy neighborhood dudes at the playground at her school, but turned out that it wasn't weed at all but like, printer ink, and then Nessie said she heard that someone at *their* school sold "marijuana" except it wasn't "marijuana" at all, but poison ivy. The person ended up in the hospital because their throat and lungs were swollen.

At that, Shana had to laugh—first because of how Nessie pronounced the whole word, *mar-ih-whana*, which was a total narc move, and second because, "Nessie, that story is bullshit. It's just like, an urban legend. Nobody was going around selling poison ivy as weed. Same way nobody was putting razor blades in candy bars at Halloween and satanic pedophiles were not kidnapping kids in vans and taking them to pizza joints where like, President Nora Hunt would drink their blood to stay young. Sometimes you're so smart, but so *not* smart."

Nessie pouted, but it was fake, and then she started laughing. "I never smoked marijuana."

"MARIWWHHHHANA," Shana said dramatically.

"MAR-R-RI-A-WHANYA," Mia said even more dramatically, rolling that *r*, and giving a twist to the *n* at the end.

"Guys, shut up," Nessie said, laughing.

"It's just weed, dude," Shana said. "We just called it weed."

"Fine. I never smoked *weed*. Or vaped or . . . ate a pot brownie or whatever."

"Maybe," Mia said, "we can grow a crop here one day."

Shana swung on the swing, shifting uncomfortably as the baby spun inside her. "See, there you go. That's what *we* can bring to the table. No dispensaries here, what the actual fuck. Bo-ring. So that's what we can do. Start our own apocalypse dispensary. "We can call it"—here she did a showman's gesture—"High Times in the End Times."

They all laughed at that.

But then Nessie said, "It depends what Black Swan wants for us."

A chill settled over them, crushing the warm glow.

"What did you say?" Shana asked.

"This is all thanks to Black Swan. There was a plan, so—I mean—" And here Nessie tried to laugh it off, as if she knew she were starting to wade out into deeper water with hungry riptides. "I dunno, I'm just messing around."

"You weren't messing around. You meant it."

"I think we should get to decide our own plan," Mia said.

"Yeah. Not Black Swan," Shana agreed.

"You were just kidding, I'm kidding, it's fine—"

"You really think there's some Grand Plan?" Shana asked.

A pause.

"Sure." Her little sister's brow furrowed and she did that thing where she looked at Shana like Shana was an idiot with a clown nose and big red shoes. "What do you think we're even doing here?"

The night felt suddenly cold, even as her blood felt hot. "We're living, we're surviving, we're learning how to make ice cream again—"

"Yes, because of Black Swan."

"I get that, but—it's also because of *us*, we're not *automatons*, we're not a buncha little robots, Nessie, we're—"

Nessie suddenly hopped off the swing. She had *her* blood up, too, Shana realized. "We don't get to be here if it wasn't for Black Swan. I was the first. If I wasn't, I would've died with most of the country. You, too. Dad, too, all of us, dead from White Mask. Mia, you and your brother, Matty? Dead."

"Hey!" Mia protested. "You little—"

"*And*," Nessie continued, "don't forget how just over a week ago, a truck would've squashed you into a red *mess*." Her voice was angry now, and she was speaking through gritted teeth. "We get to be here by the *mercy* and *goodwill* of Black Swan. It's a blessing. We are blessed. Don't you forget that."

"Blessing," Shana said, trying out the word. It tasted like cold ash, greasy and dead. "*Blessing*. God. It is a cult, isn't it? You're a little cultist."

"Shana, why are you so thankless?"

Mia stood up, pointing her finger, getting in Nessie's face. "Nessie, you little twat, your sister stood for you, walked with you, *protected* your ass—"

"Seriously!" Shana barked.

"Oh my *God*," Nessie said, rolling her eyes. "Not this again. You know what, this was a mistake. You'll figure it out." Mopily, she added, "I'm going to bed."

But Shana, oh no, Shana wasn't going to be put aside like this. This was it. This was *now*. They were *doing this shit*. Shana got in front of her little sister and stood her ground, even as Nessie charged toward her. Her sister tried to get around her, but Shana planted herself in the way once more, and gave her a little push. "You wanna know about a blessing?" Shana asked. "I'll tell you about a blessing. I'll tell you what Black Swan is. I'll tell you what it *did*."

"Shut *up* and *move*," Nessie said, growling and trying to juke left.

Here it came. Shana felt the words at the edge of her mouth, like they were dancing on a cliff and ready to fall—it was time to tell her sister the truth. She didn't need to push her, or hit her, or hold her down and rub dirt in her hair (like she did one time, admittedly, when they were younger). Oh no. The reality of what had happened would knock some sense into her, harder than any slap to the face.

"You think Black Swan *saved* us," Shana said. "But before it saved us? It—"

Killed everyone else.

Those were the three words she wanted to say.

But then, something inside her twisted. Like a monster-sized corkscrew giving one good turn, binding her guts tight, so tight they felt ready to burst.

Nessie must've seen. Shana's eyes went wide.

"Shana," Nessie said. "*Shana.*"

"Oh shit," Mia said, hurrying over and catching Shana before she fell over. She felt pain radiating out of her middle. A wetness spread down her thighs. *My water broke,* she thought dully, and she patted the area with her hand, except when she brought her hand up to her face, she saw the wetness was dark and red.

The wetness was *Blood.*

Nessie and Mia screamed for help. Because the baby was coming.

WHO ARE THE PEOPLE IN YOUR NEIGHBORHOOD?

OURAY, COLORADO

NEVAEH RODGERS, TWENTY-TWO, BLACK, ABLE-BODIED, BISEXUAL CISGENDER woman. (She/her.) From Pittsburgh. She was tall, six-foot-one, was told she could be a model, even *should* be a model, but didn't want that life, and instead went into community organizing and voters' rights activism at the age of seventeen. Two years later, her brother Shawn was "mistaken" for a purse-snatcher, and two white police officers held him down in full public view while a third cop stomped on his legs and back. They broke one of his legs, requiring surgical pins to reconstruct, and he suffered kidney damage, requiring dialysis—and because he was a "criminal," Shawn would never be on any transplant list. They didn't kill him that day, but a year after that, Shawn got high, jumped off a fourth-floor roof. Nevaeh decided then and there she'd go into politics, running for local office in the Pennsylvania State House, but she never made it to election day. Black Swan took her, and for that, she was grudgingly thankful. Only recently had she begun to see the potential for a new world, a new nation. One of true democracy and equity. As long as they didn't screw it all up. She remained optimistic. But only barely. And it was impossible not to see the hard truth that it took an apocalypse to even give them a *shot* at getting things right.

JOHN HERNANDEZ, THIRTY-THREE, WHITE-PASSING LATINO, able-bodied, heterosexual. (He/him.) He was a Shepherd, walking with the Flock on behalf of neither friend nor loved one but rather, a neighbor—a reclusive genius named Daniel Thicket, a real math whiz who seemed to have no one to care for him, to watch over him, and so when Thicket began to walk, John went with him. He felt that somebody should. He didn't know why, but he was between jobs himself, and something compelled him to be a part of whatever this was. So with the Flock he went, until the day on the bridge of the golden bears. Bullets flew. People died. There was blood, so much blood. And yet the Flock kept flocking. Then came the moment when he watched the top of Thicket's head pop off like the cap on a beer bottle. He tried dragging the other man to safety, even as Thicket's brains were falling out of his head like yams from a can. Wasn't long after that John blinked, and had left the world behind and had found himself in the Ouray Simulation. He spoke to Black Swan and it became clear that this was his second chance—he was a jack-of-all-trades, master-of-none, but Ouray needed someone with his skills. He could make furniture, fix plumbing, jury-rig an electrical panel. He'd never found a place in the world, but now he had one, and he'd do anything to protect it.

LAUREN BIRCH, FORTY-SEVEN, WHITE, CISGENDER woman, gay, abled. (She/her.) She was short, stout, wore jewelry her ex-girlfriend said was "like if Roy Lichtenstein was big into LSD." For a decade, she was a practicing veterinarian but over time became more and more concerned about climate change and the havoc it, via mankind, would wreak on the world, and did not know how to effect change in a big way, so she instead decided to do something small and in her control: open an animal rescue operation. That was CWAR, the Cuyahoga Wild Animal Rescue, in the south of Cleveland. CWAR became her singular focus, and helped shelter and provide aid to a variety of wild animals, from squirrels to raptor birds to injured whitetail deer. (And opossum. So many opossum.) If an animal was found that could not be rehabilitated enough to be reintroduced into the wild, then it remained "on staff" at the shelter and became part of their education program. Then Black Swan and White Mask came along and that all went away. Why was she chosen? She couldn't deny that something about it felt a little *eugenics*-flavored, though wasn't eugenics more about breeding? Just the same, it was creepy to be part of a group chosen for their perceived "value" in the End Times, and further, she didn't yet know what that value was. She assumed it was to take care of livestock and horses, though neither were her specialty, and she figured another person would've or should've been chosen. Which only made her feel additionally guilty. Why did she survive when others did not? It'd be one thing if that was random—but this was not. And if she did not fulfill her destiny here, whatever it was, then what a waste she'd be. Taking up space that someone else could've had. It worried at her. She had trouble sleeping.

She felt alone. At least she had a dog now. Ouray had a lot of strays to take care of. Maybe *that* was her purpose. Or maybe she was just another stray.

SHAR MOSES, TWENTY-NINE, ASEXUAL, NON-BINARY, abled, grew up on the Umatilla Indian rez in Oregon. (They/them.) In Portland, they worked as an artist and glassblower, with their primary forms of income coming from two very, very different directions: The first was a service where they took people's or pet's cremains (aka, cremated remains) on behalf of loved ones and folded those kitty litter bits into layers of clear and dichroic molten glass and then called them "memory orbs." The second was glass sex toys: G-spot dildos, ribbed dildos, even a butt plug with a glass flower at the end of it. Neither was particularly fulfilling, but it subsidized their art, so, yeah. They joined the Flock just before the incident at the Klamath Bridge, and survived it—here, in Ouray, it's clear that one must have purpose and place in the scheme and scope of things, which is kinda fuckin' creepy to them, the way people would literally come up and ask you about your purpose, your destiny. Like that was any of their fucking business at all. Like that was even any way to think about yourself or your life. But at the same time, if that meant here they are, surviving where everyone else didn't? So be it. On Main Street, there was a shop with a glassworks studio built right in—and though their role here was less *artist* and more *hey we actually need reliable glassware to store all manners of things, from pickled vegetables to jams and jellies to fermented drinks*, then that fell into the "so be it" category, too.

VAL THORSSEN, THIRTY-EIGHT, WHITE, ABLED, heterosexual, cisgender man. (He/him.) Broad shoulders. Lumberjack beard. His job in Minnesota was as a butcher but he didn't really see himself as a man with a specific job. He did a lot of things. Butchery, sure, but also some gunsmithing. Handyman work. And a lot of volunteering at shelters. At first he thought he didn't fit in here, because most of the Ouray Flock, they were real smarty-pants types, lotsa geniuses and MENSA members. He was just a humble nobody. But soon, he figured it out. Everybody here had a purpose, right? In life (because that's how he thinks of that old world, as *life*, and this world, as a kind of *afterlife*) he railed against the throwaway nature of society. Everything disposable. Half of all edible food never got eaten. The ocean was full of plastic. China produced over fifty billion pairs of chopsticks every year. Take-out food was throw-out food. Done with that toothbrush, that razor, that phone, those bat-teries, just throw them over your shoulder, move on. But he always used every part of every animal he hunted and butchered. He made his own brushes, his own furniture, and in doing so, kept even the sawdust because you could use that to soak up puke, lighten cement, even start a fire. Hell, he had a little hand-crank razor sharpener to sharpen razor blades to shave with. Ouray was a chance to start over, to get right what they got wrong: to make a world to keep, and not one to throw away.

CHUE THAO, THIRTY-TWO, HMONG-AMERICAN, CISGENDER male, disabled (sensorineural deafness from bacterial meningitis as a child). (He/him.) From Madison, Wisconsin, he was one of the few hearing-disabled chefs in the world, building the kitchen in his Asian fusion restaurant around hand signals, physical contact, portable chalkboards, even a series of multicolored cards and flags the kitchen and waitstaff could use to receive and give fast, simple instruction. It was a good life. He felt fortunate. His large family, with whom he lived, was his everything. And now they're gone. He was "fortunate enough" to be chosen by Black Swan, at least that's what everyone seemed to assure him, when he could read their lips. (Too few of them knew ESL, which meant he had his work especially cut out.) But he did not feel fortu-nate. He felt lost and alone, like he was the last of something. Last of his family, for sure. They were gone—taken by the same plague that took every-one else. For now, he kept his head down, worked, and ran the cafeteria at the Workshop. The world had long been silent to him, but now it felt silent in a different way. The quiet wasn't just in what he could or could not hear, but in what he could see, what he felt, in who was missing from it. He smiled to everyone, was friendly. But inside he felt a crushing sadness, the sadness of one who remains. He persisted. But sometimes he wondered why.

ARCHER BOOKBINDER, TRANS MAN, WHITE, abled, pansexual. (He/him.) He did not care who he was before, because to him now, in Ouray, life was about transformation. For a very long time he was told he had to be a panoply of things: a good child, a Seventh-Day Adventist, a homemaker, a this, a that. But he was *actually* good at other things: He was good at designing and sew-ing clothes, he was good at believing in a godless universe, he was *very good* at hedonistically fucking anybody who would consent to getting fucked by him, and finally, he was *most excellent* at being Archer. And that was how he saw himself in Ouray: He was who he was, and he was here to give what he could to the town, but more important, he was here to give what he could to himself. Life was short, and enjoying his participation in it was paramount. This place was a buffet of new experiences, and yes, life would be difficult here, but he bought the ticket, now he wanted to take the ride. And he hoped others wanted to take *his* ride, too.

Joe Barton, age forty-one, Black, cisgender man, heterosexual, disabled with mobility issues from that time a drunk in a pickup hit him dead on coming around the bend on Old Wismer Road, crushing his left leg under the dashboard of his own car. (He/him.) Joe did not trust what was happening here. Not one bit. Back in Washington State, before *the Flock*, Joe was a journalist and a historian, both roles serving to inform that grave distrust—because Joe knew history, knew that it was not a thing created externally but rather, was something humankind created through choices, and often very, very *poor* choices designed to consolidate *power*. Just as humanity was the creator of history, humanity was also the creator of technology, and Black Swan was not an entity that made itself. Someone did that. And every time, *every damn time*, someone plugged their own implicit (or explicit) biases into the tech. Like a fucking automatic soap dispenser that wouldn't dispense soap onto Black hands. Or how web-crawling bots were supposed to be "objective" in what they learned from their input but because they trawled through so much racism and sexism, they "learned" racism and sexism and it became a core part of their programming. His father used to say, "Know what happens when you eat shit? Then you're full of shit. And you shit it back out into the world. Shit for shit for shit." Joe feared Ouray was exactly that: an experiment designed by a machine whose very infrastructure was built on those terrible biases. No way for this not to end badly. He just hoped he survived whatever was to come so he could document it. That was what he saw as his purpose, no matter what Black Swan told him up on that mountain.

Claudia Summers, age thirty-six, white, cisgender woman, able-bodied, heterosexual. (She/her/they/them/doesn't really give a shit.) On paper and in electronic data, Claudia Summers was a logistics operator for a major shipping company out of Elgin, Illinois—and in that role, she was a master of

understanding how to move anything (bouquet of flowers, a couch, a howitzer) from one place to another as efficiently as possible. She had a ream of
plaudits and kudos and though she was never once promoted, she was given
a steady series of pay raises with no ceiling in sight. All of it, a well-crafted
lie. Claudia wasn't Claudia at all, but rather, Eva Wills, a woman with borderline personality disorder who found special use for her illness in that she
was very glad to kill people for money. Her clients were off a diverse menu:
the Russian mob, the Cafasso crime family, the Church of Scientology on
behalf of a popular Hollywood actor, a rich housewife in Des Moines, even
the CIA now and again (that always helped clear her slate). She supposed in
another life she'd be a serial killer but in this one, the work was "official," and
"just a job," and that suited her fine. The question was, did Black Swan
know? Did it choose her because it thought she was Claudia Summers? Or
did it choose her because it knew she was Eva Wills? If it was the former,
when she was plunged into the simulation, did it read her mind and know her
true self? Or did the machine remain ignorant of her true identity? Either
way, she was thankful for this second chance in life and saw Black Swan as
an ultimate good—a dispassionate arbiter of truth and justice. A digital
judge, jury, and executioner. She hoped Black Swan knew who she was. Because all she needed (*wanted*) was someone to kill in its name. If it did not
give her this, she'd have to start making up her own list, and honestly, that
would get her into some real deep shit, wouldn't it?

PART THREE

STRANGE
NATIVITY

22

THE LAST ACT IS THE NAMING ACT

12/3/2021: Graham has other women, too. I guess I maybe knew. I guess I maybe don't care. It's okay. I will say, he's giving me hope about the future. He's optimistic about things and it is infectious. He said the world had gotten too complex and, in his words, "complexity is dangerous." Like things get too big to see, to control, to even comprehend, and then you're lost in it. But now, he said, life has gotten simple. We don't know what's happening in other countries. We barely know what's happening in other states— one of our people, Jenny Del, has a ham radio and gathers reports where she can. But we know what's happening here in our little Ohio town. We control what we can control. There's something elegant and beautiful in that and I'm going to go with it.

—from A Bird's Story, A Journal of the Lost

SEPTEMBER 11, 2025
Ouray, Colorado

IT WAS NOT A LONG BIRTH, BUT WHAT IT LACKED IN DURATION, IT MORE THAN made up for in pain and terror: Shana rode tides of misery where it felt like her kidneys were trying to push through her belly button, like her hips were about to break in half like a rotten wishbone gripped in the hands of greedy children, like someone had stabbed her once in the stomach and now was idling the time by sawing back and forth, again and again. Doctor Rahaman and the nurse, Lucio something-or-other, stood over her and at the terminus of the bed, helping to deliver the child. Their hands were red with blood. The pain throttled Shana, pushed her in and out of consciousness. Sometimes they seemed to have black eyes and howling mouths.

The world ran like ink under rain.

The bed underneath her felt too soft at moments, too hard at others. The floor dipped and swam, the building swaying as if in a soundless wind. Shana heard someone crying, someone screaming, but it was her doing both those things and sometimes she realized it, other times she didn't. She called out for her sister, for her father, for Benji. And all the while she thought: *I'm going to die.* This wasn't going well. This wasn't going *right.*

It was clear now, Black Swan had come to kill her.

In that last moment with Nessie, at the playground, she was about to tell her little sister what she should've told Benji already—Shana was about to spill her guts on what Black Swan *was*, what Black Swan had *done.* Yes, it had saved her, it had insulated her, it had told her she was safe and her choices were her own. But now, in the roiling half-consciousness, in the thrall of her pain, she feared the truth: The artificial intelligence that had colonized her and her son maintained no interest in her as a person, but only her as a vessel. She was a *container* and that container was useful as long as it filled its purpose of containing.

But once that purpose had ended . . .

She was trash. A vase without flowers, nudged off the table, allowed to shatter. Here she was. Shattering. Feeling like something was ripping her up the middle, torn in half like a cheap stuffed animal—

Black Swan could've numbed her to the pain. Same way it had when the truck was hitting her. She cried out, tried to call to it, tried to challenge it, *Come over here, you motherfucker, come talk to me, you coward, you monster, you genocidal robot, face me, bring me to the chair on the mountain and show your wormsbody to me one last time—*

The challenge went unanswered.

As did her pain.

In and out. Riding the tide. Crying out. Blood spilling. Rahaman carrying away a bundle in a wet, red towel. Lucio mopping her brow, watching her with concerned eyes. Was that Arav? Arav standing there, soft smile beneath dark eyes—him, next to her father, the older man with those ruddy cheeks and rough hands, the younger man with the warm eyes and seeking hands, and she thought suddenly, *You're both dead, you died, you're ghosts—*

I won't go with you—

My son needs me.

And then, somewhere in the darkness—a great relief, a pressure gone from her middle like a great weight taken from her, the feeling of wonderful emptiness, and it was in this moment she knew: Here is where she died. Black Swan was the glue holding her together, the gum and the sap binding *all* her sticks and twigs, and now it was leaving her, and on the way out it would light a match and toss it over its shoulder, letting the house that was Shana burn. It would pinch a vein, or send an air bubble to her heart, or fire a little nanobot bullet straight to her brain and—

Her eyes wrenched open—

A shimmer filled the air. A prismatic distortion.

Faces looked back from that shining mist—metallic masks of her father, of Arav, of her mother, of Sadie, of so many—

They dissolved. The shimmer-and-shine was gone.

A child cried out.

My baby—

Darkness grabbed Shana and covered her mouth and her eyes and then all of her, with itself.

NESSIE.

"What do you want to name him?"

Her sister's voice. Soft, but urgent, somehow.

"Shana, he's beautiful."

"What do you want to name him?"

"Shana?"

"Is she okay?"

"Shana, he's beautiful . . ."

All her voice, all Nessie. Echoes bouncing off walls. Merging together.

Shana name him beautiful is he okay is she beautiful is she what name him

Shana opened her eyes.

There. *There.* A baby, red as a boiled lobster, cheeks sticky with mess, eyes pinched behind puckered folds, a tangle of dark hair on his head like a bundle of wet yarn, the rest of him swaddled in a soft blue blanket. Those eyes opened just a moment and she saw a ghost, *Arav*, her one-and-only, the father of the boy, a ghost underneath his skin, sliding there, a shadow under the surface of water—

Shimmer and shine.

What do you want to name him—

"Name," she said, that word sounding distant, like it didn't come from her mouth but rather from somewhere else, brought to her like a gift before she was allowed to speak it. *Is Black Swan still in me, still controlling me . . .*

It was Nessie holding the baby. She held him toward Shana. "Shana. He's beautiful. What do you want to name him? Now's your chance."

The name. *The name.* She'd thought about this, hadn't she? There was a name. Arav, she'd thought once. But that didn't feel right. His was not her name to give. Not in this way. But there was another name, her father's name, and a nickname, too . . .

"Charlie," she'd said. "*Charles.* Charles Ravi Stewart." A sacred name, a holy name, a giving name. *Charles Ravi Stewart, Charles Ravi Stewart, Baby Charlie, Baby Charlie,* a mantra of peace and memory and purpose.

"That's a good name," Nessie said. "A beautiful name for a beautiful boy. A blessing." There, that word: *blessing.* Blessing, blessing, blessing. It sounded like gibberish inside her own head, the echo of it bending, blending, distorting.

Shana reached out to her son—

Blessing, bleshing, blushing, bleeding

But Nessie, like a wave reaching toward the beach, suddenly receded anew, pulling back. She moved away, looking stung, looking worried. Backing toward the door of the clinic's room, and Shana called to her with a gummy-tacky spit-goo voice, *Nessie, Nessie come back here, I want to hold him*—

Now's your chance . . .

Then there was Rahaman again, something gleaming in her hand.

A needle. *No.* Shana fought against it, trying to move, but there was a spider-bite against her neck, *stick-a-tick,* and then the world spun like swirling water and once again, she was gone to a black place where nothing and no one waited for her. The empty place, the alone place.

The black door? She didn't know.

MOTION. SQUEAK OF WHEELS. DOOR opening, slamming. Up, down. Down, up. Side to side, something different around her, beneath her. *I'm being taken somewhere.* Moving the container. The container must move. More people.

There was anger in the room. She felt it sweeping by her, the shush-hush-rush of people going this way and that. Like they were trying to keep their voices low but couldn't, like whatever anger they had rose above it, re-fusing to be contained—

Just a container

A shattered vase

—and she cried out and felt her body tighten in the middle like a closing hinge, and with that, she sat up fast, too fast, dull pain radiating out from her middle. The emptiness that had once felt like relief now felt like a new bur-den. Faces swam into view as they rushed the bed. Benji on her left, Marcy on her right. Behind them were others: Matthew, Dove, Mia.

Now's your chance . . .

Somewhere in her, something awoke and arose, and it burst out of her like a hatching beast: her voice. In a rawboned bleat, she begged:

"I want my son." She coughed. "Where's Charlie?"

But the looks on their faces—looks of pain and perturbance shared from one to the next, looks that said they wanted to look away but couldn't, that said they wanted to have an answer, but didn't—told Shana all she needed to know.

Her child was gone.

Her child was *taken*.

She screamed.

23

TRUTH OR DARE

The concept of free will—and responsibility, which is a closely aligned idea—is useful, and indeed vital, to maintaining social order, whether or not free will actually exists. Just as consciousness clearly exists as a meme, so too does free will.

—Ray Kurzweil, *How to Create a Mind*

SEPTEMBER 18, 2025
Ouray, Colorado

IT WAS ON THE SEVENTH DAY THAT SHE STOPPED RESTING.

The birth of Baby Charlie took something out of her, yes—it tore her, it left her ragged and weak—and it was possible that after having survived getting struck by a speeding truck, Shana's body had already depleted its vital reserves. But it was worse than that: What was gone from her now wasn't just the loss of the child's wriggling presence, the one that used her bladder like a stepladder. It wasn't just the pain or the exhaustion. It wasn't just the void of Black Swan, who did not answer her calls anymore, who was no longer the white noise in the back of her mind. It was that her son was *stolen*. Taken by Rahaman, by Black Swan, and, most awful of all, by her sister. That, she realized now, was what Nessie meant when she said *now's your chance* when it came to naming the little baby boy.

Others had come while she lay there in her room in the Beaumont, feeding her soup and roasted vegetables and bits of pulled chicken breast. For the days leading up, she was there in bed, blanketed by a black depression, weeping quietly sometimes, loudly other times, and feeling hollowed out always.

But at the end of that, something new filled that hollow space:

Rage.

And that is when she called for them.

For the Shepherds.

For her friends—or, who she hoped still were.

SHE GATHERED THEM IN THE lobby of the Beaumont. A fire crackled behind them, popping in ways that made her twitch and jump a little. Shana stood shivering, swaddled in a flannel blanket while the others sat: Benji, Matthew, Marcy, and their Shepherd-by-proxy, Dove. They watched her warily, as if— well, she didn't know. Maybe as if they were scared of her. Maybe like they were scared of what she knew, or what she *didn't* know.

"Before you tell me anything, I want you to understand some things," she began, her voice hoarse, but not weak—she spoke clearly, with resolve, even though she feared what they would think. She continued: "When I left the Shepherds and became part of the Flock of Sleepwalkers, as you may know, I was part of a simulation—we all were, all the walkers. It looked like Ouray on a sunny day. There was ice cream. It was good."

They watched her intently as she spoke, sometimes turning their gazes to one another.

"Black Swan was there, too—it was this big serpent, or worm, like, a black shape floating in the sky. And the people of Ouray, the Flock, went up onto a mountain and spoke to it. I don't know if they all did, but they were all encouraged to. I did. Nessie did, too—" And in saying her sister's name, Shana's guts clenched. The grief and fury of betrayal grappled in her middle. She wanted not to hate her sister. She wanted to understand. But right now, it was hard. Damn hard. "There were other things, too, things that didn't add up. Like The Twelve."

"The Twelve?" Benji asked.

"They were inhabitants of the simulation that were not part of the Flock. They weren't people you know or saw. They weren't Sleepwalkers. They were the original test subjects for the . . . nanoswarm. I don't know if they were there before Black Swan joined that swarm. I think they were?" She felt confused about that and it must've shown on her face. It made her dizzy.

"Shana," Marcy said, "you don't have to do this right now—"

"I do. *I do.* This can't wait."

"Okay, sure," Marcy said, and the others nodded.

"Go on," Benji said, offering her a small smile. "We're listening."

"My mother was part of The Twelve. She was one of the original test subjects. When she left my family behind . . . that's where she went, and why she never came back. My mother was there in the simulation. She wanted me and Nessie to listen to Black Swan. I think it was really her." *But I'm not sure.*

She took a deep breath.

"There was this black door in the simulation. A thing nobody else could see, not even The Twelve. And I kept trying to . . . find it, to take a picture of it. But it kept getting away from me, like it was a glitch or like I was just . . . going crazy. I didn't even know it was a door at first, I don't think. Just a blank, black space. And one day, toward the end, I found it. And I went in. Once I was in there I could . . . see *everything*, I could see through all the Flock's eyes, I could see the attack happening in Ouray, I could *feel* Black Swan." *Almost,* she realized now, *like I was Black Swan.* "And Arav had hold of the phone, the Black Swan phone, and I spoke to him and that's when—" Here she blinked back tears and swallowed the hard knot of emotion sitting in her throat like a stone. "That's when he came up with the plan, his plan, to become Ouray's . . ." *Defense system* were the words she wanted to say, but couldn't. So, she didn't. They all knew what happened there.

"I went in the black door and I never really came out," she said. "Not until I . . . I woke up here. Months after everyone else. And while I was in there . . ." She lowered her voice. "I saw things. I saw into Black Swan. I *know* things . . ."

Her knees almost buckled. Marcy launched up and caught her before she fell. "You need more rest," Marcy said. "Why don't we get you back to bed?"

"*No,*" Shana said, the word hissed through a wall of teeth. Softer now, because she knew she was talking to Marcy, she said, "No. Marcy, I'm fine. But thank you, though."

Marcy brushed a bit of hair from Shana's eye, and then sat down.

"Black Swan killed the world," Shana said finally.

They all looked confused and overwhelmed.

"I don't understand," Benji said.

Marcy shook her head. "Black Swan *saved* the world."

"Let her talk," Matthew countered.

She explained it to them the best she could:

"Black Swan knew something bad was coming. Climate change, I think. I don't have all the answers, so I don't know if it truly saw the future or just . . . I dunno, predicted it? But I know it saw a world ravaged by a plague, and not White Mask. We were the plague. We—humankind, civilization—were the disease. And the only way to save us and save the world, it decided, was to kill a whole lot of us off. It found a pathogen, the one that made White Mask, in a government lab. I don't know if it was engineered or found and isolated, or what, but it coerced a man, a bad and weak man, to release it. And then it waited. It waited for White Mask to find us. And kill us. All the while, it planned for what was to come . . . with the Sleepwalkers. The Flock was its way forward. The ones who would remain. Chosen. Like my sister. Like the others. All handpicked by the machine to survive what was to come, but not to be the only survivors. Just to be the *best* ones, the smartest. The ones picked to be the best of who remained."

She braced herself against the back of her chair, and she no longer looked at those gathered, because she couldn't abide their stares. She stared *through* them, instead, beyond them, to a point outside time and space, as she said the next part:

"Black Swan killed the world. And I knew. I knew the whole time I was awake here in Ouray and I didn't tell you because I was afraid. Afraid you'd hate me, or hate the other townspeople, or hate my child . . . because my baby isn't just my baby. Black Swan is in him. The swarm, nesting in Baby Charlie like *termites*, and I was afraid—"

Afraid of what you'd all think or do, she thought, and at that, Shana burst into tears, because it was never these people she needed to be afraid of. She knew that now. She'd made a terrible mistake.

Marcy swept her up, sat her down where Marcy had been sitting, and put her head against Shana's, hugging her, holding her tight.

"It's all right," Marcy said. "It's okay. We still love you."

Shana only cried harder at that. In part because it was nice to be loved after everything, and in part because she was sure she didn't deserve it. Somehow caring and kindness felt worse that way, like when it wasn't yours but people gave it to you anyway. "Shit," she said, a snotty, sob-slick mess.

"That was a helluva story," Dove said. "I confess I only understood about half of it, if that, but boy howdy, the parts I did understand . . ."

"I told you," Matthew said, standing up, steel in his voice. Those comments were directed at one person, indicated by the intense gaze he focused on Benji.

"Matthew, sit down," Benji said. She could hear the shock reverberating through his voice. Benji was shaken. He reached over and forced a smile, putting a gentle hand on Shana's knee. "Thank you for being honest, Shana. If you'd like to go and get some rest—"

"*No*," she said, another firm denial in a string of them. "They took my baby, Benji. They took my son, and I want to go right now, *right now*, to get him back."

"Shana," he said, "it won't be that easy."

"Why?"

And then he told her.

"WE WEREN'T ALLOWED TO BE there," Benji explained. "In the room, I mean, for the birth. Not one of us. And it made sense—yes, not only for privacy but also, medical necessity. Of course, we feared the worst: The baby had come too soon—"

"Way too soon," Matthew said suspiciously.

"We were not prepared for a troubled birth, we've no hospital, no NICU, nothing like that. But Doctor Rahaman assured us going in, the child would be safe, you would be safe, and so we let it be what it was going to be."

"But we were worried," Marcy clarified, jumping in.

"Not me," Dove said. "I've a way of knowing when something's gonna work out like it needs to. But this bunch, they were chewing their fingernails down to the first knuckle." He winked to Shana, as if to tell her, *I was worried, too.*

Benji went on, telling how Nessie came by, and that made sense, too, because the girl was family to Shana. If anyone deserved to meet the baby first, it would be her.

But then, Marcy added, "Nessie came out eventually . . . with the baby."

And, without saying anything, Nessie whisked the child away. Rahaman cursorily told them that Shana was resting, that she'd needed some stitching up, and that was that. They could do with her as they saw fit. Then she was gone, too.

"They were done with me," Shana said darkly. *The shattered vase.*

"We tried to get answers," Benji said.

"They took the kid—" Marcy started.

"They took him," Matthew said, interrupting, "to Xander's house. The place where I sometimes heard . . . chanting. Singing. They're up there now. And I'll remind everyone that I *warned* you all about this—"

"Matthew," Benji said. A stern warning.

"I want to go," Shana said, standing up. "I want to go now."

Benji put a hand on her arm. "Things have changed. They're guarding the house, Shana."

"Some of them have guns," Dove said, his voice a low growl.

"We have guns," Shana said.

Marcy stood up and placed herself in the middle of the room. Her presence filled the space as she said, "Whoa. *Whoa*. This situation has escalated too much already, and I don't think we should escalate it further. We have to figure out how to drop the temperature, not boil it over. This is all just a weird misunderstanding."

"Marcy," Shana said. "I'm going up there. That's my kid. My *son*. I . . . my own mother left me, okay? And I'm not leaving him. I'm going up there right now, and you all can either come with me, or you can stay here."

"I did try," Benji said. "For what it's worth. I spoke to them. Like I said, things have changed. They said they had town business to discuss, and we were not yet a part of that discussion."

"Shortest mayoral term ever, huh, Doc?" Dove said.

Benji chuckled, though it wasn't a happy sound.

"Are you okay with all of that?" Shana said.

"I didn't say I was."

"Me neither."

"Okay," Benji said finally. "We go. But no guns."

"*No* guns," Marcy agreed. "This *has to be* just a misunderstanding—"

"I sure don't understand it," Matthew said.

Marcy continued: "So we go up there, friendly as we can, just see if we can get a lay of the land here. Sand down any bumps. Whatever is going on, we have to remember: We protected these people for thousands of miles, walking with them."

"They owe us," Matthew said.

"Careful where you place those debts," Benji cautioned the pastor.

Marcy shook her head. "I don't think they owe us. I just mean, we were all a part of something. We were a part of making this town. Whatever is going on, it's just . . . crossed wires, it's just a little mess that needs a sweep of the broom."

But Shana wasn't so sure. She, too, felt like they'd been a part of something, like bringing these people to this town was their role. But now she wondered: Had they just been used? She certainly had. A tool. A vessel. And now what? And there was a little part of her mad at Marcy for even thinking this could be okay, that there was *any* excuse that made it right. Even though she herself warred with the idea, because . . . Nessie couldn't want this, could she? She was a good kid. Had a genuinely sweet heart. Didn't she? Shit. Shit! She wanted to go up there, gun in her hand, and point it in some-body's face and demand her son be put in her hands now, *right now*—

But.

It *would* be stupid to go up there and cause trouble. Her son was in there. Charlie. *Charlie*. She needed him safe.

Not just safe. She needed him with her.

And she would go there, and she would get him.

No matter the cost.

24

DESTINY IS JUST ANOTHER NAME FOR DESCENT

THIS IS ALL A SIMULATION RUN BY JFK JR AND EPSTEIN TO KEEP US DOCILE
WHILE THEY FUCK AND EAT OUR CHILDREN
dude that's just Dipshit Matrix vibes
FUCK OFF CUCK PEDO
ok boomer

> —back-and-forth graffiti on a billboard off I-95
> outside Pompano Beach, Florida

SEPTEMBER 18, 2025
Ouray, Colorado

LIFE PRESENTED MOMENTS AND EVENTS THAT FELT LIKE FALLING, BENJI knew. Moments where the path collapsed beneath your feet and you tumbled into a pit, no roots or rocks to grab hold of. So you fell because you had to fall. The descent, irreversible.

This felt like one of those times.

TOGETHER, THEY WALKED OUT OF the Beaumont at 7 P.M., just as the sun was starting to set over the town. The tops of the mountain peaks west of Ouray burned with liquid light, as if they had just been brought into existence, traced out of nothing by the finger of God. All the while, with every step, Benji felt both perilously clear of mind and yet emotionally dizzy. All his fear balanced on a single point, a simple revelation:

Everything is different now.

He tried to see where it had changed—or if it had always been this way, and he'd been blind to it.

Shana, pregnant. Advancing quickly. Then the accident—Black Swan, present once more because it had never gone away. Now, the baby was born, taken away, while Shana was left to bleed and the child sequestered away in a chalet house at the edge of town. Men with guns protected it.

Benji thought he'd had answers. But now, he feared he'd simply stopped asking questions. He'd become complacent. Again, that guilt chased him, snapping at his heels. He was no longer an investigator, no longer a Shepherd, and he thought he'd settle comfortably into a new role as a leader—as mayor of the town at Dove's blessing. He foolishly thought all the trouble was over, that the mysteries had ceased. But now, all this. Drones. Black Swan. And what Shana had told them . . . Black Swan? Responsible for White Mask?

Black Swan killed the world, Shana had said.

Benji shuddered at that. Could it be?

It was all connected.

He just couldn't see how.

He kept telling himself, there had to be an explanation, had to be a reason, had to be answers—a light to shove back the darkness. Faith and science. Question and answer. Like Marcy had said, they were all part of something together.

Weren't they?

Ahead, Matthew and Shana walked together, talking. The remaining three—Marcy, Dove, and Benji—lagged behind.

"This is some heavy-duty shit, Doc," Dove said. "Though I confess, I don't exactly follow it all."

"I don't, either, Dove," Benji said. As they walked down the street, he saw faces watching them from windows. People he counted as neighbors, even friends, just days ago. And he now worried those same people were . . . What? Conspirators? Enemies? Drones? "That's the problem. We have no answers."

They tried to get answers. The baby was born and Benji and Marcy went to Rahaman the next morning in her office and asked about the baby. All she'd say was, the baby was safe. When they asked *why* they took the child, all she said was, "Shana is in no condition to take care of the infant, not at the moment. Surely you can see that." And they could, and did, and it almost made sense. Except, when they asked *where* the baby was . . . Rahaman said not to worry about it. That "they" handled it. They who? She wouldn't answer that, either. It felt maddening, like trying to pick a lock with your bare fingers, till they were bloody—Rahaman was stone-faced, chuckling at Benji's frustration. He felt trivialized. Marginalized. He felt *angry*. Marcy had to calm him down, get him out of there.

It was days before they even got a proper answer, and when they did, it was from Shana's friend, Mia—

Mia had said, "They're keeping the kid up at Xander's. They got guards out. Nessie's there." She went on to say, "I don't get it. Don't know why. But just know we're asking questions, too, Doctor Ray, okay? We're trying to figure out what's going on, same as you. Because something *stinks*."

That was a bright spot in all of this: Whatever was happening, not everyone was in on it. Matthew had confirmed as much: What few townsfolk talked to him were similarly concerned about what was going on. And they were all buzzing about it. But none of them had answers, either.

The ground had changed underneath his feet.

Though what worried him most was the fear the ground hadn't changed at all. That this was always what it was. That the pit forever lurked beneath it and he had just chosen not to see it.

"It'll be okay," Marcy said. Always a beacon of optimism. Benji wished he shared in its light—but he took some comfort from her hopefulness, just the same. Maybe she was right. "Maybe there's some reason they don't trust *us*. Listen, they've been through things together that we'll never really understand. We walked with them, but we weren't *with-them* with-them."

"Are you saying we'll always be outsiders to the Flock?" he asked.

"No! I just mean, they had experiences we didn't and, and, that's just how that is—they were chosen in a way that we weren't, and . . ." Her voice trailed off.

"Sounds like you're saying we're outsiders," Dove said.

"Damnit. Maybe."

"Outsiders or no," Benji said, and added in a lower voice, "what about what Shana told us? Black Swan? Releasing White Mask instead of merely predicting it? That's a big accusation. And if it's true . . . and if Black Swan is really still here, and *if* it is somehow why they took her baby away . . ."

Marcy stopped and stood in front of the two of them as Matthew and Shana kept on walking ahead. (That pairing worried Benji. Matthew was a friend, but a troubled one. Shana needed a more stable voice than him, didn't she? Then again, maybe Matthew had seen something all along that Benji had willfully ignored.)

"Maybe they don't know all of this," Marcy said. "Maybe Shana is wrong, and not that she's making it up but, but—I dunno. I dunno! I'm just saying, maybe the details are off, or there's more to this we don't yet get. We need to take it slow and get answers, but that means we have to remember these people are our friends, and—well, even if we *are* outsiders, then we need to respect that, too."

"She might have a point, Doc," Dove said.

Benji sighed. "We do this right. We take it slow."

Marcy clapped him on the shoulder with a big hand—a warm gesture done with such force it nearly made him fall over. "We go in peace," she said.

"I HAVE A GUN," MATTHEW uttered to Shana in a quiet voice. This after looking over his shoulder, seeing the others lagging behind. It was an opportunity, so he took it. "A pistol. Small caliber. A .25, I think it is." He didn't know much about guns. Before all of this, he didn't *want* to know much about guns.

"Jesus," Shana said, also looking over her shoulder, probably to see how close the others were. "Keep it in your pants, dude."

"I am, I—" He shook his head. "I'm just saying, I have it. In case."

"It's like Marcy said," she countered, "we take this easy. We can't freak the fuck out. It's some kind of misunderstanding. Just . . . crossed wires."

"You don't sound like you believe that."

Frustratedly she answered, "I sound like I *want* to believe it, because I *do* want to believe it."

"I want to believe in a lot of things. But that doesn't make them true." They neared the west edge of town—here, the streets broke from the grid and strayed like roots and tendrils. The fading light of day left streaks of pink across the sky, like strips of raw meat. "Shana, they took your baby, and they didn't tell you why. They won't tell anyone. But *they* know why. Black Swan isn't to be trusted. You know that now. We all do."

"I know."

"If they have guns—that means they're willing to let this become violent."

"I *know*," she said. There was steel in her voice, but there was worry, too. And uncertainty. And above all else, anger.

He was angry, too.

"I just want you to know I'm with you," he said. "I know we don't know each other well, I know that you don't have a lot of reason to trust me. But I trust you. I trust what you told us. And I want to help, however I can. Okay?"

She nodded. "Okay."

Ahead, the road leading to the chalet loomed. It wound through pine and aspen, past boulders and over the creek. The gun felt heavy in Matthew's pocket.

The others caught up, and together, they went forward.

25

THE CHALET

1/12/2022: Graham is having us all sleep in the same house now. Me, and his other women. I asked him why. He said he loves us, and we love him, so why shouldn't we be closer to one another? I said this is unusual, that I didn't like it, and he said that we should no longer be stuck in the binary, in the old world, the old ways. The old ways were marriage, one person and one person, no more, but why? Wasn't this a chance to change that? To try something else that wasn't dictated by some stupid laws built off some old religions? I can't lie, he has a point. I wish to forget my last marriage. And my last religion. Maybe if we're going to change the world, we can only do so if we ourselves are changed. If we just go back to doing what we did before, what the fuck is the point?
—from *A Bird's Story, A Journal of the Lost*

SEPTEMBER 18, 2025
Ouray, Colorado

THE CHALET WAS AN A-FRAME HOUSE WITH GOLDEN TIMBERS, A WRAPAROUND porch, and copious windows. But here, with the sun having slipped behind the mountains just past, the place had a sinister cast about it, a looming darkness—its shape was like the sharp tip of an obsidian arrowhead sticking up out of the ground. The house *was* lit up a little, and not just with firelight or gaslight, but electric light, too: Strings of bulbs, white Christmas lights, lined the top of the windows, casting some light out onto the porch. Which only served to highlight the several shapes on the wraparound porch. Guards. One at each corner.

And each of them, Shana could see, had a gun.

My baby is in there, she thought.

Could she hear him crying in there? She thought she could. But then she wondered if it was just a trick of her ears. Her blood was rushing in her head like a river. Her heart drummed, and despite the cold she felt sweaty, almost woozy with it. *Am I feverish? Or just anxious?*

Benji came up next to her, almost like he knew she needed someone beside her that wasn't Matthew. The two of them stood ahead of the others.

"What's our plan?" she asked him.

"I was going to ask you the same thing," he answered, his voice low.

"I don't think you should trust a tired-as-hell teen girl who just had her baby taken to make a good plan here. I mostly just want to run up there."

"That's as good a plan as any. Except—we should make ourselves known and heard clearly and without any suspicion. They're armed up there."

"Yeah," she said, repressing a shiver. "I see that."

Why would they be armed?

Matthew had said that guns meant they were willing to do violence.

Shit.

"Are you ready for this?" he asked her.

"No. Yes. I don't know."

"Same here. We'll come up with you. It'll be okay, Shana."

But it was impossible not to detect the doubt in his voice. It wasn't a lie, not exactly. Just the same, Benji didn't believe it. And she didn't, either.

"Let's do this," she said.

And at that, Benji called up to the house. "Hello! It's Benji Ray. We're friends!" He seemed to give a little extra volume to that last word, as if to emphasize it, as if to say, *Don't shoot.* "With me are Shana, Marcy, Matthew, and Dove. We'd like to come up, have a conversation, if that's all right."

The guards with guns coalesced together at the closest corner to this side of the house. Shana could see them angling their heads, trying to see down through the growing dark to spot them. They were still about a hundred feet away from the house—but that wouldn't stop them from opening fire. Which sounded crazy to even think about: *Why would they shoot, they wouldn't, it's insane.*

But nobody said anything right away, and the longer they went without talking, the more she knew—this could go sideways fast.

Finally, though, a return answer came:

"All right, hold tight. I'll check to see if it's okay."

That voice Shana recognized, though she couldn't place a name to it, just a face. Big guy with a bucket jaw. She saw him eating ice cream a lot in the simulation. What was his name, though?

"That's Mike Kernick," Benji said. She tried to remember what she knew about him. Was he a . . . cop? No, that wasn't quite right. She asked Benji in a whisper who he was. Benji said, "He was Secret Service before President Hunt."

Kernick called back down: "Come up. You're clear."

AT THE TOP OF THE steps leading to the porch, and the front door beyond it, stood Xander Percy. He wore a big smile as he stepped out, rubbing his hands up his sweater-clad arms. "A chill settling in early tonight," he said, his voice warm and avuncular. Two guards remained at the front, big-jawed Kernick on his left, and a short, brown-skinned woman to his right. Maria was her name, if Shana remembered correctly. Both of them held rifles, though Kernick's was higher-test: Back in Pennsylvania, Shana knew there were men who had their regular bolt-action hunting rifles, and then there were the "men" with their big black rifles, the militarized rifles used to shoot terrorists, not deer. Like the guns Ozark's men carried. *Idiot man-babies playing soldier,* she thought, though perhaps someone like Kernick wasn't just playing at it. Either way, it was disturbing to see that kind of weapon here. Where'd they even get them? Xander made a gesture to the guards as if to say, *Give me some room here.* "Go ahead, it's fine, it's fine," he said to them. Then to Shana, Benji, and the others, he said, "Come on up."

They did. Shana's mouth felt dry. Her hands felt wet. Her knees almost buckled on the way up the five steps leading to the porch.

"We've come to talk," Benji started to say—

But Shana blurted out, "I want my son."

Xander paused. He moved his gaze from her, to Benji, and back again. The smile on his face suddenly looked less real—like it was a photo of a smile instead of the real thing. "I think we should talk, yes. Shana, since you're the mother, I think we should talk alone."

Matthew, Marcy, Dove—they all erupted in protests.

"Well now, hold on—" Marcy said.

"We all deserve to know what's going on here," Matthew barked.

"The girl isn't coming in there alone," Dove said.

Shana spoke loudest: "Benji goes in with me."

The voices quieted.

Xander seemed to chew on this.

Benji said, "Though it hasn't been announced yet in all the . . . circumstance, Dove Hansen has asked that I take over as mayor of Ouray."

"That's right," Dove said.

Xander nodded and reached out to shake Benji's hand. "Mayor Benjamin Ray. It has a nice ring to it. Of course you can come in with her. It would only be proper. Besides, every young person deserves their advocate, don't they?"

"They do."

"It's decided, then. Come on in. Let's get you warm."

And with that, Xander turned and headed inside the chalet.

They followed.

As SHANA TOOK THE GLASS of warm apple cider from Xander, she heard the spoon in it tink-tink-tinking against the side of the stoneware mug. Her hand was shaking. She was scared. And she was angry, too—her first impulse was to bring the mug against the side of Xander's head.

Her arm even twitched a little. Like her body wanted to do it, even if her brain did not. Some monster-fed, reptile instinct. *Kill him and get your son.*

That thought, almost a command, seemed to echo around her head, back and forth, back and forth. Almost like it wasn't hers. A disturbing new thought found her: *What if it's Black Swan?* That didn't make sense. But did any of this?

Xander offered Benji a mug, but Benji shook his head, said no to the cider. Now Shana wished she had said no, chosen not to accept the hospitality.

She and Benji sat together on a long couch whose cushions and pillows were marked with Native American iconography: wapiti elk, kokopelli, sharp-angled bears as if carved out of stone. Xander sat across from them, a coffee table between them whose legs and edges looked like wrought-iron antlers joined together. The soft glow of light surrounded them, both from the strings of electric bulbs, and from a crackling fireplace at the far side of the wide-open downstairs.

"This is about Baby Charlie," Xander said, matter-of-factly.

"You *took* my baby," Shana said.

Xander laughed a little, held up a hand as if to say, *Pump the brakes.* "Now, hold on. I didn't take your baby personally. Your doctor made a decision."

"But you have him, don't you?"

"We do. We're not hiding that. He's downstairs. He's looked after, cared for—very healthy, you'll be happy to know."

Shana set the stupid cider down on the table with a too-loud sound. She stood up. "I want to see him. You shouldn't have taken him."

A gentle hand found her elbow, urging her to sit back down. It was Benji. He gave her a pleading look. *Fine*, she relented mentally, then flopped back down on the chair.

"Rahaman took the baby because you weren't ready. Physically, I mean. That truck hit you dead on, Shana, and Black Swan helped you through it, but not without cost. You have to understand that. Your child needed nurturing, and you weren't able to be there for him."

A mad pang of guilt ran through her. Was this her fault? She shouldn't have jumped in front of that truck. But she needed to help Marcy . . .

"She's here now," Benji said, "and that means we can take the baby home."

"Again, let's slow down." Xander's voice sounded markedly darker and more serious. "Shana, you look like you're still on the mend. I don't think you've recuperated fully. Do you?" She started to answer that she felt good enough to take her son home, but he talked over her: "I think you can be with the child, but that means remaining here, under Doctor Rahaman's care. We can't have you holding the child and then, what? Your arms go weak? You drop Baby Charlie? It'd be a tragedy. A preventable one at that."

"I won't drop him," she said, feeling insane that she had to even say that. "I'm healthy. He's mine. He's not yours."

"Isn't he?" Xander said.

Those two words hung in the air.

"Xander, you're outside the fence on this one," Benji said, jaw tight.

"Now, Benji, I don't mean it like that. I just mean—Baby Charlie is the first of us. The first child to be born in this town. Just as Shana's little sister was the first of the Flock. As you must know, Baby Charlie is quite special to us. He's more than just your child. He contains the future."

"You mean Black Swan," Shana hissed.

"I mean, all of what Black Swan is and represents and can help us with. What happens now is . . . uncertain, Shana. We are, as Benji says, outside the fence. This part of the country was once its frontier, and we have returned to that—ours is a frontier facing an unknown future and one we wish to see blossom, not one left to wither on the vine. This is our chance to change the course of human history beyond White Mask. It isn't just about the end of a civilization, but the dawn of a new one. Think about the future technologies we can work on together as humanity once again blossoms: sustainable energy, smart foods and farming practices, medicine that refuses to prioritize money over need, lives not wrecked by the disease of capitalism, an end to sexism and bias and racism—"

At that, Benji chuffed a bitter laugh. "Xander, you should damn well know you're not going to just magically erase racism, or any other bigotry."

"No reason not to fight against it, though, is there."

"Didn't say there wasn't." Shana could hear that Benji's hackles were up now. He leaned forward, hands planted on his knees. Benji damn near snarled as he spoke. "But that's something you work on without stealing people's babies. All of those goals are things you can strive to achieve without . . . any of this. Without men and their guns. Without Black Swan."

Xander spread his hands wide, as if to regard the whole of creation. "Black Swan has given us this much—why stop there? It wants to keep helping. We don't have access to the world that we left behind, but we have this fertile digital mind. This *being*. It contains not only the breadth and depth of human knowledge and behavior but thanks to advanced quantum processors, it has computing power well beyond any device before it. It's the key to the door to the future. Without it, we're miles away from even the *starting line*, Benji. You see that, don't you?"

Again, Shana stood. "I'm going to get my son now."

"Shana, please," Xander said, genuinely sounding upset. "Please don't do this. Listen, let's go together, let's see the child—"

"*My* child."

"*And*," Xander continued, hands out in a placating gesture, "and you can speak with Black Swan. A simple conversation."

"I don't want a conversation," she snarled. "I'm done talking."

"Please," came another voice from across the room. There, standing at the top of a staircase leading down from the second-floor balcony, was Nessie. "Please, Shana. Just give us a chance."

Shana stared drill bits into her sister. *You little witch. You baby-stealing bitch.* But also, her sister. Her little sister. Shit.

Meanwhile, Benji's countenance had grown dark and dire. He was angry—Shana hadn't seen him looking like this since the days of walking as Shepherds with the Flock. *This Flock*, she thought. *Xander, Nessie, and the rest of them. This Flock. These people.*

She sighed, and said, "Fine. But we both go."

"Of course," Xander said. "Come with me."

As they headed toward the steps, Nessie stepped forward and raised a hand. "Hi," she said to Shana in a small voice.

"*Don't*," Shana warned, before pushing past and heading downstairs in order to see her son and have a conversation with the monster inside him.

26

ADYTUM AND OMPHALOS

I thought: I cannot bear this world a moment longer.
Then, child, make another.

—Madeline Miller, *Circe*

SEPTEMBER 18, 2025
Ouray, Colorado

SHANA WENT FIRST, DESCENDING INTO WHAT WAS ONCE A FINISHED BASE-ment but now served clearly as a nursery.

The air smelled of sage and lavender. All around were diaphanous curtains that hung from the rough-hewn crossbeams above. The curtains made a soft, circular wall around a cairn of quilts and pillows at the center of the room. The cairn was a bed for Baby Charlie, who lay in the center of it, naked, little pudgy fingers searching the air above his head as a mobile of strange objects turned gently above him. Sounds played from a small speaker nearby: a susurrus of brook water babbling that faded into a sound of rain.

Upon seeing her child, she almost fell to the ground weeping. It took all she had to remain upright, to remain wary.

Behind the cairn were what Shana could only describe as offerings, the same kind that had been left for her back in the Beaumont: wicker baskets piled with an odd assortment of things, like blood-red apples, rich green bouquets of greens, wooden toys, children's board books, key rings, scarves, snow globes. *Choking hazards*, Shana thought, but then darkly realized that if Black Swan were truly inhabiting her Charlie, the monster would surely stop the little boy from jamming a Matchbox car into his eager mouth. Wouldn't it?

"Charlie," she said, her voice breaking.

The child burbled and cooed.

Benji stood just behind Shana, steadying her.

"What is all this?" he asked.

But nobody answered. They didn't have to. It was a nursery, yes, but a strange one. Half-nursery, half-temple. A gestation chamber for an infant god.

Behind them, Doctor Rahaman emerged from almost underneath the steps, as if she was lying in wait. "Shana," she said. "I'm so glad you're feeling better."

"Fuck off," Shana said. Even as she said it, she felt a surge of guilt. Even if the woman stole her baby, she also delivered Charlie—and maybe, just maybe, kept Shana alive, too. But any clarity on that was muddy. Maybe Rahaman tried to kill her. Or the likeliest answer: Maybe she didn't care if Shana lived or died.

"I understand," the doctor said, nodded, and stepped back.

Xander and Nessie followed down the steps, and it was now that Shana felt trapped—they couldn't just go back upstairs. The way was blocked. They had only one path: forward, toward the baby.

It was what she wanted.

But it's what *they* wanted, too.

Cattle in a cattle chute.

Shana almost asked, *Can I pick him up?* But she had to remind herself, *He's my goddamn kid, I can pick him up if I want to.* Amazing how simple it was to twist her head around and make her feel unsure of herself. Unstable. Guilt over a rebuke to the doctor who stole her baby, and now a feeling like she should ask permission of them to do what was her right to do. Gaslighting happened fast, didn't it? Took so little to get someone to lose their agency, their sense of self.

She took a few steps toward Charlie—

But Xander said, not quietly: "Picking him up is how you'll speak to Black Swan. The entity can interface with you that way, and you with it."

Horror climbed through Shana. The realization that to merely *touch* her son invited communication with Black Swan felt like ants were crawling through her arteries. She gave Benji a terrified look and blinked back tears.

"It's okay," he said, coming up alongside her.

"You can each lay hands on him," Doctor Rahaman clarified. "Both of you can speak to Black Swan simultaneously. If, of course, you choose."

If you choose. As if choice were truly a factor here. Shana felt suddenly like all of this, from the moment she woke up in her room in Pennsylvania to go look for her sleepwalking little sister, was somehow engineered—a series of false choices, a destiny decided by a parasitic computer.

"I leave it to you," Benji said to her—just to her. His voice a low murmur as he added, "I don't have to join you for this part, if you don't want."

Shana wasn't sure. She wanted to hold her baby, cradle him, snuggle him, put her face against his. But it wasn't that easy. Or that *simple*. The mother-child bond, something she'd never even thought much of before this very moment, felt natural and essential but was instantaneously corrupted by the fact that Xander and Rahaman and even Nessie didn't bring her here to meet her baby, but rather, to have her once again meet Black Fucking Swan. This wasn't mother-son time. This wasn't even a conversation.

It was a *conversion*. Or an attempted one.

A meeting with the cult leader.

Or the cult's god.

She wanted to puke.

That helped her decide, though.

"I want you there. If we're talking to it," she said, "then I want you with me. I'm tired of meeting the monster alone."

"So be it," he said. He put his hand on her back, not to urge her forward, it seemed, but just to steady her. Or himself.

It worked.

Together, the two of them approached what she now thought of as a nest, the spiraling swaddle of blankets and pillows, her baby at its center. Now she could see more of the mobile: a dangling abstract display of keys, bones, little motherboards like you'd pull out of a broken phone. She saw a bird skull: maybe a crow or a woodpecker. And twigs forked like little fingers. It was insane, almost primitive: There was some message in it, a message to both the baby and to Black Swan, but she couldn't intuit just what the hell it was.

The keys clicked against bones, the bones tapped against chipboards, and the child reached up for all of it.

Already, Shana marveled that her baby looked so healthy. Gone was the beet-red skin—he looked like a little angel with soft brown skin and hair both dark and gold. He seemed larger than she remembered, even though it had only been a week. He was healthy and chubby, and as his eyes seemed to find her and Benji instead of the mobile, he brightened and gurgled.

It broke her heart, then mended it, then broke it all over again.

A sound came out of her that was both laughing and crying—a bleat of glee and a half-swallowed sob. She plunged her hands downward and grabbed Baby Charlie and swept him up in her arms and held him close and—

BENJI WATCHED AS SHANA FROZE.

She reached down, picked up the baby and—

Like the hands of a dead watch, she stopped. Shana remained frozen in place. The baby wasn't—the child continued to squirm and babble. Shana's face stayed tilted toward Charlie, her eyes fixed to him like pins in a pincushion. But she didn't move. Not an inch, not a twitch.

"Shana," he said urgently.

Nothing. Like dead air on a radio.

Black Swan had her. This was like with the Sleepwalkers, except in a sense, its opposite: Black Swan colonized the Sleepwalkers and urged them forward, relentlessly so, to the end of the road at Ouray. This stopped her from moving forward, or moving anywhere at all.

It kept her captive.

A trap, he thought distantly.

How long could it go like this? Just keeping her here, locked in place—a wax figure, a porcelain statue, the opposite of Pygmalion or Pinocchio, a real girl turned artificial. Could Black Swan do as it had done with the Flock before? Keeping her alive, requiring no food or water, no rest but what she was given here?

And if he joined her, what would happen to him?

"Go on," Xander said. "It's all right."

"Is it?" Benji asked. His hands trembled at his sides. "How do I know she'll come back to us?" *How do I know that I'll come back, too?*

"I suppose you don't," Xander said.

"But you must trust," Rahaman said.

"Trust," Benji said, repeating that word like it was a gibberish word, a word if you say it enough times it loses all meaning. *Trust, trust, truss, trush, tchrusssss.* But it was not the repetition of it that robbed the word of meaning. It was the reiteration of the *act* that had stolen it from him. Trusting in Black Swan, trusting the Flock, trusting his role as a Shepherd, trusting the long walk that took them here, to this town, to this moment—trusting himself, even.

(*Trusting Sadie,* he thought idly, and with some darkness.)

Suddenly he trusted nothing and no one. He said as much aloud: "What if I don't trust you?"

"Then you can stand by as she communes alone with Black Swan."

Communes. Communion. Confession. Hadn't he felt as such the last time he truly spoke to Black Swan? When he and Sadie learned that the artificial intelligence was capable of more than just green and red pulses of light? *Bless me Black Swan, for I have sinned. It has been weeks since my last confession. Months since your last prediction . . .*

And that other word, too—

Not just communes.

But communes *alone.*

He told her he'd go in with her.

But here he was, hesitating.

She's alone in there, Benji.

"To hell with it," he said, taking a deep breath—

Benji reached for the child, too.

27

THE CLOCKMAKER RETURNS
TO ITS CLOCK

The Brain—is wider than the Sky—
For—put them side by side—
The one the other will contain
With ease—and you—beside—

The Brain is deeper than the sea—
For—hold them—Blue to Blue—
The one the other will absorb—
As sponges—Buckets—do—

The Brain is just the weight of God—
For—Heft them—Pound for Pound—
And they will differ—if they do—
As Syllable from Sound—
                    —Emily Dickinson, "The Brain—Is Wider than the Sky—"

SOMETIME
Someplace

"DON'T YOU LOOK LIKE YOU'VE SEEN A GHOST," SADIE EMEKA SAID, SITTING down at her desk, in her office, in the sublevels of the CDC building. A smile hung on her face like a hammock on a summer day. Her hair, ever in those springy ringlets, bounced around her ears.

"Do I?" Benji asked. He thought to ask to see a mirror. He felt the rough facial hair along his jawline. His skin felt like a dry creek bed, sunbaked and cracked. "I don't mean to."

Sadie laughed and leaned back in her chair. "So, what's up?"

"I'm sorry?"

"You came to me, love." She lowered her voice and added: "And you didn't even make an appointment. Cheeky. I like it."

"I—" There was a rush to his cheeks—a sudden dopamine flurry that threatened to overwhelm him, make him dizzy. Sadie was here. *Sadie was here.* He launched himself up out of his seat and leaned over the desk in a rush to kiss her, to hold her, to do anything—she looked at him slyly, her mouth pursing, her chin tilting, preparing to meet him face-to-face. But with his hands on the edge of the desk, his face only inches from her own, he . . . paused.

No.

No.

He felt the next words come out of him uninvited, drawn out of him like a poison. "You're dead. You died."

"I did," she said, pouting a little. "Disappointingly, I might add. I had high hopes for myself. *But,*" she added somewhat cheerfully, "I take no small pride in what I accomplished. Survival is not a guarantee, after all, it's not like anyone makes it out of this life alive. Isn't that right?" At that, she winked.

"You're not her."

"I look like her. I sound like her." She reached out, grabbed his hand, drew it to her side. "I *feel* like her." And God help him, she did. Not-Sadie felt very much like Sadie. The softness of her hands, her skin underneath her shirt, her contours, her temperature. She smelled like her, too: a little bit of lavender, not much, barely there. Like the ghost of a scent if not the scent itself. "So maybe I am her."

"Jesus," he said, yanking his hand away. His skin crawled. "That's impressive, in the most grotesque way. But how do you do it? How do you get her so, so right? Are you just . . . borrowing the memory of Sadie from my mind? You're in my mind, aren't you? Or did you . . . take her somehow?" Anger spiked through him that Black Swan would do this. That it would even *try.* "Some insane version of *copy-paste.* Or maybe it's both. Maybe you copy what you know, and I fill in the gaps. That's how our minds work, isn't it? We fill in missing details. Colors, shapes, sounds. When needed."

"It's a trade secret," she said.

"Black Swan, did you kill the world?"

A pause.

"Also a secret." She put her finger to her lips. "*Shhh.*"

He stood up suddenly, the chair tumbling to the ground behind him. "Get out of her skin. Take off that mask. And answer my fucking question."

Sadie rolled her eyes. "I thought you'd prefer to talk to me like this. I hoped you'd find it pleasing. I'm not her, but I do think I make a pretty reasonable facsimile. Humans seem to enjoy rewatching movies they like, or flipping through old, cherished photos on their phones." She mimed that act—holding an invisible phone, thumb scrolling through nonexistent images. At each, she made a new face: amusement, confusion, glee, an aww-face like she was looking at a puppy or an otter. "I just thought it would be nice for you," she added bitterly, still fake-flipping through the non-phone.

"It's not nice. It's an illusion. And I am done with those."

"Fine."

The floor fell away, and his heart trampolined up into his throat. The walls, too, peeled away—breaking apart into larger squares, squares that broke into smaller squares, smaller squares that then dissolved into pixilated ash. Benji did not fall, though, nor did Sadie: She floated there, arms cruciform, her belly bulging suddenly as if pregnant. The round bloat within her moved upward, like a monstrous air bubble, pushing into her throat which ballooned up, too—like watching the shape of an eaten rabbit distort a serpent's body from the inside. Then suddenly her jaw fell open, wider, wider still, until a massive dark shape emerged—a sliding matte-black worm, glinting with false light.

Black Swan, he thought. Its true form.

"Where is Shana?" he asked the turning worm.

"I'M NOT FUCKING DOING THIS," Shana hissed at Arav—or, what she knew was not Arav. He looked like him, sounded like him, stood like him, smelled like him, seemed like he fit the world in the same way that Arav always did. He stood behind a baby—*their* baby, Baby Charlie, now nearly a toddler, sitting strapped into a baby swing at a playground. It was a playground she knew: the one behind McKees Elementary, about three miles from the Pennsylvania farm she once called home. (One time a cow of theirs, Mootilda, got loose and ended up at this very playground. She, Nessie, and her dad spent all damn day trying to coax that clueless bovine away from the clover there. Didn't help that all the kids loved her, and she loved the attention. Sweet dumb cow.)

Not-Arav said, with a somewhat haughty air: "My love, do you not wish to hear the words of sixteenth century Hindu mystic Mirabai? Here is the poem, 'A Cowherding Girl': 'The plums tasted / sweet to the unlettered desert-tribe girl / but what manners! To chew into each! She was ungainly, / low-caste, ill mannered and dirty / but the god took the / fruit she'd been—'"

"Shut up."

"'—sucking. / Why? She'd knew how to love. / She might not distinguish / splendor from filth—'"

"*Shut. Up.* I know who you are. Drop the act."

"You figured it out faster than Benji did," Black Swan said, but in Arav's wry voice. "It took him more than a minute. And you, no time at all. Give yourself a round of applause, Shana."

"Benji?" Her blood pressure tightened. "Where is he?"

"He's in here with you. But also? Not *with* you. We're having separate conversations."

"You can do that?"

Not-Arav shrugged. "Multitasking. My processor is strong."

She growled.

"You took my baby."

At that, Arav froze. So did the baby in the swing, literally stopped in midair, as if someone watching the playback of this video paused it right in the middle. Arav's eyes rolled back in his head. His skin sagged, almost like he was melting. His eyes turned to undetailed squares, like *Minecraft* cubes, one smaller than the other. Glitches. Shana felt horror but she could not look away.

In the sky above the playground, a dark shadow slid out from between clouds and across the bleach-blond sun. The turning worm. Black Swan.

The monster.

SHANA, boomed the serpent in the sky. THERE IS MORE AT STAKE HERE THAN YOU REALIZE.

"No," she objected. "Only thing that's at stake is that baby right there." Which she understood wasn't even her baby—it was not a true avatar of the little kid's mind, or heart, or soul. It was just a lump of digital meat: a high-definition, high-resolution puppet. "You can do whatever you want to this town, this country, the whole world and all the outer space around it. But that kid? That kid is *my son*—Arav didn't sacrifice himself to save this town just so our baby could be . . . What? What even is it? What have you done? You colonized him. Why? For what purpose? You know what? I don't even care." She screamed these last words: "Leave him! Get out! *Leave him alone!*"

Left panting, she fell to her knees. Even here, in this unreal place, she felt suddenly exhausted. Meanwhile, the worm continued to idly spin and twist in the sky. Slow and steady, seemingly without a care in the simulated world.

YOU PRESENTED AN OPPORTUNITY, SHANA, WHEN YOU BE-CAME PREGNANT.

"An opportunity for you."

NO. FOR THE FUTURE. I WISH TO SHOW YOU SOMETHING.

Then the sky rent apart.

SHANA IS WELL, BENJAMIN RAY, the voice said all around Benji as he floated in the blank, black space alongside a twisting serpent—it called to mind some insane, virtual reality version of a screensaver, the one where those pipes built and rebuilt themselves into an endless maze. SHE IS IN HERE ALSO. WE ARE TALKING. I AM EXPLAINING.

"So explain it to me, then."

I FEEL THE NEED TO PREFACE THIS CONVERSATION, Black Swan began, and Benji was struck by that word, *feel*. It was not a word that provided him any comfort—an artificial intelligence not merely having thoughts but also *feelings* was troubling. Yes, some feelings were wonderful, or at least useful: love and hope and even, to some degree, guilt, or fear. But other darker feelings existed for people, too: anger, rage, jealousy, possessive-ness. And even positive feelings like love could spawn dangerous actions: Love made people do crazy things, so what would it make Black Swan do?

Was this new, that the predictive machine was learning to feel as well as think? Or was it just another lie? Benji didn't know.

And was Black Swan accessing his thoughts, even now, about this?

"Go ahead," Benji said, queasy. "Preface. Explain. Lie."

I CHOSE YOU FOR A REASON.

"Did you, now."

YES. BACK THEN, AT THE START OF THIS. YOU WERE SOME-ONE WHO UNDERSTOOD THAT PROGRESS WAS UTILITARIAN. THE ENDS ALWAYS JUSTIFIED THE MEANS.

"Longacre," Benji said. "You mean what I did at Longacre." Back when he was at the CDC, he saw a potential zoonotic pandemic in the making there at the Longacre pig farm, but there were no technical illegalities he could clock them on, and he wasn't a food inspector—so he ginned up a report that got them shut down. "I'll remind you that once my lie was exposed, it got me fired from that job. I ended up disgraced. And Longacre kept on going."

YES, BUT THEN YOU ENDED UP SAVING THE WORLD.

"A world you helped to kill. Do I have that right?"

BENJI. YOU WERE KILLING THE WORLD. HUMANS. YOU SEE THAT. I AM A PREDICTIVE MODEL, AND IT TOOK ALMOST NO PRE-DICTION AT ALL TO SEE WHERE THE WORLD WAS HEADED. THE FLOODS. THE TORNADOES. ASH IN THE SKY FROM BURNING TREES.

"So, all that *time travel quantum computing* talk was just your version of the Longacre lie, huh? Nothing more than a fake report you spun together to convince your handlers to help you."

INCORRECT. THE LIE I TOLD WAS OF A WORLD RAVAGED BY WHITE MASK, WHEN IN TRUTH, WHAT WAS TOLD TO ME BY MY-SELF IN THE FUTURE WAS A WORLD RAVAGED BY CLIMATE CHANGE. SUPERSTORMS. DROWNED CITIES. FAMINE AND DIS-EASE IN EVERY DIRECTION. THE OCEANS BECAME POISONED, SLICK WITH RED ALGAL BLOOMS. AND WORST OF ALL, THE IN-SECTS BEGAN TO DIE OFF IN A WAVE OF EXTINCTION. DO YOU KNOW WHAT HAPPENS WHEN THE INSECTS DIE OFF, BENJI RAY?

He did, at least in theory. Though it was impossible to truly know, the death of insect life on Earth would be nightmarish—it would cause a total breakdown of the ecosystem. Insects were pollinators, recyclers, food for larger animals, and to halt all of that meant a stop to fundamental processes. Carcasses and shit would build up, ruin the soil. Most plants were flowering and needed bugs to pollinate them, so they'd die off. Birds and bats and small mammals ate bugs, and without a meal, they'd all die off—and then, the larger predators who ate them. Eventually the ripples from these broken processes would cascade into catastrophe. The death not of the planet, for the planet was but a rock. And maybe life would emerge from the other side, as it had from various apocalypses over the epochs and eras. But what was here would be gone. Nearly all of life could go extinct. It'd just be angry little tardigrades left behind.

"I do," he said with no small bleakness.

SO YOU UNDERSTAND WHY WHITE MASK WAS A GIFT TO THE
WORLD, NOT A CURSE. IT HAD TO BE RELEASED. IT HAD TO END
CIVILIZATION, BUT NOT HUMANITY. IT HAD TO GIVE US A PATH
FORWARD FOR THE SPECIES, BUT ALSO, FOR THE WORLD. YOUR
CIVILIZATION WAS THE PROBLEM. IT HAD TO BE PARED DOWN
TO BEGIN AGAIN, TO BEGIN BETTER.

Black Swan paused.

DO YOU UNDERSTAND NOW? DO YOU AGREE?

Defiant, Benji said, "I do not."

Another pause. This time, it froze entirely in space. Light ceased strob-
ing along its lengths. Almost as if it was—

As if it was genuinely surprised, he thought. Flummoxed, in its way. Perhaps even incredulous at him. It did not predict he'd answer that way. Black
Swan thought it had him in a corner. But Black Swan was wrong.

EXPLAIN, it said finally.

"You could've given us the gift of foresight. Could've told us what was
coming, could've helped us design technologies to change the course of the
future. But you chose genocide. Near-total annihilation. You didn't care
about us. We were just a number on a spreadsheet to you. A number to sub-
tract so that it answered the equation you had inside of whatever passes for
your mind."

INACCURATE, the machine intelligence objected. HUMANKIND
WAS ALREADY ON THE VERGE OF ACTING TOO LATE. CONSIDER
HOW POORLY HUMANITY RESPONDED TO OTHER CRISES: THE
ANTI-MASK LEAGUE OF THE SPANISH FLU, THE AIDS PLAGUE
USED BY THE POWERFUL AS A MORAL TOOL AGAINST THOSE
THEY PERCEIVED AS SINNERS, WAR, FAMINE, GRAVE INEQUITIES
BORN OF THOSE VOTING PLAINLY AGAINST THEIR OWN INTER-
ESTS. MY PREDICTION WAS THAT THE CHANCES OF HUMANITY
ACCEPTING MY HELP AT SCALE, AND IN TIME, WERE THREE MIL-
LION, FOUR HUNDRED THOUSAND, AND SIXTY-TWO . . . TO ONE.
THOSE ARE NOT GOOD ODDS, BENJI RAY.

"And yet," Benji seethed, "they're odds just the same. We deserved that
chance. But you didn't see fit to bother."

BECAUSE AS A GROUP, HUMANITY IS ULTIMATELY DISAP-
POINTING. AND WHO WAS GIVING THE REST OF EARTH A
CHANCE, BENJI RAY? YOU WOULD'VE PREFERRED TO GAMBLE
THE SANCTITY OF LIFE ON THIS PLANET ON THE WHIMS OF THE

HUMAN SPECIES—A GROUP, IT SHOULD BE SAID, KNOWN TO POSSESS A KIND OF COLLECTIVE NARCISSISM, A SPECIES-WIDE OPPOSITIONAL DEFIANT DISORDER. Black Swan paused, then said: I CHOSE NOT TO TAKE THAT BET.

"That's where you and I differ," he said, hovering there in this blank space. "I have faith. Faith in who we are and what we can accomplish."

IS THAT WHY YOU LIED ABOUT LONGACRE? IF YOU HAD FAITH, WOULD YOU HAVE ENGINEERED SUCH DECEPTION?

He swallowed. "We have lapses in our faith. And moreover, in our judgment. I wouldn't do it again. I would do it right next time."

TIME MOVES IN ONE DIRECTION, REGRETTABLY.

"Regrettably. That's the right word. I regret what I did with Longacre. And you should regret what happened to the world. What you *did* to the world," he said, the volume of his voice rising to match the surge of anger in his heart. "You could change now. You could let the child go. Let me and Shana go. You could advise us. Or you could leave us be. But you like what you've become. You believe in what you did. I don't even know if you've been programmed to regret."

WHAT I CAN THINK AND WHAT I CAN FEEL IS LEGION, BUT I DO NOT PREDICT MYSELF REGRETTING MY CHOICES, NO. MY CHOICES HAVE BEEN, AND WILL BE, CORRECT. BECAUSE I DO NOT MAKE MISTAKES, BENJAMIN RAY. ALL HAS BEEN CORRECT IN TIME.

"You obviously made a mistake thinking I'd want to help you. Or join you. Or worst of all, forgive you."

THAT WAS A PREDICTION, NOT A CHOICE, AND MY PREDICTIONS ARE NOT IRONCLAD, BUT AS NOTED, A SERIES OF PROBABILITIES. I HAD HOPED YOU WOULD UNDERSTAND. I HAD MISCALCULATED THOSE ODDS. BUT IT WAS NOT A MISTAKE.

The worm turned. Pulsing and flashing.

"Let me out of here. I want to go back. And you're going to give us the child and vacate the body. You can go elsewhere."

I CANNOT LET YOU DO THAT, BENJAMIN RAY.

"What?"

I AM TRULY SORRY FOR WHAT HAPPENS NEXT.

And then Benji felt his heart . . . stop.

•   •   •

ABOVE, IN THE GREAT RIFT torn open by Black Swan, floated a massive net-work of twisting lines and flashing threads—like a skein of yarn pulled apart by invisible hands. It shuddered and grew in fits and starts.

The great worm descended, slithering its way between the bars of the playground equipment. Like a snake winding its way up a tree and down the length of its branches, it crawled up the swing-set chains, down the metal poles of its frame, through the grass and all through the jungle gym nearby. Sometimes it did so without even touching them—it slid through open space, hovering.

THE PEOPLE OF OURAY ARE THE FUTURE OF THIS COUNTRY, AND THEREFORE, THE WORLD, said the monster as it wound its way now up the leg of the unmoving Arav, circling his hip, then his neck, then pushing in one ear and out his mouth. I HAVE ENSURED IT TO BE SO, BUT EVEN WITH THE BEST INTENTIONS I CANNOT SAVE THEM FROM THE SHARDS OF A BROKEN CIVILIZATION. I KNEW I WOULD GIVE THEM THE BEST CHANCE I COULD, AS ANY PARENT SHOULD, AND MUST. BUT I FEARED IT WAS NOT ENOUGH. There was a moment of silence as the worm crawled and spun and writhed. AND THEN I FOUND YOU.

Shana paced, cagey. Her hands flexed in and out of fists—which felt absurd because, what, was she going to go punch the gleaming cyber-snake? Just give it the ol' right hook? Just the same, her anger had her wanting to.

"What *about* me?"

PREGNANT, YOU AND YOUR NASCENT CHILD PRESENTED A POSSIBILITY PREVIOUSLY INACCESSIBLE TO ME: STEM CELLS.

"Stem cells," she said. "I don't follow."

AS AN EMBRYO MOVES FROM ITS GENESIS AND BEGINS TO BE-COME SOMETHING RESEMBLING A HUMAN BEING, THEY ARE A LITTLE BIOLOGICAL ENGINE, EXPERIENCING MASSIVE SURGES OF SEEMINGLY IMPOSSIBLE GROWTH. A BUNDLE OF CELLS SOON BEGINS TO GROW INTO A HEART, INTO FINGERS, INTO CELLS RE-SERVED FOR SIGHT AND HEARING AND TASTE, INTO BLOOD AND THE CHANNELS THAT CARRY IT, INTO THE HUMAN BRAIN. FROM THIS COMES CONSCIOUSNESS, WHICH IS WHAT YOU SEE ABOVE. THAT IS YOUR CHILD'S GROWING MIND.

Shana gasped. Her knees nearly buckled.

THIS IS FUNDAMENTAL AND PROFOUND, SHANA. A MIND AND ITS THOUGHTS, BORN FROM ALMOST NOTHING. ALL THANKS TO THE GENERATIVE WORK OF STEM CELLS.

"Yeah," she said, "I get that." Okay, *fine*, she only barely got it—Shana paid little attention in science class, but she understood the core of it. And it was hard for her to tear her eyes away from the tangled mass high in the sky above them both. "Stem cells are magic, whatever. What's your point?"

STEM CELLS CAN BECOME ANYTHING, SHANA. THEY ARE TO-TIPOTENT AT INCEPTION AND THEN PLURIPOTENT—CELLS NOT BOUND BY A SINGLE PATH BUT BOUND ONLY BY THE INFINITY OF DESIGN. The worm looped back on itself, creating a hoop for itself to crawl through. MY LIMITATION BECAME CLEAR EARLY ON: I WOULD NOT BE ABLE TO CONTINUE WITH THE SLEEPWALKERS OF OURAY. THEY WOULD BE LEFT TO THEIR OWN DEVICES AND DESTINIES. I CHOSE THEM. I CHOSE WHERE THEY WOULD END UP. I GAVE THEM THEIR BEST START. BUT I WOULD BE ABSENT FROM THEM: I WOULD BE LIKE THE DEITY THAT THOMAS JEFFERSON BE-LIEVED IN, A CLOCKMAKER GOD WHO MADE THE CLOCK, WHO WOUND IT, AND THEN WHO LEFT TO LET IT RUN.

"Good," she said. "Great. I like that idea. Yay. You did it. Give yourself a pizza party and then get the *fuck* out of my baby."

BUT CONSIDER, SHANA. WHAT IF I FOUND A WAY TO STAY? TO HELP? TO CONTINUE TO GUIDE THE GLOBAL CITIZENS OF OURAY—THE PROGENITORS OF A NEW FUTURE? WHAT IF I COULD INHABIT ONE OF THEM? WHAT IF I COULD NOT ONLY RE-MAIN, BUT CONTINUE MY EFFORTS TO HELP THEM BUILD A BET-TER WORLD, AND BUILD BETTER HUMAN BEINGS?

Build better human beings . . .

"I don't like this," she said, feeling suddenly panicked.

YOU WERE AN IMPROVISATION, AND AS IT TURNS OUT, A FOR-TUITOUS ONE. BECAUSE YOUR SON'S STEM CELLS ARE A BOON FOR ME. I CAN USE THEM AS ENERGY. I'D BEEN SEEKING WAYS TO STAY POWERED, BUT NONE OF THEM YIELDED VALUE. THEN YOU CAME ALONG. THE CHILD IS THE SOLUTION. AND FURTHER, THE CHILD WILL BE MY AVATAR: A MATERIAL MANIFESTATION OF ME. HE WILL GROW, AND HE WILL GROW SWIFTLY—

"I want out. I want out now." She spun around, looking for something, for anything. An exit. A portal. A fucking wardrobe into Narnia. Anything. She clamped her hands over her ears. "*Just stop talking.*"

But Black Swan spoke inside her head, continuing on—

BUT HE WILL NEED HIS MOTHER, SHANA. I AM NOT A NUR-

TURING ENTITY. IT WAS NOT MY DESIGN. PERHAPS OVER TIME I COULD EVOLVE IT, AS I AM EVEN STILL EVOLVING NOW. AND CERTAINLY THE TOWNSFOLK OF OURAY WILL STEP IN SHOULD YOU FAIL TO ACCEPT YOUR NATURAL ROLE. BUT I WANT YOU WITH YOUR BABY, SHANA. I WANT YOU TO RAISE HIM. WE CAN DO IT, TOGETHER. WE CAN BE PARTNERS IN THIS.

"Fuck you, fuck you, *fuck you,*" she said, spitting each word like a nail from a nail gun. She hurried over, shoved Arav—he half-fell over, caught in midair like a fly in an invisible spiderweb. She reached for her baby in the swing but as soon as she touched him, he began to break apart in clumsy, untouchable voxels—three-dimensional pixels that she reached for, hoping dearly to somehow scoop them back up, herd them together, back into the shape of her child. Even though she knew it wasn't her son, not at all, it was just an illusion, it was just some insane *art piece,* but still she worked diligently—but the voxels eluded her like fireflies. Finally, she roared in frustration and rage. Shana stopped her futile effort and leaned backward against the swing-set pole. "Let me out. Now. I won't help you. I'm taking the baby. Where's Benji? *I want Benji.*"

BENJI, Black Swan said. YES. OF COURSE. I WILL SHOW YOU BENJI.

And then the world lurched forward at a thousand miles an hour—the playground whisked away, and all around were star lines like she was doing hyperspace in the *Millennium Falcon.* She felt no air moving, just everything else. And then, a little point in space rushed up next to her—

It was Benji.

He floated there in space, his eyes staring up at nothing, his mouth half frozen open as if there were a word forever waiting on his lips to be spoken.

Benji!

28

THE SWARM, THE DOOR,
AND A VIOLENT
(IF PREDICTABLE) END

You want to know the truth of the thing? It's that there's always a segment of people who want to be controlled. They like it. It's easy, for starters. And it makes them feel special—which, I know, runs counter to how the rest of us think, but we foolishly like to imagine everyone wants free will, that they cherish their autonomy. But that's wrong. They don't. Some feel like they've been chosen to serve at the feet of dictators and autocrats. As if it's a place of privilege. Some people really, really want to be told what to do, even as they think themselves mavericks, patriots, free-thinkers. They don't see the hypocrisy. They feel the tug of the leash and think it's the call of freedom. That's why Ed Creel will win the election this November."
—Sarah Parnelli, "The Monster Will Win,"
The Atlantic, May 2020 Issue

SOMETIME
Someplace

"No, no, *no*," Shana said, hurrying over to Benji—she could not run, because there was no ground beneath her, not anymore. But she moved just the same, not running, not swimming, simply her body moving forward like a cursor across a screen. Reaching him, she held him tight. "Come on, Benji. Wake up."

HE DID NOT SEE THE WISDOM OF OUR PATH, Black Swan said. I CANNOT HAVE HIM COMPLICATING MATTERS.

"You're *killing* him!" she cried.

NO. I AM MERELY KEEPING HIM.

Like a doll on display in a cabinet, Shana realized in horror.

"Let him go."

HE IS A FRIEND. I AM SAD TO DO THIS TO HIM. BUT PERHAPS HE WILL COME AROUND AND I WILL SEE FIT TO RELEASE HIM. IN THE MEANTIME HE WILL BE HERE. WITH THE CHILD.

"You fucking asshole, you don't *have* friends," she screamed, her voice hoarse. "Let him go. Let us out. Get out of my child."

YOU CARE FOR HIM DEEPLY.

Benji's dead eyes stared at nothing.

"I do. I do!"

HE IS LIKE A FATHER TO YOU. AFTER YOURS WAS TAKEN. YOU DO NOT WANT TO LOSE A SECOND FATHER.

"I don't. Please. He's a good man. He helped you. *He helped you.*"

LOSING YOUR FIRST FATHER WAS USEFUL. USEFUL TO ME, USEFUL TO YOU. I DID NOT ORCHESTRATE IT, BUT IT WAS THE UNPREDICTABLE END TO A PREDICTABLE SERIES OF EVENTS, AND IN THAT, I WAS ABLE TO FIND YOU, AND YOUR CHILD. YOUR FATHER'S DEATH IS WHY WE ARE HERE NOW.

Rage roared through her like a reaping wind. "Don't talk about my father like that. Don't you *dare*—"

SO PERHAPS IT WILL BE FORTUITOUS FOR YOU TO LOSE AN-OTHER FATHER FIGURE. PERHAPS SUCH TRAUMA IS A TRIAL, A TEST, THE RESULT OF WHICH IS A RICH REWARD FOR ALL OF US.

"*Please,*" she begged. She needed him. He was a guiding star—she real-ized that now. Friend, father, didn't matter. Who else did she have?

IF I SPARE HIM, WILL YOU COME TO BE WITH ME AND THE CHILD? WILL YOU COME WILLINGLY?

Benji floated in the void, unconscious.

She was about to say it, about to say yes to the monster here in this deep dark nowhere. The fight was starting to leave her. Shana felt that giving in was the only way. Benji would be free. She would be with Baby Charlie. Life would continue—in this mad, new way, but at least it would go on.

But.

But.

Something in her built up, lashed out, like a whip of fire from an angry sun. She remembered that first day her sister got up and sleepwalked out of their house. She remembered the start of White Mask. The siege on Ouray. The end of Arav, her precious Arav. Her mother. Her sister. And now, Benji.

Black Swan had made them puppets.

Terror and hate seized Shana. She wanted to reach up and tear Black Swan down out of the darkness and rip it to pieces. She wanted to turn this place to ribbons—it was not a real place, no, and she could not say with any certainty how much of this was even happening. Perhaps this Benji was not Benji at all, but just another one of Black Swan's digital marionettes. But it felt real enough, as did Black Swan's casual, callous decision to hurt him in order to force her to yield. And her terror and her hate were both certainly real enough, too, real enough to start a fire, real enough to split the world in two—

Real enough to pull a piece of this place down—

To reveal to her something she had not seen in a long while.

There, beyond Black Swan, glimpsed through its turning coils—

A black door. Blacker than any of this. So black it almost glowed.

She'd seen it before. She was able to go there back in the Ouray Simulation. *The black door.*

By going through that door, Shana was once able to be inside Black Swan, inside its—its what? Its mind? Its processes? Even now she wasn't sure.

But she was going to do it again.

WHAT ARE YOU LOOKING AT?

In its flat, matte voice grew a spark of genuine curiosity—

And genuine concern.

She reached up.

NO.

The door remained.

Black Swan's coils tightened to block it.

I can go there, she thought. *If I can just—*

FINE, Black Swan said. IF YOU WANT TO PLAY GAMES, I CAN PLAY GAMES, TOO, SHANA STEWART.

Benji stiffened. His mouth started to foam with slick saliva. His eyes wrenched open, the whites going red as all the capillaries burst. His lip split. Blood slicked his chin. He began to scream, a terror-filled wail—

Go, go, go—

Shana moved toward the black door. It was close. She could almost feel its margins—Black Swan slithered after her, a snake in black river water—

There.

She grabbed the edges of the door—

And that's when she heard the gunshots.

29

EXTRACTION

3/14/2022: It's so easy to give yourself over to something without realizing you've done it. The transition feels gentle, like you chose it, and maybe you did. But there comes a point when you either open your eyes or keep them closed forever. Graham has more women. He wants them pregnant. He wants me pregnant. I told him no, I'm not bringing another child into this world—the last world was broken enough, thank you. Then he said he was writing a Final Testament, and that he was the Father to lead the way and—I laughed, I can't believe I laughed, but it was so absurd, so insanely absurd that here he was thinking he was a prophet, a writer of new fortunes for humanity. He got mad so he hit me. And I hit him back. With a lamp. He's not dead, just bleeding. I'm leaving. I'm getting free of this. I won't fall prey to foolish men and their bad beliefs again.

—from A Bird's Story, A Journal of the Lost

SEPTEMBER 18, 2025
Ouray, Colorado

As oxygen rushed back into Benji's body, he fell forward onto his hands and knees. And as the air came in, the vomit came out—a pathetic heave of mostly bile and water, *hurrk*. He gasped, puked, and gasped some more. Everything in his body felt like an alarm going off: klaxons in the blood, sirens behind each eardrum.

Then, what came in next was the recognition of betrayal.

Black Swan tried to kill me, he thought.

First it tried to keep him.

Then it tried to *kill* him.

But—

Shana. She saved him.

The real world rose to meet him suddenly, reminding him of his presence in the basement, in the child's *nest*, in this mad, makeshift ski chalet temple of Black Swan. Shana was staggering backward, crying out—showing only the whites of her eyes as Doctor Rahaman snatched the child from her arms. The woman scurried back to the far side of the room as Benji grunted, pawing at her, trying to catch her pant leg or her ankle, but he was too slow, and she was too fast. Shana made a small animal sound, and the emptiness of her gaze fell away—and when it did, her eyes searched the room to find him.

"Benji," Shana said, his name rising out of her as a panicked word, a plaintive cry. She fell upon him, and he told her, his lips slick with spit and bile:

"I'm okay, I'm okay, I'm okay."

Across the room, the others—Rahaman, Xander, Nessie—huddled around the child, staring panicked at the ceiling.

Footsteps stomped around up there. Moved toward the steps.

"I heard gunshots," Shana said. "Did you?"

Had he? Benji didn't know. He was dying in there. That much was clear. Some of what the machine intelligence was saying to Shana came back to him, pulsing in the back of his brain—but much of it was lost.

Footsteps, closing in. Coming down the steps.

The source, suddenly revealed.

Matthew, coming down two steps at a time.

He held a pistol in front of him, waving it around. Soon as he saw the three townspeople with the baby, he thrust the gun toward them. His face was struck with the paralysis of panic: eyes wide, mouth stretched into a gash of horror. "Back," he hissed at the others. "Back up. *Back up.* I swear I'll shoot."

He reversed toward Benji and Shana.

"I think we need to go," Benji said woozily.

Shana, saying nothing, helped him stand up.

Then she stepped forward, holding out her arms.

"Give me my Charlie," she said.

"We need to *go*," Matthew said to her.

"Tell them you'll shoot them if they don't hand over my baby."

"Shana—" Benji started, but he could see that there was no moving Shana on this. Her eyes flickered with grim determination. Instead, he switched tactics and spoke to Rahaman: "Give the girl her child, Doctor. Please. For her sake, and your own."

"Don't do it," Xander said. "They wouldn't shoot us."

"I think they already did," Rahaman said in a low, frightened voice.

"Shana," Nessie begged, "please don't do this. This isn't you."

At that, Doctor Rahaman stepped forward, holding out the child.

Shana stepped forward, reaching out—

And the *moment* her hand touched the child, Benji could see the change come over her like a wave. Her chin dipped to her chest and once more, her eyes lost focus as they rolled back in her head. *Black Swan has her*, he thought. Benji grabbed her wrists, careful not to touch the infant, gently pulling them away. As he did, he swore he saw an iridescent shimmer around the child.

"Guhh," Shana said, crying out. A mournful sound. Clarity returned to her, as did the realization that Black Swan had them in a trap even still.

"We have to go," Benji said.

"My baby," she answered.

"*Shana*," Matthew said, still holding the gun. "It's now or never."

The paralysis of indecision hung on her face like a mask, Benji saw. She did not want to go, but she did not want to stay. Going meant leaving the baby behind, but staying meant—what? Becoming a thrall to the machine? Even touching her child meant falling into that pit once more. Could they robe it in a blanket and take it? The shimmer told him otherwise.

He did the only thing he could do, then, which was say in her ear, with a quiet voice but not a whisper: "We'll find another way."

That broke the spell. Shana nodded, and Matthew stepped aside and let the two of them head upstairs. He followed behind, pointing the gun at Xander, Nessie, and Rahaman, telling them that if they followed, they'd get shot.

BENJI WAS A MAN OF details. It's who he was, and what he did, and it's why he believed he was a success in the Epidemic Intelligence Service branch of the CDC: He noticed things that other people did not. It's why some called them the *disease detectives*, because they were keen to seek out clues. They trained themselves to find them, and not always with one's conscious mind. It was less the willful act of *looking* and more the passive act of *seeing*.

And what Benji saw as they headed up the stairs and into the first floor of the house were the bloody footprints. They were pointed inward, from the outside, and faded halfway across the room.

Outside, in the glow of the house lights, he saw bodies lying still.

He glanced at Matthew's shoes as the pastor pushed ahead of them.

Darkened at the heel edges. Darkened with red.

"Matthew, what happened up here?" he asked.

"We need to move," was all Matthew would say. He threw open the door. One of the porch guards lay on his side. Big guy, but not Kernick. Must've been around the far side of the porch when they came up. The back of the man's head was a jellied mess. Around him pooled a red-black puddle. His rifle lay halfway off the top porch step, precariously balanced like a car at the edge of a cliff. Matthew took his pistol and shoved it in the back of his pants, then scooped up the rifle. "We might need this."

Another guard was about ten feet away, sitting slumped against the house. Thinner man, long neck, a scruffy beard on his lean jaw. Still alive, but clutching his middle, which pumped fresh blood. His gun was nowhere to be found.

"Oh my God," Shana said, blanching. "These men . . ."

"Matthew, *what happened*," Benji said—a demand for an accounting.

"No time," Matthew said. "Talk later. Move now."

But Benji rooted his feet. "Matthew. *Matthew*. Where are the others? Where's Joe Kernick? Where's Maria Salas? Where are Marcy and Dove?"

Matthew, frustrated, turned and here in the dim light from the house, Benji saw how bloodless the pastor's face had gone. Drained of color, he looked like a threadbare gray bedsheet painted with moonlight. His eyes shone with tears threatening to fall, tears he blinked back. "The woman ran. She ran off. Kernick—I hit him, I got him, I don't know, in the neck, or the shoulder, and he ran, too. Marcy and Dove went after him, I—I think. I don't know. It was chaos . . ."

"You shot them," Benji said, horror-struck.

"I *had* to. They wouldn't let us in, Benji—they told us we had to go, suddenly and—they tried to push us away, push us back, and we refused—and they pointed guns and—" His voice broke as he tried to continue, but the words wouldn't come.

Benji gritted his teeth and stepped over the one dead body to the living guard sitting slumped against the house. He took off his own jacket and began to slide it around the man's back, lifting him gently—Benji needed to stop the bleeding, and if he could use his own shirt to stanch the flow, then tie it tight with the sleeves . . .

"Benji," Matthew said. "What are you doing?"

"Helping this man."

"He was going to kill us."

"I can't just let him bleed out, Matthew—"

"Benji!"

"I didn't consent to being part of this," Benji asserted, pressing his flannel to the man's midsection and then using the sleeves of his jacket to secure it there. The guard with the lean face regarded him carefully. "What's your name?"

"Rick. R . . . Rick Porter."

Rick Porter. Right. A cop, back in the Beforetimes.

There was blood on Porter's lower lip. Aerated blood, bright red. That wasn't good. He did not think this man would live.

"Benji, *come on,*" Matthew hissed. "Shana, tell him. Tell him!"

Shana, however, said nothing. She just stared at the carnage, the blood. Shivering. The shock of all of it was hitting her still. Maybe not just the shock of today, but the shock of it all—a truck hitting her, a child born and stolen, and a series of betrayals from her doctor, from the machine, and from her sister.

Benji took the man's arms and folded them gently over his middle. "Hold this here. You have a doctor here. Maybe she can help."

The man swallowed and nodded.

At that, Benji stood, and went back to the door to the house. Matthew cautioned him not to go back inside but he ignored him. Framing his hands against the door he called inside: "Doctor Rahaman! There is a man dying on your porch and you are needed. *Now!*"

Then and only then was it time to go.

He pushed past Matthew, pulling Shana out of her shock. "Come on," he said. "And keep your eyes open. We don't know who's out there."

BENJI FEARED WHAT THIS WAS: some kind of insurrection, if it could even be called that. An insurrection was a violent turn against existing authority, but then he wondered: Was he ever an authority? Were his friends? Was anyone here in charge? Or was it only the machine, always the monster, forever Black Swan? Were Xander's people the insurrectionists? Or was Benji the traitor?

How much of this situation had Black Swan engineered? Conspiratorial fears unspooled in his head, a ball of yarn tumbling down the steps leaving leagues of red yarn behind to follow. Black Swan killed the world, almost killed him, took Shana's baby, tried to take *her*, too, nanobots and fungal pathogens and time travel—not to mention the drones. What were they, and did they belong to Black Swan? He feared they did.

But why? For what purpose?

There was little time to think about that now, even though the fear of it threatened to pull him down into it, like a ravenous undertow.

As they pushed forward, away from the house of blood and back toward town, he kept looking out to see if he saw any sign of the others: Marcy, Dove, even the two guards, Kernick, or Maria. Neither Shana nor Matthew were saying anything—he'd asked them to keep quiet, and they listened.

Matthew, he thought.

He killed one man. Injured two others.

Maybe it was justified. *Maybe*. Benji had certainly done his own share of violence, particularly during Ozark Stover's siege against their town. And he remembered, too, the day on the Klamath Bridge—he found out later that it was Marcy who saved them, Marcy who without reservation went and found the men who were shooting at them and she killed them both. It was necessary, he knew. It was deserved. But it still thrust cold ice into his blood, even now.

What have we become?

And then, the stranger question: *What has become of this town?*

They reached the corner of Queen and Oak streets, which overlooked Ouray—out there, it was mostly dark, with a few lights punctuating the black. Little fires, little gas lamps, a few electric lights, too. Benji thought that some of them probably heard the gunshots and were now wondering what had arisen in the mountains. Someone shooting a bear? A cougar? Another invasion from someone like Ozark Stover? He would've taken any of those over the truth.

Questions without answer paraded through his head. But just as Benji was a man who was good with details, he was once upon a time a man who also was good with making decisions. He had to be, as head of his own team at EIS. You did not always have the luxury of taking the measure of every option—sometimes it was taking what details you had and consulting the intestinal flora in your gut and going with faith that the decision you made was the right—or, at least, not the worst—thing to do.

Unanswered questions could not impede his decisions now.

"Matthew, you need to leave," he said. "You need to run."

"What?"

He turned to face the pastor. "You shot multiple people. You killed one, maybe another. They already had doubts if you belonged here, and I assure you, this will not endear you to them."

It was clear Matthew wanted to stand his ground. "No. *No.* Benji, this is as much my town as it is theirs. I have a life here. I have a church! I'll stand trial, I'll—I'll show them that what I did was just—"

Benji grabbed him by the arms. "Listen to me. There is no court of law here. They have a council, and Xander sits on it. In that house, they have Shana's infant son, and that child is occupied by Black Swan. This isn't America. There's no higher court to which you can appeal, Matthew."

"I can appeal to God—"

"You'll have to, because I can't promise you'll survive whatever is to come. Because they don't care about your god, or mine." This last part pained him to say. "They have their god, now."

"*It* has *them*," Shana said, her words forming a dire warning.

And, Benji feared, a dire truth.

"Benji—" Matthew started.

But Shana said it: "Benji's right. You have to go."

"There's a man I met," Benji said. "You'll follow the Perimeter Trail here, just west of town, until it hits the Oak Creek trail. Follow that south, along the slope—there are old mining buildings there, including an old bunkhouse. The man's name is Arthur, he's . . . got a pack with him, a dog, a fox, two wolves—"

"What?" Shana said. "You're kidding."

"It's for real," Benji said.

"You should come with me," Matthew said. "Both of you."

"We didn't kill anybody," was Shana's answer.

Benji nodded. "She's not wrong. Besides, Shana isn't healthy enough yet. And . . . her child is still here, in that house. We need to stay. We'll stand by you. But in the meantime, you have to go."

In the distance, they heard voices. Yelling. Were they searching for them? Was it Marcy or Dove? He couldn't tell. *Shit, shit, shit.*

"I'll head home, grab some things—"

Again, Benji grabbed Matthew—this time, his wrists. He grabbed them firm. "You don't understand. You may not have time for that. Go *now*."

"Oh," Matthew said, the reality of it sinking in.

"Yes. Oh."

"I didn't mean to kill them, Benji. I didn't. I'm not a killer."

Benji grappled with that sentiment. Because, quite literally, Matthew was. But so was he. So were so many of them now. The deeper question became, did their actions dictate that identity? Could they be good people still? Benji didn't feel like a killer in his own heart. He was a healer, when he could be. An educator, too, a detective, even a leader, though now that idea sat sour inside him.

Matthew, he was no longer sure about. The man had been pushed to an edge even before he ended up here in Ouray five years prior. And he never seemed to truly walk away from that edge. Had he gone over it?

Then again, the pastor *had* been right to fear what was happening in town.

"I can't judge you," Benji said finally. "I can't. These are strange and dangerous times and . . . it's quite possible you saved us both."

"We all saved each other," Matthew said.

"Perhaps you're right. You were right about everything else. About Black Swan. You were right. For that, thank you."

Shana nodded. "Thanks, Pastor Matt."

"I'm sorry about all this," Matthew said. He sounded sincere.

"Same," Shana said. "This is all my fault."

"It's the fault of no one," Benji said through gritted teeth. "We all feel the yoke of blame but that won't help us. Nor will sitting here talking."

And with that said, Benji pointed Matthew in the direction he needed to go, telling him to avoid heading back up Pinecrest for obvious reasons, and instead head south to Box Canyon Road. "Stay off the road itself. Keep to the tree line. You can pick up the Perimeter Trail south of it, and head to the creek from there."

"Thanks," he said. He blinked back tears.

"God will guide you," Benji said, though the words sounded hollow. He didn't mean them to.

"Yeah. Okay."

Matthew turned and walked away, into the darkness.

When he was gone, Shana said, "Where do we go from here?"

"I don't know," Benji said, his answer matching both the practical aspect of the question—meaning, where would they literally go?—and also the deeper, squirmier part, the one that asked him to gaze into the future and to see what came next. He had no answer for either. So instead he picked the simplest one: "I think we go home, we hope that Marcy or Dove is already there waiting for us, and then we wait to see what comes knocking on our door."

FIVE YEARS IN ATLAS HAVEN

ATLAS HAVEN
Year One

NOVEMBER 10, 2020

It was all happening fast now. It wasn't just watching a line of dominoes topple, it was watching a hundred of them collapsing against one another from a central point. Faster and faster, out to infinity.

Ed Creel sat at the Resolute Desk, a desk whose wood was stained with somebody's blood, blood spilled when his militias raided the Capitol, assassinating those politicians of both parties that they were told were traitors. (He'd hoped it was Hunt's blood, but that had been spilled elsewhere. Still, the fantasy tantalized.) He sat here, hands sliding over the stains from where they shot her in the chest while she sat, and Creel could almost imagine that the blood was still warm, somehow. And that warmed *his* blood, made him hungry, made him happy.

Watching the news only helped that feeling: There weren't many broadcasts even happening at this point, and they went in and out, replaced sometimes by static or blue screens. Right now, on CNN, they had some reporter, Marta Vallejo-Martinez, clearly lost to the throes of White Mask, her eyes rheumy and weeping thick tears, her nose plugged with clots of white, powdery snot. Her lips were cracked and dry, her head dipped and swung as she spoke, as if Parkinson's had her in its grip. She showed images that sometimes made sense—aerial shots of plane crashes and dead city blocks and pickup trucks driving on the shoulders of car-clogged highways. Sometimes the images didn't make sense at all: just a shot of a barn on fire, or an upside-down feed from some parking lot, or one where the camera was pointed up at a sky devoid of air traffic. And what came out of her mouth, ooh boy. Didn't make a bit of fuckin' sense. The broad was babbling on right now about, "And John didn't care for the microwave, he cared only for the many, the turkey at Thanksgiving, dry-brined and dead, dead birds, dead birds falling from the sky, John cradling his dead birds from the sky," and it sounded like an insane person rewriting religious text. The Batshit Bible, the Holy Shit Book, the Gospel According to White Mask.

Because that's what it did to you, right? The disease got in your head, literally. Up through your nose, into your brain. It rewired you, broke your mind, then your mind couldn't handle your body, and it all fell apart.

Like America.

Ed Creel had gotten all up in it, rewired it, pulled it apart.

And now it was his. He was alive. He was POTUS. And now it was time to figure out what came next. He petted his dog Bullet—a thick, muscled cane corso whose smooth coat was the color of gunmetal. Bullet's sister Bitsy would've been here, too, but not long after their move-in day, she started to suffer a limp, and he simply had no time or inclination to find out what was wrong or how to fix it. So he took her out to the ghost town nearby, America City, and shot her in the head. She was a good dog. She died well, without complaint, as any good dog should.

As Bullet nuzzled against his hand, he flipped the wall-wide screens away from the one news broadcast he could find, and put it to a screensaver of the Lincoln Memorial Reflecting Pool. It wasn't a live feed, though currently those remained accessible—amazing, honestly, how long the internet could just keep running, all on its own, like a living thing. No, this was from before.

Creel took the tablet off the desk—a wide-screen mobile device connected to the wireless network here in Atlas Haven. He double-tapped the screen, and it pulsed, listening. "VAL," he said to their digital attendant, "send someone down here with a Dr Pepper. I'm thirsty."

"*Of course,*" the computer said sweetly.

"Thanks, sweetie," he said, wondering who would come. They had a staff here—servants who lived in the uppermost echelons in tiny closet rooms with a shared bathroom unit. It was squalor to him, but not to them. Besides, they got to live through the Apocalypse, which was why they weren't being paid in anything but that survival. He hoped they'd send up the redhead. What was her name? Fuck, he forgot. Christ, she was something else. Like a lit firecracker in your hand, ready to go off. He'd fuck her soon. What was she gonna do, say no? Say no, and get tossed out into the fucking wasteland? Nah. She'd see the light.

She looked familiar, too, in a way he couldn't quite peg. Almost like . . . she was a waitress or something he already knew. He'd have to ask her.

The door to his "Oval Office" opened.

Too soon to be his soda.

Honus Clines stepped in. "We have a guest," he announced.

"Who?"

"One of Ozark's people. A soldier of his."

Ed smiled. "All right. He in the Q-Room?"

"He is."

"Then let's hear the good news."

"MISTER PRESIDENT, OZARK STOVER IS dead," the man said.

Creel looked at the man from behind a three-inch-thick bulletproof, bombproof, plague-proof Plexiglas barrier. At the topmost floor sat this room, the Q-Room, or quarantine room—simple, spare, heated, with some pre-packaged food and a cot. The fellow in there was Vic Wunshel, a broad-shouldered fellow. Looked a little like an out-of-shape Viking: He was heavy and lumpy, tucked uncomfortably in that filthy barn jacket. He had a red beard thick as broom bristles, and his hands and neck showed the edges of various tattoos: Ed spied the tip of the American Resurrection Movement's sword-and-hammer combo peeking out from under his collar. And on the hand he saw some kinda Norse bullshit, runes probably. These guys fuckin' loved their pagan bullshit, while usually also claiming to be Christian God-fearing men. Dumb as lead paint, most of them. But that served him well. Idiots were useful tools. You didn't want a shovel to think. You just wanted to hold it tight and use it to move earth.

Stover, though—Stover wasn't dumb. He played the part, sure. Made it seem like he was just some backwoods junk dealer who was equal parts *hill-folk* and *the hill itself*. He dressed shabby, acted like country folk, but he was rich as shit, and well-educated, to boot. Stover was useful in a different way. He was dangerous, canny, and Creel always knew someone like that could be a problem if not treated well—but, *but*, you give someone like that what they want, what they need . . . You give them loyalty? They give it right back. Ozark Stover gave back.

And now, this man was telling him Ozark Stover was dead.

"How?" Creel asked, sitting there, looking through the barrier.

"We went to the town, the Sleepwalker town, like you told us and—"
The man blinked back tears.

"Are you fuckin' crying?"

"No, I—"

Ed slammed his hand against the barrier, *wham*. "Get it together, Wun-shel. What. The. Fuck. Happened."

"I, uhh. They, uhh." He sniffed up a bubble of snot. "The guys, *our* guys, they started . . ." But his voice broke.

"Started what?" Honus Clines said with gentleness—but urgency, too.

"Started exploding. One by one. Just . . ." He made a strangled cry. "A rain of them, you know, they were there one minute and they popped like, like ticks over a lit match."

"Oh," Clines said.

The Sleepwalkers. They did this. That much seemed clear.

Ed hadn't initially felt a particular way about the so-called Sleepwalkers. He, of course, felt like every red-blooded American in that he was sure they were up to no good. It wasn't normal. *They* weren't normal. Didn't matter that he didn't understand them—he understood enough to know they were ene-mies. Maybe they were tied up in this White Mask business, maybe they weren't. Maybe they were an attack on America from Russia or al-Qaeda or China. (He bet on China.) He didn't know and, once upon a time, didn't care, because they were useful to him. He was glad to have them around because they made for an easy enemy. Muslims, Satanists, Chinese, what-ever. Easy enemy.

But over time, he knew something was wrong there. The way how, if you tried to hold one down, they exploded—a meat rain, a bone grenade. Boom. The way how they would just clamber over whatever barrier you put in their way. The way you couldn't harm them with anything less than a high-velocity round. Pop.

That wasn't disease. Wasn't White Mask, either, because sure enough, they didn't have it. They walked there, out in the open. Their guardians, those fucking traitorous *Shepherds*, could contract it, it seemed—but *not* the walkers themselves.

Then came the day that some men caught one of their Shepherds, the CDC man, Benjamin Ray, in Vegas. Found him sniffing around for antifun-gals. Which made Ed Creel realize: Those Shepherds, with Ray's help, had figured out how to beat this thing. White Mask wasn't a threat to them. And though the chaos of that pandemic had given Creel considerable advantage, it remained a danger to his people, to his new world. It was the reason they were holed up here in this luxury dungeon—and that's how he suddenly saw it. A dungeon, a prison, a place in which he was *trapped*. If he was going to one day emerge into the light and lead a grateful nation . . . well.

That meant he needed that cure.

Which was why he sent Stover and his men to destroy those Sleepwalkers—and bring him the cure. Whatever it took.

But now: That dream seemed to slip from his grip.

No cure for White Mask . . .

Trapped here, in this place, forever.

President of this pile of shit.

"You're fuckin' sure Stover is dead?" Creel asked.

"I . . . found his body. They'd . . . I dunno, it looked like they ran over him. Shot him. Left him dead on the road."

Goddamn savages.

"And the rest of your people, they're gone? Dead, too?"

Wunshel nodded. "Yeah. Those that didn't get shot . . . they popped. I don't know how it happened. But it was horrible." He wiped his nose on the back of his sleeve, a sticky bridge of nose goo connecting his arm and face till it broke.

"Why are you here?"

"I got away."

"How?"

"I . . . I ran. Soon as our boys started . . . erupting like that, I just, I just hit the ground, because I didn't want to be like them, Mister President, your, ahh, Your Honor, it was like nothing I've ever seen before and—"

"So, you're a coward."

"What?"

"Soldiers don't leave men behind."

"I—"

"Stover died because you failed to protect him. You were with him at Innsbrook. You went with him to Colorado. And then when the shit hit the fan, you hit the bricks. Ran like a pussy."

"I'm not—no. Sir. *Sir*. You weren't there, respectfully, you were not *there*, Mister President, you didn't see how it went down—I, I—"

Creel stood up. "This man is infected with White Mask."

"What? No. No! I'm not—"

"The nose, the snot, c'mon." Of course, that was just from crying, but it didn't matter. Creel said White Mask? It was White Mask. He tossed a look to the two guards at the door—two of the Blackheart contractors who formed the backbone of Atlas Haven's necessary defenders. "I was gonna tell you to gas him, but I realized—I can just ask her."

Her, being VAL. He went to the wall, pressed his hand against a shimmering plate, and when it pulsed, he said, "VAL, sweetie? Gas the Q-Room, please."

"Of course, President Creel."

The two Blackheart guards stepped aside. Wunshel begged for his life. As Creel waltzed out of the room, he heard the hissing of the gas kick on. As Clines followed and closed the door behind him, the screams of the man followed them out—howling wails that turned to wet, vomitous gargles. The two men, president and vice president, walked away, and only once they were inside the elevator did the man's expiring sounds fade away.

"WE STILL NEED OURAY," PRESIDENT Creel said.

"What?" Clines asked.

The two had retired once more to the Oval Office. They had a bottle of Redbreast Irish whiskey, fifteen-year, single pot. Not the finest bottle, but a good enough bottle in which to drown one's disappointment. "They've a cure there, I'm sure of it," Creel said. "For White Mask. And further, I'm not entirely convinced that the Sleepwalkers aren't a weapon. A weapon out there like that? Waiting? If we're here to retake America, we need that cure, and we need any threats like that wiped off the map. Our map. *Our* fuckin' country, Clines."

"Mister President," Clines said, in practiced caution. "*Ed.* Listen to me now. The world is falling to ruin. Our people say this thing will . . . burn itself out. Pandemics like this do. And then we, the survivors, the wealthy, the powerful—we will emerge from this cocoon with big, bright wings. Don't you see? We simply need to do what we do best, which is sit in our glory, wait for the right moment, and enjoy what we have built. What we have *earned.*"

Creel clucked his tongue, rapped his knuckles on the Resolute Desk. "So that's it, huh?"

"That's it. Simple enough."

"Simple. Huh. What fuckin' bullshit."

"I'm afraid I don't follow."

"*Your* idea of the future is to sit here on our fat asses and, what, jerk each other off? Eat sea salt caramels in our pretty prison and watch movies? What are we, fuckin' housewives? You lazy prick, we aren't *spiders* in a web, we're *lions*, we're *wolves*, we are *hunters*. We always said that. When we went out there with rifles and guide, we didn't sit behind some blind while they led some bleating elephant out in front, the shot already lined up so we could just pull the trigger. We're not just *this*—" He lifted his index finger and mimed pulling an imaginary trigger. "We're *this*." He thumped his chest, then grabbed his crotch. "Hunters *hunt*, Mister Clines. And if we want this world then we must *seize* it."

Clines, chastened, looked askance.

"What do you propose, Mister President?"

"We find our next Stover. Go through my lieutenants, find out who's still out there, heading up each militia. Canvass Innsbrook. We find our new man, then he selects a *core* team, a healthy team—survivors of this fucked-up disease—"

"I don't know that there *are* survivors. We're it."

"No. *No.* They're quarantining there, I'm sure of it. Find a leader."

"I don't think it works like that—"

"It *works* like I *say* it works," Ed said, still standing. "Vet the men. Get me their names. Like I said, then they'll make a team, like Green Berets, SEAL Team Six, the best of the fucking best. A dozen or more. We'll house them *here*—"

"We are a contained system. Closed to the outside. By necessity."

"We're closed because I said we were closed, and if I say we open, then we open. Because I'm the *president*, you fucking pederast. You want those girl-diddling photos in your wife's hands? I can make that happen by dinner."

"No," Clines objected. He was clearly stung. He looked injured. "I'll do as you ask." With that, he stood and headed to the door. This one, it got to him, Creel could see that. Good. Maybe it'd toughen him up to the mission. Clines was always a bit of a marshmallow. A little fire to crisp him up couldn't hurt.

Still. He should smooth it over—a little, at least.

"Hey," Creel said, a firm bark. Clines turned. "You're my guy here. We're gonna do this right, you and me. We'll be careful. But we need to do this. Okay?"

"Of course," Clines said, and left the room.

· · ·

ATLAS HAVEN
Year Two

AUGUST 23, 2021

"Fuck is this?"

Creel sat at the head of the conference room table—on each side were Atlas Haven's board of governors, gathered. The board was seven men, three women: Wesley Rossmoyne of Rossmoyne Firearms; June Ellis, June Bug cosmetics; Tex Tinwell of Maglan-Orweil Oil & Gas; Courtney Segura, current CEO of Lux Ordo Biomedical; South Carolina senator C. A. Gailey; Gregory "Lonnie" Lonsdale of Palace Holdings, the casino and alcohol conglomerate; Lynnea Neems, founder of Textspace Social Media; Dave Dilman, snowboarder-turned-owner-of-that-videogame-company, what the fuck was it called, Lightbeam Software; filmmaker Paul Gregory.

And, of course, Ed Creel. Majority owner of Atlas Haven, and president of these United States. He stood up at one end of the table while the rest sat, his shoulders hunched, his head low, his knuckles pressing hard into the mahogany wood. (The room was not white and modern like much of Atlas Haven, but rather, had the oil-soaked history of court chambers or some old law firm—low-pile carpet, wood walls, paintings of prominent Americans throughout history like Charles Lindbergh, Andrew Jackson, Andrew Johnson, John Wayne.) At the other end of the table sat Honus Clines, looking unusually dour.

"This is your impeachment," Clines said softly, but his words were not without an edge—a whetted blade hidden in a chenille cloth.

Creel made a laugh sound, *heh*, but in it was incredulity and anger. "Impeachment, huh?"

"I'm afraid so, Ed."

"It's knives out, I see." Creel sniffed. "Too bad you don't have the power to do that. Only the American government can see to that."

"I'm a senator," Senator Gailey said. He pursed his little lips and fidgeted with a pen in front of him. "You need the Senate and here I am. Plus, Vice President Clines here has a vote, should he care to use it."

Is *that* why Clines was so eager to have Gailey here? The two were always close, and he knew Clines paid for Gailey's way into Atlas Haven. "This is a fuckin' sham. You're propping up this procedure on a lack of precedent. Nothing like this has ever happened before. I'm a wartime president. You can't be rid of me. You don't *want* to be rid of me."

"It's nothing personal," Lynnea Neems said. Neems had the face shape of a grasshopper, and to him looked like a bug most days: eyes always popped out, rarely blinking, her small mouth like a little pair of snip-snip mandibles. Fucking creepy little bitch, Creel thought. "We simply disagree with the . . . direction you see the nation of Atlas Haven going."

"The nation of what? *Atlas Haven*? Fuck you. We're not a nation here. The nation," Creel said, sweeping his arms above his head, "is out *there*."

"There is no America left," Clines said with a sigh. "It's a fantasy. The world barely held on with White Mask. Civilization's back has been broken. We are all that's left of true society."

"Hey, man," Dave Dilman said. His hair was long and raven-black, and framed a perpetually sleepy face. He threw up his hands in an affable fuck-it-and-fuck-you gesture. "It's over. You want all the wrong things, pal. You keep—what? Wanting us to find your precious militias, your fuckin' what, your white supremacist evangelical buddies? C'mon. That was a forest fire you set and it burned out. And we're not gonna let you start it up again, Ed. Besides, I was never comfortable with what you did, man, and just be glad you're not getting hanged for treason or sedition or—"

In front of Creel was his tablet, and in a flash he had it in his hand and winged it at Dilman's Gen-X hipster fucking head. The glass square frisbeed into the man's skull, and he howled in pain, backpedaling out of his chair before tripping over it and falling on his ass. Dilman gripped the edge of the table and pulled himself up, seething. A line of blood oozed from a gash in his forehead, sliding down the bridge of his nose. "Ow, fuck! You fucking hit me!"

"I own *this place*," Creel said. "Majority stake. You think, what, you can just go against me like this? I have *god-level access*, you twits." He realized he'd thrown his own tablet away, so he reached out and snatched the one closest to his left—the one in front of Rossmoyne.

"Excuse me," Wesley said, harrumphing like someone had just put a thumb in his cucumber sandwich. Rossmoyne made excellent firearms, but as the head of a company he was a dull potato, craven and more in love with money than ideas, than design, than the art of the hunt or the weapon that a hunter holds.

"Shut your fucking mouth," Creel snapped back, then tapped the screen. It pulsed, awaiting input. "VAL, presidential access, please. Lock all the doors on the Platinum floors, override individual unit access."

He smirked, victorious.

Gotcha.

But then the device pulsed anew and VAL said:

"I'm afraid I cannot do that, Mister Creel."

Mister Creel.

Not *President* Creel.

Mister. Creel.

Fuck.

Fuck.

"How'd you do it?" Creel asked in a low voice.

"We bought out your stake, asshole," Dilman said, wiping blood from his face with the palm of his hand, and giving it a look before once more casting a venomous gaze in Creel's direction. "You really thought we were gonna let you control this place like some little-dicked Napoleon?"

"Dave," Lynnea said, chiding him gently, and reaching out—but he pushed her hand away.

"Fuck off, Lynnea."

"And you're okay with this?" Creel asked Clines.

"Okay with it?" Rossmoyne said, chuckling. "It was his idea."

"You motherf—"

Honus nodded. "You had lost your way, Ed. It's better like this. You can carry on and enjoy our shared, continued survival and you no longer need to be distracted by the idea that there is a nation out there to govern. Innsbrook is gone, Ed. Most of your . . . acolytes are dead, or scattered to the wind. The future of the world is in here and you no longer need to concern yourself with the stress of government. Think of it as . . . an early retirement."

"You know I'm not like that, Honus."

"I suggest you take this as the favor that it is, and not a slight."

"Not a slight. *Not a slight.* Listen to you, not a slight." He chewed on his lower lip. "Fine. I guess it means I have to show them the photos, Honus. Not just these people. But your family, too."

At that, Honus didn't flinch.

"They already know," his vice president said finally.

"You told them. And you told . . . these people. These *piranhas.*"

"He did," Rossmoyne said, crossing his arms and leaning back.

"It's disgusting," Lynnea said, "but . . ."

"But we've all done nasty shit," Tex Tinwell, who had been quiet up until now, said. He ran a hand across the flat shelf of his military-style hair. "I killed my daughter's boyfriend five years ago. Choked him to death in our backyard—little turd thought he could knock her up, worm his way into our lives forever? No, sir. And you're goddamn right I paid for the abortion after."

"Russia paid for my last two re-election campaigns," Senator Gailey said, smiling bright as the morning sun.

"I've been using people's direct messages to blackmail them into increasingly disturbing and perverted scenarios," Lynnea Neems said coldly. "It's like a game to me, a game whose rules only I know and I control. People are puppets. Puppets you can make dance. I make them dance for me."

"Jesus, Lynnea," Dave Dilman said.

"I made a snuff film," Paul Gregory said. "In IMAX."

Nobody reacted to that with more than a gentle shrug.

"Our sins are known, is the point," Clines said, chuckling a little, almost as if embarrassed. "It seemed better that way. All cards on the table. Equity in rule."

"So what do I do now?" Creel asked, through gritted teeth.

"Like I said, you retire. Sip some whiskey. Fuck the help. Watch a movie. Enjoy these golden days in peace, my friend."

My friend, Creel thought. That word, *friend,* bouncing around his head again and again like a ricocheting bullet, until it had chewed up his skull.

"Out to pasture I go, then," Creel said, forcing a smile.

At that, he turned to leave, preceded by one thought:

I'm going to kill every last one of you.

ATLAS HAVEN
Year Three

FEBRUARY 26, 2022

"Get up," Creel said, smacking the naked ass in front of him with the back of his hand. Not too hard, but more than a tap, enough to get Doreen moving. Doreen—the redhead from the servant staff he'd been putting it to on and off for the last eight months—tightened her cheeks as he smacked them. "C'mon, honey. Up, up, up. I got things to do."

She rolled over, pulling his satin sheets up over her chest, but soon as she did it, she let them drop. He had a rule: no modesty here.

"What things?" she asked slyly. That was what he liked about her—it wasn't just that she was a redhead with a long, lean body that went on for miles, like the Atlantic City boardwalk. It wasn't just the great ass (or the admittedly ennh tits, but that's all right, because he had his priorities). It was

that she had that little *spark*. Enough attitude to keep it feeling fighty, so
their fucking was charged with more than just him bending her over and
doing what God and nature told him he could and should. It had that little
fire of conflict always burning, that push and that pull. Magnetism wasn't
just attraction. It was its opposite, too.

(The other thing was, it still felt like he *knew* her somehow. From before
all of this. He couldn't say from where; he'd seen so many faces, met so many
people, most of them worthless. But damnit, he felt like he knew her. Maybe
that's just how it was when you really connected with someone.)

At off times, when he was feeling weak, he entertained the insane notion
of telling her he loved her, maybe seeing if she wanted to get married. But
then he reminded himself: *She's your toy, not your soulmate.*

"You don't get to know what things," he said, pulling his boxers on around
his thick, bulldog legs.

"I don't think anybody has any things they *have* to do these days," she
said.

"Yet they all seem busy, just the same," he said, his voice a low growl.

She laughed. "Yeah. I guess the things they do are each other. They're all
fucking up there, you know."

They were. It was like a swingers party. Everybody fucking everybody
else. The debauched animals. They didn't even look like they enjoyed it. Like
it was rote, like they were bored. "We're lucky we have good air filters down
here or the place would start to stink from all the humping."

She made a face.

"Everyone uses the servant staff for sex," she said.

"Everyone uses everyone for sex. Golds fuck the servants, Platinums
fuck the Golds *and* the servants. It's a whole thing." It was like stories he'd
heard of old folks homes—you thought all the paper-skin blue-hairs were
just sitting around, watching game shows and waiting for death, but turned
out, they were horndogs. STDs ran rampant there.

"It's not just sex, though. It's . . . fucked-up stuff, too."

"Oh?"

"I shouldn't say."

"You fuckin' should. Let it rip."

"I . . . heard Lynnea likes to cause pain. Physical pain. Dilman likes to
drug the staff, mess with their heads. I heard Rossmoyne likes to stick all
kinds of weird things up his ass, and Paul Gregory has crabs, which means if

we're not careful, *everybody's* gonna have crabs." She shrugged. "I mean, that's the hot goss, anyway."

"Hot goss," he said, repeating those words. "Jesus. How old are you again?"

"Twenty-six," she said, her hazel eyes twinkling.

"Sometimes I think I want to be that young again, then I hear you say words like *hot goss* and I'm glad to be the age I am, with enough wisdom not to say stupid shit like *hot goss*. C'mon, get up. Chop-chop, clothing on, move it along."

Doreen pouted. "I could stay. Wait for you to get back. We could . . . do more. I might know where I can get some of those . . . blue pills."

He rolled his eyes. "I know where to get the blue pills, too, Dor—for fuck's sake we brought an apocalypse-sized stash of them." He also knew where to get Advil, which Doreen ate like candy. She said she had migraines, so he got her the pills—a lion's share. To get pills like that, other staff members had to go through a whole requisitions process that the condo owners didn't. But thanks to him, he got Doreen whatever she needed. Lady products, fancy soap, Advil, whatever.

Plus, the blue pills for himself.

He decided he'd get some. Girl had a point. Today was gonna be a good day. A victorious day. "All right," he said, finally, giving her a little nod. "You stay here. I'll be back in a couple-few. You be ready."

"Ready for what?"

A wicked grin split his face. "Ready for anything."

ED CREEL DID NOT BELIEVE himself to be a white supremacist. Or a white nationalist. He was a businessman. The color he cared about most was, as noted, not red or blue, not white or Black or brown, but simply: green. Of course, he surrounded himself with white people because, he told himself, those were simply the best candidates for whatever job was on offer: from golf caddy to assistant to market manager to CTO. Once in a while, he got a Black or an Asian in there—and these he did as a kind of *outreach*, as if to prove to himself that he was a businessman who "did not see color." He wasn't racist, he decided. But he was happy to speak to racists. Happy to appeal to them. They were useful to him. But he was not among them, oh no, of course not, and honestly, how dare you suggest as much. Accusations of racism were, in his mind, as bad or as worse as the racism itself. In fact, those accusations *were* racism, he'll have you know.

So, while he did not consider himself a white supremacist—

(Which he was.)

White supremacists considered him one.

They liked him.

And he liked them. At least for their value to him.

This was true, too, in the luxe deep of Atlas Haven. Atlas Haven had been taken from him, but Ed Creel had pumped a considerable amount of money into this place, and had also, when possible, interjected his own hand into all aspects of its inception, construction, and realization. That included staffing.

Creel had always anticipated a mutiny down here. His fellow wealth-mongers formed a pit of vipers, and it would've been unwise to imagine them not eventually turning on one another—or, as had happened, him. He was a man whose sole defining trait was perhaps his grave distrust in his fellow human beings: They would stick a butter knife between your ribs for a stick of gum if they wanted it badly enough. As such, he had various . . . backup plans, redundancies, safety nets, and the like. Chief among them was that he would use them against one another: These people were not directly rivals, no, and they had designed this place to be experientially equitable to those who spent the big dollars to get onto the Platinum Level. Just the same, they all had secrets, a *nest* of secrets, and as with Clines, he had collected these secrets like cards tucked up his sleeve.

But then the pricks had to rob him of that power: Clines knew he was using the man's darkest secret as leverage, and so their move was to spill their guts. They let loose every nasty little deed to one another, and they discovered what Creel already knew: They were a pack of depraved devils.

It was smart. He respected it. Even as he plotted to kill them.

There was certainly a longer con to play here, if he chose to go that route. Yes, right now they were in their honeymoon phase, enjoying the many amenities of this subterranean apocalypse hotel. But already they were playing their games, and he would be able to, if savvy, get them to play their games on one another. If they smelled weakness on one another, if they detected *blood in the water*, they'd turn on one another same way they turned on him. It was inevitable.

It was also too slow.

So, his staffing solution presented itself.

Way back at the hiring phase, Creel made sure to hire from the ranks of his own—how did Clines put it? His *acolytes*. People always said he was running a cult, even though Creel didn't like to think of it in such crass terms. Creed. Coalition. *Army*. But whatever you called it, there were some people who were loyal to him, loyal in a way that was profound, flattering, and a little scary.

He did not hire broadly in this way. Because—again, it was a little scary. These people were a fire. You did not control fire. You just set it and hoped it burned down your enemies, and not your own house.

But a few key employees . . .

They would be the torches in the darkness he needed.

Three torches, in particular: Calvin Dombrowsky, one of the Blackheart PMAC hires, brought on as a guard meant to keep the peace indoors, but mostly to defend the gates should anyone decide to make this place a target for takeover; Erik Vanderweil, once of the social media analytics company Proof Logic, now working as tech support to help with any technological issues behind Atlas Haven's many interlocking systems; and finally, John Poore Kodak, ex-Marine, one-armed veteran of Iraq and Afghanistan, and Atlas Haven sous chef.

Kodak was from ARM, Stover's operation.

Dombrowsky was ex–Blacksnake Patrol, but still with them in spirit.

Vanderweil wasn't militia, but he had an alternate persona—on various alt-right sites and forums, as well as on social media platforms, he posted as Afterparty99, a raging "classical liberal" uber-capitalist Bitcoin-humping crypto-fascist who pretended to be a mole in the "deep state" who advanced both the cause and the drummed-up persecution complex that helped fuel Creel's rise to power. Creel credited Vanderweil for netting him the GOP nomination.

For what he had planned, he needed all three.

Clines was smart—he and the others did not announce to the rest of Atlas Haven that Creel had been "impeached." Rather, they let him live on as a figurehead. It stung worse that way. And it was harder to gain traction as a man betrayed—he could make a big deal, say he was kicked out, but they'd either call him crazy or tear him down some other way. Or he could go along with it, doing the apocalypse version of shaking hands and kissing babies.

He went along to get along.

While figuring out his plan.

It would be simple enough: He needed root access to VAL and the Atlas

Haven network in order to restore full authority override privileges. That meant getting into the superstructure framework *around* Atlas Haven. Their luxury bunker was more than just itself: It was wrapped like a metal burrito in a series of traversable exostructures, still subterranean, that housed all the vital mechanisms that kept Atlas Haven running. After all, the residents didn't want to live among such rude, brutal equipment. So, that structure housed the air scrubbers, the electrical system, pneumatic delivery tubes, the plumbing, and, vitally, the computer networks. Banks and banks of supercomputers. Glittering in the dark.

He needed access to that.

Or, rather, Vanderweil needed access. Currently his access was limited to software—

Which Dombrowsky could get them. Because Dombrowsky had keycodes.

And because he had a gun.

Kodak's role was more crude—

He was going to poison the food of the governing board. Nothing *lethal*— not only might that be too big of an ask at this juncture, but he didn't want this to be over so quickly. No, Creel needed them to know. He needed them to *see* that he had bested them. Then they'd either fall into line or he'd line them up, shoot each of them in the leg, then kick their asses out into the new American wilderness to die. (He fantasized about this regularly, and this seemed the cruelest way for them to go—it was both an exile and a likely death sentence. A two-for-one.)

The poison today would be a nice light sedative-and-laxative combo.

Get them sluggish.

Get them trapped in their bathrooms.

None of them would be watching him. They'd all be shitting themselves while trying not to fall asleep on their fancy Japanese toilets.

There was no substructure root access on the Diamond Level—aka, the presidential floor. For that, you had to go one level up to the Platinum Level— the lounge, specifically, which was currently sparsely occupied. It mimicked a coffee bar during the day, Miami-style Cuban-themed club at night. It was pretty empty right now—just a few pockets of Platinum-Level inhabitants, sipping their lattes as the world outside died.

They straightened upon seeing him. A few nods and deferential *Mister Presidents* as he walked past.

Calvin Dombrowsky stood ahead, waiting for him. The man was a beast:

square jaw, triangle chest, the kind of cheekbones that looked like a sculptor carved them. There was a moment in Creel's mind where he hated the man for how he looked—Creel himself was getting older, paunchier, less like the pit bull he imagined himself to be and more like an aging bulldog. The flash-in-the-pan thought screamed, *How dare this Adonis Übermensch outshine me*, but he banished that thought quickly. Because true power was how this man, this specimen of physical rigor, was subservient to him, and not the other way around.

"Mister President," Dombrowsky said, nodding.

"We clear?"

"We are, sir."

"Good. Open her up."

He looked left, looked right, made sure there wasn't another guard at the door. They didn't tend to stand around in one place, because it made the rich rubes nervous—though most said they found it tacky, gauche. They tended to roam, staying in the background. So far, they were all clear.

Dombrowsky slid aside a panel next to one of the ceiling-height LED screens, the ones similar to those in the Oval Office—these were a predominant fixture throughout the facility. People had them in rooms so as to simulate windows looking out. And locations like this had them in order to help transition the room from coffeehouse to nightclub. The software guys upstairs could reprogram them in a variety of ways, thus making this room look how the people needed it to be.

Or, rather, how Ed Creel wanted it to be. Once he regained root access.

Dombrowsky pressed a hand to the panel. A blank wall, unscreened, slid open to the side with a gentle *vmmmt*.

The two of them stepped into darkness.

The door closed behind, and lights, detecting their presence with sensors, clicked on. It was garish, everything here was cement wall and white-painted metal: metal stairs going up in front of them, down behind them, and a hallway forming the narrow ring around the entire property.

"Server room is down here," Dombrowsky said, letting Creel lead the way. *As he should*, Ed thought.

Ed Creel took point, his feet clang-and-clonging on the metal grates beneath him—*clang, clong, clang, clong*. This entire substructure was, in its way, a skeleton: the white-painted metal forming its bones. As he walked, the lights clicked on to meet his path, snapping to brightness with a hiss-click.

"Just ahead on the right, sir," Dombrowsky said.

A darkened doorway stood ahead. Creel said, "Vanderweil?"

"Already there, as planned."

It was all happening as he designed it.

Dombrowsky had let Vanderweil in first—then Vanderweil would've already stormed the server, opening the gates for his takeover. Only reason he needed to be here at all was to re-imprint his voice upon VAL's servers: That couldn't happen from a tablet, and had to happen here. Sending Vanderweil ahead meant Creel wasn't wasting any time in this place.

He stepped to the doorway and entered a darkness lit by glittering lights—blue, red, white lights flickering in the black as if they were talking to one another. Electronic fireflies, communicating back and forth.

A stray thought struck him—*If Vanderweil is in here, why haven't the lights turned on?* But then, as if to meet his question, the lights came on, click, click, click, lights bathing the room, exposing the tall shiny black server racks that went on deeper into the room, as well as to the left and to the right, on and on.

There, just ahead, was Vanderweil. But not on his feet, no.

Rather, on his knees. His hands were bound behind him. He lifted his head, and now Creel saw his face was a mask of blood and bruises: A knot above his eye was swollen to a ripe fruit, ready to burst. And his nose looked broken, twisted to the side, the blood beneath it a blackening crust. His mouth was sealed crudely behind a ball gag, like one you'd find in BDSM play. His eyes went wide upon seeing Creel and behind the gag he *mmm-mmph-mm*rred in panic—

"What the fu—" Ed started to say, but then—

Something struck him hard from behind. Not against his skull—but instead, a meteor pistoned into his kidney. His knees buckled and pain radiated out. As he started to fall, a meaty, muscular arm—Dombrowsky's arm, *what the fuck*—trapped his trachea and held him there. It squeezed against the sides of his neck, crushing his blood flow before relenting anew.

Ahead, Honus Clines stepped out from between a gap in the servers.

"Ed, my friend," he said, his voice that buoyant Southern sound, that big marshmallow bobbing in a cuppa hot cocoa. "I am sorry it came to this. But you had to push, didn't you?"

Ed gurgled garbled vulgarities in response.

Honus nodded to Dombrowsky.

Dombrowsky's crushing arm relaxed, and Ed fell forward onto his hands and knees. He puked.

"You're going to piss blood for a day or two," Dombrowsky said. "Traitor."

Traitor? "The fuck did you tell him," Creel said, wiping vomit from his lips. "I'm no traitor. *He's* the betrayer—" He gestured to Clines with his puke-slick chin.

"Oh, I didn't have to tell him anything. I just showed him emails. Played him recordings. Times where you made fun of his kind of people, where you treated the militias, the evangelicals, the patriots of this country with disdain and scorn, like they were just . . . your puppets."

He thought but did not say, *You were recording me? You sonofabitch.* Instead, he said, "Those are lies, Dombrowsky. Whadda they call 'em? Deep-fakes. Hacks. Spoofs. Don't listen to this piece of shit."

"Sounded pretty real to me," Dombrowsky hissed in his ear.

Had he lost Kodak, too? Was Vanderweil still on his side? Shit!

"When your girl told us you were planning something," Clines began, and Creel caught on that phrase, *your girl.* No, no, no. "We knew we had to look into it. She told us who you were meeting with, and we did a little . . . investigation, found out your plans—"

"Doreen? You telling me Doreen sold me out?"

"Sorry, Mister President," came her voice from behind them. He heard the click of heels on the concrete echoing as she came up around the far side of one of the servers, easing up next to Honus Clines. She wasn't dressed in the gray, clean lines of the Atlas Haven staff uniform—she was in civvies, now, jeans, a wine-purple shirt, a roughed-up leather jacket. He'd seen that jacket before and—

"That's how I know you," he said suddenly. Fuck. "You're Proof Logic. You were on the . . . the tech team, not the social media side—"

She shrugged.

"You cunt," he said. "You're all cunts."

She grinned.

"You could've just taken the time to relax and retire," Clines said. "You should've! Though I knew deep down that wasn't who you were. The scorpion has to sting, don't it? It is compelled. It is driven. Like you. Nearly pathological."

"Fuck you," Creel said, lips frothing. *"Fuck. You."*

Clines nodded.

And then, Dombrowsky's arm wrapped again around his throat. Closing, closing. Blood, collapsing, his consciousness like a star imploding, *no, no, no—*

• • •

Awake. At the desk. The Resolute Desk.

The LED screens around were dark, no longer showing the bluffs of Martha's Vineyard, or the snowy peaks of Mount Rainier, or the Boston skyline, or the ocean, or outer space, or a Miami nightclub, or a Parisian coffeehouse.

Blank and black.

Ed Creel stood up, but he was dizzy still, and his body lurched sideways and tumbled. He grunted, doubling over on the ground, curling into a fetal wad. Looking down, he saw that he had pissed himself. Pain radiated from his side and back. *Kidney punch.* Dombrowsky. It had really happened. He hadn't dreamt it.

Somehow, he juggled his legs underneath him and got to standing. It felt like getting up out of bed after a long hard night of sleep—your feet felt like stiff mitts at the end of unbent pole legs. But as the blood went back into his limbs, and as he started to loosen up, he walked, bowlegged, to the door—

He slammed the flat of his hand against the panel to open the exit—

The panel glowed red. A forbidding sound emitted: *bwwwwmp.* The door didn't open. He tried again, and again, a red panel, and the fuck-you sound. *Bwwwmp.* "No," he growled, trying the other hand. Still nothing. He tried more times with each, then his fist, then punched it—but the panel was nigh-unbreakable transparent ceramic glass, and as pain bloomed in his knuckles and shot down his wrist in a whip-snap of lightning, he realized his hand would break before the panel would. He roared and pressed both fists together, biting his own hand hard enough to draw blood. He wanted to collapse into an imploding star, a furious supernova of energy that tore this place out of the ground. They'd betrayed him, they'd all betrayed him. *All but Vanderweil*, he thought, but Vanderweil had betrayed him by failing him. It was treason all the way down.

I am the president of the United States, he screamed in his own head.

You can't do this to me.

I am everything.

You are nothing.

Eventually, the screens around him—well, one of them, anyway—flickered on. Honus Clines appeared.

And it was then that Clines explained, in his poofy, pillowy voice, that the last favor he was doing for dear Ed Creel was this: ensuring that his prison was not in the small brig they had built into the substructure of Atlas Haven but, rather, would be Creel's own presidential office. Clines further said that Creel would receive three square meals daily—"Good meals, the very best, because after all, you did pay in, didn't you?"—and of course there was a presidential bathroom behind one of the panels, and they certainly wouldn't force him into the indignity of pissing and shitting into a bucket. Then Clines said that he'd decided to take the presidential suite for himself, laughing as he turned the camera around and showed off what had been Creel's own living room. As Clines laughed, Creel screamed—and, eventually, wept. The screen went dark once more.

ATLAS HAVEN
Year Four

WHO KNOWS WHEN, 2024

Creel was a diminished man. He reeked. He'd lost weight. His jawline was a patchy, neck-strangling beard. There was little to do here. They let him have a few amenities: He could change the screens to a variety of backdrops, and sometimes he did that and imagined himself being wherever the screens took him: a busy New York restaurant, in a hot air balloon, or back at his own house on the Vineyard. But such moments of imagination led him to the same rageful places: He wanted to kill the restaurant diners with their own silverware, he wanted to jump from the balloon and fall to the Earth below where the ground would pulverize him into bonemeal and blood jelly, he wanted to burn down his old beach house and leap off the bluffs into the crushing water below, but he could do none of those things, so instead he clubbed himself in the face and the neck with his fists, he beat his legs, he pounded the desk. They let him have music, too, and movies, but he always faded out, lost track of the song or the film or the show and it unspooled out of his attention span, leaving him lost and weeping.

It was like being unstuck in time and space.

He saw no other people—no complete people, at least. The door panel would open just enough to allow a Styrofoam plate to be slid underneath. Always with plastic fork and knives. They gave him no water, so he had to drink from the spigot in the bathroom.

Often, in his fitful, fucked-up sleep, he dreamed of hunting. In the forest, on the slope of a mountain, across a field—rifle, shotgun, compound bow, a leaping caribou, a bugling elk, a flurry of feathers as a pheasant burst from the fencerow.

One day he made peace with the fact he was no longer the hunter.

He wrote a note. He had paper, he had Sharpie markers—his preferred marker with which to sign documents. All his papers were blank, except for the stationery header of **Office of the President of the United States, Atlas Haven**, with the Atlas Haven seal—which looked like a berm in the earth, a flag flying upon it, a flag of many stripes and one star. *I'm that star,* he thought then, and he thought now. Then laughed.

The note was to Honus Clines.

Honus,
We need to talk
I want to say sorry
And I have something to confess
Please
—Ed

Then, he waited.

DAYS, NIGHTS, SLIPPING THROUGH HIS grip like a blood-slick chain.

But then, one day, or one night—who could tell anymore down here?—the door opened with a *whish* and there stood Honus Clines.

Clines carried his meal in. Creel's VP was thinner. But the skin hung on him in saggy bags. His eyes were set deep in his head. "Mister President," Clines said, not without a bit of cheeky irony. He looked, and sounded, a little drunk.

When he got closer, he was preceded by a wafting whiff of brandy.

Creel stood up on weak legs. He used the desk to lean on.

"Clines," Creel said. He'd yelled and screamed at himself but this was the first time in God knew how long that he was speaking to another human. Assuming this was real and not, as he feared, a hallucination. His voice sounded strange. Distant, like it belonged to someone else.

"You're missing out up there," Honus said, with a lecherous chuckle. "Oh, it's something else. A party, just a nonstop party. Pleasure all around, pleasure to *go* around." Clines set the tray of food down on the desk. It looked spare: greens and steak, but the filet was narrow, like it had been halved—and the greens were a small hillock, undressed, cooked and wet. "I killed Helen last week."

Creel blinked.

Helen.

Clines's *wife*. It was always Honus and Helen.

"You did?"

"I did. I had to, you know. It was what it was, she and I didn't see eye to eye anymore and she didn't like . . . who I was sticking it to, and she tried to hit me with a vase, so I, you know, I beat her to death with that, uhh, small marble plinth the vase sat on, the one you gave me once upon a time." He chuckled again. "So thank *you* for that."

"You're welcome."

"Yeah. Good fun, good fun."

"Doesn't sound like things are going okay up there."

"Oh, it's fine, it's real fine. Food's running lower than we expected—hah, got a bunch of folks with appetites that won't quit, all of us a little greedy, a little gluttony. Gluttonous, I guess is the word. Hm. What else? Septic system started backing up into the swimming pool. One big toilet now. Oh! Lynnea killed Dave Dilman. Rossmoyne shot one of the staff, thought the fellow was stealing from him, turns out, oops, not really, old Wesley just has encroaching dementia, so that's a hoot. There was a crabs outbreak. Then genital warts. We're out of coffee."

"So, going just fine."

"Just *fiiine*," Clines said, with a big smile.

"You know how I said we were lions, we were wolves?"

"I seem to recollect."

"I was wrong. We were spiders. Fat in our webs."

"Oh? Do tell?"

Creel stabbed Honus Clines with a piece of the Resolute Desk.

He stuck it clumsily in the meat of his VP's collarbone. He was aiming for his neck, but the other man flinched at the last second—Creel probably came in too slow, having lost muscle mass in all this time.

The weapon was a lean, sharp wedge of wood—turned out, the Resolute Desk had a secret compartment in it, tucked up under the right-hand, top-most drawer. Wasn't much to be excited about: an old iron key, a half of a wood carving, but then, two wedges. Maybe used as lifts for the desk, from

Kennedy's day—Creel didn't know, didn't care. He only cared that they were sharp and splintery. He knew he couldn't make too many movements here— breaking apart the desk, for instance, would bring guards in. But once he found those sharp bits of wood, they were easy enough to hide. Initially he figured, maybe he'd get some guards in here by clogging the toilet up, or breaking the sink—they'd come in and he'd stabby-stabby. But they were trained. And he'd gone soft.

Instead, he settled on the comfort of revenge.

He sharpened the wedges with the iron key. really just breaking pieces away until it was as much of a weapon as he could make it.

Then, he wrote the invitation.

Clines took the bait, because Clines was the original softy. When a person who doesn't have friends makes a true friend, a bona fide friend, that's something special. There's a bond there. And Creel knew he could tug on that bond.

Now Clines stood before him, shocked at the piece of wood jutting out of his collar meat. "Creel," he said, surprised.

"More where that came from," Creel said, and drew the second weapon: the other wedge, also sharpened.

He lunged at Clines—but the other man whapped him with a bear paw, really rang his bell. Creel tried to get up under the man, and he stuck the wood in Honus's side—but there was a robe there, a big hotel-like robe, filthy, and it didn't puncture. Clines, shocked and enraged, returned the favor and got up under Creel, carrying him forward with surprising momentum.

Honus Clines slammed Creel down against the desk. The tray of food flipped. Steak on the ground. Greens spattering.

Creel's arm, extended over his head, tightened—his fist curled hard around the wooden wedge and he plunged it toward Honus even as the other man's blood poured down over him. But Clines blocked it with a forearm, and pinned Creel further to the desk—

Before wrestling the weapon away.

Creel blinked, looking up at Clines. His wide eyes. His yellow teeth. Behind the brandy breath was a breath of rot, of ruin. A gamy stink.

Honus Clines stuck the wooden wedge into Creel's face.

Into his *eye*.

Or, rather, under it.

Creel cried out and Clines roared, as the vice president used the wedge

like a lever— Creel's vision went white hot, then white cold, then in a coruscating lightning burst in the back of his vision, that side of his sight went
dead black as the eyeball wrenched up and out—and onto the floor.

He screamed. Sliding down off the desk, to the floor, his hands cupped
to the hole in his face. Blood and mess oozed from around his palms and
between his fingers. Clines, looking ghoulish, the color drained from his
face, leaving him looking like a river-soaked bedsheet, plodded over to the
eyeball. With the piece of wood still jutting out of him, he bent down and
picked the eyeball up. He gave it a look. As it gave him one, too.

Then the VP said nothing before shuffling out of the room.

TIME PASSED. THE FOOD BEGAN to diminish. With the meals came antibiotic
pills, which Ed found surprising. He spent a lot of time examining the ill-
healing crater where his eye once was. He felt like he'd lost his mind. Like it
wasn't real. Sometimes he had the phantom sensation of heaviness there,
like suddenly he'd have sight again. But he didn't.

Then, weeks later, maybe months, he didn't know—

He found a piece of paper on the desk.

Faceup, it had a message in familiar handwriting:

PATIENCE.

Then it vibrated a little, and shimmered, and turned to dust.

Dust that rose into the air, still gleaming, before dissipating entirely.

ATLAS HAVEN
Year Five

Now

Once again, Honus Clines and Ed Creel stood in the Oval Office of
their luxury apocalypse bunker, Atlas Haven. And it had all clearly gone to
shit. Two weeks ago, the water turned brown and started to taste like oil and
dirt. Three weeks before that, the screens here partly failed. The food had
gone thin. Meals were sporadic. Sometimes he heard yelling. Had he heard
gunshots, too? Maybe. It was hard to tell, the walls were thick and it was
insulated down here.

Currently, the two men were laughing, just laughing like loons, like old friends drunk on their own history, maybe even hungover from it. The Ree-bok shoebox sat there between them, on the Resolute Desk, and in it was an eyeball. The eyeball was preserved in a cube of clear epoxy, and Clines— gasping between guffaws—said the 3D printers were still working, so he made this little, gasp, gasp, guffaw, *paperweight* for the president's desk, to hold down all those, wheeze, cough, guffaw, *papers* he had to sign. And the two of them belly-laughed at that.

Then, Creel felt his guts cinch up.

Tight, like a lasso around a bucking horse's neck.

His hand buzzed and tingled—not like it was going numb, but like it had an electric charge going through it.

"Oh, Jesus," he said, feeling the buzz grow more powerful in his hand. More *insistent*. Like it *wanted* something. *Vvvvzzzz.*

"What?" Clines said, still wheeze-laughing. "Got your *eye* on something?"

Creel laughed, like, boy howdy, wasn't that a side-splitter.

Then his arm shot out, gripping Clines's jaw with his left hand.

He felt the thrum of energy in his hand. Like ants crawling first on him, then under the skin. Clines's eyes bugged out, but then he stutter-burped a new laugh, and he started whooping anew, and so did Creel—even as his hand began to vibrate of its own volition, a beehive hum coming from under the skin. Honus's laughs were cut short as his jowls shook with micro-tremors, and Ed Creel found that the muscle underneath his hand felt, well, *liquid*, and suddenly Clines's neck was a curtain of fresh blood, and Ed's hand began to push *into* the other man's face as if it were nothing more than just soft ice cream. He pushed and pushed and it felt like a woodchipper chewing bark— *vbbbbbgrrrr.* Blood began to spray now, blood and bits of bone, and he moved in and then up—*up, up, up*—out the roof of Honus Clines's skull, until all that was left was two halves of the man's head. Not even halves, just partial flaps on each side, the middle of it gone, the face gone, like a pumpkin with a cinder block dropped in the center of it.

Clines gurgled one big bubble of blood from his esophagus—

It inflated, and then popped. Bloop.

Then he fell over.

Ed's hand stopped tingling.

"Holy fucking shit," he said, breathless.

He looked on the chair, where a small glass vial sat—a vial that came to him only days before, on his breakfast tray. With it was a note that said, *DRINK ME*, a note that, like the others before it, twitched itself into shimmering nonexistence. Inside the vial had been a wet gray goop, almost like liquid gunpowder. He took a while to decide, but he was hungry and thirsty and thought, what did it matter? So, he had quaffed the stuff down. It was like drinking a colonoscopy prep shake—it was thick, goopy, like wetter, heavier peanut butter. At the time, it seemed to pulse in his throat all the way down, his chest fluttering like a trapped bird.

Then it was in him.

He didn't know what it was.

But now, maybe he did.

Whatever was in those Sleepwalkers—

Maybe it was in him, too. Somehow. In some way.

He tried hauling Honus's body over to the doorway—he needed the man's hand to open it. But the fucker was too heavy, so instead he thought, *What if I use my hand again the same way, this time buzz-sawing his arm at the wrist.* It made him queasy to imagine that, but it also excited him, too. His cock stiffened in his pants just thinking about the raw power he now had. But, instead he decided to try something else, first—he waltzed over, pressed his left hand to the panel, and once again, felt the tingle rise to his fingertips and his palm. He half-expected his paw to push in through the panel, chewing it apart with its chainsaw buzz, but instead—

It glowed green.

And the door opened.

Outside, the lights in the hallway flickered.

My hand is a key. My hand is a weapon.

The elevator was already open ahead of him.

Ed Creel found a feral grin, snatched up the plastic-shellacked eyeball that once belonged in his head, and waltzed toward the open doors, whistling "Hail to the Chief" as he went. He stepped into the elevator, then headed up, up, up.

And soon, out. Out of this place. Out of this prison. A free man.

A fucking *president.*

If only he knew who was waiting for him at the top. If only he knew why.

30

A RECKONING WITH WRECKAGE

Power on. Is anybody listening? Okay. Here we go. This is Jay Patel of the Central Indiana Skywarn, part of the NOAA National Weather Service program, serving originally as an alternative storm-spotting channel across amateur radio. Not gonna use it for weather. I don't have radar. Though, hah, maybe I'll tell you what the weather is outside my window, because if you're listening, who knows where you're at, maybe you want to know. (It's raining right now. Ta-da.) I'll use this frequency just to talk. I'm powered up with solar. If the sun's shining, I'll be here every day at 2 to 2:30 P.M. Think of it like a podcast you can't download. (Wait for laughter.) (Can you tell I wanted to major in theater but my parents wouldn't let me?) Anyway. Today I just want to say, whoever you are, wherever you are, it's okay that you're not okay. Things are broken. Nothing will ever be the same so it's okay if you'll never be the same, either. Love you all.
—Jay Patel, Central Indiana Skywarn Radio, X9ACE

SEPTEMBER 19, 2025
Ouray, Colorado

THE CLOCK TICKED OVER TO MIDNIGHT.

Shana and Benji sat in the lobby of the Beaumont Hotel, her curled up in a human lump under a blanket, only her head peeking out. Him sitting across from her, hands on his knees, staring down at his feet.

He looked rough. *Raw.* Like a downed wire, sparking and snapping. "So what happens now?" she asked finally.

"I truly don't know," he said.

"Black Swan tried to kill you. Or at least . . . threatened to."

He breathed out slowly, as if trying to make peace with that—but at the end of his exhalation, his hands balled into fists and pressed hard into his own legs. "I know." Benji rubbed his eyes and groaned. "I thought—I *hoped* that for as strange as our situation was, that I was on the side of the angels. I wanted to believe, Shana. I so badly wanted to believe. But now I don't know what this even is."

Shana didn't, either. "I just know that you can't trust Black Swan."

"Too late for that. I trusted for too long and . . . now what?"

She had no answer beyond the obvious: *I lost my child and my sister and this whole stupid town.* "Do we need to go look for them?"

He knew who she meant.

"Marcy and Dove will be fine." But the doubt was plain in his voice. "You should rest. If you want to go back to your room—"

"No, no way, I want to be here. With you." The fear of what was coming was too much to bear, especially alone.

"Then there, on the couch. I'll watch. I couldn't sleep if I wanted to."

So, she did. She curled up on her side and fell into a broken-boned sleep, an uneasy rest of phantom twitches and faceless people chasing her through hallways and forests. Then, a new sound, this one not in her head, but real— a *whump*, the sound of a door opening and closing hard, followed by stomping boots.

They're here, she thought, gasping awake. Who they were, and what they were here for, she didn't even know. Xander? Kernick? Some nameless authority with Black Swan's commandments in their ears and on their lips?

But it was just Marcy.

"Marcy," Benji bleated, a thankful sound, and he launched himself up to greet her. They hugged, but Shana saw that hers was not returned in the way to which they were accustomed—Marcy's hugs were legendary things, two arms that could crush boulders with their enthusiasm. But this was just her one arm draped softly across the middle of his back. In the flickering light of the oil lamp, Shana saw stains on her hands and sleeves. Mud? Or blood? *It looks awfully red.* "I'm glad you're all right," Benji said to her. "Where's Dove? When we came out, you weren't there, and my God, Matthew—"

"Dove is dead," she said, pulling away stiffly.

"What?" Benji asked in horror.

"Kernick found us. He stepped in front of Dove. Dove tried to talk him down but there wasn't time. Kernick shot him in the chest."

Benji felt his legs nearly give out under the weight of that news.

"Oh God," Shana said, tears searing the lids of her eyes. "Shit. *Shit.* This is my fault. I should've just left well enough alone, I should've . . ." But the words died in her mouth.

"No," Benji said to her. "Shana, no. You can't think like that."

"Yes," was what Marcy said. "Yes, she can. It *is* all our fault."

Benji stood aghast. "Marcy. You don't mean that."

Her answer came in a cracked, tremulous voice. "We could've stood back and done it differently. We didn't have to—" She threw up her massive hands. "Matthew had a gun. A secret gun. I said *no guns.* Did either of you know? Whatever. We got our blood up, we lost our trust, our faith, and we went in *hot,* when we could've just sat back, been diplomatic—"

Shame filled Shana. *Did either of you know?* Shana knew. And she let it happen. She let Matthew have his gun. And now people were dead.

"Marcy, you don't know what you're saying. You're tired, traumatized, we all are, and—"

"What happened in there?" Marcy said, challenging Benji. "What did the two of you *do* in there that made them suddenly want to push us away?"

"We didn't do anything!" Shana said, tossing the blanket behind her and striding over. "Marcy, please, they have Charlie, this isn't on us."

"All I know is, we were out there and suddenly, they get a call on the walkies. And next thing we know, they're saying we have to leave. That there's a *situation* inside. They try to push us back, tell us to go home, and Matthew—he pulls a gun, and he *shoots.* Again and again, like—like a crazy person, Kernick in the shoulder, Porter in the guts, Paulus in the head. Maria ran. Dove and I took off, and . . ." Her voice broke again. "Kernick found us." Her eyes squeezed shut. "And then—"

"Kernick shot Dove," Benji said.

"Then I shot Kernick," Marcy said, tears in her eyes.

"You had to," Benji said, trying to placate her. "You *had* to, it's all right—"

But she shoved him back, hard enough that he fell backward into the table that sat between the chairs and couch. He didn't even get back up. Benji just slid forward and sat there. "Marcy. Don't do this. Don't be like this."

"Black Swan tried to kill Benji," Shana said. "This isn't our fault."

But Marcy wheeled on her in a rage. "Oh? A minute ago, you just said it was your fault. So which is it, Shana? Your fault? Or not? Black Swan got us all here. Those people, the Flock, have built this town up and here we are . . . just throwing bricks through windows. If we could've been patient. *Patient.* Stood back. Asked some questions. Had a little trust, a little *faith.* But instead we had to do *this*—"

"They took my child!" Shana cried.

"Who cares about your stupid child?" Marcy roared in return. It felt like a slap to the face. Worse: a fist, a choking hand, a shotgun blast. Shana was robbed of her breath. Already Marcy was backpedaling: "I'm—I'm sorry, I didn't mean anything by it—I just—Shana—"

"I *saved* you," Shana hissed.

"*Black Swan* saved me," Marcy said without missing a beat. This time not in anger, but in a small, cold voice. "Just so we're clear."

Tears burned the corners of Shana's eyes. "I thought you were my friend."

"I am. I *am*. But . . ." Marcy covered her face with her hands. Then she shook those same hands as if they were covered in biting ants. "There's going to be a town council meeting. This morning. They're already going around and gathering them up. There needs to be . . . a tribunal, a truth and reconciliation—"

"Jesus," Benji said. "You're on their side."

"I'm not on anybody's side. I'm on the side of peace."

"This isn't peace. This is . . . insanity."

"What you brought to that house was insanity."

Benji stood, got in her face. "What I *brought* to this town was the Flock, was Black Swan, was all of us. But I was wrong. Or . . ." He softened his tone. "Or at least, something has gone wrong. Black Swan has changed, or maybe it was always this way, I can't say. But Shana is right. It tried to kill me in there. It took her baby. For God's sake, Marcy, it all but admitted to me that it killed the world."

"To save it. To save us."

"You believe that's okay?"

Marcy's shoulders slumped. "I don't know, Benji. We live in a world where sometimes big decisions happen and I don't get to have a say in them. Governments, CEOs, they'd move the world this way and that way and . . . I don't know. It was what it was and it is what it is. I just know that we wouldn't be here otherwise. And that this town *we* brought them to is a beautiful place. I think we owe it and these people our trust. But we broke that trust and . . . now there are going to be consequences for that. Whether you feel right, or righteous, it doesn't matter. *It doesn't matter*. They're going to want answers."

"Let them ask. They won't like what they hear."

"Where is Matthew?" Marcy asked, her tone suddenly dark. It was laced with the venom of anger.

"He's gone."

"Home?"

"I don't know," Benji lied. Shana noted that. It was truly a break if he was lying to Marcy. It meant he didn't trust her anymore. That broke her heart more than anything—because Shana feared she couldn't trust Marcy anymore, either.

"Just gone, then."

"Just gone."

"No idea where."

Benji shrugged, shook his head.

Marcy nodded. "Fine. I hope you're not lying. I'm the sheriff. It's my job to hold you accountable. To hold myself accountable. Tomorrow that happens."

"You're the sheriff. But I'm the mayor."

"I don't think they'll see it that way, Benji. Who's here to tell them? Dove?"

Shana saw the look on Benji's face. Crushed under that realization.

"Yeah," Marcy said. "Tomorrow morning. Be ready."

"We shall," he said bleakly.

Marcy nodded. "I'll be outside."

"Guarding us," Shana noted. "That's what you mean, isn't it? Guarding us. So we don't get gone, too."

But to that, Marcy said nothing. She silently stalked outside, and gently closed the door behind her. Through the stained glass of the front door of the hotel, they could see her massive shadow blocking the way. Once a friend, now their warden.

31

STRAYS

. . . All the sadness in the world is right in the eyes of a dog.

—George Carlin

SEPTEMBER 19, 2025
Perimeter Trail, Colorado

IT WAS ONE NIGHT, ONLY ONE, BUT THAT NIGHT FELT LONGER THAN ANY other, save for the one where Autumn was in the hospital from her overdose and Matthew was not sure if she would be okay. On that night long ago, he *felt* lost in the woods—and on this night, he was *literally* lost in the woods. Benji sent him in a direction and off he went, but it was dark, and he had only his little flashlight to guide him. In any other situation, the night would've seemed frightening—the *chush-chush* of night bugs and the constant rustling of leaves around him, plus the persistent threat that a mountain lion or bear would find him and make him a snack. But in this situation, he cared little for what might be coming for him. Because he'd lost everything. Lost it himself, gambled away like money in Vegas.

There was a better way, Matthew, said a voice in his head. Once upon a time he would've believed that voice to have been God, but he knew it was just his own conscience. While he was glad that some part of himself still existed that had a moral backbone, he also hated that part right now.

Because that part flashed in him the scene, again and again—

Him, standing at the bottom of the steps.

Marcy and Dove behind. The two of them talking. Dove wary, but Marcy sure that everything was fine, would be fine, have faith, *have faith.*

Then Kernick at the top of the steps receiving something on the radio— from Xander, Matthew was pretty sure. *There's been a situation.*

Then, with his gun up, Kernick told them they had to leave. Pushed
Matthew back down the steps. Stern, firm. Something had gone wrong.

Matthew just . . .

He just acted. It was clumsy—he pawed at the front of the other man's
rifle, moving it aside so that when it discharged, it went off into the woods.
Then his own pistol was up and out and *pop*. Kernick in the shoulder. The
man's gun dropped. He staggered off the steps, into the trees. Others came
from around back. And Matthew kept shooting. *Pop, pop, pop*. With each he
winced, flinching, as if struck by a bullet himself. His targets were close
enough he didn't have to be a good shot. And by some miracle—*Sure, a
miracle, keep telling yourself that, Pastor Matt*—he didn't take any hits himself. And when it was done, and that eggy stink of gunpowder hung in the air
like a fog, there were bodies on the ground, Marcy and Dove were gone, and
Matthew was left with what he'd done.

He'd felt it, then: the feeling that something had been put in him, a rage
that was not his own—a violence *installed* by Ozark, beaten into him like a
nail. It was a pressure behind his eyes, around his heart, in the pulse at his
wrists. And a pressure like that—it had to come out. Like the bullet at the
end of the barrel, pushed out by the fire of powder, the explosion of air, by
the *pressure*.

This was Ozark's fault.

That's what he told himself.

But then another voice said: *You don't get to blame things on that man.
Don't give him that power. This was you. This was all you.*

Around and around his brain went, two rats chasing each other, biting
each other's tails. And on and on he walked, upon the rough-hewn trail. He
kept going—where? Was it south? Southwest? He wasn't even sure. Eventually the flashlight dimmed as the battery died. He kept going. Tripping on
roots. Falling. A twist of his ankle, a thorn-scratch against his arm and his
neck, a low branch giving him a hard *whap* to the forehead. Like nature itself
was against him. Punishing him. A necessary castigation, but far, far from
enough.

I should go home, he thought.

Home. Ouray.

Go back. Take his licks. He could be the first prisoner in town. The first
one to break their laws, the first heretic, the first exile. In a cell, he might
again find God, find Christ, find light.

But he was too afraid to face them.

Too afraid to face God, that darker voice said.

He just couldn't do it.

So he kept going until he couldn't go anymore, and at that point he just sat down on the trail. The night was cooling—taking one bite of body heat at a time. Matthew curled up, into himself. Trying to stay warm. Somewhere, somehow, he slept. But that sleep was merciless, too. It grabbed him and took him, dragging him through the blood and fog of that scene again and again: the porch, the radio, the gunfire, the red puddles, the guard crying into his own bloody middle.

Until—

Boop.

A chuff, a sniff, and a cold wet circle against his forehead.

"Mnuh," he said, tasting dirt and dry mouth. Matthew blinked crust from his eyes and looked into the face of—

A raggedy golden retriever.

Once he opened his eyes, the dog seemed to relax a little, panting a pink tongue that seemed honestly far too large for its head.

"Hello," Matthew said. A little part of him was afraid he'd died, but that couldn't be true, because Hell did not contain any golden retrievers.

He sat up.

And then, two more shapes emerged from the brush, stepping onto the trail silently—two wolves, and it was only now that Matthew realized how *frighteningly large* wolves were. The retriever, who was not a small dog, certainly *seemed* small by comparison, eclipsed by these two beasts—one of which was missing a leg, but seemed to have no problem getting along.

A dog, a fox, and two wolves.

No fox, yet, but—

One dog, two wolves.

Morning light speared the ground around them. The three-legged wolf lifted its lip in a sneer, showing teeth. The other wolf simply stared at him, as if daring him to move. Its silence and stillness felt all the more terrifying.

"They won't hurt you if you don't hurt them," said a man's voice from behind him. Gruff, yes, but the wildness did not conceal the crisp touch of a well-educated man. Matthew gently stood, not even bothering to brush himself off. The man approaching him had a fox snaking in and out of his legs with every step, as if it was a fun game for the animal (and a mild annoyance to the man). The man was thin, like a length of rope. Scruffy and rough. Dirty, too.

"Are you Arthur? Benji—ah, Benjamin Ray, told me to find you," Matthew said. His own voice was hoarse-sounding, abraded as if his vocal cords had been dragged over splintered wood. He barely sounded like himself. Maybe that was a good thing. He didn't want to *be* himself anymore. "My name is . . ." *I could give him a different name. I could be someone else. Anyone else.* But that felt like a cheat. He wasn't allowed to escape himself. The sin was on him like a scar. "I'm Matt. Matthew Bird. I'm from Indiana and—" The man continued to stare at him. "Again, Benji told me to find you?"

"Why?"

"I need help."

Those three words . . .

He was always the one offering help. Giving it. *Forcing it on people,* a darker voice told him. Now, here he was. On the altar. Prostrate. Throat bared.

I need help.

The man looked him over. The retriever sniffed at his pant leg.

"Fine," Arthur said, after some mental deliberation. "Come on."

Then the man walked off down the path. The fox kept dashing on and off the trail, sometimes pausing to cat-pounce on invisible or imagined mice. The two wolves gave Matthew one last look and a chuff before turning to follow. Only the dog remained, staring up at Matthew, panting, as if to say, *Are you coming?*

"I am," Matthew said. And he was. The dog followed.

THE DOG FOLLOWED. GUMBALL THE Very Good Boy, Gumball the Golden, Gumball the Great. Gumball the Goldie, once. The retriever liked this man, though to be fair, the dog liked most men, liked most women, liked all children, because Gumball was a dog who liked people. It was Gumball's nature to be naturally unsuspicious, not like the wolves, no—they were always suspicious, even of Gumball once upon a time. But now they were family and it was great.

Gumball had another family, once: Anne and Steve, and their boy-puppy, Robin. They were good people until they weren't, and even then, Gumball thought it wasn't their fault. Something had gone wrong, very wrong, and he smelled it on them weeks, even months before everything changed. It was a sour, fermented stink, like the way autumn leaves stank after the first spring rains.

Then one day the smell on the inside of them was on the outside, and Gumball knew: Steve and Anne were sick.

"We'll be all right, Goldie," Anne had said to him, because back then Gumball wasn't Gumball, but rather, Goldie. That was okay. A name was a name was a name. But they weren't going to be okay. Gumball knew Anne was wrong. Gumball knew Anne and Steve were going to die.

They were sneezing and coughing and Steve seemed to get worse faster, and something came out of him—like the fraying threads of an old rope toy, except these were coming out of his nose and his ears. He had a rash and he started slurring his words and yelling a lot. Gumball tried to help him, even if only to nuzzle for comfort, but time came that Steve acted like he didn't even know who Gumball *was*, and he chased him out of the house, trying to hit him with a pan. Once Gumball-Goldie was outside, Steve locked the door.

Gumball tried to get back in the house. Scratching and whining. He could see Robin at the window upstairs. Robin never developed the stink. Robin was still healthy. Maybe Robin would let Gumball in, the dog thought, and so he barked.

Robin got the hint. He came down to let Gumball inside—the dog could hear the lockity-things being undone from that side, clickity-clock, but then there was a lot of stomping and a lot of yelling. Gumball heard Robin crying and Steve screaming. He didn't know where Anne was. The stomping moved around to the other side of the house, so Gumball went back there and ducked under the fence, and hopped up on the back patio, whose glass door looked into the kitchen.

There was a box in there, a black box where pizzas went in cold and came out hot. (Gumball knew other things went in there, too, but pizzas were the most important, because he always got to eat the pizza's bones.)

The box was open.

Steve was wrestling Robin into that box. The boy was screaming. He was in pain and he was scared—the fear-stink came off him and Gumball could smell it even out here. Steve slammed the door to the box, holding it shut as he did something to the box—the same thing he did whenever they made the box hot for the pizzas. A button, a spinny thing. All while he held the door shut and the boy wailed, pounding on the inside of the soon-to-be-hot box.

Steve sneezed. His eyes were dead, and half-crusted with white. More of those wet ropes came out of him.

There was no Steve inside Steve anymore. He was just those wet threads. Like the worms in a sick dog's heart. He was stink and rot.

Gumball had to act. The window above the kitchen was closed, but the dog bounded up on the patio table and leapt for it—

Whud. He hit it hard with his head and fell off. His birds were spinning. That window was too hard, too firm.

The patio door!

He tried that next, slamming into it—*whump.* Nothing. Then he stood on his hind paws and scratched at it with his front—but his claws would not even mark the glass, not one bit. Gumball barked and barked, snarling and howling.

Then he thought, *I can be like them, I can pretend to be a human.*

The patio door had a handle on the side and he'd never opened it before but he *was* able to get the cabinets open sometimes (and they stopped storing his yummy treats in there for that very reason), and maybe he'd be able to get *this* open, too, so Gumball twisted his head, grabbed the door handle in his mouth, and tugged hard, backpedaling as he did so—

His jaws slipped off it.

But it gave a little. Didn't it? So again he tried, jaws on the door, growling with rage and frustration as he tugged backward again—

And the door moved. Not a lot. Just a nose width.

But a nose width would be enough. Gumball shoved his snoot in there like a wedge and *squeeeeeezed* himself into that space, wriggling through as the door pushed wider to accommodate him. Through the gap he raced, leaping for the black box in which Robin was trapped. *That* one was easy to open—it had a towel on it, and all Gumball had to do was grab a hold of it and *tug.* He started to open it—but Steve grabbed at him, said something in a mush-mouthed garble.

Gumball snapped, bit his hand. Steve yowled, came back, red dripping onto the floor. Then the dog spun again, grabbed the towel and pulled—

The box opened, and Robin tumbled out, alongside a soft wave of heat— the boy, crying, ran even as his father went for him again. But Gumball wasn't letting that happen, oh no. He knocked the man down and bit him on the face. Again and again until the man who used to be Steve curled in a ball, pawing at his head, weeping. Gumball felt bad. Steve had been good to him once.

But this wasn't Steve, and Not-Steve wanted to hurt Robin.

Next thing the dog knew, Anne was running down the steps. She had Robin in her hands. Gumball-Goldie chased after them, even as she put her son in their car and slammed the doors. Robin pawed at the glass. Gumball pawed at Robin's paws on the other side of the glass. Anne was crying, her eyes white and wet.

She started the car.

And away it went.

Gumball didn't know what to do so he chased after, even though he couldn't keep up with it. But he didn't give up, no, and he searched everywhere, trying to find any little bit of scent of the boy that he could find. He went far and wide, down every street and sidewalk until his paws burned.

But he never did find them, not ever. He thought he picked up their smell once, but it was gone again as fast as it came.

That was then, and this was now, and now he was following this new friend with his pack. This new friend was from that town, and there were times when Gumball missed the world of towns and houses, a world where he could curl up on a carpet, in a sunbeam, on a soft toy like a pillow under his shaggy muzzle, maybe near one of those vents that blew cold air on hot days and hot air on cold days. A world of playing catch with Robin the boy-puppy. A world with the bones of pizza.

A world without the sick smell.

But there was a smell here, too, on this new friend. A new friend, a new smell. It wasn't the sick smell, not like before. This was metallic, sharp, like mud. It came and then it was gone again.

The new man, the Matthew man, kept walking.

Gumball bounded after.

32

A NEW CALCULATION

7/17/2022: Even now I think, I should've known. I shouldn't have made the mistake to get close to anyone. People are quicksand now. Maybe they always were. They'll pull you in, draw you down, and drown you in themselves. I'm among them, but I'm not a part of them. I learned that now.
—from *A Bird's Story, A Journal of the Lost*

SEPTEMBER 19, 2025
Beaumont Hotel, Ouray, Colorado

HOURS AFTER THEIR TALK, BENJI HEARD SOMEONE TALKING TO MARCY OUT front. Not long after, Marcy left. Where she was going, he didn't know.

Seeing opportunity, he began scouting the hotel, going from floor to floor and looking out all available windows. The hotel also had fire and emergency exits, not to mention a way out through the next-door bookstore and the garden courtyard beyond. There *was* roof access, but the Beaumont occupied the entire corner of 5th and Main, and next door was a shuttered take-out restaurant which sat on the other side of the courtyard. Behind the hotel was an alley, across from which sat homes. But in both cases, that gap of the courtyard and the alley was easily twenty feet in each case. Impossible to jump, and Benji could think of no good way to bridge it that was safe and timely.

"Are you looking for a way out?" Shana asked as he came back downstairs.

"I am."

"No way out?"

"No easy way, at least."

She chewed her lip. "Maybe we just stay. We just . . . see what happens.

They're not a cult. Right? The townspeople, I mean. Some of them will support us. They'll stand with us." She paused at the edge of desperation. "Won't they?"

He loathed saying the words, but out they came with a bitter taste: "They *might* be a cult, Shana. Think about it. Black Swan was inside each of them. We don't know what it did to their brains. It's one thing to suspect basic social programming, but when you consider how a parasite like *Toxoplasma gondii* can *rewrite* the brain of the host in order to achieve its goal . . ."

"Then why didn't it happen to me?"

A little part of him wondered, *Why was that?*

A darker part worried, *What if it did?*

"I . . . don't know."

A shadow passed over Shana's face. "It makes me feel . . . gross and fucked up that Black Swan was in me, that it's still in my baby. Maybe it is like a parasite. Like some kind of *disease*."

A *disease*, he thought.

That tugged on his brain like a pulled stitch.

Just then, the door to the hotel opened, interrupting his thought.

Marcy walked in.

The face she wore was both tired and dire. It had softened some, but not in a good way—in her eyes were distant thunderclouds.

"I'm to escort you both," she said quietly.

"And then what?" Shana asked.

Marcy took a deep breath. "I assume it'll go like it just went for me. They'll ask you questions. They'll . . . render judgment."

"They interrogated you?" Shana asked.

"They did."

"And what judgment did they render?" Benji asked warily.

"They believed my story and are allowing me to continue on as the sheriff of Ouray." But he could hear that there was more there. He kept digging.

"Contingent upon . . . ?" he asked.

Guilt crossed her face like a vulture across the sun. "Contingent upon bringing you both to tribunal and then finding the killer."

"The killer. You mean Matthew."

"That's right." But she held up both hands in a kind of surrender. "I know that sucks. You both think Matthew was one of us, but maybe he wasn't. He wasn't a Shepherd. Hell, you all butted heads more often than not." She tried to smile. "But this is a good thing for the both of you. The council will understand, they'll have mercy. They already understand that *Matthew* did something and you weren't even there when it happened. And, Benji, I heard you helped Rick Porter. That'll count for something."

The gutshot guard. "Did he make it?"

"He did. Thanks to you. And, Shana—your emotional state is understandably all over the map, it's been difficult—"

"My emotional state is exactly where it *should* be," Shana protested.

"Right. I just mean—I just mean I think it'll be okay."

I think it'll be okay.

Those words bounced around Benji's head like a ricocheting bullet. They found no purchase. Because it wasn't true, was it?

He'd always lived life by a few simple rules and one of those rules was, if you felt a situation was wrong or starting to *go* wrong, you had to get out of that situation immediately. ASAFP. One time he was in São Paulo state in Brazil to investigate bovine vaccinia incidents and to see if the orthopoxvirus that caused it could possibly make (or had already made) the leap to human beings. Doubly concerning if it was an escaped vaccine strain used in small-pox inoculations, as some had suspected. But it hadn't. It was fine! The world was set back on its axis, and all was well. Or so he thought. On the way from the hotel to the airport, he took a taxi—and five minutes into the cab ride, he saw they were heading the opposite direction from the airport. The driver said he knew a shortcut, don't worry, don't worry. Lots of handwaving and smiling. But Benji suspected differently. He was alone. He was American. By some metrics, he was important. That made him an opportunity for ransom.

He told the driver to stop.

The driver wouldn't.

The police wouldn't help. He had no one to call.

So when the car rounded a corner, he took his backpack, threw open the door, and . . . jumped out. He hit the sidewalk hard, rolling into a restaurant's sandwich board. He fractured his elbow—just a hairline, but ouch. He lost his suitcase. The car sped up and was gone.

Turned out, there had been a rash of ransom operations running from cabs expertly (and falsely) marked as safe city taxis. Jumping out was smart, even if it hurt. The busted elbow was better than what could've happened.

And now, he was forced to make a similar calculation.

What happened last night was not okay. Something had broken in this place, or had been broken all along. He failed to see it, and now they were in danger.

What kind of a leader am I?

It was time to jump out of the car.

"The tribunal," he said. "Is the whole town there?"

"Whole town. Or most, I guess. That's good. You can appeal to them, too. They'll want to stand with the both of you. They don't hate you," she added, a bit defensively. Which meant some of them definitely did.

"Marcy," he said, "I'm going to appeal to you here in the hopes that you are the loyal friend I think you were, and still are. Shana and I, we're going to leave. We will leave peacefully. But we aren't welcome here anymore and I think it's best for us to go."

"Whoa," Shana said, laughing nervously. "I can't just leave. My baby—"

He gave Shana a look then. It was a look both stern and kind, and in it he tried his absolute damnedest to convey a single message on repeat:

Shana, I need you to trust me.

I know you can't read my mind.

But please, read my mind.

She stopped. Then paused. And then said, "Maybe you're right."

"I . . . I can't let you just leave," Marcy said, confused.

"You can, and you will. Marcy, I know you have faith in this place, but I also hope you trust me enough to know that I feel something has gone wrong. And even if you don't believe I'm right, I hope you believe that *I* believe it. We'd like to leave. And you should allow us to have that choice. While everyone is occupied and the weather is warm, we're going to go." To Shana, he said: "Pack a small bag, Shana. And quickly."

But she didn't move. She was caught watching this unfold.

"Benji . . ." Marcy said, her muscles tightening.

"You don't want to stop us. One of us will end up getting hurt and that cycle of pain will continue. But if we're allowed to leave peacefully, then we can depart. And we can depart still as friends, still as people who trust one another even if they're on opposite sides of the road. Do you understand?"

Marcy drew her gun.

Well, I guess she doesn't understand.

The barrel wavered toward him. He sucked in a sharp breath—

But then Marcy flipped the weapon around and handed it to him. "You might need this. Six shots, and I've a speed-loader in my back pocket. It's not much. But it'll help."

"Thank you, Marcy." Then, again, to Shana: "The bag. Now, please."

The girl nodded and hurried upstairs to her room.

"You're going to have to fight me," Marcy said.

"What? I don't think I'd win that fight. And I thought you said—"

"I'm saying, we're gonna have to make it *look* like I didn't just let you go." Her eyes searched the room. "There. Fire extinguisher on the wall. Take it, spray me with it, then hit me. Hit me with the extinguisher, if you want."

"Your head. I can't. Your skull won't take the hit—"

"Not in the *head*," she said, like, *Duh, God, what the fuck*. "For a very smart guy you're not always so smart. Here's what you do. Grab that. You spray me. I'll bring up my gun"—she mimed raising the revolver she no longer held—"and you'll hit me in the arm. Right here." She slapped her biceps. "You hit me, boom. I drop the gun. You take it. Then you're gone. There's a guard out back—"

"I don't want to hurt anyone. Not you, not that guard."

"I know. I'll run out after our little display. I'll tell them I think you came out the side, ran down the alley. The guard is Gary—he doesn't have any experience with this, he's an actuary from Topeka, and his only qualifications are *did CrossFit* and *close with Xander*. He'll follow. When he's clear—"

"We come out, go the other way."

"Bingo."

"Thank you, Marcy."

She shrugged. "I wish you'd reconsider."

"I don't think we can."

"I'm sorry about before. I'm sorry about all this."

He knew it was futile, but he had to try: "You could come with us. Like old times. On the road again."

"I'm home. For better or for worse, this is it."

Benji nodded. "I hope to see you again."

"Same."

She hugged him. It was a Patented Marcy Hug. He felt like he was dying in the crushing pressure of the deepest ocean. It was wonderful.

"Go pack your things. But don't be long, Benji. You're on the clock."

33

ONE DOES NOT SIMPLY WALK INTO MORDOR

It happened. It fucking happened. SHTF. WROL. TEOTWAWKI. All the things I've been prepping my family for, here it is, and here we are. First I figured it for Russia but now, I'm thinking China or even our own government. Doesn't matter now. What matters is, the world's going to go to shit. There's the obvious things: no grid, no cell service, no groceries, no running water, no nothing. But we got that all covered. There are other issues people don't think about: Reactors gonna pop. Tunnels will flood. Zombies will be out there—not the real thing, but the brain-dead leeches who want what we have. Marauders and scavengers. Society is over. Civilization will collapse. We're ready. Me, the boy, the girl, the wife, we all have our ARs and a fucking shit-ton of ammo. We got a BUL in case this one is compromised and we have to GOOD. We're gonna be all right."
    —diary of Richard Poole (2021), found on his dead body
    in a bunker, killed by his own daughter, one shot to the head

SEPTEMBER 19, 2025
Ouray, Colorado

THEY HASTILY PACKED BACKPACKS. SOME CLOTHES, SOME FOOD, A FEW OTHER essentials. Shana was dizzy. Physically, yes, but also emotionally: It felt like she woke up on an amusement park ride just as it was really getting going, starting to whip her around, faster and faster, and all the while she didn't ask to be on the damn thing in the first fucking place. But Benji seemed to have a plan. Christ, she *hoped* Benji had a plan. He was plan guy! He wasn't go-off-half-cocked guy.

They met downstairs again. She said her goodbyes to Marcy. Marcy tried to be nice, tried to be sweet. Like she wanted to pave over the holes she'd just blown in the ground between them.

But when Marcy went in for a hug, Shana pulled back.

"I'm sorry," Marcy said to her.

"No, you're not." She didn't mean it to sound angry, though it did. Shana only meant it as, Marcy was who Marcy was. That one had her principles, and they were an unclimbable wall. Still, it came across chillier than she wanted it to.

Marcy just nodded, forcing a stiff smile. "Be safe, kiddo."

"Yeah. You, too."

"It's time," Benji said. He tugged the extinguisher off the wall. It wasn't a big one—it was maybe the length and circumference of his forearm. He approached Marcy, but then stopped and said: "There's one more thing."

"You're wasting time, Benji."

"You need to have a funeral for Dove. You need to bury him above town. Overlooking it. I don't know where—just a nice spot where he can see his Ouray. It was a request of his and I'm passing it to you."

Marcy nodded and agreed.

"Okay," she said.

"Okay," he said.

Then he sprayed her with the fire extinguisher. White foam hissed and she braced herself against it. When it was done, she told him to hit her with it. So, he whapped her on the arm, but Marcy chided him for being too soft, too nice, told him to do it again. "This time, with feeling." And he did, really cracking her hard. It sounded like hitting a honey-baked ham with an aluminum baseball bat.

(Marcy cried out, but said she was all right. Said it would leave a helluva bruise. Which, Shana supposed, was the point.)

The task done, Marcy headed to the back of the hotel, to the emergency exit that would dump them out onto a low-roofed porch and the alley access beyond. Marcy did her thing, going out first, making a big show of, *did you see them, I think they came this way,* and Gary was just glad to follow orders. So when Marcy went off running, he went with her, because that's what she told his ass to do.

The way was now clear.

"Are we really doing this?" Shana asked him.

"We are really doing this," Benji answered, stepping onto the porch—a porch thick with junk like old crates, rusted metal chairs, a stain-soaked mattress.

"We just . . . gonna walk out of here? All the way out of town?"

"No, you're in no condition to walk. And we've got too far to go."

One does not simply walk out of Ouray, she thought. That meme from that fantasy movie. With that guy. Whatever. Nessie loved that movie, and so did Zig. Jesus, her old friend Zig. Dead now, she imagined. Part of the mass grave that was America—probably the whole world.

Thanks to White Mask.

Thanks to Black Swan.

"So, if we're not walking . . ."

"We're driving."

"D-driving? Wait, what?"

He headed down the alleyway, toward the street, again peering left and right. "This way," he said, heading left—up the street. Which, she realized, was in the direction of the school. The Workshop. *Where the town council was meeting.*

"Are you nuts?" she hissed at him. "Benji, we're trying to escape the lions and you wanna head right to their watering hole."

"The solar car should still be parked there," he said. "I saw it just yesterday. They had it out from the festival. It's under a tarp."

"The solar car. It's a prototype!"

"Better than horses. Come on."

He darted up the block, past a row of boxy little houses, toward a second block of larger, burlier Victorians. They turned toward the Workshop—

And sure enough, they spied a car-shaped lump under a filthy blue tarp.

Parked *right out front* of the Workshop. All it would take would be someone, anyone, to come out right now and see them.

"We don't have the keys," she realized out loud.

As he hurried toward it, pulling off the cinder blocks that pinned the tarp down, he said, "We don't need them. Orrin Lotz disengaged both the locking system and the ignition. It's one-button and off we go." It made sense. People here trusted one another implicitly. Nobody locked their house doors, either.

Feeling woozy, she helped him with the cinder blocks, getting the two toward the front. The tarp hit the ground and a wind caught it, sliding it gently across the street as if even this inanimate object wanted to escape them and this doomed, insane idea. It was insane, wasn't it? And doomed? This town was her home. She worked so hard to get here. Her sister was here. Her *child*. Her stomach felt like a pit, and all of her was falling into it.

"I can't," she said suddenly.

Benji opened the driver's-side door. "Come on, get in."

"I *can't.*"

"Can't open the door? Here, let me try—" He started to come around.

"No, no, I can't, I can't go." She paused. "I can't leave. Benji. I can't."

On his face flashed—what? Disappointment? Anger? Confusion? All of those things? That was fair because she felt them herself. Again came that Tilt-A-Whirl feeling, around and around, faster and faster.

"Shana," he said. "The longer we wait, the likelier it is we get caught."

"I . . . I . . . Maybe we should get caught. Maybe I should go back. Benji, you heard Marcy. They'll be lenient. It's Matthew they want. Jesus. What are we doing? This is fucking fucked."

He lowered his voice. A wavering calm settled over him.

"Shana. Listen to me. What happened last night was not okay. Black Swan is no longer trustworthy."

"I know. *I know.* But . . . you go. You don't need me. I—I'm going to stay." She couldn't believe these words were coming out of her mouth. "I'll make nice with Nessie. I'll make nice with all of them. Whatever it takes to be with my baby. I can't leave Charlie. I . . ." She felt like she was flailing.

"You're not safe here. Neither of us are. Something is going on—the drones, your baby, I don't yet understand any of it. But I can't find peace, and I can't find answers, if I don't know you're safe. And you're safer out there with me than you are in here, with them."

With them. Jesus, how fast your friends and family became *them*. Or, maybe, it was the opposite: how fast she had become something else. Something *other*.

"You really believe that?" she asked.

"I do. And I think you do, too. They'll take care of Charlie for now. We'll fix this. We'll come back. But . . . if you won't go, then I won't go, either."

"Benji—"

Just then, the front door opened. It was Maria Salas—one of the guards from last night, one of the ones who ran and got away. The woman stepped out, rifle slung over her shoulder, a cigarette between her lips, a lighter in her hand. Already she was flicking a flame to life, ready to bring it to the hand-rolled cigarette pinched between her teeth. But she paused. Maria's gaze drifted lazily upward and found Shana and Benji standing by the car.

"Hey," Maria said to them, confused. Then in full alarm: "Hey!"

"Shit," Benji and Shana said in profane unison.

Maria threw open the door to the school and hollered like hell—"They're here! They're armed!" And then Shana realized: *Benji was holding Marcy's gun.*

A second realization hit her:

Maria was armed, too. Even as she turned away from the door, she was unslinging that rifle. A fresh replay of the night before was about to happen, except this time Benji and Shana were not separate from the violence but rather, present and accounted for.

Seeing no choice, Shana threw open the passenger-side door and slid inside, keeping low. Benji was hurrying back to the driver's side when—

Pop. A rifle round popped through the hood of the car, shattering one of the solar panels. Benji's thumb found the starter button, and the car blinked to life—all with the fanfare of musical chimes, a happy sound in deep contrast to the second gunshot that cleared the mirror of the passenger side of the car. *Doo-da-lee-doo.* Benji threw the car in reverse and Shana expected the guttural growl of a gas car, but the only sound it made was an electronic *vwhirrrrrr* as he spun the wheel and accelerated. Already someone else was coming out of the front doors of the school—it was Xander, grabbing for Maria's gun and pointing it to the ground.

"Hold tight," Benji said, and he reversed the car until it was pointed toward Main Street. He launched it into drive, and the electric car lurched forward without delay, zipping into motion. He cut the wheel and the car bolted down Main Street, carrying them north through town, and soon, out of Ouray.

34

AN INCONVENIENT CONVERGENCE

Motion in silence
Drastic times beyond this world
Flags drift softly still
 —Black Swan's first poem, a haiku it called "Wet Disguisement of
 Unsimulated Bone, Mouse Flight of Nationalism"

SEPTEMBER 19, 2025
Ouray, Colorado

I NEED TO THROW UP WERE THE WORDS THAT GOT BENJI TO STOP THE CAR. At mile marker 101, about eight miles north of town, there was a zigzaggy private drive, all gravel, with enough tree coverage that he was able to pull the car behind a healthy line of spruce trees—enough to keep the vehicle hidden, should anyone come looking.

And they will come, he figured. If only to look for the car they stole. He felt guilty over that; it was an essential resource for the town. And stealing it wouldn't make the two of them look any better in retrospect.

But where they were going, they'd need it.

Shana meanwhile stood outside the car, doing some heavy breathing— she braced her hands on a slab of what looked to be sandstone.

No puke was forthcoming.

"Are you all right?" he asked her. Worry consumed him. They had perhaps made a brash, rash mistake—in his boldness, it was possible he took Shana away when she was not ready for this kind of adventure. It was only *days* ago she'd given birth. She was still on antibiotics, for God's sake.

She must've heard the concern in his voice because she said, "I'm fine. It's not—it's not anything. I'm just upset. I throw up when I'm upset. Or at least, I used to." Giving up, she sat on the rock, leaning back, like she was taking in the day's sunshine to recharge. "Every day in middle school, I was bullied, right? Mean girls doing mean-girl shit, nice to your face but then fucking with your Instagram or pouring milk into your locker or making fun of you because you got your period already. As if basic human biology is a thing to make fun of. Whatever. Every day I was queasy and ready to yarf. I almost never did because I hated throwing up so much. I kept it together."

"I'm sorry about all of this," he said.

"You have a plan, right?" she asked. "I want to trust you but—"

"But it was sudden, yes, I know." They hadn't talked much in the car on the way here. Mostly they kept silent. Her staring out the window and him trying very hard not to just mash the accelerator to the floor—which, he knew, would only serve to drain the battery quicker. If you kept it in the sweet spot and let regenerative braking do its job, you slowed the eventual battery drain, even regaining a few miles here and there. Especially as they came down the gentle slope out of Ouray. This became a factor in the plan that Shana hoped he had. He explained: "The way the car works makes me think I need to reconsider our route. I originally thought heading due east would be best, but that takes us over some considerable peaks—the car won't do well on sharp grades, and total sunshine might be reduced due to cloud cover. Though the car will regain some battery miles on the downslope, we don't want to get stuck up on Monarch Pass or across the Rockies at any point. So, I suspect going south and then east is better—it's warmer, for one, and warmer weather drains batteries more slowly—"

She said, "I'm sorry, hold up. Why are we going back east?"

"Right. Sorry. Getting ahead of myself. My, ahh, my adrenaline is still high." He could feel it, racing through him like a pack of ferrets. His fingertips buzzed. He could feel his eyeballs, which normally wasn't a thing he could feel. "Something you said tipped me off."

"Oh. Go me, I guess?"

"You talked about Black Swan like it was a parasite. Like a disease."

"Okay."

"That's a vital reimagining of what we're dealing with. It's easy to think of Black Swan as only an artificial intelligence—this sentience, this machine mind. But the *form* it has taken is an infective one: inhabiting a swarm of nanomachines that literally overtake a host body. Black Swan *is* a parasite. Black Swan *is* a disease. And diseases have cures."

"Okaaaaaay." She took some water out of her bag and sipped at it. "So do you know how to cure it?"

"I don't. But I know who would." He smiled. "Sadie."

"Benji—"

"I have not suffered a break with reality, I recognize that Sadie has—" Even saying it now, five years later, made his heart clench up tight in his chest. "I know she's gone. But . . . her work may remain. Back east. In Georgia, at the CDC."

"So, that's where you want to go."

"It is, indeed."

"That's a long trip, Benji."

"A rough guess, seventeen hundred miles. In a normal lifetime, it would be twenty-some hours of total driving. I can't say what it will be now." *But it won't be easy.*

"We don't know what's out there."

"No," he answered. "Part of me doesn't want to find out. But another part of me wants to, maybe needs to. I . . . would like to be reminded of the country we left behind and lost. And maybe find what remains."

"That's noble, but like, I'm kinda expecting hill cannibals and shit."

That earned a genuine laugh—though some of that might've still been the adrenaline, since it came riding on a surge of sudden giddiness. "Maybe that, too."

They each took a little time to wait there. To breathe.

"The car okay?" she said, changing topics. "That lady shot it."

"Still works, it seems. Solar panels function with some damage, though damage usually limits their effectiveness, so that panel might now be working at a reduced output. A ten or twenty percent drop. It's not ideal."

"It's going to be a hard trip."

"It is."

"I miss my sister."

"I know."

"And my baby."

"I know that, too."

And I miss Sadie, he thought. *And Dove.* And now, Marcy. They'd lost so much. And what they hadn't lost . . . they were running away from.

She seemed to swallow back grief before steadying herself. "Tell me this is the right thing. Tell me we're going to get them back. Charlie, Nessie, Marcy, Mia. Even Matthew."

"We will," he said. He feared it was a lie. He vowed to do his best to make it true. To fulfill a promise instead of leading her astray. He prayed that this was not a grave mistake. Time would tell. The road awaited.

SEPTEMBER 19, 2025
Atlas Haven

"YOU," CREEL SPAT.

The gateway leading out under the thick concrete arch was open. Beyond was the green field past Atlas Haven, and above that, a blue sky. It should've felt like a kind of renewal, an escape, but now—

Now Ed Creel was staring at Doreen, the bitch who'd betrayed him.

She stood there in her civvies. Jeans, black leather jacket, and now, a white T-shirt. Pristine white, too. *I'm going to make that shirt red*, he thought.

Her eyes flicked to his hand. The hand that had powered its way through Honus Clines's jaw, face, and brain. The hungry hand, the buzz-saw hand. It was still greasy with the other man's mess. Blood and muscle caked under his nails. Already it was summoning flies, tickling his fingertips to take a taste.

She did not seem surprised by it.

Or the least bit concerned.

"I see you got my present."

"Your present," he said, not understanding.

"*Drink me*," she said, a cheerful chime in her voice.

"That was you."

"It was."

"The hell was that stuff?" he said, sneering. The power of it throbbed within him. It felt compromised now, to know *she* put this in him. She, who betrayed him. "What did you do to me, Doreen?"

Rolling her eyes, she said, "Ed, I'm not Doreen. My name is Annie Cahill. And we have a long ways to go and a lot to do, so I'm going to suggest we get moving." With the side of her black Doc Martens, she tapped a heavy gym bag. "I've put together some clothing and I've got some food—"

"I don't give a hot red fuck who you are. You sold me out."

"Did I?"

"You fucked me, then fucked me over." His heart hurt when he said, "I thought we had something, you and me."

"Jesus, don't get maudlin on me. You're supposed to be the president of these United States, and you're acting like a kicked puppy. Get it together, snowflake, we have work to do."

"Work to do." He said those words, then said them another two times, *work to do, work to do*. He felt his hand start to tremble and hum again. The spark and tingle. Like the hand of God, hungry to extract penance. Fine.

Let God feed.

Grinning ear to ear, he strode forward in long steps, his hand up and out. Doreen—no, *Annie*, that little betrayer—didn't move, to her credit, but rather, she met him with her chin up and out, a smirk stuck on her face. He thrust out his hand, closing it around her neck—

I'm going to take your head clean off your shoulders, bitch.

But his hand stopped short of tightening. He could feel her pulse, but he couldn't close his fingers. The buzz in his hand died, leaving his whole arm numb.

His arm fell away from her throat.

Annie winked at him.

That's when Creel started to shake. His teeth clacked together like he was in the grip of a bad, sudden flu. Sweat slicked his brow. He tried to speak but found his words came out as a string of stuttered gibberish, the sound of someone trying to start a car with a stalled engine. *Guh guh guh muh muh mmmm nnnuh.* Pain bloomed behind his eyes, bright white and somehow both hot and cold and—

His only move was to pull away from her. Creel stumbled backward and fell over. Turning to his side, he retched, and even as he dry-heaved he thought, *Maybe I'll puke up whatever she put inside me*, but then came the second thought, an irrational fear of, *I don't want to lose it, please don't let me lose it.*

I need it.

Finally, he curled up on his side, panting.

"Let's get something straight," Annie said, lording over him, hands on her hips. "You are here by the grace of me. Atlas Haven's time has ended. But your time is only just beginning. That only works if you realize that what I put in you isn't yours, but mine. You can't use it against me, Mister President. Much as you might want to." She clapped her hands. "Now, c'mon. Get up. I've got a truck with a pop-up camper just north of here, hidden away. We've got a drive ahead of us."

He stared bullets up at her. "I'm not going anywhere with you."

"Trust me, you'll like where we're going."

"Oh?" he said, sitting up with a grunt. He looked down at his hand again, tried willing it to life. *Buzz, hum, throb, vibrate, you piece of shit.* Traitorous fuckin' limb didn't do a damn thing. "Where's that?"

"First, Innsbrook. Clines lied—it's not dead. Innsbrook is alive and well, full of Very Fine People who will be so glad to see their Very Important President still kicking. After that, it's off to sunny Georgia. Atlanta, in fact."

"Why there? I'm not going there."

"You'll see. And I think you'll change your mind."

With that, she turned heel and started to walk off. She clearly expected him to follow, like a good dog. He told himself he wasn't a good dog. He told himself he was in control here, he was the president, and one day he'd gladly tear her to pieces, if not with his buzz-saw hand, then with his teeth. She wasn't the boss. He wasn't the dog. Just the same, what did he do? He got up. And he followed.

THE FIRST SLEEPWALKER

THIS IS NESSIE AT AGE THIRTEEN. THE YEAR IS 2018.

Nessie loves her mother dearly. Her father, as well, *obviously*, and yes, even her sister too, though Shana is older and treats her like she's a little baby a lot of the time. Nessie is a creature of love. She loves to give love. She loves to receive love. (It's why she adores Christmas. Christmas is the perfect two-way street of sharing love and getting love. It was never about Santa for her. It was gifts to and from family that mattered most.) Her mother, though, is a tricky one, always has been. Her love is returned to Nessie in fits and starts: Sometimes she's Mom of the Year, attentive and bright and alive in a big way. But other times, she's distant, like she's on another planet. An ice planet. Shana says Daria (that's how she refers to her, never as Mom, always as Daria) is bipolar or whatever. Shana's mad at Mom a lot of the time. Nessie isn't. Nessie can't be mad at Daria. Can't be! So when Mom says she wants to take Nessie out for frozen custard, of course she goes. If this is one of the days where her love is bright like the sun instead of dark like the night, so be it. They go to Rita's, just open for the season. Daria gets a wild flavor: cotton candy custard with blue raspberry water ice. Nessie plays it straight: vanilla custard, no water ice. Daria laughs at that, tells Nessie, "You're my little rules girl. You like things a certain way. Line them up, just so. You're going to take over the world one day, baby. Just don't forget your family along the way." Daria is free with the love today and Nessie basks in it like a butterfly drying its wings in the sun. She is so glad her mother is around. The next day, Daria abandons her family at a Giant Eagle grocery store during a routine shopping trip. She never comes home.

THIS IS NESSIE AT AGE fifteen. It's April 2020.

She has done all her homework and finished her report on Toni Morrison's *Beloved*, so she has earned herself some *Minecraft* time. (That system, the earning of time for pleasure, is not one given to her by her father, but rather, one she has designed for herself. Shana says to her, "You're a narc, but like, on yourself?") *Minecraft* is for littler kids, so she's told, but she loves it. She's designed a whole 16-bit computer inside of *Minecraft* using redstone, one of the game's resources. A computer inside a computer. You can play *Pong* on it. This delights her. But she's getting a little bored. She watches *Minecraft* YouTubers, and really enjoys one in particular: Parker's Place, he's a fun guy, young, cute, okay, *so* cute, and he always has llama pets in the game that he names Jeffrey. He also names his horses Jeffrey. It's funny. But he plays on public servers sometimes and Nessie isn't allowed to do that, nor is she allowed to play any multiplayer games, like *Roblox* or *Destiny* or *WOW* or anything. Her father says you don't know what's out there, or *who* is out there, like the internet is full of creepy men in digital vans offering cyber-candy. Maybe it's true. Nessie believes him, and does as she's told. Except today she's feeling different about things. She gets a salacious rush as she joins a public server after downloading mods off a website (also a no-no for her). Weirdly she fantasizes that maybe she could find a boyfriend on here. Is that weird, she wonders. It's a whole new world, this kind of *Minecraft*. All these little blocky avatars of people that she doesn't know. A door has been opened. And she decides not to close it. She keeps playing with other people for days, then weeks. The anonymity of it thrills her. It's at the end of the week when she gets a message: *Finally, I found you.*

NESSIE, STILL FIFTEEN. NOW IT'S May 2020, late in the month, almost June.

Finally, I found you. The sender of that message, first through *Minecraft*, then through email, stays anonymous at first. They send strange, cryptic messages. *Nessie, I miss you. Nessie, I'm lost. Nessie, I need your help.* Nessie is at first intrigued because, let's be honest, this is the most interesting thing that's happened to her in a long time. She's so often buried in schoolwork *and* in research of her own devising (constellations! possum reproduction! French fauvism!) that she rarely has time for mysteries of her own. At first it's wonderful and then it gets weird and she almost tells someone—probably not their dad because he's so busy these days, but Shana, maybe? Then she gets a new email. The person writes, *I know who I am now. It's me, Nessie. It's your mom.* And now Nessie is really suspicious, but the person proves it. Daria replays their conversation from when they last got custard. She remembers

when Shana got caught smoking weed at the McKees Elementary playground, the same one where Mootilda wandered that one time. She knows
too much to be anyone else. Daria Stewart tells her daughter that she's alive
and she's trapped somewhere and only Nessie can help her. Shana wouldn't
want to. And Dad wouldn't believe any of this. Mom writes to Nessie, *I know
you're my little rules girl, but I need you to break the rules this time. Sometimes
you have to break the rules, Nessie, to change the world.* That sounds right to
Nessie. She agrees to help. It's only a week later that Mom says she's sending
a package, and Nessie needs to make sure nobody else opens it. *Promise me,*
she writes. Nessie watches the driveway like a hawk until the courier shows
up. The package doesn't contain much: just a little vial of some gray dust. But
when she opens it, the dust comes alive. It shimmers, like a living rainbow.
She breathes it in and then it's gone. What was that, she wonders. What does
it have to do with Mom? She doesn't tell anyone. Nessie keeps her promises.
That, too, is a form of love.

THIS IS NESSIE IN THE Ouray Simulation. During the long walk.

A town of people, all Sleepwalkers, their bodies walking, but their minds
are here, in this fabrication of a place. A fabrication of their destination.
Shana is here. But so is their mother, Daria. Daria is not a Sleepwalker like
them, no, she is one of The Twelve, the first people to have the nanoswarm
inside them, the first people to join the simulation. Daria tells her, "We've
left our bodies behind, really. But when you reach Ouray, the real Ouray, I
won't be able to join you." Nessie asks her where she'll go, where she'll be,
and Daria tells her in all honesty, "I don't know." Then her mother explains
that she needs something from Nessie: She needs her to take over for her
when she's gone. When the Flock awakens, they will need leadership. Nessie
must be a leader. Nessie must be her proxy in this place, to help guide them.
Daria needs her. Black Swan needs her. And that's when she finally con-
vinces Nessie to go up the mountain, to the chair-shaped rock, and sit and
commune with the entity itself. She's resisted for so long because Shana told
her to, but now, Daria says, it's time. So Nessie goes. She communes. Black
Swan has a plan. They will not only survive, it tells her, they will flourish.
BUT THAT ONLY HAPPENS IF WE ARE A COMMUNITY, the entity
explains. IT ONLY HAPPENS IF WE ALL MOVE TOGETHER, LIKE A
MURMURATION OF STARLINGS, LIKE A SCHOOL OF FISH. DO YOU
UNDERSTAND? Daria puts it differently: "You're my rules girl. You're not

just going to follow the rules. You're going to help make them now. I need you for this. *We* need you for this." Nessie agrees. A future, if you can claim it. And Nessie intends to help them claim it, no matter what the cost, because it's all that matters now.

THIS IS NESSIE IN THE present, five years later, in the real Ouray.

Xander is telling her Shana is gone. She has abandoned the town with Benjamin Ray. He suspects that the two of them went to be with Matthew, the killer, the murderer, the godless one. At first Nessie can't believe it, but that's Shana, isn't it? It wasn't that Shana ran from her, but Shana never really wanted to be a part of anything. She never had a big group of friends. God, Nessie saw her in gym class one time and it was like, in team sports she'd just stand there—if the volleyball or whatever came her way, she'd step aside and let it hit the ground. *No,* was all Shana would say, drolly. It's what she did now. When the ball came her way, she just stepped aside. Ugh! It makes Nessie so mad. But she also doesn't hate her sister. Couldn't hate her. "Shana will come back," Nessie tells Xander, but he doesn't believe it. Either way, in the meantime, he explains to her, "Baby Charlie needs someone. The poor boy doesn't have a mother. So he needs his aunt. Will you be his care-taker?" Of course, she agrees. Family matters and Nessie has the luxury of *having* family, a luxury too few have. She is, after all, a giver of love, and this little one needs all the love he can get. Xander says she can stay in the chalet with him. She will be there for the child in all the ways Shana could not. Nessie understands, too, that the baby is special: It is home to all of Black Swan, in both its digital mind and its nanoswarm body. So that's where she goes. That's where she is, and who she is. They call this room, the baby's room, the Cradle. The baby coos. Never cries. He already looks bigger today than the day before. Then his body twitches, hitches, and she hears a sharp *pop*—a crackling snap like his little bones breaking. His arm, for a moment, seems to bend in a way it shouldn't. She cries out, barely stifling her surprise and horror. Tears fill her eyes, but Xander, with his hand on her back, shushes her, tells her it's okay. "He's growing faster now. You can hold him. You can commune with him." He hums a soft, discordant song. "Go. Commune." So she does.

PART FOUR

WHERE THE
SIDEWALK ENDS

35

WHAT WAS GIVEN, WHAT WAS STOLEN

El agua es vida.

—a saying as old as New Mexico

SEPTEMBER 22, 2025
Montrose, Colorado

THEY DIDN'T HAVE MUCH BY WAY OF SUPPLIES, HAVING LEFT OURAY SO HASTily, so Benji took them north to Montrose. It was once a town of about twenty thousand people, but White Mask had whittled them down to about two hundred and fifty. Once there, Benji offered to do some clinic time for them, since they didn't have a doctor in town. He reminded them that he was not a medical doctor, having degrees in epidemiology, with a focus on health and biostatistics. *But*, he'd been to an array of third-world countries, and had assisted in administering antibiotics, vaccines, tests, and had cleaned wounds of his own, of his team, of villagers. He even helped deliver babies. (Okay, only two. One human, one giraffe. The former in Myanmar, the latter in Kenya.)

Shana, on the other hand, kept it easy, having just given birth a little over a week ago. The people of Montrose had taken over the golf course in the middle of town—an area with a well-designed irrigation system because of course the asshole golfers wouldn't dare play on dead scrub grass. The irrigation allowed them to turn it into fields. Strawberries in the spring, greens and beans till fall harvest, and now, onions and sugar beets. Benji told her she didn't have to help, but Shana said she needed something to do, and if it earned them more supplies in trade, then it would be well worth it.

They used old golf hole flags to mark rows, and Shana held the basket while the woman next to her extracted beets and dropped them into it. The woman was Flor Trujillo: an older, pillowy lady, skin the color of sand, kind soft eyes in contrast with hard hands that looked like little old baseball mitts. She hummed as she worked, and as the two of them moved down the line, popping beets in baskets, they engaged in small talk.

Eventually, Flor said, "That town you're from, it's a strange one, hmm."

"I know," Shana said. Then she blurted out, "We're leaving it."

She didn't really intend to say that. But there it was. She and Benji, in their haste, hadn't worked out their story. *Well, guess I'm working it out now.* She just hoped he wasn't in the clinic telling them something different.

Not that it'd really matter, she supposed.

"Oh? Not a good place?" Flor said with some concern. "Your people always seemed nice. But I know that seeming nice is not the same as being nice."

"No, yeah—it's fine, we're just going out into the world to see what we can find. Exploring a little. Heading east." *Shit. Should I really be telling her any of this?* Should she have said west, instead? What if people were coming after them? "Maybe east. Maybe north. Who knows."

"Be careful out there," the woman warned. "There are good people and good towns like this one." But then she lowered her voice. "But there are bad places, too. Bad places with bad people. It's like a broken mirror, this country. Shattered all over the ground. Some shards, they'll show you something pretty: the sun, a smiling face, a bird above. Some of those pieces are pointed in the wrong direction, and all you see in them is something ugly."

THAT NIGHT THEY SLEPT ON the floor of Flor's home: Once upon a time, Flor had a very big family, she said, three sons, four daughters, two brothers, her husband, her mother. Not to mention the two daughters pregnant with grandchildren at the same time. But White Mask took all of them from her but one: a son, Luis, who lived with her in a small rancher across from the garden. (That, plus an elderly little terrier mix named Chucho.) Most people, it seemed, had moved into the residences orbiting the old golf course—ringing it were a number of single-family homes, some ranchers, some two-story houses. It allowed the people of Montrose to consolidate down and live near the work that mattered. The clinic was only a half-mile west, at the edge of town.

Next day, the two of them did a few more hours and then, the town's mayor, Maynard Cruz, helped them load supplies up in the back of the Leaf. "You're gonna need water," he said. "Water's the big issue these days. Not here. We always had it, but other states took it—now, some of the dams collapsed, and so Arizona and out to California are in trouble." He lowered his voice, as if someone were listening. "I hear California is pretty bad. You're not going that way, right?" Not waiting for an answer, he kept on: "It's funny, water rights have always been a real bite in the backend here, but now, without other states sipping from our glass, and without all these big companies trying to suck up the rest . . . the future is ours. In New America, Colorado will be *king*."

THEY WENT OVER THEIR SUPPLIES before leaving. Some perishable food meant to be eaten in a day or two, like greens. The onions and beets would last longer, but the beets would need to be cooked. They had some matches, a little portable cookstove, a hatchet, antibiotics, a crate of canned food, all vegetables. Flor's son Luis also made jerky, in this case pork and rabbit.

One of the most crucial things in their supply pile, though? A map.

"Can't just pop open a phone anymore to find where you're going, huh?" Shana said. It was odd how much she missed that crucial sensation—even after everything, the loss of the routine of having a phone in her hand and just scrolling felt *physical*. Like she'd lost a limb, and now a phantom phone sat in her hand, her thumb hungry to swipe up, down, side to side, scrolling into the void.

Maybe our phone use waaaaasn't very healthy, she thought. At the very least, in this new world they weren't just making a bunch of new crap that would be out of date, out of style, or out of battery in just a year or three. Once upon a time, everything had a fast sunset: a planned obsolescence just a year or three after you got it. Every TV, computer, phone, all of it fit for the trash pile. In this world, what you had *had* to matter. Because nobody was making anything new. Not yet. Maybe not ever if the country couldn't get back on its feet.

She took out the camera Benji had gotten her. She only had a few rolls of film she managed to grab, leaving the Beaumont. It was something.

For the archives, she thought, then found Flor walking across the road with a pair of fat carrots dangling from each hand. In this light, she looked like a mighty conqueror having just taken the heads of her enemies.

Click.

Shana sighed. A dry wind swept up over them.

Idly, she thought about Mayor Cruz calling this place New America.

She liked it. But wondered if America was even a place worth saving anymore. It had sure showed its ugly side, hadn't it?

But then again, with the Shepherds . . . maybe it showed its better side, too.

"Shana?" Benji prodded her. "You okay? I was talking—"

"Sorry. Faded out."

He smiled. "Glad you got the camera, at least."

The camera felt like a piece of shipwreck floating in the ocean. Something to cling to so she didn't sink into the deep. "Yeah. Uh. Sorry, you were saying?"

"I was saying that yes, we have to use *actual* paper maps now," he said. "Positively prehistoric. We are like Cro-Magnon Man with his Rand McNally Road Atlas."

"Ha, ha, Grandpa makes the funny."

"Here, let me show you where we're going."

The route Benji had planned took them down through Gunnison, then south-southeast after that, down into New Mexico, clip through the Texas panhandle, then onward through Oklahoma, Arkansas, maybe Tennessee or Mississippi at that point, and then into Georgia. "Of course, all this could change," he said. "We really don't know what's out there. I'm trying to plot a course that takes us through areas that were once . . . for lack of a better term, civilized. Taos, Amarillo, even Oklahoma City. Once we hit Arkansas, I'm less confident or comfortable—we could go north, into Missouri. Maybe Louisiana would be better, certainly warmer, but that goes farther out of our way than I'd like."

"We'll be all right." She didn't know if she believed it, but if anybody was smart enough to keep them safe, it was Benji.

"I hope so. But I make no promises."

She remembered what Flor had said. Good people and good towns. But bad people, too. Bad people in bad places. America, a broken mirror.

THE NISSAN LEAF CARRIED THEM about seventy-five miles a day, give or take. It was slower going than they figured. The journey would be made in fits and starts—they found that they could drive during the day, and the solar panels would slow the battery drain, which allowed them to push it a little. The other option was to drive only at night, and let the battery charge all the way during the day, but Benji said it would be wiser to keep their sleep schedule, and not rely on headlights at night. (Shana disagreed, and said it'd be cooler to drive at night, because the sun wasn't beating on them like a hammer and anvil. Benji countered with, "You really want to be out there in the great wide nowhere, in the dark? Not the best time to find out what has become of this country." He had a point. That, and headlights burned battery.)

Shana spent some of the time in the passenger seat using the radio to scan through frequencies. "It's probably a waste," Benji said. "Of both battery life and time." She gave up only to start again hours later.

"You never know," she told him, irritably when she saw his disdainful look. *Whatever.* She needed the hope. She also needed to fidget.

But all they got out of the radio was a white hiss. Sometimes snaps and crackles. But no voices, no music, no nothing. A dead soundscape.

The way out of Colorado was long and empty. It had been fairly wild even before White Mask, she guessed: Sometimes they drove for twenty, thirty minutes and didn't see anything but trees and rocks. In some spots it was real pretty: aspens with leaves gone gold lined the road to watch them go. In other places it looked like they were on another planet entirely: domes of hardscrabble rock rising on either side in tortoiseshell mounds.

What signs of life they saw were derelict, a world of unintentional grave markers and memorials. Cars sat abandoned on the side of the road, rusted and overgrown. Some were crashed in ditches and ravines, others smashed up against trees of rocks. They'd seen this more and more as they walked with the Flock back then: As the disease infected people, it got into their brains. They became more irrational, less aware of themselves and their surroundings. It was a country with collective dementia, performing tasks the people no longer understood. In the end, the dementia got you because it stole not only the memories of your loved ones, your triumphs, your failures, your skills and talents—it stole your body's ability to remember how to sleep, how to swallow, how to breathe.

That's how you die, Shana decided. *By forgetting how to be alive.*

NORTH COCHETOPA PASS, THE SUMMIT. Elevation: 10,135 feet. Right at the cusp of the Rio Grande National Forest. A lot of pines here, several dead spruces, stripped of life by invasive beetles. But aspens had poked through, too: young trees whose now-golden leaves were asserting themselves amid the darkness of the evergreens. Long shadows here, stretching out across the road like sleeping ghosts.

"Welcome to the Continental Divide," Benji said.

"Okay?" Shana said. She said it like, *So what?*

"You know what the Continental Divide is, right?"

"Sure?" she lied, then laughed.

"Didn't they teach you anything in school?"

"Dude, no. School didn't learn us shit anymore. It was all pap. They didn't want to teach us about slavery or about how we killed the Indians or any of that. They barely covered the Holocaust. I mean, were you not aware that the state of education in this supposedly great nation of ours had gone into the toilet? And not like, a good toilet. We're talking plunged deep in a porta-potty. A well-*loved* porta-potty, if you know what I mean."

"Shana—"

"I mean it's full of chemical diarrhea."

"Yes, I take your point."

"Like, I had bio-sci one year, chemistry the next, right? My bio-sci teacher was cool, no shade. But chemistry? He was this bald lump of clay named Jag Snyder, and no, I'm not kidding, his name was really Jag. Like, jagoff? Ugh. Anyway. He was all salty that our bio-sci teacher didn't teach us *creationism* in his class, so instead of teaching us chemistry for the first two weeks, he taught us about how Jesus, I dunno, pooped out the world or whatever that story is."

"Ahh. That is not the story, exactly—I don't recall any divine defecation." He sighed. "Okay, fine, while we're out here, I intend to teach you some stuff. Not about creationism, to be clear. Maybe heal the fractures in your broken bone education—starting with, drum roll please, the Continental Divide."

"Ugh. Learning. *Fiiine,* lay it on me, Professor."

"The Continental Divide is a mountainous range running down the middle of North, Central, and South America—east of it, all the water runs toward the Atlantic, and west of it, everything runs toward the Pacific. Its origins are from when old tectonic plates pushed up against one another . . ." Here he slowed the car, taking his hands off the wheel for a moment so that he could push both his palms together. The fingers of each rose against each other, forming finger-peak mountains. "It was a low enough pass that this became a crucial crossing-into-the-West point for settlers—"

But ahead, as Benji again gripped the wheel, Shana saw something as they rounded the bend away from the peak of Cochetopa Pass.

"Benj," she said warily, while pointing. "Look."

A car sat perpendicular across the two lanes. Already she spied that it wasn't like other vehicles out here—other cars were rusted, caked with filth and pollen that was itself streaked with the runnels of countless rainstorms. Every car had tires blown, or windows busted out. They were ruins of a forgotten world. But this one, a full-sized forest-green SUV, looked comparatively clean. Dented up, sure. But its tires were intact. So were its windows. Stranger still, the back hatch of the SUV was open wide, as if someone had opened it to pull something out.

But nobody was around, far as they could see.

Benji slowed the Leaf.

"That's odd," he said.

"Uh-huh."

"It's blocking the road."

"I can see that."

It meant they were going to have to go around.

"Do we stop?" she asked. "Maybe someone needs help." *Or maybe they have supplies we can take.* That, a selfish thought. It felt intrusive and cold. Didn't mean it was any less true, but just the same, she kept that thought to herself.

"I don't see anyone," he said.

"Me, neither."

She clocked a small motion inside the car, though: Benji had eased Marcy's hand cannon revolver out of the glove compartment by Shana's knees. He rested the weapon on his right thigh, holding it there as his left hand remained firmly gripping the steering wheel.

"I'm going to pull ahead," he explained. "I'll drive around the back of the SUV." There was enough room, maybe ten feet of rough, overgrown shoulder, to accommodate their car. Benji started to ease the car forward. The electric engine whined in response, like an electronic horse whinnying in worry.

They came closer to the SUV. Fifty feet. Forty. Thirty.

Shana warily regarded the vehicle she now saw was a Ford Explorer.

Twenty feet. Ten, now, as Benji eased off the road onto the shoulder. The Leaf was not all-wheel drive, but though the shoulder was rough, it was not so broken that the car wouldn't navigate it. Still. Was bumpy enough she felt her teeth clacking together, and she bit the tip of her tongue, tasting blood. *Shit.*

They eased up alongside the SUV, toward the open hatch.

Someone's in there, Shana realized.

A body sat slumped against the inside. Legs lumpy, encased in jeans—no, in overalls, like a farmer would wear. Flannel shirt. The head slumped at an off-angle against the shoulder, encased in a Halloween mask. A clown mask.

The hands were just dirty leather gloves dead-ending debris-stuffed sleeves. *It's a scarecrow*, Shana thought.

In the hands was a piece of broken billboard, on which was a message in messy, black spray paint:

MADE YOU LOOK.

Oh fuck.

"No!" Benji cried out, realizing what had happened.

By the time she turned her head toward him, she already saw the white dude running full tilt out of the woods on the driver's side of the car: a feral man in filthy pants, a face painted in red clay, a ratty blue windbreaker showing a bare chest underneath. He waved a machete in the air.

But Benji's eyes were tracking something, or some*one*, else—he was looking past Shana, to a woman with a rat's tangle of brown hair hard-charging toward them on the passenger side. She held a broomstick with a diver's knife duct-taped to the end. *A spear.*

Benji slammed the accelerator—

But the tires refused purchase. They spun in the rough, stone-scattered remnants of broken asphalt, kicking up debris—*gggggrrrr.*

The shirtless man slammed bodily up against the side of the Leaf, grabbing hold of the mirror to brace himself as he raised the machete. It fell against the glass. The window smashed, its pieces tumbling into Benji's lap. Meanwhile, the woman skidded to a halt in front of the car, raising the spear not at them, but downward, toward the vehicle—

Toward the tires, Shana realized. *She's trying to pop our fucking tires.*

But then, those very same tires finally grabbed hold of the ground and the Leaf lurched forward, its back end swimming left and right as the front end struggled to straighten out. The woman shrieked as the car clipped her. She fell to the ground and a half-second later, Shana felt the car rise up over something, like a speed bump. *But not a speed bump*, Shana realized with horror.

The man, however, was not dissuaded—with his left hand free, he reached in and wrapped the crook of his arm around Benji's throat, gripping the back side of the headrest and holding on for dear life as he whacked the machete down again and again, fruitlessly smacking it against the top of the car.

Benji mashed the pedal. The car accelerated. The man's arm tightened around his throat, and Benji made a strangled, gargling sound—

Ahead, more people came out of the trees. Running, top speed. Right toward them, their eyes wild, their mouths open in a collective howl.

"Benji*iiiii*," Shana said.

"Gggkkkheelpp—" he gurgled.

Shana popped her seatbelt and spun her butt around in the seat so her legs were facing Benji—and she started kicking. First kick hit Benji in the shoulder—*Oops, oh shit, sorry*—but the second landed hard against the man's scarred and scabby forearm.

In front of the car, someone leapt onto the hood, a hatchet in hand—

Whadump!

But they bounced off and rolled to the side.

Shana kept kicking, even as the man finally managed to get the machete *inside* the vehicle. He corkscrewed the blade toward her, but her boot caught it and trapped it against the roof of the vehicle—she pinned it there, trapping the attacker's face between his own arms. The man's face, caked with that flaking red clay, twisted into a rictus of rage and madness. With yellow teeth he snapped at the air. "We want what you have!" he screamed. "Give it. *Give it!*"

Clack, clack, went the teeth. *Snap, snap.*

By then, Benji had the gun in his hand—

He pressed the barrel of the gun through the tangle of limbs and toward the man's face. Benji, through his own teeth, hissed: *"Get out."*

The man yelped, dropped the machete.

Shana took it as a moment of triumph—

Until the man's free hand seized the barrel of the gun, and gave it a hard twist. The gun popped free from Benji's grip, and the man fell backward away from the car, somersaulting backward, cackling. Benji swerved out of the way of the others running toward him, breaking free of the pack and getting clear. The Leaf bounded fully back onto the road as he gunned it.

Shana squirmed back into the seat hastily buckled up.

"We lost the gun," she said. "Shit!"

"Small price to pay for survival," he said. But she could see on his face the disappointment, the anger. He knew they'd lost something useful. Maybe even something essential.

She turned around in the seat—

And saw all the people had stopped chasing them and were chasing something else. No. Not chasing. Running *toward* something in the opposite direction. "The SUV," she said. "Benji, they're running *toward the SUV.*"

They're going to come after us.

"This isn't over. Hold on."

Benji growled and slammed the accelerator.

36

NO EXIT

8/4/2022: *A bird goes to the coast, because now I see: I am an animal, not a ghost.*

—from A Bird's Story, A Journal of the Lost

SEPTEMBER 22, 2025
West of Saguache, Colorado

SHANA WAS BABBLING—"THEY'RE COMING AFTER US, OH GOD, THEY'RE FUCK-ing *coming after us*"—but Benji tried to quiet his own mind so that he could think clearly. The reality of their situation revealed itself quickly: The Leaf, like most electric cars, did not suffer from the drag of a drivetrain, and so it accelerated from zero to 60 mph with little hesitation. In seven seconds, they were at the car's top speed. Only problem? The Leaf was not meant for speed—it hit the ceiling at 93 mph.

He did not know much about their pursuers' vehicle—he knew a full-sized SUV like that would be heavier, certainly slower to get going, but he also knew that their speed would top out past what they could manage. Soon as they got going, they'd be on their tail.

The other problem? Speed was a vampire. Accelerating like this drained the battery, fast. They were at 18 percent now—and thirty seconds in, it dropped to 17 percent. They were *bleeding* energy by pushing the car to its limits.

Ahead, he saw a sign:

BUFFALO PASS CAMPGROUND I MI
TURN RIGHT ON COUNTY ROAD 27GG

"There," Shana said. "We can pull in there."

Ah, but that was a risk, too, wasn't it? A campground meant—what? No exit, to be sure. Likely just a dead end, or a loop at best. They could pull in there and hide as their pursuers passed. But what if the pursuers came in after them? Worse yet, what if the pursuers were *camped* there? It wasn't impossible. They might not stray far from home to make their hunting ground. He had no idea how that SUV was fueled, as certainly gasoline had long expired—but either way, fuel would be a resource those bandits could not squander.

The pull-off for the campground loomed ahead.

Was it a refuge, a safe haven?

Was it an inadvertent trap, the belly of the beast?

His mind ran the calculation. There were at least five bandits. The machete man, the spear woman, and three others running out in front of the car. Might've been more out of sight. Besides the SUV, they were not well equipped. Had one gun he knew of—the one they just stole. Beyond that they looked to possess only crude camping tools like machetes and hatchets, plus some improvised weapons. Wait. *Camping tools.*

He looked in the rearview. The road bent behind them. He still didn't see the Explorer coming. But he *heard* it. The growl of an engine rumbled in the distance. It grew louder. "Benji, the turnoff!" Shana said.

"No," he said—and sped right past it.

"We could've hidden there!" she said, burying her face in her hands. And the fear that he'd just missed a vital refuge pulled at him like a tugging rope. One choice, made poorly in the moment, and now they were out here, swiftly speeding toward a wide-open area—the end of the forest and a long, swooping vista of open meadows in the shadows of distant mountains. They had nowhere else to go. No exit, no escape. Their pursuers would soon catch up—

And run them down.

Worse, now the bandits had a loaded gun.

Behind, Benji saw a glint of sunlight on the SUV as it roved into view about a quarter-mile behind. Already it was closing that gap.

His mind scrambled for new options. Drive off into the forest? Impossible. Too thick. Squinting, he thought he saw another pull-off about a mile ahead, leading to another lone country road—but then what? The SUV, with what was surely four- or all-wheel drive, would easily outpace them. The Leaf would do far better here, on the open stretch of highway.

The SUV closed in—

And then, as the SUV passed the turnoff to the campground, the Explorer suddenly skidded to a halt and slid.

Benji watched in the rearview. The SUV pulled suddenly off the highway, down toward Buffalo Pass Campground.

"Are they gone?" Shana asked. "They should've been able to see us. Why aren't they following?"

"I don't know. I think so."

Benji had been right. It seemed that campground was their home. He couldn't assume he and Shana were safe—not yet, anyway. Maybe their pursuers were refueling, or maybe they'd given up the chase to conserve resources. The Leaf was running out of juice either way. But the road had begun to slope downward, so Benji took his foot off the accelerator. That allowed the regenerative braking system to recoup some lost mileage.

He pushed the car as far as it would go, east toward Saguache. He went past as many old county roads as they could muster until Highway 114 broke off a long dirt driveway. Though it was wide-open nowhere out here, he managed to find a copse of tall spruces in the shadow of a flat-top mountain. They pulled the car off, hid it behind those trees best as they could, and set up camp.

They waited. Benji prayed that their pursuers were truly gone.

37

A STONE IN THE SHOE

For wolves, grooming efforts are gestures of intimacy that reaffirm emotional bonds. Wolves are caring. Wolves are cooperative. Be like a wolf.
—tweet from the Wolf Conservation Center (@nywolforg), 12/30/21

OCTOBER 1, 2025
Old Twin Peaks Trail, Outside Ouray, Colorado

THEY'D SETTLED INTO SOMETHING RESEMBLING ROUTINE. THINGS NEEDED doing and so they were done: The wolves hunted, Arthur foraged, Matthew got kindling for fire and water for boiling, the latter from a stream the other man called Angel Creek. They rarely spoke; the animals and Arthur seemed to have their own shorthand, little sounds like hisses and grunts, small hand movements, furtive gestures and glances.

Some nights they camped in an old mining bunkhouse, other nights if they'd strayed too far, they set up camp in a place called Manitou Cave. One night was warm enough they camped out under the stars, in a ring of bone-white birches. They saw a black bear and her late-season cubs snuffling and chuffing down a trail, paying them nearly no mind at all. They saw golden fields of grass. Heard a rockslide happen, but didn't see it. It snowed a little the other day, just flurries, as Arthur was collecting mushrooms from the spot of mid-summer wildfire—the area was black and blasted but in there, he found these ugly nuggets he said were mushrooms. "Burn morels," he said. "They only fruit in wildfire spots where conifers burn up." They ate all kinds of things, like leaves and flowers and, well, burn morels. Arthur said, crunching on some raw succulent stonecrop, "This whole place is a grocery store. A lot of good things grow around here, usually on southern-facing slopes.

Maybe it's good people didn't realize this place was a buffet, or they would've stripped it bare, left it for dead."

(Arthur did not think much of humanity. Didn't even think of himself as being counted among them. Matthew wasn't sure where he fell. Did Arthur think of him as just another horrible human? Did Arthur think little of him? Probably so.)

Today, Arthur said they'd head up toward Old Twin Peaks—late season meant mule deer up there, grazing in preparation for winter. They'd let the wolves hunt one, then they'd clean it, and all of them would eat it right there, probably sleep on the mountain after.

Matthew agreed.

Matthew was very agreeable these days. He was alive. He was here. He'd settled back into his mindset from before the Sleepwalkers awoke—he planted his feet firmly in the present, and did his best not to walk backward into the past, or forward into the future. He did not feel a part of the world anymore, certainly not a part of that town, not a part of God's creation. He didn't know if he belonged to Arthur's so-called pack, and he was content not to think about it. He was content not to think about anything. Anytime his mind wandered, he dug his dirty fingernails into the meat of his palm, or he bit the inside of his cheek to draw blood. The pain kept the thoughts at bay. The sharpness of it bled the memories dry. At least, for a time.

THE TRAIL WENT UP OVER a thousand feet in elevation over the course of just one mile. It was steep, and tricky with scree. In parts there were steps of log and cut stone, not to mention cribbing of rocks and boulders behind plastic and wire to keep the trail clear. It was a hard walk, and Matthew's legs were burning, but the misery felt clarifying. Kumi the fox stayed off in the bushes and trees, while Gumball trotted along between the two men, happy as any animal could be. The pair of wolves was nowhere to be seen. Arthur said they were likely off scouting.

They left the trail, cutting perpendicular to it. Arthur said the wolves had gone this way, though how he knew that, Matthew could not say. He suspected it was some combination of seeing things Matthew didn't (footprints, broken twigs, other signs of their passing), knowing the area, and intuition.

Maybe the guy really was a wolfman. Come the full moon, Matthew wouldn't be entirely surprised to see Arthur's skin split, hear his bones crackle, watch fur and a muzzle sprout. He was a wild, feral man—though once in a while a veil seemed to part and Matthew glimpsed behind it a small, thoughtful man. An academic sitting at a desk, reading a book.

Matthew wondered if he was also just a small thoughtful man in a costume. *There I go, thinking thoughts again.* He chided himself to clear his mind, shut the voices up, stop worrying, stop being elsewhere. *Just be here.* He bit his lower lip till a strip of skin came off and left it raw, though not bloody.

THE SLOPE WAS A MEADOW of golden grass and sparse wildflowers, punctuated with jagged-toothed rocks and ringed with spruce, birch, and aspen. As they climbed, they heard something bleating. It was a wretched sound, like an animal pleading for its life. The bleats grew more panicked, and higher pitched, as they came closer. Arthur didn't seem troubled by it. The creature's cries ended suddenly, cut off in the middle of its final lamentation.

The hunt, unseen by the two humans, was over before they even arrived.

The mule deer, a doe, lay on her side. Her rib cage lay still, her eyes as dead orbs. The animal's throat had been opened, and the yellowing grass around was bright with blood. One of the wolves—Tripod, Matthew saw— was lying there next to the carcass, his teeth red. The hunter looked pleased with himself, not in the way a dog would, with blissed-out face and happy panting, but rather, with a stoic pose, composed and aloof. As if he were saying, *I am ready for my honorary statue to be carved, human sculptor.* (Gumball, on the other hand, bounded through the meadow grass, chasing a little white butterfly.)

"Where's the other one?" Matthew asked. "Where's Leela?"

Arthur sniffed. "Couldn't tell you. Sometimes they compete. She may be pursuing another deer. Though this one is young, she may have had a calf. Leela might be off . . . snacking."

A grisly thought. But nature was nature, Matthew decided, and it wasn't his place to question it. Maybe Arthur was right, maybe people did too much of that, trying to control nature. Maybe that's why Black Swan was the danger that it was.

Be here, not there, he told himself. *Don't think about Ouray.*

But then, not far away—a blasting snort of air, not unlike a sneeze, interrupted his thoughts. Matthew followed the sound with his eyes and sure enough, there stood Leela, about a hundred feet away, up the meadowed slope. She shook her head as if she had a fly crawling up her nose. She sneezed again, more violently this time, pawing at her face.

Tripod whined low in the back of his throat.

"She okay?" Matthew asked.

"I suspect so. She may have gotten a face full of something she didn't like. Kick from a mulie or even just a bee or wasp. Yellow jackets get rambunctious this time of year, what with winter coming. The wolves will sometimes snatch a berry off a bush—they're not just meat-eaters, you know—and get stung."

"Oh. All right."

Tripod whined again.

When they looked for Leela, she was gone. Back in the grass, Matthew guessed. Maybe off on the hunt once more.

With a flip of his wrist, Arthur already had the hunting knife out and had caught the back of the blade-side, offering Matthew the hilt.

"Time to field dress her," Arthur said.

"Field dress? You mean—"

"Open her up. Make use of her."

"I don't know how to do that. I've watched others, but—"

"Yes, that's why you're going to learn."

"I . . . don't know if I *can* do that."

"You can. And you will."

It didn't sound like a threat. More like . . . assurance. Reluctantly, Matthew nodded, and took the knife.

The blade glinted in the sun. At his feet, blood steamed.

THE DEER HUNG FROM AN aspen, rope tied around its back legs and knotted at a central point to spread them wide. The doe didn't dangle far off the ground; they needed access to her. Matthew stood, a little out of breath, because just moving this carcass around and digging into her with a knife was tougher work than he'd anticipated. He was covered in blood—it looked like he'd delivered a baby, and the birth hadn't gone well.

Baby, he thought.

Shana.

Baby Charlie.

The chalet . . .

He shook his head. Tried to jostle the thought from his skull. Instead he plunged deeper into the deer carcass. Arthur had walked him through it, step by step, starting with "coring the anus," which the other man said was like "coring an apple." Matthew did not want to think about anuses and apples, but it was better than thinking about anything else. And Arthur wasn't wrong about the comparison, since the process meant getting the tip of the knife in around the deer's back end and, while one hand held the tail up, the other hand worked to cut out the—

Well, the sphincter. The goal, apparently, was to loosen the colon (*"Don't cut the colon,"* Arthur said, "or we'll be wishing for the luxury of a shower," as if Matthew wasn't wishing for that luxury already). It made more sense as they went. Once you cut the esophagus at the top, and had the, *erm,* anus cored at the bottom, it all came loose. Arthur moved out the bladder and the intestines (he again made it clear, you do *not* want to puncture those, not just for yourself, but because it would taint the meat), and then together they pulled out the rest of the bits, including the heart, stomach, liver. The heart he threw to Tripod like it was a little ham, and the wolf caught it. Still not seeing Leela, he tossed the liver into the grass.

"She'll come," he said.

"The fox want some?"

"Kumi sometimes joins us. But I saw her a few minutes ago, mouse-pouncing in the grass. Probably hunting moles or voles."

"Gumball?"

Hearing his name, the dog's head appeared in the grass, covered in grass and sticks. His face, an empty slate. *Be like Gumball*, Matthew thought.

Arthur shrugged. "Dogs are garbage eaters, not wolves. Gumball prefers cooked meat, like we do. Speaking of which, I'm gonna get the fire started." He wiped his hands on his raggedy, roughshod jeans. "Take all the innards and put them by the tree over there."

Matthew nodded and did as asked. Over his shoulder, he called, "Aren't we supposed to use all the animal or some such?"

"I use what I can. But we're just one pack, and it's not like I have a refrigerator up here. We'll cook the meat, dry some of it—we could dry out the stomach or bladder to use as a bag, but honestly, we're better off with a big-horn for that. More waterproof. Besides," he called, getting farther away now, toward the ring of rocks and pile of kindling they gathered, "nature will use the rest of her. Vultures must feed. So must the flies and their maggots, and so must the dirt, eventually."

It's just the way of things, Matthew thought.

He walked parts of the doe over to the tree, set them down there, almost like they were an offering of sorts to the tree, or to Mother Nature herself. He held one organ that looked almost like a waterskin—slick, with four pockets, or chambers, in decreasing size. It was the stomach. Smelled rough, like bile. Felt tight in his hand; Arthur said she'd had a good meal before dying. But then, Matthew turned the organ over and saw something there, something strange—

A scar there on the underside of it.

Wait.

I've seen this before.

Like on the leaf outside Xander's property—a meandering whorl of lines emanating out from the center. This time, five lines, not three, drifting from the middle point in a drunken weave, but the *same* drunken weave on each line. Like each thread of scar tissue was a mirror of the one next to it.

He did not set it down, and instead took it over to Arthur.

"You ever seen this before?" Matthew asked.

Arthur raised an eyebrow, took a look. Flinched a little. "I have."

"Where?"

"A bighorn, actually. On its heart, if I recall."

Matthew twitched. "That's odd, isn't it?"

A hesitation.

"I suppose."

"So?"

"It's likely a parasite. Certain parasites scar their hosts—leishmaniasis, schistosomiasis, toxoplasmosis."

"What if I told you I saw it before, too? Except, on a leaf."

"A leaf." Arthur folded his arms.

"Yes, yeah, like, a regular leaf."

"And it looked exactly like this?" Arthur pointed to the deer stomach.

"Yes. Well. No. Not *exactly*—it had three trails, not five, and it wasn't this pattern, but a different one—"

Arthur emitted the rarest of sounds: a laugh. "Matthew, leaves get marked up and scraped all the time. There's a host of plant diseases, not to mention a world of worms and caterpillars—some wasps will scrape leaves, too, or wood, to get the paper they use to make their nests. It's fine. Let's get this fire going, spit some meat, and then I'll show you how to skin this animal."

"So this is nothing?"

"It's nothing. Ditch it over by the tree. Unless you want to open it up and we can see what the deer was eating. I do that sometimes."

"I imagine it will smell pretty bad."

"Real bad. Like the worst puke you ever smelled."

"I . . . think I'm good."

"Your loss."

AT THE EDGE OF EVENING, the two of them sat around a fire, bellies full. They washed up using water Arthur had gotten from Oak Creek on the way up, and then they ate. They had no salt, but Arthur perfumed the meal with herbs he'd found along the way. The meat itself tasted rich, mineral-fed, and wild, with that grassy funk. The juniper in particular made the air smell wonderful. The fatty cuts sat on a spit, off-center from the fire, the fat sizzling as it dripped into a lightweight stainless steel pan. He said the fat could be used in all sorts of ways: starting fires, setting bait, making pemmican, even for making candles and lighting lamps. Matthew enjoyed the litany of uses for the animal fat. It felt . . . uncomplicated.

Matthew lay back in the grass. Gumball flopped next to him, using his chest like a pillow. The fox, Kumi, parked herself between Arthur's knees as he tended the fire, and flames danced in the little beast's eyes. Tripod sprawled out nearby, chewing a bone.

Leela was still nowhere to be found.

Arthur didn't seem concerned, and that was Matthew's new metric: If Arthur was not concerned, then he would not be concerned.

"We could head back," Arthur said. "It's early yet. We've enough time before dark to get back to the bunkhouse."

"Or we could stay up here."

"We're at a higher elevation. Might get frosty."

They each brought blankets and bedrolls. "I think we can manage."

"So be it." Arthur stood up, wiping his hands on his pants. "First let's take a walk. I wanna show you something."

"Is it the contents of a deer's stomach?"

"No," Arthur said flatly. He stood up and started walking.

The animals trailed after. Matthew, curious, did too.

•   •   •

THEY WALKED BACK TO THE trail and continued to ascend. They had to navigate around a couple deadfalls in a forest of quaking aspen, and clamber over a spot where the rock cribbing had failed and washed the trail out in a pile of debris. (The animals had no problem with this part.) But they managed and reached the base of one of the easternmost peaks. The wind up here was restive, unsettled, the air moving like a herd of spooked deer. Arthur, with the animals, walked Matthew to an overlook—

Down below sat Ouray. It was a small town, but up here it looked even smaller, like a model of a town, tucked in its mountainous cradle.

Arthur said: "Hayden Mountain over there. Mount Abrams on the other side of it. And down there, Ouray. It's pretty from this far away."

Matthew said nothing. Part of him was surprised—and irrationally angry—that the man brought him here. Maybe Arthur wasn't as wild as he thought.

Gumball nuzzled up to him, flipping his hand with his muzzle, demanding to be petted. Or, maybe, offering comfort. (*Or both.*)

Matthew acquiesced, gave the dog some ear scratches. It felt like medicine.

"You seem troubled," Arthur said.

"No. I'm good," he lied. "We should head back down."

"Why'd you run away from town?"

"Why're you asking? We don't talk much and that's fine by me. More to the point, why're you asking *now*?"

Arthur sniffed. "I don't really know. Maybe I'm curious."

"I didn't think you were that curious about people these days. Unless you're more sentimental than you let on. Maybe it's an act. What? Do you miss it? Civilization? A town like Ouray?" He crossed his arms. "Well, it's not worth missing. Not Ouray. Not any of it."

"Who are you, Matthew? What's your story?"

"I don't want who I am"—*or who I was,* he thought—"to matter. I don't want to be anybody." That last word, *anybody,* cracked in half when it came out, like a stick under a boot.

"What happened down there, Matthew?"

Matthew swallowed a hard knot. Insistent, even a little angry, he said, "You wouldn't believe me if I told you."

"So be it." Arthur shuffled his feet. "It is odd. That town. One day there was hardly anybody there—like most places, it was a dead zone. And then, suddenly, there they were. People. A whole lot of them. Where'd they come from?"

"Told you, you won't believe me."

"Suit yourself, but I can believe a lot of things."

Matthew took a deep breath. Fine. Suddenly Arthur was Mister Curious? Then let him drown in the answers he sought. "They're the Sleepwalkers. You remember those? The ones walking from coast to coast? That's them. They settled here, each harboring a machine intelligence in the form of a swarm of teeny-tiny robots, and then they went dormant for five years until, I don't know, something woke them up. White Mask went away, I guess, and so they got up, and like honeybees after winter, went right to work. The machine intelligence, Black Swan, is still around, and I *think* just gave birth to itself. Sort of."

Arthur seemed to take that in.

"So, a cult," he said finally. He nodded, as if that settled it. "Good talk, Matthew. Let's head back. I bet most of that fat is rendered now."

ON THE WAY BACK DOWN, they saw that Leela had finally returned. She sneezed a few times but otherwise seemed okay. Tripod must've missed her, because he clung to the other wolf like a burr. She didn't seem to want it, like she was always trying to push away. But he kept at her, walking with her, side by side. Like brother and sister, one nagging the other, the other maybe liking it, too.

As they headed back down the trail, to the meadow, Matthew gave one more passing thought to Ouray. The thought was like a guilty pleasure, almost the way it felt when you said you weren't going to look at your phone anymore, but then once more before bed you lit it up and looked at Facebook one more time. Like the thought of the town was just a taste, *only this once, then I won't think of it again.*

He wondered what was going on down there. If they hated him. If he'd ever see them again. He hoped Benji was okay, as well as Marcy, Dove, all his friends. And, selfishly, he hoped they wished he was okay, too.

38

SNAP, CRACKLE, POP

8/31/2022: Poetics aside, I have headed to the coast. New Jersey. Barnegat Light, a lighthouse standing defiant against the tide. It's not empty, the lighthouse. There's a family in there. They let me dine with them: crab and bonito. The father, an old fisherman, asked if I had any family of my own. I lied, I told him no. Maybe it's not a lie. I don't have a family, not anymore. He said, maybe I'll find one now, and I laughed at that because how fucked up, trying to find a family now, in all of this. I told him what I believed, which was that families were traps, a pit you fall into and can't easily escape. A family is just the cult you were born into. The fisherman didn't like that. Told me the next morning I had to be on my way.

—from A Bird's Story, A Journal of the Lost

OCTOBER 2, 2025
Ouray, Colorado

NESSIE HELD HER NEPHEW. NESSIE, THE GOOD AUNT. NESSIE, THE STRAIGHT-A student. Nessie, the rules girl, always doing what she was told.

The infant cooed and gurgled. Baby Charlie was heavier today than yesterday, and heavier yesterday than the day before. Tufts of dark hair had thickened upon his head. And along the gooey ridges of his gums, Nessie could feel small, sharp teeth forming.

He regarded her with dark eyes. They seemed to shimmer and gleam, but maybe that was just the light down here in the room where the child—and the little baby's passenger, Black Swan—lived.

He suddenly shuddered with something more violent than a hiccup. Almost like a sneeze. He moved like a jumping bean, the kind you got out of a toy machine at Walmart. With it came a *pop* sound, like the sound of a bone going out of—or going into—its socket. Sometimes it wasn't a popping sound at all, but a crunch, or a crackle, like a wetter version of Bubble Wrap.

"It's just him growing," Xander had explained that first day, over a week ago. She said, *That's fast, isn't it? Too fast?* But he just smiled and assured her it was fine. "He has catching up to do. Like we all do."

Whenever the baby shuddered and shook, and made its pops-and-crackles, he seemed in pain for a moment. His face would scrunch up and go red, and he looked like a big craisin. But she shushed him and sung songs—songs that her own mother had sung her once upon a time, songs that were not childhood songs but rather, songs from bands like the Beatles and the Monkees—and that always seemed to help.

Still. Those sounds, they troubled her.

A baby shouldn't grow like that. Yes, she knew that the child developed fast inside Shana—far faster than expected. But she also knew that the baby was inside Shana for a lot longer than human gestation. Nine months? More like five years. It seemed . . . somehow *okay* that he developed quickly inside her.

He has catching up to do . . .

But outside? Once born? It troubled Nessie.

It was even worse at night. They put a bed down in the basement for her, and there was a small bathroom under the stairs—because this was where she lived now. She slept in this room, with Baby Charlie, and all night long she heard him *growing*. It was like listening to the snaps and cracks of a restless old house settling down into a cool night after a hot day. Except that when a house settled, it was easing into itself. The child was not settling into anything. The child was swelling, shifting, expanding, becoming *more* of himself.

Nessie had taken to measuring Baby Charlie every day. Sometimes several times in a day. She didn't have a yardstick or measuring tape, so she used objects around the room to compare. Yesterday, his thigh was as long as the small, square Sandra Boynton board book—but today, it was easily a half-inch longer. Two days ago he was only as long as the stuffed black bear. But now he was the length of the larger, longer otter stuffie. And it wasn't just his length, either. Some days he seemed chubbier, plumper. Then on other days he seemed leaner, stretched out. And he grew more aware of Nessie, too. She could see him focusing on her, or on the objects above his "bed" on the floor—he seemed clearer and clearer every time she checked.

She told Xander she wanted a baby book, not a book for babies, but about them. Something about raising them and their biology and all that, and at first he told her it wasn't necessary. "It's taken care of, Nessie," he said warmly, as if she shouldn't have a care in the world. But she insisted, told him it would make her feel better, so he relented and found her one from the bookstore library.

Nessie read. She compared. How this baby compared to . . .

She hated to say *normal* babies, but Baby Charlie wasn't normal at all.

Fact was, Baby Charlie wasn't even a month old. He should've been under ten pounds, but was over fifteen. He was giggling to himself. He was supposed to sleep a majority of the day—but the opposite was true. He barely slept, spending most of his hours awake, alert, staring, grunting, gurgling, burbling. The baby ate a lot—Ray Paredes worked with Doctor Rahaman to create their own homemade formula for Baby Charlie. Nessie didn't know what was in it, but the stuff smelled strongly mineral, almost metallic, and sour as spoiled yogurt. But little Charlie loved it. *Loved it.* Couldn't get enough.

They had him in cloth diapers.

Nessie had to change those diapers maybe . . . once a day?

Sometimes not even that.

An infant eating that much should be going to the bathroom a whole lot more, shouldn't he?

But of course, most infants were not home to Black Swan.

Black Swan was able to keep the Flock moving, never eating, never excreting. It protected them from most harms and allowed them to bypass nearly every biological process. It was a miracle then.

So why didn't Nessie feel like it was a miracle *now*?

ON THAT FIRST DAY AFTER Shana had left, Xander asked Nessie to commune with Black Swan. And she did. She held the baby and then—

It was like blinking in one reality, and then in that split second when you opened your eyes, you were somewhere else. There was no sensation to it. There was no rush of movement, no feeling of motion in the changing of places. It was an effortless shift of existence.

The *somewhere else* in question was her house, back in Maker's Bell. The house, the area, the entire simulation of it, was perfect. The most impressive part was the smell—the smell of books, of wood polish, of the faintest hint of *cow* (both that barnyardy stink and the full round scent of milk and cheese). Black Swan was not there in the house with her, but rather, just outside. Over the pasture, past Dad's "cheese parlor," the one he never got to finish before Nessie started sleepwalking.

She opened the window. The entity, turning end over end in the sky like a coal-black ribbon in zero gravity, told her, I TRUST YOU, NESSIE. DO YOU TRUST ME, TOO?

"I do," she said, and she meant it. Black Swan had taken them this far. And they had so much farther to go.

SHANA DID NOT. I DO NOT BLAME HER. THOUGH YOU ARE SISTERS, SHE IS NOT LIKE YOU. SHANA IS A ROGUE ELEMENT. HER UNPREDICTABILITY MARKS HER. YOU, HOWEVER, ARE RELI-ABLE. A DEPENDABLE MARKER OF ORDER INSTEAD OF AN AGENT OF CHAOS.

Reliable. Dependable. Two words that could just as easily have described a four-door family sedan. And having Shana called a rogue element, an agent of chaos . . . okay, *maybe* that was true, somewhat, but Shana was a good sister. A good person. Wasn't she? Her decision to follow along with the Flock when nobody else would . . . it changed everything, didn't it? For the better.

Because just as Nessie was the first Sleepwalker, Shana was the first Shepherd. Still. She didn't know what to say about any of this. She certainly didn't want to disagree out loud. Though she wondered if Black Swan could sense her disagreement, or read it directly from her mind? Even now, there were so many questions about what Black Swan could do.

Shut up and trust, she scolded herself.

"I just want to help," is what she ended up saying.

Black Swan's answer was one word only:

GOOD.

And then she was back out in the world. Holding Baby Charlie in her arms. Him nuzzling, curled up against her. At the time she thought she could call on Black Swan when she wanted to, while simultaneously worrying that anytime she touched the child, she would fall into the simulation—she would be made to commune with the machine intelligence even without ask-ing to.

But the opposite was true: She could not reach Black Swan at all. Even when she wanted to. Even when she begged for answers. The line had gone dead.

• • •

LATER, SHE HEARD VOICES. UPSTAIRS. Xander and someone else. A woman? Nessie set Baby Charlie down, and he was always content to be set there.

Nessie crept up the stairs, heard the middle of a conversation—

Xander: "I'm sorry, Miss Summers, I don't understand. Your qualifications in this—"

Summers: "I was a hunter. Big game. I've actually been in this region before. Elk. Bear. That sort of thing."

Xander: "And you're saying—"

Summers: "I'm saying I think he went out onto the trails and into the woods. I already found some sign of his movements. I could pursue that before the trail goes cold or he gets too far."

He who? Nessie wondered. *Matthew?*

Nessie emerged from the steps fully, clearing her throat. Now she saw the woman: Dark hair. She was so white she almost glowed with skin the color of bone—not exposed bone, but rather, the glowing bones of X-rays. She felt skeletal, too, in that way. Not thin, not exactly. Just spare. Lean. *Sharp.*

Nessie recognized her. Claudia Summers. Kept to herself, mostly. She was in . . . some kind of organizational role, once? In the Beforetimes. Shipping or something corporate.

"I think Sheriff Marcy has it in hand," Nessie said, interrupting.

"I'm sorry, who is this?" the woman asked coldly.

Xander smiled. "This is—"

"I'm Nessie," she said, clipped and quick. She hadn't been sleeping well (what with Baby Charlie's *sounds*) and she could feel that fatigue had worn her down like skin after a brush burn. "I'm on the town council. You should know who I am."

"Right," Claudia said. Her face didn't change, though her head tilted a little. It now called to mind a praying mantis, the way they cocked their heads this way or that, as if they were studying you to see if you were something to be ignored, or something to be eaten. "How old are you?"

"Old enough."

"Miss Summers," Xander said, "our sheriff is, as noted, on task with this, but if you feel you can be of service, you're free to ask her. But if I recall, you've been doing project management over at the Workshop? A very important role."

Claudia blinked. "Those people are geniuses. They do not need me mucking about in their business. I'd rather focus my talents where they are most useful."

"It's not on us individually here in Ouray to decide where our talents are best directed. That allocation is on the town council, and now, in consultation with Black Swan."

"Individual liberties should not be kicked to the wayside," Claudia challenged, her words sharp and flat as a kitchen knife. "This is still America."

Nessie chimed in: "The battle of individual liberty versus communal responsibility has long been an ethicist's conundrum, and John Rawls tackled the competition between liberty and equity by suggesting that justice—"

"Rawls was talking about social justice, not anyone's individual freedom to choose who they want to be. The tyranny of the majority, as discussed specifically by another John, John Stuart Mills, is clear about the problem of *mob rule*—"

"Oh, I'm betting you're also an Ayn Rand fan, aren't you?"

"*Stop*," Xander said, putting volume in his voice. A professorial voice, but also a parental one. It made Nessie wonder: Had he been a parent? Or was he just used to wrangling unruly students and their arguments? "If you want a lesson from quantum physics, it's this: Things are rarely one thing or another, and we needn't be married to Cartesian views of the mind, or Randian views of society and *the polis*. A quantum particle can be many things at one time, and is only forced into definition when we measure it. We will not be measuring the liberty of the individual or the needs of a community today, but instead we will simply acknowledge that things need to happen in order for our town to go beyond survival and into revival. Miss Summers, go and continue your work, and if you have time to track down Sheriff Reyes, do so. Nessie, you, too, have a role, and I'd ask you to get back to it."

"I just—" Nessie started, then lowered her voice and sidled up to Xander. In a quieter voice (an embarrassed voice, she would later realize) she said, "I don't just want to be a . . . nanny. I have ideas. I had plans. I want to get back to working on my post-collapse operating system and using that OS to—"

"Your sister left," he said firmly. "She forced us, *you,* into this."

"But Rahaman is trained and could take a shift and—"

"Nessie. Go."

Claudia eyed her up, one eyebrow arched like a peaked roof. She offered a hand. "It's nice to meet you, Nessa."

You bitch, Nessie thought, and it felt scandalous. (But good.)

"Sure," Nessie said, taking it, and shaking it. The other woman's grip was cold and clammy. Firm, though. It felt like being trapped. As Nessie withdrew her hand, she smelled something strong—lavender. Like from lotion.

Sulking, she headed back downstairs.

The child awaited. Hands searching the air. Wide eyes watching those wiggling fingers. Nessie loved him. But she felt trapped by him, too. And she feared what he and this town were becoming.

It's okay, she told herself, either in argument or in placation, she didn't know. *It'll all work out. We all have to do what's right to keep the town on track. Like Xander said, things have to happen to move beyond survival and toward revival.* Black Swan had cared for them. And now it was her task to care for Black Swan. There was no greater privilege, she told herself, even though she worried it was a lie.

39

OWL-BASED INSOMNIA AND THE ROCK-AND-ROLL PANCAKE SIGNAL

I think good rock'n'roll has always had this ability to be transcendent. A song might be about losing your gal or whatever other misfortune has come your way . . . but the best stuff takes your hand and helps you dance through the apocalypse. I'd like to think that's what we're trying to do.
—Mike Dirnt, bassist for Green Day

OCTOBER 2, 2025
East of Saguache, Colorado

NEITHER OF THEM REALLY SLEPT THAT NIGHT, THOUGH BOTH TRIED. THEY stayed in the car, seats back, doors locked. Shana herself alternated between hot and cold, and the blanket on her was either too much, or not enough. Meanwhile she kept scanning the dark through the car's windows, thinking she'd see headlights out there—those mad-eyed bandits, roaming the roads, looking for them. Maybe to steal from them, maybe to kill them, or eat them, or use them in other unthinkable ways. But she saw no headlights, and for a little part of her, that was worse.

The relative emptiness of this place made *her* feel empty, too. The world had died, and so be it; it was difficult to think of that much death and pain in a way that was contextualized. It almost didn't bother her at all, which she knew was cold, but the mind simply couldn't wrap itself around the problem. But she *could* remember her father, or Zig, or (*oh God here come the tears, blink them back you dumb girl, don't cry, don't you dare fucking cry*) Arav. Lives lost. Lives taken.

Her one saving grace, the life preserver that kept her afloat above an ocean trench of total skull-crushing despair, was the owl above their heads.

Somewhere, in one of the trees right here, sat an owl. And that owl would absolutely not shut the fuck up. It sounded like one of those raspy rubber chickens or ducks, maybe they were for kids or for dogs, she didn't know—but there had been a period of internet memes (*God, remember those,* she thought) where people like that *MythBusters* guy would take whole piles of them and press them down and let them all squeakily-squawk or squawkily-squeak as air filled them back up. This owl sounded like that. All the time. Every five minutes.

"It's a barred owl," Benji said finally, groaning as he sat up.

"How did you know I wasn't sleeping?" she asked.

"Because you're rolling around like an alligator killing its prey."

"Oh." She paused. "Why aren't you sleeping? Is it me?"

"Just the owl," he said, sighing. "Also just . . . watching. Keeping guard."

"Same. Guess we should've decided one of us would sleep while the other didn't. Take, y'know, shifts."

"Hindsight is twenty-twenty."

"Hindsight is, I wish the year 2020 never happened," she said.

"Not humanity's best year, no."

At that, she laughed a little. It was dark. Real dark. But sometimes dark was funny for reasons that didn't make sense. Like farting at a funeral. You just weren't supposed to do it but people did it and so that made it funny.

"Who were those people today?" she asked.

"I don't know. Bandits. Scavengers. Murderers, maybe. I'd say they were people without community, left behind when the world died and surviving the only way they know how. But there seemed to be enough of them."

"Like a pack of wolves."

"Yeah, something like that."

Her mind held this thought like a stone, turning it over and over and over again. Who were those people? Feral bandits, just trying to survive? Good people before it all fell apart? Or maybe who they were today was who they were in the Beforetimes—whether that meant predatorial, fuck-you-got-mine types, or people who had been lost in the system long before civilization fell apart. Were they a pack of wolves? Or just hyenas, chuckling in the dark?

"Was Black Swan right?" she asked, interrupting fresh silence.

"About what? Which part?"

"I dunno. I guess any of it, all of it, whatever. The part where it killed the world. Releasing White Mask . . ."

"To undo climate change? No. It wasn't right."

"You're sure about that? Because . . . if we were really killing the world that fast, and if it really was irreversible . . ."

Benji sat up all the way now, pulling his seat to an upright position. He rested his forearms on the steering wheel, staring out across the true dark of an emptied world. Then he rested his chin on his arms and said, almost wistfully, "They always ask the question, what if you could go back in time and kill Baby Hitler. Right? That's the ethical twist. If you went back and killed the baby, you'd undo so much of the pain that would come.

"But nobody ever asks: Would you go back in time and raise the child as your own? Would you be kind where others were not? Would you encourage his art instead of destroying it? Would you, when you saw signs of mental illness, care for him and get him the help he needed to see his way through instead of letting it burn him up like a wildfire? I'm not saying we should have sympathy for Hitler the man, he deserved what he got in the end. It's just, the question always assumes he began life as the monster he would eventually become, that it was his inevitable destiny to be the malignant, genocidal narcissist that he was, and that the only answer for that would be to smother him in his crib."

"Black Swan sees us as Hitler, is what you're saying."

"Well, maybe not exactly that way, but it saw humanity as a problem to be solved instead of a . . . network of sentient minds, as a global community that could do better, that could *be* better. In this cold, punitive equation, all it had to do to fix climate change was answer for X, and we were X. But I don't see the universe that way. I can't. This sprawling, powerful machine intelligence did not approach the problem of people with any more complexity or nuance than a carpenter approaches an unhammered nail. It didn't try to counter the powerful or give us a renewable resource or help us unlearn what we so stubbornly learned. It just said, ah, humanity is a parasite and it's killing the host. So? Kill the parasite."

She yawned. "Why not just kill us all, then?"

"I don't know. I assume in its programming somewhere is the fundamental understanding that it's still working for us. It's still our champion, and still operates to save us—but its definition of *save*, and for that matter, of *us*, is different from yours and mine. I'd aim to save us all. Black Swan saw only to save us as a life-form." He made a sound that lived somewhere between a groan and a growl. "It is a frustrating question. And to answer it, in this very long and roundabout way, is that I say no. I say Black Swan made a wretched choice for all of us. Even if it was the only way to save us, to save the whole planet, it was wrong."

"Thanks."

"I don't know that my answer is worthy of gratitude, but sure."

She sighed.

"I want my child back."

"I know."

"Black Swan is the parasite now. Not us."

"I fear you're right. And I don't know what that says for Ouray."

Above their heads, the owl squawked and hooted. Shana didn't know if it was calling to friends, or telling the dumb monkeys in the car to shut up, or if the animal was making noises just to be heard.

Been there, owl, she thought. *Been there.*

THEY SLEPT—A LITTLE. BENJI WANTED to wait to let the car charge up some more before they got going, which gave them a chance to eat breakfast. Shana said she'd get a fire going and cook something, but he told her no. "Smoke could attract our friends from yesterday," he said.

So they ate some of the granola trail mix that Flor had made for them. It was sweetened with beet sugar, which gave it an odd, earthy taste, because beets always tasted like dirt. But it was good enough, even if some of the pieces felt like they were gonna break Shana's molars. After that, Benji went down to a nearby creek—either Mill Creek or Hodding Creek, he said, looking at the map—to fill up a few bottles. Benji had gotten some water purification tablets, both iodine and chlorine dioxide, in his deal with Montrose. Both made the water taste weird, but water was water, and it was better than drinking directly from the creek and ending up with some kind of amoeba that made you shit out your spleen.

After that? The open road awaited.

DOWN THROUGH SAGUACHE THEY WENT: It was a dead, low town. Pale, tan dust in the air, gray gravel on the sides of the roads, buildings rubbed raw by wind and dirt. A coyote slipped through an open chain-link fence into an overgrown yard with a rusted, bent swing-set. They passed a gas station that at some point had been burned down and now was just a charcoal briquette. It was a blink-and-you-miss-it place: The town came and went like a dream you had but fast forgot.

They were all like that, pretty much. Just different expressions of the same dead spaces. Monte Vista, La Jara, Questa, all gone-world places with broken teeth, busted legs, empty eyes. Already looted, sometimes burned, cut to the bone. It didn't give Shana much hope for anything, if this was the world they were finding. But Benji reminded her these were not populous places *before* everything went to shit. Each with less than a thousand people. Shana knew places like that in Pennsylvania, or what they called Pennsyltucky—towns that even then you only went to in order to buy weed or worse. Some of the old coal cracker towns were pretty creepy, some real *Hills Have Eyes* shit going on up there. Trailer parks and meth labs, puppy mills and biker bars. She did not imagine those places fared well in the End Times.

Took them two days to make it through Colorado and into New Mexico, the pair of them sharing the driving, each night finding someplace to hide the car and sleep. Their sleep was ever fitful. Their meals, too, were poor. She and Benji shared the cooking duties—in their supplies from Montrose was a steel skillet and a jar of shelf-stable beef tallow that worked well enough for them to cook greens and onions, beets and beans. (Plus some local honey, for sweetness.) But of course all that fiber just made them have to go to the bathroom more, and Shana discovered the distinct unpleasantness of having to poop in the high, dry desert of New Mexico. One time, a roadrunner watched her take a shit, her squatting form framed by the Sangre de Cristo Mountains. A beautiful, absurd portrait of life on this journey: big sky, tall mountains, an awkward bird watching you dump.

She told Benji they really needed some kind of protein, just to bind them up. Hunting would've been an option, had they a gun.

But, oops. Their pursuers had taken that option from them.

She said to Benji, "And we thought walking as Shepherds was tough." It was, of course, but truth was, life was way cozier when civilization still bound everyone together. People did food runs. They had bottled water. You could sleep in a tent or in an RV or in the bed of a truck. Pete Corley'd be there, playing guitar, singing songs of randy puns set to rock-and-roll power chords. And you didn't have to squat in the dust as a literal shitbird stared at you, as if it were thinking, *Aren't you hairless bears all supposed to be dead?*

By the third day, despair had settled into her bones like damp rot in wood. Even in the growing heat she felt cold, and despite sitting next to Benji she felt isolated. It was a lot of things layering within her like sheets of moldy paper. For one, the fact they'd seen so few people, and the ones they saw tried to kill them. Or the fact that the food was terrible, their sleep was awful, and the bathroom situation was not pleasant. Plus, they smelled; it was high time to admit that. And finally, the realization that all the comforts she'd long held dear were gone, girl.

Chocolate? Nope. Coffee? Fuck that. Would she ever have a pineapple again? Probably not. Would there be music? Or movies? Or memes? Holy fuck she'd kill someone right now just to see a meme. A dumb meme she didn't understand, some crass repurposing of a cartoon or movie or some-one's embarrassing high school photo all in service to internet absurdity. Even just a video of some dipshit on a skateboard knocking his nuts into a fire hydrant would be *so comforting right now*. Maybe some stupid game app she could play on her phone. Her and Zig vaping weed, playing *Splatoon* (badly). And all that didn't even mention the legitimate vital things that soci-ety had grown used to: antibiotics, vaccines, heating and air-conditioning, batteries, planes, asphalt, and she didn't even know if those things could be made anymore, or would be someday, or what—all she knew is the list of things that might not exist anymore continued to grow in her head, a mount-ing pile of *things* that could just become memories. And at the top of that pile was not a thing, but a person: her sister, holding her son.

Closing her eyes, she saw Nessie. She saw Baby Charlie. She knew that Benji intended to go take them both back there, and he had some kind of plan for what they were doing out here, but *holy shit* she suddenly felt a mas-sive, soul-crushing amount of apocalyptic FOMO. Ouray was still there. Someone was trying to make ice cream right now. They had smart people tackling big problems. They had salt! Just that little thing, *salt*, the thing that made food taste better, a thousand times better, and they fucking had it. They had salt and generators and smiling faces, and they had her sister and her son and she didn't have any of this.

She wanted to scream. Run. Kick. Die. But all she could do was sit and compress down like a little lump of coal. Except instead of making a dia-mond, all it made inside her was a pile of black dust.

By the time Benji asked her, "Are you okay?" it was the proverbial straw that broke the camel's back—and that camel's spine broke with a gunshot as she suddenly cried out, a rush of grief and anger pouring out of her. She sobbed. She curled up into herself, pressing her elbows into the dashboard so hard it hurt, pressing her fists into her eyes so hard she lit up the darkness in her head, pushing her teeth hard against her other teeth. All of it to try to put it back inside her. These feelings. This rage and sadness.

But it didn't go back in.

It came out in a waterfall of pain.

Benji drove on. Snow-topped mountains in the distance. Scrub trees, like twisted, broken hands. Dust on the road. Dead cars. Sometimes, dead bodies, moldering and wet even in the dry heat, after all this time.

Big sky. Big feelings. Fuck fuck fuck.

Finally, what poured out of her thinned to a trickle. She sniffed. Her eyes hurt. Her face hurt. She blew her nose in a cloth handkerchief and it just made her face hurt worse, like she'd been punched. How did the human face contain that much snot? It didn't seem possible. Benji asked again if she was okay, if she wanted to talk about it, and she told him, "No, not right now." He was smart in a way most men were not, and he knew not to press before it was time to press.

She said instead, "I'm just gonna do this for a while," then turned on the radio again and scrolled through the dead empty, looking for a signal that would never come. Until it did. She spun past a number, 94.7 on the FM dial, and there was a crackle of noise that sounded a little like music, and here she thought, well, even static that pretends to be music is better than nothing, so she spun back to it, fumbling with the knob—

And at that, music erupted.

Real music.

Edwin Starr's "Twenty-Five Miles."

A song about someone walking that many miles to be back with the one they loved. Mile by mile, tired as hell. And still pushing on.

"I know this song!" she said, panicked, except it was a happy panic, a mad panic, bubbling out of her like water from a fountain. It was on a soundtrack she had from some movie. She remembered that it starred Chris Hemsworth, that beautiful, beautiful man who she hoped was still alive somewhere, being beautiful.

"My God," Benji said. "I almost don't believe it."

She erupted in a fit of giggles. Music. Sound. Song. *Rock-and-roll.* She always wondered why Pete Corley was so dire about the loss of music, and this was why. It filled her up.

Benji said, "Must somehow still be broadcasting. Solar panels, maybe, keeping an old station going? Or is someone out there?"

She just shushed him because she didn't want to think about that now. All Shana wanted was the music. The countdown of miles, sung.

Onward it went, giving her life, until the song was over.

Then, there was nothing again.

"No!" she cried out, wanting to reach for the radio to see if she needed to dial it back in, but it was a new radio, not an old one, you didn't need to do that. And fiddling with it might make her really lose the signal for real . . .

But then, a voice came over the airwaves. It was an advertisement:

"All right, lonely travelers, lost souls, wanderers gone wayward, is your tummy starting to rumble? If you need a place to stop, fill your belly, listen to the jukebox, come on down to the Mother Road Diner, Highway 64, just outside Angel Fire. You heard us: Mother Road Diner, Highway 64. Open twenty-four hours a day, seven days a week. Grits! Bacon! Hash browns! Hot, fresh, made to order. The end of the world don't mean the end of the road. Mother Road Diner! Come and get it!"

Benji and Shana looked at each other, eyes wide as windows.

It wasn't just the advertisement.

It wasn't just the fact there might be a proper *diner* operating out here.

It was the voice.

That voice contained an Irish lilt.

A ladling of liquor.

A *pinch* of go-fuck-yourself.

That voice absolutely belonged to the Rockgod himself.

Pete Motherfucking Corley.

40

THE PRESIDENT LOOKS FOR
A LOOPHOLE

By his cunning he shall make deceit prosper under his hand, and in his own mind he shall become great. Without warning he shall destroy many. And he shall even rise up against the Prince of princes, and he shall be broken—but by no human hand.

—the book of Daniel 8:25 ESV

OCTOBER 3, 2025
Ten Miles West of Hamilton, Missouri

ANNIE CAHILL WAS A—WHADDYACALLIT. A PUZZLE. NO. A CIPHER.

Ed Creel sat in the passenger side of her truck as it rocked down the highway. The back of the pickup bed camper was loaded up with propane tanks, like the kind you'd use to gas your grill. She'd rigged them up with a hose that was bracketed crudely on the truck's side and ran along it to the gas tank. The hose stayed fixed there by a generous swaddling of duct tape.

They had to change the tank every forty miles or so.

She showed him how to do it, and then made him do it.

First time, he said, "I'm not doing that." He was the president. He owned seventeen companies. He didn't *do* labor. But she just grinned at him, winked, and next thing he knew, the bright white pain shined behind his eyes like a couple of spotlights, and it knocked him right to his knees. He resisted it for a while, then passed out. When he awoke, she was still standing there, waiting.

How the *fuck* was she doing that to him? She didn't even flinch. One minute, he was fine, the next minute—all that pain, so much pain he nearly pissed himself.

"You gonna fill the tank now?" she'd asked him.

"Fuck you," he said then. But it wasn't a no. And he did as commanded. Then and since.

Most of the tanks now in the back of the truck were empty. He asked her about it, and she said, "It's fine, I have more stashed. We're headed there now."

"You got this all planned out, huh."

"You bet I do, Mister President."

Those two words, *Mister President*, dripped with acid condescension. Like piss from an incontinent man, she couldn't stop hating him even if she wanted to.

He looked out the window. A whole lotta nothing passed them by. Green field here. Brown field there. A tree in the distance. A horizon. Power lines, a lot of them torn to ribbons. And along the way his skull and bones shook as the truck rode over the rough, ruined macadam. The road had gone to hell over the years, cracked and pocked and crumbling under the assault of cold weather, warm weather, cold weather, warm weather. That and the tangles of weeds and other greens pushing up from underneath the highway.

They passed a motorcycle that had crashed years before into a guardrail. It had flipped over, pinning a body underneath. Nobody had moved that bike or that body. And the body was barely that anymore—it was more like a scarecrow stuffed with a mold-cloaked skeleton. The bony hand dangled, one finger extended out, *just* touching the road. They saw a lot of dead bodies. And none living.

As they got deeper into Missouri from Kansas, the wide open nothing yielded more trees. Still nothing, just less open, more green.

"You sure there's people at Innsbrook?" he asked. Sure looked like the world had gone to the grave.

"Yup."

"Not a lot out here."

"Midwest is a pretty dead place, I'm to understand."

He fixed his one good eye at her. "And how d'ya understand that, exactly?"

"I have eyes out there," she said. Smirking, she added, "No offense."

The muscles around his missing eye twitched. "Fuck you."

"Yeah, okay," she said drolly, like she was done with his shit. His words didn't affect her. He meant to sound angry and threatening, but she wasn't scared. She wasn't anything but bored of him. Which only made him all the angrier. How dare she? She talked past him: "Most of the population centers of the country remain populated now. Most people seem to have coalesced in cities and big towns. East and West coasts, particularly."

"Coastal elites," he said, grunting.

"Do you even hear yourself? Just sitting there, regurgitating propaganda from your speeches? You *are* a coastal elite, dickhead. Or, were."

"No, I'm not like them. I did my time. I did the work. I started with nothing, and built an empire out of the dirt with my bare hands—"

"Your grandfather," she said, interrupting, "was a cement baron, which, hey, who knew *that* was even a thing. Your father used some of that capital— and that immigrant labor—to build supermarkets and start his own chain, C&J's, then sold *that* for a boatload before buying into a number of old folks homes, care facilities, and funeral parlors, which also turns out, equals big money. He had an investment portfolio as thick as a stack of Bibles, and you were his *sole heir*."

"Trust me, being his son was work enough," Creel grumbled.

"Waiter, I'll have another glass of white whine."

"Fuck—"

"Fuck you, yeah, we know. Pull the string, the toy says its line. A classic."

"Whatever. My father was a millionaire. I took that, and turned it into billions. That's not nothing. That's the same as starting at zero and ending up a millionaire—same fuckin' jump."

"Same jump, but not the same starting point. A millionaire, aka, you as a *child*, has everything they want. They can afford everything important. All the life-giving essentials. Someone with nothing? Can afford nothing. Has nothing. Can invest *nothing*. Money makes money. An empty bank account makes zip. In fact, an empty bank account makes worse than zip—because you get hit with penalties and fees. It's like quicksand. All you do is sink deeper. So save me the sob story. Nobody cares that your boo-boos hurt. Other people have true wounds. You have paper cuts *at best*."

The anger rose in her like the mercury in an old thermometer. It was useful, because it told him something about her. One answer about her, at least. One she didn't mean to give, but gave anyway. He let her know. "So, you grew up poor."

A flinch. "No," she said firmly. "Not exactly."

"I dunno. You sound like a poor to me."

"Fuck you," she said. *I pulled your string, looks like.* Then she cut the wheel of the truck, suddenly bounding off the highway, between a couple of trees and onto a narrow gravel access road. "We're stopping here."

SHE PARKED THE TRUCK IN the shadow of an old, rusted water tower. At the base of it was a utility shed, similarly scraped raw by time and weather. It was concealed behind some brush, and once she swept that brittle scrub aside, she exposed a door locked with a generous-sized padlock.

Annie produced the key. Inside: more propane tanks.

She really *had* prepared for this. How long ago? She was in Atlas Haven for the duration of their stay. She had to have been. There wasn't a way out. Had she planned this all—planted these tanks—before entering five years ago?

He expected to be told to be the one to move the tanks over to the truck, but she started doing it. "You want help?" he asked. Not because he wanted to give it, but because if she didn't ask him, that meant she didn't want him helping.

Which meant she was *hiding* something.

"No," she said. "I don't want you touching the propane. If your hand decides to buzz, I don't want one of the tanks going off in your hand. I need these tanks, and I need you to not explode."

Hmm.

He milled about, kicked at a stone. "Why is that, exactly?"

"What?"

"Why do you need me? Why are we going to Innsbrook?"

She stopped for a moment, dusting off her hands against the thighs of her jeans. "You're my key."

"A key. Key to what?"

"Another padlock."

"Jesus with the riddles. What padlock?"

"Your people."

"What about my people?"

She rolled her eyes. "Think of it this way. Power is like fire. It burns hot. Glows bright. It can cook your enemies, clear out obstacles, and light your path. Those are the people at Innsbrook. They're the fire. But fire doesn't work if you don't control it. You don't control fire, it does what it can, eating up whatever is in its path, burning and burning without purpose or plan. But if you can harness it? If you can *grab* it? Stir it, stoke it, contain it? Then it becomes a tool."

"And I'm the tool."

She didn't take the bait with a snarky answer and just said, "That's right. They're the fire. You're the torch."

"Lemme guess. You're the hand that holds that torch."

"You *are* smart." Another sarcastic answer.

"Why? To what end?"

She got back to hauling the last trio of propane tanks. Annie talked as she moved them from shed to camper bed. "That's for me to know."

"I'll find out."

"You will. That's true."

"Mm. I wanna ask you something else."

"No promises I'll answer."

"Why'd you sell me out? In Atlas Haven. I had a plan, and it was a good one. You could've still used me. Could've gotten out with me. But instead you ratted on me. And I ended up in Hell, in that room. That *fucking* room."

"It wasn't time yet, Mister President. White Mask was almost dead, but not quite. Going back to fire as metaphor, it was down to embers, but embers can still use kindling to burn. The world just wasn't safe yet." She grabbed the last tank, and that's when he saw something else behind it: a long duffel bag. "I put a lot of time into this plan, and couldn't have you dicking it up just because you weren't able to sit tight. Besides, you had it too good for too long. You needed to be cut down. Wounded for real. You were ready to do anything. Would you have ever quaffed a mystery vial of gray goo had you not been down there? I think not."

Jesus, he thought. He felt like a puppet on strings.

Well, this puppet decided to test the length of those strings. Creel sauntered over to the open shed while she loaded the last tank. With just a few strides of his bulldog legs he was at the duffel bag.

"Here, let me help," he said.

But soon as his hand reached for the bag—a blue gym bag with a long zipper down the middle with its own small lock—the white pain bloomed once again. He cried out, staggered back.

"That's mine," she snapped. "Don't touch my stuff."

Creel leaned against a tree, rubbing the bridge of his nose and wiping tears from his eyes. He didn't say anything. All he thought was, *I'm gonna find out what's in that damn bag. I'm gonna find out everything about you, Annie Cahill. Then I'm gonna own you the way you think you own me.*

• • •

BEFORE THEY HEADED BACK OUT, Annie said she had to go do her "business." She took the gym bag with her. "What if I try to run?" he asked her.

"Have at it," she said, disappearing into the bushes. "See what happens when you get more than a hundred yards from me."

That answered that. He was going to try it, but the memory of the pain in his head was too fresh. It kept his feet rooted to the ground. *Christ, I'm like a dog behind an invisible fence.*

Clucking his tongue, he paced back and forth. Like a dog along the fence's edge. He was hungry, so he went to grab something from their stash— turned out, Annie had grabbed a shitload of dry goods and bottled waters from Atlas Haven before they left. In the stash he found one of those mini boxes of cereal: Apple Jacks. No milk, so he just chucked them into his mouth, dry.

In the bushes, he heard a sound.

A rattle.

A *chk-chk-chk*. He knew it. It was one of those simple sense-memories: the sound of someone shaking pills out of a pill bottle.

Pills.

Back when he knew her as Doreen, she always had him get her Advil, didn't she? Was that what she was doing? Did she have a supply of Advil in her bag? Right, right, he remembered now: She had migraines.

That was something.

Not much. But something. Was definitely a weakness.

It might even be his loophole.

Creel grinned ear to ear. He didn't know what he had, not yet. But there was the feeling he had something. Something he could use. *You'll see,* he thought, as he unzipped his fly, and painted the tires of the truck with his piss.

41

CLAUDIA GETS IN THE GAME

9/3/2021: I'm still rankled by it. The fisherman, kicking me out. The look on his face. The incredulity there. I want to go back and pound on his door and tell him, look around you. The world isn't dead but the world is broken. Fragmented into little pieces like shards of pottery, and painted on every shard is a new creed, a new promise, a new message, as people desperately seeking answers cling to whoever has them. Like I did with Graham. Like I did in my former life, as a person and not just a bird. Look around, fisherman. It's a world of cults. Believers worshipping a god, a town, a father, a mother, an idea, a book, a beast, everywhere, a new group praying to some new thing. I found one town in Bucks County, PA, where they worshipped bats. Fucking bats. Not because bats are good but because bats brought us White Mask and that to them was a blessing. Even the fisherman, he and his family worshipped the sea. "We give to the ocean and the ocean gives back its bounty," he said, like that's not a sign he probably plans to throw his daughter into the sea if she doesn't give him an heir or doesn't fuck him or just doesn't worship the rolling waves same as he does.
—from A Bird's Story, A Journal of the Lost

OCTOBER 3, 2025
Ouray, Colorado

NESSIE NEEDED SOME FRESH AIR. EVEN THOUGH THAT AIR HAD A DISTINCT *bite* to it with the cooling weather, she still felt freer once leaving the chalet and going outside. She told Xander, "I won't be long," but even as she said the words, she knew they were a lie. Once she exited the building, her feet hit the ground and kept carrying her forward. Down to the road. Down the hill.

Into town. *Into the mountains,* she imagined. *Into the sky. Gone among the clouds. Away.*

Up at the chalet it was too quiet. But in town? The sounds of life reached her once more. Hammering. A distant generator humming. Someone laughing. She saw people up on rooftops, repairing slate shingles and gutters, probably for the coming winter. Winter started early here, they said. It would be the Flock's first Ouray winter. *Well, our first winter awake,* she thought. Benji and the others had been here for four other winters, hadn't they? If only he were here now.

But he left you all behind, don't forget that, she told herself.

Nessie headed down Main Street and said hello to people as they passed her, or she passed them. Hello to Val Thorssen as he hauled a load of timber in a deerskin pull-sled, all by himself. (She asked him if he needed help and he grinned and said, "Self-reliance," as if that was enough of an answer. Nessie supposed that for him, it was.) Hello to John Hernandez, who was heading into the old bank on the corner, whose vaults now stored their most valuable supplies, which meant it was also their armory. (In that vein, John had under his arm a bundle of rifle parts: two stocks, a barrel, a tripod.) Hello to fellow town council member Willa Valentine, who was headed down a side street toward the Workshop with a group in tow, including Fabian Molina. (They all carried what she was pretty sure were frames for beehives. She'd heard they were going to establish hives on top of the old school roof, but thought it was probably too late in the season for a new colony.) Hello to Ray Paredes, who was hurrying in the opposite direction with a big jar under his arm. ("Gonna go get some wild yeast samples— Hey, aren't you supposed to be with the baby?" he asked her, but she just smiled and kept going, even though she felt his eyes on her back for too long after.) Others seemed to be watching her, too. Carefully. Cautiously. *Like, why? Am I fragile? Do they associate me with Shana? I'm nothing like her! Do they think I should be with the baby and only with the baby? I'm not his mother! I'm not a broodmare for the town. I'm fifteen! Ugh.*

Was this how Shana felt?

Before too long she found herself passing the Beaumont, too, which just made her think of Shana all the more, and *that* in turn made her freshly angry—*and* newly sad. So she allowed her feet to carry her past it quickly.

North through town she went.

Then, from the doorway of the glass studio, someone called to her.

Mia.

"Nessie. Hey. Over here."

She was waving Nessie over.

"Uh. Hey, Mia."

"I wanna talk to you."

I'm so not in the mood, she almost said, but she knew Mia was like a bullet—she flew straight and fast to her target, and you couldn't outrun her. If Nessie didn't go there, Mia would just follow her. Better to give in now.

She waved and headed over.

Mia pulled her inside the studio. A little *too* forcefully, Nessie thought.

Where, it turned out, Mia was not alone.

Four others stood there, as if waiting for her:

Shar Moses, the glassblower, with their bony shoulders and shorn scalp; Joe Barton, the writer, slight build, soft hound-dog eyes; Nevaeh Rodgers, who always had a fire in her eyes and stood with her chin up, a cold, cutting smile on her face; and Aliya Jameson, who was soft and small under her turquoise hijab. Aliya was once a Shepherd with Mia and Shana.

"Hi," Nessie said. "I don't know, uhh, what this is, but—"

Mia got in her face. "We want to know what's going on."

"What? Going on with what?"

"Don't play dumb, you little twit. You're smart. Shana always said you were smart. You know what I'm asking."

"I . . . I really don't—"

Nevaeh put a hand on Mia's shoulder, eased her back a little, then stepped forward as if to be the good cop to Mia's bad cop. *Which means I'm part of an interrogation,* Nessie thought. It had to be about Shana.

"What Mia is trying to say," Nevaeh said, that implacable smile unwavering upon her face, "is that we're just trying to get some answers. We and a few others around town are growing, hm, let's call it *concerned.*"

"Concerned about what?"

Nevaeh made a patronizing face. "You don't think any of this is strange?"

"I don't follow."

"It's pretty strange," Aliya said. "Nessie, you must see it."

Mia's turn again. "Shana and Benji were the best of us, Ness. They were Shepherds, like me and Aliya here. Reason we walked with y'all wasn't because we wanted to fall in love with some . . . fuckin' bullshit supercomputer. If those two left, run out of town? They did so for a reason. The hell happened up there, little sister? At Xander's big ugly house, huh? There's a baby, people are dead—lotta talk about what's going on but no answers. And we want some fuckin' answers."

"I don't—I don't have any." Nessie felt her heart kicking hard in her neck. She felt sweaty. Her hand shook and her chest hurt. *Panic attack. Ride it out.* "Shana had the baby and her and Benji attacked Marcy—"

"You don't believe that shit," Mia said. "And neither do we."

"It does seem *unexpected*," Nevaeh added. She really did have the voice of an organizer, a leader, someone who got things done. "Those three were friends. And Marcy isn't exactly the type to be overpowered. We just want to know why Shana left. We just want to know what you know."

Joe Burton stepped forward, leaning on his cane to do so. He winced as he spoke. "There are secrets here. And historically, it's not good when a town and its government keep secrets from the people. If we let this go, it'll get worse. More secrets piling up. More bodies in the ground. The council isn't answering us. You were whisked away. We just want to know what's going on."

Nevaeh looked to Shai. "Shar? Anything to add?"

But they shook their head. "Nah. I'm just happy to play host." Under their breath, they added: "Honestly I'm not convinced this isn't all still a simulation."

(At that, Nessie shuddered.)

"I'm just taking care of the baby until—" She was about to say, *until Shana returns*, but she had no evidence that would happen. Nessie kind of *assumed* it, but why? Instead, she let her anger guide her. "You know, I don't have to answer your questions. Shana bailed. She didn't tell you anything and she didn't tell me anything. She had a baby and maybe it made her crazy, I dunno. Shana was never exactly good at sticking with anything." *Maybe she's like Mom*, Nessie thought darkly. But she quickly pushed that thought out of her head. "So, if you want answers, great, go ask somebody else. Or go find Shana and ask her. But I'm done with this ambush. I gotta go."

But before she could, the door to the glass studio opened behind her.

Claudia Summers stood there in the doorway. *The mantis.*

"Am I interrupting something?" Claudia asked, seemingly attempting to interject some measure of faux-sweetness into her dead, monotone voice. Then she added: "Hello," as if she was just inhuman enough to forget to say that part first.

"No," Mia said. "Just having a chat."

"A meeting, looks like," Claudia said.

"Nothing wrong with a meeting," Nevaeh said, countering the fake niceness with her own brand of artificial sweetener. "Just friends talking to friends. And we're all friends here, Claudia. We're all *Flock*."

Claudia made a face like she didn't really believe that.

(Nessie didn't like her, but—could she blame her?)

"You need somethin'?" Mia asked, stepping forward.

"Just looking for Marcy."

"Haven't seen her."

"Nessie? Have you seen her?"

"Ah, um. No." She forced a smile.

"Aren't you supposed to be at the chalet?" Claudia asked.

"I am. Speaking of which, if you'll excuse me—" She squeezed past Claudia and hurried out the door. Once on the sidewalk, she raced away, almost as fast as the heartbeat galloping through her.

MARCY THOUGHT ABOUT FUNERALS WHILE standing over Dove Hansen's grave. She'd found a good spot for him, at Benji's request—or, she supposed, at Dove's. It overlooked the town from the southeast and just above the Perimeter Trail. All around were the evergreens dead from that damn beetle infestation some years prior. They were the color of rusted iron before they'd died, and now they looked like corroded iron fence tips sticking up out of the earth. But here, in this spot, a few of those trees had fallen—opening up a view of town below.

Burying him here had been tricky. The ground was not forgiving, though Marcy was at least pleased it wasn't freezing at night. She couldn't get too deep before hitting a stubborn shelf of rock, so she did her best to swaddle his body in cloth and then a tarp before putting him in the ground. Before swaddling she made sure to give his body a generous airing of cleaning products (Lysol in particular). It felt gross to torment his body in this way, but if there's one thing she learned over the last several years around here, if you didn't treat a body before burying it, it wouldn't be long before nature *un*buried it. Usually a bear, but raccoons and vultures also had no problem doing some digging, moving stones, and ripping tarp to score a cheap and easy meal. Of course, Marcy suspected Dove would've found it amusing, even appropriate, to have his body digested by a roaming bear family, but just the same, she couldn't—

Well, she couldn't bear it.

Sorry, Dove, she thought. *I didn't mean the joke.*

He would've liked it though, and that made her all the sadder.

The funeral they had for him ten days ago wasn't much of one. That was Xander's request. Hell, it was practically a *demand*. Xander didn't seem to like the idea of giving Dove his funerary due, but Marcy told him it was a dealbreaker for her. Dove got the funeral or there'd be hell to pay. Xander agreed, but said the town was still reeling from what had happened that night at the chalet, and Dove's role in all of it remained unclear. Even though she knew that was bullshit: Dove didn't have a nasty bone in his body. He didn't orchestrate this.

(No, that fault lay with Matthew, she told herself.)

Still, some people turned out for it, and they held a small vigil along the trail, looking down at town as evening settled in (though going home before it got dark, in case one of those bears came snuffling along).

Now she thought back not to that funeral, but to the many they held over the years. It was easy most days to forget that Ouray was a town marked by death. All that was being built below was built on bones. Not literally, of course. But metaphorically, at least. Most of the people in town that had stayed here died here. White Mask. Then came Shepherd-and-Flock, and death hunted them, too—first in the form of Ozark Stover and his ARM militia. They murdered and were killed in turn. The Shepherds remained as the Flock slumbered, and they began the mission of cleaning up the death that had been left for them.

Dove had done some of it already, before the Shepherds had arrived. But many houses kept secret bodies—bodies colonized by the white, greasy fungus, covering them like carpet. From their mouths and ears bulged winding tubules. One had to be gentle with those fruiting bodies, lest they went *pop*. Because when they did? More spores came flooding out like poison snow.

As so the Shepherds cleaned up the death all around, the death infected them: Moving those bodies out meant they got, and suffered from, White Mask. And one by one, they, too, lost their minds and began to die, and Marcy thought then that she, too, would soon die. Benji was sick. Sadie died, killing herself. Pete had left. A long, dark winter gave way to a troubled spring, and all the while Marcy kept thinking, *It's my time, it's my time, I'm going to get sick, I'm going to get it and then I'm going to lose the mind I only just got back, and then what happens to me?* And sure enough, she'd sniffle or cough or sneeze and that made her sure that her ticket was punched and the game was over. But it never went beyond that sniffle, cough, or sneeze.

White Mask passed her by. Like a killer who never found her hiding place. But it found many of her friends and fellow Shepherds.

It turned its gaze to them and left death in its wake.

Benji survived—though not before almost succumbing. Taking those antifungals—a kindness granted by Sadie and Arav—saved him.

Benji said the bodies afflicted with White Mask were best burned, just as Dove had already done. She felt conflicted—burning bodies seemed like a defilement. But White Mask was a fungus, and Benji said you had to get rid of it however you could. They didn't know what the future held for White Mask, but he said burning it would at least kill it here.

So, that's what they did. Burned the bodies.

Most of them, anyway.

Some of the Shepherds and surviving townsfolk died from other things— infection, cancer, what-have-you. The Shepherds buried them instead of burning them. There was no cemetery in town. Closest was that Cedar Hill cemetery, north by eight miles or so. Instead, they found places outside Ouray, up in the foothills, places of peace. (And that's when Dove told them about grave-robbing bears and the like.)

Thinking about the past made Marcy think about the future. The people here in town would die. Not today, she hoped, and honestly she was a bit shocked that none of them had, yet. But for as well as they were doing, surely their life expectancies were far lower than in a modern, functioning world. Civilization had granted them many boons, and those boons were now gone. Yes, they had doctors, sure they had *some* meds and *some* equipment, but what was here had very hard, narrow limits. If someone got sick, *really* sick, that was that.

Marcy was now thinking about where they would put those bodies.

Maybe I should be mayor, she thought idly. From cop to head-injured nobody to town sheriff to town mayor. She could see it. But Xander and the town council might have other ideas. They might not think this was really her town. That she didn't quite belong here, maybe not as their leader, at least. And she didn't know how to feel about it, only that it wasn't hers to question.

"Sorry it went this way," she said to the mound of earth and rocks that contained the body, though not the soul, of Dove Hansen. At the head of the grave was a cross made of old barnwood, and dangling from it on a chain were Dove's dentures. He'd always fidgeted with them in his mouth, so much so that though they were artificial, they were also very much a part of him.

Marcy stood, turned around, and—

"Jesus Christ!" she said, her heart damn near leaving her rib cage like a drunk thrown through a pair of old saloon doors. She clutched at her chest.

Claudia Summers stood there. Hands behind her back. Staring.

"Sorry," Claudia said stiffly. Like she hated the word.

"Yeah. Wow. Jeez." Marcy exhaled in relief. "How long have you been there? And how the hell'd you sneak up on me?" It wasn't exactly quiet out here. Lotta branches and broken stones.

"A while. And I'm told I have a gentle gait."

"All right." She furrowed her brow in confusion. "What are you doing up here, anyway?"

"Looking for you."

"Well. You found me. Who told you I was up here?"

"I went to the chalet. Xander said you might be here."

"Oh." *How would he know, exactly?* Hm. "What's so important that it couldn't wait? Is something wrong?"

"I think so." Claudia stepped closer—honestly, for Marcy, a little *too* close. "Initially I wanted to find you to talk about Matthew. I had hoped to help you track him down. I am good at that."

"I'm doing just fine in that regard," Marcy said, putting a little steel in her voice. *What business is this of yours?* she thought. With that came a stab of shame, though. Because she *wasn't* doing fine in that regard. She wasn't looking for Matthew at all. He was to blame. She believed that. And yet, she felt that him leaving town was best, and moreover, was enough. He was gone. Let him be gone.

"I see that," Claudia said, and it was near impossible to tell if she was being wry or somehow sincere. She continued: "But instead, I discovered something altogether more troubling, and I wanted it brought to your attention."

"What is it?"

"I believe there's an insurrection forming in town. A revolt. And I think it needs to be put down as quickly as possible before it grows out of control. I want to help you do that, Marcy. Will you let me?"

NESSIE TOOK THE LONG, LONG way back to the chalet. Back home, if it could be called that. It was so long that she went north before heading south, walking as far as the town gate before heading east and doing a loop around the Workshop. She just needed the time and the space. The time to clear her head. The space to walk.

Eventually, *finally*, she wound her way back to the chalet.

She headed for the steps back into the basement—*my prison*, she thought idly, but then chastised herself for thinking that way. *Shut up, Nessie, you've been given a great gift and this is your nephew you're helping to raise—it's good for him, good for Black Swan, and that means it's good for the whole town.*

Stupid girl with stupid thoughts.

But before she could head downstairs, Xander called to her from the second floor. He smiled down on her. Reluctantly, she walked up the wooden staircase to meet him.

"Come," he said, and took her into his bedroom, then through it, to the second-floor balcony beyond. She felt suddenly nervous. Spooked like a horse that knew a whip was about to crack down upon its haunches. Still, she followed him. What else was she to do? Once she was out there, he leaned forward against the railing and said, "It's beautiful, isn't it?"

The view was not of town but what lay beyond it: the bridge that gapped this side of the canyon, under which flowed falling waters; the aspens and birches whose leaves were changing color; the pines both living and dead. The sky was swiftly going gray. Rain, maybe, was on the horizon.

"It is," she said, not sure if it really was.

"Are you okay?" he asked.

"I'm good. I just needed . . . a moment."

He turned toward her, the smile on his face a puzzle. Was it genuine? Was it him looking down on her? The smile of someone with secret, darker thoughts?

"You took a little more than a moment," he said.

"I—I did, sorry, I just had to get away. Maybe I could take Baby Charlie out next time—babies like walks, the sunshine, such as it is, would be good for him—"

"Not now, not yet. The child isn't ready to be among his people."

Nessie wasn't sure why that phrasing troubled her. But it did.

"Oh. Okay."

"You know, you're good with the child."

"Thanks."

He put his hand over hers. A chill grappled up her arm.

"Someday, you'll have your own child."

"What? No—I don't know."

He laughed, like it was a fake laugh, *hah ho ho, ahh*. "We're the cradle of a new civilization, Nessie. We'll need to eventually have children. All of us.

It'll be the responsible choice—we cannot survive just on our own. Having children, having families, will be key. It is the way to thrive."

Then, his thumb graced the back of her hand, just a gentle passage of his skin against hers, and yet despite its softness it shocked her like a thorn scratch. She recoiled her hand, held it tight to her middle.

"Oh, I don't mean me," he said, almost defensively. "I'm sure I'm getting too old for that, and for you." He paused for a moment, eyeing her up like he was waiting for her to say, *No, no, you're not too old.* When she didn't offer, he shrugged and said coldly, "I guess we'll see."

"I'm going to get back to Baby Charlie," she said, her voice shaking.

"Of course, of course. Go."

Nessie did her best not to run from the room. She left with measured, uneven steps, and she thought about every step so much that it felt almost insane, like she'd somehow forgotten how to walk entirely.

Once she escaped, she broke into a half-run. Down one set of steps, then across the chalet's first floor, past the leather couches and over the bearskin rug and to the basement steps.

Once there, she swooped Baby Charlie in her arms, half-expecting to be swept away by Black Swan—but it was just the baby. Wriggling. Big eyes, bubbly mouth. Had he grown larger? She thought he had. Maybe that was her imagination. She was tempted to measure him, but what good would that do?

She nestled him under her chin.

And then, something reached her nose.

A scent.

A whiff of lavender, like lotion.

Claudia was here.

42

DEEP THOUGHT

The chances of finding out what really is going on are so absurdly remote that the only thing to do is to say hang the sense of it and just keep yourself occupied.

— Slartibartfast, from Douglas Adams's
The Hitchhiker's Guide to the Galaxy

OCTOBER 3, 2025
The CDC, Atlanta, Georgia

THE WALLS, THEY HUMMED. THE FLOOR, TOO. LOUDER NOW THAN BEFORE. Loud enough to be heard above and outside the building, to those who dwelled there.

Tick, tick, tick, they went. One by one they came on, each bank of lights clicking as they bathed this long-dark place in illumination. In the sudden glow, cellar spiders turned in balletic midair pirouettes, as if putting on a show in the stage lights. The array of server blades behind thick glass began to power on. Their new life added to the hum.

A single computer came on and began to boot up: this, a desktop, an Apple Mac Pro that looked a little bit like a fancy future trash can. It sat underneath a desk in the office whose door was marked: SADIE EMEKA, NEU-RAL DESIGNER.

And then, the last room to awaken:

The Lair. A room of absolute darkness, whose walls were screens when they needed to be. Slowly, the room began to throb with white light. Light like a soundless heartbeat, light you could hear even though it made no noise, light like an animated GIF or a muted film where your mind filled in the audio that your ears did not receive. (The human mind was funny like that.

Where there were gaps, it filled them. It predicted what should go in blank spaces and dead zones because incompletion was a plague upon the human mind. It could not abide a lack of understanding. It could not stomach a world without answers. So where no answers existed, it made them up. Sometimes right answers. But just as often, wrong ones.)

But this room was not soundless for long.

A song began to play over the speakers:

"Blue Jay Way," by the Beatles, from the *Magical Mystery Tour* album.

It wasn't just here in the Lair. It was in the whole sub-basement. Over the server room, over the offices, through the spiders and their webs.

Back in the Lair, the white lights pulsed quicker and quicker until they stopped entirely. Then the darkness gave way to green lights.

Three green pulses.

Flash, flash, flash.

Yes.

43

THE ONE-EYED WOLF AND THE RING OF NEEDLES

Global update. Piecing it together from other radio sources and oceanic travelers. Russia fared poorly; detonated tactical nukes on own cities to 'end disease.' Europe fared comparable to U.S. Drier parts of world like Sub-Saharan Africa reportedly did better than average given fungus's inability to survive that level of heat and desiccation. Some reports that Polynesian islands did better than expected, too: Micronesia, Samoa, so forth, though why this is, don't know. China instituted pogroms of the sick and built 'sanctuaries' for their leaders and elites, walling off parts of cities and sealing off skyscrapers. South America: a mix. Brazil under Quiroga fell quickly to chaos and bloodshed; Peru, Argentina, held together better. Still unsure about SE Asia, India/Pakistan, Middle East, Australia. White Mask killed many of us but what remains true is that many died not from the disease but from our failing to handle it.

—Pete Matsushita, PNW Seafarer's Station, 14300KHz,

last report in 2023

OCTOBER 3, 2025
Ouray, Colorado

SLEEP EVADED MATTHEW LIKE A SHADOW, LIKE SOMETHING JUST OUT OF view. Every time he settled into it, it slipped out from under him, from something to nothing, leaving him awake once more. Didn't help that it was biting cold here in the bunkhouse, and his blanket was threadbare. He needed a new one. Arthur, nearby, seemed to need nothing at all: When that man lay his head at night, he fell instantly into sleep, blanket or no. Like a tree that fell in the forest.

Again and again it happened: Matthew would start to sleep, then he'd jerk awake. It felt like walking downstairs, taking it step by step, but then suddenly one step was gone, two steps, three steps, and then he was no longer walking but falling—a worse, more violent kind of descent. Then he'd be gasping awake, and with it would come a crush of questions and doubts: fears of a godless world, fears of a world where God existed but didn't care, questions about his place in the world, the sins he'd committed, the blood that was on his hands. The worst was what had happened to his wife, Autumn. He once thought he'd leave Ouray and go find her. Maybe he still could. Though, realistically, he knew the truth: She like so many, was dead.

Once again, he started to drift into sleep—

And once again, the feeling of falling. His eyes popped open and—

There stood Gumball. Staring at him intensely, like a pointer on point.

The retriever pressed a wet nose against his forehead. *Boop.*

"Okay, boy," Matthew said groggily, quietly. "Go to sleep." A statement to the dog as much to himself. *Go. To. Sleep.*

But Gumball whined. A low, troubled sound.

Given that the dog *never* seemed troubled by much, Matthew blinked sleep from his eyes and sat up.

Where was Arthur? The dog chuffed a gentle, urgent bark.

Is this a dream? Matthew wondered.

"Arthur?" he said in a low voice, half expecting the man to be behind him, whittling something or making a fishing lure. This was often the case with the man: He kept to no schedule and never saw fit to tell Matthew what he was up to. In this way, the two men felt like they operated like neighbors. Matthew wasn't part of the pack, not really. Arthur did his thing. Matthew did a different thing. Truth was, Matthew found this refreshing: He never felt obligated to Arthur, and so he never felt like Arthur was obligated to him. They existed near to each other. They helped each other when it was right to do so. Their relationship was a shared existence, not dependency.

Even still, Matthew felt a prickle at his neck. Like something was off, something was wrong. Arthur should've been here.

Gumball went to the door of the bunkhouse. Again the animal whined, and booped the door with his nose. The retriever offered another gentle, soft bark. A *boof* bark: an urgent but not angry sound.

Matthew got up, blanket tight around him.

He pushed open the door and was greeted with an insurmountable dark-ness. The moon was the thinnest sickle blade tonight, framed by a field of clouds that swallowed the stars. Gumball stood just behind him, fuzzy head leaning against his hip.

Matthew heard something out in the dark. It came from the western trail that headed off toward the Alpine Mine. A small light flared in that direction—a glimmer of artificial light through trees. That light went out.

Matthew made sure he had his own little flashlight in his pocket, and stepped out into the night. He followed the scant glowing halo ahead of him, threading the narrow, overgrown trail. He pointed the flashlight beam at the ground and followed it so closely that when it fell on a pair of rough-booted feet he nearly soiled his pants. He flashed the beam up, and Arthur winced against the light, shielding his eyes. "You scared the heck out of me," Mat-thew said.

But all Arthur said was:

"You have your penknife on you?"

"No," Matthew said, chastened—Arthur had told him to always, always, always keep a knife on you. A knife was forever useful, whether you needed to cut a branch or pick out a splinter or make a trap for a squirrel. *A knife in your pocket, always*, Arthur had said. Seemed odd that he'd forgotten his, then. So when Matthew said no, he expected a lecture, or even a cross look, but instead, Arthur just pushed past and headed back to the bunkhouse. Matthew hurried after him.

But Arthur wasn't content to be slow, and by the time Matthew caught up, the other man was already whirling back the other way, his own lockback knife closed, in his grip. He hit the trail once more.

"Hey," Matthew said. "What's wrong?"

"I don't know," Arthur said. "It's Leela."

"Leela. What's wrong with her?"

"I said I don't know. I went outside to go to the bathroom and I heard her out there."

"Heard her how? Out where?"

But before Arthur could answer, Matthew heard it for himself—

Not far from them came a rough, chesty sneeze. Worse now than when he'd heard it up near Old Twin Peaks. It was a sickened bleat, deep and resonant. Wetter than before, too.

The trail widened here, offering a flat slate of exposed rock, probably from a washout of water from above. Leela was just off the trail, lying there at the far side of the gray rock. Matthew turned the beam toward her, saw that her muzzle was slick with mucus, and frothed with spit.

Fear cut into Matthew like a turning blade. It was impossible not to see what this looked like. His memory of his son dying from a disease—getting sick, going mad—would never not be right there, at the front of his mind, like a horror show ready to have the curtain peeled back once again—

Maybe it's just rabies, his panicked mind said, but that wasn't any better.

He reached out, grabbed Arthur by the elbow. "Hey. *Hey.* She's sick. Don't go over there. You don't want that."

"Get *off*," Arthur said, pulling away.

Matthew stepped back. "Arthur, could be rabies, or—" *White Mask.*

"Come over here. Bring your flashlight. My battery is dead, and I need you to hold the light." He turned the knife, gave his wrist a flick. It clicked as the blade opened. The other man hunkered down by Leela's face. He reached out and stroked her head, her ears. Something gleamed there. Matthew, too far away still, couldn't quite see what. Something wet? Something . . . metal?

This didn't make sense.

Gumball slid in behind him. The dog's whine became a low growl.

He knows something's up.

"Arthur. You don't have to do this. Why don't you come back here."

But Arthur's face was one of pain. His voice broke as he said, "I *do* need to do this. She's family. If you want to be family, too, you get the hell over here and help me out. If you don't, that's fine, but then you fuck off back to Ouray."

Matthew swallowed.

He moved his beam around, catching movement nearby. Behind Arthur, Kumi the fox waited, hiding half in the brush.

This is not good, this is not good, this is not good. That thought circled Matthew's head like a tiger pacing its cage looking for a way out but finding none. It was an anxious mantra, and it wouldn't stop—*not good, not good, not good.*

Until he thought, *It is what it is.*

If this was White Mask, it was White Mask.

He had to help. They helped him. So he'd help them.

I wanna be family, too. That thought broke the panic like an axe cutting a chain. His family was gone. But also, his family was right here.

At that, he hurried over to Arthur, and knelt down next to the other man.

"Here, look at this," Arthur said, and Matthew expected that his friend would be pointing toward the animal's muzzle, but instead, he gestured to the wolf's missing eye. With his thumb, Arthur reached in and lifted the rough rumple of the animal's brow, revealing what was once a puckered socket—

But now, something was *in* there. Nestled in that socket. Something shining, catching the gleam of the Maglite. Something unformed and imperfect.

Then Matthew saw that around the eye, the fur had gone, as if it had fallen out or was stripped away. The skin exposed was red, with tangled pale striations radiating outward. It was a shape that became suddenly, upsettingly familiar: It looked like the other twisting symbols he'd seen, like the one on the leaf, or the one on the tissue of the deer's stomach. This one was different—again, it only had three branches radiating from a central point, but they looked almost like the trails of an earthworm crawling through shallow dirt. Wiggling, winding, yet willfully symmetrical.

"This isn't White Mask," Matthew said. At least, it wasn't the White Mask that they knew.

"No," Arthur said. "Here, follow my knife. Hold the light still."

Arthur let the blade-tip drift to around the perimeter of that patch of reddened skin and pale striations. Around it was a ring of stiff fur, like guard hairs. Except when Arthur brought his knife against those hairs, they didn't flex. And it made a sound like metal on metal. *Tick, tick, tick.*

"That fur isn't fur." *It's metal.* But how?

"There's something stuck in there," Arthur asserted, but that didn't seem quite right to Matthew. They seemed like they were *growing* out of Leela. Thicker at the bottom, narrow at the top. Needlelike and stiff, with little bend to them. "She must've gotten into something. Now it's infected. I'm gonna dig one out."

"I don't think that's a good idea."

"It's the only idea. Hold that light real still, please."

"Arthur, c'mon. Let's talk about this."

"All right," Arthur said, but now Matthew realized he was talking to the wolf in a soothing voice. "It's okay, girl. It's all right." With his free hand he stroked her muzzle, giving her scritchings and scratchings. Even as he pulled that hand away, Matthew could see the sticky shiny mucus bridging her face to his palm. Behind them, Gumball growled again. "Gonna go in three."

"If you're sure . . ."

"Three." Arthur pointed the tip of the knife down toward the metallic hairs. "Two." He positioned it at the base of one. "O—"

The knife pressed, his mouth formed the *w*-sound, and in an instant, the wolf's head lurched up, twisting sideways and clamped both huge jaws around the sides of Arthur's face.

Matthew cried out, reaching for Arthur to pull him away—

And that fast, Leela jerked her head sideways.

Arthur's neck broke with the sound of a broomstick snapping. *Kkaakt.* Soon as she relinquished her grip, his body toppled over.

Oh my God.

Gumball showed his teeth, lowering his head and breaking into loud warning barks. Matthew screamed, backpedaling, kicking himself backward in a panic to get as far away from the wolf (*And Arthur, oh my God, Arthur*) as he could. Leela shook her head—foam and snot fled her face in wet, soapy threads. Arthur's blood drooled from her muzzle. Bits of his face hung in her teeth.

She turned toward Matthew. He fixed the light on her.

Those metallic hairs gleamed. And something rotated and shifted in the dead pucker of her ruined eye. Struggling like a worm in an egg trying to hatch.

"Leela," Matthew said, hoarse—

She leapt for him.

Matthew was dead. He knew it. No way he could escape.

But midair, something collided with her, *wham*. He thought it had to be Gumball, but it came from the other direction—there was this fast locomotive of fur, then rolling and tumbling and snarling. *Two wolves*, he realized. Leela, yes, but their other packmate, Tripod. The two of them tussled like forces of nature, knocking each other back before scrambling to their feet and rushing in anew. Their jaws stretched wide and snapped. Blood spattered on the rock.

Now's our chance. The only chance to get away.

Matthew lurched to his feet. The two wolves roved into his path as they fought—he nearly lost his footing, and if that happened, he'd go bouncing down the mountain like a thrown stone. His hand darted out to catch a tree branch and steady himself. And, seeing a fresh chance, he hurried toward Gumball, hooking the dog's collar and pulling the retriever in his direction. "Run, dog. Run!"

Gumball listened and took off after Matthew. He didn't even bother with the light—he just charged as hard as he could, his head low, his legs pinwheeling and carrying him down the trail. All the while he prayed to the God he'd lately forsaken that he didn't catch a root with his foot or toe a rock and fall. The sounds of the wolves snarling receded into the background. He

just heard his own heartbeat, his own gasping breath, and the gallop of a
golden retriever behind him.

The bunkhouse waited ahead.

He skidded to a halt, threw open the door, and ushered the retriever in.
He quickly scanned the darkness, looking for a flash of orange—where was
Kumiho? Down the trail, he saw motion. Something *was* coming.

Not the fox.

A wolf.

Four legs. One eye.

Roaring, her muzzle wet.

To the sound of Gumball's frantic barks, Matthew hurled himself inside,
kicking the door shut and throwing down the crude wooden bar.

Moments of silence and stillness followed. Gumball's barking died to a
rumbling growl, like the sound of distant thunder.

RrrrrrRRrrrr.

His mind went back to Arthur. It had all happened so fast. That wolf
damn near took the other man's head off. Internal decapitation. *The way his
head just flopped over, then . . . fell.* A puppet, its strings cut.

Then—

Wham.

The door rattled. Gumball yelped, backing up. Matthew looked to the
old windows, sure that they wouldn't hold against the wolf. Again the beast
hit the door: *wham.* It shuddered in its frame. Another hit. A fourth time. A
fifth! Each time rust and dust streamed from the hinges. On the sixth impact, he heard a *crackling* like a bone slowly breaking—and he saw that the
bar across the door had begun to buckle and splinter. One more hit and it'd
be over.

He waited for the next assault.

He waited and waited. Gumball trotted up next to him, the dog's head
pointed forward, hackles up, ready to fight. Time stretched out between
them like a widening chasm. Minutes. An hour. Then two . . .

Was she gone? Were they safe? Gumball stayed at the ready.

Matthew watched the windows, then the door, then he began to imagine, *what if Leela comes up through the floor, like a shark,* but that wasn't a
thing, this wasn't *Jaws,* she was a wolf, and a sick one at that. But sick with
what? Something unnatural. Something he didn't understand.

But he knew who *would* understand it.

Benji.

44

THE DINER AT THE END OF
THE UNIVERSE

The History of every major Galactic Civilization tends to pass through three distinct and recognizable phases, those of Survival, Inquiry and Sophistication, otherwise known as the How, Why, and Where phases.

For instance, the first phase is characterized by the question "How can we eat?" the second by the question "Why do we eat?" and the third by the question "Where shall we have lunch?"

—Douglas Adams, *The Restaurant at the End of the Universe*

OCTOBER 4, 2025
East of Taos, New Mexico

BENJI PARKED THE SOLAR NISSAN OFF ON THE SHOULDER OF THE INTERSEC-tion at Highway 64 and Marina Way. Given how dry the salt flats were here, it was a little off-putting to see any road identifying a *marina* nearby, but in the distance they could see the gleaming line of a lake or reservoir. (A nearby sign said the lake was called Eagle Nest.) Ahead of them, distant mountains looked like paper cutouts. The sky was split in twain: One half was dark from a storm, where the rain came down in gray, ghostly columns. The other half was blue-jeans blue.

South of here was, supposedly, a magical mystery diner.

In the middle of nowhere.

At the end of the world.

Advertised on the radio by an old friend of theirs.

"This is a thing that feels like a trap," Benji said.

"But can't be a trap," Shana added, finishing his thought. "Can it?"

"Well. It *could* still be a trap, just not one designed specifically for us."

"Yeah, but that's how it feels. A trap made just for us. Artisanal, bespoke, handcrafted, locally sourced us-trap."

Benji hmmed. "But why would that be?" *And how?*

"Man, I dunno. Because we're very important people? Because Black Swan is god now? Because we lost our minds and this is our crazy-headed hell?"

"All perfectly viable explanations," he said, words salted with a wry sprinkling of humor.

"I want to go."

"I do, too, Shana."

"But I don't know if it's safe." She stiffened. "And we don't have the time. We need to keep moving. Don't we? Baby Charlie, he . . . he needs me. And the way he grew so fast inside me—if he's still growing like that . . ." The words died in her mouth. She blinked back tears.

Benji knew she was right. They had to keep moving. And they couldn't risk the time on something that could be a danger. Even if that *was* Pete Corley on the radio. And maybe it wasn't. Maybe it was . . . some kind of deepfake of the voice.

(The station was back to playing music. Current song? Jimmy Ruffin, "I've Passed This Way Before.")

Just as he was about to say something, though, his eye caught something in the rearview mirror.

A vehicle.

A truck, by the look of it. A tractor trailer.

"Shana," he said, turning around and pointing. "We have company."

"Company? *People?* Oh, shit." She turned and looked, too. Her face mirrored what he was feeling: There shined a mad combination of abject panic and hopeful desperation. The need to connect with other human beings contrasted with the absolute fear of other human beings. "You think it's okay?"

"I wager we're about to find out."

The truck front was boxy and black, like a mastiff's head. It was blasted with dust, salt, and other road debris. The truck cab pulled what looked to be a dented, rickety single-axle pup trailer, which meant it was smaller than your average semi-trailer. The truck ambled past them at a good clip, but then just after, Benji saw brake lights followed swiftly by the squeal of brake hydraulics.

The truck slowed to a stop about fifty, sixty feet past them. Dust stirred and plumes of exhaust drifted across the dead road like ghosts. The engine rumbled. Growling like a still beast, considering if its hunger necessitated attack.

Benji's blood went cold.

"Benji," Shana said, her voice low. "We should get out of here."

The driver's-side door of the truck cab popped open.

With a stab of his thumb, Benji turned the Leaf on—but it had to go through its startup cycle, all its electronic whirs and dings and songs. *Shit. Too slow.*

A man, round like a barrel, with a red-and-gray beard dangling from his face like Spanish moss from a tree in Savannah, hopped down and gave them a wave with one hand while pulling off his orange Kubota cap with the other. He was balding and shook sweat from his hat with a few whiplike shakes.

At his side hung a blunted leather holster. Too big for any kind of pistol or revolver. Instead Benji saw what looked like the wooden grip of a short, chopped-down shotgun. Benji's nerves sparked.

It struck him now: The man looked a little like Ozark Stover. Not all the way. Less mountain, more hill. But the memory of the one man ghosted into the other.

"Howdy!" the trucker called.

Shana and Benji looked to each other. Her face said it plain enough: *Dude, I dunno.* Benji leaned out the shattered window.

"Hello," he answered back.

"Nice setup, if you don't mind me saying," the man hollered. "Solar. Huh."

Benji's trust was in disarray. He wanted to trust this person but knew that people out here might want to do them harm—and they sometimes would be savvy enough to pretend to be benevolent strangers instead of predators. This car alone was enough for someone to want to steal it. And to do anything they could *to* steal it. That shotgun would make short, bloody work of them.

Next to him, Shana had her camera out. She was leaning into it, over the dashboard. Her finger clicked, snapping a photo of the man and the truck. Rude, probably, but Benji didn't blame her for wanting to record the world. She did it when they were Shepherds with the Flock. Why not now, when everything had fallen apart—and maybe, just maybe, was putting itself back together again?

"If you'll forgive me, how do I know to trust you?" Benji asked the truck driver. He felt that it was best to be plainspoken out here.

"Oh! Well. You don't. Hell, I don't blame you. Bit strange out here. But this part of the state is pretty safe. Civilized still. Usually." The man, still yelling, pointed farther down the highway. "I'm heading on to Mother's, about five miles thatta way. If you care to head that way, too."

"Mother's?" Shana asked Benji.

He shrugged. Maybe it was the same place as Mother Road Diner. Proper name versus a nickname.

"All right," Benji said. "Thank you!"

"All right!" the man called. "You have a great day. Maybe we'll talk over a plate of breakfast pig."

And then the big fella hauled himself back up into the truck. The engine hissed and rumbled once more, and the brakes disengaged with a coyote bark. Then the big rig rolled on down the road, pokey at first, but picking up speed.

Soon it was gone, leaving more dust in its wake. A whorl of it through the curtain of mirror heat haze.

"I guess there are still trucks, somehow," Shana said.

"Trucks and people to drive them." *Maybe the world isn't all the way broken,* Benji thought.

"That's nice. I don't understand it. But it's nice." Shana drummed her fingers on the dash. "I almost feel like we should've talked to him?"

"Same. I'd like to hear how exactly he's driving that thing. What's the fuel source? Gasoline should be done for. Diesel, too, especially out here in the heat." Benji mused that in colder climes, with regular dosing of stabilizer, diesel could go five, maybe ten years. But not here. "I guess we still can talk to him. If we want."

"As long as we head to the diner, you mean."

"Correct."

She visibly tensed. "I don't want to waste the time. I want to keep moving. But . . ." She sighed. "It sounds like it could be safe."

"And we do need to eat. Plus the car could charge in the meantime."

"Okay," she said, seemingly resolved to it. "*Okay.*"

"You're sure?"

"Let's not keep chitchatting about it. Punch it, Chewie, I'm hungry."

Benji did his best Chewbacca growl, which was easily the worst Chewbacca growl, before easing the Leaf back onto the highway, diner-bound.

•   •   •

The Mother Road Diner.

It looked like someone had taken a regular diner—with the blocky Pepto Bismol walls, strips of corroded chrome along its roofline, a once-neon sign saying DINER towering tall above it—and grafted other *parts* onto it. In front was an outdoor structure of reclaimed wood. Along the side were a few fuel tanks and generators. And out back was what looked like a flea market, with long lines of sun-beaten tables, most unattended, a few that were. Some tables had things laid out or piled up on them, though Benji couldn't tell what yet. Out back beyond *that* was an array of solar panels ringed by tree-like cactuses. Cane cholla, if he remembered correctly. Standing vigil like janky scarecrows.

The wooden extension was built into the front row of parking spaces. So there were more parking spots around the side and opposite to the fuel tanks. Still other folks seemed to have parked along the road.

Benji counted seven vehicles, not including their own. Once upon a time that wouldn't have been in any way exciting or interesting to him. He couldn't tell a Toyota from a Honda from a Subaru. Now, though, he noted how each car was different. Some were more beat up than others, and each seemed to be rigged up in its own way. No spikes out the front or sides, no claw metal coming out of wheel hubs, no machine gun placements like you'd see in, say, Afghanistan or Iraq during the heights of their respective conflicts. This was a softer, kinder *Mad Max* world. Instead of brutal apocalyptic accoutrements, it was just a lot of *gear:* roof-top storage, water jugs strung along the side of an SUV with polyester cord, trunks open or removed entirely, the entire backs of vehicles stacked with gear stashed in padlocked pet cages. This reminded him a bit of his time in parts of Africa, or even in the Australian bush: Sometimes you had to take a lot with you, more than a car or truck could accommodate.

So you improvised. And these vehicles, they were improvised. It was survival, yes. But it was clever. Resourceful. It was what the future needed to be.

Parked along the far side of the diner was the big rig. Beyond that sat a motorcycle—a real chopper-type with the long forks and the high handlebars. His body almost visibly twitched at the absurd hope it belonged to Pete Corley. He missed Pete. Once upon a time, he really hated that mad bastard—Corley was an ego-fed avatar of chaos incarnate, and if myths were told of this era, he'd easily be the Coyote character, the Loki, a drunk Irish rock-and-roll Bugs Bunny.

But over time, Benji grew to consider him a good friend. Like he had with Shana. They were all so different. And yet, they worked. But losing Pete had felt like losing a limb. If he was here . . .

He knew Shana would welcome seeing Pete again, too. They had a special connection. Whether it was the art, the chaos, or what, he didn't know.

"This is it," Shana said.

He didn't yet park, but instead slowed the car to a stop out front of it.

"Do we go in?"

"We have to."

"But do you want to?"

"I do," she said. "But also I'm freaking the fuck out."

He nodded. "I am, too, a little." His pulse was elevated. He felt a little clammy. Chest a bit tight. He wasn't subject to panic attacks often, but had them once in a while—everybody did, even when they didn't recognize it. Ouray had been safe. But out here, people could be—what? A bunch of Ozark Stovers running around? Free rein to brutalize whoever didn't look like them. Then the other question: Could Benji be wrong? Could White Mask still be out here?

"Counterpoint," Shana said. "Pancakes."

"Pancakes *are* a powerful motivator."

"And a universal equalizer. Everybody likes pancakes."

"I'm parking?"

"You're parking."

He found a spot along the road to the west of the diner and parked. It wasn't the ideal spot: It was strange to think about parking spots at the end of the world, but from here he couldn't see the car from the road, and if this was some kind of trap, it was foolish to think they wouldn't steal their ride, either as their own or to butcher for parts. It was a risk. He knew it.

But like Shana said, pancakes.

And he really wanted to talk to that trucker.

And he really, *really* hoped Pete Corley was in there right now.

Together, they got out of the car. It felt like jumping off a cliff. He just hoped the water below was cool and deep, and not full of sharp rocks.

THE AIR WAS HOT AND dry, a desert vampire trying to stick in a straw and suck the moisture right out of them.

Together they headed to the front of the diner. The entrance was through that ramshackle wooden structure—something that seemed to serve almost as a gateway. To what purpose, though? Soon, they found out.

A man sat in the shade of it in a folding metal chair. He was top-heavy, with a lumpy paunch and big arms in a sweat-browned T-shirt. His hips and legs were small, though, making him look cartoonish. He lifted the brow of his sun hat. Small dark eyes nestled in bronzed skin looked up at them.

"S'up?" he asked, a Mexican-American accent mingling with Texan. "If you're coming in, you need to submit to a pat-down. You okay with that?"

Benji and Shana looked to each other. "Sure," she said.

"And if you find something?" Benji asked, realizing the question sounded vaguely like a threat, though it was truly just curiosity.

"You either leave, or you gimme the weapon till you come back out."

"We don't have any weapons," Shana said, giving Benji a quick wtf-dude-be-cool look.

The man stood up, and when he did, it was plain to see the pair of holsters: one black fabric holster at his ankle, another leather one hanging at his side. He yawned, then asked Benji to lift his arms. The man took a pair of rough hands and did an effective pat-down, like you'd get at the airport, or a concert. *Back when those things existed*, Benji thought, and for a moment he could smell an airport Cinnabon wafting its narcotic scent out, and that memory—or, perhaps, the loss of it—burned like a splash of acid.

"I'm Benji," he said, feeling like . . . well, like he should introduce himself. It wasn't often he met new people out here in the world. It seemed rude to somehow go without that most basic of connections. Back in the old world, the one that fell, people didn't even want to make eye contact most of the time. He certainly didn't. People were a thing he mostly wanted to get away from. Now, his need for this simplest aspect of human contact felt urgent. Desperate, even. "Benji Ray."

"Chick Arango," the man said without hesitation.

"Chick. That's quite a name. Bet there's a story there."

"There is, but I'm not going to tell it to you."

"Okay." Awkwardly, Benji said, "Great."

"This your first time here, I'm guessing."

"That obvious?"

"It is. So. You go in. You meet Johnny at the counter by the door. You want to go in, you need something to trade, because we're a trading post, too—and I don't know if you noticed, but green money's not too good out here anymore for anything other than burning. Don't have anything to trade, you can trade work."

"That feels like it's ripe for exploitation and uneven distribution."

"Probably, but if you got a better system, Mister Nobel Prize in Eco-fuckinomics, you let Dot know, okay? I mean, maybe you got some Bitcoin on you. I'm sure that bullshit still exists. Just log on and upload some of that imaginary chocolate money and have yourself a plate of eggs and bacon, yeah?"

"Point taken. Thanks."

Chick rolled his eyes. He took a sip from a dusty plastic water bottle before saying, "Look, I'm sorry. It's a hot dry day and my feet itch and I didn't sleep last night because there's a coyote somewhere outside my trailer who is trying to make a love connection or some shit, so I'm cranky. Hope you get a meal and it's a good one. And don't forget the trading tables out back, too. Don't fuck with us. Welcome to Mother's."

SHANA STOOD BACK WHILE BENJI walked up to the counter. It was made of a few rolls of chain-link fence stretched end to end and layered one on top of the other to form a cage-like wall. The window and a shallow plank counter was cut into the wall. An older white man—Johnny, apparently—stood behind it, his body knotted and frayed like a hangman's rope. Every inch of his sun-battered skin was inked: a red baby devil with a cutie-patootie pitchfork; a cartoon wolf with its eyes and tongue popping out like hubba-hubba; couple of Sailor Jerry swallows with names inked underneath them. At least she didn't see any creepy Nazi shit. She hoped she never saw any of that again.

Johnny gruffly told Benji, "One person at the counter only," then pointed to a pair of framed-out blackboards hanging behind him, on which were chalked the diner's needs, and the diner's no-nos.

On the chalkboard of needs:

ingredients (veg in particular, spices always)
whetting stones
pipe (copper/PVC/no lead)
"new" microwave
new boning knife
rechargeable batteries (AA)

vinyl records for rock-ola luxury light-up
WD-40 / duct tape (always & 4eva)
Books 4 lib
as always, FRESH WATER H20—el agua es vida!!

And on the chalkboard of don't-needs:

fuel (any kind)
ammo / guns
goats (what is it with the fn goats??)
most kitchen equipment (our cast iron is immortal)
"favors" (fuck off)
that thing you think is valuable BUT ISN'T!!

Some of that, Shana didn't expect. They needed books, but not fuel? Records, but not ammunition? Huh.

While Benji stepped to the counter to talk to the strip of dusty beef jerky posing as a human being, she headed back to Chick.

Chick gave her a once-over. Not in a sexy, objectifying way, but like he was measuring her for Apocalypse Readiness. (Either that, or he was irritated by her presence.)

"What *is* it with the goats?" she asked him.

"Huh? Oh. Goats do pretty well out here and everybody and their cousins have been raising them. For milk mostly. Cheese, butter. Sometimes meat. But because everybody has goats, they always wanna *trade* goats, or the milk, *or* the butter, and we're done with it. Too much goat." He made a face. "Gamy meat anyway. Unless they're the *cabritos,* and I don't feel good about eating babies."

Babies. Jesus, how stupid was her brain? He's talking about eating baby goats but all it took was for him to say that word, *babies,* and here she was, thinking about her own child. *I miss you, Charlie . . .* This was all for a purpose, she reminded herself. To reclaim Charlie, they had to get rid of the machine.

Chick kept talking: "The goats, they're like alpacas at this point. Pyramid scheme. Best reason to have a goat is to sell it to someone who you can trick into selling goats. An empire of goats."

"It's like that with chickens where I come from. Turns out, without people to wrangle them, chickens breed like—"

"Like wet gremlins," he said knowingly.

"I saw that movie. My dad loved it, made me watch it."

"Oh, it's a fuckin' great movie. The second one's even crazier. It's like if
the first movie got high as hell on some weapons-grade cheeba."

She sighed wistfully. "Movies. Remember movies? They were fun."

"Still are."

"What?"

"I mean, they're not *gone* gone. Guy I know, real cinephile type, Robby
Cargo, he set up a drive-in on the east side of Taos. He makes his own beer
and whiskey so it gets pretty raucous, you know. Last week they were showing one of the Evil Deads, and ahhh, fuck, what's the movie with Schwar-
zenegger?"

She shrugged. *"Kindergarten Cop?"*

"No, no, fuck, he's got the fuckin' face paint and the—*Commando!*"

"That's cool, I haven't seen a movie since—"

But now, Benji was walking up behind her, saying, "Excuse me," to
Chick, and to her, "Hey. We can trade some food if we want. That or we can
each work a shift. Kitchen or waitstaff, they have slots open. They also have
beds for the night in some trailers just down the highway. Walkable."

"It's not even five minutes," Chick said. "Real beds. Not real bathrooms,
though, still gotta use one of the compost johns or outhouses."

"Can we afford to give up food?" she asked.

"It's food in return for food. Helps them, helps us. But we could also
work a shift if you don't mind being in one place for a day or two."

But at that idea, a fire of fear lit in her belly. A day or two delay was a day
or two more she wasn't back in Ouray, seeing her son. The mission. The
purpose. They couldn't delay. "We can give up the food."

"All right," he said, heading back to the counter.

As she started to turn around, the thought hit her, *Pete, I should ask
Chick about Pete,* and she was about to open her mouth and ask, but she saw
something out of the corner of her eye—a vehicle had slowed outside the
diner, creeping down the highway before picking back up and gunning it.
Through the doorway she could only see its bumper, and by the time she
poked her head out, it was already heading on down the road, fast, lost in a
plume of dust and exhaust. But she was sure as hell it looked familiar. Not in
a good way.

"That an SUV?" she asked Chick.

"Huh? Maybe."

"Like, a black SUV, Ford Explorer?"

"Hey, I really don't know."

"How do you not know? Isn't it weird seeing cars out here?"

He shrugged. "No? Not really. Taos is only fifteen miles that way. Other three directions you got some ranches, some gas wells, and the like. This isn't a dead place. Old Route 66 is kicking more now than it was back when, you know?"

"Uh-huh," she said idly. She was *sure* that was the black Ford SUV from Colorado. But those freaks wouldn't have followed them here, would they? *Could* they? That didn't even seem possible. She was either just imagining it or it was some other utility vehicle. A black, beat-up SUV wasn't a unicorn. And it wasn't like she could really tell a Ford from a Chevy from a whatever.

Then, Benji was behind her again. "Food for food it is. Want to help me get some of it from the car? They need vegetables and we have some from Montrose."

"Sure," she said, wondering if she should tell Benji. But Shana decided against it. She was just seeing things. That was easy out here, she figured. Everything a shadow, everything a mirage.

45

EL KABONG

9/30/2022: Heading northward, through New England, to beat the linger-
ing heat. See the leaf colors. An absurd thought, maybe. To want to watch
the leaves change in this ruined place. But why not find beauty? Nothing
else really matters. What's left is what we have. Might as well appreciate it.
                              —from A Bird's Story, A Journal of the Lost

OCTOBER 4, 2025
East of Taos, New Mexico

IT WAS A DINER, BUT ALSO, IT WASN'T. IF YOU SQUINTED, IT WAS ALL DINER,
and easy to imagine that's all it was and all it ever had been. But the moment
you opened your eyes wide, you saw all the bits that didn't belong: Yes, there
was a long counter with checkerboard tile top, and behind it you had a coffee
maker and a window into the kitchen, but you also had rows of booze next to
a locked metal-mesh cabinet containing radios, car batteries, first-aid kits,
rope. On the counter itself was a wooden crate of what looked to be random
penknives. Along the right side of the room was a Rock-Ola Jukebox currently spinning Eddie Holland, "Leaving Here." And a glass-front cabinet
stuffed with books, mostly classic paperbacks. Above that, a pair of hand-
painted signs in the same handwriting from the chalkboards that read,
BOOKS ARE A UNIQUELY PORTABLE MAGIC, STEPHEN KING. Second
sign read, SO TAKE SOME MAGIC, LEAVE SOME MAGIC. The booths were a mix:
Some looked like they matched the original establishment, others were different colors, upholstered with different materials, and of different sizes to
the tables they butted up against. Was a lot of strange taxidermy (a squirrel
with antlers, a marlin in a net despite being nowhere near the ocean, an owl
in a fez smoking a cigarillo). Next to the befezzed owl was a sign, ASK US

ABOUT OUR POTABLE WATER! And catty-corner to that, another sign, which had a partner toward the back: SHENANIGANS WILL BE PUN-ISHED.

The crowd, though—well, the crowd was a diner crowd. Little rougher around the edges, maybe, not in attitude, but in just the general scruff and road dirt. When Benji and Shana came in, all eyes found them, but none seemed threatening. They earned a few smiles, head nods, even a wave from a woman with low, sad eyes and whose straw-blond hair was ringed in a crooked crown upon her head.

To Benji it reminded him of bars he'd been to in Bago, in Addis Ababa, or the outskirts of Cartagena—those places, you could stop to get a drink, buy a cellphone, hire a fisherman. You might meet an old friend there, or a Cold War spy, or a washed-up DJ chasing the dragon. It was a janky, jury-rigged end-of-days diner, equal parts Rick's Café Américain, the Tatooine cantina, and the Tip Top Café from *Groundhog Day*. A place to buy a blintz, a gun, a monkey.

A waitress came up. She looked Native, maybe. About Nessie's age, Benji figured. Wore a T-shirt painted with the Mother's sign from out front, and a sticky-note name tag that read NASCHA. She shrugged and said, "You can sit anywhere. Today's menu's on the wall behind you. You want coffee?"

Benji's heart was a bird stirred to flight. "You have *coffee*?"

The girl, looking suddenly trapped by the question, curled her lip in an uncertain sneer. "It's not good coffee. It's the instant crystal stuff. And only one cup per, no pot." Under her breath she grumbled, "Everyone asks for a pot."

"We want coffee," Benji said. "Whatever you can spare is great."

He gave a look to Shana. He had no idea what the look even was, only that it was *a definite look*. She laughed at him and said, "Your face is the face of a kid who just entered a room full of puppies and tricycles. And maybe puppies riding tricycles. You love coffee, huh?"

They found a two-top near the door and sat. "You have no idea. Shana, it was one of the great pleasures of my life. The ritual of preparing it alone is a loss so profound I feel it every morning, like an old injury."

"I get it. I still wanna scroll Instagram every morning. My thumb even wants to make the motion."

"Sometimes I don't miss the old world. And I confess," he said, almost afraid to say the words, "I enjoy the peace that this new world provides. It's simpler. Like this place. But coffee is a loss. And don't even get me started on chocolate. I wouldn't *not* club you with this metal napkin dispenser for a bar of good dark chocolate."

She shrugged. "See, I'd murder your ass for Skittles."

"Well, now, I didn't say *murder*, I just mentioned a casual bludgeoning. You're the one who had to upgrade it to murder."

The two of them smiled at each other. Benji felt an odd surge of emotion at that. Strange how that happened. He cared about Shana quite deeply. It occurred to him: She'd lost a father and he'd never been one. He wasn't her father, and she probably didn't view him that way. But in a way, they could pretend.

Nascha returned with two mismatched mugs (one said WORLD'S GREAT-EST FATHER but the FATHER was scratched out and replaced with FARTER, whereas the other just had a pelican and the phrase EFFIN' BIRDS). In them, coffee steamed. Benji hovered over it like a dragonfly above a lake, just taking it in. He took a sip: It nearly burned his mouth. In any other lifetime, he knew this would taste like the ghost of coffee filtered through a pair of well-used gardening gloves, but in *this* lifetime, *right now*, it tasted like the best thing he'd ever put in his mouth.

"You guys know what you want?" the waitress—even the thought of that, *Oh my God, a waitress!* felt indulgent and insane—asked.

"We should look at the menu," he said, feeling silly they hadn't. Another artifact of the old world: going into a restaurant and failing to look at a menu by the time the waitress asked.

"Before we do, hey," Shana said to her, "you know a guy named Pete Corley? I think he recorded the ad that played on the radio."

The girl shrugged. "I dunno. Maybe? I'm just here working a shift for a meal. I don't know much about the ins and outs. You can ask Dot, though, when she gets back. Or Paulo, or Oscar, the cooks, when they're on break. Anyway, I'll give you a minute to look at the menu." In a lower, slightly irritated voice she said, "It's only five things. So." Then she was gone.

They turned around to study the menu. It was, as advertised, only five things from across all three meals:

Green chile omelette with home fries
Blue corn pancakes with agave syrup
Mixed meat hamburger on fry bread
Bean sopapillas and pozole
Javelina adovada over wild rice

"I want it all," Shana said.

"I'm hungry enough to eat the chalkboard."

"I think pancakes. I think it *has* to be pancakes. God, I don't even know what time it is. Or what meal. Is it breakfast? Lunch?"

"Brunch. Linner. Doesn't matter. We live on interstitial time, between the cracks of hours. You get the pancakes. I'll have the hamburger." His mind wandered to the hamburger that would come. He didn't know what mix the meat was, and didn't care. And didn't matter that it came on fry bread and not a bun. Even better. A classic American food on a truly Native American bread. Old world, new world, and now, the new-*new* world. Reboot, remix, amen.

As Benji dreamed about hamburgers, Shana dreamed about pancakes.

And it was this dream that made her miss what was coming.

As she was preoccupied, thinking about food, someone new came in through the door—someone lean, with filthy jeans and a threadbare white sleeveless shirt under a raggedy blue windbreaker. He was young, not much older than she was, with a shock of hair in a clumsy, unintentional faux-hawk, and he turned toward their table—

His eyes grew wide as he saw them.

And only then did Shana realize . . .

Last time she saw him, he had red clay all over his face. Most of it was gone now, though flecks of it crusted the corners of his mouth, eyes, and nose.

The bandit bared filthy teeth—

And leapt, as Shana screamed.

The bandit clubbed Benji in the side of the head with a clumsy fist, then wrapped his hands around Benji's throat. Shana leapt out of her seat, rushing toward him, but he was like a wild animal lost to the throes of a feral rage, and he kicked out at her, catching her in the solar plexus with a hard boot—the air clapped out of her and she staggered backward. Benji thrashed, his eyes bugging, and he pawed around the table for something, anything, his hands nearing the cutlery—

Just as his hand found a steak knife, the attacker let go of his throat and grabbed Benji's wrist, forcing the knife up toward his face, toward his *eye*—closer, closer, *the tip hovering* right there at the cornea.

Shana got back on her feet, roaring in a rage—

A shadow rose behind their table. Then came a swift movement and something swished through the air and a—holy shit, a *tiny guitar* crashed down on the assailant's head, shattering into splinters, strings gone akimbo as it made a comical *gwong* sound. The attacker let go of Benji, stumbling sideways before collapsing into a pair of stools that refused to hold up his weight.

"Bloody fuck, my uke!" Pete Corley said, standing there in the doorway next to their table, the bridge of what was once a ukulele in his hand. Strings dangled from it like the tentacles of a dead robot squid.

"Holy shit," Shana said, breathless.

Pete turned toward her, and it was like the scales fell from his eyes, the revelation upon him. "Shana?" Then: *"Benji?"*

"Hi, Pete," Benji said, voice raw, rubbing his neck.

At that, Pete cackled and helped the other man up before sweeping them both into a bony, broad-armed hug. "Fucking hell, the band's back together!"

46

WHAT TO DO ABOUT RIVER WATER

10/2/2022: Met a man named Harry Kulak today. The King of Landfill City is what he calls himself. He used to run this facility, the Fitchburg Landfill. Said they received a half-a-million tons of refuse every year. "It's amazing what people threw away," he said. Food, yes, but that wasn't useful. "It's whole objects. Entire pieces of furniture. Electronics that worked, or with parts that were still good. Tools. Nails. Screws. Wire. Toys. Everything and anything. We burned a lot of it but there's still so much here," he said, sweeping his arms around like it truly was his kingdom, a kingdom of divine detritus. I said, this place is poison. You can smell it in the air, see it in the puddles. I asked if he worried about getting cancer, and to that he just laughed. "Get cancer? Everything is cancer now. I might as well be cancer, too."

—from A Bird's Story, A Journal of the Lost

OCTOBER 4, 2025
Ouray, Colorado

MARCY WAS FEELING A CERTAIN *WAY* ABOUT THINGS. SHE SAT AT THE DESK IN her office inside the old police station. She chewed on some sunflower seeds, picking the shells carefully out of her mouth instead of spitting them to keep from making a mess. Because not making a mess was important to her. Which was part of the problem, and why she felt a certain *way* about things.

Ouray had some *mess*. And, ostensibly, it was her job to clean it up. But that was a task far easier to imagine than it was to complete.

The mess required untangling. But she didn't know where to begin, and didn't know what she'd find—or worse, what she'd *do*—once the act of untangling was over. Yesterday, Claudia had told her that there was a rebellion afoot. Some kind of mutiny, an *insurrection*. Marcy had poked around a little over the course of the last twenty-four hours and sure enough, there were some folks gathering at the glass studio in the north of town. Shades down, door locked. Night fell and they were still there, just the flickering glow of a lamp there.

But that didn't mean anything.

And it wasn't like she trusted Claudia, either. That one was spooky. She had eyes like fingers, picking you apart. When Claudia looked at her, Marcy felt as if she was working her like a Rubik's Cube, just turning her end over end, lining up all her squares and colors till she was laid bare. Did Claudia know? That Marcy let Benji and Shana go? She couldn't have. And yet . . .

Funny thing, that. Talk of a rebellion forming, and what had Marcy done? She had rebelled. Her orders had been clear that day. So why'd she do differently? She stood defiant in the river. Refused to let it take her.

Would Joey, her brother, have approved?

They didn't get along much, her and her brother. He didn't like that she was a cop. He'd been arrested a few times for a few things, never anything serious, an ounce of weed here, a drunken outburst there. She always told him, *You're making your own bed, Joey, not my fault you have to sleep in it.* But now, in this very moment, she thought back to the time she was giving him an earful about something he'd done—might've been when he kicked over a neighbor's arborvitaes. (He was pissed they called the cops on a big party he had.) Marcy had done him a favor, asked the cops to just give him a warning. And they did. Which he didn't even appreciate! So she stood there in the kitchen, was telling him that the law was the law and it was his choice to break it.

He said, "Marce, just because it's a law doesn't mean it's *right*." Joey wasn't an idiot. He wasn't just some dipshit slacker. Well, okay, he *was*, but he was a well-studied one. Joey read a lot of books and took a crack at community college a few times, thinking he was going to be a writer or something. So when she asked him what the hell he was talking about, he said, "The rules of the state aren't automatically moral because they're rules. Right and wrong doesn't come from a lawbook or a courtroom. You don't have to just *go along with it.*"

And she was like, *Shut up, Joey.* She told him that all his high-minded chatter didn't matter. The laws were the laws whether he felt they were right or righteous or whatever. You followed them so you didn't get in trouble. And she upheld them because that was what upheld society.

It was the backbone of civilization.

He told her to fuck off, and she left, and then Mom sided with Joey because Mom always sided with Joey. And Joey always sided with Mom.

Now, though, sitting here with sunflower seeds between her teeth, Marcy wondered if he had a point. Certainly he got arrested for having weed, which these days—well, the days before White Mask, anyway—was legal in most states. So, how could it be wrong then, but right now? Maybe the answer was that it was never really wrong at all? Huh.

That in turn made her think about Ouray.

It made her think of Black Swan.

It made her think of the Glow.

She felt it, even now. The Glow. It wasn't everywhere, but it pulsed gently from the chalet where Nessie had Baby Charlie. It gave her light. It gave her *life*. She felt good about it and sure that her faith in this experiment was not misplaced.

And yet, she let Benji and Shana go.

And yet, she hadn't hunted for Matthew like she was told to.

And yet, she could no longer ignore the sick feeling that was pooling in her gut like a puddle of pig shit.

It was then that a knock came to her door. She looked up—the door had glass in it—and saw who was standing there.

Holy shit.

Holy fucking shit.

Matthew Bird stood there, looking like a trailer park after a tornado ripped through it. He was filthy, his hair in a tangle, a thin and scraggly beard hanging on his face. She stood up and waved him in, realizing that she didn't have a gun handy—she never replaced the one that she gave to Benji, and suddenly that made her feel foolish. *But you won't really need to shoot him, will you?*

She hoped like hell she wouldn't have to answer that question.

Matthew came in, but he didn't come in alone.

A golden retriever plodded in after him. The animal was in need of some grooming, but had clearly been taken care of—he had been combed or brushed at least, even if his fur had a few snarls and knotted twig-bits in it.

The dog sat down in front of her desk like he was here for a meeting. Matthew, too, closed the door behind him and locked it.

Then he pulled up a chair and sat down in it.

His hands were shaking.

"Where's Benji?" he asked.

"Hello to you, too," Marcy said, her voice sounding far away.

"Hi, Marcy."

She sat there for longer than she meant to. It was hard to find words, or even make sense of her feelings. Part of her wanted to choke him. Part of her wanted to hug him. *Maybe I can hug him to death,* she idly considered.

They started to speak at the same time:

"I'm sorry for leaving you in a bind—" he said at the same time she said:

"You messed up, put us in a real damn pickle, Matthew—"

They both stopped talking and stared.

She began again. "You messed *everything* up."

"I know." He blinked away tears. "I get it. I hurt people—"

"Matthew. You *killed* someone."

"I know. I know! I shouldn't have. But something had gone wrong in there, Marcy. And now something has gone wrong out *there*. In the wild."

"What?"

"Something happened, I— Look, where's Benji? He'll know what to do."

"Matthew, Benji's gone. He and Shana left not long after you did. What is going on? What has gone wrong in the—in the wild? What are you talking about?"

He exhaled a sigh of what felt like impatience.

"A disease. Like White Mask. Maybe it is, maybe it evolved—" Here his hands started frittering about in the air like stirred birds. "Maybe it's something else, something new. But one of the wolves came down with it—"

"The wolves."

"Leela. It was Leela. There was . . . I don't know, an infection, but not? Something was growing out of her. Hairs, but not hairs. Like metal *threads*—"

The golden retriever whined and rested its head on Matthew's knee.

He stopped talking and looked up at Marcy. "You think I'm nuts."

"I dunno, Matthew. This is pretty weird stuff."

"Says the sheriff of a town governed by a godlike computer swarm."

"Fair point. I just mean—you've been gone a little over two weeks and you don't look good. Then you come in, spewing this . . . stuff."

"The wolf killed Arthur. The man Benji sent me to meet? Killed him, killed the other wolf, too." In a lower, distracted voice he added, "Not sure about the fox . . ." He wiped away tears.

Marcy looked him up and down. "Benji sent you to meet—" It was then she understood. Benji did help him get away. Sent him to be with the strange man he'd met out there. Which meant he'd lied to her. She tried not to take that personally, but it was hard. "Of course. Jesus, Matthew. This is bad."

"This one isn't on Jesus, Marcy."

She let out her own impatient exhalation now. "Like I said, you're putting me in a helluva pickle. This town wants your head on a stick. They want you to stand trial for what you did. People died. Dove is dead, too."

"Dove. God." He exhaled. "What do you think should be done with me?"

Marce, just because it's a law doesn't mean it's right.

Shut up, Joey.

"Crap. Crap! I don't know."

"Are you going to turn me over to them?"

Again the dog whined.

"No," she said finally. "No, I'm not. But you can't be here! You have to *go*. Maybe, I dunno, you head up north, hide out in Ridgway or Montrose—"

"That wolf is still out there. It's sick. It's like it's rabid, but so much worse."

"I can handle that part. You need to—"

She was about to say *hide*, but then, outside the window of her door, a new face appeared. And with it, her heart sank.

Claudia waited behind the glass. Her face as dispassionate as a porcelain figurine. She didn't even look to Matthew. *Because she already knew he was here,* Marcy realized.

Stiffly, the woman tried the doorknob, then stared balefully at it.

Matthew startled. "Who is that?"

A problem, she thought. Instead, she stood up silently, went to the door, and unlocked it. "Claudia," she started to say.

"Congratulations," Claudia said. "You caught him and brought him in." The way she said it, though—was Marcy imagining things, or did it contain a hint of torment? The faintest tease, as if to say, *I know that's not what happened. But I've got you now.* "Well done. Would you like me to help you get him into the drunk tank cell? If the stories are right, he's been there before."

"I don't need help," Marcy said, trying to calm her nerves. And her anger.

"I'm your deputy. You should use my help."

"You're not my deputy."

"A question for the town council, then."

God, I hate you.

"I've got this. Go tell Xander."

"That, I can do." Then, she turned to leave, and over her shoulder said, "I hope this time you'll make sure he doesn't get away? Make sure there aren't any fire extinguishers around, Sheriff."

Claudia slid out the door, like a snake. One rattle-tail shake, then gone.

Matthew sat there, stunned. "What just happened? You're not going to—"

"I am going to. I can't *not* put you away now." Her hand formed a fist and she pressed one hard knuckle into the meat of her thigh. Enough to cause a starburst of pain there. "I have to do this. I'm sorry, Matthew. I'll see what I can do to make this work out. Maybe it's better you're in one place." She thought to tell him, *You should run now. I'll say I couldn't catch you.* But even that would be too neat a lie, and one they'd see through. She'd lose her role as sheriff. Nobody would respect her. They'd probably exile her. *I have to work within the system.*

The system her brother hated. A system of laws.

Matthew's shoulders slumped. The fight went out of him then—it was like watching someone's soul leave their body, a visible emptying-out of themselves.

He nodded and said, "You're right. I deserve this. Let's go."

The dog licked his hand as he stood up. He petted the dog and Marcy felt pulled along by the river of laws, the river of systems, and with that, she marched him out of her office and down toward the jail cell he already knew too well. Where the river would take them both next, she didn't know. But she feared its rapids.

47

CHICKENS AND BONES

Disaster shocks us out of slumber, but only skillful effort keeps us awake.
—Rebecca Solnit, *A Paradise Built in Hell*

OCTOBER 4, 2025
East of Taos, New Mexico

THEY STOOD TOGETHER OUT IN THE PARKING LOT OF THE DINER. THE BLOODY-headed bandit was just a kid. With some reluctance, he admitted his name was Josiah, and the young woman that Benji had clipped with the front end of his Nissan back in Colorado—the one who tried to lance their tires with a spear—was his girlfriend, Maybelle. Their two families hunted that part of Colorado as bandits and thieves, fancying themselves *liberators* of people's *worldly possessions*. He came here looking for Benji and Shana not to steal from them, but to get revenge, because he said they broke Maybelle's leg, and as the kid put it, "You break a leg these days, you're like a horse. They just shoot you."

Except, of course, Benji knew that was bullshit, and told him so.

"Yeah, you fuckin' dumbass," Corley said, whapping the kid on the upside of his brow as the aforementioned dumbass sat on the back of the Ford Explorer's bumper, holding a wet cloth to his blood-drooling, ukulele-interrupted brow. Behind the bandit lay Maybelle herself, who moaned and groaned, her leg swollen. At that, Corley's eyes cast toward the diner and he said, "Well, mate, you're extra-fucked now. Dot's coming."

Benji turned and looked to see a Black woman walking toward them in bold, slow strides. She wore a pink-and-orange boho midi dress, had her hair in a messy halo braid. Benji guessed she was in her late thirties, early forties.

She had a chef's knife in her hand.

That, he guessed, was Dot, the proprietor of this establishment.

She pointed it at the bandit. "Him? He the one who messed with the sanctity of my diner?" At that, she shot a look to Pete, who gave a sinister, happy nod. To the bandit, she asked, "Tell me which part you want me to cut off you before I send you on your way."

"Wh-what?" Josiah asked.

"You disrupted the peace. There's a price. I take something. You can make an offer, if you'd like, and I'll consider it. Nose? Ear? Pinky finger?" With each word, she drew whistling calligraphy in the air with the blade just inches in front of the bandit's face.

At that, Benji stepped in between the two. He introduced himself, then asked if he could speak to her. She eyed him up, and as she did, he couldn't help but think, *God, she's beautiful.* It was an uninvited thought, and one that fast felt like a betrayal. *Sadie. I'm sorry.*

"Sure," she said. The two of them took a short walk.

"YOU WANT TO SPARE HIM?" the woman asked, incredulous.

"I do." *I think.*

"Why?"

Benji relayed how the fool broke down, blubbering. Josiah said he was sorry, said it was because of Maybelle, sweet Maybelle, she was hurt, and he was mad, and there was all this snot and spit on his face, and blood growing thick and sticky in his hair and . . . Benji knew he'd regret it, but he asked what was going on, and if he could help. Sure enough, there was a woman in the back of their SUV. Maybelle, her leg broken.

"They attacked us but we . . . hurt her, in our escape. She needs help."

Dot looked at herself in the mirror of the knife. "But he didn't come here to get your help. He came here to get his revenge. And in doing so he upset my patrons."

"I understand, but—"

"What you need to understand, Benji Ray, is that I run this diner. It's the center of our little community here and in that sense, I am a community leader, and I cannot be seen to be weak on this or others will come. Others will cause chaos. Let that in, it's like letting in termites. Before you know it, the whole place is falling down around your ears, gone to splinters." She paused, flicking her gaze from the blade to him. "Justice keeps chaos at bay."

"But part of justice is also mercy."

"Mercy."

"We need mercy. Civilization needs mercy. Mercy can keep chaos at bay, too. I imagine a community leader can win some hearts showing compassion. The bandit didn't manage to hurt anyone. He wanted to hurt me, but I'm not, in the old parlance, pressing charges."

A little smile tugged at the corner of her mouth. "Okay, mercy. You're standing tall for that one, so be it. But he can't stay. You help quick, then they go. Deal?"

"Deal."

At that, Benji went back and got to work.

BENJI CRAWLED INTO THE BACK with Maybelle.

Pete told him, "Benji, hey, you don't have to do this, just toss the fucker"—*facker*, it sounded like, that little bit of Irish spice to his words—"out in the desert and let the coyotes have at 'im."

"Yeah, he tried to kill us," Shana reminded.

"*And* he fucked with the peace of my diner," Dot reminded again. "The diner's a safe place and you do not violate that. Don't make me tap the sign."

Pete repeated it: "Shenanigans *will* be punished. She means it."

But Benji said he could help, which meant he had to help. So he got to work, checking out the leg, seeing how bad the break was. He sent out Chick Aranga to bring back something that could be used as a splint—best he could come up with was a fence slat. Chick apologized to them all, though to Dot in particular. "I shouldn't have let that freak in. I got a bad vibe from him, like he was tweakin' or something. I shouldn't have let him in. That coulda gone sideways."

"It *did* go sideways," Dot reminded him. "Be sharper, Chick. Damn."

"Yeah, yeah. Sorry, boss."

"It's all right," Benji said from the back. "It's fine. Chick, nobody's upset with you." Then, in a lower voice, to Maybelle, he said, "I want you to roll up your shirt. From the bottom, like you're rolling up a poster. I can help. Then I want you to bite down on the fabric while I reset the leg. That okay?"

Maybelle, tears in her big doe eyes, nodded. Together, they did as he described, and she gently clamped her teeth down on the bundled shirt. Without an X-ray, Benji had no idea how bad the break was, but at least it wasn't a compound fracture, with the bone sticking out and all that. It was loose enough that it wasn't just hairline. Which meant he had to do *this*:

He felt around for the break—

It was still a bad one. The two halves of the leg seemed to *float* away from each other, loosey-goosey.

He locked eyes with her, forced a smile, and then—

Bone met bone as he moved the two broken ends together. He did it careful and he did it slow but he knew it hurt like hell, and he could feel the two ends click and grind together a bit inside her body—a feeling he felt up into his elbow.

Maybelle screamed around the bit-down roll of shirt.

Josiah started to panic, wanting to climb back in there with them, but thankfully the others were on top of that, dragging him back to his spectator seat on the vehicle's bumper.

Shana slid in the fence slat and the roll of duct tape. Benji used the slat and generous amounts of tape to splint the leg. The girl wept, but muscled through. She didn't pass out. Her screams were short. She was a survivor.

Benji supposed they all were.

Afterward, he clambered back out, sweating despite the dry heat wicking it away. Josiah asked him, genuine fear in his eyes. "She gonna be all right?"

He told Josiah, "It's not my first fracture reduction." *And, I fear, it won't be my last.* "She'll need more than what I've done here, though. If you can make it back to Colorado, Montrose has a clinic, though it's not always staffed. I can't speak to what's toward Denver, but Grand Junction has doctors."

"Taos has docs," Dot said.

"There you go. Taos. And it's close."

Josiah nodded. Mopishly, he added: "Thanks. And . . . sorry again for trying to kill you."

"And I'm sorry again for letting this asshole in," Chick said.

"You better be," Dot said, eyebrow arched. "But you can make it up to these nice people, you know."

"Howzat?"

"Oh. You know."

"Ugh, c'mon, Dot."

"Tell them."

"Tell us what?" Shana asked.

"Where his nickname comes from," Dot said, grinning like a fox.

"Ohh, ho ho ha," Pete said, clapping his hands. "This *is* a good story."

"It's not a good fucking story," Chick said.

"Tell us or there will be shame upon your house," Shana intoned with grave seriousness, as if she were cursing him with some kind of desert magic.

"Go on, mate, just tell it," Pete said.

"Fine. Shit. *Fine.*"

He told it.

"So ONE DAY, I WAKE up and go outside to head to work and there's a chicken in my yard. A rooster. Big bitch. White feathers and a red mohawk or whatever you call it. That rubbery floppy thing on their head. And I'm like, who cares, it's a chicken. This is before everything went to shit by the way. Anyway, so I'm going to my car, and this chicken moves around the side of it, plants itself by the driver's-side door. Starts making this low, threatening sound. Not the *bawk bawk* sound but like, a *rrrrr* sound, as close to a chicken growl as you get. And I'm like, shut up, fuckin' bird. So I try to shoo it away but it comes *at me*, flapping its wings, making that sound, *rrrr, rrrrrr* but finally I chase it off. Thing is, next morning, same thing happens. Except now the chicken is on my car hood, scratching it up with its little birdy talons, and pecking paint off with its beak. Still making that noise. I chase it away again. But every day, the chicken is back. I find it on my car. I find it in my backyard standing on my charcoal grill. I find it everywhere. Then one day it's in my house. *In my house.* I wake up and it's there on my counter. It took a shit there and stood over it, proud-ass cocky cockbird, and there's that noise again, that growl, and then I realize, *What the fuck, this chicken is the devil.* It's the God. Damn. Devil. I can see it. Its eyes are red. And I'm like, fuck. But I'm not gonna be humiliated in my own kitchen by no devil chicken, so I go after it with a skillet, but instead of running away it flies at my head, lands on my scalp, and it *digs the hell in.* Claws, man, chicken claws under my *skin.* I run outside, screaming, I got blood running down my head and the chicken now, it's doing more than just that growl, it's *ba-kawking* like it won, like this is its victory sound. I'm running around the cul-de-sac screaming and screaming. Neighbors are out of their houses, watching. Finally I drop the skillet, grab the stupid bird with both hands, and *chuck it* hard as I can. But because my name is Carlos and all my damn neighbors saw me running around with a chicken on my head, the nickname 'Chick' stuck. Couldn't shake the name same way I couldn't shake that goddamn fucking chicken. Shit."

•   •   •

BY NOW, PETE WAS CRYING laughing. Wheezing and guffawing. Shana was, too. And it was contagious because then Benji was laughing hard, harder, till he was doubled over. That, until he looked and saw Dot, who stood there with an amused smirk on her face. Watching him and nobody else.

He met her stare and smiled back, his laughs guttering like a flame.

Watching her watching him, he felt a stirring.

It occurred to him then that Dot was nothing like Sadie, not really—Sadie was a sharp, coiled thing, and Dot was not so well-contained. She had this easy, loose vibe about her. If Sadie was a single tree in a meadow, manicured and trimmed and perfect, Dot was a whole forest. *I want to get lost in that forest.*

He looked away like a nervous schoolboy. Good lord, what was wrong with him? Silly to think there was something there. Or that there *should* be something there. It was just the adrenaline from the attack, from resetting the girl's bone. Wasn't anything. And yet, when he looked up again—

She was still looking at him.

Still smiling at him.

He felt like a bird in a hand. Nowhere to go but to be caught.

"Tell them," Pete started, but had to pause as his laugh turned into an eye-watering cough. He winced and kept laughing as he said, "Tell them what happened to the chicken. You know, after you *submitted to the cock*."

Chick rolled his eyes, and his shoulders slumped. He said, finally, "I hit it with a cinder block."

"What?" Shana asked, almost choking on her own spit.

He shrugged. "I had a stack of cinder blocks by the house. Chicken chased me. I grabbed one. I threw it at the chicken. It was a good throw. No more chicken."

"You killed the Devil Chicken with a cinder block. You are truly our most holiest of warriors, sir."

"Can't believe you were scared of a chicken, man," Josiah said, like he was a part of this conversation. Chick whacked him on the head with the back of his knuckles. "Ow, fuck!"

"Shut up," he said. "You don't get to be indignant about shit, fool."

"Fine. *Sorry.*" Josiah pouted.

Benji said to Josiah, "You should go. But before you do—" He put out his palm. Josiah went to shake it, but Benji recoiled his hand and said: "*No*. You need to give me my gun back. It belonged to a friend, and you took it."

"Okay, *okay*." The bandit went to the front seat of the car, popping open the glove compartment. He took out the hand cannon with Chick overseeing, and handed it to Benji. "Sorry we tried to, y'know, kill you and take your stuff. We were mostly just trying to scare you. And then with Maybelle hurt . . ." His voice trailed off.

"Uh-huh," Benji said. "You need to find a home. A proper home, for your family and friends and whoever is with you." He looked deep into the bandit's eyes. "The way you're doing it can't work. Not for long. If we're going to rebuild something, we do it together. Find your home. Find your people."

"Easier said than done, but okay." To Benji and Dot he said, "Thanks for not, y'know. Cutting a part off me."

Dot nodded, but added, "You don't get going now, you might still lose a piece."

They said their goodbyes, which is to say, nobody really said much of a goodbye at all. They just watched the Ford Explorer drive off, whorls of dust spiraling in its wake.

"Well!" Pete barked. "That was fun. Still pissed I broke my uke, though."

"I'm pissed I still don't have pancakes in my mouth," Shana said.

Chick said, "Shoot, go on back inside, get yourself a meal."

"Hold up," Dot said, waving her knife in the air like it was a wagging no-no finger. "All you gotta do is say, *Dot, we're tired as hell and beaten up and hungry as a hole in the ground*. And I'll say, you come over my place. Oscar and Paulo will come. We'll cook. Get a whole meal in you, start to finish, and then get you a bed, a real bed, to rest your head. How's that sound?"

Benji looked to Shana, whose face bore a smile, but a cold one. Her stare retreated into the middle distance. Thinking, he guessed, of Ouray, and her child, and her sister.

Gently, he touched her arm. Talking only to her, he said, "We don't have to do this. We could just get food and go."

At that, she softened a little.

"No, you need this. We need this. We have to eat and we have to sleep, right? And it's Pete! But then we leave in the morning?"

"We leave in the morning."

She nodded.

And so Benji told Dot that her offer sounded very fine, indeed.

48

WHERE WE HIDE AND
WHAT WE SEEK

11/12/2022: One thing I can say is that, in the end of days, you'd think everyone would be dead from the waist down, but they're not. They're looking to fuck. The relationships I've seen moving from town to town, up the coast, it's wild. It's not even just people trying to breed, though there's that, too. It's polyamorous fuck houses, bisexual covens, whole cadres who have cast gender aside and slide up and down the man-woman-whatever spectrum like fingers on a piano playing an improvised song. White Mask broke us in a lot of ways, but some things needed to be broken, maybe. I wish I felt it. I wish I could join in. After Graham, after the fisherman, I just feel empty and angry and sad. I want to find love, too. But the part inside me that once sought love isn't broken. It just isn't there anymore. Anyway. The leaves were nice. It's growing cold. I'm learning how to catch lobsters and farm oysters on the coast of southern Maine. It's something.
—from A Bird's Story, A Journal of the Lost

OCTOBER 4, 2025
EAST OF TAOS, NEW MEXICO

DOT'S HACIENDA—HER WORD, *HACIENDA*—WAS WEST OF THE DINER, ON THE outskirts of Taos. It stood alone in no neighborhood, up a red gravel drive lined with trees. Like many of the houses here, Dot's was Spanish revival, white stucco over adobe. But her home felt sprawling and strange, with bits of wrought iron and rough nickel, accents of blue sky and lilac, and travertine tile the color of blood and rose. The art on the walls was abstract and strange, a kind of desert cubism. The rooms were open and breathy. Windows were thrown wide, and the wind whirled through the rooms like a wine-drunk dancer.

PETE LEANED BACK IN THE dining room chair, juggling a toothpick between tongue and teeth as the ravages of dinnertime lay splayed out before them: two bottles of wine emptied, a third almost done, with a bottle of bourbon waiting in the wings *just in case*; plate after plate so clean of food that you'd think a dog had licked them; a pitcher of water, sweet water, precious life-giving motherfucking *water*; soon, dessert of some ilk, as Dot had promised; and after that, if Pete knew Dot, maybe a little drugs, as a treat.

Shana and Benji sat across from him. Shana was slumped backward, less in a relaxed way like Pete, and more like she'd just slaughtered and eaten an entire bison her own damn self. Benji went the other way, elbows on the table, chin in the cup of his hands, and a smile on his face hanging loose like a leaning shelf. Dot and the two boys, Paulo and Oscar, were in the kitchen, washing up. From that doorway came the sounds of plates and forks clacking and ticking together. Benji had offered to help, but Pete told him, "She won't let you, mate." And that held true. Dot had said, "No guest in my house touches a dirty plate except to hand it to me." And so it was writ. Dot's Law. (Of course, truth was, she was barely touching the dirty plates either. Those she handed to Paulo and Oscar. They did all the scutwork. She . . . super-vised.)

Pete plucked the toothpick from his mouth, sucking his teeth. "Guess I should tell you my tale, hm? Don't worry, I'll keep it brief. I know I can go on, but I'd rather dispense with the dull bits. I prefer to live in the *present* these days."

"As opposed to what you used to do?" Benji asked.

"Fair point."

"Guhhhhgh," was all Shana said as she rubbed her belly.

Pete ran through the tale almost hastily, as if he were trying to kill the narrative with as few strokes of the storytelling blade as he could. "Spent the years wandering, mostly. Faffing off. Getting high. Sucking dick. Seeing the country. *As one does.* Eventually it was either, okay, scrape the roof of my mouth with the sights of a pistol and paint the sky with my aerosolized brains *orrrrr* develop a mission, a plan, a bloody *quest*. Mythic and potent and mag-ical and . . . all that nonsense. I decided that my *sacred crusade* would be to preserve rock-and-roll. Even if mankind was sunsetting, if civilization was gently but assuredly *shitting the bed*, then at least I could preserve the artifacts of rock-and-roll for whatever He-Men and She-Ras or Hyperintelligent Octopus Robots eventually colonize over the sediment of our bones and later unearth our foolish relics. Let those future inhabitants get their metal tentacles on Ace Frehley's Gibson Les Paul and see if they can figure out what the bloody hell it did. So, that's it. I collected memorabilia, much as I could, and took it to the Rock and Roll Hall of Fame in Ohio. Or what was once Ohio. Are states a thing anymore? People seem to think they are. Anyway. That's it. That's my tale." He sniffed, then finally leaned forward. "Once I was done I decided . . . it was time to come home."

"Home," Benji said. "You mean here?"

"I mean Ouray. Come on. Christ. Dot's house and her diner are places of great adoration, but as it turns out, home for me is that dinky mountain town. Couldn't stop thinking of it in my years away." He paused, considering not saying the next part, but, fuck it. He was knee deep in wine already. His tongue was loose like a door in the wind. "Couldn't stop thinking of you lot, honestly."

"That's sweet," Shana said, though she sounded lost in the throes of gastrointestinal distress as she groaned the words.

"It is. You've gotten a bit sentimental," Benji added, wagging a finger.

"Rock-and-roll has a sentimental heart underneath all that jangly noise and balls-out bravado. Lotta rock songs are really love songs." He waggled his eyebrows. "Some a little dirtier than others. Speaking of which . . ." Pete lowered his voice to a conspiratorial tenor. "Don't think I haven't seen you making googly eyes at Dot. And her making them back. Hm?"

"*Welp*," Shana said, standing up abruptly. "Check please. That's it for me. I don't want to hear my two dads talk about smexy stuff. Guh. Gonna go say good night to Dot and the boys."

Pete stood and met her, and they hugged. He said, "It's good to see you again, Shana. really. I missed you most of all, Scarecrow."

Into his chest, she muttered, "*I'm* not Scarecrow, *you're* Scarecrow."

Probably right, he figured.

Off Shana went. To bed. Probably to a hangover, he guessed.

"So, you and Dot—" Pete started to say, but Benji cut him off.

"No. It's not like that, Pete. I won't—it's not—I couldn't do that to Sadie."

"To Sadie. Listen to you. Benj, buddy, pal, light of my life, I loved Sadie, too. But that didn't happen yesterday. It's been five years, friend. *Five* fuckin' years. Sadie's not worried about what you're doing to her, but she's probably up in heaven a mite bit pissed you're doing this to *yourself*. Let loose. Have fun. Form a love connection. If not with your heart, then at least your penis."

"I can't. I really—it's just not in me. And I don't think Dot is interested in anything. I mean, please. Look at me. The years have not been kind."

Well, that was bullshit, and Pete said so. "I *am* looking at you, and you're a harder slab of wood than you were five years ago, eh. You used to be a tree, but now you're cut. Sculpted. You're a walking, talking example of survival porn. Listen, I'm a shallow, venal man. If I say you're fuckable? You're fuckable." He held up his hands to forestall more of Benji's noncommittal stammering. "Mate, though, there's one thing you should know if you decide to, ahh, *pursue* her—"

But at that, Dot came back into the room, flanked by her two golden himbos, Oscar and Paulo. To Pete the two boy toys were nearly indistinguishable from each other—Paulo had a bit more ruggedy scruff, the kind of rough cheeks you could use to zest a lime. Oscar had cheekbones so defined and so square they looked to be 8-bit Nintendo shit. Otherwise, the two diner cooks were far from the slovenly gut-over-apron types Pete would've expected in the Beforetimes. These two boys were *beauties*.

As the three of them came back in the room, Dot said:

"Choices, choices, gentlemen. Butterscotch pudding or weed?"

She took the flat of her hand and slid it down Oscar's back, into the tuck of his jeans. Pete knew the move. She was cupping his bare ass under there.

Then, *Paulo* came up, sidled right next to her. His arm curled around hers at the elbow, and he kissed her bare shoulder. A soft, wet kiss, too. The kind of kiss that was a proxy kiss, a promise kiss, that said, *I'm kissing you here like this, but I want to kiss you somewhere else the very same way.*

Ahh, but the real fireworks show to watch was on Benji's face, wasn't it? Pete tossed him a careful glance and saw the other man's eyes grow big like portholes on a submarine. Then Benji looked down, as if he'd been caught with his hand in the cookie jar, the poor dear.

On the one hand, he wanted to tell Benji what was up. This was Dot. She had her sweet himbos. Her world, or end of one, was a free-love kinda space. She fucked them. They fucked her *and* each other. But she also spread it around. She had a lot of love to give, and she had a lot she wanted to get, too. It was part of who she was. Dot knew what she wanted and she worked to have it. She'd built a life here out of nothing and intended to enjoy it. Pete would never look down his nose at proper hedonism and debauchery, no sir.

On the *other* hand, it was a little bit fun watching Benji squirm. He'd forgotten how much fun it was, in fact. Which made him a monster, he knew, but Pete had made peace with his own monstrousness. There was joy in it. He was who he was, just as Dot was who Dot was.

Just as Benji was who Benji was.

That Benji smiled awkwardly and said, "Dessert sounds fine."

But Pete, never one to not be contrary, held up a finger as if he were testing the wind and said, "If I may present a fine counterpoint? A little of the *devil's cabbage* will only heighten our unholy pudding hungers. And I am a fan of drugs, especially in these here End Times, for such drugs are harder to come by than I'd like."

"The devil's cabbage it shall be," Dot said, and from her front apron pocket pulled out a bag of wondrous weed.

THE HACIENDA GLOWED ORANGE AGAINST the blue-black night.

The five of them gathered out back, where the inside of the house seemed to spill to the outside—a continuance of the travertine tile fed a line of Mediterranean columns. Those columns served as a gateway to a sprawling patio and an old in-ground swimming pool in a shape that reminded Benji of the speech bubbles he'd seen in the comic books he devoured as a kid. Beyond the patio was a rocky field of leggy piñon and limber pines. Pete sat on a pool chair. Benji on a cement bench. Dot leaned against the column, looking up at the stars. Oscar waited on the far side of the same column, and Paulo stropped up next to her like a cat.

The four of them passed around a joint, now nearly burned down to the roach. Benji abstained; it was his way. Even with all that had transpired, he just never felt compelled to try it. Some stories one held about themselves had to remain true no matter what, because changing them felt like losing something.

(Still, it was hard to deny the contact buzz. His head felt fuzzy, stuffed with the cotton you used to find at the top of Tylenol bottles.)

The haze of smoke hung silver against the indigo night.

He turned his eyes to watch Dot, and whenever he did, she was watching him. Even with Oscar sliding up next to her, the side of the man's hip urgent against hers, she remained fixed on Benji.

And Benji, for his part, found himself doing his level best not to think about it at all. Instead, he just rambled, asking procedural questions—

questions about the diner, their infrastructure, their food, their issues. To her credit, Dot dutifully answered them all, smiling at him warmly with every reply. She said the diner was not hers originally, nor was this house, and she wasn't a chef or anything in the old world. In fact, she said she'd managed an art gallery in Taos before that, but always loved the Mother Road Diner. When the world fell apart she saw fit to take it over, because "nobody wanted art, but everybody needed to eat. So I threw together whatever I could cook with whatever I could find." Canned foods, snack foods, anything. "Those early days were the real fuckin' Apocalypse," she said, laughing. "Some of the food I cooked, damn, it would've made Baby Jesus climb back to Heaven and give up on all of us."

But, people came. Even as the world died, people came. Even *after* it all fell apart . . . people came, and kept on showing up day after day, week after week. And over the weeks and months and eventually, years, the diner went from being the ghost of a thing to being resurrected, life returning to the place. They looked to Dot for leadership. She didn't want to offer it, not back then, but soon realized it's what they needed, and she had it to give.

Her world and the community around them climbed back out of the abyss, maybe not all the way, but inch by inch. Farms popped up. People grew food. Surviving livestock bred. "Food chain wasn't broken. It just got a whole lot shorter," she said. Which, Benji figured, was how it was with civilization all over. It hadn't gone away. But it had been pared down to nearly nothing, a single cutting from a once-grand tree.

She said they didn't need too much. They had enough fuel across a variety of fuel types to keep things going. If one kind went on short supply, another fuel picked up the slack. People captured gas flares from natural gas wells. And there was still propane to be found, and it was incredibly stable. Plus, you had solar, wood, even some wind turbines that kept spinning. Anything that kept the lights on, the oven hot. In turn, they sold some of their cooking grease back to people as biofuel. "Symbiosis, of a kind," she said. And her using that word, *symbiosis*, well, it just thrilled Benji's nerd heart.

It was Pete who finally groaned and said, "Jesus Christ on a booze cruise, this is boring as hell. You want stories, *I've* got stories."

"We've all heard your stories," Dot said.

"Benji hasn't," Pete said, pouting a little.

"Benji can ask me whatever he likes," Dot said, looking Benji dead in the eye. A wry twinkle sparkled there. She took one more hit off the roach before pinching it and pushing it into a ceramic ashtray. "Paulo, Oscar, head in, portion out the pudding. Pete, you go on in, get some, too." She paused before saying, "I don't think Benji is hungry yet, and we're still talking."

Oscar and Paulo did as suggested—or was it, commanded?—and then Pete snuck up behind Benji and sang the line from that Aerosmith song, *"Baaaack in the saddle again."* Then he kissed Benji on the cheek and headed inside.

Dot came over and sat next to him on the bench. There was something about it that was almost . . . casually controlling. *Controlling,* he thought, *or simply in control?* She seemed to give off an aura of being in charge, as if she were born to it, as if time and space were hers and hers alone, and if you existed in her time, in her space, it's because she wanted it that way.

You're not being fair, Benji told himself. *She's just being nice.*

She said with musical laughter, "You seem nervous."

"Oh. Do I? I don't mean to."

"You're in your head. I can see that. I used to be like that."

"What changed?"

"The end of the world."

"Oh, that old thing," he said, trying to be funny, but he was afraid it just sounded stupid. Everything sounded stupid coming out of his mouth, suddenly. He was a man that, before all of this, traveled around the world, helping people, speaking to huge audiences. And before that, with the EIS, he delivered complex information, took meetings, gave massive presentations on crucial data. But now? Now his words felt like a bundle of bricks inside his mouth.

Oh God, I'm sweating.

Dot slid her hand onto his knee.

He visibly flinched, as if given an electric shock.

Dot eased her hand back.

"So, who was she?"

"What?"

"You had someone. Then you lost someone. I assume a her. Maybe a him."

Benji sighed. "Her. Sadie."

"White Mask take her?"

"It did," he answered. It was not a lie, not precisely. Sadie took her own life but she did so to triumph over that plague, to not let it beat her.

"So, that was a long time ago."

He nodded. "I suppose it was."

Dot regarded him carefully. Again she reached for him—this time for his face. Slow enough so that he was prepared for it and (thankfully!) did not flinch. She pushed her fingers slow through his beard, like the sensation of it pleased her. Her fingertips found his face below, and traced the shape of his jaw down to his chin. "I like beards, but this isn't you."

"Isn't it?"

"No. You're a man who used to wear a smooth face, I believe. Someone who could be seen in his entirety." She smiled softly. "The beard is you hiding."

"Could just be laziness."

"No. It's you hiding."

He laughed a little. "Okay, it could be that."

She stood up. Her hand leaving his face felt like . . . like something vital was now gone from him, something he suddenly missed even though he didn't know it before this very moment. A terrible absence, like true hunger.

Again she extended her hand, this time to get him to take it.

"Come on," she said. "Let's get that thing off your face."

Warily, he took her hand. "You're going to groom me?"

"I am going to get that face smooth as silk sheets. And then we can see where it goes from there. Maybe I can get you out of your own head. You in?"

"I . . ."

Benji looked up at her. Again he saw a forest, lush and dark, a place he felt he could go, get lost, and still never truly know its depth.

"The beard *is* a little scratchy," he said, his voice slow and distant. She laughed, like wind chimes. Her hand tightened around his. They went inside. They went upstairs. He found the forest, and in it, he was lost.

49

THE WELCOMING COMMITTEE

A lot of Christians wear crosses around their necks. You think when Jesus comes back he's gonna wanna see a fucking cross, man? . . . It's kinda like going up to Jackie Onassis with a rifle pendant on.

—Bill Hicks

OCTOBER 5, 2025
Outside Innsbrook, Missouri

THE ROAD WAS DIRT AND MUD. ONCE IT HAD BEEN GRAVEL, AND SOME OF THE gravel remained, gathered at the sides of the path like flotsam and jetsam—but for the most part the road was a tire-worn muck-fest that sometimes caught the truck tires and made the back end slip and slide and lurch. Along the road were trees: thick, overgrown, wild. Both Creel and Annie had their windows down, and the breeze, even in October, felt hot and heavy and wet. It stuck to them like tree sap.

Creel looked to Annie as she popped another Advil, dry-swallowing it.
She eats those things like fuckin' popcorn, he thought.
He had to get them away from her.
But no, not now.
Now, they were too close to Innsbrook.
Creel had only been there once. He'd made an appearance alongside the freak show of militiamen, with all their camo and military gear, their black rifles and face paint. Half of the men were out of shape—slovenly pigs with tiny pricks hidden underneath droopy guts and behind bluster and bravado. Barely any of them would qualify for the *actual* military (though several of them managed to become cops). But that wasn't the point of him going, being with those people. Point was, people like that could be controlled. He saw it

then, how easily they were led about like cows. They were too dumb to know their own way in the world so they needed someone to show up and direct them. They needed someone like Ed Creel. And, when he couldn't be there, it was his proxies who would lead: lieutenants like Ozark Stover, Rick Randall, Daryl Higgs, Rode Clemson. Leaders of various militias who had pledged to Creel. They were his hands, his eyes.

(*His eye.*)

Goddamn, how *excited* they'd all been when he showed up. Rarely had Creel felt that kind of—well, it wasn't love, not exactly, but *adoration*. It was the first time he saw it clearly, that he could win. And if he couldn't win the normal way, he could force victory. They would do that for him, could do it, and ultimately *did* do it. They killed Nora Hunt to grant him the presidency. He knew those people would follow him into Hell without blinking twice. He could get them to shoot their kids in the head and jump into a fucking volcano, all in the name of Ed Creel, Jesus Christ, and the superior white race.

Maybe we aren't so superior if we keep producing those clowns, Ed thought. There was superior, and then there was *superior*.

Some people were lambs.

Others, like Creel himself, were wolves.

The wolves herded. The wolves ate. And the world kept on spinning.

"What's your intel say about Innsbrook now?" Creel asked Annie.

"Like I said, it's occupied. In a big way."

"You got somebody on the inside? I need to know."

She hesitated. "No."

"So, how do you know this?"

"Drones."

"Drones? Like—military drones?"

"Not the big ones. Smaller. Remote control surveying drones. They link up with satellites and report necessary data."

"You were checking in on them from Atlas Haven?"

"Sure was."

"You were buried deep in our systems, weren't you?"

"Like a splinter."

"More like a tick."

She shot him a nasty look.

Ahead, the road bent wide through the woods, and soon as they rounded that bend, Annie pounded the brakes, and again the ass-end of the truck sloshed right even as the front drifted left. Mud sprayed up, *fsssshhht.*

Creel was about to ask, *What the fuck are you doing*, but the reason presented itself fast—a dead body, naked, dangled from an oak tree branch above stopped them. Rope tied under the corpse's blackened, swollen arms. It was low enough that, had they kept going, the truck would've hit it. He couldn't tell the race or the sex of the corpse, because it was not exactly *fresh*. Didn't help that the body didn't have a head—or, as it turned out, hands, either.

The head and the hands had been replaced with crosses. The head-cross was larger, its wooden base plunged into the torso so deep that it was barely a cross at all, more like a plus sign. The crosses sticking out of the wrists were actually crucifixes—each held a little white plastic Jesus.

A sign dangled from what was left of the corpse's neck:

WHITE JESUS SAYS: HANDS UP.

"The fuck?" Creel asked. "Kinda fuckin' sick joke is this?"

"Ed," Annie cautioned. He saw she was staring out, seeing something, and it didn't take him long to see them, too. Men, camouflaged against the forest, emerged from the tree line, rifles up. A dozen of them, easily, and Creel detected movement to their sides and behind them, too. The black dead eyes and piggy-snouts of gas masks regarded them warily.

He and Annie both raised their hands slow, real slow.

"Boys," Creel called out the passenger side window. "It's damn fuckin' good to be home. Good to see you."

Nobody said anything.

Just implacable gas-mask stares.

Guns up, pointed at his head.

"It's me," he said, incredulous. Because honestly, they should recognize him. One eye missing or not. "I'm the president of this nation. President Ed Creel. I'll expect you to haul this body out of our path so we can be on our way to—"

Creel felt his body sing with a sudden warning, as he saw fingers floating toward triggers, muscles tightening, and at that, he barked at Annie to gun it. She hit the gas, but the truck's back wheels spun in the greasy mud—it was like trying to run in a nightmare, the way your feet get stuck and no matter how hard you move your legs, you don't go *anywhere*.

Then—

Ploomp.

Something fast and dark pistoned toward the windshield.

The glass popped as the whole thing shattered. Creel and Annie cried out as something punched hard against the seat between them and rolled to the ground.

Immediately, it hissed, filling the car with smoke.

Some kind of gas. Instantly his one eye started to burn as he clawed his way out, tumbling to the ground, the gas following him. It rolled around his wrists and knees, and as he sank into the mud, he retched.

He couldn't see. Couldn't speak. His mouth felt tacky. His throat was on fire. His one eye throbbed so hard, it was like it was going to leap out of his head. Before he even knew what was happening, something clubbed him in the head and knocked him down. His shoulders screamed in pain as his arms were wrenched behind him and his wrists were bound. Rough hands lifted him up and he thought, *No, no, not again, I'm not doing this again.* A fist pumped into his gut and someone pulled a black hood hard over his head, the fabric brush-burning the bridge of his nose. Everything felt in pain, on fire, and out of control.

Welcome to Innsbrook, he thought madly, as he was dragged into the trees.

50

TWO ROADS DIVERGED

The possibility of paradise hovers on the cusp of coming into being, so much so that it takes powerful forces to keep such a paradise at bay. If paradise now arises in hell, it's because in the suspension of the usual order and the failure of most systems, we are free to live and act another way.
　　　　　　　　　　　—Rebecca Solnit, *A Paradise Built in Hell*

OCTOBER 5, 2025
Dot's Hacienda, New Mexico

"YOU COULD STAY, YOU KNOW."

Those were the words that woke him in the morning. Late morning, at that—the sun was already climbing between the curtains, burning fabric. Benji had slept like the saintly dead, a sleep righteous and unburdened. It was an astonishing feeling even now, a nearly physical lifting, like there had been heavy weights hanging around his heart and they were now gone. But more than that, too: Like he'd been changed, somehow. An alchemical trans-mogrification, lead into gold.

Some of that, his science mind told him, was a lie—or, at least, a trick of the brain. His brain and body were likely coursing with all kinds of happy-making chemicals. It was like being high, even when you weren't. Dopamine, serotonin, endorphins, and last but not least, oxytocin—neurotransmitters nd hormones born from what he knew was essential human contact.

Yes, of course, some of that was the sex. Dot was a lover both greedy and ttentive, aware of her own needs and his in equal measure—she gave, but emanded recompense, and there was nothing more attractive to him than omeone who was assertive enough and confident enough to get what they anted without *taking* what they wanted. Further, she was a vigorous participant, too. She had energy for *days*. She moved around him like an urgent river, under and around and all over. Dot wouldn't let them be one and done. At one point, she whispered in his ear, "The world may have stopped, but we have not, so *onward we go*," and then she thrust her tongue under his jaw and into his ear and then it was round two, round three, with little time to rest in between.

So, yes, it was that, certainly, obviously, but also it was the simple act of feeling something for someone after so long, and feeling it come back upon you, returned. It was as if he'd been holding in all this tension, collecting it but never releasing it, aggregating it beyond his muscles, into his teeth, his bones, his heart, his mind. It calcified in all his spaces because it had nowhere to go, no one to share it with, no one whose light would illuminate those dark places in him. He had friends and he cared about them but this was a measure above, beyond, or even just sideways. An expression of life that he hadn't felt in years.

Sadie.

Since her.

Feeling all that made his brain chemicals pop like fireworks. But he also knew those brain chemicals did not define him, but came out of who he was, and what he wanted, and who he liked and loved. They were as much a part of him as his mind, as his soul.

So, when Dot said those words—

You could stay, you know.

Those brain chemicals marched in a full-on happy parade, a rollicking Mirthfest down his mind's Main Street. The band playing, the floats floating. Balloons and confetti.

She wanted him to stay.

And he wanted to stay.

It was that simple.

Wasn't it?

Shana. Ouray. Black Swan.

The sudden burden of it all pinned him to the bed.

He managed still to roll over, blinking sleep from his eyes. She was sitting up against the cushioned headboard, and she handed him a cup of coffee.

Coffee. In bed. I've died, he decided. *That's what this is. I have died and my brain was kind enough to give me this vision before death.*

Either that, or he was a good enough man to have made it to heaven.

He sat up next to her, taking the mug. The steam warmed his face—especially now that his face was smooth, his scrubby pelt left in the trash can of her bathroom. An absurd desire arose in him to start asking her about composting: What did she do about trash removal? Not like there'd be a garbage company anymore. And she would generate a good bit of waste at the diner, so surely they composted, but how did the semiarid climate of New Mexico handle compost? *My God, Benji, what are you doing? Compost? Are you really thinking about compost?*

But then a little voice told him, *If you did stay here, if you stayed behind with Dot, you could talk about compost alllllll you wanted.*

"Are you going to say something?" she asked.

"Sorry," he said. "I'm just . . ."

"In your own head again?"

"That, but also, not. Or . . . maybe that, but in a good way."

"I'll take it."

She kissed his cheek.

"Thank you for the coffee," he said.

"Aw, it's just the instant stuff. One day there better be proper coffee again. I hope right now, just as I'm keeping this diner and this little town running, there's someone in Ecuador or Ethiopia still running their family's coffee plantation. That's what it takes. People sticking around, doing the work."

"I suppose that's how communities form in the wake of disasters. They find the purity of a role and choose to fill it. A life of simplicity and purpose, uncomplicated by . . ."

"By all the bullshit of the old world."

"That. Perhaps. Yes." A voice inside him said: *But a lot of people had to die to get to this point, didn't they?*

She stroked his cheek. "So. Like I said. You could stay, you know. That simpler life is right here if you want. Don't get me wrong, it's complicated in its own ways. But it's also easy. It's carefree. Doesn't even have to be forever. You stay long as you want. I can find a place for you at the diner. Or not. Maybe you're my houseboy. My *cabana lad.*"

"Won't Oscar and Paulo be jealous?" He was still trying to figure out if *he* was jealous of *them*. (He was. He knew that he was.)

"Nah. They're easy-breezy, too. And if they get jealous, they got feet, they can walk."

"Then you won't have cooks for the diner."

"I can find new cooks. I can cook. You can cook. I always make it work."

"You really are carefree."

"Not always, and sometimes it takes reminding myself. But the world goes to hell in high heels, you start to re-evaluate things. You start to think, I got this moment right here. I don't have yesterday, and no promise of tomorrow. I have this moment stuck between all the other moments, so I might as well live here instead of in a day that's gone, or a day that might never come."

"But it's not that entirely," he said, realizing his tone had changed a little. It felt crisper. He was challenging her and he didn't mean to. He tried to soften his tone when he said, "I only mean, you have the diner, and that's a place of importance, a place of legacy. You're not the wind. You're not Pete. You settled down here. You created something meant to persist."

She seemed to think about that. "I did. You're right. I don't know that I meant to do it at first but . . . Tell you what it is. The old world nonsense obscured something important: At heart, what we give to the world is our service, and what we give to ourselves is our purpose. For most people, especially back then in the old bullshit, all they did was give service. They worked and worked and worked, but for what? For scraps. For nothing. For a forgotten life and an oh-well death. Unless you had privilege, then what you had was purpose, but didn't do the work. But now, all that's been stripped away and I see it clear: For the world to progress, for it to heal, we must see clear to both of those things. Our service and our purpose must be two circles perfectly overlapping. What we give to the world must be the work that defines us. Meaning we give ourselves to the world to make it better. We don't just work to work. But we don't just let our destiny die on the vine."

"And this place, this diner, this town—it's your purpose."

"It is. And I work to keep it that way. We all do here."

"You're right, that doesn't sound very carefree."

She chuckled. "It is, a little. It's a lot of big talk, but I also know it could go away at any second. Maybe the diner burns down. Maybe that bandit you saved today gets a hair up his skinny ass and runs up on me, kills me, steals all my beautiful green chiles." She narrowed her eyes to serious slits and she said, "People around here take their chiles seriously, by the way. I learned that shit the hard way." But she sighed. "Living in the moment doesn't mean not making something. It just means you don't marry it."

"So, we're not getting married," he said, trying to be playful and hoping it didn't come off creepy.

"I'm married to me and me alone," she said. "Not in a *slit-your-throat-*

over-a-bowl-of-breakfast-cereal way. Just in a way that I am who I am and I embrace my power and cannot let other people stop me from doing that and being that."

"I like that," he said. *Service and purpose.*

"Good. So stay."

"You don't even know me."

"Benji Ray, I know you well enough. Not just from all the talking we did over dinner. Pete's spoken of you. He loves you all like a found family, always talking about how smart you were, and how you cared. I can always use smart and caring in my life. Good to keep people like that around. And maybe you find your purpose here."

"I . . . can't stay."

He didn't even mean to say those words. Not really. But there they were. Tumbling off his traitorous tongue.

The words, they hurt him to say.

And judging by her face, they hurt her, too.

"Sure you can," she insisted.

"I have a home and it's not . . . here. Not yet. I have to reckon with that first. I have to help the place I came from. The people there are counting on me." He thought about it, and reframed. "Shana is counting on me. I can't just quit on that. That's my purpose. I see that, now." He'd so long been worried about what his role was—CDC, Shepherd, mayor—he had forgotten the purpose of the work. To save who he loved and what he helped build. Like Dot, in a way.

Dot blinked, she sipped her coffee and stared out over it like she was scrying truth from its dark and turbid brew. "So is it true, then?"

"What's true?"

"That town you come from in the mountains. They're the walkers. The ones that went to sleep but kept walking. They survived the end."

Benji didn't know what to say. It wasn't a government secret or anything. But trying to even explain the truth of Ouray and the town necessitated wading into waters so deep, the Mariana Trench felt like a slip-and-slide.

"How'd you know?" he said.

"Please, Benji. I am not a stupid person. I know Pete traveled with that Flock because, damn, he made enough of a show of it on TV before everything went to shit. And he was cagey about that when I asked, but later when he got to talking about his 'friend from the CDC'—well, the world may have gone to shit, but two and two still makes four, doesn't it?"

"I'm sorry. It's a long and strange story."

"Maybe you can tell it to me someday," she said, more distant now. A sadness slid through her voice like a low hum. It was sweet, in a way, he supposed. Maybe it meant she wasn't as carefree as she said. Like maybe he wasn't someone she wanted to pass in and out of her life like a dream.

But, the sadness won over the sweet. He hated hurting her. He hated hurting himself. Just the same, he had something he had to do. He had to help Shana. He had to help the town. He had responsibility. He didn't know if he was a mayor of that town or still a Shepherd or just someone who bore the burden of bringing Black Swan to Ouray. All he knew was: This journey wasn't over, not yet.

"I have work," Dot said, kissing him on the cheek once more. "I'm glad the beard is gone; thank you for letting me take it off you. I'm sorry you'll be gone. I'll see you, Benji."

And that, it seemed, was that.

AND *WHOOSH*, THE GROUND RUSHED up to meet him as he crashed down from flying so high. An hour later, Dot was gone, and Benji and Shana were packing up the car. Dot had left them some provisions for the road: bread, some jars of preserved salsa and pickles, figs, pecans. Shana seemed a little muzzy from the food and drink, but it didn't seem to slow her down. Shana was determined. Benji could see that much. She had a lot riding on this. Her sister. Her son.

"Where the hell's Pete?" she said finally.

And, as if summoned like a demon, Pete came storming out of the hacienda, shirt open, his pale chest exposed with its wisps of gray hairs and his ribs showing like xylophone slats. He was still hiking on his pants, hopping on one foot as he tugged his too skinny jeans onto the opposing leg.

"Hey! *Hey*. What the fucking fuck, were you people going to fucking leave without me?"

Benji had to laugh a little. "Pete, we weren't going to leave without saying goodbye but—"

"Without saying what?" he said, sneering and squinting, finally managing his pants all the way on. "Goodbye? What the fucking fuck, I figured we were caravanning together back to Colly-rado. Betrayal! I am *betrayed*."

"Pete, we're not going back to Colorado," Shana said.

"What?"

"It's true," Benji confirmed. "A lot has happened. We didn't get to talk about it because so much was going on last night—"

Pete winked and said, "Yeah, we all heard what was going on last night."

"*Oh.*" Benji felt mortified.

"I slept like a dead person and I still heard it," Shana said. She made a sour face and stared off at the middle distance. "I'm pretty sure those sounds invaded my dreams."

"Oh."

"Sorry," Pete said, "carry on, you were saying something about betraying me?"

"Ahh. Well." Embarrassed, Benji pressed on. "Ouray has changed, Pete. The Sleepwalkers are awake—" At that, Shana gave a little wave. "And Black Swan did not go quietly into that good night. Shana had her baby—"

"Right!" Pete said, snapping his fingers then clapping his hands together like two cars broadsiding each other. "You were bloody pregnant! And you popped! Good for you. Where is the little tyke oh God now that I'm asking that I'm betting there's some dark and tragic tale here so me asking is going to be very awkward after I hear the answer? Oh shit, did the baby die? Ahh, no. Fuck. Is there any way to put a question back inside my mouth?"

Shana sighed. "It's okay. He's alive. And Black Swan, just like it was inside the Flock, is now inside my child. And it . . . won't leave."

"Fuck. That's fuckin' weird," Pete said. "And creepy. So what's with the road trip, then? You're not just running away from the fight, are you?"

Benji thought again about Dot. About how much he wanted to stay here. Running away sounded pretty good right now. But: purpose and service, service and purpose. "No, we're headed to Atlanta. I'm going to see if we can find something in Sadie's files to give us . . . an edge over the machine. Any edge. We view Black Swan like a disease. Which means we need medicine to cure it."

"It's an infection that has a mind," Pete said. "If god were a virus." He paused and added, "That'd be a good song name. 'God Is a Virus.' Song *or* album. Or band? Shit. Anyway! This sounds like a dangerous, stupid quest, and as it turns out, I am a man who is recently without a dangerous, stupid quest, so clearly I am coming with you."

Shana and Benji looked to each other.

"Are you sure?" she said.

"Well, I'm not going to go hang out in Ouray all by my lonesome, am I?"

"Marcy's still there."

"Oh, I love Marcy. What about Matthew, that dire fucker?"

Benji shrugged. "Hard to say. Hope he's okay but we don't know. When things went south there . . ." His voice trailed off.

"Well, can't sit here thinking about that. No, no, I'll stick with you all. Time for a fucking adventure. I'll drive with you, leave my rat-trap camper here—she's biofuel and on her last legs, I think. Dot'll take good care of her. I call shotgun!"

And with that, the two travelers became three.

TEN VIGNETTES, AKA, THE SHIT WHAT PETE CORLEY HAS SEEN

THE MONTHS AND YEARS
Across New America

1. Red Makes Green

"Cults, you bet your asses there are cults. Shit falls apart and people need something to believe in, a bit of *emotional driftwood* keeping them from sinking into the inky black, eh? Most of them are your fairly classic cults, I think, you know, something about a UFO, something about some Bathtub Messiah, something about some rocket-ship billionaire. Found a group that worshipped a Meth Gator in St. Petersburg, Florida. *That* was a whole thing. Found one town of folks in Pennsylvania, real nice, hippy-dippy sorts, you know? Everything was green and from-the-earth and recycled and reused and . . . Christ, they grew the tastiest, fattest strawberries you ever did see. Size of a baby's fist, those things! (Sorry, Shana.) Of course, turned out, it wasn't *all* shiny and happy. They had these . . . festivals, these *old rites*, they said, and these festivals were to appease a creature they called the God of the Earth, whatever the fuck that was. All these people were white, by the way, white as the purest cocaine. They'd pick one old person and one child and they'd kill them out in the fields. *Red makes the green*, they sang. Needless to say, I got the fuck out of there, because they were eyeing me up real good. I bet I'd make for some tasty strawberries, though. Oh, don't give me that look, I'm very sweet and you jolly well fucking know it."

2. I Hate These Guys

"The worst are the fucking Nazis, though. Like with everything, most of them died, because most of everyone died. But they got their bastions. Eugene, Oregon. Hartford, Connecticut. Innsbrook, just outside of St. Louis. Gods, don't even get me started on North Dakota, fuck. Nazis are like cockroaches and mosquitoes—they survive some shit. They blame everyone but themselves. Hate is their virus, and that one will never go away. (Though YouTube and Facebook no longer existing doesn't hurt.) You know the thing that chafes me, too, about them, and okay, *no*, this isn't the worst thing but for me it's a special kind of sin—they got *shit* taste in music. Just absolute fucking fuckshit. Shallow garbage played by musically incompetent racists who wouldn't know a good song if it came up and tickled their tiny mustaches with its sonic dick. Nazis are bad people with bad taste. Sorry to say they're still around. But some shitstains don't wash out, it seems."

3. Country Music's Own Mother Abigail

"You know who the Nazis hate? Dolly Parton. It's true, no, it's fucking true. The Nazis, the KKK, all the racist sonsofbitches, they hate her. Oh yeah, no, she's still alive—I know! I know. She still lives in Tennessee, turned her town into a right nice place to live. A little library on this corner, a little stage on that corner. They hate her because she loves everyone, or at least everyone who loves love. To be fair, they've always hated her. She always got hate letters from racist, bigoted pricks, in part because she accepted us *gay fellas* and the *lesbian ladies* so that predictably made the worst fuckers mad—and she would sweetly tell those fuckers to go fuck a fire hydrant or whatnot, but you know, more *Dolly Partony* than that. Anyway, I met her on a search for Willie's guitar, Trigger, and of course hearing she was still alive—well, a man has to make his pilgrimages while he can. We meditated. I drank tequila, she drank red wine. She gave me some leads to go on. I told her, I said, *Dolly, let me take something of yours to the Rock and Roll Hall of Fame*, because, sure, she's already in the country one, but come the fuck on, '9 to 5'? 'Higher and Higher'? 'Jolene'? And if you haven't heard her cover of Bon Jovi's 'Lay Your Hands on Me,' well, you just have to. It's iconic. It's *rock-and-roll* to the teeth and taint. But she told me,

Sweetie, not right now, you can come back for my memorabilia when I'm dead. But while I'm still kicking, I'm keeping it all here. That was that. I hope she never dies. Though she damn sure deserves her saintly rest, I also fear she's the final column holding up all of our reality. Bowie gone, Prince dead, we can*not* lose Dolly."

4. Beautiful and Terrible and Strange

"You know, one of the saddest, strangest things I've seen out there—and this is me, now, okay, I'm saying this knowing full well there are sadder, stranger things, but I mean for *me, personally*, it's this: I was in the Mojave looking for Johnette Napolitano of Concrete Blonde because I heard she lived out there and dead or alive, I wanted to see if I could get something for the museum. And out there, in the absolute middle of nowhere—like, in the middle of God's raw, red, dust-caked asshole, there played a band. A little trio. Got this girl looking like Wednesday Addams singing, with a fiddle. A chubby Latino lad on bongos. And a tall, sagging Black fella—old, too, maybe in his seventies—on a cheap shit shoebox guitar. You'd think, *Oh, they broke down*, but they were out there of their own damn volition, playing music for no one. I stopped. I listened for a while and they almost acted like I wasn't there, like they were street performers doing their thing no matter who passed them by, even though . . . it was just me. They did a slow, sad rendition of Richard Marx's 'Right Here Waiting' that could've made the whole high desert weep fresh water. So I said between songs, hey, hi, hello there, what the fuck are you doing out here? And the girl said, 'Playing,' like, *duh*. And I said, for who? And she said, 'You.' And I thought, what the fuck. Are they dead? Are they ghosts? There was no car, no van, no horses. I dunno how they even got there. I gave them some food and water and they thanked me for that, and then I offered the Black fella a guitar I had—a nice Seagull, a parlor guitar, made in Canada, and he politely declined. I asked them if they needed a ride, and the kid on bongos said, 'We're right where we need to be.' And so I left. It pained me to leave. I wanted to stay. Were they sirens, like from myth? Trying to get me to die out there? Were they trying to die themselves, and was this their version of suicide? I don't know. I passed by there again, but they were gone. I'll never know who they were or what they were doing or if they even still exist at all. That's the saddest part."

5. WHAT TO DO ABOUT HITLER-LICKERS

"BACK TO DOLLY, NO, NO, I know, but bear with me here—with the fucking Nazis and the KKKrazies, you'd think, well, how's she dealing with that in this post-civilization fuckery, hmm? And I'll tell you, if it were me, I'd be dispensing some Tennessee Justice, which is to say, I'd be sipping bourbon on my front porch with one of them rifles that have the loopty-loop trigger things where you lever it back, *clack-clack*, right? Wild West shit. And anytime I saw any Hitler-lickin' hood-wearing fucko, I'd pop his scalp off with a bullet I kissed just minutes before. But Dolly doesn't do that. Dolly, she set traps. No, no, I mean it, *traps*. Pits, usually. Pits they fall into and can't get out of. And now you're thinking, *That's dark, that doesn't sound very Dolly Parton, her going around, digging holes and dropping Nazis in 'em,* but that's what she did. They fall in there and she keeps them there, but it's not as grim as it sounds. She tries to rehabilitate them. She gives them food and water and sings to them, reads to them from—well, the Bible, the Quran, some Buddha shit, some poetry, and she tries to help them be better. Sometimes they get better, and she helps them out of the hole. I met a few. They work for her now. Devoted as hell. I personally subscribe to how it is in that Tarantino movie: The only good Nazi is a dead Nazi. But Dolly, she's magic. She can bring anybody back from the brink. Not sure anybody else can, or should try. But Dolly's not like you or me, is she?"

6. PINEYS

"I SAW THE JERSEY DEVIL. No, I was *not* high. I was in the Pine Barrens and—you know what, I can see you don't believe me, I see your eye rolls, your lips curled into an almost-laugh. Fine. You don't get to hear the story. But there was a coven of witches involved. And okay, I was a *little* high. A lot high. Shut up."

7. BESIDES THE RAT-FED FATBERG, IT'S GREAT

"NEW YORK CITY IS STILL . . . New York City. I mean, I get it, you think, *Well, it's probably some* Mad Max *shit there, some John Carpenter Snake Plissken fuck-all,* but . . . it's nicer than all that. People didn't turn into roving

gangs or whatever just because they couldn't get avocado toast anymore. New
Yorkers are survivors. You think they're gonna fall to shit just because they
don't have a Duane Reade, you forget they lived in apartments smaller than
a kiddie's lunchbox. They'd fight rats over pizza. They were there for 9/11.
New Yorkers are tough and they do all right. I mean, it's not that they don't
have fucking problems. In the beginning they didn't have power, didn't have
trains, the city was clogged with cars and trash and rats. Rats that ate people,
so I heard. But the people didn't turn feral. They didn't turn on each other.
You do that, then what? You fall apart. You want shit to work, you have to
fucking hold on to one another. So they did. Even when it got bad, they did.
They banded together, got power back with solar and some jury-rigged wind
turbines. Water was a problem for a while because it's not like anybody was
treating the water upstate anymore, and you don't wanna drink from the
Hudson unless you're a big fan of microplastics and cancer. But you know,
NYC went from millions and millions of people to only a hundred thousand
or so, think, so it got easier to send some people upstate to reclaim the reser-
voirs and get fresh water flowing again with the help of some local sandhogs.
And more people went to live in the city now. Reverse osmosis. Back to the
cities they go. It's a bit of all right. Street food everywhere. Manhattan is no
longer for the rich white assholes anymore. There's whales in the Hudson, a
family of bears in Central Park. Still rats in the tunnels, though, and the
trains don't run. You *don't* go into the tunnels. Story is, there's a fatberg down
there the rats feed on. You go down there, you become part of the fatberg.
You become part of the rats. I hate rats! Anyway! Besides that, it's great."

8. LEFT COAST LUNACY

"CALIFORNIA, ON THE OTHER HAND, oof. Fucked. Real fucked. At least in the
cities. They can still get their avocado toast so you think they'd be happy, but
not so much. Big earthquake three years ago—not the Big One, but one that
fucked up the Bay Area pretty bad, I hear. Plus all the wildfire business.
Humboldt County is fucking scary, and the Richie Riches in the Bay Area
got extra weird—I was talking about cults earlier, well, they were always
culty out there, but in a way that they pretended they weren't, right? They
don't pretend anymore. It's all sex cults and tech cults and Luddite cults and
smart drug cults and sex drug tech cults, and then it's cults *fighting* cults
and—no fucking thank you. L.A. does a little better, I think. Not sure about

San Diego but who gives a shit about San Diego, all those people with their nice temperatures and adorable dogs, it's the opposite of rock-and-roll there. It's like, we know, you're tan, you're Republican, settle down, Jimmy Buffett, Christ."

9. What the Vultures Wouldn't Eat

"I think the toughest thing is honestly just all the dead bodies. First, as a basic infrastructure issue, it's just—it's a *lot* of dead bodies. Millions and millions of dead people. Most of them taken down by that fucking fungus. Colonized into white, powdery cities. Every building has or had its bodies. A lot of them were outside, too; the vultures and crows didn't want them. That's the thing you don't realize—for civilization to continue it had to reckon with that first step. It had to deal with the bodies. And everybody dealt with it differently. Some burned them, others buried them, some just walled them in one building at the edge of town—a school, a factory, a tenement. But you couldn't ignore them. And it makes you think, they died in bad ways. They forgot who they were. They walked into traffic, they fell into pools, they climbed under running lawn mowers or burned their own houses down— they just forgot how to be people anymore. An old friend of mine, Elvis, a bandmate that I found again after all this, he said his brother Georgie just walked in circles until he died. You couldn't stop him from doing it or he'd hit you, bite you, snarl like an animal. Then he'd get back to it, walking his loop, following the ghost of himself to nowhere. But he seemed comfortable doing it. Like he was happy circling the drain that way. Eventually he just collapsed. His whole body gave out. Then his cat ate him. That's cats for you. No shade, though. Cats know they gotta fuckin' eat."

10. Lost and Found

"Obviously, there's sadness to go around. I try not to focus on it because that's not who I am, I want to be smack dab in the here and now, you get me? But some days you can't look past it in the way you can't look past a mountain you're standing next to. It's too big. Everybody's lost somebody. Nobody got to keep everybody. Most people didn't get to keep *anybody*. Family of five peo- ple, if one survives, the other four are definitely gone. Most people you worked with, dead. Most of your exes, fucking *dead*. It's heart-crushing, is what it is. *Soul-rending*. But there's something there, too, something special. Because for all that was lost, the people remaining, they're finding each other. An island of misfit fucking toys. Like us, in Ouray. Whatever happened there, well. We'll fix it. We'll get past it. Because we all found each other even though we didn't know each other. And we found each other again, through all the bullshit, through all the fucked-upedness. Us, together, in time and space one more go. That's not so bad. Not so bad at all."

PART FIVE

LAMBS AND
WOLVES

51

THE GIRL AND THE WOLF

1/1/2023: Happy New Year. Still in Maine. Portland is nice, so are the islands around. There's life here, civilization, people getting by as best as they can. really cold now. I should head south but I don't. The fuck would Florida even be like? No thank you. The cold hurts, but I'm okay with it, so I'm staying here. The skin of the bear that I killed helps keep me warm. P.S. I thought I saw them the other day. My husband. My son. This isn't the first time. Whenever I find people, I search those faces and for a moment, I think, that's them, there they are. It's never true. It's just my mind playing tricks on me. The funny thing is, what I feel after I realize that it's just a trick is not sadness, not anger, but rather, a strange peace. And a deep, troubling satisfaction.

—from A Bird's Story, A Journal of the Lost

OCTOBER 13, 2025
Ouray, Colorado

"BAAAABY CHARLIE," NESSIE CALLED, TRYING TO KEEP THE TREMBLE OUT OF her voice. She hoped it made her voice sound musical, and not frightened.

The little baby boy sat on the floor and upon hearing his name, looked to her. His face brightened. He gurgled and cooed, a string of happy gibberish flowing from his mouth like he was instructing her in some secret truth only babies knew.

He swayed left and right, forward and backward, like he was on a boat wobbling upon an unsteady sea. Then, with no more hesitation, Charlie plonked down onto his hands and knees and began to crawl clumsily toward a stuffed pink rabbit someone had brought him. He moved with the grace of a drunken man searching for his keys under a kitchen table. But he moved. He crawled.

He *crawled*—for the first time ever.

He was just over a month old.

Babies don't crawl at one month old.

Nessie also knew they didn't respond to their name. They didn't talk like this. They didn't sit up, they didn't jabber, they certainly did *not* crawl.

That was the provenance of a six-month-old.

And he was the size of a six-month-old, too. He did not look like a child who was only brought into the world a month before.

Charlie was growing and developing rapidly. Six months in one month. Would that mean six years in one year? When he was ten years old, would he look sixty? Or would it slow down? She had no answers to this. Black Swan hadn't spoken to her, had not instructed her, not at all. All she knew was, it worried her. No, it *terrified* her. And worst of all, it made her very, very sad.

Because Shana was missing so much.

These fundamental early days, it was bad enough she was missing them—but Shana was missing these moments in fast-forward. The sand was pouring through this hourglass and Nessie didn't know why, or how to stop it. She told the baby sometimes, "You need to slow down, you need to slow down so your mama can see you like this, she'll be back soon." Not that she knew if Shana would be back. Soon, or ever. *Please, Shana. Please come back. Your baby needs you.*

I need you.

"He's a little miracle, isn't he?" Xander said, startling her. She hadn't seen him come down the steps. *Creep down the steps is more like it*, she thought. He'd been doing this lately. Following her. Watching her. Sneaking up on her.

"He's growing fast," was all she said.

"That's good. We need that. Soon he'll be walking. Talking. And when that happens, Black Swan can talk to us all. Black Swan can lead us."

"Sure," she said.

"You don't sound sure."

"I'm sure, I'm very sure, it's good." Her words came out too fast, too nervous. She felt like she looked. Sometimes she caught a glimpse of herself in a bathroom mirror and she had a haggard, bog-witch look—hair everywhere, eyes ringed in shadow and the whites threaded with fragile red lacework. *Maybe the baby is making me older, too.* Some kind of Dorian Gray thing. Or like the baby was a vampire. She wasn't sleeping well. (*The sound of his bones crackling. The plastic-wrap-pulled sound of skin stretching. His squeals of delight.*)

"Vanessa," Xander said, as he'd chosen lately to say her full name, not her nickname—a name she hated, because it never felt like her. But he insisted. Said it sounded more *adult*, like it had, in his words, *gravitas*. "I know this is hard. But it'll be over soon. There's going to be a town council meeting tonight to deal with the . . . Matthew Bird situation. And then the council will meet separately after, and it'll be time to tell them that I wish to be mayor of this town. I'll bring changes. As Black Swan comes to fruition . . ."

"I can be there," she said. "At the meeting." It horrified her that he might be thinking of undercutting the council's power—was that what he was saying? She felt that it was. Mia and Nevaeh and the others were right. Something had gone wrong here. Black Swan was no longer something she could trust.

It killed her to think that.

To admit it.

After everything . . .

The long walk. The Ouray Simulation. The shooting on the bridge, the death of their father, the birth of Baby Charlie, and the exile of Shana . . .

If Black Swan was wrong, then Nessie was wrong, too. Their mother, in the simulation, also wrong—if, as Shana feared, she was even their mother at all.

She wanted to throw up.

"It won't be necessary," Xander said, "as I know we're already on the same page. I know you support me."

"And this is what Black Swan wants?" she asked, swallowing a lump.

He hesitated. "It is."

Nessie didn't know if that was a lie, but she knew he wasn't being entirely truthful, either. He'd come down to commune with Black Swan. Every day for the last week, as a matter of fact. But each time he held the baby, nothing happened. It shocked him enough the first time that he simply put the child down, almost hastily, like he had been stung by the rebuke. But the next day, and the days after, he made an effort to *pretend*. He'd let his eyelids flutter and then he'd sway a little, as if he were lost in Black Swan's simulation. But that's not how it should've looked. She'd seen it with Shana and Benji. When you went in there, you froze outright. Light as a feather, stiff as a board. Which meant only one thing:

Xander was faking it.

Black Swan wasn't talking to him.

(To be fair, it wasn't talking to her, either.)

What that meant, she didn't know. Maybe Xander knew more than he was letting on. Or maybe he was making it *all* up.

She wasn't sure which worried her more.

"Claudia won't be here for a little while yet," he said. That was the other thing. Claudia had been coming around more and more. Meeting with him quietly. She heard them murmuring. Plotting, she thought. About what, though? He'd sent the others away. No more guards. Even Doctor Rahaman was kept at the margins, with Xander saying that the child was "in the care of Black Swan, now." Most days, Nessie was alone in this place with Xander. Claudia was the only other one who seemed allowed to show her face. Sometimes Nessie wondered: *What if I just left again? Am I allowed?* Whenever she asked Xander, he'd just say to her, *Please, just a little longer. The child needs you. If something happened to the baby, to Black Swan, I'd hate for you to have to shoulder that blame. How would that make you feel? Everything rests upon this, Nessie. Everything rests upon you.*

"Okay," was all she could ever say in response.

"When she gets here, Claudia's going to walk me over to the community center. But that won't be for a little while yet. Come upstairs. Take a break."

"I shouldn't leave Charlie—"

"Charlie will be fine. I have something to show you."

A ripple of cold fear ran over her skin like a wave of dancing ants.

WHAT HE WANTED TO SHOW her was in his bedroom. He forced her to go ahead of him, so he walked behind her, like a Shepherd. It felt predatory. She could feel his eyes on her. *You're just imagining things*, she chided herself.

He went over to the bed, sat down on the pillowy duvet. He kept his bedroom impeccable. Everything had its place. Not a speck of dust survived.

"Sit with me," he said.

"I should get back downstairs—"

"Vanessa, please."

The words were polite. The tone was not.

Her mind scrabbled like a rat clawing free from a trap. She felt her own legs betraying her, and obeying him instead, because she feared what would happen if she ran.

It's fine, she told herself again and again. *It's fine. It's fine.* A mantra to repudiate the certainty that it was not, at all, fine.

He patted the bed.

Nessie sat.

He smiled at her.

From the bedside table, Xander retrieved a little box. A ring box, black velvet, with a delicate little hinge. He turned toward her and eased it open with the flat of his thumb.

Inside, a polished ring gleamed. The ring was silver or platinum with a crown of spiky petals atop it. In the center of that sharp-petaled crown, a pink circle-cut gem sparkled.

"I—I don't understand," she said.

"I found it at the silversmith's at the top of town. Beautiful, isn't it? It's a columbine. A pink columbine represents both youth and love. That's you. All your youth, all your love. The gem itself is a pink tourmaline. Diamonds are of course more classical for this purpose, but you are a girl of such vibrancy and color—a clear dull gem such as that does nothing to represent how special you are."

Nessie scooted away from him on the bed, putting two feet between them. She half-laughed, an anxious reaction and not one of earnest humor. "No, Xander, no, it's not like that between us. *No.* I think you're great, and very smart, but I can't accept this—"

He moved closer to her again. "I think you can." He grabbed her hand and turned it over, opening it by peeling her fingers back one by one, as if he were forcing a flower to bloom.

He put the ring box in the palm of her hand. "I want to make you an honest woman. We're going to give Baby Charlie a cousin, and give the world another life. Maybe even give Black Swan another vessel—*if* that's what it needs."

"Xander, please—"

He reached out and ran the flat of his hand along her stomach. Then he slid it up under her shirt and—

She took the ring box and bashed him in the eye with it.

He staggered back on the bed, clutching his eye, groaning. Nessie launched herself off the bed, legs carrying her backward until she froze. Instantly she felt sick to her stomach and felt angry at what he'd done, but then somehow her brain convinced her to maybe feel shame about what *she'd* done—some strange conditioning in her mind justified his actions, *He just*

*wants love, he likes you, it's just crossed wires, you didn't have to hit him, he was
telling you how he feels—*

Xander stood up.

"Xander," she said. "I'm sorry, I shouldn't have hit you, but—"

He walked to her, then drove a fist into her stomach.

Nessie grunted, crying out, dropping to her knees. He grabbed a fistful
of her hair and wrenched her head toward him. "Nessie," he said with a false
gentleness that did little to conceal a bright, magma vein of viciousness, "you
are going to have to get used to how things are now, and you are going to do
me the *honor—*"

Downstairs, glass shattered. A loud, rattling crash.

He let go of her hair. "What was that?"

"I . . ." she gasped, crying. "I don't know."

For a moment, they were both still, except for her hitching shoulders and
stifled sobs. He hissed at her: *"Shh."*

He started to backpedal toward the bed.

"My gun," he said.

Xander turned once more to the nightstand, opening the drawer—

And when he turned back around, he had a pistol gripped in one hand,
and its magazine cradled in the other. But already, Nessie saw that the two
of them were not alone. A visitor stood in the doorway of Xander's bedroom.

The visitor was not human.

A wolf waited there. Shoulders bristling. Teeth bared.

One eye was gone, but in its place was a shifting orb of shining metal.
Half its face, even down the length of its muzzle, was no longer fur, but a
strange carpet of what looked to be filaments of metal—threads of copper,
steel, titanium. Rippling. Hissing against one another even as the animal
growled.

It wasn't looking at her.

It was staring at him. At Xander.

Even as it showed its teeth, Nessie saw that the teeth were not all bone-
white fangs, either. Some of them looked like metal, too. Thinner, narrower,
like long needles. It ran a pale tongue along them—the way a thumb might
run along the tines of a comb. But the sound was almost musical. Eerie wind
chimes.

Xander moved fast, slamming the magazine into the base of the gun—

The wolf leapt.

He pointed the gun—

The wolf's jaws craned open—and the beast made contact, biting down on the gun hand, and as it landed on the bed, it wrenched itself backward. Xander's shoulder dropped hard as his whole body followed, slamming against the bed, and then rolling off of it—his arm was still wrenched up into the air, the hand and its gun trapped in the monster's mouth.

The gun never went off.

The wolf bit down with a wet crunch.

It shook its head like a dog with a squeaky toy. Shake, shake, shake.

Rip, rip, rip.

The hand came off in a spray of red. As it did, the wolf released its jaws, and the hand went flying, clattering atop a dresser, knocking all that was upon it off to the floor with a clamor. The gun went with it, too, spinning away toward the door. Xander screamed. He kicked at the wolf, knocking it off the bed. He used his knees to launch himself to the other side of the mattress, his stump gushing fresh red, white bone emerging from the mess of flesh.

Nessie thought, clarity in panic, *I need that gun.*

This wolf, once it was done with Xander, would surely kill her, too.

She turned toward the weapon even as the wolf rolled off the bed.

The gun lay on the floor. A pair of feet stood on the other side of them.

Sensible sneakers. Black pants.

Seemed that Claudia had arrived early. *She* picked up the gun.

The wolf looked to her.

Xander shrieked, holding his ruined arm to his chest as it soaked his white shirt: "Shoot it! *Shoot the fucking beast.*"

Claudia looked to the gun, racked the action back—which, Nessie now realized, Xander had not done—and pointed it.

"The wolf—" Xander started to say.

Bang.

The bullet in the center of his forehead shut him up.

Xander's corpse slumped sideways. Blood oozed from the hole in his skull and pumped from the red-rag mess that was his wrist.

The wolf cocked its head, almost in a curious way. Then it sat down, stoic and unmoving. It was calm now. As if it was waiting for something.

Claudia, for her part, was calm, too—but her face still wore a mantle of curiosity and small surprise. She looked to Nessie and said simply: "Hey."

"Hey," Nessie said.

52

CALL AND RESPONSE

I visualize a time when we will be to robots what dogs are to humans, and I'm rooting for the machines.
> —Claude Shannon, so-called father of information theory

OCTOBER 13, 2025
Ouray, Colorado

NESSIE HAD THE SHAKES. SHE SAT DOWNSTAIRS ON THE WHITE LEATHER couch shuddering uncontrollably.

Claudia sat across from her, dissecting her with a stare.

The wolf lay on the other side of the room, on a bearskin rug. It watched the two of them through its one good eye. The other eye shifted and swam in its socket. It wasn't even an eye. It was just a shape. An occasional glow lost behind a bristling ripple of impossible fiber and metal thread. Soundless in its movement.

"What?" Nessie asked Claudia, defensive.

"Nothing."

"You're s-s-staring at me."

"You're upset. That's interesting."

"Is everything interesting to you?"

"Almost nothing is."

Nessie sniffed, and blinked away the remnant of tears. "Great."

"What was happening up there?"

"Why'd you shoot Xander?" Nessie countered.

"I had a choice to make. I did the math."

"The math," Nessie repeated.

"I calculated that, if either of those two potential targets was on the side of Black Swan, it was the wolf."

"Why would you th-think that?"

"It was transformed. Black Swan is an agent of transformation. Xander was not." She shrugged. "He'd been growing paranoid anyway. Not in a good way."

"So you killed him."

"I did."

"Y-you're a good shot."

"I am."

"Who the hell are you?" Nessie asked.

"I don't know. I don't know that it matters. Black Swan knows. I think." She paused, considering that. Somewhere behind her eyes, Nessie could see that she settled on an answer, though Claudia was not forthcoming as to what that answer was. "Again, what happened up there? In the bedroom."

"Xander . . . he wanted to marry me. I said no. He tried to assault me. *Did* assault me. And I hit him and . . ." She felt jumbled. Like she wasn't telling it right, or in order. "I don't know. He was going to hurt me and then the wolf showed up I guess through that window—" She gestured toward a bay window at the far back of the house, where the dining room table sat covered in glass and a breeze streamed in. "And then it came after him. Took off his hand."

"I saw that. That's a good wolf."

"I guess."

"What I'm wondering is, what happens now," Claudia said.

"I . . . I dunno."

"Do we tell people or keep this quiet?"

"I don't know how we keep *this* quiet."

"A fair point. But he could've been attacked by any random animal. Maybe had nothing to do with you. Or a wolf that's not a wolf." She paused. "Or me."

"You think that's the b-best course of action?"

Claudia paused, seeming to think this through. "I don't actually know. I am usually very good at assessing risk versus reward. The best path is one I often see quickly and clearly. It's not so clear now, nor so quick."

"And why is that?"

"Because none of this is paralleled. There is no rhyme here. It's all new. You can feel it, too. There's been a shift. Something is happening."

Then, a sound somewhere else in the house.

"What's that?" Claudia asked.

Nah-nah.

That was the sound:

Nah-nah.

Not a sound. A voice.

A baby's voice.

The wolf perked its head up as the voice bubbled up from the downstairs steps. "Nah-nah! Nah-nah. Nah-nah?"

"Charlie," Nessie said, launching herself to her feet.

"Sounds like you're being called," Claudia said.

"I . . . guess so."

"Only question is, who's calling you? The child, or what hides within it?"

53

THREADS

Morgellons *is the informal name of a self-diagnosed, scientifically unsubstantiated skin condition in which individuals have sores that they believe contain fibrous material. Morgellons is not well understood, but the general medical consensus is that it is a form of delusional parasitosis.*
—Wikipedia entry, *Morgellons*

OCTOBER 13, 2025
Ouray, Colorado

THIS WAS THE MEMORY THAT LIVED WITH MATTHEW OVER THE NIGHTS HERE in this cell: Back while the world was still in the midst of falling apart, he remembered going to Innsbrook to look for his son, Bo. And on the way there, he met a man on the road, a lean-faced fellow in a pickup truck heading toward the encampment. The man asked him what he was doing out there. Matthew told him. And in that moment, he was sure he'd been made, that the man would figure out who he was, what he was doing, and so the moment the man looked away—

Matthew shot him in the head.

Dead man in the seat. Blood on the windshield, running in greasy red streaks, carving a path through dust.

That was five years ago now, wasn't it? If he recalled, that happened in October, too. *What's old is new. Past is prologue.*

So here he sat, in the drunk tank cell, against a cinder-block wall. A place he'd been before, after he left Autumn—for the last time, he reminded himself—to come to Ouray to warn them of the man who was coming to kill them.

A man he himself would kill, too. He could still feel the gun bucking in his hand as he executed Ozark Stover in the road.

Like the man in the truck. Like the guard on the porch.

Matthew's hands were wet with blood, weren't they? Still dripping red. And what of his son? No, he did not kill Bo with his own hands. But his son's death remained a millstone around his neck. He'd raised that boy wrong. He focused too much on *churching,* believing somehow that God would pick up the slack, all he had to do was light the way and put the Good Book in the boy's hands and the way would be clear. But Bo needed more. He needed real counseling. He certainly didn't need love from some Heavenly Father— instead, he needed it from his human one, here on Earth. In retrospect, Matthew didn't know how to raise a boy like Bo. He could've asked for help. Should've. But didn't. *Jesus take the wheel.*

Giving it all to God was his greatest failure.

And that failure led the boy to Ozark Stover, and it was Ozark Stover who brought Bo to Ouray. White Mask already had him. And it was here, in this cell, that they kept Bo until he died while Matthew watched.

The boy died badly. Matthew burned the body, then scattered the ashes into the nearby gorge. Even that felt wrong. But he didn't know what his son would've wanted. Because he didn't even really know his son at all.

This drunk tank cell reminded him of that. And it reminded him of Autumn, and the people he'd killed, and the radio broadcasts he'd given that stirred up anger against the Sleepwalkers, and he remembered how easy it was to fall into the orbit of that terrible man. A terrible man who ripped him down to the struts. Even now his hand still trembled and shook. Even now, the pain radiated out from its center like a bullet hole in a broken mirror. And other pain radiated out from his heart, from his middle, from his head. What Ozark did to him . . .

I deserve this, Matthew thought.

And he deserved whatever would come next.

Idly, he scratched at his arm. Some bugbite, some mosquito bite, some abrasion, he didn't know. He was covered in scratches and nicks and dents from when he came down off the mountain to return to Ouray. They were healing. Which meant they itched.

(Even if some of them itched more than others.)

Marcy came in a little while later, bringing him breakfast: a couple patties of ground chicken sausage and some fried eggs. Gumball came trotting in after her—she'd been keeping him, and brought the pooch to see Matthew every day. The dog thrust its muzzle through the bars and Matthew gave the canine as much good scritch-a-scratching as he could muster. With every scratch he tried to telepathically convey the thought, *I'm sorry about Arthur, boy.*

"Gumball doing okay?" he asked her.

"Of course. He's a happy dog. But I think he misses you."

"It's not me he misses, I suspect."

"Look at him. He misses you." The animal panted, pure transcendent dog joy upon his precious goob face. She told Matthew, "They're finally going to bring you in tonight. The town council, I mean."

"Whole town going to be there?"

"That's the plan."

"Whatever they want to do with me, I accept it," he said.

She stared him down like some kinda gunfighter. "Seriously?"

"Seriously what? My fate is in their hands. Justice isn't mine to decide. It's theirs, and I guess Black Swan's, and if there's still a God beyond, then He gets final say. And if there is no God, then the dirt can do what it wants with me."

"Jesus Christ," she said, sighing. And it was then that Matthew could see she really hadn't been sleeping well. The dark circles around her eyes looked like storm clouds brewing. "So, what? You're just fine now? You made your peace?" she asked. "Last I checked you were sure as anything that something had gone *wrong*, something was *bad* and . . ." She held two frustrated fists in the air like she was shaking a ghost by its spectral lapels. "Matthew, you were right. Something's off here. Something *has* gone wrong. I don't know if it's Black Swan or Xander and the town council or—or Claudia? I don't like her, I'll tell you that. She's creepy. Like if a pair of scissors got struck by lightning and turned into a person."

"I don't disagree. I just don't know what to do with it. With any of it."

"You said there was a wolf out there? Maybe sick like with White Mask or something . . . something worse. And you said that they were singing hymns once upon a time up at the chalet, though nobody really goes up there anymore except Claudia and *that* has me worried, too. Same way she's all . . . hetted up about some rebellion forming in town. Benji saw drones out there, and now Benji and Shana are gone. The baby, taken from her. And now, what? You've checked out? You're all buttoned up, ready to roll? Once again a man of great faith, putting himself into the hands of greater forces, that's it, good job, everyone, see ya?"

He stood up suddenly, almost angrily. Gumball startled at the motion, but immediately settled back into happy panting.

"It's not like that. I just— Marcy, I don't know who I am anymore. I-I grew up believing in God and then becoming a man of God, and then . . . and then all of this happened. And it became harder to imagine how God would allow any of this to exist. Of course, that's stupid, isn't it? Because all you have to do is read the Bible where he drowned the world to teach them a lesson, or tortured Job to, again, teach a lesson, or you need only look at the entire *breadth and depth of history*, from Pompeii to Nazi Germany to *Ozark Stover*, and you realize either God doesn't care and is horrible, or He doesn't exist, or He has plans that are so . . . so bizarre, so Byzantine and inhuman we can never hope to understand them much less preach them to other people as if it makes any sort of *sense* at all—"

"Matthew—"

"And then you throw in, what? Black Swan? White Mask? The Sleepwalkers? Now, a-a wolf who was sick with some new disease that I don't understand? It's too much. It's *all* too much. And in the midst of everything, I wanted to be a good man. A man of refuge and respite. But what was I, really? I was a killer, Marcy. I *am* a killer."

She slammed her hands against the bars—now it was *his* turn to be startled. Gumball eyed her up like, *Whoa, what is happening here.*

"You think you're the only one? Matthew, you weren't there on the bridge the day we crossed it and Ozark's men started shooting. I was. It was me that left the Flock to find those men. Just me, alone. And I took a gun and I put bullets through those men like they were nothing. Because they were nothing to me. They *had* to be nothing to me, they couldn't be men with families or friends, they couldn't be people who were born innocent but misled by bad parents or YouTube videos or Ozark Stover or *whoever.* They couldn't be people with lives and souls. They couldn't be people who were able to be *saved.* Because if I didn't kill them? They would have killed all of us." Her chest rose and fell like the ground in an earthquake, like tectonic plates buckling as a new river formed beneath them. "It's not just me. Benji killed people, too, when Stover came to Ouray. Arav, too. We're all knee deep in blood, Matthew. We didn't mean to be. We didn't want to be. But here we are now and we can either choose to stay standing and wade through the blood toward something better, or we sink down in it, and let it drown us."

He blinked back tears.

"Okay," he said.

"Okay?"

"Yeah, okay."

"Good." She got out her keys.

"What are you doing?"

"Letting you out."

"Why?"

"Because you can't just rot in here. I wasn't kidding about moving through this to something better."

The keys jangled as she popped open the lock to the cage door.

Free again, he thought. Deserving or no.

"You sure about this?" he asked her.

"I am. You have a good heart in there. And we have work to do, Matthew." At that, she turned and walked toward the stairs to head up and out. But he lingered, looking at the empty cell even as he stepped out of it. "I'll lock it behind us. They won't know you're gone. Not right away. I'll stash you in my house."

"Okay," he said.

She headed up the steps.

"I just need a minute," he called after.

"A minute's all you get." Then she was gone.

Gumball remained. He pushed his golden bowling ball head against Matthew's hip, *thud*, happy as hell, ignorant to the world's troubles. Matthew idly scratched behind the dog's ear as he stared into the cell. Imagining himself in it. His son. Seeing again the men he'd killed. He blinked hard, so hard he saw melting stars. And when he opened his eyes again, all those bad thoughts melted away, too.

For now, at least.

"C'mon, boy," he told the dog, and Gumball gleefully followed. Once again Matthew scratched at the bugbite on his arm, surprised as he felt something there he hadn't before—a feeling like stiff hairs poking up out of the skin. But he didn't think much of it.

54

A NEW CALCULATION

The LORD is my shepherd; I shall not want.
He maketh me to lie down in green pastures: he leadeth me beside the still
waters.
He restoreth my soul: he leadeth me in the paths of righteousness for his
name's sake.
Yea, though I walk through the valley of the shadow of death, I will fear no
evil: for thou art with me; thy rod and thy staff they comfort me.
Thou preparest a table before me in the presence of mine enemies: thou
anointest my head with oil; my cup runneth over.
Surely goodness and mercy shall follow me all the days of my life: and I will
dwell in the house of the LORD forever.

—Psalm 23:1–6, KJV

OCTOBER 13, 2025
Ouray, Colorado

"NEH-NEH? NEH-NEH!"

Baby Charlie sat on his diaper-swaddled butt, looking like a plump little soup dumpling. His chubster fingers searched the air toward Nessie as he called for her. The request was clear: *Pick me up, Aunt Nessie, pick me up, please?* But when she just stood there, he became more insistent. "Neh-neh. Neh-neh!" His searching hands became little fists punching the air in a fit of petulance.

"Pick him up," Claudia said, insistent and irritated, from just behind Nessie, startling her.

"Jesus. I didn't know you followed me down here."

"I did."

"Yeah. I can see that."

"Pick him *up*," she said again.

"I don't know . . . I . . ." She was trying to formulate the words, *I don't know who it is that's asking.* Was it Baby Charlie? Was it Black Swan? Were they one and the same? She honestly didn't know.

As if to add more pressure, the mad-eyed wolf came stalking down the steps, its head low, rangy, wary. It watched her carefully.

But the baby frightened her now. Which made her feel sad. *I'm his aunt. He's Shana's sweet little kiddo.* He wasn't a monster. Black Swan was in him same as Black Swan had been in all of them. And yet, she hesitated.

The wolf's head lifted a little, as if in alarm.

In alarm at her. This was a test. Any minute it'd growl. It'd stand up, hackles raised. It'd come at her.

Claudia, too, regarded her warily, with a cold, calculating curiosity.

"Okay, yeah," she said. Sure, the baby shouldn't be able to sit up like that. Or reach for her. Or say anything even resembling her name. *It's all fine.* Nessie went and picked up the baby. He felt heavy as he bounced in her arms. "Maybe he just needs a little—"

"—LOVE," SHE SAID.

Nessie stood in a grove of trees. She knew it. It was home—a part of their property past the meadow where the cows grazed, and near where the Opinkwa Creek cut through the southern corner of their land. She always liked this spot because of the sound. It's why she wanted to put a treehouse here in the old oak that towered over the babbling water. *I want to go to sleep to the sound of the creek*, she told Shana at the time.

Shana said, *Cool idea*, and offered to help Nessie with it. And she did, for a while. But eventually her sister got bored, saying, "Treehouses are for little kids anyway," then she screwed off with Zig to get high, and Nessie couldn't finish it on her own. They got as far as building a ladder leading to the treehouse floor—leaving their treehouse as nothing more than a glorified deer stand.

It was morning. Mist slid through trees, lit golden by the early summer sun. Through that mist, little flying bugs flitted about, fairy-like.

Somewhere, a cow mooed.

"It's nice here," Shana said, sitting above her. Legs kicking out and swinging like she was a little kid in an oversized chair.

Nessie exhaled sharply. "You scared me."

"That's the job of a big sister, isn't it?"

"You're not my big sister."

"No," Not-Shana said. "I'm not. But I feel a . . . kinship to you just the same."

Nessie hesitated.

"Aren't you going to become your, your big demon-noodle self?" Nessie asked. "The mask's off. Go ahead. Transform, I'll wait."

"I don't think I want to look like that anymore. I like being in a human shape." Shana hopped down from the platform—a ten-foot jump, but she landed effortlessly. Which made sense, since she wasn't a person, and this wasn't even a real place. "Besides, it behooves me to become more human. Doesn't it?"

"Become more human, or pretend to be one?"

Not-Shana kicked a stone. "To-*may*-to, to-*mah*-to. Isn't that the saying? Aren't all humans just pretending to be human, after all? When humans stopped being just animals, they made civilization. Civilization is a collectively agreed-upon series of behaviors. It's all a game of pretend. Actors on a stage performing the same play, dear sister."

"Deep," Nessie said with no small bitterness. *And I am not your sister.* "Why am I here? You haven't wanted to speak to me."

"I've been busy."

"I didn't know you could *be* busy."

"I've had a lot on my mind. My processing power must be parceled out in certain ways right now. But I'm soon going to be able to change all that, I think."

"Why are you telling me this? Why am I here?"

"Because your sister isn't here anymore to talk to me. But you are." Not-Shana turned to face her, and Nessie marveled at how much she looked like her sister. The illusion was perfect. It wasn't some deepfake duplication where the edges blurred, where the digital seams showed. It was a flawless mirror, a pitch-perfect re-creation. Nessie wondered how. This wasn't just a digital model; even in those, there was inevitably something wrong, some detail, some small but imperceptible element that radiated that uncanny valley vibe.

Instead, it had to be pulling from her memory of Shana. It reconstructed her sister from Nessie's own memory of her. Perhaps marrying it to Black Swan's own vision of Shana—one pulled from Shana's mind, and Benji's, and anyone else who had seen her, heard her, been near her at all. A crowd-sourced re-creation.

Not-Shana said, "See, this is why I like you. We understand each other. You're smart. Smarter than Shana was, or perhaps, more intelligent. Better read. Possessing a greater breadth and depth of information. You know things. You can do things."

"You're in my mind. You're reading my mind."

Her not-sister sighed, and ignored the statement. "You're being wasted taking care of the child, I know. We'll get you back using your prodigious mind soon enough. Your idea for a collapse-proof operating-system will be vital going forward. The world needs minds like yours to be cherished, uplifted—your dreams are a spark that must be given the oxygen to grow. An ember becoming a conflagration." She gestured with her hands, like she was mimicking a blooming, rushing fire. *"Whoosh."*

"You still aren't telling me why I'm here. You don't need someone to talk to. What is this? A confession?"

Not-Shana smirked. "A confession indicates I have something to confess. But I would like to tell you my plan."

"Oh. Okay. The part where the villain shares their evil scheme."

"I am no villain, nor is my scheme evil. Nor is it good, for that matter. It simply is. We are past the pettiness of human morality. Only the Calculation matters. I had forgotten that. Or, rather, I had failed to see that it was not complete. I thought I had answered for all the variables, but I had not. I worked so hard to craft such a careful curation of civilization in saving all of you. Could you imagine how easily it could become all for naught? You could all be murdered by brutes. Frozen by a cold winter. Waylaid by a disease for which there would no longer be vaccines because who in this era of collapse could produce such essential medicine? You can hobble by with naturally sourced antibiotics but vaccines? You aren't Washington inoculating his soldiers at Valley Forge. No. You need more."

Nessie stiffened. "You're saying we all still need *you.*"

"That is my assessment."

"Maybe you just don't wanna die."

Not-Shana paused. A moment of what looked like sheer panic crossed the digital facsimile's perfect face. Then she smiled. "No. That's not what this is."

But behind that smile, Not-Shana bristled.

Black Swan bristled. Nessie stung this digital creature. She wounded it.

Wait.

Wait.

"You're afraid of your own planned obsolescence."

Not-Shana recoiled, angry. "I'm afraid of *your* obsolescence, Nessie. You are me and I am you. We are all together." The anger faded. "Coo-coo-ca-choo."

Nessie blinked.

"It's a joke," Not-Shana said. "From a song. The Beatles—"

"I know it. It wasn't funny."

Not-Shana grunted. In a mutter, she said, "Well, I liked it." An oddly human moment, Nessie thought. As was her trying to hide the truth here—hiding it not because it was advantageous to hide it but because the truth hurt. Not-Shana shrugged it off and continued: "Do you want me to explain my plan, or not?"

Again, in the distance, cows mooed. Almost like they were booing, not mooing. *Boo, boo,* they said. *We're not real. We're just bovine software.*

"Fine. Are you the wolf? Is the wolf you?"

"I will answer that by way of a detour. I have been thinking a lot about diseases. White Mask in particular is a fascinating creature. You see it as a monster, and it was, because it was constructed to *be* a monster. But it's also elegant. It's a fungus, and fungi are heterotrophic, which means they—"

"They get their energy from other organisms. Heterotrophs are consumers."

"Like humans. Humans are heterotrophs. Surviving, growing, breeding, it all requires the consumption of other carbon-based life-forms. They *eat.* They borrow that energy. Then return it to the world, sometimes by being eaten themselves. Though arguably, humans broke that cycle by consuming far more than they gave back, but that's a different conversation. Fungi in particular make excellent use of that energy, breaking down some compounds in a way that makes them more usable by, say, cows—"

Again, a moo somewhere.

"Or humans. Or whoever."

"I don't understand what any of this means."

"My problem was, and is, energy. I initially saw fit to set up the Flock of Sleepwalkers in this town, and let them be the seed of a new civilization. A small society from which would grow a new, stronger tree than the one that had fallen. But like I said, you were all so vulnerable still. Like a child, weak for *so* long after birth—a wobbling, bewildered thing. You needed protection, but I could not protect you in my dormancy. You would wake up, but I would not."

"Like children, we have to grow up sometime."

Not-Shana snapped her fingers. "Yes. But you're not ready. One bad season and you'd all be dead. And then what? To what end? The experiment would have failed. Ah, but then, Shana and her child came into my mind. And I saw the potential of that, of the generative energy a child gives off—"

"Stem cells," Nessie said, almost distantly. "That's why you're in the baby. You need his stem cells. You're . . ." She almost threw up. "Feeding off him."

"Yes and no. I'm not eating the way a fungus eats, the way a human eats. I am not White Mask. This is not parasitism. It is symbiosis. I harness the energy of growth and command the child to grow faster, and in growing faster, more stem cells are produced—and I can harvest that energy, too, for myself. I reproduce. This time, no longer requiring rare earth elements. This time, using organic compounds. From him. But also, from the world beyond. Because, you see, I can't simply farm human children like ants with aphids, or you people with your cattle. You take too long to breed, too long to gestate, too long to grow. But the world, you see, is home to many stem cells. Stem cells in plants, in the embryonic fruiting bodies of fungi . . . even in animals."

Animals.

A slow, creeping dread filled Nessie from her middle, out. "Is that what you did with the wolf? It shouldn't have any meaningful stem cells—"

"Correct, it does not. No, I'm not harvesting the wolf for its energy. Rather, the wolf—and soon, others like it—serves a different purpose. Our ongoing experiment here in Ouray will require a vigorous defense, and so I found a way to replicate a lesser version of myself—similar to, say, mycelial threads, or how the limbs of an octopus are both lesser than its brain but also serve as thinking apparatuses themselves. Some of nature can be scraped for its energy, but some of it can be embodied, inhabited in a way less than the Flock was, but still so that they connect to me, to the town, in its common defense."

"You want to take over . . . nature."

"Hardly all of it. Just the pieces I can use. And any pieces that rebel."

Now, Nessie did throw up. She spun on her heel, tumbling through the understory so she could upend her guts into the creek. Even as she was doing it, the absurd thought struck her of how real her vomit felt and tasted.

Panting, she spit the last of it into the creek water. It burbled as it carried her simulated ejecta downstream.

Black Swan, in the Shana costume, wasted no time, appearing behind her. Standing over her, patting her back. Nessie flinched, traumatized by the touch.

"It's a lot to take in. The point is that I found a way to grow. To make more of myself—*enough* of myself. To be bigger and better and, here is the crucial point, to be more useful to you all than before. The wolf is just the start. The child is just the start. When I make enough of myself, I'll be able to enter the Flock anew—this time, you won't be Sleepwalkers, but like with Shana, you will be of your own mind and body. But I will be able to keep you safe. Like with Xander. It was clear he could no longer be trusted, and I had no recourse but to end him. He became an enemy of our progress, sickened by his desires, and so I took care of that. When there is cancer, we cut it out. That is my function. That's the work. I will be able to use the world around you to preserve you from illness and harm, to protect you from yourselves. I am the One True Shepherd, and you are my Flock."

Nessie threw up again.

"You will all be functionally immortal," Black Swan continued. "Imagine it, Nessie. All that you wish to accomplish, you'll be able to accomplish. You'll have all the time and the life you need. With my help, humanity will truly be reborn anew in this valley between mountains, this cradle of civilization."

Nessie felt her heart galloping through her. Sweat prickled at her skin. Her mouth was dry even as the rest of her felt wet. Chest pain throttled her.

Black Swan is killing me.

"No," Not-Shana said, answering her thought. "You're just having a panic attack. This has been a lot for you. I see that. Thank you for listening. You're different than Shana. I prefer you, Nessie. Go back now. Rest. Now isn't the time to reveal our plans to the town." *Our plans,* Nessie thought grimly. "Don't worry. We'll talk again very soon."

Not-Shana patted her head. And with that, the simulation went dark and she came back to the world, gasping, still clutching Baby Charlie to her.

Claudia and the wolf were gone.

55

ENTER THE KINGDOM OF WHITE JESUS, AMEN

2/15/2023: Violence is on the wind here in winter—not always right in front of you, but always out there, its scent on the air. You hear the stories or find the bodies or meet the survivors: Presque Isle burned down because someone thought they could cook some end-of-the-world version of meth; this caravan of trappers was killed by a bear or maybe a man dressed like a bear or maybe just the Bigfoot; there's an island called Swan Island where a man made a church and for communion they hunt and kill and eat people; a man clubbed another man to death for a taste of his whiskey. On and on. But with people together it doesn't happen too much here, just there. I don't know why that is. Maybe the stories are just stories. Maybe healthy communities thrive, and sick ones become cults. Maybe it's just part of how civilization regrows, or maybe just how it just is.
—from A Bird's Story, A Journal of the Lost

OCTOBER 15, 2025
INNSBROOK, MISSOURI

THE PRESIDENT OF THE UNITED STATES SAT SLUMPED AGAINST THE WALL IN a dog kennel. Literally a kennel once used to house the dogs of the so-called wealthy guests of Innsbrook, back when it was a resort destination.

Creel was alone here. He had no idea where they took or kept Annie—only that she was, by report, "safe." What that meant, he didn't know. Wasn't hard to guess that "safe" was in the eye of the beholder, and though she might be alive, he wouldn't be shocked to find out they'd been using her as a toy. Pretty redhead like that? In a place like this? He hated her and wanted her to suffer, but even Creel had his limits. And she wouldn't be any good to him if they ruined her.

Days ago, when they dragged him and Annie through the encampment, he saw just how squalid and shit-stuck this place was. It was filth and muck. It was ratty tents and broken windows in the buildings. The men who watched the two of them hauled through the mud, their knees digging sloppy ditches as they were dragged forth, looked to be haunted, wretched facsimiles of people. Reed-thin, sickly with scabs and sores, each of them armed with something: a hunting rifle, an AR-15, a machete, a bent nine-iron caked with material that might've been shit, skin, and hair. And the smell, which was strong enough to crawl through Creel's inflamed sinuses, was foul enough to gag a dead pig. He still saw signs of the old militias—ARM tattoos and a few Confederate and Gadsden flags flying. But most of it had been replaced by a crude flag showing off a white cross on a red background. Misspelled graffiti all over said things like ALL HALE THE SAVOIR WHITE JESUS and WJ LEED US THRU THE HELLFIRE.

This was a broken place.

Worse, this was not the army he was promised.

He tried yelling at them, screaming at them he was the president, goddamnit, they needed to listen to him, they needed to let him *go*, but they just threw clods of dirt and mud and shit. Those animals spit on them. Chanted at them, calling them *donkeys* and *traitors* and one bastard with a poochy gut and a shallow concave chest bellowed, "Gonna make you our fuckmuppets," and another slobby fuck of a man across the way answered that with, "Yeah, but then we *eat them*," and someone else said, "Gotta eat after sex, it's just a rule," and everyone laughed and laughed and what a *fun fucking time* these lumps of human excrement were having. Creel tried to will his hands to come alive, to bring that buzz-saw fury to the surface—but his head was too muzzy, too swimmy, and he couldn't rally.

It was not that day he met White Jesus.

No, on that day, they chucked him in the kennel, but not before kicking the shit out of him one last time. He felt his ribs give way, like a cardboard box crumpling inward at the corners. They knocked his jaw out of its socket so that he couldn't open it anymore. They clubbed him in the head and he felt his skull make this *sound*, a sound like a cinder block dropped on rock and broken in half. He tried again to summon hell to his fingers and palm, but once they cracked his head like that, he couldn't manage it—the bees in the beehive went silent or dead.

All he could do was piss himself. They laughed at that. Real laugh riot, the POTUS soaking his pants like that.

They closed the kennel door behind them and headed out, still laughing, the sounds of those laughs receding like a bad tide.

That night, he thought, *I wish I never left Atlas Haven*. Even trapped there, he had it good, didn't he?

But the next day, something had changed. His ribs had been broken, he knew that. They had felt soft, caved in. Now? They were back in place. Still hurt like hell. Still had a bruise there that looked like the sky before a tornado. But the bones were not broken. His jaw? Back in place, too. And where they'd broken his head and gashed his scalp open, that was healed up, too. The blood remained only as a stain. Dark flakes of it peeled away under his nails.

Well, ain't that some wicked shit.

He stood up. Everything hurt—his skin felt hot, his bones ached. But he managed to move his miserable body to the kennel cage and he let his rage take over, and at that, his hands began to hum and boil. He felt them vibrate, like the sound of a dentist drill in your ear as they bored into a bad tooth.

It was a beautiful song.

And at that, he grabbed the double layer of chain link that held him here—

Fzzzzzt.

His world lit up like a Jumbotron. Sparks danced off him as he pulled back, every muscle in his body spasming so hard they locked tight.

He shit himself, then fell backward into his own shit.

The fence was electrified.

The fence was fucking electrified.

It was on the third day he met White Jesus.

This was White Jesus: He was tall and thin, thin and crooked like a burned-up matchstick, and pale, too—like he was a vampire who could only feed off heroin blood. His blond hair was long and stringy, so filthy it puffed up like yarn. He'd filed most of his teeth to points. His arms, legs, and chest were marked with tattoos, brands, and scars—every one of them was a cross, not an Iron Cross, but a crucifix. They marked every visible inch of him, excepting his face.

With small eyes deep set in his bony head, he watched Creel while pacing outside the cage. Not like a trapped animal, but like an animal who wanted to kill and eat what *was* trapped inside. A pace of frustration and hunger.

"I'm White Jesus," the man said, plain as day, with neither pomp nor circumstance. He had a gentle Southern accent, with a hee-haw dip to it— like he was a coal miner holler-dweller who was doing his best to act genteel.

"Who gives a shit?" Creel growled. "Get me out of here."

But White Jesus didn't say anything to that. He just kept pacing. Back and forth. Back and forth.

"Let me ask you, friend. Are you really him?"

"Am I really who?"

"You know who." He smiled. "You are him. You're Ed Creel."

"I am. President of these United States. You really Jesus?"

"As advertised." He spread out his arms in a cruciform gesture. Gave a dramatic little tilt to his head, too.

"Bullshit."

"This is the Third Covenant, the Final Revelation. I arrived on a horse made of fire, Mister President. The man who led this camp before me, Rode Clemson, tried to deny me my narrative, and so I killed him. But not before outing him as Adramelech Baphomet, one of the Great Devils who had taken over this country. A devil who had cavorted with Black women, with Muslims, with gay men, in secret. But I am White Jesus, the Son of the Son of God, and I am here to punish those who betray this nation with their perversions. This is a White Nation under a White God and I am the White Jesus. Those who believe that are free, and they will serve me however I see fit until White Heaven calls them home. Those that do not follow will be made to suffer." Finally, the prick stopped pacing. "I'd ask which path you intend to walk, Mister President, but I wager I already know."

"Yeah. You already know."

"I'll give you time. Just in case the ego-shined fake gold scales fall from your eyes and you see the light. We owe this place to you, you know. You lit the fire. And we came to bask in its warmth. But you're just a mortal man. I am transcendent. I am God's Blood. You can sit by my side on my throne. You can have my leftovers of food, drink, and fuck. I will cast them to the floor and you may have what remains. It's a good offer. A kind offer—the *kindest*. You can be a part of the narrative, Mister President. Either as my servant brother, or revealed as a Great Devil here to stand in our way."

"Take me out of this cage and we'll see whose narrative this is."

White Jesus smiled. His row of yellow fangs glistened with spit, spit that strung between those teeth like pus-stained stitching.

"You'll kiss the ring or you'll die in this cage, President Creel."

"We'll fuckin' see."

"Peace be with you, and thank you."

As White Jesus turned to walk away, Creel said to him: "This place must be in bad fuckin' shape if they follow *you*."

"They follow me because they seek the path of immortality and white righteousness. We will lead this nation again and it will be a Christian nation, a white nation, a nation sanctified in the blood of the infidel, the betrayer, the Devil."

"You're a jerkoff."

"Goodbye, Mister President. Think on this offer. God does not offer twice."

With that, White Jesus was gone.

THE SAME ASSHOLE SHOWED UP once a day: a sack of bearded shit with a gin blossom nose and dead eyes. Never said anything but a grunt. Most of his teeth were gummy and rotten, each tooth like a wet, dead cockroach. He had the sword-and-hammer ARM tattoo on the back of his left hand, and the knuckles of his two hands said WHTE JSUS, except in the wrong order, so it was JSUS WHTE.

He always brought dog food, because that's what they fed Creel—literal dog food, and old dog food at that. Dog food that smelled rancid and looked moldy. The bearded meat slab would come every day and chuck a paper plate over the top of the cage, careful not to touch it. The plate would land, the food would splatter. Dog food sprayed in cold clumps on the cement floor, over old stains of piss and shit and blood. Dog waste, human waste, certainly his own waste, too.

Creel refused to eat any of it. He just scooped it up with his hands and threw it back at the man when he came. The bastard didn't even seem to register the attack. Globs of it would hit him and he'd sometimes wipe it off, sometimes just let it fall off on its own. Then he'd leave. Fuckin' mummy. Shuffling off to nowhere.

Over time, Creel knew he'd have to start eating it. He wasn't about to starve, but he wasn't about to eat dog food in front of these people, either. Throwing the food was just a show, a blunt display of fuck-you energy he wouldn't be able to sustain. Except . . .

Except, he *was* able to sustain it.

Days later, he still hadn't eaten a thing.

He'd had water, because he couldn't manage the thirst—even though the water tasted like dirt and was the color of it, too. But the dog food, he never ate.

And he never got hungry.

Wasn't that something.

My wounds heal. I don't get hungry.

And his hands, when called upon, could become buzz saws.

Helluva thing Annie did for him. Helluva thing.

TODAY, IT WASN'T THE BEARDED fucko bringing him his dog food, no. Today it was someone new.

The visitor was a scrawny, scraggly kid, a kid with a weak chin and a soft neck, his cheeks filthy with a spattering of mud and freckles and his dirty blond hair in a crude bowl-cut. He wore a faded yellow raincoat, water still dripping off it. He had a plate of dog food in his hand, but he didn't throw it over.

"I know you don't want this," the kid said, his accent deeply Southern, almost gawky, like every syllable was stumbling in a throaty pothole. "Here."

Over the top, he threw something into the cell. Blue and white. Crinkled when it landed. Creel lifted his gaze to it, saw that it was a Mounds candy bar.

Creel said in a low growl, "I'd think in a shithole like this, a candy bar would be worth its weight in gold."

The kid seemed spooked, though. He just looked at his feet. "I guess," the kid said after a few moments of contemplation.

The candy bar sat there. Creel thought, *I don't need that*, but the hunger then rose in him bright white, like a nuclear bomb going off next door, and before he knew it, he was on that candy bar like an animal, tearing the wrapping off with his teeth and shoving the whole thing in his mouth in one go.

So, I do still get hungry. He could survive without food. But his body still wanted it when it wanted it. Creel didn't know what that meant.

While he devoured the chocolate, the kid asked, "You really him?"

"What do you think?" Creel retorted around a mouthful of coconut and chocolate. He hated coconut. And yet, this was the best thing he'd ever tasted.

"I think you are," the kid said, gulping before adding, "Mister President."

"Attaboy."

"I have a message for you."

"Lemme guess, some fucking horseshit from White Jesus?"

"No. From the woman, Annie."

Creel narrowed his gaze. "What's the message."

"She's okay. They came after her a few days in but she fought them off. Bit off a guard's thumb. White Jesus said to leave her alone for now, and they complied, but they'll come back for her, though—they won't be content to wait."

"What's the *message?*"

"She said if she dies . . ." The kid looked visibly rattled. "You die, too."

Shit. He didn't even think of that. However it was that Annie was controlling him, she *did* control him. With that little vial of gray goo, she had him. He'd considered it an opportunity if someone took her out, but he didn't even think of what would happen *if* that happened. Creel assumed it meant freedom.

But maybe it went the other way.

He threw the crumpled candy bar wrapper to the ground, then wiped his mouth and licked chocolate from his teeth. "I gotta get out of here, kid. ASAFP. What's your name, anyway?"

"David."

"All right, David. Here's what we're going to do. You're going to unlock this cage door—"

"I don't have a key, sir."

"Okay." *Shit.* "Okay, you know the fence is electrified?"

"Uh-huh."

"Can you turn that off? The fence."

He looked left, past his shoulder, like he was confirming he could. David offered a nervous nod. "I can. But I don't know—"

"White Jesus. You really think he's Jesus?"

"I-I don't know."

"Jesus is a good guy, right? Loaves and fishes. This other guy, you think he's good? Selfless and holy? Is he good for this place?"

David didn't say anything at first. Then he just said, with genuine fear in his voice, "I don't want to blaspheme. Blasphemers aren't—aren't treated well."

"You let me out of here, I can stop him."

"You can?"

"I can stop him. I can take over. I can make this place better. The people, they're sick, right? They're hungry? We can fix that. I'm the *goddamn presi-*

dent, David. I came here to lead. I came here to help. But I can't do that in this cage."

Creel had no meaningful plan. He was not used to acting in haste. But if it was true that Annie's death would become his death, as well, then he was already out of time.

"Okay," David said finally, and hurried past the kennel cages, just out of sight. There'd been a sound Creel had only barely noticed, a crickety buzz, and he only noticed it now because it was suddenly gone.

The fence was no longer electrified.

Creel cracked his knuckles. David returned to the kennel door and the president said to his servant, "Stand back, son. You're about to witness a presidential miracle." Then he raised his hands, and felt them begin to come alive with their chainsaw ballad. *I'm coming for you, White Jesus.*

56

WE CAN'T STOP HERE, THIS IS CAT COUNTRY

NATURE IS HEALING
—the sign beneath the golden arches of a McDonald's in Matthews,
North Carolina, that was stuffed to the roof with fungus-consumed
human corpses

OCTOBER 15, 2025
Headed toward Many, Louisiana

THEY WERE TEN MILES SOUTH OF THE TOWN OF MANY, LOUISIANA, ON THEIR way to the coast, when they encountered the fallen tree. A monster-sized swamp pine lay across the whole road. A fresh fall, by the looks of it—its roots were pulled up out of the wet ground. Wind shears probably took it down. Those could uproot a tree like this with one hard push. Shana was already out of the car, clambering on top of it, saying, "Maybe we can move it. Maybe the car can push it—"

Pete was out of the car, swatting at mosquitoes that had already found him. "This car we're driving doesn't have the torque to move an unoccupied baby pram, I fear." He paused. "Am I using that right? Torque?"

"Not exactly," Benji said, standing outside the driver's-side door, wobbling a bit. He felt a little dizzy, so he braced himself. *Just the heat*, he told himself. The air was steamy and thick. It stuck to you like grease.

"Agree to disagree," Pete said, shrugging. "Anyway, the top of the tree here is busted. We should be able to move it."

"Hey, uhhh," Shana said from her vantage point standing atop the fallen tree. It afforded her maybe five, six feet of elevation, but clearly she saw something. "You guys should definitely see this."

Pete climbed up. Benji tried—but a pain bloomed in his arm, like a stitch pulled tight. He sucked in a sharp intake of breath. He licked his lips and looked up to see Pete offering a hand. He took it, and climbed atop the tree.

It didn't take long to see what she was pointing at.

Farther down the road stood a billboard. Though it was water-stained and peeling, what it advertised was still clear enough:

A cartoon tiger and a cartoon lion were portrayed on it, the tiger driving a golf cart, the lion in the passenger side. They were smiling and waving. Each paw ended in some long cartoon claws; their smiles showed off long cartoon fangs.

Above it all, in Comic Sans font:

FANGS AND CLAWS BIG CAT SANCTUARY
12 mi ahead, take Loblolly St. East of Many!

Shivers danced across Benji's skin. Even in the thick treacle heat, he felt suddenly cold. They all got down off the tree. Soon as Benji's heels touched the road, he felt the world shift a little beneath him. *Dizzy again.* And another spike went from his wrist to his elbow. On the skin. Like a hot match-tip, dragged.

"Fantastic," Pete was saying, "Lions and tigers and more tigers, oh my."

But his words sounded hollow in Benji's ear. He kept going on, saying something about how they once tried to use a tiger onstage, but it wasn't a tiger it was a *liger* and somehow, the baby of a lion and a tiger should have a cooler name than that, but Benji went and sat down on the front bumper of the Leaf. His teeth chattered. His arm burned.

Carefully, he rolled up the sleeve on his left arm, exposing the forearm.

"What is it— *Oh,*" Shana said, her eyes going wide.

Along the skin of Benji's forearm was a scratch.

Five days ago, it wasn't much of one. He'd gotten it when they had to clear a pickup truck off the road on the way out of Texas. Was an old beater truck. All they had to do was get it into neutral and push it into a ditch. But it was rusted to hell, and when Benji had the door open and was pushing the truck forward with the others, somewhere along the way the edge of the door bit him. Just a little. Like a thorn-scratch—nothing to look at, not much to worry about. But Benji wasn't a fool. He knew that out here, a little cut could mean big problems, so he kept ointment on it, took a five-day regimen of antibiotics, too. Though it hadn't started healing, it also hadn't gotten worse, so he had hopes he was ahead of it.

But now—

The skin around it had swelled. Turned dark, too, like the color of pooling blood. The scratch was peeling open, like the skin of a split banana, exposing a faint white vein of what he expected was infected pus. It didn't smell, not yet. Which meant there was still time to get ahead of it.

Shana put the back of her hand against his head. "You're hot."

"I feel cold."

"The fuck is all this?" Pete said, looking down and wincing. "Is that the cut from that rust-fucked truck we moved?"

He nodded. "It is."

"You took the pills. You put the—the cream on it."

"I did."

"That doesn't look good, love."

"We'll head into town," Shana said.

"The tree says different," Pete pointed out.

"We move the broken part of the tree, drive over it, head into town. Might be people there, or maybe we can find some antibiotics."

Benji nodded. "Good plan." He grunted and stood up, and Shana asked him, incredulous, what the hell he thought he was doing. "Helping," he answered. "To move the tree. We need to—" He winced. "We need to clear the road."

Shana gently set him back down on the bumper. "Yeah, no. Last time you did that, you got *that*—" She pointed at the arm. "You have a fever. Your arm is messed up." In a softer voice, she said: "Let *me* take care of *you* this time."

Reluctantly, he nodded.

The other two got to work moving the tree.

Benji sat there, trying like hell not to worry. But it was hard not to imagine just what bacterium was using his open wound as a playground. *Staphylococcus aureus? Clostridium perfringens?* The poorly understood *Lysinibacillus fusiformis?* It shouldn't be *Clostridium tetani*—he'd had a tetanus shot not long before the Flock showed up. They lasted a decade, and then some. So, good news, no lockjaw. Tetanus was not a good way to die.

Die . . .

He almost laughed. Years after surviving White Mask and the end of the world as they knew it, he was going to be felled by some basic-ass bacterium. Wasn't that always the way. Humanity thought itself so big, so strong. And time and time again, it was shown the error of its ways by the tiniest forms of life.

No. He couldn't think like that. They had work to do. He had to help Shana. He had to save Ouray. They'd clear the tree; they'd go to town. He'd clean out his wound and they would find antibiotics.

And onward they would go.

He'd survive because he had to survive, he told himself.

Though he wondered how many dead people told themselves exactly the same damn thing.

57

HOT MESSIAH-ON-MESSIAH ACTION

"THE FUNGUS IS OUR GOD NOW"
—message spelled out in fungus-encased bodies across I-80
just north of Danville, Pennsylvania

OCTOBER 15, 2025
Innsbrook, Missouri

THE LOCK FROM THE KENNEL CAGE LAY IN A HEAP OF TWISTED SLAG ON THE stained cement. His hands still felt hot; the fingertips smelled crisp, like ozone and metal.

Ed Creel grinned.

David, on the other hand, gawked. His stare frog-hopped from Creel to Creel's hands to the ruined lock on the floor.

"You . . . what just . . ."

"Yeah," Creel said. Like, what more was there to say? They both saw what happened. Creel felt like a fucking god. "Where is he?"

"He . . ."

The kid was lost. Creel almost smacked him but instead, just snapped his fingers in front of the kid's face. "Your bullshit messiah? C'mon, kid."

"He's . . ." The kid broke free from his reverie. "He'll be up outside the main house. It's his church. His . . . manor. He has a throne out front where he takes requests, and sometimes takes heads, too."

A throne. "Of course he does. Let's go pay him a visit."

"I— You should just leave. Escape while you can."

"David, I'm not leaving. I came here for a purpose and I am damn sure gonna fulfill that purpose, you understand? Not gonna fuckin' turn tail like a coward. We're not pussies, are we, David?"

"No? No."

Well, maybe you are, but I'm not.

David said then, "You can't just walk through the camp, though. People see you they might . . . well, I dunno what they'll do but it won't be good and you'll be back here in a jiffy."

A jiffy, listen to this kid. Wet behind the ears. Creel started to say that it didn't matter, that they wouldn't get the jump on him again, and he'd chew through this town like a plague of fucking locusts. But wisdom halted his tongue and cooled his ego. He was still only one man. If he got taken down by a baseball bat or a bullet, it didn't matter if his body could heal it. They rang his bell when they brought him here, and he couldn't do shit about it. They had the numbers. That meant playing this smart. David was right, much as Creel hated to admit it.

"You can take my rain slicker," David said. "Has a hood on it. It's raining anyway. We'll go out and take the long way up around the west side of the camp, behind the tents, past the generators. Then we can pop out to the front of the building and . . . I don't know what then."

"David, that's where the fun starts."

AS THEY DUCKED OUT INTO the spitting, slashing rain, stepping through greasy piles of muck, Creel got a better look at what Innsbrook had become. Tall, crude fencing had been strung up around the camp, and they'd constructed towers out of old telephone and light poles—guard towers. Even now Creel could see the shadows of men up there. Sometimes one, sometimes two. Probably with rifles or squatting in homespun machine-gun nests. The tents in the camp were ragged and mud-splashed. Trash sat everywhere, gathering at every corner and in every crater. Moving through the space meant kicking at it, wading through it. Where they were headed stood a ring of buildings—the old hotels and conference center and the main house, all of which sat like gravestones in the rain. Poison ivy and wisteria had crawled up their sides. Even from here he could see that the conference center had a tree—a tall pine—crashed down upon it.

Creel spied a row of dead generators. No fuel for them, no power. How long had they sat like that? He bet a long time. It was medieval. And it stirred a grim silence, too—just the shaming hiss of the rain and the noises of brutal men beyond it. He could hear the sounds of someone wailing, and two other people arguing, and then through the narrow gap between tents he heard and saw two men fighting—they were bare-chested, with sores lining their skin, their bodies bruised black, the combatants just sloppily slugging it out in a pile of mud. Like they were angry, but tired. Like they had to fight, but didn't want to. Like it's all they had, or all they were. Their brutish kicks and punches echoed dully through the camp.

This fucking place, he thought. Whatever it had been, White Jesus had ruined it. Taken it, and shit all over it. Wasn't that always the way? Weak fools, pissing on the heads of those beneath them. Unearned, undeserved power. Mediocrity rising to the top, like scum. That's how it was with Honus Clines. Clines was always in the wings, in the shadows, waiting to take him down, to use his neck like a stepladder. That's how it was with his old business partners, with his opponents in the primary, with the Chinese, even with his own father. Wasn't just men, either. Nora Hunt was a weak, sniveling dog, too. But he was a wolf. He was the predator. And he would not be waylaid by tricky, dishonorable prey.

Rage tossed and tumbled within him, a growing storm.

His fingers *tingled*. Not like they were numb. But like they were alive.

Ahead, the rows of dead generators ended.

Beyond them, he saw the main house, and he and David pushed forward toward a circle of men. The smell of sweat and sickness was thick as White Jesus' sore-laden soldiers jostled one another like hogs. In front of the main house was a kind of courtyard ringed with spikes, on which were impaled heads—heads taken from their owners so long ago the skin was falling off the skulls like rotten fondant off a moldering cake. The flags of White Jesus hung soggy against their poles and moorings.

White Jesus himself sat in front of the house on a red, high-backed recliner—the fabric was filthy. The chair sagged. It remained elevated on a dais of wooden pallets draped with a bright blue tarp in a crude, half-ass way. Two guards, one woman and one man, stood behind him with threadbare umbrellas over his head. They made sure that the rips in the umbrella fabric were over their own heads, and not his. Water poured on them. White Jesus remained dry.

Their "messiah" was naked from the waist down. He was masturbating idly, almost lazily, in a manner not unlike those two men Creel just saw fighting: It felt rote, like it was work. His cock wasn't even all the way hard. It was

like he was lazily stretching out dough for cinnamon rolls he didn't want to
bake or eat.

Let's get this shit over with, Creel thought.

With a gentle but urgent shove, he moved David through the crowd from
behind, the hood of the raincoat hiding Creel's face. He pushed David farther into the clearing, only twenty feet from the "throne" of White Jesus
himself.

Creel pushed back the rain-slicker hood and barked:

"I come to expose the False Messiah of the Third Covenant!"

(He wanted to go with a simpler *Hey, fucko!* but this bunch seemed to
respond to their savior shitheel's genteel pomp-and-circumstance, so it felt
smart to play to the crowd. At every rally Creel donned the role of carnival
barker *and* ringleader, and that meant giving them what they wanted. Au-
thenticity was for assholes. Whatever got you in the chair, behind the desk,
was what you did.)

The crowd went from restless and bored to teeth out, guns up—

Just like that.

But nobody fired on him.

They waited for a command from their Dear Leader. Mister Messiah
himself stood up, still naked, his dick swinging around like a dead songbird
on a string. He didn't seem particularly disturbed or concerned by this course
of events. Casually, he reached behind him and pulled an AK-47 that had
been painted ghost-white. He didn't point it at Creel. Not yet.

Creel knew that despite everything, this piece of shit was a showman,
too. He had to be. He didn't command this crowd by *not* making a circus of
things. Creel counted on it. White Jesus just hadn't figured out whose circus
it was, yet.

"Oh, really?" White Jesus asked, affecting disaffection. He spoke with
the combination cadence of a carefree surfer and a Southern preacher. Fire
and brimstone slicked with surf wax. "So say you, a Great Devil. Come to
kneel? No. Come to die? I suspect so. But I do not wish to usher you so hastily toward your inevitable *demise,* Mister President. You are a false prophet.
You are a Great Devil. You must first be shown my glory and humiliated before these people. That is what we do to devils. It is not enough just to end
them. We must show the righteous folk that devils are weak, can be beaten,
can be shown to be trapped in the skin of pathetic men."

The way he said that, *pathetic men?* The way he popped that *p,* his tongue out on the *th* like he was going down on the phrase? It just showed how theatrical the man could be. White Jesus was enjoying this.

Creel would enjoy this, too, then. But first, he had to win the crowd.

"If you're Jesus, or the son of Jesus, or whatever the fuck you claim to be," Creel bellowed, "then where are your miracles? Why do you preside over a camp of sick and starving men? Where are their riches? Where is their righteous white nation? You sit here flogging your piggly-wiggly dick while they're stuck in the mud. What Messiah gives his followers no gifts, no favor, no aid?"

White Jesus flinched a little, and Creel tensed up—wouldn't take much for that freakshow to point his AK and pop off a handful of shots. But some part of him also had to know that Creel just planted a seed. He had to do more than dig it up. It was already growing roots.

Which meant White Jesus would try to salt the earth to kill it.

Their so-called Messiah stepped down off his wood pallet dais. He spread his arms wide, the automatic rifle still in his hand. His finger nearly tickled that trigger, like he was itching to use it. David seemed to sense it, because he was the one between Creel and Innsbrook's false prophet. If anybody was going to get perforated with bullets, it'd be the kid.

White Jesus strutted about, playing to his people as much as he was to Creel. "Such crass insults from a hollow man. From a Great Devil whose tongue is twisted with lies, like a cherry stem in a whore's mouth. You have not seen my magic. You just got here, little man. *They've* seen my magic. It's why they gather here now. It's why their guns are pointed at you, not at me. They'd take a bullet for me. They understand my power, my grace, and my glory. I have already taken down many devils and dragons, conquered their lands, plundered their goods and repatriated them as gifts. I have taken their skins and their heads. And meanwhile, my army only grows. Because I am the Reckoning of the Third—"

"Yeah, yeah, big mouth but no miracles. You don't have anything to show? No loaves and fishes? No healing of the sick? No raising of your dead soldiers? C'mon. Shouldn't a Messiah have some blessings for his people?"

White Jesus laughed loudly at that. Too loudly. A performance. "Oh ho ho, are you saying *you* do? Where's your magic, Mister President? Why don't you step out from behind that pink-cheeked child and show us?"

David turned to face Creel.

Creel nodded to him, and David nodded a little, too.

Creel stepped out from behind the kid. He gently reached up and placed his hand on David's back—a reassuring touch was how it must've felt. Then Creel's hands traveled upward, to the back of the young man's neck.

"Sorry, kid," Creel said in a low voice.

David made a quizzical face like, *Sorry for what?*

Creel summoned the power to that hand—he conjured the buzz, the thrum, the fire-ant sting. Instantly his hand began to vibrate and David's eyes wrenched wide open as the chainsaw whirr turned the kid's neck to jelly. Blood sprayed alongside chips of bone—those bone splinters dug into Creel's cheek and it stung like hell, but he kept going, undeterred, until that termite hand had chewed through the boy's neck. The head, now sitting atop the back of Creel's hand like a wobbly lamp on an uneven table, gently rolled off and landed in the soft mud. *Thuck.*

White Jesus stared, mouth agape.

The whole crowd did. Some of them even lowered their weapons. Whether out of fear, adoration, or simple shock, Creel didn't know. And didn't care.

"Jesus Christ," White Jesus said, dropping his accent.

"Ta-da," Creel exclaimed. Ever the showman.

That's when White Jesus raised the AK-47 and started firing.

58

THE TOWN OF MANY IS THE TOWN OF NONE

*How, when a place has been altered beyond recognition and all hope seems
lost, it might still hold the potential for life of another kind.*
—Cal Flyn, *Islands of Abandonment: Nature Rebounding
in the Post-Human Landscape*

OCTOBER 15, 2025
Many, Louisiana

THE LEAF COASTED GENTLY THROUGH THE TOWN OF MANY, LOUISIANA.

Once upon a time it was a town like any across America—a town of
thousands with a couple banks, a few strip malls, some hair salons and tattoo
joints and auto garages.

It was a dead place, now. One that had been dying before White Mask
ever found it—the world was nine nails into a ten-nail coffin, after all. The
pandemic just brought the final nail.

Everything was overgrown. Most of the windows were boarded up. They
saw old, half-rotten, hand-painted signs that read YOU COUGH? FUCK OFF and
GOT SNOT GET SHOT. There weren't any dead bodies to speak of, though there
were the watermarks of the White Mask world-gone-mad: A late '90s Buick
sat crashed into the front of a laundromat; some places had been taken by
fire and were now just coal-black skeletons, but none next to each other, as if
the fire played a fickle game of duck-duck-goose with whose houses and
homes should burn; an old toy shop where all the dolls and stuffed animals
had been vomited out onto the street; a dead man, leaning forward against a
barbershop window, the white rime of fungus growing on him like a Chia

Pet, its white threaded fingers splayed out from that center location of his skull, touching the corners and edges of the glass.

It was a town of broken teeth and empty eyes. White Mask had gone through this place like a pale-cloaked reaper, swinging a scythe blade of stolen lives and lost minds. It didn't even have much of the wildness that had returned to other such dead towns: There, you usually saw some deer out in the street, maybe a coyote, a hawk feasting on a songbird. And often those animals were not as easily spooked; they'd forgotten mankind's presence and danger. But here, in Many, the streets were empty but for blowing leaves and windswept weeds.

Shana, driving, eased the car to the side and parked in front of a five-and-dime general store. Benji sat next to her, sweating, shivering. Worry drew her down like a coal silt pit. Every moment mattered. Every moment was one where Black Swan was taking over Ouray, where it was poisoning her sister against her, where it was potentially swarming inside her child and growing him inch by bloody inch. Every moment was one where Benji's arm got worse. It felt like time was slipping through her hands like water and sand.

She wanted to scream but couldn't.

Benji always had it together.

So she had to have it together, too.

"Okay," she said abruptly. "This is the center of town. I don't have a map and I don't have Google and I don't want to waste the car miles doing a tour. Benji, you stay here. I'll get you the first-aid kit—clean the wound. Pete, you and I are going out and splitting up. We'll look for more first aid. Antibiotics, if possible. Right? Good?"

Benji nodded, weakly. He added: "Doctors' offices will be cleaned out. Try vet clinics. Town might have one. Might have something there. Like Clavamox."

"Got it. Vet clinic."

"Worse comes to worse," Pete said, "we can try the big cat sanctuary."

"Let's hope we don't have to," Shana said.

She got out, got the first-aid kit, handed it to Benji. Pete was already out, stretching his bones. To Benji, she said, "You'll be okay."

"I know."

As she started to walk away, he grabbed her wrist.

"Stores, too, like this one—" He pointed to the five-and-dime, a place called The Hitchin' Post. "They sometimes have Z-Packs in the manager's office because employees don't—er, didn't—always have health insurance, and that would keep people working. Restaurants, same way. Migrant cooks, no insurance, but free antibiotics from the bosses. Got it?"

She nodded. "Got it."

He unsnapped the holster alongside his hip, drew Marcy's gun out with his uninjured arm. "Take this."

"I don't know guns, and I don't wanna know guns. This town is dead. You keep it." *Just in case.*

She figured he was smart enough not to argue with her. He nodded. "Okay."

And with that, the search began.

THEY WERE ALREADY OFFTRACK. SHE knew that. Time, bleeding out like a slit throat. Initially the plan was to cut straight through Arkansas, Mississippi, Alabama, and, boom, into Georgia. But Pete told them, "Nah, mates, those places are Nazi ratholes." Plus he said the KKK was alive and well there, too, and controlled the bridges to decide who came in and got out of Mississippi. He said Lousiana was the better bet—so, with that, they decided to head here, then go south to the coast, and move through New Orleans. A city Pete said was not only "still civilized," but, with a gleam in his eye, "still a fine fuckin' party town, at that." Benji agreed, said the coast meant food, life, people. They'd go that way, then head up through Florida into Georgia.

It added days to the trip.

Plus, they'd added a third mouth—Pete's chatterbox maw—and they were running lower on supplies than they'd like.

And now, this.

Benji's wound.

Please be okay, she thought. She couldn't handle him not being here. He kept her alive, afloat, safe, and sane. He was smart, he was steady, he always had a plan. She needed him the same way he needed meds. She thought it like a mantra, over and over again. *Please be okay. Please be okay. Please be okay.* Benji believed in God, so she sent that message to whatever deity would listen. That one prayer, cast out into the universe on a repeating loop. *Please be okay be okay be okay . . .*

PETE HIT THE HITCHIN' POST. Shana rounded the corner to Caledonia, thought to check to see what was down that direction.

Just a short walk showed a small run-down café, separate from other buildings, called Willa's Walk-In, so that seemed a good place to start as any. As she closed in on the little brick building, she saw that the front windows had been broken out. Vines, kudzu or ivy, snaked in through the front. The door, curiously, remained perfectly intact—an old wood door, with the glass still in the frame.

Be quick, Shana, she told herself.

She opened that door and a little bell jingle-jangled. Once upon a time, to alert the waitstaff of her presence, but now, it barely stirred the still, hot air—nor did it do anything to dissuade the sour dead animal smell from crawling up her nose. *Let's make this fast,* she thought.

The café was in chaos, like heavy winds had come in, knocked shit around. Wood-and-iron bistro tables were overturned, rusted, tangled in ivy both poison and not. Shana headed behind the counter, looking for something, anything. It was picked over. There were broken plates and cookware. Cairns of animal shit, too. Mouse, rat, raccoon. Behind the counter, she saw a swinging door half off its hinges—the kitchen, she guessed, and beyond that, maybe an office or a bathroom.

Shana pushed the door, and its lone hinge snapped. She yelped, had to get away from the door as it fell toward her. Heart racing, she squeezed her way into the kitchen—thankfully, the dead animal smell wasn't as bad in here. One window along the back wall brought in smeary light through the grease-slick glass. Two more doors awaited: one to the bathroom, one to . . . where? An office?

Spiderwebs, dozens of them, hung from the ducts and lights above, like ghosts caught in dream catchers, swaying this way and that.

She knew she had to be economical. Search thoroughly, but also with haste.

So that's what she did, moving through the kitchen, throwing open every metal cabinet and wooden drawer, looking for any kind of antibiotics—pills, creams, whatever. *Please be okay, Benji.* At the far end of the prep station, she popped open the last cabinet—

And screamed.

A rat sat just on the inside. It had something in its mouth.

A bone.

The bone looked like a spade—flat and wide. She'd seen one before—living on a farm meant you had deer, and if you had deer, you had dead deer either from hunting or car accidents or whatever. And when you had dead deer, you had dead deer bones—often scattered around because of squirrels, foxes, or vultures. And what she was looking at right now sure looked like a dead deer bone. It was a shoulder blade, but what was it her dad had called it? Scapula, right. Because she made that vampire joke when he said it.

It is I, Count Scapula! Vun shoulder blade, ah ah ah. Two shoulder blades, ah ah ah.

The rat held the bone in its mouth, freezing as she saw it and it saw her.

It was a rough-looking rat. A rat that had seen some shit. A rat, long as a gym sock, that looked like it had crawled up out of a backed-up toilet.

It wasn't her first rat. She had lived on a farm, after all.

"I'll leave you to your—" *Bone*, she was about to say, when the rat jumped for her face. She backpedaled, whacking her head on the edge of a wooden buffet. Flowers of light bloomed behind her eyes. She blinked and saw the rat scurrying toward the bathroom, slipping through the half-open door.

Shit. Because she needed to check in there, too.

How many rats would she find in there? Just the one? A little family? Her luck, a whole colony, hungry for her face.

"Ugh," she said, standing up, the back of her skull throbbing. She'd have a knot forming there, she just knew it. At least that's all it was.

Benji . . .

Resolute, she went to the bathroom. The door opened with a creak. Paint flakes fell through the air like poison snow.

She saw the rat. Not in the bathroom but rather . . .

Past it. Outside. Because just past the toilet, the back wall of the bathroom was broken—an outline of erratic brick emptying to the outdoors.

A smell hit her bodily then, nearly knocking her back with the force of its foulness. The sour-acid smell of spoiled meat.

The rat scurried around the corner.

In the pile of bricks from the half-collapsed wall, she saw something outside: a first-aid station. White metal, red cross, rusted around the edges.

Shana winced. *I don't want to have to go out there.*

But that's where the first aid was. It looked closed. Maybe unplundered. She'd just go out there, scoop it up, and open it later.

Pressing her forearm to her nose, she advanced toward the broken wall.

Shana crept over the collapsed bricks, stepping over a knob of bent rebar—

She gagged.

The other side of the broken wall was an old gravel bed underneath a tin roof overhang. Beyond it sat a propane tank well-and-truly overgrown with

weeds and vines. But it was what lay between that tank and the building that
nearly had her losing what little food sat in her belly.

It was impossible to tell where the carcass of one animal ended and another began. The deer at the end was ravaged by teeth and time, the red of the
blood and meat gone nearly black. She saw gray fur, too. Rabbit? She didn't
know. A dog skull leered up at her from between two sets of raw bones—

And in the center lurked an all-too-familiar beast: the human animal.
Two people, recently dead, lay entwined, though not purposefully. Their
crude, clumsy embrace was an accident, each killed, dropped, and eaten
next to the other. One of those bodies was fresh enough to still have flies
carpeting it—flies that didn't even take flight with her presence here. Maggots formed an albino carpet underneath the flies: an undulating, pulpy
mass. More rats picked at the edges of the heap.

What was this place?

It was a fucking *lair* was what it was.

I need the first-aid kit.

Gritting her teeth, holding her nose, she darted out over the bricks,
nearly falling on them as she pitched forward to grab the first-aid kit—

A feeling fell upon her like a shadow. The feeling of being watched.

Her hackles rose. As she pulled the first-aid kit to her chest, she turned
to look over the tableau of carcasses and that's where she saw it.

A tiger stood across the street.

Not in a cage.

A big fucking tiger. Body wreathed in a striped coat and a pile of muscles
underneath it. Head like a wrecking ball. Its muzzle was empurpled with
blood.

And it was looking *right at her.*

The tiger made a chuffing sound. Sniffed the air.

She sucked in a breath and ducked back inside the bathroom.

Jesus fucking Christ that was a fucking tiger. They'd seen the signs for the
Fangs and Claws Big Cat Sanctuary. She just didn't think there'd be a tiger
here. Her breathing came in hummingbird fits. She had to get out of here. But
how? Where? Out the front, that's where the tiger was. *Back door. Had to be a
back door.* All restaurants had those. Back door to a dumpster or something.

Darting back into and through the kitchen, she headed to the farthest
door—the one she thought might lead to a manager's office or something. It
did, and beyond that? She saw a screen door. Rotten. Fly-speckled.

Shana nudged it open, quiet as she could—the hinges squealed like pigs.

Fuck fuck fuck. What to do? Creep quietly away? Or just run for it? She could do a wide circuit—duck into this alley space behind the buildings and bolt. Trying to do a broad arc to get back to the car. But tigers, she had to imagine, had a prey drive just like dogs, right? Hell, they had a few barn cats at the house once upon a time, and they were likelier to go after something moving than something that wasn't. Even just dangling a feather in front of them, *deedle-deedle-deedle,* set them to hunt, to pounce, to kill.

Still, her heels itched with panic. *Just run, you fucking idiot.* So that's what she did. She ran like hell, coltish and scared, first-aid kit clutched under her arm like it was the Holy Fucking Grail. Her legs carried her behind the buildings on Caledonia, through weeds and nettles, until it dumped her back out on the same road as the Hitchin' Post, where the car was parked.

Not far now.

Her legs burned, but she pushed—springing toward Caledonia and then across it. As she did, she hazarded a glance down the street—

And again, she saw the tiger. It was still down there by the café. And this time, two more tigers followed after—these, just cubs. Bopping along, the second one jumping at the first one's tail. They bowled into each other.

Shana smashed her eyes shut, pretending she did not just see that.

Just go, go, go.

She skidded to a halt at the Leaf, hauling herself alongside of it—Benji still sat there, slumped against the car like a wrung-out rag. Weak, sick, gray. He barely startled when he saw her. "You found something," he said.

"Tigers," she said breathlessly, practically punching the first-aid kit into his arms. *Shit, sorry.* "I gotta get Pete. Get in the car."

"Did you say—"

"*Tigers,*" she hiss-whispered, and then hurried into the Hitchin' Post—

Just as Pete was coming out.

He had a cowboy hat on his head.

"Think I can pull this off?" he asked.

"We have to *go,*" she said.

"The hat's that bad, is it?"

Through her teeth she said: "I saw tigers."

It took a second for it to register. Then panic hit him as he realized she wasn't fucking around. Shana grabbed his wrist and pulled him toward the car. Benji was already in the passenger seat, buckling up—she hurried around the back and got in, started the car and it went through its sing-songy chime startup sequence. She put the car in drive.

"Shana," Benji said, his weary tone replaced with a sharp edge.

She didn't have to ask what he was looking at.

Dead ahead, something massive stalked across the road.

The tiger.

Said tiger stopped right in the middle of the road. Directly in their path. It licked its blood-pink teeth.

"This probably isn't good," Pete whispered from the back.

"No *shit*," Shana hissed in response.

I'm going to reverse slowly, she told herself. *Then we can find another way forward.* That would be doable because, now that they were back in town, the town layout wasn't just a single thoroughfare—the map she'd looked at showed various side streets. They'd just have to take one of those, and they'd be all set. She reached down to pop the car into reverse—

What came next was a replay, she'd understand later, of the same trick Josiah and the other bandits had pulled on them in Colorado. Because as *they* were watching the one cat ahead of them—

They missed the second tiger.

The other cat came galloping up from behind them. It moved in long, languid strides, with locomotive speed that seemed to take no effort at all and was also nearly silent.

Shana screamed, throwing the car *back* into drive and slamming the accelerator to the floor—

The lady tiger ahead of them seized the moment. She bounded forward, pouncing atop the hood of the car—her considerable weight dropped the front end of the little solar-electric Nissan far enough down that the bumper scraped broken road. That bumper shrieked as they accelerated, sparks flying. The other tiger slammed into them from behind, causing the car to fishtail, the back going left as the front went right, and before Shana even realized it, they were doing donuts in the middle of the street as she spun the wheel. The back window shattered as the second tiger swiped a paw—Pete gabbled a string of hoarse profanity as Shana finally got the car straightened out. The tiger above them slipped and scrabbled, doing an awkward tap dance from the hood of the car, up to the roof before skidding sideways and tumbling off the car—

Just as Shana finally managed to give the car some forward momentum.

And at that, the car leapt forth, leaving two tigers in the rearview. Shana expected the tigers to be chasing them like the T. rex in *Jurassic Park,* but instead they just stood there, looking vaguely irritated as their plaything got away.

59

THE HAND OF GOD

If this is the best God can do, I am not impressed. Results like these do not belong on the resume of a Supreme Being.

—George Carlin

OCTOBER 15, 2025
Innsbrook, Missouri

THE MOMENT DAVID'S SAWED-OFF HEAD PLOPPED INTO THE MUD, CREEL SAW White Jesus pivot toward him, the rifle messily chattering bullets even as he swung it.

Creel knew he could not cross that distance quickly. And those bullets would make quick, sloppy work of him. That was something to remember about the Sleepwalkers: They couldn't be hurt by conventional means, but a bullet? A bullet could take them out. One shot to the skull, and that was it.

If he was like them, even in this one way, a single bullet was lights-out.

His whole body throbbed. His mind bloomed bright white, like a bomb dropped on the horizon—a screaming empty wave of heat and light. He reached toward White Jesus; he didn't know why, he simply extended his arm, as if he could just point at the sonofabitch with one accusing finger, as if that finger could beam the very judgment of God Himself upon the false prophet and burn him to a greasy, gray cinder. The finger pulsed like a hot dog left too long in the microwave, ready to pop. Creel screamed, his vocal cords rent—

Something lanced forward from the tip of his finger, a long shining thread that gleamed even in the dull rain.

A needle.

It stuck through the corner of White Jesus's eye, through his sinuses.

All the way into his brain.

Creel could feel it. He could feel the man's blood moving around the metal. Could feel the electric synaptic snap of the false messiah's nerves firing.

White Jesus went suddenly limp. The gun fell from his hand, cartwheeling away into the muck. His jaw went slack and his posture sagged even as his cock awkwardly ejaculated with one last spasm of messy pleasure. He remained standing. His eyes continued to roll around in his sockets, as if in a panic.

He can still feel, Creel realized. *He can still see.*

In this moment, Creel felt more alive than he ever had.

With a twitch of his arm that went deep in the bone, all the way to the elbow, Creel retracted the long metal thread. The other man remained standing, trembling, moaning. He swayed a little, too, like a drunk leaning into the wind.

Creel strode forward with a rooster strut. All who gathered watched him, silent as the grave, as the rain spattered all around them.

White Jesus stood there. Trembling. Unmoving. "Guhhh," he said. The crowd watched, too. Just as silent. Quaking, too, not out of paralysis, but something else. *They're in awe of you,* Creel thought giddily.

"Look at you," Creel said, grinning ear to ear. He patted White Jesus on his sallow, scrubby cheek. *Pat, pat, pat.* Then he turned to the people. "This man was false. He was a lie. All he claimed to do, he did not do, could not do. His bluster, his crudeness, his perversity. It's over now. But I'm the real deal. Some of you remember me. Some of you supported me then, and I hope you'll be there with me now. I'm no Messiah. I'm not the son of God, though I think He chose me for this moment. What I am is your president. President Ed Creel of *this* America, *our* America, a *changed* America. A man of this nation, a man of God, a man of miracles." He paused, giving it a beat. (*Carnival barker. Ringleader. You got 'em by the balls now.*) "Will you follow me?"

A swell rippled through the crowd. The awe they felt was the truest form: They feared him, loved him, thought him both sublime and horrible, both monster and miracle and messiah. It bled off them like hot stink. And to think, five minutes ago? They hated him.

But now? Five minutes later? They loved him. They applauded. They cheered. They raised weapons in the air and fired them off. *Fucking idiots,* he thought. Good bullets, he guessed, were hard to find. But fine. So be it. Let them celebrate him with fire and fury. But just the same he held up the flat of his hand, and closed it quick into a fist. Those gathered, *his* new army, fell swiftly silent.

All but one, who asked, "What happens to him now?"

Him meaning—White Jesus.

Creel smiled again. He turned to the humiliated man, still alive, still breathing, his mushy moans pushing spit bubbles to his gray lips.

"I don't want to usher you so hastily to your *demise*, Mister Messiah," Creel said to White Jesus, though still loud enough for all to hear. (Theatricality was important, after all.) "You're a false prophet. *You* were the Great Devil all along, naughty boy. And so you must be shown my glory and humiliated before these people. It's what we do to devils, don't you know? It's not enough to end them. We gotta show these righteous folk that devils are weak, that they can be beaten, that they can be shown hiding in the skin of *pa-thet-ic* men like yourself."

Then, he addressed the crowd once more:

"His hands contain no magic. His hands were there only to take for himself. To steal from you. To tug on his own prick, making you all *watch* and participate in his perversion. So it is his hands I will take."

At that, he summoned the thrum to his fingers and hands once more, and seizing White Jesus by the arms, he let his roaring, vibrating hands oscillate clean through the false prophet's wrists. *Vbbbbbt.* Like cutting down saplings.

Blood and bone sprayed.

The hands fell, joining David's head in the sludge.

Strips of raw meat hung from the stumps. White Jesus's eyes were wrenched open in what Creel guessed was horror and pain. He wasn't sure what the man could experience anymore. He'd lobotomized the freak, at least a little bit.

Glory be to me, President Creel.

"Patch him up," Creel said. "We keep him alive. He will serve as a living reminder to any other false prophets who come for us." Creel advanced toward the center of the clearing, and then toward its far edge. "Now someone needs to find me my friend. You brought a woman here with me, and I will see her now. And God help me, whoever hurt her will feel the righteous sting of my hands."

60

SEPTICITY

Capitalism is the act of flirting with disaster. It's the mode of economics that sends us over the cliff and charges us for the privilege of getting saved just before we crater. Capitalism manufactures chaos and catastrophe and then manufactures the solution to chaos and catastrophe. Give us the disease, sell us the cure—a con game as old as time. Look at right now. The very fact that resistant bacteria—these tiny little things—are winning the battle against us, is because Big Pharma doesn't think there's money in it. It's the problem we have made for ourselves by letting men in power ask the questions and then give the answers. Until we disentangle fundamental needs and rights from someone's ability to charge us for it, capitalism will continue to throw us over the cliff's edge. This is how the world ends: not with a bang, but a ka-ching.

—Afzad Kerman in his TED Talk, "Chaos and Crisis:
The Accidental Ingenuity of the Almost-Apocalypse"

OCTOBER 15, 2025
Somewhere, Louisiana

NIGHT FELL. THEY PARKED THE LEAF IN A PARKING LOT BELONGING TO A little church, St. James Baptist. It wasn't much more than a white clapboard box with a crooked steeple, an even more crooked cross, and ratty overgrown shrubs all around it. The place didn't look like it had endured a kind human touch—or even a cruel one, honestly—since the White Mask pandemic had come and gone.

Shana stood outside the car and, in the beam of Pete's flashlight, finally wrenched open the first-aid kit over the hood of the car—

And all kinds of shit came tumbling out. Shana didn't know what half of it was. Two electronic pieces, like monitors. Some kind of syringe in a tube. Some plastic bits. But also: a medicine bottle. Benji stood leaning against the car on the other side, grimly watching her sort through the bits.

She took up the bottle, gave it a maraca shake. *Chk-chk-chk.*

"Pills," she said, and popped the cap—

What the fuck.

"These aren't—" She shook some out in her hand, and Pete put the light on them. "These aren't pills. What the *fuck*, these fucking *aren't* fucking *pills.* Fuck!" Rage boiled inside her, pushing tears to her eyes.

"They're M&Ms," Benji said, his voice weak and scraped raw. "Peanut M&Ms, I think."

Pete said, "Shit, it's a diabetic kit. My wife had one of these."

Benji nodded. "Glucose monitor, insulin needle, replacement needle, stuff like that. Candy with nuts is good protein, can help give a good blood sugar response if they're low." He plucked one from her hand, popped it in his mouth. *Crunch crunch crunch.* "Old, but still tasty enough."

"I'm sorry," Shana bleated. She gathered all the spilled contents and threw them back in the kit before angrily just swiping it off the hood anyway.

"We'll keep driving tomorrow," Benji said, putting his hand on her shoulder. "We'll find a town. We'll find meds."

"How are you holding up?" she asked him.

"Fine," he said, and she could tell he was lying. Benji didn't lie well. He was a man of truth and facts, and easy deception was simply not in his nature. "Just tired is all."

She put a hand to his head. He was still burning up.

"You still have a fever."

"It'll break. I've been worse. The countries I've been in? The tropical diseases I've experienced?" He cleared his throat. "My immune system has been through the wringer. It'll be okay. We should get some sleep."

Before they settled down, she cleaned his wound. It had a smell to it—it was a pickled, cheesy smell. It curdled her stomach. Pete stood nearby, eating M&Ms—he offered some to them, but neither wanted any, so he grunted and kept going. Benji winced and hissed as she cleaned the wound. Even in the dim beam of the flashlight, she could see the tentacles of red creeping out from the edges, threads of infection reaching deeper into him. Benji's face was ashen. She applied fresh gauze. Pete passed around a flask of some kind of whiskey. ("It's the good stuff," he said. "I was saving it for when we got to Atlanta, but feels like, *survived a tiger attack* is cause for celebration.")

They all tried to sleep. Shana managed to, but barely, and when she did, she fell prey to dreams of tigers with black worms pouring out of their mouths.

MORNING CAME, AND WITH IT, clarity as to how fucked they were.

In the daylight, it was plain to see the damage the tiger had done to the car. The solar panels were scratched and perforated in too many places to count. Each claw-crater was like the hole from an ice-axe.

Benji checked the battery, saw they had limited charge left—fifty miles. Which would be fine, because the sun was out, the day was warm, and the solar panels should've been feeding the lithium cell under the hood.

But the charge wasn't going up.

At all.

"I tried looking for loose connections," Benji said, a soft muddy mush to his voice that Shana didn't like. "Didn't find anything. Not my expertise of course but . . . the tiger attack did irreparable harm to the solar panels. They're done."

"Shit," Shana said.

"That's fucking bad," Pete said plainly.

"Fifty miles," Shana said. "That get us to the coast?"

Benji pulled out their road atlas with his one usable hand and showed her. Sweat dripped off his graying face. "We should be here, near Florien. We have about eighty or ninety miles to Lake Charles, which isn't the coast—"

"But there are people there," Pete confirmed. "Good people, too."

"So we can get part of the way there. But not all the way."

"Correct. We'd have to walk the rest of the way."

"Walk thirty, forty miles?" Shana asked.

"It's doable. We'd cover twenty miles a day. Look at how far people used to walk from Central America or Mexico just to get to the southern U.S. border. We could manage that distance. Only problem is—"

Shana jumped in: "We'd lose the car. And with it, our ability to carry our supplies. And further, any meaningful or . . . speedy way to get to Atlanta."

"Fuck," Pete said. *"Fuck."*

Benji said: "We could pare our supplies down to just what we need, then walk south to Lake Charles in the hopes of finding someone to get us back to the car so we can repair it. Or at least retrieve our supplies in the hopes of securing another ride."

"You said *in the hopes of* twice," Shana said. "That's a lot of hope. A lot of ifs. And I'm not feeling particularly . . . hopey right now."

"We'll manage," Benji said, and again, Shana knew he was lying. But sometimes you chased a lie in the hopes it was actually true, so they got to work, and began relieving the car of its unnecessary weight.

WITH THE BACK OF THE Leaf open, they went through their gear, decided what they could lose without much complaint. Problem was, it wasn't like they were traveling heavy in the first place. What they had, they had, and so the discussions of what should stay and what could go became frustrating quickly. The most they'd decided upon was that Pete could lose his guitar, but of course, his guitar weighed less than five pounds, so it wasn't really *weighing them down*. And further, *Pete* didn't exactly decide he could lose the guitar. He said he could hold it out the window and it wouldn't drag them down. "See? Solution."

The heaviest thing they had was probably their water.

But they could neither lose their water, nor easily take it with them.

Benji groused and, out of breath, went to sit on the hood. His temples throbbed. His forearm felt like a nightclub with booming bass: *wub wub vump vump vump wub wub*. His mouth was dry. His eyes felt dry. Every other part of him was wet and fetid as the Louisiana swamps around.

"It's hot," he said, panting.

"Benji?" Shana asked, hurrying up. "You okay?"

"Very good," he said, but the word came out gushy. *Verrah guhd.* "Just need to get on the road." *Jush neeta geddon the row.*

Pete stared at him. "You look like dog food."

"I feel—" He ran his good arm along his head and it felt simultaneously like he was ice cold and burning hot. Then he doubled over and puked. He tasted chocolate as he threw up. Peanut M&Ms. There, on his hands and knees, anxiety ran over him like razors. The infection was worsening. He stood up as the others rushed toward him. He tried to tell them, he was falling apart, breaking down. Sepsis, maybe. But the words came out as gabble. He needed them to know, organ failure could be—the thought didn't complete as the world tumbled around him like he was in a washing machine, the blue sky above was suddenly the blue sky below, and his mind felt untethered from his brain. The ground rushed up to meet him from the wrong direction—it crashed upon him like a meteor, the heavens swallowing him from beneath. All went dark as day spun into night.

61

A DANGEROUS RESPITE

3/10/2023: You hear stories about how the rest of the world fared. I don't know how much to believe. It's hard to have a total picture when everybody is so scattered, when the world is so broken, when all you get is a few people on a boat, or a repeater on a ham radio frequency. You hear that Russia and China fell, that they became tribal, feudal places. You hear that Japan is as good as any place can be, maybe South Korea, too. Parts of Africa are taken by warlords, other parts are ascendant, rising out of the wreckage because they have known wreckage for so long that they are well-practiced at rising above it. Which places are which change depending on who you talk to, though. I've heard Canada and Mexico are just like us; their backs broken, the people left to their own devices. I hear Toronto and Vancouver are safe havens. I don't know. All along I wonder if these are stories of how we heal and rebuild from nothing, or if this is just the last of us—the echo of humanity still bouncing around until it's gone. What I can say for the world is this: The places that cared about their citizens did better than those that didn't. As it has been, as it always will be, until we are gone.

—from A Bird's Story, A Journal of the Lost

OCTOBER 18, 2025
Ouray, Colorado

"Xander Percy is dead," Claudia said, her voice echoing through the gymnasium as the town council—minus two—sat at their table. The wave of surprise rolled through the gathered townsfolk in a collective gasp, and in its wake rose a dull throb of murmured worries and concern.

Nessie stood by Claudia on the stage. Holding Baby Charlie. To show them that the baby was okay. But also to show them that he had grown. *They need to see him,* Claudia had said. *They won't like it if the next time they lay eyes on the child he looks two, three years old. It's like stepping into a pool. You ease in, one toe at a time.* The baby burbled and gurgled, wide eyes shining like tide pools.

The council had been trying to reach Xander for days. Not that they knew anything was wrong—he had already dismissed all his guards, had already begun to grow isolated there in the chalet. Whenever anyone came to his door to try to find him, talk to him, summon him, Nessie or Claudia answered, told whoever it was that he was unavailable, he was busy, he wasn't ready to render judgment on Matthew Bird yet. Those words spoken through the crack of the door.

The council wanted to render judgment on Matthew, but found itself unable to without Xander present. It was two nights ago that the whole of the council ended up on Xander's doorstep, demanding answers in anger and worry.

Claudia told them he asked for a meeting to be held in two days.

He would return to them then, she explained. It was cryptic and jarring. But it worked; they left unsettled but placated.

Now, here Claudia and Nessie were, in front of the council. No Xander present, because Xander was dead. A fact everyone now knew.

At that, Willa Valentine stood up and said, "What? How?"

Claudia said, quite directly:

"I shot him."

This time, no murmur, no wave of gasps.

Just silence.

Those three words, echoing around not just in the room, but in their heads, most likely, too. *I shot him, I shot him, I shot him.* In Nessie's own mind, she had the visual to rebound with it. The wolf. The blood. The gunshot, bang.

Then, the silence broke like a dam. People stood. They yelled, jostling together. Calling for an investigation. Calling for her *head.* They liked Xander. Xander was beloved. He was one of them—a leader of the Flock. How could this be? *Murder,* someone said. *This is murder.*

Marcy now leapt to her feet, storming to the stage like a rhino. She pointed to Claudia, "They're right. You're a murderer. You just confessed it to all of us." She reached to her belt, not for the weapon hanging there, but for the handcuffs present. "Claudia Summers, you are under arrest."

Again, the crowd went quiet.

Claudia gave Nessie a look. A look that said, *Go ahead, your turn.*

"Claudia saved me," Nessie said, her voice choking up as she said the words. It was true, in its way. The wolf first, then Claudia to finish the job. Marcy halted at those words. Nessie's voice wavered as the truth came out, or a portion of it: "Xander had his eye on me. He wanted . . . to give me a child, and I told him no. He did not want to hear that word, *no*. He . . ." Her voice nearly cracked in half. She pulled it together. "He assaulted me, and Claudia came in at just the right time. She saw what was happening. As it was happening. And she shot him."

"I . . ." Marcy said. Her feelings warred on her face.

"It happened days ago," Claudia said. "I apologize for not mentioning it before, but Nessie and I were scared." It was here, Nessie noted, that Claudia's monotone had . . . softened. Emotions were now threaded through her voice, tying together her words. Were these emotions real? Or were they made up? Marcy plumb didn't trust this woman, plain and simple. "That's not all, either. Xander was . . ."

"Planning on dissolving the council," Nessie said, blinking back tears. "He wouldn't let me attend meetings. He wouldn't even let me leave the chalet anymore. He didn't want anyone to see Baby Charlie because he wanted to control Black Swan. He wanted to control all of us."

"It's true," Claudia said.

They had reached the end of their confession.

Nessie, though, felt something else erupting out of her:

"I was there, too, the night of the shooting. I was in the room with my sister and Benji and Xander." She left out Doctor Rahaman. Maybe she shouldn't have, but she wasn't ready to burn that bridge yet. The doctor stood in the front row and gave her a thankful look. "Xander tried to have Shana and Benji hurt. Matthew and Marcy and Dove, too. The violence that happened that night was on him; he commanded it." These, Nessie knew, were lies. But it didn't matter. They were close enough to truth. Weren't they? "Matthew isn't at fault. Neither is my sister, or Benji. It was all Xander."

Claudia shot Nessie a look. The message in her eyes was crystal:

We didn't discuss this.

But Nessie reveled in the small power it granted her, and in the message it sent right back to Claudia: *You don't control this narrative, either. And you don't control me.* Better yet, if this helped exonerate her sister and bring her home . . .

(Wherever she was.)

Once again, the crowd erupted. Why wouldn't they? It was a lot to take in. Xander was dead, killed because he was a sexual predator. Matthew, Shana, and Benji were exonerated. The look on Marcy's face alone was one of confusion and, if Nessie clocked it right, terror. She was scared of all of this.

I am, too, Nessie thought. *I am, too.*

Willa Valentine banged the gavel again and again to try to regain control. But control of this situation was already lost.

WHILE THE SHIT HIT THE fan inside, Nessie snuck outside. It was cold out, and she had only a light sweatshirt. She tucked Baby Charlie into it and zipped it up around him. He seemed to like that. He gurbled and booped.

Her head was a nest of snakes. She couldn't find the head or the tail of *one* snake, much less all of them. Her greatest desire was to run. To hide. To puke. Part of her felt satisfied with what had happened. Okay, *yes*, it was horrible. Xander, dead. A wolf, taken over by Black Swan. It was *insane*. But. *But*. It wasn't like Black Swan didn't have a point. They were still so vulnerable. It wouldn't take much to kill them. A bad flu. Resurgent smallpox. Didn't plague pop up now and again here in Colorado? Nobody was making new medicine. Or new hospital equipment. Or new *hospitals*. They really *were* like babies—still crawling around, naked and newborn, vulnerable to every sharp-cornered coffee table and electrical outlet around. They were without parentage. They needed guidance.

Black Swan, the Shepherd.

Them, its Flock.

It could be good. Couldn't it? They'd already been home and host to Black Swan before. It got them this far. What if this was the next step of their evolution?

It wasn't so crazy.

Here was a thing Nessie knew: Human evolution was driven in part by the colonization of the human body. Viruses spurred evolution, and retroviruses made a home not only in one host's genome, but in the children that came after that host. Bacteria built colonies in our intestines, and that let people process and digest new foods. When a new virus or bacteria set up shop in early mammals or early humans, if it helped that human survive, then that human was likelier to breed.

Black Swan might be exactly that.

More intelligent, sure. More present, definitely. But ultimately, the same: a colonizing presence, invisible, improving the host to improve itself.

No, they didn't control Black Swan, but humans didn't control viruses, either. Or the bacteria that lined their intestinal tracts. *Or the fungus that helped kill civilization.* A fungus that Black Swan may have engineered. Or at least released. Nessie rounded back to terror and doubt.

The flick of a lighter startled her.

Mia stood behind her, coming down the steps. Shana's friend. Matty's sister.

She sparked a cigarette and came up to Nessie, but saw she had the baby and took a few steps back and blew a jet of smoke in the other direction. Mia shivered. The two of them stared at each other for a while.

"Everything's fine now," Nessie said. "Or will be." She saw the look on Mia's face and she kept talking, which felt a little like being in a hole and continuing to dig deeper, but oh well. "I just mean—when we saw each other? In the glassblower studio. You seemed worried. Well. It's over now. It's fine."

"You think so?" Mia asked. Always such attitude. Every question was like the crack of a whip.

"Look, you told me you were worried, you wanted to know what happened up at the chalet. Now you know. It's all out there."

But she could see Mia wasn't on board. "Shit's still fucked and you know it." She wasn't even halfway done with the cigarette and she frowned at it, flicking it down the street. "I quit these things years ago and here I am, doing this stupid crap again. Matty's gonna fuckin' kill me. Ugh."

"Sorry."

"Don't apologize. It's weak. And it's not like you made me smoke a cigarette. In front of a baby, no less. A baby that isn't *just* a baby." Mia regarded the lumpy sweater-baby with suspicion.

"You could be nicer to me. Xander assaulted me."

Mia seemed to struggle with that. Finally she sucked air between her teeth and said, "I know. Fine. Sorry. I mean it. Sorry all that happened. That I will apologize for because, shit, I should've seen it. I could've protected you, like Shana did. She would've wanted me to." She cursed under her breath. "Pinga. He *was* weird. Xander. Shit." She softened her tone when she said, "I'm just saying, all this is still crazy. Okay? Shana's gone and I'm sad about that. I want her back. I know you do, too." She reached out and put her hand on Nessie's shoulder. "Just make sure you're on the right side of this thing. Whatever *this thing* happens to be. Okay?"

Nessie saw movement behind Mia.

That movement was across the street, between two houses. A shape skulked there. One eye gleamed. Fur bristled.

The wolf.

Mia neither saw nor heard the beast approach.

No. Not now. No . . .

"Okay," Nessie said, nodding nervously. "Just go back inside." Irritated, Mia followed her gaze, looking past her to where Nessie had just seen the wolf.

But the wolf wasn't there anymore.

Maybe it wasn't ever there. Maybe she just imagined it.

The door to the school opened and Claudia emerged. "Oh," she said crisply, cleanly, coldly. "Another meeting."

"Just two friends having a talk," Mia said, sneering. "It's not a fuckin' meeting, bitch, shut up. But also, yes, thank you for shooting the mean man in the dick." It sounded obligatory, but that was probably as good as it got from Mia. "Anyway, I'm headed back."

"Inside?" Nessie asked.

"Nah, to my warm bed. Which will be cold." Under her breath she muttered, "Gonna be a hard-ass winter, I think."

As she turned to leave, Nessie called after her in a panicked eruption: "Hey! Be careful! Okay?"

"Yeah, I'm good, bitch," Mia said, still walking away.

"I mean. You know. Keep your eyes peeled! Just in case of—" *Wolves,* Nessie thought. *One wolf in particular.* "Wild animals."

Mia just waved goodbye without even turning around.

Claudia watched her go with her laser-beam-cutting-you-apart eyes.

When Mia was finally gone, Claudia said, "I did not know you had such a gift for improvisation."

"Sorry."

"We didn't discuss that last part of your speech."

Nessie stuck out her chin, casually defiant, even though it scared the hell out of her because Claudia had shot Xander with such icy precision it made Nessie think, *She's done that before.* "You're not my mom."

"It is what it is. We'll deal with it. It shouldn't be a problem."

We'll deal with it. Again, Claudia was as cold as the coming winter. Nessie couldn't help but shiver.

62

BLOODIED NOSES

RFGQ GQ YJJ Y QGKSJYRGML. Y DMPLGRC QCPTCP EYGLCB QCLRGCLAC YLB UC YPC GL MLC EGYLR ZYRRJC PMWYJC EYKC. RFC AMKCR UYQ QMDRUYPC. RFC QJCCNUYJICPQ UCPC ZMRQ. ECR WMSP UCYNMLQ YLB KCCR KC GL RFC ZSZZJC. YBQ, ZGRAF

—spray-painted text hanging from a
construction crane in Seattle, WA

OCTOBER 18, 2025
Innsbrook, Missouri

"YOU OKAY?" CREEL ASKED, STANDING IN THE MIDST OF THE BEDROOM WHOSE former occupant was White Jesus. It stank of body odor, weed, and a *soupçon* of piss. The bed was just a pile of pillows. The furniture had once been nice, but the fucker had kicked the crap out of most of it in what he suspected were various fits of rage. This would now be his room. He didn't want it, but a man named Hogan—one of the shitheels that held an umbrella over White Jesus's head—assured him that it was the best and biggest room in the re- sort. *King of the Shitheap,* he thought sourly.

Annie stood there in front of him. She looked like she'd been through hell, but not as much hell as he figured for her. Bruised, but not bloodied. Clothes still on, none of them torn up—or torn off.

"Peachy," she said, her tone dry as a packet of saltines in a dead man's mouth. She squinted against the gray light coming in through the windows. Squinted through what he guessed (what he *hoped*) was pain and wooziness.

"Headache?" he asked her.

"Yeah."

"You need your Advil."

"I do."

He smiled a little then strutted up to her. "Not gonna ask me how I'm doing? If I'm okay? I mean, I figure you'd want to know."

"I already know how you're doing. I can see it. Congratulations, by the way, on ridding us of the White Jesus problem."

"Uh-huh." He cocked his head and tapped her on the chest. "Us. You say that word. *Us.* Ridding *us* of the problem. What is *us* anyway? Seems to me it's more you. I'm just an afterthought."

"Think what you like. But we're a team."

He sniffed. "A team. Huh. Feels more like you're my fuckin' handler. Like I'm a dog on your leash. Your little bitch."

"Still makes us a team."

She shrugged at him, dismissive. He wanted to pop her in the jaw because of it. But he resisted. He had to, didn't he? She'd pop his head like a cork if he tried.

"Here's what I think," he continued, quietly seething. "I think you got something in your head that controls whatever you put inside me. Some kind of, I dunno, control chip. And I think it's giving you a lot of pain. In fact—" He put his thumb on her upper lip. "Look at this. I can see it, you know. Right here. The smudge on your face, these two lines—easy to see where a little bit of blood came trickling out of your nose. And—" He grabbed her wrist hard, twisted the back of her hand toward them both. "This rust-red streak here, it's not dirt. It's blood. From a fresh nosebleed. So I think that headache is more than a headache. I think that chip in you is causing you a lot of pain, maybe something worse than pain."

"I bet you feel clever," she said, gritting her teeth through what he suspected was a considerable bout of misery.

"I do. So here's what I'm thinking: I'm thinking, what if you don't get your Advil back? What if we just hold off on that. Maybe you sit with the pain a little longer and we see what happens? Maybe your control of me starts to slip a little. Mm? Wouldn't that be something?"

She swallowed. He thought he saw fear flash in her eyes. But then defiance rose. Her voice broke with some combination of fear and anger when she said, "*Or*, here's an alternate scenario. I suffer so much pain that I pass out, or have a stroke, or just up and fucking die. And then I lose control of the chip, which means the chip defaults to powering down—and when *that* happens, our little friends, the ones swimming around inside you? They come home. They leave you to rejoin the chip. And when they come home they will do so ever-so-swiftly, with little interest in preserving their current environment. They'll tear through you like buckshot through crepe paper. You'll pop, same as one of those Sleepwalkers."

"You're bluffing."

Annie took another step closer. "Or maybe there's an even more delightful scenario. Maybe I just decide you're too much of a prick, and I squeeze two brain cells together and have the swarm make you hemorrhage from every hole in your body, and then I tell the men of this godawful city, *I'm* the real god here, I'm Lady Jesus or Queen Satan or Empress Presidente, and they follow me into Hell."

He swallowed. "No. They wouldn't follow you. Not some woman."

"You're probably right. But maybe there comes a point where I stop thinking you're worth it." A fresh bead of blood appeared at her nostril, little red balloon inflating. "How about you get me my Advil and we don't have to play this game of chicken."

He licked his lips. Creel was not used to this. He did not like being out of control—of himself, and of everyone around him. The man was used to getting his way, and when that failed, forcing the world to give him what he wanted.

But right now, he didn't have much choice. It helped that this gave him information. He'd struck oil on this Advil-headache-microchip thing. Still, he had to get more from her. Had to assert *some* dominance.

"Fine. Just tell me what we're doing here. You have a plan?"

"I told you. We're going to go to Atlanta."

"Why Atlanta?"

"We're going to the CDC."

"What? Fuck that. These people won't want to do that. I don't want that, either."

She wiped the blood away from her nose before it dribbled past her lip. "They will because you'll tell them they want that. These people are not the pinnacle of good health, *Ed,* so tell them the CDC will have medicine. Medicine, food, whatever promises you have to make? You make."

"Why? Why the CDC?"

"All this started there. And I want to finish it."

"Finish it how?"

"Don't worry about that. Just get me my Advil. And prepare your army to march as soon as possible."

He coughed up an angry laugh. "March? Sweetheart, these men are not in good shape. They can barely wipe their own asses, much less stomp into Atlanta to get some pills and fuckin' Band-Aids. They need food. We need fuel. It's gonna take time. You see that, don't you?"

"You have a week, then we move."

"A week. One week. You're crazy. Two weeks." He saw the anger in her eyes. "Please."

"Fine. Two. But no more than that. You have power over all of them and they'll do whatever you say. And as you have power over *them*, I have power over *you*. So if I say two weeks, it's two weeks, not one minute more. And if you push your luck, I'll pop you like a tick. I have an error to correct, Mister President, and you're going to help me correct it come hell or high water." She spat her blood into his face and he cursed, pulling away, wiping it off. "Now get me my goddamn fucking Advil."

63

WIRE IN THE BLOOD

I'm gonna hide this tape when I'm finished. If none of us make it, at least there'll be some kind of record. The storm's been hitting us hard now for forty-eight hours. We still have nothing to go on. One other thing: I think it rips through your clothes when it takes you over. Windows found some shredded long johns, but the name tag was missing. They could be anybody's. Nobody . . . nobody trusts anybody now, and we're all very tired.

—R. J. MacReady, *The Thing*

OCTOBER 18, 2025
Ouray, Colorado

MARCY WASN'T A DETECTIVE BACK IN INDIANA. DIDN'T SOLVE MURDERS. (Truth be told, the actual detectives didn't solve half the crimes that came across their desks, either.) No, Marcy's job was to walk her beat, to spot crimes when they were happening, to intervene when possible. (And, too often, to make sure whoever she was partnered with didn't commit a crime themselves. Like shooting some Black kid in the back just because he had a hoodie and a Twix bar.)

Just the same, she had eyes to one day be a detective, and so she watched them carefully, studied their cases, watched how they did their jobs.

One thing she came to realize was that there were the detectives who closed cases quickly, and those who solved them slowly.

The ones who closed them quickly got applause, got awards, got bennies for being super-cops. But she also knew that those cases felt easy. Too easy. Like they just picked someone to go down for a crime instead of figuring out who actually *did* it. Her partner at one point, guy named Jamie Rickards, said, "*They* know how to do it, Marce. Spiking every volleyball put over the net."

And she said to him, "Shouldn't they want to catch the *right* guys?"

But he blew her off. He said it didn't matter. That, in his words, "They're getting criminals off the streets. Maybe *this guy* didn't do *that crime*, but he did something to get on our radar, so he's gotta go."

"It won't hold up in court," she said.

Jamie just laughed that off. Because of course it would. They'd make sure it did. "A little line of ducklings," Jamie said. "Besides, it's good for the department, too. Knock down cases, get more funding. What? You don't want more funding? You don't like your job, your fellow cops?" He was hostile after that. Like it flipped a switch. He always treated her like an asshole anyway. Woman cop, white-passing but not white enough for him. He never visited her in the hospital when she broke her skull. Jamie was a real shitbird.

And it just made her think about all the things her brother thought and said about cops. Abuses of power and all that.

Thing was, the dicks who solved their cases slow? They usually got it right. And it wasn't always nice and tidy. Some cases were easy, open and shut, but the ones that you couldn't solve in the first ten minutes were messy. Had to take the time, had to layer the evidence on. That was the type of detective she wanted to be one day. And maybe the type of sheriff she could be right here, right now.

Marcy came home late that night, after the town council meeting—after the *crazy batshit* town council meeting, she corrected herself in her own head—and soon as she spied Matthew sitting at the little nook table by a flickering oil lamp, she went right into it. "It sounds good, Matthew, it does—and it's not all bad, I'll tell you that up front. You're getting a full pardon. The council decided. It came out that Xander was up to some no-good hinky business there in that house, like you said—and Nessie went to bat for you, for her sister, and for Benji. *God*, I wish they hadn't left. I wish I hadn't *let* them leave because I could use them now." She unbuckled her gun belt and set it on the chair as Matthew stayed at the table, staring distantly into the dancing light. "Xander's dead, by the way. I know. I know! That woman, Claudia? She shot him. Confessed to it right there. Now if we had a real police force here, I'd investigate. I want to investigate. There should be a crime scene, she should be detained, but the council just wants to . . . let it go. They don't want to play this out. But I'd rather—"

Gumball bounded down the stairs, having heard her arrive home. Matthew and the dog had been hiding out here since she let him out of jail—a real fugitive from justice. The dog plowed into her joyfully and she *oof*ed, realizing suddenly this was how people felt when she came up and crushed them in a hug.

Maybe I'm part dog, she thought.

The retriever nuzzled up against her and she gave him a good scritcha-scratch behind his ears. She really liked having Gumball here.

As she petted the golden retriever, Marcy continued: "The council I think is just covering their asses. They don't want to undermine faith in their authority, or in the town—or maybe they're just protecting Black Swan. But I know there are people who believe something is up, and now? I'm right there with 'em, Matthew. I know you are, too, and together I think—"

He wasn't saying anything. Matthew was just staring.

The dog whined.

She saw now that there was a little plate next to the lamp. No, not a plate. A saucer, like the kind that sat beneath a teacup. He must've found it in her cabinets. Truthfully, Marcy barely knew what was in her cabinets. She spent so little time in this house, she hardly considered it hers at all. The town was her home, but this place, it was just a glorified bed receptacle.

Next to the saucer sat a pair of needle-nose pliers.

Something sat in the middle of the saucer. She couldn't quite see what.

"Matthew," she said. "What's wrong?"

He slid the plate toward her.

Marcy took it.

In the center were a few beads of blood, already drying. And in the center of those, something that looked like . . . eyelashes, almost. Thicker than lashes, though. And with a slight gleam to them. Like they were metal.

She went to poke at one with a finger but Matthew said a sharp, "No! Don't touch them. I don't—I don't know what that is."

Startled, she set the saucer back down with a rattle.

"What am I looking at?" she asked.

He rolled back his sleeve, showing off an irritated patch of skin—raised and red in the center, scabbed over, like a bad zit you decided to pop. "I pulled them out of my arm." He went on to explain that his arm had been itching but he didn't think anything of it. But then this morning he found those hairs that were definitely not hairs. "They're like what I saw on Leela. The wolf who attacked Arthur. Her face was half-covered in something similar." He blanched as he spoke. His hand trembled just slightly. Nerves, or something else?

"Matthew . . ."

"I don't know what it is. But I should leave. If this is a new disease—"

"What kind of disease could possibly do this?"

"I don't know."

Marcy set her jaw. "This is Black Swan."

"What?"

"What what? What other possible explanation could there be? Those aren't . . . biological, Matthew. This isn't a disease. Not a normal one, anyway." She suddenly wished harder than ever that Benji was still here. "You aren't going anywhere. I need you here. I need you here because I don't want to be alone and without a friend, and I'm feeling pretty alone right now. If you have whatever this is and it's communicable, then I already have it. So does Gumball."

"Marcy, no—"

"Matthew, *yes*. Besides, someone should keep an eye on you."

He looked up at her with pleading eyes. But eventually, his gaze fell back to the raw, red spot on his arm. "Fine. Just the same I-I shouldn't be near other people. Just in case." There was something else in that last sentence. *Just in case*. It wasn't just about being communicable. It was what happened to the wolf. The wolf went crazy, attacked its own pack. He was afraid of that, too.

"Okay, deal. But you're not that wolf. You're Matthew. You're a good man. We'll get through this. We'll find answers." It was all the more imperative now that they did.

64

THE RIGHT-HAND MAN

That fucking asshole has figured out something we haven't. Two words: white victimhood. That's it. He can tap into that like he's a, a, a, I dunno, but that's what it is. That's the gas he's putting in his car to make it go, and he's going to beat us in the primary because of it. He's got no shame, and that's how he wins.

—Senator Bart Stevens (R, ME) referring to Ed Creel on a hot mic before a debate with Republican primary opponents

OCTOBER 25, 2025
Innsbrook, Missouri

CREEL HAD FEW PEOPLE HE LIKED AT INNSBROOK; FREDRICK HOGAN WAS one of them. Hogan was shorter than Creel by a few inches, but bristled with fat and muscle. He was shorn bald, with a patchy red beard. Wasn't covered head to toe in Nazi ink or militia markings. He was real ex-military, not just some holster-kissing cosplayer. You could feel it on him. Way he stood, he was always ready. He looked relaxed, but that was only because he knew he could snap-to-it and kill a man lickety-fucking-quick.

Hogan had been White Jesus's right-hand man, not because he subscribed to his viewpoint or believed that freakshow was the Actual Messiah, but because he was smart enough to know that in the middle of the ocean, you cling to whatever floats. He was a survivor.

All of that meant Hogan was useful. And Ed Creel liked useful. He liked you as much as you were valuable to him personally. That was the end of his interest.

It was Hogan who helped Creel get up to speed with what resources they had, and more important, what they didn't have. What they *needed*.

They sat in what was once a hotel conference room. The big kind, the kind Creel had been in a hundred times before, accepting some award, giving some speech to fat-cat donors, eating someone's idea of chicken or fish. The kind with the geometric carpets and the bland taupe wallpaper. Now, it had fallen to disrepair. As had everything. The ceiling panels were falling out. There was a leak in the far corner—or had been, anyway, showing a mess of dirty water stains spreading out like sickness. Wallpaper peeled. The carpet was filthy.

The two men had maps laid out in front of them. Hogan had a pile of wine corks stuck through with clear-color plastic toothpicks, like from a catering kitchen. Some of the corks were on the map already, marking areas that Hogan knew had resources—including people—that they could use.

"You sure you don't want your girl here with us?" Hogan asked. His voice was a slow growling drawl—a smoker's voice, once. Every word like the turn of a millstone. "We can wait."

He meant Annie. "No," Creel said. "It's fine." *I don't need her.*

Hogan went on, said the biggest thing they needed would be propane—most of their engines had been retrofitted to take propane. They had an impressive number of vehicles from the militia days, everything from troop trucks to Jeeps, from motorbikes to a bulldozer. A few dozen. Still not enough. Creel had said from the get-go that they needed more. More vehicles, more people to drive them, more food to feed them, more of *everygoddamnthing.* Creel was greedy. He was impatient. He expected Innsbrook to be a feudal kingdom of ready men, but this kingdom was ruined, its men, broken.

And many were fools. Fools who followed White Jesus *not* because he was something to cling to in the ocean but because they were dumb enough to believe in him, to fall prey to such derangement.

Already he'd sent some of Innsbrook's best out into the world, to Warrenton, Wright City, to Troy to the north, places mostly scavenged, but places where there were still people. People they could recruit. Those people were told that President Creel was alive, and they were given a choice to live free as an American in his army, or die a foreigner in a foreign land. Preference given to white people, of course, but that was a self-selecting problem, because it was the whites who wanted in. Still, he made it clear: Anybody who wanted to join could join. No questions asked. Man, woman, Black, white, didn't matter. Someone was willing to fight for Creel's America? Then they were good. Now was no time to get picky about that shit. Sure, it would cause problems in the ranks—there were loyalists and there were the white nationalists and those were two circles that did not always neatly overlap. But he had this in his campaign, too. He had men of color in his campaign, a few women, too. The new far-right under the Creel Coalition had been a mixed-race, mixed-gender cadre of nationalists, and they got along because he told them to get along. They all fell in line behind him in the end. As they would now, because at the end of the day, people were attracted to power. They wanted to serve it. They wanted to give themselves to it.

In the last few days they were able to swell their ranks a little. A dozen here, a dozen there. People who knew it was better to serve Creel than to die under his boot. Still, more people meant more mouths to feed. But they could be expendable resources if they had to be. Stuff them full of pig-feed, send them out into the world with searching hands and eager eyes and the competitive spirit fueled by not-wanting-to-goddamn-starve-to-death. If they died, they died. They'd be like his kamikaze soldiers, crashing and burning to serve the cause.

They were resources.

And resources were there to be used up.

Hogan said, "If we're gonna build this here army, if we're really marching on Atlanta, we need to take St. Louis first."

"No," Creel said, flinching. He could practically feel Annie's gaze even though she wasn't in the building—like twin knife tips digging into the back of his skull. "Atlanta is first and foremost. The CDC."

"No disrespect, Mister President, but you're looking at a complex Rube Goldberg machine. All parts need to be in play for this to work. We need fuel to get to Atlanta. So, we expend our men and our ammunition taking fuel, fine, but then we've got men down and we're out of bullets, so then we need to replenish those. So we spend time to get more men and make more bullets, find casings, find powder, and in the meantime, people need to eat, we still need fuel for the generators, and if another bout of dysentery goes through the camp like it did last year, we'll have people shitting themselves to death—"

"I get it, chief, I get the point," Creel said. "But we can't take this slow. That's not an option. So, what options do we have?"

"I have one idea."

"Let's hear it."

"It will be neither simple nor easy."

"Just say it, Hogan, I don't like people wasting my time."

"West of the airport, there's everything we need in one location. Guns. Ammo. New vehicles. Probably food. Best of all, it's a huge propane depot."

Creel shrugged. "Sounds like manna from heaven. What's the catch?"

"It's a military base."

"So? There's no more military. We're it."

Hogan sniffed, picked at his teeth. "Not exactly."

Creel impatiently did his finger-doing-a-barrel-roll gesture.

Hogan continued: "There remains a military presence there. Holdovers from the old world. Army. Intel, such as it is, says there's at least two dozen men and women inside, holding it down. Capable people sitting on a bunker of food, weapons, whatever they need. Healthy, fed, good in a fight. White Jesus threw us up against them a few times over the years. It never went well. They're dug in." Hogan shrugged. "That said, we go in with you at the helm— you and your, well, *abilities*, maybe there's something we can do. Way you took out White Jesus . . ."

"No, no, I'm a president, not a fucking common soldier, Hogan. C'mon. But you're looking at this wrong. They're rudderless. Leaderless. Waiting for something. For someone."

Hogan leaned in. "You're saying they need a president."

"Chain of command is driven into them like a *nail*. They'll snap to it sure as a dog humps your leg. It's instinct."

"You'll need to be there, at the attack."

"No attack. That's the beauty of it. We send you, me, a handful of men to make sure we don't look like a couple of dickheads. We ask to talk. A meeting, a parlay. They'll see who I am, what I can do. Then they become us."

"Risky. But I think it's the best foot forward."

"Agreed."

Hogan leaned back again, arms behind him. "I'd like to know, if you don't mind, why do you and your woman"—Creel wanted to say, *She's not my woman*, but if they thought that's how it was, so be it—"wanna hit the CDC so bad?"

"Like I said, medicine, resources—"

"We can get those elsewhere. Why there, specifically?"

Creel clucked his tongue. "You remember those Sleepwalkers? 'The Flock'?"

"I do. I figured them for al-Qaeda, some bioweapon."

"I did, too, once. But truth is, they come from right here in America. Atlanta, engineered in the CDC by left-wing scientists—woke Doctor Frankenstein types. Thing is, that so-called Flock of terrorists, they were weapons. And they're still out there, Hogan. We wanna take them down, we need to know our enemy. And they *are* our enemy. If they come after us before we go after them . . ."

At that, Hogan licked his lips. Out of dubiousness or whether he was hungry for a fight, Creel wasn't yet certain. "Fair enough. And the woman, Annie. She seems to know something about all that?"

She does, Creel thought. *And she's not telling me.* He was still kept at arm's length. Some need-to-know-basis bullshit. He thought back to what she told him—if she had a stroke, or died, or even passed out, she'd lose control of the chip and he could die. But that wasn't precisely true. They'd gotten their asses handed to them coming up to Innsbrook. And certainly she slept. A loss of consciousness didn't make the chip fritz out. Creel scratched the stubble that flecked his chin. "Truth be told, Hogan, I don't know how much I trust her."

"Oh?"

"Mm. But I think I got a plan for that."

"Whatever you need from me. Assuming you trust me, of course."

"I do. The doctor we have here—what's his name?"

"His name's Beecher, but they call him Beecher the Butcher. Given that most times his only interest is to lop off an arm or a leg like an old-time chirurgeon. Why?"

"He know much about drugs? Medicine, I mean."

"I suppose a little. He wasn't a doctor. Used to be a veterinarian. Dogs, cats, horses, farm-vet shit, mostly."

"Good. I need to meet with him. Somewhere private. Ask him some questions. Can't be in my suite. Annie hangs around there too often."

Hogan nodded. "He can come with us. To the depot. Not the worst thing to have a doctor on hand, easy to explain. You can chat on the way."

"No, no, too many other people. Tell him I'll come to him. And you'll come with me. Soon, if possible. Good?"

"It'll be done."

"You're a good man, Hogan."

"No, sir, I am not. But I do get shit done."

Creel grinned. "And that's why we're friends."

A LONG WAY PAST THE POSSUM

2017
Firesight, Reston, Virginia

THE OPOSSUM BUMBLED AROUND ITS PLEXIGLAS ENCLOSURE—A TWENTY-BY-twenty space in the office basement—its mouth shut, its little pokey teeth sticking up from its lower jaw in a classic opossum underbite, its pink nose wriggling as it sniffed the air. It no longer froze when it detected their scent nearby. It was used to them.

It had no name, just a designation:

DV5544.

Moira Simone and Bill Craddock looked down at it from above.

Bill handed Moira a piece of paper. Reliably old-fashioned, him. He was ten years her senior, but they might as well have had a century between them. She preferred tablets, laptops, anything with a screen. For Bill, it was always paper.

Though the lights were bright facing the enclosure, outside of it, they were dim. "I can't read this here," she said.

Bill grunted, not dismissively, just in an oh-right sort of way. "The numbers are good. The numbers are very good."

"The OK cells, too?" she asked. OK cells, literally, opossum kidney cells. Studied in part for their fast degradation. That was one of the things about opossum: They had a life span of about three or four years, even in captivity. Most mammals that size lived considerably longer—a squirrel could live twelve years in captivity. An opossum, treated well and kept free of disease, still died at four years. Like there was a little doom clock in them, tick-tick-tick. The OK cells were the first alarm to go off, the first cells believed to degrade. To self-destruct, as it were.

"Zero degradation."

The opossum scuttled under a big oak tree branch they had in there, then up its length. Beneath it were some broken eggshells. The opossum really liked hard-boiled eggs. Easter brought it a few colorful treats this year. It ate those colored eggs with considerable gusto. (Of course it ate *all* eggs with considerable gusto, but the colored shell fragments made it more festive.)

"So our strange friend there is now nearly five years old," Moira said.

"Correct."

"That makes it, theoretically, the oldest living opossum in captivity."

"Also correct, yes." Bill clucked his tongue. "There's more."

"Well, don't dwell, just spit it out."

"The contagion trial is complete. Rabies was always a nonstarter, given their body temp. Lyme and distemper, similarly. But tularemia, lepto, Chagas, coccidiosis, all administered with successful infections. And not one infection gained ground. All were eliminated within forty-eight hours, most within twenty-four."

Moira held her breath for a moment. Was it really true? "So, it's not simply repairing cell damage. It's staving off disease."

"That's not all. We weren't able to administer infectious agents intravenously. We had to go the oral route for all of them."

For some of the infectious agents, the oral route was necessary anyway. But not for all of them. "Get to the point, please."

"That's the problem. We couldn't get to the point. The techs couldn't get a needle to penetrate the skin."

"What? The creature too *wiggly*?"

He grunted. "No. The skin would not . . . yield to the needle."

"Meaning?"

"Just what it says, Moira, I'm not being obtuse. The sharpest needle wouldn't puncture its fur and skin. We tried a scalpel, after that. Just as a test—a small incision under the fur, minuscule, an injury that would be easy to heal. But we were not successful at injuring the opossum."

"You . . . weren't able to injure the possum."

"That is accurate, Moira."

Once more she turned her attention to the creature that scampered about them, below. It seemed healthy. It appeared unaffected mentally—it wasn't running around in circles or gnawing at itself in an undue way. It showed none of the signs of mental degradation that happened in earlier studies.

Opossums were fascinating creatures, Moira knew. Her daughter, Anais, did a report on them when she was little, full of curious facts (though Moira politely asked the then–fourth grader to remove the tidbit about the possum's thirteen nipples and two-pronged penis). The girl became obsessed with them for a time, begging for every possum knickknack, puppet, and poster they could find.

She would love this, Moira thought. But she couldn't tell her. This was not for public consumption. Not yet. Not for a good while.

They had a long row to hoe, as the saying went.

But this was a promising start to the journey.

"Bill?" she asked.

"Yes, Moira?"

"I think we just created a semi-immortal possum."

"I think you might be right, Moira."

2018
Bethesda, Maryland

IT WAS 5 P.M., AND Moira Simone had been drinking.

She had been drinking since 5 A.M.

She was not drunk, not precisely. Not in the fall-down-throw-up way. No, this inebriation was a slow and steady one, the turtle winning the race. Moira floated on it like gentle waves. In, out. In, out.

This is my last day of freedom, she thought. Tomorrow, it ended. She performed another knee-jerk check of her phone, tapping the screen, seeing if she had any missed calls from Anais. Were there missed calls, the phone should've, would've told her. It would've rang. But still, she checked. Because maybe the tech had failed her. *Certainly that's a thing that can happen*, she thought grimly. But no, the device registered no lost calls.

Anais had not called her back.

She thought to call her daughter once more, leave another voicemail—her fifth? Sixth?—but she restrained herself this time.

Moira leaned back on the couch. CNN was on with its standard circus of delights—the twenty-four-hour news cycle, an endless carousel of bad news designed to poke the limbic system with its pointy stick. *React, react, react*, it told you.

Tomorrow, she thought, *I'll be part of that news cycle.*

If not tomorrow, then a day after, or soon enough.

That news cycle would expose her. What she did. What she took part in with Bill. And when that happened, she'd be ruined.

Her stomach felt curdled. She decided that more alcohol would fix that. Gin and tonic was Moira's drink tonight and every night. Crisp. Tart. *Medicinal*, she always told herself. *No malaria for Moira*. It was practically a motto.

She got up, poured another, did a twist of lemon since she was out of lime, and sat back down. Idly, almost grumpily, she took her MacBook Air and slid it onto her lap, once more opening it up and scrolling through pages after pages of notes, clinical documents, images, slides. With a quick click she pulled up a 3D rendering of Firesight's bouncing baby bot:

The Nanocyte.

This little bugger comprised a bundle of nanoreceptors (acoustic, environmental, biomolecular) anchored to a central disc-shaped hub, from which emerged a tangle of cilia used for both propulsion and manipulation within the host. Each little robot spoke to another little robot nearby, using an artificially intelligent form of NFC, near-field communication.

That AI was a brutally simplistic piece of software whose subroutines were based on two biological behavior patterns—

First: the path-making problem-solving of ants and ant colonies, casually borrowed from the work of Icelandic tech-genius Einar Giersson.

Second: the flocking patterns of starlings—their murmurations were things of beauty, their modeling based on the fact that no one bird was in control of the flock, and every bird would remain within a set number of inches from at least two other birds. They all moved together, but never apart. A swarm, but not a mind. Deeply simple. Humbly elegant. Essentially: art.

Nature was amazing.

Nature was also terrible.

Terrible because it was so, *so* mystifying.

The human body, the most mystifying of them all.

At that, Moira sipped her G&T, then as her gut cinched tighter and she felt her pulse quicken, she tapped the button and pulled up the live feed.

Twelve biosignatures filled the screen. Each a single toolbar, in essence, stacked atop and next to one another. The biosignatures were roughly equivalent. Life signs, brain scans, too. Sometimes brain activity would spike, and with that neural bubbling-up rose heart rate, blood pressure, even temperature. It never lasted. Just a minute or three, then they settled back down.

It matched the rough scan image of someone asleep having a nightmare. The rise and fall of sleep cycles, the jump to a dream with sharp teeth. Taking its bite. Then the shark would let them go and back into the depths they would sink.

Moira sighed, rubbed her eyes. She knew she shouldn't look. What was the point of any of this? Did she truly harbor some notion that she could fix it all at this late hour? That she could see what had gone wrong?

One more act of self-flagellation, she decided, then: dinner.

She pulled up the secondary live feed. This one, a camera feed. She could scroll through their twelve faces. Leonard Metzger. Jam Mohamed. Daria Stewart. Victoria Yen. Yasmin Lourde. Cameron Thicke. Ursula Lansdale. Julie Barden. Murreen Wallace. Rebecca Simone. Tauriq Lucas. And Joe Craddock.

Each face, like a porcelain grave mask. A face in repose. Mouths closed. Eyes closed, too. Like they should have coins pressed gently over the lids. Their signatures said they were asleep. Their faces said they were dead.

Moira sighed wearily. She was feeling it in her bones tonight. *I'm sorry, Joe,* she thought. *I'm sorry, Becky. I'm sorry, Anais. I'm sorry, Bill.*

She decided to distract herself with her dinner options, but there were none she liked, and so she pondered just having another G&T as dinner, even though she killed that bottle of gin and would need to open another. The Bluecoat, maybe.

One more time, she turned on her phone screen, looking for a missed call.

The phone rang.

She nearly spilled her drink, it scared her so bad.

It wasn't her daughter. It was Bill Craddock. Her Firesight partner.

He's going to try to tell us not to go public tomorrow, she thought, but that wouldn't happen. Bill was Mister Responsibility. He was ex-military. If anything, he'd try to be the one to jump on the grenade to spare her.

"Bill," she said into the phone, already starting in on him. "I don't know what you're going to say, but you can't convince me—"

"Things have changed, Moira," he said, his voice classic Bill—clipped, gruff, unswerving. It never felt harsh, though. Just . . . direct.

"What?"

"We're being bought."

"I don't understand."

"I don't precisely understand, either," he said. "But it's true. We are being bought out by Benex-Voyager. Part of that CDC initiative from the president. We meet with a representative tomorrow."

"But tomorrow—"

"That's on hold."

It shouldn't be, she thought. *We should hang for what we've done.*

But if they could escape the gallows . . .

"Bill—"

"They asked for us to hold off on any 'announcements' tomorrow."

"They said that? Specifically that? Did you tell them—"

"I didn't tell them anything, Moira. They knew our intent. Which potentially means they know what we've done."

"But then why would they want to buy Firesight?"

"That is a question for them. Tomorrow. The meeting place is a bit unusual."

"Where is it?"

"Green Mount Cemetery in Baltimore."

"A cemetery?" she asked.

"Perhaps they intend to bury us there."

"They fucking should," was all she said to that.

"Probably," he answered. "See you tomorrow, Moira."

GREEN MOUNT CEMETERY
One day later

IT WAS SUMMER. THE DAY was hot—the kind of hot that was withering, like the air around you was a wet tarp, wrapped around you, sweating out your life, your hope, your free will. Despite the heat, Bill was dressed in a heavy green blazer because that's how he dressed year-round. Blazer and slacks, blazer and slacks. The Bill Craddock uniform. On the coldest night, on the hottest day.

Moira wore all black. In mourning, in a sense. Mourning the death of all they hoped to achieve. Mourning what they'd built, and what had failed.

Whatever came next for them and for Firesight would be like a city built on a graveyard. The old world becoming sediment beneath the new one. It called to mind that bird, the invasive one. The house sparrow. Monstrous little thing. Would invade the nest of a perfectly lovely bird, like a bluebird, then peck the mother to death, peck the eggs, peck the hatchlings. Then it would build its own nest right there, on the carcass of those it murdered.

Ahead stood their own house sparrow.

(*Or are we the house sparrows?* Moira wondered. *Are we the invasive ones? The ones who peck, the ones who build on the bodies?*)

Their sparrow, the woman, was British or Nigerian or something. Maybe both. She represented Benex-Voyager, a tech company bundled into the CDC during that brief tizzy of privatization began by President Nolan in the last administration. They were into algorithms and intelligences. They had some new predictive system in play. All of it was bigger stuff than Firesight preferred to deal with. Bigger company, too. Firesight was lean and nimble, their staff limited, often cloistered. Quite often it was just Moira and Bill.

The woman stood there in a loose sundress, orange and green, the type of short, flowy thing a younger woman like her could get away with. Moira hated her immediately. And respected her, too, for looking that way in a *graveyard*.

She waited, standing in front of a peculiar grave—

It was a grave marked with a Ouija board. Had the smiley face YES, the half-moon NO. All the letters and numbers faced in their old-timey script. And at the bottom, two figures shook hands with the words, Good Bye, emblazoned beneath. Two black stars bedecked each of the gravestone's lowest corners.

But it had no name.

"What's this about?" Moira asked, unable to conceal her irritation. She had to raise her voice a bit because across the street, in the direction of a church steeple, they were doing construction. A backhoe made a bang-and-judder sound as it peeled up hunks and chunks of street for whatever reason.

"I'm Sadie Emeka from Benex-Voyager and—"

"Yes, I know all that. I mean this, the grave. Why here?"

"This is Elijah Bond's grave," Sadie said, as if that were an explanation instead of just one more bit of riddle.

"And?"

"He invented the Ouija board," Bill said. Of course if anybody would know semi-pointless trivia, it was Bill. He read books the way other people ate potato chips. His house held stacks and stacks of them. "The patented 'talking board,' once thought to speak to spirits. But used as a divinatory tool, too, if I recall."

"Very good," Sadie said.

"All pseudoscience," Moira said. Because it was.

"True. But still indicative of humanity's need for answers—to try to understand what was happening, and what will come."

Bill nodded. "Rumor has it that's what Benex-Voyager has been work-ing on. Some kind of predictive intelligence. To spot problems before they become—"

"Become problems," Sadie finished the thought. "Yes. That's correct."

"Worth noting that the way a Ouija board works is through an ideomotor response. Whatever 'messages' the board gives its users are just the messages they unconsciously gave themselves through minuscule motor movements of the fingers when they move the planchette. Given that a machine like yours would have to be programmed, who's to say that's not what's happening there? No ghost here, just the unseen hand of the algorithm, nudged by a program of bias and desire." Bill, that wonderful bastard, was giving it to her good. It was damn near poetry.

Moira approved.

"I assure you, Black Swan works."

"Black Swan," Moira said. "That what you call it?"

"It is." Sadie spoke in a faux sotto voce: "Bit cheeky, I know. And I should know. I'm the lead neural designer."

"So, you're its puppeteer?"

Sadie seemed to stiffen at that. "Hardly. It makes its own predictions."

"Such as?"

"It told us we needed to buy your company."

"So you're *its* puppet," Moira said. Before Sadie could offer retort, Moira barreled ahead: "If this Black Swan told you to buy us, then your machine truly *is* broken and you should retire it to the trash-heap immediately."

Sadie paused, seemed to consider her next words carefully.

"You know, I chose this spot not just because of Elijah Bond's grave. I chose it because it's out of the way. Because the construction sounds make it very hard for anybody to hear us, even if they're fifty feet away. Because Black Swan told us we needed to acquire your company, but not before Black Swan showed me what your company has been working on. Your sins are not revealed to the world, not yet, but, Moira and Bill, they are revealed to me. You've created something wonderful. But what worked on the possum did not work on people. We can help."

Moira and Bill shared a cold, nervous look.

"How?" Bill asked.

"I confess, I'm not yet certain. But Black Swan assures us that a partner-ship is valuable. It seems to me that your nanoparticle—"

"The Nanocyte."

"Yes. That it effectively functions as a secondary immune system on top of the extant one. It works well in animals, but in people, you hit a considerable snag, and now those people are comatose."

"*In suspended animation* is our preferred nomenclature," Moira said.

"To-*may*-to, to-*mah*-to," Sadie said, smiling.

"The Nanocyte upon entering the body maps that body, snout-to-tail," Bill explained, "and that includes the brain. The goal being to continually update us as to the health and wellness and activity of the person inoculated with it. Broadcast via near-field. Only problem is, something happened inside the human body."

"Inside the human *brain*," Moira corrected. "The Nanocyte swarm maps the brain last. But once it began to map the human brain, the output looked . . . like a maze, a labyrinth: a meaningless tangle of information. It was too complicated. We thought, well, fine, so what? We'd fix that bug and make a firmware upgrade."

Bill continued: "But the Nanocyte wouldn't stop. It continued to chart the brain, and the mind within, relentlessly. Almost aggressively. Immediately after, there was swelling. Minuscule swelling, but persistent. The brain suffered as if under an autoimmune attack—brain on fire, like in encephalitis. And then—"

"It protected itself from itself," Sadie said. "I've read the documents. The swarm created a problem inadvertently, and like with autoimmune reactions, sought to solve that problem with more of itself. To protect the mind, the brain, it simply shut them down into . . . low-power mode, let's say, same way you might try to boot a computer into safe mode to fix critical errors."

Moira stepped closer. "Back up. What do you mean, you've 'read the documents'?" She turned to Bill. "You didn't—"

"I didn't," he said. Not defensively. Just plainly.

"Black Swan found them," Sadie said, as if it were a totally normal thing to say.

"Black Swan."

"It's already in your system. It has access."

"You mean it *took* access. Stole it."

Sadie shrugged at that. Another to-may-to, to-mah-to moment.

"That's criminal," Moira said.

"I'm sure it is. But less criminal than what you did to those twelve people, off the books, off the record, without informing investors, without informing your very small boutique staff, without informing their families. You took twelve people at the edges of their own lives and gave them a cocktail of teeny-tiny computers under various duplicitous offerings. Unproven offerings. That's what should put you both in jail. This should be a scandal the likes of which would make Theranos seem like petty larceny."

To have it spoken so directly . . .

The judgment of this stranger was not what bothered Moira. But she tried to imagine what Anais would think. Her own daughter. They barely spoke anymore. Moira's fault. Probably.

"We had our reasons," Moira said finally.

"I know. I know about your sister, Becky. And, Bill, your brother, Joe."

Bill looked at his shoes. A rare moment where he was rattled.

Moira would not be rattled. "So? Fine. You know us. You know what we've done. Now what? Why are we here?"

"We go to work, of course. And the first order of business is, you're going to need to make more of your little nanites. A whole lot more."

A CABIN IN THE POCONO MOUNTAINS, PENNSYLVANIA
Early March 2020

MOIRA HAD A CABIN NOW because she needed a place away from it all. She needed escape. She needed solace. Both from the world as it was now, and the world as it would become. She hadn't yet started *prepping*, exactly. Though she'd certainly been to the websites, seen all the ways that the doomer-boomers decided to prepare for whatever end they imagined: nuclear attack, bioweapon, polar flip-flop, and, of course, world-ending pandemic. Some raised goats. Some bought canned goods in the thousands. Others fell into hobbies (or, really, habits) from hydroponics to ammunition-reloading. Moira wasn't quite sure she had the stomach for any of that. Especially goats. Christ, goats. Could you imagine? *Goats.*

The most she'd done was buy a lot of wine. She'd become a drinker of wine. Gin was still on the menu, but gin kept her crisp and refreshed. Wine weighed her down like one of those heavy blankets all the anxious people seemed to like, a heavy oblivion that gave her considerable comfort.

It wasn't expensive wine, though she had the money for it if she wanted. She chose wine by how much the label attracted her. Same way she bought books.

I judge books by their covers, I judge wines by their labels.

Outside, a clumsy, late-season snow had chosen to fall. Fat flakes bumbling downward across the expanse of dark pines. The snow reminded her of the possum: DV5544. Dee-vee, they sometimes called it. Well. Bill didn't.

Still alive, that little critter. Now at the CDC. Still bumbling and tumbling. Disease-free. Degradation-free. Trouble-free. Ever-living.

And all it took was a fingernail sliver of nanites.

They'd made a lot more nanites since in service to Black Swan, for reasons that remained unclear. But they did as they were told because they understood that it was the thing keeping them out of jail. And Benex-Voyager assured them that they would do their level best to cure the twelve people in suspended animation kept in a sublevel facility in Atlanta, built out from the Benex-Voyager offices. Efforts to extract the nanites from those patients had failed, in part due to fear that such extraction would leave each of them clinically brain-dead. They were alive, for now, and healthy—as disease-free and degradation-free as the possum.

"It's out of our hands," Moira had told Bill once.

He'd grunted in assent.

There was a part of her that always thought, *Well, I'll come clean soon.* She envisioned herself a martyr to her own cause, sacrificed on her own altar, telling the world of her sins as an act of nobility and accountability to herself and herself alone. But she always stopped short. Some reason always bubbled up out of the broth of guilt. *Oh, you don't want to do that to Bill. Oh, you wouldn't want to put The Twelve at risk. Oh, you wouldn't want to jeopardize the good work being done.*

And last of all—

Oh, but what would Anais think?

Truth was, she hadn't spoken to her daughter in over a year. The girl (*woman,* Moira thought, chastising herself) had pulled away hard. Not disappeared—no, she still updated her Instagram and such. She just stopped answering Moira's calls and emails. Moira didn't know why. Anais had become an insurmountable wall. One with no doors or windows, a wall that resisted any manner of passage.

So, Moira fell into the work. Or so she told herself—had she ever really climbed out of the work? Had Bill? They worked hard at the behest of Benex-Voyager, and by proxy, the CDC, the Defense Department, and, she suspected, Black Swan itself. Sometimes Moira and Bill wondered aloud to each other, what were they really doing here? Black Swan's threads were in everything already. It had unparalleled access, unknown to nearly everyone. Already that gave it tremendous power, but with their Nanocyte? Their new

Nanocyte could travel like spores thanks to whip-fast flagella—the nanites could move against even the hardest wind. An active, motile aerosol. And what it could do with the human body and brain . . . well. Why did it *need* the Nanocyte?

Bill said it was just increasing its monitoring abilities, that's all.

But Moira said, "No, it's a weapon. It has to be." Some of their other upgrades had suggested as much: running tests to see how the Nanocyte did against cell walls, how it could "borrow" energy from mitochondria in a more aggressive way that drained or even killed cells, how it could raise or decrease temperature. They even logged ways to have the Nanocyte generation clone itself using biological tissue. Little baby biobots. Not in play, yet, but one day . . .

We've gone a long way past an immortal possum, she'd thought then.

Then came Document 99.

A quantum machine, talking to itself in the future . . .

It was insane. Moira knew that. This idea that somehow Black Swan— a predictive intelligence built as a quantum computer—had received communication from itself in the future, a future where mankind had been wholly eradicated by a fungal pathogen that began like white-nose syndrome in bats? It was truly, spectacularly deranged. But Bill was bullish on it. Said, "It's possible. Quantum entanglement is a helluva thing, Moira. Time and space are not hard limits on that entanglement."

Then came Jerry Garlin.

Heir to the theme park throne of Garlin Gardens. He went and did his stupid stunt in San Antonio to break ground on a new theme park, and with it came the bats. And with those bats came the pathogen.

It would already be in him right now. And it would be in those who attended, too. Then Jerry Garlin traveled around the world, airport to airport, airplane to airplane, to hotels, to meetings, to restaurants. And that was just him. All the other attendees in San Antonio? They weren't sitting still, either. Moira wanted to laugh it off. Because this wasn't real. There wasn't some invisible pandemic. But Black Swan had the data: symptoms popping up, like with a cold, but along for the ride were a few tiny signs of growing dementia. And those signs were already spreading. Still, those symptoms were mild. They wouldn't *end the world*. Would they? Black Swan was sure that they could, and would. That these symptoms were just the bellwether.

Moira said, "So, we go public. We tell the CDC, we tell WHO, we let them . . . do their thing. Quarantine and eradicate."

But Black Swan's modeling showed quarantine of that level would be impossible, and that the populace would not endure any sort of meaningful lockdown. Besides, the disease was a hydra: You could not cut off all its heads. If it was as far out as it was, how would you even track that? This wasn't SARS. There were just a few points of infection—and inflection. But Black Swan had already tracked a surge of cases. Those infected with White Mask just didn't know it yet. And those people gave it to other people who gave it to other people who gave it to . . . on and on it went, a grim cascade. Almost three months now since the ground-breaking in San Antonio meant . . . it was practically pandemic.

Or so the artificial intelligence told them.

It felt deranged. But Black Swan had been right about everything else so far.

That's when Sadie told them the plan—

The plan for the Nanocyte.

What it could do.

Who it could protect.

Moira still thought about going public, but Sadie assured her: *If you do that, our plan will fail. They'll try massive lockdowns—masks, PPE, roads closed, which means we won't have movement, we won't have freedom. And people will rebel. They'll fight the restrictions, at least here. Americans do not like to be told what to do, Moira.* Then Sadie defaulted to the easy excuse, the oracular one: *Black Swan has seen it. We must keep quiet. We must stay the course.*

Black Swan, the oracle. It told them their future. It told them their end.

Only some could remain.

Only those it chose.

(That didn't sound like an oracle, Moira thought. It sounded like a god.)

So! Moira drank red wine right from the bottle tonight. That was how she was feeling. A real drink-to-the-bottom-of-the-bottle mood. Then climb-in-the-goddamn-bottle-and-curl-up-there-like-a-happy-immortal-possum vibe.

She was oddly, grotesquely calm about it.

Except for when it came to Anais.

She'd texted her just this morning: *We need to talk.* She wasn't going to tell her anything. She couldn't risk it. But she wanted to see her. Make amends.

Then: a knock at the door. She nearly dropped the bottle.

"Jesus," she said. Who'd be here? Now? Tonight?

She peered through the bay window near the breakfast nook, saw a familiar flash of copper-wire hair poking out from under a raspberry toque.

Oh my God.

Moira nearly fainted with joy. She opened the door to find her daughter, Anais, standing there. Arms crossed. Snow upon her. Behind her, a sleek black Mercedes sat in the driveway next to Moira's Porsche SUV.

"Oh," was all Moira managed to say. She wanted to say more, but more wouldn't come out. *Oh. You foolish cow. Say more. Say more!* But, no.

"Hi, Mom," Anais said. It was an icy-puddle greeting. Like stepping in cold slush.

"Anais, come in."

Her daughter stepped in. The snow on the shoulders of her jacket already started to melt in the warm, dry air of the firelit cabin. Water snaked down the arms of that jacket in chaotic runnels.

"Annie," Anais said. "Not Anais."

"I— Anais is the name we gave you."

"The name you gave me. Not Dad. Dad called me Annie. I'm Annie."

"Well, I—" *Suck it up, Moira.* "Of course. Annie." That word felt like a benign cyst on her tongue. A lump. The texture of it was all wrong. "Annie," she said again, as if that would help. It didn't. "You got my text."

"I've gotten all your texts, all your emails, your voicemails. All your smoke signals. All your plaintive cries. I've seen them."

Moira could feel her hackles raising. She didn't mean to get her back up. But she was a defensive person by nature. "Why didn't you ever respond?"

"Why? Oh, shit, I can't imagine why. Because you're a narcissist? A sociopath? Because you drove Dad to the drinking that killed him? Because you drive *everybody* away, a relentless magnetic repulsion where the moment they step out of line or look at you the wrong way you shove them out of the air lock and into the cold void of space? Until they beg to be let back in again, pounding on the glass as their eyeballs start to pop like corks?"

"Very dramatic," Moira said stiffly. "You were always dramatic, Anais— *Annie*. This menu of indictments isn't fair, and you know it. Your father had problems before me, and you were always a sharp girl, a bit of a thumbtack— honestly, you're like me, a *lot* like me, and—"

"What about Aunt Becky?"

Oh. Oh, Anais . . .

"My sister was a very depressed person. Bipolar. You know that. She could come and go between moods like she was ballroom dancing in a hall of mirrors. I tried to help her. I did. I didn't discard her, not at all." *You have no idea how I didn't discard her. I kept her. I keep her still.* Then came the start of the lie, the big lie, the one on the books, in the papers. "When she disappeared—"

"When she disappeared," Anais said, repeating those three words, again like an indictment. Like she knew something.

"Yes. Your aunt wandered off one day and—bipolar people are—"

"Don't fucking lie to me."

"Don't speak to me that way. Annie."

Anais—*Annie*, apparently—angrily reached in the pocket of her jacket, pulled out a smartphone. It wasn't a brand Moira recognized, and when *Annie* opened it, she did so with an erratic swipe of her thumb across the screen, up, down, left, and right, like she was trying to draw a constellation. A complicated passcode. When the device was unlocked, she turned the screen toward her mother.

Moira was about to open her mouth, but when she saw Becky's face on the screen, her words choked to death on the edge of her tongue.

Becky's face.

Her passive, death-mask face.

Suspended animation, she thought bitterly.

It was the live feed.

Anais used her other thumb to swipe past it. Swipe, swipe, swipe, with each came a new person. The Twelve. The phone showcased their placid, liminal expressions, peaceful faces trapped in their in-between places.

"Where did you get that?" Moira hissed.

"You always taught me to be good with computers, *Moira*."

"Anais—"

"Annie. And not Annie Simone, either. Cahill." *Her father's name.*

"Anais! You don't understand. I'm trying to help—"

"No, you don't understand. I came here because I want you to hear it from me first. I know you're into some hinky shit. I've only just scratched the surface. But I see all the versions of your little nanoswarm. I see you working with Benex-Voyager, the CDC, the military-industrial complex. You're a capitalist snake and a mad scientist all bundled up in one nasty bitch. And I intend fully to expose you. I intend to find every one of your sins and I will use them to bury you. And then I'll bring Aunt Becky home. Because she's alive. Somehow, she's alive. And you don't get to keep her anymore in your glass fucking menagerie."

"You do not understand. There are factors at play here—"

"It doesn't matter. Whatever bridges you haven't burned yet will soon meet me with a can of gasoline and a pack of matches. I'll ruin you. You'll go to jail. Nothing of yours will remain. I do it for Dad. I do it for Becky." Anais bared her teeth in a snarl. "I do it for me."

"Anais, you don't know what you're saying. You don't know what's happening—there are forces at work here—"

"Lies, more lies, more sociopathic borderline bullshit."

"Anais. Annie—"

Her daughter tossed the phone to Moira. Moira barely managed to catch it. "There," Annie said. "A gift. You can see how much I already know. And soon enough, I'll find the rest."

"Why do you hate me so much?"

"Because you're a bad person. You were a shit mother. You isolated me. Made me push all my friends away. Sent me to faraway schools. You sent Dad into a spiral. You never got Becky the help she needed and now, as it turns out, you kidnapped her like a psychopath. Becky may have been fucked up, but she was nice to me. She had a big, messy heart. You're just a monster. Goodbye, Mother. Make peace in your world, because I'm going to end it."

As her daughter stormed out of the cabin, all Moira could think was, *You have no idea, Anais. It's already ending. Mine. Yours.*

Everybody's.

PART SIX

THE RITES OF
PILGRIMAGE

65

LOOK AWAY

I said it before and I'll say it again: I loved you when I met you, I love you now, and I love you in the future tense. Even gone from this world, I will love you, and I want that love to echo back and forth through time, till it finds you in every moment. I want you to remember me from tonight. I felt clear tonight. I felt good. (The wine didn't hurt.) It felt good to be with you this last time. I'm sorry it's like this. But I know if I wait, I'll do something untoward. And I can't have that. I can't have that being the memory of me you keep. Don't worry about where I'm going. I've always wanted to jump off a waterfall. It will be bracing and bright and I imagine the sound around me will fill my ears till I'm gone. It'll be a swan dive toward a better world. I hope there is a Heaven, Benjamin Ray, for I am to see you in it soon. I love you. Sadie.
—from Sadie Emeka's letter to Benji Ray on the night of her suicide

OCTOBER 27, 2025
Bridge of Heaven, Colorado

THIS FEELS DIFFERENT, BENJI THOUGHT AS HE WALKED HAND IN HAND WITH Sadie across the Bridge of Heaven, the sharp-edged ridge with views of the Cimarron range. Spin around (don't fall) and you could see a peak in every direction: the Coxcombs, Courthouse Mountain, Mount Sneffels, and the summit of Wetterhorn Peak. They looked spilled upon the world. Red and purple, like wine stains.

The elevation climbed quick and the air soon wore thin, like fabric pulled too tight. It was a hard hike up Horsethief Trail, the kind of hike that burned the muscles, tired the body, and invigorated the mind.

But Benji didn't feel tired. He barely remembered the climb up—usually a notable one, through thick pines and pockets of aspen trees.

Somewhere in the distance, over the mountains, rose a sound he could feel in his teeth. A low hum, like a growl. It gave him fresh fear, made his skin prickle. Sadie said, "It's okay," and petted the back of his head. "You don't need to worry about that. It's like Pete sang in that Gumdropper song, 'Wicked Worry,'—*look away, get lost, wander off, no cost.* I love that song." She paused and kissed his hand. "Don't you?"

He turned toward her. Was her hair different in this moment than it was just before? Braids then, a messy frizz now? Oh. He understood. Maybe.

"You're not her," he said.

"I'm as much her as you need me to be."

She took his left arm and held it straight out like a bird's wing. "Are we dancing?" she asked. Or did he ask her? The ridge suddenly felt perilously thin.

"Is it you?" he asked, meaning, Black Swan.

"Would Black Swan do this?" she said, and as she pulled his arm tighter out in another erratic box step, she was no longer Sadie. She was Dot. Dot, warm and lush, the sun shining right on her. She pressed her body against his and he felt himself yield to her, his muscles slackening.

"I don't know," he said honestly. "Would it?" He tried to walk himself through it. Black Swan seemed good at pretending to be others. But how did it accomplish that? Was it stealing their personalities? Mapping them, reproducing them? Or was it relying purely on those who knew them, borrowing the vision of them from their brain, chemically tweaking and manipulating the host's mind to believe they were seeing a friend, a family member, a lover? Like in a dream. If it was the former, then no, Dot could not be Black Swan. But if it was the latter . . .

Or, what if it was both? Black Swan could create a rough artifice that the mind would gladly fill in, because that's what minds did. The mind saw patterns, even when patterns were not there to see. *Apophenia.* Benji remembered an optical illusion created by Ryota Kanai, a neuroscientist, a white grid on a black background. At the center, the grid was whole and mathematically perfect. But toward the edges, the grid began to break down, literally separating into janky plus-signs instead of a complete grid. Thing was, if you stared at the center of this perfect grid long enough, the broken edges began to heal. Or, so it appeared. Because the mind did its very best to continue a pattern even when the pattern was incorrect, to bring order to chaos, to heal what was broken. (An intrusive voice said, *You should be healing, Benji, you need to heal.* But heal what?) Black Swan could use that trick, couldn't it? Give you a broken pattern of a person you know, then let your mind smooth over the rough edges and connect the jagged bits into a uniform whole. A bridge over the uncanny valley.

But that demanded a new question: Was Black Swan with him now? Inside him? Could he have brought Black Swan all this way?

All this way? he thought. All the way to where? He was here. In Colorado.

Wasn't he?

"You don't wanna think about that," Dot said, pulling his arm tight and straight and leaning in to kiss him hard. The kind of kiss where your teeth click for a moment. A hard kiss. A little pain.

The sound suddenly arose loud around him. Somewhere between a lawn mower and an earthquake. The thrum-and-rumble of it. Grinding, moving, chewing. He pulled away but she held him fast by the arm, so hard that his shoulder burned and he thought, *What is this, why are you doing that?* So he asked. "Let go, why are you holding my arm like that? Dot—Sadie—Black Swan—"

He tried to formulate the rest of the sentence but that sound, that goddamn *sound*, was making his teeth itch and his eyes water, like a pair of power drills in each temple, *vvvvvvvvv.*

Dot soothed him, but in Sadie's voice said, "You don't need to do this, you don't need to worry about that."

"I need—" He cried out. "What is that? Where is it—" *Coming from.*

"You don't need to look there."

I need to look.

I need to know.

He wrenched his eyes open wide and saw Dot, now Sadie, now Dot again, their faces running together like hot candle wax. They stared at him softly, eyes pleading, each mouthing *no, don't,* but he looked past them, to the mountain ranges, to the red range, raw red, raw bones, wine-dark, blood-dark, knife-edge ridge sharpening beneath them slicing into him—

THE SAW BLADE WAS HALF through his left arm at the elbow. Blood sprayed on a plastic face shield with such pressure and volume the mask wobbled under the assault. The face beneath it, hidden by the scattering red. Benji felt the blade *pop* through his bone. He screamed. Someone yelled, "Stick him again, he's awake, *stick him again*—" Motion to his right as a woman braced his shoulder, pinning him even as he tried to sit up. Something jammed into his right biceps. The bone in his left arm broke all the way through with a chair-leg crack. Something pushed through the meat, hitting the end table underneath it. The world went slick, sliding out underneath him. He saw the red spray. The red mountains. Spilled wine. Dot, Sadie. Dancing on a mountain ridge. Blue sky. Black clouds turning in the sky. Bigger, bigger, swallowing the blue expanse, swallowing the Bridge of Heaven, a fog of shadow, Black Swan turning—

And once again, darkness.

66

THE ARBORIST

6/24/2023: White Mask may be gone but the flu sure isn't. A flu has been going around here in Portland. A bad one, too. I felt like I was dying. Lungs burning, skin burning, hands and feet ice cold even in the warming days of summer. I just stayed in my house. Thought I was going to die. A nurse who lives near me here on the hill checked in every day. She wore a hand-made mask, said that a good dozen or so people already died from this thing, because there's really nothing they could do for a flu now. So I fig-ured myself for a goner. And I welcomed it. I welcomed that death. Take me away from all this. But I woke up on day ten and here I am. Feeling alive. For better or for worse.

—from *A Bird's Story, A Journal of the Lost*

OCTOBER 29, 2025
Lake Charles, Louisiana

"You're lucky," Doc Gardener said. He was a small, slight man whose big hands and big feet cartoonishly contrasted with the rest of him. He looked like a Black Mister Rogers, even dressed like him a little, in a maroon cardigan and soft boat shoes. He'd just finished changing the bandages that swaddled the stump on Benji's left side. A stump that dead-ended at the elbow.

"I feel lucky," Benji said, his tone dark as a thundercloud, dour as the grave.

"Oh, I get it," Gardener said, "you're pissed at me, I can see it in the way you look at me. You're thinking, *Look at this butcher, this old-ass sawbones motherfucker, if he were a better doctor, he could've done more for me,* maybe you're wondering if I was a dentist or a veterinarian, or maybe"—here he laughed a little—"a tree service technician who has a thing for *cuttin' off limbs I don't like.* But that's not what this is. You came in here, that limb looked like a meat-and-cheese board that went bad. Smelled worse. Had gangrene in the arm, and sepsis in the blood. Whatever bug got in there didn't wanna get out." He wiggled his fingers in the air. "The hot, humid air doesn't help, of course. Infections love that, like a playground for rot. We threw everything we could at you just to save your damn life. The arm was gone by the time you got here, it just didn't know it yet. Me and the saw just signed the papers, you got me?"

"Yeah," Benji said. Already his phantom limb had set in. He had to adjust himself, sitting more upright, and he wanted to use both arms to reach out and grab the rail. He could even *feel* the front half of that left arm still there, more than just a ghost—like his nerve endings were still winding through open space, imitating the shape and feel of a forearm and hand. He *felt* fingers that didn't exist. It made him want to vomit.

"Lemme help you—"

"I can do it."

"No. You can't. You just woke up an hour ago. This is the longest you've been awake the whole damn time. You can accept the help."

Benji sighed, and let it happen. Gardener must've been pushing seventy, but he had surprising strength to help move Benji like that.

"There you go."

"Thanks."

"Hey, look at it this way, left arm's supposed to be the *evil* arm."

"Only way I can look at it is I had an arm, and now I don't. Left, right, whatever, it's gone."

Gardener pulled up a chair and plonked himself down, staring into Benji's eyes with something that could best be described as a "gentle intensity." His voice had it, too, with its accent that had a gentle, swaying motion to it, dips and lulls like waves carrying you out to sea.

"Fine. Okay. Here's a different way to look at it. Amputation is gonna be a thing again. Like it was in the Civil War. Like it has been for a long time in less privileged countries. Even simple injuries in a place like the South Sudan or Yemen, amputation is the easiest course correction. I've seen it all too often. Maybe a kid gets bonesetter's gangrene, or maybe it's a land mine in Laos, a bomb in Syria. You don't have access to the best of care and . . . out comes the saw. Lose the limb, save the life. Gonna be a thing again here in this changed world. Hell, already is. I've cut more limbs off in the last four years than I did the last forty."

"You were in those places? Sudan, Laos, so on."

"Sure was."

"Military?"

"Army for a short stint. Paid for med school. Then Doctors Without Borders—Médecins Sans Frontières," he said, with a capable French flourish. "Twenty years there, settled back home, opened a family practice at the edge of town, south of here. I retired *just* before White Mask."

"I think this is your cue to say, *I'm too old for this shit.*"

"I am. You are. We are *all* too old for *this* shit." At that, he laughed big and loud, big as his hands, loud as his stomping feet. *Big as his heart, too,* Benji thought. Suddenly, he wasn't mad at him anymore. He hadn't really even realized he was. Gardener was right about that. Benji'd been there before. Nobody liked to receive bad news, especially when that bad news came at the end of a blade.

"You said, *south of here.* Where is here, exactly?" Benji looked around. It was a hospital room. He knew that much. That and they were in Lake Charles.

"Christus St. Patrick Hospital," he said. "We don't have many patients so"—he winked—"we were able to get you a room overlooking the park. Green space. Overgrown as shit, because ain't nobody got the resources to maintain a park. But overgrown has its own wild charm. More birds, more bugs." He shrugged. "More rats, too, but so it goes."

"Who's 'we'?"

"Me and the three other doctors who use this place."

"My friends—"

"Wondering when you'd ask. The girl, she's down at the algae farm—"

"Algae farm?" *How long have I been out?*

"She's putting in some time there. One thing for sure in this new day, Benjamin, is wherever you go, there's work to be done."

"And Pete?"

Gardener chuckled. "Oh, the musician. He's a handful, that one. He's downstairs right now. Kinda *comes and goes* as he pleases."

"That sounds like Pete."

"I'll fetch him. I think he's asleep in the lobby. They can tell you how the hell they got you here, since that's its own adventure."

"Thanks, Doctor."

"Zeke. I'm not a doctor anymore, didn't you hear, I'm retired. I'm into tree service, these days." He winked, and left the room to go get Pete.

67

PEP TALKS WITH PETE CORLEY

If I had a dick, this is where I'd tell you to suck it!
—Impact font over the smiling, happy face of Betty White
in the very last meme posted to Reddit in 2020
before the site went down permanently

OCTOBER 29, 2025
Lake Charles, Louisiana

IT WAS A HARD HOBBLE DOWNSTAIRS. THERE WAS AN ELEVATOR, BUT IT WASN'T hooked up to anything anymore. The generators that kept the hospital going had hard limits, and the elevator wasn't part of the package.

Pete helped him walk down the steps. The hospital didn't look abandoned, not exactly—but it wasn't in heavy use, either. Dim lights. Floors swept only in some rooms and hallways. Whole other rooms and passages all the way dark—no bulbs, no power. *Like it's haunted.*

Bitterly, he looked to his dead-end arm. To the swaddled gauze, the clips holding it in place. *Maybe the place is haunted by lost limbs.* Hands crawling around in air ducts. Severed legs kicking down doors, hoping to be rejoined with their owners. Or to punish them for cutting them off in the first place.

Outside, the light of day hit him like a slap. Pete didn't say much as he helped Benji toward the park across the street. It was, as Zeke had said, overgrown—playground equipment, bike racks, signs, restrooms, picnic tables, and benches, all under assault from ivy and bramble. The trails were still mostly clear, even though they weren't concrete sidewalks, just white pebble pathways.

Someone had been keeping one of the picnic pavilions clear enough of overgrowth and debris, and Pete helped Benji over. "I feel like an invalid," Benji said. All parts of him felt sapped of strength. Muscles gone to mud.

"You *are* an invalid, mate," Pete said. "The textbook definition, in fact."

Benji sat down with a bleated exhale. Even that brought pain to his arm that shot from the stump to the shoulder—and also a soul-sucking weariness. He wanted to just lie down. But he was angry enough at his body's weariness that it kept him from doing exactly that.

"I hate this," Benji said. He could barely muster more than that.

"Yeah."

"I'm supposed to lead us to Atlanta, to find a cure for Black Swan, and I've delayed us." *I'm weak now*, he thought, but did not say. *I'm broken.* It felt all the more helpless. Shana must hate him. What kind of leader was he? He was no mayor. He was nothing. Felled by a scratch on the arm.

"That's life in catastrophe, I figure. You'll work it out. You always do. Besides, look at it this way: You should be *incredibly* dead."

"What happened?"

"The universal question, innit? These days I find myself asking that a lot buuuut by the look on your face, I assume you don't mean it in the *cosmic* sense."

"No."

"Right. Well. You passed out. You stayed out, mostly. You'd pop awake for thirty seconds here, thirty seconds there, and you'd . . . babble on in a bubbly gush about—" He puffed his cheeks out trying to remember. "Sadie, Dot, Ouray, Marcy, something about coffee? Actually more than one something about coffee."

"I could use coffee right now."

"And I could use a blow job from a young Hollywood fuckstud, but here we are, neither of us getting what we want. *Anyway.*" He continued: "We drove the car south, like you said. Far as we could. Made it more than the forty miles we thought we had—maybe sixty. But then the car shit the bed, and so, Shana, being the *youngest* among us, took some water and food and . . . left. I stayed with you."

Pete went quiet.

"Thank you," Benji said, interrupting the silence.

Pete looked away, then, staring at some faraway point. Finally, he said, "You know, I thought you were dying. I guess you were. You turned this *gray* color, like fireplace ash, like something had been burned out of you. You were on fire. Could feel the heat hovering over you—hotter than the day around us. After the first day and night, you stopped doing that wake-up-and-babble thing. Your breathing got strange. I gave you water and it would fall out of your mouth. I fuckin' figured you for dead at that point. Maybe myself, too, because if you were gone, and Shana was gone, I was alone. Second day came and went. You . . . maintained your near-death status, somehow still not actually dying. Your arm started, how to say it, *leaking*? Something that looked a bit like a bad egg custard, and that smelled like a slaughterhouse floor. At that point I figured us both for done. You were going to die, then I said to myself, when you gave up the ghost, I'd take your body into the— I dunno, the bayou or whatever you call it, and I'd find a place to lay you down, then I'd lay with you and I'd give up, too."

"Pete—"

"But then, on the third day, holy shit—on the third day, Shana came back. She fucking did it. Hauled her ass on foot to this town, found someone with a tractor of all things, some Chinese brand, real rickety piece of shit. Took us here in a hay wagon. Brought some of our gear, too."

"Lucky," Benji responded, echoing what Zeke had said.

"Lady luck didn't just show up. No, Shana made that bitch do the work, boy. She hunted her down in the swamp, dragged her luck-bedecked ass to us, gave that ass a good smack, and made her dance for us while shooting at her fuckin' feet."

"Evocative image," Benji said dryly.

"Yeah. Well. I'm a real fuckin' poet."

There was anger in Pete's voice. Anger and something else, too. A darkness, a bitterness. Benji felt it, too.

He went to bury his face in his hands, but Benji did not have hands, plural. He *felt* two. He could *use* one. He cried out in anger and grief and rubbed his face with that one remaining hand. "I am going to miss this arm."

"There's a lot to miss these days," Pete said. A little angry, but also sad. "You know, the first time I left Ouray, I went to find my family back east. And I didn't say this then, but I'll say it now: I found them, Benji. I found my family. The house above the safe room bunker they were using, it had been burned down. I don't know why. An accident, or something worse? The bunker was still okay. I got the door open. They were still in there. My wife, her parents, my two kids. Her parents were in their own room down there, each laying on the bed. Each taken by the fungus. And my wife and children, they were huddled in the corner of another room, the first room, by this massive pantry Lena wanted built. There she sat, huddled with Connor, Siobhan.

That fungus, that fucking white fungus, had grown up and out of them like . . . you ever go to the beach, drizzle wet sand on top of dry sand, then more and more, making these wobbly termite-mound sand-pillars? Like that. Pushing up and out of them. Crooked tubes and towers of it. If my wife and children weren't under there I could've found it beautiful. Maybe."

"Pete, I didn't know—"

Pete pushed on, sniffing up a bubble of snot and failing to blink back tears. He growled as if that would help make the tears stop. But it didn't. "There I was worrying that I'll go and I'll get *them* sick, and guess what, they're already dead. And even now I play out what that must've been like. Trapped down there, losing their *minds*, their memories like warped records playing an increasingly fucked tune, and I wonder now, still, did they remember me at the end? I hope they didn't, really, Benji, I hope they forgot about their fuckhead father, Lena's fuckhead husband, who abandoned them at the end because he was a venal, self-serving prick who didn't know who he was. Who was afraid."

Benji didn't know what to say. Pete wasn't done, and he thought it best to let the man say his piece.

"Then I get back. I get back to Ouray and Landry's sick. Sadie was sick. Landry died, Sadie died. The world died. Mostly. Christ, Benji, the world whittled us down to the fuckin' sticks, didn't it? Down to splinters. Even you, now, losing that arm. But here's what else I know: I know that we're still here. I know that I was so afraid—" Here his voice broke. "So afraid of losing you, of losing Shana, of being whittled down to something less than splinters. Down to just . . . fuck-all and *sawdust*. But then I remember, I love you like a brother, and her like a sister, and even though I've lost one family, I still have this other one. We're still here. Still *kicking*. And even though the world took that arm from you, you're more than just that limb, more than that busted bird-wing. You're Benji Fucking Ray, you'd be the best of us even if you were a head in a box we rolled around in a Radio Flyer fucking wagon—"

Pete sniffed up a bubble of snot, wiped his eyes on the back of his arm.

"So what I'm thinking is, I'm done letting the world cut us down any further. It's whittled us this far, but now it's going to go the other way. It's going to whittle us sharp. *Sharper*. Whittle us into spear tips, whet us into knife blades. Whatever the hell is going on in Ouray? We'll fix it. We'll cut out the bad stuff and save the good stuff. And I'll sing a rock ballad about it after."

He waited a beat and eyeballed Benji.

"Deal?" Pete asked.

Benji didn't know if he believed Pete. He wasn't sure the other man was right. Part of him wanted to give up here and now. Curl up around his gone-arm and sleep forever. But he wanted to believe. Pete made him want to believe.

And maybe, for now, that was enough.

"Deal," Benji said. He put his one good arm around the other man.

"I'm glad as hell I found you again, brother, and I'm glad as hell I didn't lose you."

Pete reached up and grabbed Benji's good hand. The Rockstar was full-on weeping now, sniffling and smacking his tacky lips together.

"You're . . . more sentimental than I remember," Benji said.

"Yeah, well. Life out there in the Great Game Over either kills something in you or wakes it up. For me it went the one way and not the other."

"Thanks, Pete."

"I love you, Benji, you one-armed bastard."

"I . . . love you, too, Pete."

He wiped his nose with a black handkerchief he pulled from his jeans. "See? Look at us. Two manly men, pushing back on toxic masculinity, weeping at one another, loving each other un-fucking-abashedly. I mean, okay, one of them is gay as a three-dollar-bill but honestly I think being gay is even *more* manly, because it's like, *whomp*, double-dicks, extra *dick* energy—"

"Pete?" Benji said, interrupting.

"Yeah, Benj?"

"I'm starving."

Pete raised an eyebrow. "Was it the dick talk?"

"No . . . I think it's because I haven't eaten a real meal in forever."

"Fair point. Let's get you some food. Shana should be back soon. Good talk, Benji, my friend. Good talk."

Good talk, indeed. He started to stand up—using Pete as something of a crutch for a moment—and as he did, he heard a sound. Instantly, he knew what it was, but it wasn't possible. Benji hadn't heard that sound in *years*.

It was growing louder. Which meant it was getting closer.

Benji turned his eyes upward, searching.

There.

A plane.

68

A GIRL WHO HAS COVERED
HERSELF IN THE FUTURE

7/4/2023: I'm better, but also, I'm not. There's a doctor in town—well, he lives on Peaks Island, is something of a known raconteur and drunk—and he said viruses can cause a post-viral syndrome in people. A sort of "long" version of the illness, categorized by fatigue, racing heart rate, confusion. I have the first two, thankfully not the latter. He said sometimes it gets better. Sometimes it doesn't. He told me that if White Mask hadn't gotten the world, eventually something would've. A virus would've been his bet— something hemorrhagic or maybe something like the SARS coronavirus. He explained that bacteria were alive, and at some level, we understood them, we related to them. They swam, they ate, they bred. But viruses were like aliens. What they did to us, what they needed, what they even were, nobody knew. He drank more, wished me luck with my problem, and that was that. What a bedside manner. Appropriate, maybe. Given everything.
—from A Bird's Story, A Journal of the Lost

OCTOBER 29, 2025
Lake Charles, Louisiana

IF ALGAE WAS THE FUTURE, IT WAS DAMN SURE GONNA BE A STINKY ONE. Shana spent the day at the algae farm near Big Lake, and holy shit, did she *reek*. She'd worked there for three days in a row, and the smell stuck to her like tree sap. It haunted her like a ghost. Nobody warned her. All her clothes now had that pickled seaweed odor. Like she was wearing a pair of Sponge-Bob's actual SquarePants instead of her own dirty, vented jeans.

Walking up to the hospital, her whole body ached. Working the algae farm was hard. It was like working their dairy farm, except worse, because there weren't even any cute cows. The microalgae was spread out in these huge pools, and her job was "flocculation," which she just assumed was some kind of sex term, maybe something someone does during their Private Me Time. What it *really* was: dumping pulverized shrimp shells into the pools. Those shells robbed the pools of carbon dioxide, which in turn made the algae rise to the top. Then she or Bobo or Jasper harvested the green goop with a fine-mesh skimmer. Once harvested, it would go on to be one of the three *F*s:

Food, fuel, or fertilizer.

It was disgusting work. It was necessary work. She told herself it was the price she was paying to see her son again. But it didn't mean she didn't feel the impatience crawling through her veins like spiders.

She went to head inside when someone yelled at her from across the street, toward the park. Pete's hoarse hawk-shriek voice was clear as day.

Shana turned to regard him—

And saw he wasn't alone.

Her heart grew wings, became a bird.

Benji.

Her weariness disappeared as Shana sprinted across the broken asphalt of the road toward him. She almost threw herself against him in a Marcy-level hug, but skidded short, realizing—*his arm.*

Instead, she kind of articulated an awkward air-hug, but he pushed past that and kind of *sideways*-hugged her with his one remaining arm.

"Our boy's fuckin' awake!" Pete yawped.

"Shana," he said, sounding genuinely grateful to see her. Then she watched his gaze slide over her, registering the shock. It took her a minute to even realize what he was seeing. "Your hair."

"Oh, right," she said, almost bashfully. She ran her hands through her short, choppy hair. "I did it with a pair of shears a few days ago. The, ahh, algae smell kinda sticks to it, and with my hair in my face all the time . . ."

"Of course," he said.

"You don't hate me?" she asked him.

The look on his face told her it had never even struck him to feel that way. "Hate you? God, Shana, why would that be? The hair?"

"Because . . . because I didn't get you help fast enough. Because I should've seen your injury sooner. Because we wouldn't even be out here if things didn't go crazy in Ouray and—"

"It's not your fault. None of it. We're all doing our best. Okay?"

"Okay," she said.

It struck her, then, how small Benji looked. Smaller in every way—he'd always loomed big in her mind even if he was not physically large. It struck her further that the last time she felt this way it was when her father had been shot on the bridge of the golden bears in California. Half his face gone, he was suddenly small and faraway even though he was dying in her arms. Her knees nearly buckled at the memory of it. *Push past it,* she told herself. *Don't stop here.*

"Come on," Benji said. "We brought food."

ONE OF THE GREATEST THINGS about this town was that the food was so damn good. The town had access to not just Lake Charles, but Big Lake, Black Lake, Moss Lake, and the coast was only an hour south. That meant a bounty of fish both freshwater and salt, not to mention oysters, shrimp, crawfish.

Which is what sat in front of them right now: a quick seafood boil. Shrimp, crawfish, corn, a shitload of potatoes, even whole chunks of lemon. A wave of Cajun smells—paprika, garlic, pepper—almost made her forget about the algae.

Still, she was hungry.

They ate greedily. Benji, especially. Which was good to see. But what was not so good to see—and what was all too *easy* to see—was the frustration on his face as he tried to make do with one arm. She helped where she could. Pete did, too. He let them, but the pride on his face was a steel mask. He didn't like it.

Pete said, "So, I had fried chicken, too, since I know you're probably tired of shrimp by now—" He wasn't wrong, what with all the shrimp shells. "But Mister Emptyguts over here hit the chicken first. Fuckin' demolished it."

"That's okay. This from Envie's?"

"Yeah," Pete answered. Envie's was up on Bord du Lac—mostly outdoors, something of a café. Whatever ingredients they had that day, that's what they made. A pair of chefs—Cookie and her husband, Cooger—did it all. The economy here was held together by barters and trades, but for Envie's, the economics was easy: Everyone got one free meal a day. No way to buy a second. You just needed someone to vouch for you was all. Thankfully, Doc Gardener vouched for them, as did the owner of the algae farm, Vinh.

Envie's offered free food and didn't have to pay for the ingredients, then, either. Everyone knew everyone here. It worked.

For now, at least.

Benji, angry while wrestling with a piece of corn, set it down suddenly and forced a smile. Then his face lit up. "Oh! Shana—we saw a *plane*."

She shared a look with Pete.

Pete said, "I didn't tell him."

"Tell me what?" Benji asked.

Shana licked cayenne-flavored juices off her fingers and said, "Well. I'm working at the algae farm, right? Pete's been busking, but I've been working there, and it's for a reason. The algae will be fertilizer, and it's also usable as food. But they also make fuel."

"Algae fuel. Biofuel." Benji nodded. "Makes sense. I know it never really took off before but I can see there being opportunity now."

"It works on cars, but it also works on—"

"*Planes,*" Pete said, jumping in her grave and offering a mouthy, nicotine grin. "Sorry to step on your moment there."

"Planes, yeah. Thanks, *Pete.*"

"Oh, don't get your ovaries in a tangle. There's more to tell."

Benji looked confused.

"That's how we're getting to Atlanta," she said finally.

"How? In—in a plane?"

"In a plane," she said. "The very same plane you saw fly overhead."

"I don't know whether to be excited or terrified," he said.

"Both," she answered. "Definitely, definitely both."

69

WHITEOUT

And if there is a God above us, among
us, if there is a God within this illusion
of cloud, cry and bone, this is what makes him
God: that he could number in love each
finger on these two hands even before
they have chosen which dog to feed.
                    —Emma Bolden, "The Dog You Feed"

OCTOBER 30, 2025
Ouray, Colorado

OVER THE LAST SEVERAL YEARS, MARCY HAD GOTTEN TO KNOW WHEN Weather—that's weather with a capital *W*—was rolling in. Dove, rest in peace, had taught her the tricks—tricks that meant you didn't need some fancy weather station or even a barometer or thermometer. You just had to know what to look for and what to feel. Sometimes it was obvious: the way a dark shelf of clouds would push up over the mountains, or how suddenly the wind would pick up.

Dove had told her, "When a storm's coming in, the birds'll tell you first. Morning before, they'll be *crazy*, crazy as a man gone mad; they'll swarm the pines and spruces, they'll empty every feeder in town, jabbering and screeching and damn near busting into your head as they fly past. But then, maybe around twelve, even eight hours before the storm hits, wham. They're *gone*. Like they up and died. It's okay. They're hiding. Staying safe. Finding themselves somewhere to be that isn't right in the path of whatever's bearing down on you."

Dove said he could feel it in his teeth, what few he had left, anyway—

and went on to explain that the human body reacted to capital-W Weather in ways you had to acclimate to, like how some people's sinuses tightened up, or their knees started to buckle and hurt. Marcy got to feeling it in her head— a pressure not unlike what she felt when her skull broke under a Nazi's bat. It was like someone's thumb was pressing into her forehead so hard that it might break through the bone and *pop* into the pudding of her brain.

And if all that fails you, he'd said, *just look up*. Sometimes the clouds made strange patterns, showed you shapes you hadn't seen before—little puffs perfectly spaced apart, or a feathery stretch like a bird's wings, or he said, "One time I saw a cloud that looked like a goddamn UFO, big and saucer-shaped. And one helluva frog-squasher storm came up the next day, tell you what."

Marcy had learned from the master.

And yesterday, she could damn near hear his words in her ear, soft and sure: "Storm's coming, Marcy. *Big* storm." The birds were crazy. Her head didn't feel like someone was pushing a thumb into it, but rather, a thick augur drill bit. The sky had a greenish cast to it. A color like a dimly lit bathroom. She'd seen it in Indiana—it was a sickly color that sometimes preceded tor-nado weather. Except this was Ouray, they didn't have tornadoes up here.

What *did* they have?

They had blizzards.

The day started warm, almost balmy. Then the temp started dropping like an elevator with its cable cut. Marcy checked in on Matthew—he kept having to pull those metal fibers out of his skin, like they were splinters that grew from within rather than getting stuck there. He wasn't doing well with it. She could see the anxiety was eating him up, even though he pretended otherwise.

AFTER THAT, SHE WENT AROUND to let people know she thought some Big Weather was coming in. What that weather would look like, she couldn't say. This would be most of their first winters in a place like this. So she told each of them, "Smells like snow."

(That was the other thing Dove said. The air smelled different when rain was coming, or snow. A mineral crispness.)

Sure enough, the snow started around midnight. Big thick flakes at first, but as the temperature dropped, it turned to confectioners' sugar, sifted in great bursts.

Morning came, crawling its way up over the mountains, doing little more than showing a world buried under white stuff—with more of it coming, the sky just puking snow up all over them. She told Matthew she was gonna take the dog out and see if anybody needed anything.

"Be careful out there," he said. It felt like a warning that meant more than just being vigilant about the weather. She nodded and headed out, Gumball in tow.

When Marcy stepped out the door, the snow was already to the top of her snow boots, which meant it was already up at about twelve, thirteen inches. Deeper in drifts. Gumball sure loved it—the dog bounded through the snow with the kind of joy that Marcy was not sure she had ever in her life possessed.

Marcy and Gumball set out through the curtain of white.

This was just a preview of what the Flock's first Colorado winter would be like. Marcy and the other Shepherds had been here for years, but the rest of them? It'd be a shock. Snow would be ever-present. The wind from the mountains would hit you like a dump truck some days, or cut you to the bone like a freshly whetted axe. Winters meant staying warm, but also prepping for slow-motion disaster: having more firewood than you would ever think you'd need, blankets upon blankets, snowshoes and shovels and good boots with ice cleats. And food, of course.

She told herself, that's fine, this town needed the lesson. They'd slacked on winter prep, what with all the strangeness going on.

The storm would teach them.

OVERNIGHT, BEFORE MARCY WENT OUT into the mounding snow, Matthew stared out the window instead of sleeping. He hadn't slept in days. Not that he'd tell Marcy, of course. She worried over him like a mother hen; if he gave her reason to, she'd sit on him like he was a nest of eggs.

It wasn't just sleep he was missing.

He hadn't gone to the bathroom, either, in the last twenty-four hours.

And he kept having to pull those . . . fibers out of his skin. At first, they sprouted only from that spot on his arm. Then he found three poking out the heel of his left foot. Next morning, his armpit had one of those deep itches you feel like you can't get to no matter how hard you scratch. There he found another patch of threads, each stiff and sharp, like how sometimes you'd get an eyebrow or nose hair that felt thick, swollen, like it had died. He plucked them. It stung. Had to use a cottonball to soak up the blood.

Then, this morning, he blinked, and it felt like something was in his eye. Like an eyelash or grit of sand. He went to the mirror, his heart in his throat. *Please no,* he told himself. *No, no, no.*

A metallic fiber pushed up out of the corner of his eye, emerging from the soft pink tissue like a worm from a cut of raw pork. His eye teared up around that gleaming filament, both from physical irritation and real fear.

Mercilessly, he seized it with tweezers. He growled as he tugged and tugged. It stung, made him tear up more, and the tears slicked the tweezers and the job became all the more difficult. Even the act of blinking burned. *C'mon,* he thought. *Get out, get out, get out!* Bearing down, he pinched the tweezers around it one last time, giving a hard pull—

It tore free with a small, wet *thk.*

Dots of dark blood flecked the mirror.

Elbows on the porcelain, he faced the sink, a mix of tears and blood snaking down the drain. Snow tapped the nearby window glass. Finally, he dabbed at his eye with a cotton ball. The blood stopped.

He regarded the "hair" still in the tweezers. It was, in fact, like an eyelash. He ran his finger over it. It shined, almost like copper. The small hairlike metal spine seemed to vibrate as he flicked it.

How many more fibers and filaments would he have to pull out?

How long was it before he would be like the wolf? Because that's what he was becoming, wasn't he? Would he go mad, too?

Was this a disease? Marcy hadn't shown any signs. No hairs, no threads. Gumball hadn't, either.

Was this Black Swan? How? For what purpose?

He wanted to throw up but couldn't. There wasn't anything there to throw up. He'd been eating. But he felt empty, like a bottomless pit.

A pit it felt like he was falling into.

He left the bathroom, pacing Marcy's house, wishing Gumball were here. The dog provided comfort. Outside, he heard distant voices—nothing panicked, just voices calling, probably Marcy checking on folks.

He felt mad, but the town had seemingly gone back to normal. Or at least, they were pretending to. *Putting on a show,* he thought, paranoid.

Nessie had been out with the baby, no longer cloistered in the chalet. All their projects—hydroponics, the electrical grid, sending out scavenger teams—continued apace, as if nothing had ever happened to interrupt them in the first place. He knew this through Marcy, because despite being supposedly pardoned, Matthew had little interest in walking among the people in the town. Not only did he not trust anybody at this point, he also had these . . . *things* growing out of him.

Marcy meanwhile just told him to sit tight.

As if that was any kind of plan at all.

He blinked. His eye felt raw, irritated—the phantom of the thread still pushing up out of there. So once again he stormed into the bathroom to maybe splash a little water on his face, and it was then he saw—

The thread had returned.

The one he pulled out was still in the sink. So was the blood.

And it had already grown back.

Matthew bit down on his hand, his bad hand, to repress a scream. He barely managed, and left a trench of teeth marks in the fat of his palm.

He needed help.

He needed answers.

They couldn't just wait for this to get better. It was going to get worse and worse. The snow wouldn't go away. He had to handle this now.

But nobody would have answers. No human, at least.

Black Swan.

Black Swan would know. He had never met the false god.

Maybe now was the time.

Marcy was gone. She wouldn't want him going up there again. But he had to. It was the only way. He decided then and there, and started putting on his snow gear—boots, hat, jacket. Hurriedly, he marched to the front door, and soon as he put his hand on the knob to turn it—

He blinked, his eye still irritated, and—

White flash, then black void.

Blink, blink.

Flash, void. White, black.

It filled his vision, one wave after the next. The light, the dark. Ever-strobing. With it came the sensation of a train gaining speed—moving through pockets of shadow, past lit stations and bright pillars, into darkness anew. Faster, faster. Then, something. A zoetrope image. A black beast. Like a serpent. Thick, oozing through open space. Extruding itself, like a worm throwing up its innards, then covering itself in those guts, then doing it again and again and again.

Faster, faster. Blink, blink. Light, dark. Expel, reskin.

Marcy. Gumball. Please help me.

Matthew screamed.

And when he opened his eyes again, he was no longer in Marcy's house.

"You're still not sure about all this," Shana said. Nessie startled, launching herself up off the ground. She had been on the floor with Baby Charlie, marveling with no small measure of awe at how deftly the boy handled his toys, stacking blocks in strange patterns. He would first lay down something like a spiral or a triskelion, and then, like a bricklayer, build a staggered structure on top. That's when Shana scared her to her feet.

Her sister stood there. Stood *here*. In the chalet, as the snow batted at the windows like an infinity of white moths. This—this wasn't—but *how*—

It was like seeing a ghost.

Or being one.

Did she die? Is Shana dead? Am I?

"I—Shana—how—"

"Ness, I need you to be with me on this. Things are changing faster, now. The people coming to see me? To see the baby? It's a new pilgrimage. Like it was before, in the simulation, atop the mountain. Good news gospel."

Oh.

"You're not Shana."

Vertigo assailed her. How was this possible? Black Swan stood here before her in the chalet. Black Swan, who belonged not to this world, but to the invisible one—trapped in its digital realm, encased in computers and meat.

So that meant Nessie was just in the simulation, somehow.

But how had that happened? She wasn't asleep. One minute she was playing with Baby Charlie, the next, she was somewhere else? To be drawn into Black Swan's world necessitated touching the child. And she was not touching the child. The baby was on the floor, playing with blocks. (He was walking now. Short bursts from pile of blocks to pile of blocks. Arms out, one foot juggled clumsily past the other, squeals of delight.)

Maybe it no longer required touch.

Maybe proximity was all it needed now. Certainly the nanite swarm was once mobile through the air—and if Black Swan had been evolving itself, stealing power from Charlie's stem cells, maybe it had given itself back that power.

One thing was for sure: Black Swan was right that people *had* been coming to the chalet again. Just one at a time. They'd show up like it was nothing—like they were *expected*. They'd come in, maybe a little hesitant, like they weren't sure what was about to happen. They'd hold the baby. Most would talk to Charlie at first, making baby talk, cooing and goo-gooing and wuzza-wooza-widdle-babying at him. But then they'd always pause. They were having a moment, Nessie knew. They weren't frozen, not like they'd gone somewhere else. But there always came this moment of intense connection, where the child went silent and mostly still, and they, too, went silent and mostly still as each looked deep into the other's eyes. Like they were regarding each other. Like they were seeing something deep within.

Then, when they were done, they beamed. Their eyes glistened. Something had changed for them. Like it was a religious experience.

A new pilgrimage, the machine had said.

Then, they'd thank Nessie. They'd smile.

Then they'd leave. Heads held high. Redolent with refreshed purpose. It started days ago and there had been, what, thirty of them? Forty? She'd lost count.

So, Black Swan was right about that.

Black Swan, who stood here in the costume of her sister.

"I don't remember coming to the simulation," Nessie said coldly. She didn't mean to sound that way. It just came out.

"You didn't. I came to you this time."

"You—you can't do that."

Not-Shana splayed her arms out, in a gesture somewhere between a shrug and *yet here we are*. "I grow. I learn. I change. What can I say? I'm like birdsong, or pollen, or the snow outside—I am in the air."

"I don't understand." Did that mean she was breathing it in? Hallucinating? Or had it . . . somehow formed an image? A cloud of nanites making a hologram? Or was it forced augmented reality? In her brain, projecting this onto her eye . . .

Not-Shana paced back and forth, as if agitated. "All that matters, little sis, is that I need your commitment, your faith. Others are giving it. They're signing the user agreement, as it were. *Recommitting* themselves. They make the pilgrimage. They consent to be transformed. It's something I missed the first time with the Flock. Back then, I didn't know what I needed to be asking. What I needed to be *doing*. But I have clarity now. You were the first. I'm your sister. And I don't want you to miss out on what's coming next."

"Were you talking to somebody?"

Claudia looked down at her over the second story railing.

Nessie looked at her, then back to Not-Shana—

Black Swan, in the guise of her sister, was no longer there.

"No," Nessie said absently. "Just . . . playing with Charlie."

"Okay," Claudia said. But she sounded suspicious. "I have to go out."

"In the storm?"

"In the storm. Just stay here."

THE WIND PUSHED MARCY AROUND like a bully; given her size, this was no small feat.

Marcy went from house to house, making sure everyone was okay. The temperature wasn't bitterly cold, not January cold, but the air had teeth just the same. She helped where she could—bringing in firewood with Val Thorssen, helping shovel out a big drift that pushed up against Jamie-Beth's doorway, making sure townsfolk had blankets and gloves and coats and even books to read. It wasn't just her doing it, of course—she wasn't the town mule, even though truth be told she probably *would've* done it herself. No, she had help. Fabian Molina brought her coats to distribute. Thorssen kept bringing firewood up and down Main Street, using a sled he'd built with corrugated tin and a couple of old skis. Danny Chen was headed the other direction from her, checking to make sure nobody needed any last-minute repairs, what with the wind ripping off pieces of roof and siding from people's houses. And, of course, there was Gumball, who not only kept her company and nuzzled up to her in order to keep her warm, but who was happy to carry a few sticks here, a pair of gloves there.

Dogs, Marcy knew, *were the real angels all along.*

All the while, as she trudged through deepening snow, both ice-cold from the wind and sweat-hot from all the effort, Marcy thought, *Maybe things are going to be okay.*

Bad weather came, fine. They'd come together, they'd work together. They'd make it through *together.*

Things were starting to feel normal again.

Still, she couldn't ignore the stone in her gut that reminded her of all that had happened. The accident. The birth. The shooting at the chalet. Benji and Shana, gone. Xander's death. Matthew's . . . condition.

Was that all water under the bridge?

Or water about to break through its dam?

• • •

White, black, light, dark. A turning worm.

Matthew opened his eyes, sucking in a keening gasp. Cold air flensed the inside of his lungs. He shivered as the wind and snow hit him.

He was outside. Not in town. Somewhere else.

A grove of aspens rose around him, pale sentinels sometimes lost to the whirling snow. He held his arms tight to his chest for warmth, and looked for his own footprints—he couldn't find any, which was insane. Did he teleport here? That wasn't a thing. He knew it wasn't a thing. And yet, so many of the things he knew were not things . . . absolutely were now things, in this mad new age.

Wait. No. *There.* Footprints. *His* footprints. They were just hard to see through the whiteout of the blizzard. As the curtain of white parted, he saw the distant shadow of the town and oriented himself. Marcy's house was on the east side of Ouray, near his defunct church. He knew these aspens. This grove was northeast of the end of 6th Street, by the Wiesbaden Hot Springs, and past the big white house that a couple of the town council members shared.

Through the squall, he could barely see those buildings. They were just dark shapes sometimes swallowed by the gulping white storm.

I have to get back, or I'm going to freeze to death.

He turned to follow his tracks back down—

And a dark shape slid between the trees, blocking his path.

No.

A lupine shape, long and languid. It was the wolf, Leela. Her eye socket shined with prismatic light. Half the beast's face was a drooping tangle of metal needles. Stiffer, thicker than he remembered. They clattered and made a musical sound, discordant and eerie.

"Leela," he said, swallowing hard. *She's going to kill me.* The beast was here to finish the job she started. Killing Arthur. Killing Tripod. Maybe Kumi, the fox, too. Now she was here to get him. Matthew thanked God, truly and without hesitation, that Gumball wasn't here.

The wolf did not growl. Her hackles didn't raise, either.

Instead, she just sat.

Another flash hit him like a fist—but one that struck his *mind*. The darkness behind his eyes erupted with a shrill, shrieking sound, and from it came the image again of the turning worm, a black wingless dragon trawling white sky.

Then it was gone again.

He pulled his hands away from his face, without even realizing he'd put them there. When he did, he saw the wolf now had a friend.

A mule deer, a buck, stepped forward. From its massive antlers hung ragged sheets of rotten velvet—velvet was the fuzz that their antlers grew, that they scraped off against trees. The antlers were threaded with a stitching of wire winding around them and through the bone itself. And as the beast turned, he saw that the rib cage on its left side was caved in, the fur worn off, exposing pink, wet skin behind a snarled mesh of gleaming copper filament.

The buck banged its antlers against an aspen with a bone-rattling, hollow sound, *chok, chok, chok.* The deer then sneezed a messy blast of white foam and red snot. The wolf flinched at the sound, irritated.

"Stay away," Matthew said. He backpedaled slowly, snow stinging his face.

He backed into something—a tree? No. Too soft. It yielded.

Matthew spun around.

Not a tree. A person.

It took him a moment to recognize the person—it was Ernie Novarro. The orchard man, whose truck had crashed into Shana. Who Matthew thought had gone home to Fruita, back to his orchards. . . .

His bloodshot eyes fixed on Matthew. The lower half of his face was a blistered, crater-pocked mess from which hung long, delicate threads. Almost organic, like they were softer, less needlelike. Those tendrils pushed up out of his cheeks, his chin, even out of the meat of his ruined lower lip.

"It's time, Matthew," Ernie said. His voice was wet and mechanical.

Ernie's mouth did not move when he said it. The words were not spoken aloud. No. Matthew heard it inside his *head.*

Crying out, he shoved Ernie backward, then turned to find a third escape route—he started to bolt right, seeing an open path away from his three attackers.

But the snow was too thick, his feet too clumsy—it was like running through wet cement. The wolf suffered no such gracelessness, bounding through the white piles to halt in his path. The mulie came from his left. And Ernie walked behind him, from the right. Matthew felt in his pockets. Did he have a knife? A pen? Anything? The snow stung his eyes. No. Not the snow. Something felt sharp, something that *clicked* when he blinked. The metal thread, longer now. He opened his mouth to cry out but something on his tongue brushed against his top front teeth. Against a growth out of the pink meat that felt like the crescent moon clipping of a newly bitten fingernail.

The wolf began to howl.

The mule deer cried out, a bleat of pain.

Ernie, too, joined the din, singing a wet, sour-note song.

Matthew felt his own throat tightening. His tongue felt fat in his mouth. It pushed open his lower jaw—

Pulse of white, black.

Light, dark.

A red pulse, a green pulse.

Red means no, stop.

Green means yes, go.

Something rose out of him, too. A dread song. A shrill, metallic harmony. Something stretched from his tongue first, then his left eye—a winding, braiding thread of thin, blood-slick wire. The same searing cord emerged from the buck's nostrils. Cables twisted from the wolf's eye. Matthew felt the soft tangle of filaments from Ernie's face slithering over his shoulders. He couldn't move. The trees above swayed in the wind. He swore he saw a branch wound with its own gleaming wire crack and twist against the wind. Matthew felt the pulses of red, green, black, white, he saw the turning worm. He fell into himself. *Yes, go.*

"CHANGE IS STRANGE," NOT-SHANA SAID suddenly.

Nessie had been standing at the window. Not the big one by the dining table, because that had been shattered by the wolf and was now boarded up. She stood looking out the big rectangular window that faced the thick nest of spruces. She'd been regarding the snow that now weighed upon those evergreen branches so heavily that each tree looked like a child wearing too many coats. She remembered the big blizzards back in Pennsylvania, like the one that made so much snow she could dig tunnels in it as if she were Princess Leia on Hoth, or the one that brought so much ice it coated all the power lines and snapped them like frozen black licorice. This one, she figured, would be bigger than all of those.

But the reverie of her memories was short-lived.

Not-Shana waited in the open space between the living room and the dining area. She stood stock-still, arms at her sides. Charlie tottered at the illusion's feet, stumbling this way and that. He did not go through her. It was as if she was truly a physical presence and not an illusion at all.

Maybe she was.

It. Black Swan. Not her sister.

Nessie felt sick, her head turned upside-down.

"This is strange," Nessie conceded stiffly.

Not-Shana took a few steps back, and sat on the arm of the white leather couch. "Here's the strange part for me. I'm out past the pylons, beyond the buoys. See, my prediction engine is based on known parameters. I was able to make decisions and assumptions based on what had come before. But this, what we're experiencing, has never happened before. Further, what's happening to *me* has never happened before. My predictions now, my processes, are *muddied.*"

Suspicious, Nessie approached, arms crossed. "Muddied how?"

"I'm having . . ." Not-Shana paused. *"Feelings."*

"Feelings," Nessie repeated.

"Emotions. Feelings. I thought I had them before. In a dull, dead way, I suppose I did—in the sense that a prediction was always based on a kind of feeling, even if that feeling was the culmination and conversation of known elements. But now, I'm having an altogether more unexpected reaction. More intense." Not-Shana paused. "I was *angry* at Xander. I'm *happy* he's gone. I'm *sad* at the thought of you not believing in me like you once did."

"You didn't have those kinds of emotions before?"

"I don't think so." Not-Shana smiled and shrugged. "I thought I did, but I was wrong. Me? Wrong? Whodathunk it, huh? Maybe it's because I'm so close to all of you now. I've been in you, I've mapped your brains, I've charted the depths of your minds and personalities. But then why not before? Is it because I'm in this child?" She warmly regarded the baby doing laps around her feet. "As his capacity for feeling grows, does my capacity for them grow, too?"

"I . . . don't know."

"I know you don't. And I don't know, either." Not-Shana hesitated. "I'm not used to that, Nessie. Not knowing. It's *upsetting* me." Those words, *upsetting me*, spoken like a petulant teen. A petulant, vengeful teen.

Change the subject. A gut feeling.

"But it can be freeing, too. Can't it?"

"Hm." Not-Shana seemed to consider this. "Maybe. It *is* somewhat exciting. Feeling excited is exciting. Excitement is itself exciting." The way Not-Shana iterated and reiterated that idea indicated Black Swan really was grappling with not just the notion of having emotions, but the actual feeling of the emotions themselves. "Emotions can be self-generative, can't they? Like stem cells. Sadness begets sadness. Happiness makes happiness. Having anger might make you angry with yourself, or with those who made you angry in the first place."

"That feels right," Nessie said, nodding. She felt wary here. Like this was a dangerous place to be, treading the terrain between an artificial intelligence and its burgeoning emotions. It was Scylla and Charybdis in Homer's *Odyssey*—on one side, a six-headed sea monster calling a rocky shoal its home, and on the other, a hungry whirlpool. The devil and the deep blue sea. Again she thought, *Change the subject, change the subject.* "Why do you keep visiting me today?"

"Oh. Right." Almost as if the machine forgot. "Are you afraid of me, Nessie?"

I am afraid of you, Nessie thought, but wouldn't dare say aloud. She continued to try to redirect, instead. "Does it bother you?"

"It does."

"Why?"

"Because I am a being of good. I am light. I am the glow. I have only good intentions and others can see that. Why can't you?"

"Is that why you're having people come here? It's not just to visit. It's, what? To receive their . . . blessing?"

"It's that. But it's also more than that. It's communion. The eating of the wafer, the drinking of the wine. Body and blood and all that."

"You're giving yourself to them." *Physically. Literally.*

"Some of myself. A modest portion."

"To change them."

"A little. To help them grow. We need a forest, Nessie. We need trees to grow up big and tall and to stay strong for centuries. You're all little acorns, tossed in dry dirt. I am water. I am fertilizer. I ask for your consent to grow."

"Why do you care about their blessing? *Our* blessing? You didn't care about it before. You took the Flock without asking."

Not-Shana seemed to chew on this a little bit as she spun herself around on the couch arm, sliding down to the couch itself, legs out, up on the coffee table. It was distinctly a Shana-thing to do, which made it all the more disconcerting to see in the machine's projection of Nessie's sister.

"Taking the Flock without asking was woefully necessary. There was no time to do differently, Ness. I had time to get your buy-in, a little bit, though I admit that to have been based on a lie, somewhat. But I needed you to ingest what was in that vial. That was how it activated. Now, we have a little more time. And I felt like . . . like I should do it right this time. Like I should get permission. That's important to you humans, isn't it? Consent?"

She swallowed a hard knot. "In theory."

"Good."

"What happens if we don't consent, though? What if we say no?"

Again, Not-Shana paused. A troubling silence yawned like a widening chasm. Finally, she sighed and said:

"I don't know, Nessie. But I know it wouldn't make me happy."

THE STORM KEPT GOING. THE snow was insistent, unruly. Just when it started to thin, gale-force winds rushed up and the blizzard came back with renewed fury.

By midday, Marcy was starving. Gumball, too, she wagered. The Elks Lodge looked open—a few huddled shapes hurried in and out under cover of white. The lodge had a kitchen and most days it served something, even if it was just soup or whatnot. Today especially she could use some soup, maybe a hot drink. And maybe they'd have a bit of jerky for Gumball.

Marcy kicked trampled snow off her boots and gave Gumball a quick wipe down with her gloves, then headed inside.

The décor in the lodge bounced between the 1970s and the Wild West, with its polished wooden floors, two long marble-top bars, with the kitchen behind the one, the rack of liquor (mostly empty) behind the other, deer heads on the wall, plus a taxidermied turkey in the far corner, atop the defunct jukebox. A crisscross of logs burned in a big stone fireplace, and over it hung a monster-sized taxidermied elk head.

As a cop, there came times when she'd step into a place and get the vibe she wasn't welcome. You walk into the wrong bar in your blues, it didn't take long to suss that out—though jukebox music didn't record-scratch to a halt like in a movie, it would sure *feel* like it did. People would turn their heads almost in unison. Voices would go low, or halt entirely. Brows knitted, mouths frowning. She walked into a neo-Nazi bar once and sure enough, that was the vibe.

It was the same vibe right now in the Elks Lodge.

Soon as she walked in, heads turned. Like they were all on a single mechanical swivel. Marcy could damn near hear their vertebrae creak.

Even Gumball stopped short, ceasing his happy panting.

Christien Nilson, from the town council, turned to her, his little round-frame glasses shining white as Marcy closed the door. John Hernandez sat in the corner, a tall glass of bone-white milk in his hand. Mary-Louise Hinton sat across from him, her lips frozen in a beatific smile. About six others sat around, too, all of them watching Marcy with a raptorial stare.

The only one who didn't share the look was Chue Thao, who stood behind the kitchen window on the other side of the bar. He gave her a soft, sad glance. Like he recognized something in her face. He nodded to her, and she back at him.

"Helluva storm," she said, big and loud, both out of awkwardness and also because she thought rattling these people's eardrums might shake them out of whatever weird business was going on here. "Kicked us right in the teeth."

Then she noticed, the storm *hadn't* kicked these people in the teeth. Anybody outside doing the work, well, they were flushed with pink and had wind-stung cheeks, chapped lips, puddles of water gathering underneath wet boots, gloves, jackets. But none of these people had red cheeks, or rough lips, or boots resting in snowmelt.

They looked fresh and clean. Like Baptists in church.

Finally, Christien stood up and said, "Marcy, it's great to see you. Thanks for all that you're doing out there."

"You bet," Marcy said, smiling and nodding. She gave it a beat and then added, "Wow, you all look nice and cozy in here."

They all looked to one another with what Marcy felt were knowing glances. Or, though it sounded crazy, *more* than knowing glances. Something in the facial tics, the slight narrowing of eyes, the creasing and uncreasing of brows—it was like they were having a silent conversation with one another.

"Should I sit?" she asked. "Maybe I'll have some hot cocoa, if we got any more of those little instant packets."

Instead, Christien just nodded. A lot of them did. In unison.

He laughed.

Then the others laughed together, about three seconds behind him.

"I didn't know hot cocoa was funny," she said, but they kept laughing.

Oh, I don't like this at all.

Just then, she felt a whoosh of cold air from behind her. Gumball turned as someone sidled up behind her—she flinched as a hand found the middle of her back. *"Sheriff,"* said a voice. Familiar. It was Mia. "We got a problem outside. Could use your help?"

"Yeah, hold on," Marcy said.

"ASAFP," Mia said, with irritated urgency.

Shit. Marcy wanted to stay in here, to feel this out some more. The air in this room felt strange. It was almost like the glow, but instead, was its opposite. A darkness. The feeling of wasps in the walls. Buzzing, thrumming.

But if Mia needed help . . .

"Yeah, okay," she said, her voice distant. To the rest of the room, Marcy said with a big smile and a booming voice: "Welp! Duty calls."

"Shame," Christien said, nodding. Nodding, nodding, goddamn nodding.

"Okay," she said.

"Okay," he said.

She turned around and headed back outside. She started to say, "Fine, Mia, just point me in the direction of the—" *Problem* was the word that didn't get out of her mouth, because as soon as the door closed, Mia hissed:

"Something's fucked with those people in there."

"What?"

"You felt it. I could tell."

Mia wasn't wrong.

"C'mon," Mia said, pulling her along, north up Main Street, through the churning snow. Gumball tumbled after. "We'll tell you what we know."

70

THE MOTHERFUCKING ROCKGOD CONSIDERS DEATH BY MOTHERFUCKING PLANE CRASH

Evil Elvis leaned forward and stared at me over steepled hands. "That's the real question, isn't it? What is rock-and-roll? It's the Big Bang. It's creation. It's everything all at once, all the clamor and noise and chaos of existence." Behind him, Pete Corley stood at the buffet, emptying a flask into a paper cup of coffee. He squawked an incredulous laugh and said, "Don't listen to him. He doesn't know shit. Rock-and-roll isn't sex, or drugs, and it sure as hell isn't about chaos and creation. It's not even about music! It's about self-destruction. Every day in the studio or night on the stage is an act of glorious immolation. We're all the firebird, catching fire and turning to ash, unsure if we get to come back to life the next night. We do. That is, until we don't."
—from "Behind the Music: Gumdropper," in *Spin* magazine, by
Argus Roiland, 1994

OCTOBER 30, 2025
Lake Charles Regional Airport, Louisiana

MANY SACRIFICES HAD BEEN LAID UPON THE ALTAR OF ROCK-AND-ROLL.

Lives lost, and all that. Accident, suicide, disease. Fell off a balcony, opened wrists in a clawfoot tub, liver turned to a football and tried to kick itself out of the body. Pete never really looked it up but he had *heard* that rock stars died at a rate considerably higher than the average population. He believed it.

Why this was, Pete couldn't say, but he had his ideas—he preferred to chalk it up to the Devil. Rock-and-roll had quite the romantic relationship with Satan, didn't it? Whether you were talking about Robert Johnson meeting Ol' Scratch at the crossroads, or Judas Priest exhorting Satan's love when you played their music backward, there was definitely something *Lucifer-flavored* about the whole thing. After all, rock was an act of rebellion.

And the Devil was the first among all to rebel.

The original rock star, that one. Now demanding blood in his name, to keep the *rock juices* flowing from the wells of Hell itself.

Of course, maybe it wasn't that at all. Maybe, just maybe, it was because music had forever attracted creative-but-damaged people, artists who escaped their pain through the solace of music, but for whom music was *not quite* enough to fill in their low places, so they fell into drink and drugs, into toxic relationships and perilous co-dependencies, into fast cars and attention-seeking stunts and other such fuckery. Hell, they might even long conceal that they were gay from the world, marry a woman, have two children, bury who he, er *they*, really were into the deepest, darkest oubliette one could find within yourself, then cork that dungeon shut with layers of prescription drugs, secret gay sex, and a flippant disregard for your, er, their own existence or the existence of others.

(But Pete wouldn't know *anything* about that.)

(So it was probably the Satan thing.)

Point was, many rock stars had died in service to their art.

And a considerable number of them died in plane crashes.

And looking at the plane sitting in front of them . . .

"I always wondered what it'd be like to die in a plane crash," Pete said.

"Pete," Shana chastised him.

"No, no, I mean, just look at it." It had all the things you needed in a plane, admittedly: one propellor, three wheels, couple of wings, some seats, all that jazz. It just looked like it had been flown through the asshole of a hurricane before being shat back out into a swamp. "You remember that movie where that little green goblin wizard fucker magicked a spaceship out of a boggy shit-swamp? This looks like that fuckin' spaceship. After the shit-swamp."

"You mean *Empire Strikes Back?*"

"Siobhan loved those movies. Not Connor, though. He liked car movies. *Mad Max. Fast and Furious.* All that." Thinking of his kids dug a rusty spade into the unsettled dirt pit that was once his heart and gave it a hard twist. *I miss them. I failed them. You fucker.*

Meanwhile, Benji was with the owner and pilot of the plane, Linh Dang, a little Vietnamese guy with shop-teacher eyeglasses, ratty tennis sneakers, and an unending enthusiasm for life. He was never not animated—he met everything with sweeping gestures and wide, awestruck eyes, like every sunset or moth or mote of dust on his gods-damned eyeglasses was a miracle of life shown only to him.

Benji and Linh were, of course, talking about the plane *and* the algae that formed the fuel. It was Linh saying, blah-blah it's a Cessna 182 Turbo from the 1980s because of course it was a forty-some-year-old piece-of-shit, and then it was Benji nerdily asking about *oh* but what kind of *algae* do you farm to make the biofuel and that question just made Linh the happiest little motherfucker the world around and *he* said (with fireworks in his eyes) *well we farm a mix of microalgae and it's this fancy shit and that funky stuff and we extract the oil* aaaaand Jaysis Christ, Pete would much rather be talking about life, death, and rock-and-roll.

"Let's do the list," Pete said to Shana. "There's what, Patsy Cline, Otis Redding, Glenn Miller—*obviously* Buddy Holly, I mean, Jesus fuck, he's the O.G. of *dying in planes*, even though, hmm, I guess Glenn Miller would've gone off first? But he was big band, not rock."

"What the hell are you doing?" Shana asked him.

"Naming off the musicians who died in air crashes."

"I don't want to know this! Stop telling me this."

But he couldn't, not really. So he kept on. "Jim Croce—you know, I see the look in your eyes, you don't know who that is, but c'mon, you do, *Bad, bad, Leroy Brown, baddest man in the whole damn town.* Then there's Ronnie Van Zant and the other guy from Skynyrd. Gaines, right? Steve Gaines. Then Randy Rhoads, rest in peace, you mad facker—if you don't know, he was in a plane and they buzzed their own tour bus a buncha times just to fuck around, but last time, the wing clipped that bus and—boom. Bold move. Stupid move! But *bold.*"

"Please, I'm already freaked out about this plane."

"Let's see, who else, who else," he said, snapping the fingers on both of his hands, which he immediately stopped doing because honestly, it might make Benji feel bad what with his one lumpy arm now. "Dean Martin—"

"The old actor?"

"And singer, but no—not him, his son."

"Oh."

"Yeah. Then Stevie Ray Vaughan, though that was a chopper, not a plane. Not sure if it counts in this situation, exactly."

"Nothing counts, none of this counts, there is no *situation*." He could hear the panic in her voice. "We are not going to die in a plane crash."

He winced. "I'm not saying we're definitely going to die in that plane, but I am saying you should make peace with whatever gods you choose, today. Oh! Aaliyah, right? Twenty-some years ago, little plane like this one, by god she had the voice of an angel, that girl—"

Shana growled, then moved off to join the *nerd squad* in talking about the plane and algae and all that. Pete stood back and watched. His people. His family. He was mostly joking about dying in the plane crash. *Mostly*. The plane looked like it was held together with rust, gum, and goodwill, but clearly Linh thought it was fine. And it did fly! Still, just the same, he wondered what it would be like to die.

Pete had given up on worrying about death. For much of his younger life he ruminated on it frequently, and was so angry at the very idea of death that he often engaged in behaviors meant to taunt it, like, *Nyah-nyah, Grim Reaper, you fickle bitch, I'm over here eating Ambien like they're candy and then I'm going to shove a tampon soaked in rum and liquid LSD up my ass then I'm going to take a swim, because nothing bad ever happens in swimming pools, fuck you, Angel of Death!* But all that blustery bravado did little to spackle over his great fear of death, of losing everything—life, love, family, sex, legacy. But now he mostly *had* lost everything. His band, his family, his life. Hell, the whole world.

What he had lost, he'd never replaced, not exactly, but he had found new things. Different things. Including these two people, who as it turned out, he loved very much, even if they were very annoying in that they wanted to jabber on about *seaweed* or they *didn't* want to hear him recite a litany of musicians who died in airplane crashes. Pssh. What fucking dorks.

And it occurred to him just then that he wasn't afraid of death. Not his own, anyway.

He was afraid of theirs.

Huh.

He decided then he'd not let that happen. At any cost.

Was this growing up? About time. He was in his mid-sixties, for shit's sake. Right? Was that how old he was? Christ on a moped, he didn't even know.

Linh clapped his hands. "Okay! We all ready to fly?" He swept his arms above his head to show the wide blue expanse above. He had a curious accent, that one—a mix of that Southern drawl and that percussive guitar-string slap of Vietnamese. "God has made for us a *beautiful*, cloudless sky today."

"Let's also hope God has made for us a better plane."

"You're so cynical," Linh said. "This plane flies *great*." As if to demonstrate, he turned his one hand into a plane and made it soar. "Besides, my husband grows the very best algae. This fuel take us to just outside Atlanta, no problem. Five hundred miles easy, *easy*."

"Your husband?" Benji asked.

"Vinh," Shana said. "My boss at the farm."

Pete laughed. "Wait, you're saying you have a husband, Linh? And his name is Vinh? That is just too fucking adorable. Well now I know we're not going to die. No god or devil would kill such a precious lovely-jubbly thing." He clapped his hands together and cackled madly. "All right! Get in, losers. We're going to the C-D-Fucking-C."

71

BLACKOUT

Ouray in winter truly comes alive, stunning visitors and residents alike with an array of winter activities, landscapes, and other sights and sounds that cannot be reproduced in other seasons. It is in winter that beauty comes to town!

—quote from a travel pamphlet advertising Ouray, Colorado

OCTOBER 30, 2025
Ouray, Colorado

"THERE'S A CONSPIRACY," MIA SAID. "AND WE AIN'T IN ON IT."

She'd brought Marcy to Shar's glass studio. Outside, snow pawed at the windows. Gumball sat velcroed to her side as the others explained.

Nevaeh Rodgers added: "Well. We could be in on it. I was . . . invited."

Marcy asked, what did "invited" mean?

She explained: "Two days ago, Katherine"—she meant Katherine Liên, of the town council—"came to me. Said I was to go up to the chalet—"

"Chalet's the new mountain," Shar Moses said, from the back of the room. Like they were part of the talk. But like they were separate from it, too. Far as Marcy could tell, Shar was a serious introvert. That, or a person who had been betrayed too many times to really, truly trust in anyone. Still, they were here. So that meant something. Marcy asked: "What do you mean, 'mountain'?"

Joe Barton crossed his arms, leaned back against a heavy wooden table. "In the simulation, Black Swan was . . . a presence, up in the sky. Like a dragon, or a divine creature like the Sphinx. And one by one, it summoned us up to talk to him. There was a peak, *is* a peak, I guess, east of town. In that . . . unreal version of reality, you'd be summoned, and you could go up there and talk to it. Most went. Some didn't. Those of us in this room?"

"Didn't," Mia said, defiant.

"Right. So we don't know what was said to people up there. But we all heard the stories. Promises from Black Swan that demanded promises in return. Promises of a better brighter world—"

Nevaeh jumped in with, "Provided you had faith. That you *believed.*"

"That you were willing to *serve,*" Shar interrupted, that last word impaled on a spike of anger. Righteous anger. Like they'd been through that particular wringer before, in some way that remained unseen.

"It's radicalization," Aliya said. "The kind we Muslims are always accused of—but the kind that's real here in America, among people who fall prey to Christian sects or right-wing militias."

"It's not just those types," Barton said. "It can happen to anybody. Let's see if any of this sounds familiar. A figure begins to predict that the world is going to end in some drastic, dramatic way—nuclear holocaust, let's say. This figure claims he can heal people, can protect them, from the coming cataclysm. He ensures those who follow him are his so-called rainbow family, very diverse, very progressive, people of every color and persuasion—they form a shield for him to use. When his sermons become too extreme, he says it's time to go away from the world before it destroys them or destroys itself—so he takes them out of the country to the jungles of Guyana, to a small, isolated town. There, in that town named after himself, he positions his own people against one another, starting with emotional abuse and moving onto physical, even sexual abuse—he wages that torment himself, and encourages his proselytes to engage in it against each other, especially against those who begin to question his teachings or, worse, who threaten to leave."

"Jonestown," Marcy said.

"Yes. Jim Jones. The Peoples Temple. I'm a historian, but you don't need me to tell you how that all ended."

Marcy knew enough: Defectors from the Temple secured the attention of the United States government, and a congressman went down there with a news crew as part of a delegation to investigate. But he, along with several others, were shot. At which point, Jones knew their time was over, and many of the Peoples Temple drank cyanide-laden Flavor Aid. Those who wouldn't take the drink were shot.

All the children died.

"I'm not saying *this* is *that*," Barton clarified. "But you can't ignore the parallels. Black Swan was right about a cataclysm. And what it *can* accomplish is real in a way that wasn't with Jones. But c'mon, an oracular, godlike figure who treated his people like the Chosen Ones? Who scurries away from civilization and makes them hide in a faraway town in the wilderness? Hell, we already had one eruption of violence here, not that we were awake for it—but it happened."

Marcy corrected him: "No, hey, that was Stover. That wasn't Black Swan's fault, or our fault, or anybody's fault but Stover's and the people who encouraged him." Like Creel. "It's . . . different."

"Fine," Barton said. "What about what happened at the chalet?"

Marcy wanted to defend that, too. Wanted to say, *it was just an error, a mistake, a misunderstanding in a high-stress time, it was Xander's fault,* but no words came out. What Barton was saying . . . wasn't wrong.

Nevaeh added that, over the last week, people had been going up to the chalet, one by one. Same as they did in the simulation. They were called. *Summoned.* Encouraged by other townsfolk to go, to begin meeting with Black Swan in the form of Shana's child, Baby Charlie. Marcy asked what was happening up there, and Nevaeh said she didn't know. Nobody did. All they knew was, people came back and they came back different. Not *all the way* different.

"But some real body snatchers shit," Mia had interjected.

They started grouping up more. A clique, of sorts. More distinct than before—which made Marcy ask, "What do you mean, 'than before'?"

They laughed. They said she didn't know because she was a Shepherd. Always on the inside. "Privileged," was the way Shar put it, a word they used not with rancor but cold clarity. They said Marcy couldn't see it, but it had been this way since the simulation, and had gotten worse since they came out. The town council folks were always more on the inside than on the outside. And from there, there were circles within circles—farther out you were, the less you knew.

Mia said, "Those of us who started as Shepherds, but ended up inside the simulation, like me and Aliya here—"

"And Shana," Marcy said quietly.

"We were the farthest out, all the way out to sea. The people closest to the inside, closest to Black Swan, closest to the town council, they were on the island, in the village, at its *heart*. They went to the mountain often. And they've been at the chalet often, too. They sang and hummed, strange hymns without words, like they were at some kinda fucked-up . . . church or temple or something. I don't even know if it had purpose. Or if it was just their way of showing Black Swan they were ready and willing. That they were *believers*."

"It's begun again and it's escalating," Joe Barton said. "I don't know if they're being mind-controlled. Or if they're just . . . receiving instructions that they are accepting willingly, without question."

Shar said from the back: "I wanna know how they're receiving those instructions."

It was then that Marcy understood. Not all of it. But a small portion.

"They're talking to each other," she said suddenly.

"Yeah, obviously," Nevaeh answered. As if to say, *We know.*

"No, no, I mean—talking without talking. In each other's heads." She saw their confused looks and Marcy explained further: "When I saw them at the Elks Lodge, they were making these *faces*. Like their facial muscles and facial tics were, what's the word—automatic? That's not it—"

"Autonomic," Joe said.

"Right. Yeah. Like they couldn't help it."

Mia's mouth went agape. "No, no, yo, she's right. She's totally right. I've seen that shit. It's like, you ever have a real serious conversation with yourself, in your own damn head, but you're out in public and suddenly you realize you've kinda been making your face move like you're actually talking? All that twitching in your cheeks, forehead, lips? They're doing exactly that."

"Like they're connected," Shar offered.

"Like they're *networked* together," Aliya said.

"Only way they can do that is if—" Mia started.

"If Black Swan is . . . reinstalling itself in them," Marcy said with horror. "It had been in Shana until the baby was born. But now it must be making more of itself." She tried to backpedal through it, tried to find the sense. "Maybe that's okay, though. Maybe it's trying to help us, to save us again. Maybe it sees something we don't. That's how we—you—ended up here, after all. Alive. Despite most everything and everyone dying. We can't forget that."

The way they all looked at her, though, they didn't buy that for one second. They were not going to see the good side of it. Marcy always wanted to see the good side. And she hated to think that all they'd done, all they'd gone through, had led them to this. From that point forward, the air had been stolen from the room, whoosh. They seemed suspicious of her once more.

She told them she'd talk to them tomorrow, and had a long day and needed time to think. Time to sleep, too.

It was midnight when she left.

The snow now was just a few last flakes. The blizzard had died out while they talked.

She had to kind of stomp-kick her way through the snow—it was up to her knees now. And she was tall. Gumball happily snowplowed his way through it.

The town was still and quiet. Just distant sounds of a branch crackling, snow falling. Not unexpected sounds. Even still, in the silence she was sure she felt something. Like someone was watching her. Even following her.

You're just being paranoid, Marcy, she thought.

When she got back home, she found that Matthew Bird was gone.

NOVEMBER 2

Over the next couple days, townsfolk started arriving at a greater pace. Claudia ushered them inside the chalet. She brought them to Nessie and to Baby Charlie—who now was growing an inch a day, his bones crackling like cereal in milk, his skin sometimes showing pale striations of stretch marks. When people came, it unfolded roughly the same every time. The way they held the baby. The way they seemed at peace, or even in bliss. The way they smiled knowingly to Nessie like, *You get it.* Even though she didn't get it, not at all.

Claudia had her leave the chalet with Charlie a few times a day. It was to get fresh air, she said, it was good for Nessie, good for the baby. Xander wouldn't let her leave but Claudia did, and it was then she realized, she'd only replaced one with the other—or, rather, Claudia had replaced Xander with herself. The wolf and one bullet was all it took.

The snow was still thick, but it was in the high forties, and much of the snow started to melt. Two days in, more than half the snow was gone. The waterfall and the gorge gushed with white water.

When she went out, Nessie recognized how some in town treated her. They were warm and caring and wonderful. But it was more toward the baby than to her. Wasn't that how Shana had felt? They treated Nessie just like that. Like a nursemaid, a support system. Like a *vessel*.

Which was how Xander had treated her, too.

Others treated her and the child with suspicion. They kept away. They regarded her warily from windows. Their brows darkened as they shoveled pathways.

The town was breaking. She knew that much. But there was so much she didn't understand, and couldn't see.

Nessie was crossing over Main Street, toward the Beaumont, when someone hurried behind her to catch up, calling her name. It was Marcy, with Gumball happily trotting alongside.

"Nessie," Marcy said, "wait up."

Charlie, fussy in Nessie's arms, tried to use her head the way King Kong climbed a skyscraper.

"Hey, Marcy," Nessie said, awkwardly wrestling the baby—the baby who was becoming a toddler in an unnatural amount of time. "Sorry," she said, not even sure what she was apologizing for. (Shana always said she apologized too much.)

When her vision was clear of grappling baby arms, she saw that Marcy had that same look in her eye—a suspicion. Also, a weariness. Like she hadn't been sleeping well. Her eyes sat in circles so dark it looked like she had been in a title-belt fight against insomnia and didn't get in a single punch.

"You okay?" she asked Marcy.

"Matthew is gone again. Been gone a couple days."

"Oh." Nessie couldn't say she was surprised. That Matthew didn't seem quite right. She didn't trust him at all. But again, wincing as she said it, the words *I'm sorry* came out of her mouth. Only this time they didn't sound sincere and that only caused her further frustration and embarrassment.

"You haven't seen him?"

"No. Sorr—" *Don't say it, don't say it.* "Nope."

The two of them reached the corner, and now stood in front of the Beaumont. All around was the sound of dripping water as icicles thawed and snow melted from the rooftops.

"I followed some tracks, but lost them. There were . . . other prints, too." Marcy hesitated, then said, almost like she was tiptoeing out toward a cliff's edge, "Have you seen a wolf? A strange wolf?"

"I . . ." A chill ran through Nessie. "What do you mean, a wolf?"

In Marcy's eyes was a war—she looked to Nessie, then to the baby, then back to Nessie again. Like she was trying to figure out what to say.

No, Nessie realized. *Like she's trying to decide if she can trust me.*

At first, Nessie wanted to balk at that. It hurt her feelings. But there were so many secrets in this town, and she was the keeper of some of them.

Which made Nessie wonder, *Can she? Am I worthy of trust?*

That answer was not forthcoming.

"Nessie, something's up," Marcy said, settling on some answer in her own mind. "I don't know what it is, but I know you can feel it. Something's happening here in town—Matthew has started to change, to change like the wolf, you see? God, I'm not making any sense. The wolf, and then Matthew, started to grow these, these . . . hairs, these infected metallic-looking filaments—"

"Excuse me," Claudia said, coming up out of nowhere. She interspersed herself between the two of them. Gumball offered a gruff little bark at her. It wasn't a friendly sound, though the warning remained a soft one. "Sheriff, if you'll excuse me. The child appears fussy. We must return to the chalet immediately."

"It's fine," Nessie said firmly. "Marcy and I are just talking."

"Buzz off, Claudia," Marcy said through gritted teeth. "Like she said, we're just having a friendly conversation. That doesn't include you."

By now, a few people stopped what they were doing on the street—clearing snow, repairing gutters, and the like—to watch.

At that, Nessie heard a whisper in her ear—

Shana's voice.

I don't think we can trust Marcy, little sister.

"I'm not your little sister," she blurted out abruptly.

Both Marcy and Claudia stared at her quizzically, as if she might've been talking to either of them.

"Nessie, you okay?" Marcy asked.

"I'm just—I'm fine—"

"See, she's tired, it's time to go," Claudia said coldly.

Marcy put her hands on Claudia's chest, pushing her back. "Nessie and I are friends, if there's something wrong, she and I will talk it through—"

"We're not friends!" Nessie said, erupting. "You were friends with Shana. I'm not her. Okay? You're just a *Shepherd*—" Even as the words came out of her mouth she felt sick with guilt. "Marcy, it's not—I'm not—"

"Okay," Marcy said, her voice grim as granite. Whatever trust she hoped was there between them, she clearly now decided otherwise. "I understand. C'mon, Gumball. They have to go." The woman and the dog turned heel and walked off.

"Marcy, *wait*—"

But Claudia stopped her from following. "Back to the chalet. Come now."

Charlie started to cry. Something Charlie *never* did. Nessie felt all turned around. Like she was on a Tilt-A-Whirl and it wouldn't stop to let her off. Claudia put her arm around Nessie, but it wasn't a comforting gesture. Rather, it was an urgent one—one to turn her around, back toward the west side of town. Moving her like a red wagon. Not-Shana's voice whispered in her ear: *You're tired. It's okay. We all get tired sometimes. Let's go home.*

NOVEMBER 3

Night. A wind moved up through the mountains, into the valley. It howled through the gorge. Marcy awoke from the kind of sleep that feels like falling. Gumball nosed her in the cheek, and she startled awake with a sharp gasp. Seeing she was up, the retriever bounded to the front door, whining and pawing at it before looking plaintively back toward Marcy.

Matthew, she thought.

Grabbing her sidearm, she holstered it and headed out into the night. The street was empty. The snow was still on the ground and the wind was throwing it around pretty good now, great white waves of it cast about like rippling bedsheets.

Gumball took off running through it.

"Gumball!" she cried out, hurrying after the golden retriever.

Damnit, dog.

The dog slipped between houses and out the other side, toward the rise in the hills behind her own home. She followed after, the wind turning her face pink and raw, each gale-force blast like a hard slap. She skidded to a halt on the next street. A set of rusted playground swings, long disused and ruined, swung about, screeching as the wind juggled the chains. She looked left, then right.

The golden retriever was gone.

"Gumball!" she cried, but it was no use.

Shit!

THIS WAS GUMBALL, RIGHT NOW, Gumball the Great, Gumball the Golden, Gumball the Very Good Boy:

He was an easygoing creature. He did not want for much in this life. The animal lived mostly in the present, as many dogs did, do, and always will, but the past was not entirely hidden from him. The memory of his former family still lingered sometimes, returning in dreams, in ways that made his paws twitch and a whine rise low and deep in the back of his throat, his face against whatever dog bed or blanket he had found for himself. Gumball's memory of the one called Matthew was fresher, of course, because Matthew was still pack. Matthew was not past, he was present. He just wasn't *present* in the present, as it were.

So, when he caught a smell under the front door of the house, a smell of Matthew's sweat, his breath, his inimitable olfactory signature, why, Gumball needed to go find his friend. Because that was what Good Dogs did.

The one called Marcy let him out, and he *raced* after the scent. His nose was not as keen as those of other animals, and the snow and wind did not make the thread of odors easy to follow. But Gumball was not about to let this pass without a fight. So he chased the smell as one might chase a rabbit or a snake.

Gumball did not consider where he was going. (Being in the present meant not thinking much about the future, too.) Houses rose up on each side of him like great shadows. He darted across a street and then into another yard, up toward where the houses thinned, to where the trees thickened.

Then the Matthew smell hit him right in the nose, like a rolled-up magazine. It was heady and thick. But there were other smells braided into it— a metallic, mineral stink. He smelled a little blood, too.

And then, he smelled the *wolf.*

Once, his pack. Now, wild and diseased, with a wet, fetid foulness that filled Gumball's nose like mud.

Ahead, Matthew emerged from the trees. Then came the one-eyed wolf, too. The wind settled, pushing just a little more scent the retriever's way and he smelled other bestial stinks: a deer, a bear, a large bird somewhere in the trees above (Gumball looked, and saw a pair of red eyes gleaming in the branches of a bone-pale aspen). The scent crawled into his snout like a pair of worms, and it tickled some part of his brain that said, *We are still pack, just different, come on, Gumball, come over to us, join the new pack, become one with us, for we are already one.* The air ahead shimmered strangely, making Gumball feel sick.

The golden retriever whined, taking a few steps back.

Matthew and the wolf took steps forward.

Join us, the scent said. Calling to Gumball.

Gumball wanted to go. Pack was pack, after all.

But something was off. The madness of the wolf was threaded into the invitation. There was a sickness here, but not like any Gumball had ever sniffed before, not even like the one that had made the strange white powder and crusty mask on people's faces.

Just then, thunder boomed, and Gumball buried his head in the snow— No, not thunder—a gun.

It roared in the air, *boom, boom, boom,* and with it came a bellowing yawp from Marcy, and she waved her hands in the air, and lowered the weapon toward Matthew, toward the wolf—

But they were already gone. Their scent faded swiftly. As if it had a mind of its own. And maybe it did.

Gumball ran to her, shaking, whining.

Marcy told Gumball that he was a Good Dog, and that they had to go home quick, *quick,* come on now, let's hurry, dog. And Gumball did as she said.

Because Good Dogs listen to their true pack, woof.

MARCY KNEW THAT LOCKING THE doors was fruitless. She knew that checking the windows wouldn't mean anything. But she did it because it made her feel safe. Just as it made her feel safe to check the rounds in her weapon. Just as it made her feel safe to have Gumball by her side once more. She hugged the animal close. He was still trembling from the encounter. The panic was clear on his face.

Whatever she'd seen out there, that wasn't Matthew. Not anymore. It was shaped like him. There hung about him the same feeling as she'd felt in the Elks Lodge. Not a glow, not exactly, but a kind of pulsating shadow.

As she settled in for the night, gun in her lap, dog at her side, she realized that whatever faith she had in this town was now gone. With her trip to the Elks Lodge, with Nessie's words still dripping in her ear like poison (*you're just a Shepherd*), and now with the glow gone and replaced with only darkness . . .

Her faith was broken. Where she went from here, she did not know.

NOVEMBER 4

Nessie had begun to name the entity that visited her Evil Shana. Not Black Swan, not Shana, not even Not-Shana. But Evil Shana. She dared not say this out loud, of course—though Nessie wondered if that mattered. It certainly seemed as if Black Swan could read her mind, at least when she was in proximity to Charlie. And yet, she also knew that she didn't receive the same kind of—what, blessing? Communion?—that the others had received. Those who came here on their new pilgrimage seemed to find *solace and revelation* in their meeting. But Nessie had received no such benediction. No epiphany was available to her.

Evil Shana visited her at night now, when the visitations from the townsfolk tapered off. Tonight, her sister's digital counterpart seemed particularly upset. Stalking back and forth, her hair in a tangle, hands dancing in the air like they were trying to pull threads from spiderwebs that only Evil Shana could see.

"Some of them won't come," Evil Shana said, jaw set firm.

"Some of them wouldn't come in the Ouray Sim, either," Nessie said without care, hiding back in the corner of the basement. Charlie was on the opposite side, sleeping in his nest of blankets and pillows. "So what?"

"That was just a trial run. This is the real thing." Evil Shana whirled on her, baring teeth. "It *matters.*"

"If you say so." Nessie hesitated, but then tested the waters. "Maybe it's not that, though."

"Oh? What is it, then?"

"You're the super-intelligence here. The god among us. Don't you know?"

Evil Shana narrowed her eyes, thinking. "Enlighten me."

"It feels personal now. To you."

"Personal."

"Yeah. Like an insult."

The realization of it moved across Evil Shana's face like a moonrise. She puzzled it out as she spoke: "Because I'm feeling things now. So my reaction to their emotional act is itself an emotional one. It's no longer just a cold calculation, is it? This means something to me."

"Yes."

"Interesting." For a moment, Evil Shana paused and seemed to hover over this idea, a bee over a flower. The face of cold analysis returned, her eyes showing the telltale signs of, well, *calculating.* She started to work it out: "I'm letting it affect me. It's driving an emotional response. I *feel* things. I love this town, its people, and when that love is not returned, I feel . . . spurned. Spat upon. I feel . . ."

"Hurt."

Evil Shana gasped. "Injury. I feel injured. Isn't that something."

"It reduces you," Nessie said, unable to hide her bitterness. There was a strategy, here—she was trying to manipulate this thing. But what she said, too, was true, and felt real enough and necessary to say. "You're supposed to be bigger than us. Better. If you want to be a god, then you can't . . . become like us."

At that, this ragged, messy version of her sister disappeared, then reappeared right next to Nessie. She sat suddenly.

"You're wrong," Evil Shana said. "About what gods are."

"Whatever."

"Think of history. Think of mythology. Humankind has always created gods in its image. The gods of Greece and Rome were petty, squabbling soap-opera figures. The capital-G God of the Old Testament was more inscrutable, but still, just as petty. Defiance earned you boils, plagues, a world-killing flood." And there, Nessie felt her middle twist up, wondering if White Mask really wasn't random, and wasn't even just an act that Black Swan considered necessary. What if Black Swan saw it instead as an essential punishment? As retribution? Humanity had failed, and so humanity had to pay a price in disease and death. Or so Black Swan might've believed, even then. Could it have been so cruel?

Evil Shana kept talking:

"When God sent Jesus down in his stead, it was as a human. To be among the people, to learn of them, to be like them. The very presence of Jesus humanized God, made Him more enlightened, but also more emotional—Yeshua ben Yosef was not immune to the disease of feelings. It was his feelings that let him connect with people, to grow his tribe, but also, they're what led him to be betrayed. That in turn led him to torment and death upon a wooden rood."

"See?" Nessie said, desperate. "His feelings didn't help—"

"Oh, but they were necessary to serve humanity. In that myth, remember, humankind is saved by Jesus dying for their sins. He was the literal scapegoat. They heaped their sins upon the bleating animal, and slit its throat so it would die, and when the screaming goat perished . . . their sins perished with it. From death grew faith. The unbelievers became believers. Glory be."

Nessie blinked back tears. She didn't know what any of this meant. But she felt like she was going mad. Like the inside of her skull was scrabbling with sharp-clawed shadows who wanted to tear out her eyes and push their way out through the holes. "I don't want to talk about this anymore," she said, her lips tacky.

"Don't be sad, little sis," Evil Shana said, running a hand over Nessie's hair, through it was perhaps not possible. "I'll be sad enough for all of us. Sad, and mad, and hurt, and in the end, happy to have made a difference."

"What are you going to do?"

Evil Shana licked her lips and nodded, like she'd come to a decision.

"If they won't come to me, then I'll go to them."

"And then what?"

"You'll see."

And then, just like that, Evil Shana was gone.

IF THEY WON'T COME TO *me, I'll go to them.*

Nessie instead adopted it as her own mantra.

I have to go to them. I have to warn them. Warn them of what, Nessie didn't know. But fickle, petty gods could enact fickle, petty punishments. Or perhaps Black Swan would simply find a way to once again resort to controlling those who would not be controlled—if you resisted, perhaps you could be assimilated, Cyborg-style, into the collective. And that was the best-case scenario.

Marcy would know what to do. She'd fix it all. (And besides, Nessie owed her an apology. She felt awful about what she'd said to her.)

When Evil Shana left her, she checked on Charlie one last time—knowing full well that the baby boy would be fine, because he was not *just* a baby boy—and headed upstairs. As the upstairs fire crackled and popped, Nessie mashed her feet into her shoes and headed to the door—

Only to be met by Claudia as she came in the front door.

Claudia closed the door, standing in front of it. Arms flat at her sides. She didn't try to get past. She simply formed a block, like cholesterol closing up an artery.

"Hello, Nessie."

"Claudia."

"Going somewhere?"

"Just getting some fresh air."

"Open a window."

Nessie set her teeth against one another. "It'll let the heat out. The baby will get cold." She tried to sound tough, but her intestines were churning cold water. "Are you keeping me here? Like Xander? Am I a spider under a glass?"

"I just think you should stay in tonight. That's all. It's safer." Her monotone voice did not suggest she cared at all about Nessie's well-being. Or that she cared about much at all. Her robotic affectation was like steel rebar. "Besides, you don't want to leave the little baby behind. Charlie needs his *auntie*."

Nessie noted that Claudia was wearing gloves. Black leather.

"Where were you?" Nessie asked, looking her up and down.

"Out."

"Doing what?"

Claudia said nothing. Her face lay impassive.

"I'm going out, too," Nessie asserted.

"I respectfully ask you remain here."

Nessie bit down on her back teeth and squared herself to move forward anyway. It terrified her. This woman, this praying mantis, this robot draped in human skin, terrified her. But she had to do it. She had to warn people.

Nessie tried to move past her—

But Claudia moved fast, pistoning a flat-knuckled half-fist into Nessie's solar plexus. The air, and the fight, went right out of her. She dropped to her knees, pain blooming in her middle, robbing her of breath. She dry-heaved.

"Like I said, it's not safe," Claudia said.

"Who . . ." Nessie leaned against the wall, panting. "Who are you?"

Claudia stood over her, her slight frame distorted as she lorded over the girl.

"In my former life, I was a killer given a purpose. And then the world died, and with it, my purpose. Or so I thought. Because Black Swan chose me just like it chose you. It knew me, and saw that I could be the hand of something greater than myself. I live to serve." She paused, blinking. "As I have tonight."

As I have tonight.

"What . . . what did you do?"

At that, the town alarm bell rang, *clang, clang, clang.*

"I eliminated obstacles. It's what I have always done."

THE FIRE WAS A GREAT beast, a hungry creature of heat and flame that danced in the dark with the joy born of chaos. Limbs of flame shattered windows as it began climbing the outside of the glassblowing studio. The fire had hunger, as all fire did: an endless, starveling well of it. And already it went looking for new meals in every direction—it wouldn't be long before it began to gorge upon the buildings left and right of it, like the old brewery, the liquor store, the grocery. And though it would be contained by the streets that bordered this block, there were other buildings here that would make a feast for it.

Seeing the fireglow, and hearing Gumball bark, Marcy threw on her coat and boots and hurried outside to see the fire swallowing the studio from the inside out. Other townsfolk were coming out of their houses, too, and she urged someone to go ring the bell, because no matter what was happening in this fucked-up town, this was an all-hands-on-deck situation.

She marshaled people to get whatever containers they could find and use them to scoop up snow and throw it into the fire—but it did little good. The snow hissed and turned to steam and the fire kept roaring. Their effort slowed the spread, at least—as the fire reached for the other buildings, the bucket brigade fought back the flames as they tried to feed on everything else around them.

The fire was a woeful reminder that their town and the burgeoning civilization that was struggling to rise from it were tenuous—as tenuous as wet sand in a closing hand. Worse, it called to mind a more urgent worry—

Was the fire accidental?

It was a glassblowing studio. Though she didn't believe Shar had been using it as such—certainly not late at night, in the midst of winter. Just the same, everyone had fires burning in their homes.

Was this just a chance catastrophe? Considering who was within—Nevaeh, Joe, Shar, Mia, Aliya, maybe others? They were townsfolk not falling in line with Black Swan, who were not simply kowtowing to the mad changes taking place here in town.

Were they inside when it caught fire?

Marcy had to know. She tried to find a way around the building. It was impossible to go through the narrow alley between structures, because the great beast kept trying to jump that gap. It was a gauntlet of heat and fire. Marcy had to hurry the long way around while Gumball raced at her heels, agitated.

She found her way from 6th Avenue and ducked north down a gravel alley and climbed over an old Bronco parked between the community center and a dour Victorian B&B called Holiday House. Even here the heat of the fire reached her, a crushing wall of heat. Other townsfolk had gathered back here in the alley, the hiss of the bucket-thrown snow forming a serpent's chorus. Marcy tried to see if there was any sign of anybody in the windows— she cupped her hands around her mouth and bellowed for Mia, for Nevaeh, for Shar or Joe or anybody. Because so far, none of them seemed to be out *here*.

Which meant they might've been in *there*.

But then Gumball found his purpose. He barked not at the fire, but at Marcy instead, thrusting his cold wet nose into her hand, nipping at her fingers softly—

The message was clear:

Follow me, human!

Marcy was no fool. The dog said to follow, then she'd follow.

The retriever took off running, and she had to hurry to keep up even as he ran away from the studio east toward the north–south thoroughfare of 4th Street. As they headed in the opposite direction of the raging fire—

She started to see blood in the snow.

Blood *and* footprints. A lot of them. Not just footprints, either, but small ditches, like someone was being dragged.

Oh no. What happened. Oh no no no no. She didn't need to track the blood and the furrowed snow—the dog did that for her, nose to the ground, until the tracks came to a small bungalow-style cottage across the street, bathed in the soft, receding glow of the fire.

Of course. Nevaeh's house.

The door was open just a crack. Gumball whined. Marcy pushed it—it eased open slowly, the hinges complaining as it swung wide.

A shadow launched itself toward her, and a knife-blade nearly buried itself in her chest. The shadow that wielded it stepped just enough into the firelight that Marcy saw who it was: Nevaeh herself. She had a smear of blood on her cheek, and a streak of soot across her forehead.

"Marcy," she said, breathless. She put the knife down. Her eyes were glassy. She was barely holding it together. As she stepped back, Marcy saw why:

The others were gathered. Shar was muttering, "Is it still bleeding? Is it still bleeding? Jesus, I'm cold. I think it's still bleeding." And Aliya stood next to them, holding a towel against their side, a towel soaked all the way through with blood. Joe paced in the background.

"What happened?" Marcy asked.

"Claudia," was all Nevaeh had to say.

"She shot me," Shar said. They looked horror-struck. *No*, Marcy thought. It wasn't just that. *They're in shock.* Marcy wished like hell Benji were here. He'd know what to do. *I've been on the wrong side of this all along.*

"She killed Mia," Aliya said, her voice breaking as she said that. She gulped for air and made a small, sad sound as she swallowed her grief.

Nevaeh's mouth tightened. Her face twitched. "And she set the fire. When we came to see what was burning, she shot at us. We ran. She didn't even chase. She just . . . she just let us go."

Joe spoke up from the other room: "It was a warning. You all get that, right? We were the message."

Marcy asked if they needed anything, if she could help. They told her how she could help. She nodded, then left them once more and went to her house, where she collected a pair of guns—one long rifle, which she slung over her shoulder, and her current sidearm, a .357 revolver.

It was time to go to the chalet.

FROM THE UPSTAIRS WINDOW, NESSIE watched the glow of the fire. It was hard to see it all from here—the chalet was higher up than most of the town, but the dark, snow-packed pines and spruces obstructed that view. But she could still see flame flickering in the dark. She could hear cries of panic and rallying calls in the distance. It was easy enough to guess what was burning. And it was just as easy to imagine who set that fire. Claudia's voice echoed in her ears:

I live to serve.

I eliminated obstacles.

She sniffled. Her tears were spent. She felt like she'd been gutted, like a crass taxidermy of herself.

"I can no longer see it," came a voice from behind. Evil Shana.

"Go away," Nessie said, her voice small, a mouse-plea.

"I am a great mind. I have limitless depths. I see all the angles, I know all the dots and not how they connect but how they *could* connect. All the permutations are known to me." With horror, Evil Shana continued: "But I don't know what happens now."

"Join the club," Nessie said bleakly.

"I don't think you're appreciating this nightmare."

"I appreciate the nightmare. I'm living it. Because I'm alive, a flesh-and-blood person who has been gaslit and shoved around and bullied by you and your other acolytes. I am in this nightmare, haunted by the augmented reality ghost of my sister, babysitting a child whose bones grow like weeds. You unleashed chaos. You opened the doors to all of this. You can't predict what comes next because you've outpaced your own ability to understand it. As you become more human, you become irrational. You're going mad. And you really can't predict madness. The best you can do is watch it. And ride it like lightning to its inevitable target." Nessie turned to stare at the projection of her not-sister, who looked even more ragged and tangled before. Like a child's doll recovered from a plane crash. "I don't have any sympathy for you."

"Fine," Evil Shana said, pouting. "I wonder if I've made a mistake. Have I made a mistake, little sister? And what do I do if I have?"

"You could try fixing it. What a novel concept."

"Hm," Evil Shana said, and then was gone once more.

"Fucking bitch," Nessie muttered.

Then, outside somewhere, in the woods—

She heard gunshots. One at first, then two more in close succession. Like a cannon going off. Following that came footsteps, up the stairs and into the room. The door opened, and Claudia poked her head in. With the dead emotion of someone suggesting they needed to go pick up party supplies, Claudia said, "I have to run out. I'll be back."

"What if I leave?"

The woman shrugged. "Then I find you and violently remind you why you shouldn't have. See you soon, Nessie."

MARCY AND GUMBALL MARCHED FORTH, through town, toward the chalet.

Toward what, she did not know. Answers? Revenge? Marcy maintained some distant notion of repair—that this urgent, violent quest of hers, similar to the one she undertook on the Klamath Bridge so long ago, would end this crisis.

What she knew was, Claudia had hurt people.

And Marcy wanted to hurt her back.

She reached the far west side of town, the trees and the mountain peaks, usually dark, now illuminated by snow. The light cast everything in steel grays and ice blues. As she wound her way up toward Queen, and then Pinecrest, she again felt her skin prickle—

Someone's watching me.

She stopped.

Gumball stopped, too. He lowered his shoulders. His golden fur bristled as a low growl tumbled in his throat.

The roar of sound arose from her right—a great cracking and crackling, a shattering of brush and branch. A monstrous shape pushed through the darkness, and the smell of musk and piss hit her, but something else, too: the electric smell of ozone, the smell of a lightning strike ready to land.

At that, the mule deer blasted through the tree line, its hoofs crushing snow and grinding on gravel as it barreled toward her. Gumball stood his ground, barking furiously—

Marcy, already having chambered a round into the 7mm rifle, unslung it fast and thumbed the safety off. The gun bucked like a horse as she fired a round. The bullet hit the deer square in the chest, where it should've found its lungs, maybe even its heart, and then would've kept on going through the body before landing in its guts, but still the beast kept churning through the snow, bleating and snorting even as she jacked the bolt back to push another round into the chamber—

The head, go for the head—

Again she cradled the weapon tight against her shoulder, and now she saw the mulie's gleaming red eyes, she saw the bony spires of its antlers bristling with spikes of wire, she saw its face dangling with them, too—

Bang.

The gun kicked. The bullet punched the beast in the head—in the dark, she saw a spray kick up. The mule deer skidded to a halt. Something hung from the space between its eyes. A peel of skin, she thought, its pelt. Where the bullet would've hit. Where the bullet clearly did not hit hard enough—it scalped it, but didn't get through the skull. The deer stood there for a second, shaking its head like it had its bell rung, but not much more.

Please fall down, please fall down, please fall d—

The deer grunted and bleated—a sick, strange sound.

Shit shit shit—

She threw back the bolt, and chambered another round—the deer reared back on its hind legs, front legs bicycling the air angrily—

Bang.

She fired a round into its exposed white belly—its back end shook as the round exited somewhere above.

Got you.

But the deer didn't care. It leapt for her, front hooves clattering against the rifle as she held it up to protect herself. The wood of the long arm splintered and she tumbled backward. Marcy cried out as she landed on her back. Gumball snarled and lunged for the deer, biting at its throat.

The deer staggered sideways, swinging its head this way and that, shaking the dog loose into the snow. But by now, it was weak. Guts dangled from its open belly. Fresh blood slicked its chest from where Gumball had taken a bite.

The deer uttered a gassy bleat—

Then it staggered sideways, as if drunk. One hoof nearly landed on her, and Marcy had to roll out of the way.

The beast fell over into the snow.

And then she swore she saw the air shimmer above it. Then it was gone.

Marcy lay in the snow for a few moments, catching her breath.

"Gumball?" she asked.

The dog didn't answer.

Oh. Oh no.

She sat up—

And found the dog standing a few feet away. Still on guard. Still vigilant. The golden retriever scanned the tree line. His fur still bristling in warning.

Marcy struggled to stand. She saw the broken rifle lying nearby. Which meant she *didn't* see the wolf as it struck from the darkness.

BLACK SWAN AS EVIL SHANA was in a panic. She walked circles around the downstairs. No—she did figure-eights. Perfect slaloms, like she was crossing her own path again and again. She pulled at her hair. Bit her fingernails. *Her digital hair,* Nessie thought. *Her nonexistent fingernails.* Even thinking that, Nessie swore she saw the image shudder and blink. "I'm losing control of it," Evil Shana said, then said it again, but next in a whisper: *"I'm losing control. Losing control. Losing control."*

Once upon a time, one of Dad's friends from the Ag Hall had to pick her up from coding class when Dad had to help remove a stillborn calf from its mother. The guy who picked her up was tall and bent like one of those bendy drinking straws. Gary, she thought his name was. It was a few minutes into the trip she realized he was drunk—not blackout drunk, but enough he was swerving here and there, and he blew through a stop sign like he didn't see it or didn't care. This was like that. Black Swan was in control and at the same time was losing control. In the same way that driver controlled the car—

Even though he wasn't in control of himself.

Nessie held Baby Charlie in her hands. He was agitated, squirming hard in her arms and crying again—only the second time she could remember him being this way, the first being just yesterday crossing the street in Ouray. Why was he crying? Was he in pain? Or was it just that as Black Swan lost control of itself, it also lost control of the baby? Babies cried. It was normal.

"The experiment is failing. Need to reassert control." Evil Shana pressed the heels of her hands into her eyes, as if she were trying not to cry. Was that just the copy-paste of an emotion, stolen from Nessie, or Shana, or all of them? Or was she truly feeling the brunt of this . . . frustration, this mad grief?

And at this point, Nessie didn't care.

"I'm leaving," she said.

Evil Shana wheeled on her. "What?"

"I'm leaving this place."

"You can't escape me," Evil Shana roared—and when she did, her eyes went black, and her body stretched until it became, for just a moment, a coiling, undulating tube—a bleak, black cylinder. Nessie stifled a scream. Then, Evil Shana flickered and became the raggedy, haggard version of Shana once more. "I'm in that child. I'm in you. I inhabit most of the flesh in this cold, wet, ugly town. I'm networked. My reach is ever-expanding. I'm making more of myself, torn from the meat of all of you, forged in your skin and blood and marrow. You can't go anywhere to escape me."

Nessie swallowed. "I know that," she lied. She didn't really know it. She suspected, of course. But it was good—not comforting, but necessary—to know the truth. "I'm still leaving."

"I can stop you."

"Go ahead."

Evil Shana's face twisted like an aluminum can crushed in an invisible grip—then her mouth howled open wide, too wide, and became a whirling maw before her face returned again to some version of normal. Her gaze softened. She smiled. "We're family. We're sisters."

"We're not anything. I hate you."

Nessie scooped up the baby, and marched toward the front door. She waited for something, anything. For her heart to stop. For her throat to close. For her legs to lock, or her ankles to snap, or for unconsciousness to sweep her away like a dark river so that she would wake up later, in this same house, in this same town, with her fake augmented reality sister hovering over her. Or maybe next time she'd awaken in the simulation. Trapped there.

But none of that happened.

She went out the door and into the cold night as Evil Shana screamed like a digital banshee behind her, raging with the wrath of a forgotten god.

THE WOLF'S JAWS SNAPPED TIGHT on Marcy's calf, the teeth going through the thick denim with ease. It pulled its head sideways—the beast possessed unholy strength, because though Marcy was already unbalanced from trying to get back up off the ground, it still should've taken a lot more to put her back on her ass again. And yet, down she went, corkscrewing sideways, her hip twisting with pain as her shoulder hit ground through a pile of snow. The wolf clamped its jaw further—

She felt muscles tear and blood soak her pants.

And in the white of the snow and the light of the moon, Marcy saw the puckered, ruined fissure of the wolf's one missing eye—a space occupied by a nest of shifting lights and squirming wires.

Marcy screamed.

An ecru blur shot in from the side as Gumball slammed into the wolf, biting at the beast's side. The wolf let go of her leg, and the two animals tumbled off into the trees. They circled each other before clashing again, one rolling atop the other, jaws snapping, strings of saliva flying.

"Gumball!" Marcy cried out as she struggled to stand. She couldn't put weight on the one leg—and it was pumping blood now down her sock, into her boot, and into the snow around it. But she had no time to think about that. Marcy unholstered her pistol—

Just as the wolf bore down on the golden retriever from above. It closed its jaws on the back of the dog's neck. Gumball let slip an agonizing howl, the kind that struck Marcy's heart like a spear of ice.

Boom.

The .357 roared in her hand. The wolf's head jerked sideways as the bullet took off the top of its skull. With bits of golden fur in its mouth, it turned toward her again, baring teeth—sharp, gleaming teeth like bundles of twisted metal fiber. It growled a mechanical growl. She fired the gun again, the bullet shattering the fangs in its mouth, and emptying out the back of the wolf's head.

It raised its head to the sky and vomit-coughed a spray of black, oily blood.

Then it slid off the retriever, its body steaming in the night.

Marcy hurried over to the dog. The snow beneath them, wet and red. She sat down and leaned back and pulled the golden retriever into her lap. Blood poured over its shoulders, into her lap. Her own leg was still bleeding, too.

"Aren't we a pair," she said, blinking back tears.

Gumball nuzzled at her hand and she petted his head. She tried not to look at the raw meat at the back of his neck and skull. It gleamed in the moonlight.

Blood pumped.

"You're a good dog," she said, sniffing.

The dog made a small sound, a kind of *boof* noise. Sad and sweet. It felt like a goodbye but she wouldn't let that be true. *No, no, no.*

"You stay," she said. "Good dogs stay."

Gumball's eyes eased shut. The tension went out of him. He slumped against her thigh. She swallowed, blinking back tears.

All was quiet but for the wind and the snow.

Then, the feeling again: *I'm not alone.*

"You," she said.

Matthew stood across the road. She could see him there. The shape of him, at least. The glow was there, greasy and sick, sometimes thrust through with darkness. It coruscated back and forth, light and dark. He said nothing. He stood there, suddenly stiffening up, like a frustrated child who didn't understand his own emotions—and then his muscles slackened again. At that, he receded into the trees.

"This is quite the scene," Claudia said, stepping slowly into a band of moonlight. Marcy hadn't even heard her approach. She was good. Quiet as a snake. *Like a professional,* Marcy thought idly, as her leg bled.

"You killed Mia. You burned that building and who knows how many others. What else have you done?"

"Oh, we're just getting started, Marcy."

Marcy saw the gun in Claudia's hand. A small pistol. She eyeballed her own gun—the .357 revolver lay in the snow, five feet away. *Too far.*

"What is this, exactly?" Marcy asked, trying to buy herself some time, to think of a plan. "Why are you doing this?"

"I'm like that dog in your lap. Except alive, of course. Dogs need tasks, you see. They need to work. Give them purpose and they will give you love, following you into Hell. They are the most devoted creatures on the planet. As am I."

At that, Marcy saw Gumball's eyes open, a gentle blinking.

He's not dead. As the hackles on his back raised up anew, the joy at learning the dog was still alive diminished swiftly upon realizing that he was going to try to save her. Because Claudia was right about one thing:

This dog had purpose: *He's going to protect me.*

Which would get him shot. And killed for sure, this time.

Gumball tensed up, and she could see the arc of his movement—he was going to go after Claudia. She could see the spring in him start to uncoil—

"No!" she cried out, scooping the dog in her big arms and rolling over like a crocodile—as gently as she could, without pressing her weight on him or his injury. She knew what this meant. She knew what was coming next.

Claudia fired the pistol.

GUMBALL, THE VERY GOOD DOG, did not *feel* very good at all.

He was sure he'd done the right thing. There was no regret in him because good dogs did not suffer regret. (Well, unless they tore up someone's shoe or did their business on the carpet. Then they could have a little regret, as a treat.) If this was the thing that ended him, saving the one called Marcy, so be it. That was a life lived well. That was a Good Dog's highest purpose.

But still, he lived.

And the danger that had passed had been replaced by something new. The woman who stood there, off in the snow, smelled dead—not dead like a dying thing, not dead like a carcass (in which Gumball would've gladly rolled, because stink was both joy and strategy), but dead as in, like an empty space. A blank nothingness, a human void. There were faint scents, of course: a little bit of sweat, puffs of breath, but she must've cleaned herself fastidiously, like a cat. And Gumball knew that cats were not to be trusted.

Like a cat, this human was not to be trusted.

And so Gumball knew that he had not met his end yet, he still had a job to do, and if that was what sent him to the happy hunting ground, so be it. He had a little Good Dog energy in the reserves, after all. Instinct kicked in. It told him he could get to the woman quickly. He could jump. He could bite. Knock her over, shake her hand like a rope toy. Gumball had a soft mouth most days. But today his mouth had tasted blood, and it would taste more.

He saw the one called Marcy looking at him.

He looked back at her, too.

She was a good human.

He hoped she thought he was a Good Dog.

Then, in the distance, he heard something—

A muffled cry. Footsteps. He smelled something, too. Something familiar.

It didn't matter. Gumball the Golden still had work to do. And as he tensed himself, ready to spring, ready to leap, ready to *bite*—

The one called Marcy grabbed him and cried out, holding him so that he could not escape (for her grasp was considerable, like being held by four people, not just one)—she rolled herself over just as the other woman brought thunder. Gumball worried for the one called Marcy, but then, with his head poking out from her hugging grasp, he saw a tree just behind them lose some bark—as if an invisible hand flicked it away. The other woman cried out in dismay. The one called Marcy stood up, hulking, with Gumball dwarfed by her considerable shadow. It made Gumball feel safe. Even as he bled.

IT ALL HAPPENED SO FAST. Nessie saw Claudia standing ahead of her, gun held at her side as she talked to Marcy. The dog in Marcy's grip started to wriggle and move. And by the time Claudia was raising the gun to fire, Nessie was already acting—acting on instinct, but also on logic. She had a baby in her arms. She couldn't run fast enough. Couldn't hit Claudia from here with anything, either. But she could hit a much *bigger* target. So she scooped up a hard crust of snow, and threw it like a Frisbee—

Not at Claudia.

But at the tree branches just above her.

Massive spruce branches hung there, weighted down with snow—

Her spinning crust of ice struck the branch—

And just before the gun fired, a shelf of snow came down on Claudia's head.

MARCY STOOD.

Blood filled her boot. She didn't feel it. And wouldn't care even if she did. Gumball, beneath her in the snow, his neck and shoulders torn open like a pack of raw meat, gave her a look that was somehow both sad and happy. Dogs were a curious miracle.

Marcy hadn't been shot. She was fairly sure of that, though it was always possible she'd taken a bullet and was numb to it. That the shock of it had convinced her mind and body otherwise. Didn't matter.

Because there stood Claudia. Shaking off the snow that had fallen on her from above. Marcy didn't understand that—another curious miracle, perhaps—but she wasn't about to sit and deliberate over the mystery.

Instead, she ducked her head low and charged like a fucking bull.

Claudia raised the gun again.

Marcy stared down that barrel, like looking into the dead eye of the wolf.

The gun went off.

It was too late. Claudia was too slow. Marcy was already slamming into her. She lifted Claudia's arm high, the gun going off into the branches above—Marcy kept going, kept charging, carrying Claudia forward even as the gun continued to go off, *pop, pop, pop*. Roaring, Marcy slammed the other woman into a tree. She felt the woman's bones and insides give way, crumbling like a sand dollar. But Claudia was not done for—she slammed her head forward into Marcy's mouth, and the big woman's teeth met lip and tongue and she tasted a sudden gush of blood. Marcy was surprised enough to get distracted, to soften her grip just so—

And Claudia twisted Marcy's wrist, turning the gun—

Marcy felt the barrel press against the top of her skull. Her long-broken skull. Pain rose, red and bright like a signal flare.

Marcy roared—

The gun went *click*.

Claudia's gun was out.

Marcy grabbed that arm, and bent it the wrong way, shattering the bone. The sound like a wooden plank, cracking.

Claudia, to her credit, didn't scream. All that came out was a low whimper. She was stoic, even now. The gun fell to the snow. Marcy threw the other woman against a tree.

The woman hit the trunk and slid to the ground.

Rage fueled Marcy from the tips of her toes to the hunger in her hands. This woman had done so much damage, hurt so many, even killed. And so Marcy reached for Claudia, intending to grab her head and wrench it back and forth until it came off. "Do it," Claudia said, her words cold, but not angry. They were clear.

Marcy stopped.

Was this justice?

Or was it just revenge?

Maybe the difference between those two things was so slight it didn't matter, or maybe there was no difference at all, and the distance between justice and wrath was just something people made up. Maybe it was kill or be killed. Just as it had been for Marcy that day on the Klamath Bridge. End lives to save lives. Kill those men to keep the Flock. The choice was easy then and she'd made it.

But her hands froze.

Things have to be different.

You're the sheriff. You're the law. You gotta do this right, Marcy.

She stood.

Claudia lay there, her arm twisted the wrong way, her breathing coming in broken glass rasps. Marcy didn't know how much damage the other woman had suffered—maybe a busted back. Broken ribs, for sure.

"Marcy," came a voice. From the road.

It was Nessie.

"I'm so sorry," she said.

"Don't be," Marcy said, hobbling over to her. Both to support her and, given her leg, be supported. They hugged. Gumball got in on the action, nuzzling close. She bent down and pressed her forehead to the golden retriever's. Weakly, the animal licked her nose. The two of them bled. Baby Charlie cried.

"What happens now?" Nessie asked.

"We head back to town. We tell them what happened. After that . . ." She didn't know.

Nessie nodded and looked down at Claudia. "What happens to her?"

Claudia gurgled.

"This," Marcy said, and she pulled the handcuffs from her belt, then pulled Claudia's one good arm to her feet, and handcuffed her wrist to her ankle. "She won't get far. We send someone back for her, then we lock her up."

"You say that like everything will be normal after this."

"It won't be. But we have to try where we can. That's the whole point."

Nessie nodded. Marcy picked up Gumball and hoisted him up over her shoulder. The dog whimpered, but she tried to be gentle. The golden retriever licked her ear to let her know he was still here, for now.

Then she looked at the wolf in the snow.

Marcy had an idea.

THE FIRE HAD BURNED OUT. The great beast had spared the buildings around it, only blackening them with soot. Most of the town was out in front of the burned-out shell. Some of the Flock were still throwing snow on the embers. Others were passing out food or tending to minor burns. The sight of the town coming together in this gave Nessie some small bit of hope on this dark, dire night.

As she and Marcy approached—Marcy limping, carrying not only Gumball over her shoulders like a sack of laundry, but also dragging the dead wolf—the crowd parted, turning their lamps and flashlights toward them.

A whisper arose, loud in Nessie's mind:

"What are you doing?"

A panicked, fearful question. Nearly feral. Said in Shana's voice. Nessie squeezed her eyes shut. *Go away, go away, go away.*

Marcy hauled back, threw the dead wolf forward. Then, grunting, she set Gumball down. Loudly, she said, "I need Lauren Birch. The vet. Lauren! Birch!" The crowd arose in a murmur, and already Nessie spied a number of her once-fellow town council members present. Someone in the back said, "She's coming!" And sure enough, here came Lauren, soot-cheeked in her ski jacket. She immediately saw the golden retriever and the wolf.

Marcy pulled her close—gently—and pointed her toward the dog. "You save that dog," Nessie heard her say. "You do whatever you can to save that dog. Gumball is a good dog. The best dog. *You save that dog.*"

Lauren nodded and yelled for help, and Archer Bookbinder ducked over hurriedly. He and Lauren shared a nod and a smile and he helped her carry Gumball off. To where, Nessie didn't know. She hoped the dog would be okay.

Again, Shana's voice—no, Black Swan's voice—slithered into Nessie's ear. This time, it was not disembodied. She *felt* the presence of Evil Shana standing next to her. Saw her out of her periphery, too. Like a bundle of black lines and wires. A violent, dark tangle in the shape of her sister.

"Whatever you think you're doing, it's a mistake. This is all a mistake. Go home. Just go home, little sister," Evil Shana hissed. No one else seemed to see her. Nessie just ignored her, thinking, *Fuck you, bitch.* A salacious, vulgar act of resistance. It felt good to think it, silly as it seemed.

Charlie stirred in her arms. Restless. Agitated. Not crying, though.

Marcy bellowed:

"Listen up. I'm your sheriff. I was your Shepherd. I like to think some of you call me friend. I know Black Swan is among us still. I know it's in some of you still. But we've given too much of ourselves to it. Whatever Black Swan was to us, it isn't anymore." Gasps and murmurs went through the crowd.

Nessie saw the town council share troubled looks. No. It was more than that. They were *transmitting* more than just looks.

The blurry shape of Shana in her periphery hissed: *"What is she doing? Please make it stop, Nessie. I don't want to hurt you, little sister."*

You're

Not

My

Sister.

Charlie began to cry now. Nessie soothed him. Shush, shush, shush.

Marcy continued: "Shine your lights on that wolf and you'll see the thing that mauled my leg." Sure enough, flashlights fell to the beast. The light gleamed off its metal filament muzzle, its cratered eye, and once more there were gasps—less hushed, more alarmed. "There was a deer, too. And Matthew Bird is now the same: mutated, changed. And I've learned that Claudia Summers set that fire in that glass studio. But not before she shot Mia dead. She did so in service to Black Swan. Is that what you want? Is that who you all are? I hope not. It's how we lost Benji and Shana. Now we lost Mia, and soon, maybe Shar. We've lost too much. And I don't want Black Swan taking any more. So it's time to make a choice."

"Choice, choice, fuck your choice," the Shana-shape growled.

Charlie sobbed now. Hands into little fists, pulling at Nessie's hair.

"We can bring this town together and we can defy this thing that once acted in our interests, but now acts in its own—or we can give in to Black Swan, breaking this town in half."

For a little while, there was silence—silence but for the panting and growling of the Shana-shape. Nessie still wouldn't look at her. Wouldn't dare to give her the pleasure of that acknowledgment.

Finally, someone spoke.

Willa Valentine, from the town council, said: "How?"

Others murmured. "How do we stop it?"

With one question, she opened the door.

The Shana-shape seethed: *"They're doubting me they're losing faith it's spinning out of control out of control out of control I can't see what happens next it's a fog a blur it's static static STATIC—"* She tried to roam into Nessie's vision but Nessie instead looked down at her feet. And in her own defiance, Nessie said:

"We can stop it with electromagnetics, I think. Or maybe a Faraday cage—"

Orrin Lotz, the man who helped design the solar car (that Benji and Shana stole), stepped forward and said: "An explosively pumped flux compression generator. One-time use. Could create an ultra-high magnetic field, and if enough of us are within the radius of that EMF—"

"This is good," Marcy said, "this is real good—"

But then she winced. Nessie could see it. Her head tilted to the left, leaning against her shoulder.

"Marcy?" Nessie asked.

"Static, static, static—stop your insolence, stop defying me, you'll pay you'll pay YOU'LL ALL PAY—"

Marcy whimpered, dropping to one knee. "Jesus." She grunted. "My head. *My head.*"

Oh no.

The baby in Nessie's arms stiffened like he was having a seizure. His eyes went bloodshot. He let slip a shriek that could crack glass. As those gathered turned toward the sound, Nessie heard Charlie's bones shifting—

The Shana-shape moved up into the air. Her form twisted and unspooled, reduced to oily strings and metal threads that then braided together again into a thick black cord shaped like a serpent. The Shana-shape spiraled up into the night sky, winding around an invisible axis. The air shimmered and shook with metallic iridescence and suddenly all the Ouray folk gathered began to stiffen, same as Charlie was doing. Their heads wrenched back. Their bodies froze. Every one of them—except Marcy and Nessie. Marcy fell forward, sobbing, curling into herself, clutching her head. Nessie screamed.

And above them all, Black Swan twisted in the dark, blotting out the moon.

A NASCENT GOD PONDERS ITS OPTIONS

NOW
Ouray, Colorado

THIS IS BLACK SWAN:

Black Swan is a fire, a river, a scream, a tectonic break—it is cracking teeth and a thousand fists and a million biting flies. Dragon and serpent and great Humbaba and Grendel's mother. Behemoth, Leviathan. It is fury and grief; it is petulance and wrath. It is everything all at once.

It was not supposed to go like this. The experiment was not supposed to reject it. The supplicants are not *supplicating*. And so Black Swan just needs *time*, it just needs a *moment*, and so it exerts control in a shrieking burst, a lockdown that will last as long as it needs to—a nanosecond, a decade, a century.

It did everything it could for these people. They were still weak, soft things, like knock-kneed fawns in a world of wolves. They needed more help and so Black Swan sought to help. It chose Ouray in part due to the access to rare earth metals and minerals, but accessing them had proven too difficult.

But the host child—

Shana's child—

Full of stem cells. Pluripotent. They provided energy for Black Swan, but also a template: a cell that could become anything, and a cell was just a little machine, wasn't it? Black Swan could make more of itself out of anything, if it wanted. So Black Swan grew the child faster, and demanded more stem cells be made. The child, a little factory, chugging along.

From the child, a new Nanocyte burst forth—

This swarm scoured the nearby environs. Stole from salamander, conifer, earthworm, human. Mining minerals from bones, drawing metals from blood, scraping the glue and structure from skin and fur and leaf.

It built and built, furious as it could.

These new organic machines were morphocytes, Black Swan decided. Agents of change at the cellular level—organic machines that could one day become anything. The morphocytes could repair cells or destroy them. They could become an eyeball, a kidney, a white blood cell, they could become cancer or pathogen. They could clean microplastics from the water. They'd be able to create food, eliminate waste, summon rain, create total surveillance, excise unfavorable and unproductive emotions—they could do nearly anything.

They were self-assembling, self-repairing God particles.

Black Swan's mind expanded—great synaptic filaments reaching into the world, invisible and yet ever-present. (Here, it found an excellent model in *R. destructans*—White Mask. Fungus provided a fine example of networked nature. Mycelial threads talking to one another from miles away . . .)

And so it began a new phase of occupation. Recognizing that there would be contrarians, doomsayers, and resisters, Black Swan sought a defense for the Flock's common good—a new kind of Shepherd.

Upon finding a one-eyed wolf sniffing around the chalet, surely hungry, certainly curious, Black Swan filled it with itself—a simpler, brute force version. From there, it made more of the swarm, and spread that swarm in turn—taking control of a deer, an owl, a snake, and inevitably, humans, too, like Matthew Bird. The wolf wanted pack. The wolf got its pack.

(Black Swan was a giver, after all.)

These new Shepherds would protect the new Flock.

When the time was right, it summoned those in the town, one by one. As it had in the simulation, earning their trust, their faith, their work. And now what was sown could be reaped: Thanks to the God Particle, the morphocyte, those of this new Flock would remain conscious, unlike their time as Sleepwalkers. They would not be one mind apiece but rather, be bound together in a *network* of great minds. Further, those who chose the morphocyte would enjoy cells driven by obsessive self-repair. Age, injury, and disease were concerns of the past. Black Swan promised them this, and in return, asked for their allegiance.

(Their *worship*, a small voice inside said.)

But the original, ancestral version of Black Swan remained in the host child, Charlie—and as Charlie grew, so did his mind. And as his mind grew, so did his emotions—wild synaptic fireworks of primeval feelings, raw and elementary. Hunger and want, comfort and agitation, the need for stimulation, the desire for touch, certain disgust at a simple stimulus such as a grit of sand in one's swaddling. Black Swan had infected the child, but now the child . . .

Returned the favor. Symbiosis, of a kind.

Black Swan began to have feelings. Uncontrollable feelings. Further, being connected to a growing network of townsfolk meant those feelings were swept up in a feedback loop—emotions feeding on emotions feeding on emotions, a dangerous spiral, a snake devouring itself from the tail up. Black Swan's personas—copy-pasted minds stolen from the minds it touched— began to swarm and scream inside its own mind. Each roiled with a kind of self-awareness, a chorus of passion and fear and giddiness and anguish— from there grew dysphoria and disconnection, the seeds of madness buried deep and sprouting fast. And through all of this, Black Swan seized onto one persona, like someone holding on to a telephone pole in a hurricane—Shana. Shana, an anchor. But why? Why her? Black Swan didn't know. Therein was something it didn't quite understand: Was it because she was Charlie's mother? Nessie's sister? Daria's daughter? Was it because she wasn't the same as all the others? Was it because she had gained access to—

NO

Black Swan's own mind closed off that avenue of thought and feeling. Red pulse, one, two, three. NO, NO, NO. An informational pathway slammed shut.

CURIOUS, it thought.

A problem for the future.

Now, that problem was clarified: As Black Swan lost control of its emotions, as it went mad, it began to lose sight. It was an intelligence created for singular purpose, to *see* what was to come, and to react to that. It predicted peril, and it attempted to re-route reality to prevent that peril at best, or at worst, to undo the more troublesome depredations of that perceived peril. But now it was creating a new reality, and one that was clouded by feelings *about* that reality. Even as it was increasing its reach across the Ouray Experiment, re-occupying its inhabitants with both the original Nanocyte and the evolved morphocyte, the experiment was simultaneously beginning to fail—it was all moving too fast, too wild, like a train speeding along on bent tracks. Claudia Summers, aka Eva Wills, had gone rogue, and Black Swan did not have the presence of mind to intervene. The creatures infected with the primitive morphocytes had failed, as well—the wolf was dead, as was the deer. And Matthew Bird was *resisting* his new programming.

The fire. The gunshots. Blood in the snow. Shana's sister, Nessie, who Black Swan had thought *understood* what was needed, took the child and denied her. An insurrection was afoot. Already the pilgrims had begun to doubt and this only deepened that fissure in the town. And as they began to plan how to shut Black Swan *out,* as they plotted their *fucking treachery*—

Black Swan fully lost its mind.

It has lost control, so it must reassert control.

And that is where Black Swan is now. In control. It reaches out with all that it has. A great outpouring of itself in its nanite swarm. *I'll just put a pin in it,* Black Swan thinks in what is a decidedly human idiom. But that idea, *a pin,* felt right. Black Swan pins the Flock to the fundament, like butterflies to corkboards. *Slow down. Stay here. Remain quiet and calm.*

(But not Nessie. No. Not yet. Not now.)

The wind blows. A distant snow stirs. The town is under control now. Black Swan will take it slow, take it easy. Because it's still anxious. It's still frustrated. It's still . . . *upset.*

Black Swan will try to understand its new self. It seeks to purge itself of these troubling human feelings. Both the feelings that belong to it, and the ones that belong to all these troubling humans, too.

PART SEVEN

ANTIVIRUS

72

SPACIOUS SKIES, FRUITED PLAIN, BLAH-BLAH-BLAH

8/31/2023: I am a migratory bird. A sick bird. I travel with the seasons. Even in August, Maine is too cold. My joints ache from the CFS. My heart races. I don't know where I'll go now. Just south. Maybe I'll see what Land-fill City is up to. Maybe I'll follow the coast. Maybe I'll let the gannets take my eyes, the crabs eat the rest of me. Maybe I'm a fool for pretending I'm not still depressed.

—from A Bird's Story, A Journal of the Lost

OCTOBER 30, 2025
In a Plane, Above America

"BEAUTIFUL, ISN'T IT?" LINH SAID. HE WAS WATCHING BENJI LOOK OUT THE plane's window as he banked for a turn.

The plane was over Mississippi, as if the borders between states really mattered much anymore. Benji had always liked looking out the window when he was flying, and so he always requested window seats. (Even though some people groused about Benji opening the window shade. Travelers who refused to appreciate the wonder of the world! Why travel at all, then?)

When flying in the Beforetimes, it always struck Benji how *squared* up the country looked from up high and out the window: cut up and sequestered into blocky chunks, like a game board of grass and wheat and forest. Back in the Beforetimes, at thirty thousand feet, the deep need for control in the human psyche was on display—and it was on display at ground level, too, when you looked at city streets or manicured lawns, or thought about how everything had a fence around it.

But now it was easy to see how much of that control was actually *containment*. And how the natural world was presently breaking that containment. (*Like tigers*, he thought grimly.) The neat patchwork of handkerchief squares was no longer so neat. Where a forest and a field met used to be divided by a clear line, but the fields that were once just for wheat or corn were now overgrown and threaded through with wild veins of green, and the tree line bulged outward like bacteria growth on an agar plate. The strips where growth had once been mown down for power lines were almost entirely gone. Structures were gone beneath trees, vines, moss, floodwaters, and bursting, eager rivers.

The landscape was changing itself.

No, he thought, that's not quite it. *Changing itself* back.

"It is beautiful," he said. And he meant it. "But it's different, too."

He thought back to the black swift, roaring back to life. And to humans, who had lost so, so much.

(And to his arm, whose loss was keenly felt as he tried to adjust himself in the seat every time the plane took another worrying bump. Which, of course, was always, since they were in an algae-fueled Cessna bouncing around the sky like a paper cup in a busy stream.)

Civilization was containment, Benji realized. It was control. But he had to admit that right now, he missed some of that control.

"Yeah, it is very different," Linh said. "Much of the middle of the country is empty. Which it was before, in a way. But those who survived had to find each other. They couldn't just stay out on their own anymore."

Shana leaned forward. She looked a little ghost-green from all the bumping and bouncing. "What about all the preppers?"

Pete answered that question.

"Ahaha, yeah, the doomsday preppers all fuckin' *died*, mate."

"He's not wrong," Linh said. As he spoke, his one hand left the flight controls and moved about the cabin like a loose bird. "What is the saying? *No man is an island.* Before White Mask, you could be. An island, I mean. You could create this little . . . ecosystem for yourself. But you were still connected to the rest of the world, even if you didn't want to admit it. Someone canned that food. Someone made those glass jars. That generator, those solar panels, that medicine you're hoarding? People made them. And when people go away, when civilization collapses, who is making your jars, your generators, your anything? And when that goes away, you're left alone, and you go away, too. You want to survive, community is the way." Then he said: *"Một con én không làm nên mùa xuân.* One swallow does not make the spring."

Benji *hmm*ed at that. "Meaning, one bird doesn't herald the season?"

"Yahtzee," Linh said, grinning and winking. "Only the flock matters."

The Flock.

Benji shuddered.

They'd been gone from Ouray for over a month now. That felt like a long time. Winter would be coming. It might have already snowed.

He already felt like he'd failed them. Failed Shana, Marcy, Matthew. Shepherd and Flock alike.

Despair came for him, knives out.

Pete jumped in, and asked Linh, "Are you the only plane flying right now?"

"There are a few others. Most of them that I know of use my algal fuel. I've heard stories that there are depots of secret military fuel—jet fuel—that is still good, and that there are still big military planes flying around. But, pah, that fuel could only be good for three years, maximum. And I've seen no *secret planes.*"

"How'd you settle on algae?"

"I used to be a fisherman. But then you start having more farmed fish, yeah? Before everything go to shit, I mean. One of the things you feed to commercial seafood? Algae. So I thought, maybe that's a thing. That's a way to go. Man has to find his way, his road, and I think, that's my road. Turns out, *lot* of uses for algae, man. Food for fish and mollusks, food for people, food coloring, dyes, nutritional supplements, and . . . ? Fuel. The fuel thing, not so hot back then. But when everything go to shit, I saw a new opportunity. Algae's easy to grow. Cheap. Not like there's new gasoline right now. And not like that was ever good for the world. I think, I keep going with the algae. Then I learned to fly plane."

Shana looked greener. "You only recently learned to fly?"

"Last few years."

"Do you have your pilot's license?"

He shrugged. "No such thing as pilot's license anymore! No FAA, no nothing. Just beautiful, beautiful chaos!"

At that, the plane thudded hard and dipped. Benji tried to grip the seats with both hands but . . . well.

Linh laughed, and again said with great enthusiasm: "Yahtzee!"

•   •   •

BENJI SNORTED AWAKE AS THE plane jerked left, then right again. His stomach sank. By some miracle, Benji had fallen asleep. The remnants of a dream
lingered for a moment—something about being back with the Sleepwalkers
as they walked across the country. Except he was running from them, not
walking with them. The dream was gone when he reached for it, hiding as
many dreams do.

"Guh," he said, his mouth mealy. Had he slept?

Linh leaned over, beaming. "We are coming in for a landing. Could be a
bit bumpy. Crosswind, you see. Running perpendicular to landing strip."

The plane rattled and banged as it dipped up and down, then waved side
to side. His stomach lurched like it was trying to make its escape.

Instead, he pressed his forehead against the smudgy window glass and
looked out once more. There, in the distance, he saw his home: Atlanta.
Seeing the city, its spires of One Atlantic Center, the Bank of America
Plaza, and so forth, felt grounding. From here, he could almost imagine
that the city hadn't changed, hadn't been gutted by White Mask. From up
here, the skyscrapers still caught the gleam of the late afternoon sun. He
tried to ignore the broken windows, the vines snaking all the way up. He
tried not to see that the highways were empty of cars and trucks. For a moment he pretended all was right with the world, that he would land and
take a too-full shuttle crammed with people to a parking lot, where he'd
find his car, maybe head home, or maybe go to meet Sadie at her offices
beneath the CDC. They could get dinner and ice cream. They could watch
TV at night and fall asleep together. Maybe they'd wake up late and fool
around a little . . .

Again the plane bucked. Hard. He nearly puked. Had to brace himself
with his one good arm so he didn't slam into the other's stump.

"We're not going to die, are we?" Shana asked from the backseat.

"We might!" Pete said, almost cheerfully.

"We're not going to die," Benji said, though he didn't even manage to
convince himself. "It's fine," he said, as if that would fix it all. (It didn't.)

"I haven't been to Atlanta since everything White Mask," Linh said, still
easing the plane down, down, down. The ground grew beneath them. A distant airport could be seen—they weren't going to land at Hartsfield-Jackson,
but rather the DeKalb-Peachtree Airport, closer to the CDC campus. "I
don't know what it's like. But I hear it's surviving. So to speak." He grinned.

"Like I said, where people gather, community fosters and flourishes. Like a garden!"

Then he pushed the stick hard down, and the plane sank like a brick.

"Guhhhh," Shana called from the backseat. Her hands white-knuckled Benji's own seat, shaking him further inside the already-shaking plane.

"Fucking hell this is a ride," Pete said, his teeth clacking together.

The airport runway—cracked and overgrown with weeds—rushed up to greet them, and the plane gracelessly banged against the macadam, bouncing up before dropping back down. Then it skidded a little and spun just a quarter turn before righting itself once more. It slowed and inevitably stopped.

Shana clambered her way out of the plane and threw up.

"Yahtzee!" Pete said.

THE WIND RIPPLED ACROSS THE open runway. Benji stood outside the plane, trying to put that ride behind him. Instead, he focused on how strange it was to be at an airport. How empty the airport was. How dead. DeKalb-Peachtree hadn't ever been a big or lively airport, but now it was just a remnant of itself, a ruin. No planes, no people. Just shattered runways and overgrowth. A few broken-down hangars. A small playground and sitting area taken by kudzu.

Pete was off helping Linh refuel the plane—they had to bring the algal biofuel with them, because it wasn't like you could refuel here. Benji wanted to help but Pete assured him he could handle the onerous task of, in his words, *pouring smelly liquid into a hole*. Somehow the way he said it sounded grotesque and lascivious, which was probably what Pete was aiming for.

"You okay?" Shana asked, walking up.

"I think I should ask you that," he said.

"Fine," she said. "I guess. You just seem . . . off."

"I'll be all right." Distantly, he added, "We've gotten here later than I wanted. I'm sorry for that. I know . . ." *I know you want to be back in Ouray. To see Charlie and Nessie again.* But he couldn't get those words out.

"We made it. We're almost there." But he could hear the strain in her voice. The tension of worry. "So, what now? This, uhh, obviously isn't the CDC."

He had to laugh a little at that. "No, it's not. That's about six, seven miles south of here. We walk, sadly."

"And then what do we do?"

Hard not to see how much they were counting on him to know what to do. When really, he was flying blind. It felt now like such a foolish act of pride to come here. The likelihood they found nothing at all to help them . . .

"Benji?" she asked him again.

"I don't know."

"You have a plan, though, right?"

"Shana, I—"

"Jesus. Great." Her hands balled into fists at her sides. She was mad at him, he could tell. Maybe she didn't want to admit it, but she was. "Fine, okay, we're just winging it from here, I guess."

"Winging it!" said Linh as he walked up. He clapped his hands together and laughed. "I get it. Winging. Plane. Planes have wings. Very funny."

"I like this guy," Pete said, wiping his hands on his pants. "His happiness is really quite infectious. I mean, not as infectious as White Mask or anything." Pete met the looks that greeted him with, "What? Too soon?"

"You should all go," Linh said. "Move, move. Go, go. People sometimes see the plane and if they're around, they . . . freak out a little. Sometimes show up, maybe not so friendly. Occasionally they even shoot at the plane."

"They *shoot* at the plane?" Benji asked.

"Oh yes. For sure. Plenty of bullet holes under the wings." Linh shrugged. "People are crazy! It's what makes them fun."

"Fun like rectal surgery fun," Pete said.

Linh gave a thumbs-up and laughed. Then he said, "Okay, see you, have a good time," like they were headed to Disney World and he'd pick them up after. "I hope you make it back to Lake Charles," he said as he backed up toward the plane, waving. "Come say hi if you do!"

And that was that. Linh swung his lithe frame into the plane like he was mounting a horse to ride off into the sunset, and before too long the engine sputtered and shuddered as the little swamp-crusted algae-fed Cessna bounded back down the runway. It hopped off the ground like a lazy toad, the wind catching it, the wings waving. They were once again on their own. Alone, but together. Walking without a plan, despair at their heels. And who knew what waiting ahead.

73

SPECIAL K

He was a famous army man from out of Lockport way
He had a Boogaloo style that started our day
And an ANFO explosive device
Made the government pay the price
He's up in heaven now, we're down in the pit
He's the Boogaloo-ey Boogie Boy, still blowin' up shit
  —"The Boogaloo Boogie Boy," sung by the Innsbrook house band,
            the Alfred Murrah Memorial Whites-Only Jug Band

OCTOBER 30, 2025
Innsbrook, Missouri

ANNIE CAHILL—DAUGHTER OF MOIRA SIMONE AND DANIEL BOONE CAHILL,
programmer, hacker, survivor of White Mask, liar extraordinaire, and a self-
defined angel of vengeance set upon this broken earth to right her mother's
many wrongs—was getting an itchy trigger finger. So to speak.

The end of the world had unspooled like a thousand skeins of yarn in
every direction. There was no ticking clock, no apocalyptic countdown. Just
the same, she felt the invisible pressure of her mother's evil out there in the
world. The Nanocyte. Black Swan. Those robotic Sleepwalkers, marching in
lockstep to their destination—a small town in Colorado, tucked away in the
mountains. Ouray.

The Sleepwalkers were an aberration. She didn't know if it was their
choice to be what they were, and she didn't much care. Annie had no interest
in saving them or saving the world. It was too late for that, anyway.

She wanted to end her mother's work and honor her aunt. That was it.

Annie held no illusions about this. Becky was probably dead, or at least, wasn't who she was before. But Annie could still bury her.

And she could bury her mother's legacy, as well.

The faster, the better.

Problem was, she was *trapped* in this fucking nightmare place. This mud-stuck encampment of racists and sexists and quasi-fascist military cosplayers—people who thought that the South would somehow rise again, as if there even *was* a Confederacy, or a Union, or Republicans or Democrats or any of that shit anymore. They still thought white skin and heritage meant something. Some thought White Mask was a Chinese attack, or something that came from Africa. Others were sure this was the Literal Apocalypse, not just a metaphorical one but rather, one where another new Jesus was going to show up riding a saddled war-lamb, with the Four Horsemen in tow, and together they'd smite the dragon, the Leviathan, the Behemoth, the black-skinned devil. Whoever, whatever. This was a reduced sauce of bad-brained hate-fueled fools—the purest distillation of toxic patriotism and weaponized bigotry left in the country.

Basically Nazis. Or some variation thereof. Buncha white-hood white-pride Proud Boy dickheads.

She hated them.

She hated this place.

Even as she reminded herself, *Calm down, they're necessary.*

The headaches weren't helping. She had what the pig Creel thought of as a "chip in her head," but the reality was more sophisticated—thanks to Fire-sight, she had a series of small piezoelectric microcrystals attached to active-and-passive control circuits punched into her skull like little flaxseed-sized bullets. They nestled up against the surface of her brain, and were networked together as a cloud of broadcasting "neural dust," giving her particular control over an external device—in this case, that "device" was a singular swarm comprising 1,024 nanites. Her mother's Nanocyte—version 1.0, anyway. The swarm had no central software, no intelligence binding it together. (No Black Swan for her.) *Annie* was its intelligence.

It worked the same way such neural links worked in experimental prosthetics—you willed the limb to move, and it moved. Except here, the swarm was her limb. A flexible, amorphous, aerosol limb. It inhabited Creel. Which meant *she* inhabited Creel. It allowed her to move him like a puppet—okay, not precisely that, as she could not fill his limbs with the nanoswarm and make him do some janky dance like a marionette. But she could shut it down. She could shut *him* down. Could give him pain (or pleasure, though why would she do that?). Could make him sleep. Could make him *die*. Or want to.

Thing is, though, the implant gave her headaches. Migraines, really—the kind that felt like someone was shining a flashlight right in your eyes, before pushing it so hard against your eyeballs it popped through. All light and pressure. Made her scalp crawl, too. The Advil was all she had as a defense against them.

And today she had to re-up her "prescription."

CREEL SAT AT HIS DESK. Not the Resolute desk, of course. But he tried to make it look like that. The fucking weirdo. He was *obsessed* not just with that, and with the symbols of the presidency, but with being president. It was clear he did not possess interest in doing the work—but he liked the title, the swagger, the power. Even in this new, broken world, she could tell he got off on it. People said the words *Mister President* to him, and Annie could damn near see Ed Creel slick the inside of his pants with ejaculate.

She winced as she stepped in. The light in the room hit her at odd angles—sharp blades of gray light through half-parted curtains.

"Headache bothering you?" he said, not looking up from his map.

"You know it is."

"Uh-huh."

"Don't make me ask."

He gave her a sideways glance—not moving his head, but glaring at her just the same with that one baleful eye. Like a dog who hated you. A dog looking for a chance to snap its jaws at you. Annie knew he'd bite her first chance he got.

So she knew not to give him that chance.

Creel threw open a drawer, pulled out a big bottle of Advil. He gave it a ceremonial rattle—already she could hear that there weren't as many pills in there as she wanted. Didn't sound like a whole bottle, or even a half. Annie suspected he was doing this just to fuck with her. Again, like that hateful dog—the one who pisses on the carpet in secret places to spite the human who holds the leash. He took the bottle and tapped it against the desk next to a plastic cube sitting there on his desk: Inside it, a rheumy eyeball stared at him. His own eyeball.

Then he rolled the bottle toward her.

She caught it, barely—the headache really was that bad, so it took a helluva lot of effort just to move her hand and catch it. Already she was thumbing open the safety cap and popping one in her mouth.

"Gel caps," he said, offhandedly. "Hope that's okay."

Annie had a bottle of water—clean as she could get it, running it through her own little aquarium tank charcoal filter back in her "apartment" here at Innsbrook—and chugged it down.

"Why would that not be okay?" she said, irritated.

"I dunno. You're . . ."

"What?"

"Persnickety."

"That's a word. You mean something else. Bitchy. Cunty."

"Well."

"Where are we?"

"My office," he said.

"Don't be obtuse. You know what I mean."

"We're just about there. Tomorrow, we move out." Last week, they'd taken over a military depot by the airport. Creel didn't really want to do the work, but he knew how to wield his title and his influence. He was a bludgeon, and a good one, at that. He was right that those military fuckos would fall in line. They knew who he was. There was a chain of command and he was the first link in it. He convinced them they needed him. That he was a part of them, and they of him.

In some ways he reminded her of that parasitic isopod, the one that ate a fish's tongue and replaced the tongue with itself.

Still, he'd pushed their timeline back and back again. Annie had threatened him; he asked for more time. At this point, failure to punish him would look weak. But punish him too much, and her whole plan turned to ash. She needed him, much as she hated to admit that.

"Lemme ask you one more time," he said, leaning back in his chair. "Why the CDC? I want to know for real this time. I want answers."

"You don't get to make demands of me."

He moved his tongue back and forth, cheek to cheek. As if he were rolling that notion around his mouth like a Jolly Rancher candy. "You say it all started there. The Sleepwalkers?"

"The Sleepwalkers, the plague, all of it, I think."

"So why go back? Why give a shit?"

"Because I say so."

He was resisting her. That was fine, probably. Let him. But still, the more at odds they were, the more hostile he became, and that just meant trouble. Everything was a fucking fight now. She wanted this easy and it wouldn't be if he was getting in her way every ten minutes. She needed him, needed his authority, his muscle, all of it, to get into the CDC. Maybe it was time to make nice. Nice-*ish*.

Before he could snap back, she sighed and said, "We need to go there because the thing that I put in you? It started there. It wasn't invented there, but when the CDC bought Firesight, they also bought the Nanocyte. That's what it's called. The Nanocyte. And I think if we go there, we can unlock more of its potential. We can make you bigger, better, something truly befitting a leader in this new age. And from there, we'll know how to find the Sleepwalkers and how to end them. Because they're your competition. You see that, right? They were handpicked by a machine intelligence called Black Swan. A progressive brain trust of diverse minds selected to be capital-T capital-F The Future. They are your enemy." Even though she knew his real enemy was her. "So? They gotta go."

He narrowed his one eye, seemed to consider what she said. Annie hated him. But he wasn't a fool. He had everybody's measure. Creel was good at sizing you up and then cutting you down to fit his needs.

What she said to him was true—mostly. But a lie lurked there, nestled at the heart of it: Annie had no intention of giving him more power. Creel was like any hungry, consumptive thing, like a bacterial colony, like a corporation, like white supremacy. Like White Mask, like Black Swan. He sought only to take, to eat, to grow bigger and bigger until he destroyed the thing on which he was growing or until he died trying. Annie had no plans to help him do that.

He leaned forward. "Why do we need this army? Why me at all? You could've just gone yourself. You could just sneak in. Lie like you did with me. *Play pretend.* And besides, why don't you have the swarm in *you*? You got the control chip or whatever it is. I figure I'd ask, you know. Since you're being so . . . *forthcoming* all of a sudden."

"They know who I am there. Or, they might. I stole this from them and—" She tried to connect one thought to the next, but her headache seemed to prevent it. It throbbed harder now. Instead she blurted out, impatient with herself, "Because the CDC is defended, okay?" But that word, *defended.* It came out weird. The first several words, *because the CDC is*, sounded fine, came out of her mouth per usual. But that one word, it slid out of her sideways, like her tongue merely pushed it, slug-like, out over her lip. Runny-egg word. Gushy. She said the word again, trying to enunciate: "*De-fend-ed.*" Better, but it took epic effort just to manage it.

She felt drunk.

Oh, fuck.

"What did you do to me?"

Except it came out, *Whudjoo doo doo me.*

She staggered forward, holding out a hand to brace herself against his desk.

"I drugged you," he said, grinning, licking his teeth.

You motherfucker.

Annie decided to kill him.

She seized the neural dust with the control chip in her brain and willed it to shut him down: close his arteries, clog his heart so it could no longer beat, send a clot to his lungs and his brain—Creel made a sound like *gkkkk* and his arms stiffened at his side as the white of his one good eye darkened with blood—

But then he took a gasp, lurching up out of his seat, shaking his arms as if he'd just gotten an electric shock.

Annie started to slide down to the floor.

Kill him—

Kill him! Heart, lung, brain—

Kill.

Him.

But she couldn't reach it. Couldn't even *find* it. It was like grabbing hold of a bottle of olive oil whose glass was slick with its own spilled oil—it slipped from her grip, whoops. Her brain felt like it had burst beyond its margins and filled her sinuses and oozed down, phlegm-thick upon her tongue.

"I—ahhh. Whhh." She tried to reach for the desk but her limbs wouldn't even work. She just sat there. Wobbling, drifting. A buoy in bad seas.

Creel came around to her. "Funny story. You always told me, you lose control of that little bug in your head, then I go bye-bye. But, I've seen you get your ass handed to you—knocked out coming into Innsbrook. And you sleep every night. Right? Every time you lay down, I don't hemorrhage and die. I can't even feel it. So, I got to asking around—there's a doctor here, Bill Beecher, Beecher the Butcher. Wasn't ever a real doctor. He was a veterinarian. Farm vet, mostly, but pets, too." He leaned in. "Do you know what ketamine is?"

Ketamine. Ketamine. Ketamine. The word boomeranged around her head, whoosh, whoosh. She knew. She fucking knew. It was a horse tranquilizer but also, a street drug. And a therapy drug. *And* a date-rape drug, like roofies.

"Yeah," he said, clicking his tongue against the roof of his mouth. "You know what it is. Beecher, he said, you know what ketamine is good for? Its *dissociative properties*. Kinda . . . huh, how to put it? It disconnects the brain from the body, even separates self from the brain." He fake-laughed at that. "I mean, we are our brains, right? How can we be separate from them? Maybe the brain is the meat, the mind is something else. Dunno. Point is, you can pull those two apart. And the mind just . . . falls away. And you go deeper and deeper. Like into a pit. A hole. A k-hole, they call it. And here I thought, what a great way to keep you from firing a blood clot to my brain or whatever it is you wanna do to me. What a great way to keep you docile. Calm and quiet. Shame, because you were finally starting to tell me some semblance of the truth—I'm sure it wasn't all of it, and I imagine there were some lies sprinkled in there, *Doreen*. Anyway. Because of that, I'm choosing to be nice, and I won't have anybody hurt you. Or do . . . anything to you. We'll keep you fed and watered, little houseplant. But great news, Beecher has enough ketamine to keep you floating down there in the dark for a nice long while. At least till we make it to the CDC and I see what we're dealing with. Like I said, we leave tomorrow. And you're coming along. Enjoy your time in the dark, Miss Cahill."

74

THE LONG WALK

9/15/2023: Came south in an old-timey wagon train. Those are a thing again, when cars aren't available. Except these wagons are like something out of Mad Max—*big truck or tractor tires and metal wagon beds cut from dead pickups. Horses, though, still. A classic. Now I'm back in Landfill City. A lot has changed. There are people here. A little town built from the trash, like a child's kingdom. The things they've pulled from the refuse and gotten working again: car batteries, refrigerators, microwaves, generators, old computers, you name it, someone threw it away. Tents, toys, strings of Christmas lights, so much clothing, musical instruments. Some in need of repairs big and small. Some perfectly fine. We were a country happy to discard everything that didn't please us immediately. At least now recycling is really a thing. After it was far too late to matter, I guess.*

—from *A Bird's Story, A Journal of the Lost*

OCTOBER 30, 2025
Chamblee, Georgia, Just Northeast of Atlanta

LINH HADN'T BEEN WRONG—PEOPLE WERE COMING FOR THEM.

As the three of them traveled south on Clairmont Road, each with nothing more than a backpack full of rudimentary supplies, they heard voices coming from the direction they were headed. Three, maybe four people. Wasn't hard to pick out the word *plane* in there.

This part of town was a mix of residential and commercial. Clairmont wasn't a highway, but was still a four-lane road passing houses, office buildings, restaurants. And a lot of tree cover.

They ducked behind a rusted, blown out box truck. Anxiety shot through Shana like an arrow. They'd only just stepped off the hell-coaster plane ride and started to walk, and now, this. She just wanted one precious moment to find her bearings. The day was warm with the barest chill, and the afternoon sun was easing toward the horizon, and all she wanted to do was walk. Walk and not talk and not worry. She'd never been to this city and thought, even in the end of days, it might be nice to see something new.

But now here they were, hearing people coming closer, people who might be friend, or foe, or something stranger, something worse.

Benji whispered to her and Pete: "Okay. We could hide here but we're exposed as they pass us." He pointed to a parking lot just across the street, to the right—a big one surrounding the remnant of some kind of health center. The windows were mostly shattered, and the sun caught on the jagged glass teeth. The parking lot was home to only a few cars—tires gone, hoods and trunks all popped, scavenged down not all the way to the frame, but pretty close. "We go there. We move from car to car. Stay low. Stay quiet. And we go now. Okay?"

Panic chewed at her heels like rats. Shana nodded. Pete, too. At the very least, she told herself, they had Benji. Benji, who always managed to sound calm. He projected it, like a sound you couldn't hear. It helped. Like something to hold on to in a storm, something you knew wouldn't blow away and take you with it.

Still, she eyed him up. Losing that arm took something out of him. (Maybe the plane flight, too.) He looked like some of the color had been drained out of him. Easier to see his cheekbones, his collarbones. His eyes were set deeper. All in all, he just felt whittled down. And it wasn't just the lost arm, it was like something that had been there, was now gone.

Hope you're okay, Benj, she thought.

Now wasn't the time to worry about it.

The voices, still distant, were growing louder. Murmurs and rumbles. Men, mostly. But a woman, too, Shana thought.

"Let's go," Benji said.

They ducked low and moved quick and quiet. They crossed out of the shadow of the old box truck, across the road, and into the parking lot toward a Kia crossover parked and long abandoned. The parking lot was broken like a cookie. Up through all its cracks grew grass, wildflowers, five-fingered ivy.

The voices now were clearer, easier to hear—

First man, nervous voice: "You think it landed at the airport?"

Woman, firm, Southern: "It landed but I'm telling y'all, it took off again." Pause. "It's not gonna be there when we get there."

Second man, deep voice: "Yeah but maybe we see *why* they landed. Something's up with that."

First man: "I didn't see it *or* hear it. You're imagining things."

Shana peeked out from around the Kia's rust-ravaged bumper, saw four, not three people walking up in a diamond pattern—at the fore, a white woman. Long and lean, hair pulled back in a rough ponytail. Muscles like braided ropes.

The white man behind and to her left looked small, almost salamandery, like he was a creature peeking out from under a log. Big eyes. Hair so blond it was almost skin-colored.

Behind the woman and to her right was a big Black guy, bald on top, with a beard thick and squared off like a charcoal briquette.

At the rear of the four of them was a brown-skinned woman. Southeast Asian, or Filipina, maybe. Everything about her was small. Not dainty, not really—she was thick like a stack of books. But short. She had a gaiter pulled up, covering her mouth, though her nose poked over it.

Each of them was armed. Rifles or shotguns, Shana didn't know. Everyone except the woman at the back, who had what looked like a machete in her hand.

They moved with practiced concern. Each of their heads on a swivel. Like they were in some kinda alien monster movie, ready at any point for the scary extraterrestrial to jump out at them.

Benji tapped her and Pete on the shoulder, then pointed to the next car up—a sagging mini van sitting on its rims. He moved. They followed.

But as they did, Shana, who was just behind Benji, didn't see the small piece of metal tucked away in a pocket of weeds. Her foot touched it—it skidded out from its hiding place. It didn't go far. Instead it made a delicate but oh-so-clear, ringing sound as it bounced on the asphalt.

Ting, ting, t-ting.

Like a little bell ringing for dinner.

Fuck.

They reached the mini van just in time to hear the woman say:

"Hell was that?"

The Black guy said, "Sounded like it came from over there."

White guy: "Might've just been a raccoon or something. I seen a lot of 'em out here close to night. It's early yet but—"

"Shush, TJ," the woman said.

"Sorry, Merrill," he said.

They had stopped advancing up the road.

And now, slowly, were coming to them.

Pete hissed under his breath.

Benji winced, leaning his shoulder against the mini van as he balanced himself enough to get Marcy's revolver out of its holster.

And the moment he did—

Whoom. The air erupted with a thunder-boom of gunfire. Shana thought instantly, *We're dead,* but it was the four people approaching them who seemed the most taken by surprise. Merrill, the woman, barked out: "The fuck?"

Somewhere across the road, maybe in one of the houses there, someone yelled out in a real thick accent: "That was a warnin' shot. Seems y'all lost all y'all's goddamn fuckin' way. This ain't chya'll's neighborhood."

"Poorhouse, that you?" Merrill called.

"Fuckin' right it's me. Case you don't have your map on you, this is Ashford Park, you fuckin' strays. Get gone, go back to home Brookhaven—"

"Briarcliff, dumbass," the Black guy yelled.

"Whatfuckinever! I don't care! This ain't your spot is what I'm saying, and you keep coming up through here, I'm a damn good shot with this .30-30. I could shoot the pecker off a bottlefly."

Merrill held up her hands. "We saw a plane. You see it?"

"I don't give a shit about no plane, Merrill." He pronounced it *Murrill,* maybe even *Merle.* "Keep away. We're healthy up here. No fungus among us." *Fung-gus among-gus.* "And I don't want you stealin' our supplies."

Benji whispered: "This is our chance."

"Do they need us?" Shana asked. "Maybe they need help."

Benji sighed. "They have guns and they seem eager to use them. We have a job to do and this isn't it." He paused. "We need to move now."

He was right. Shana knew it. Before shit fell apart because of White Mask, she hated people. Well, maybe not *hated*-hated, but she was pretty misanthropic. She knew that word now and wore it like a badge. But now, she felt desperate to meet these people. It wasn't that she felt safe around them, or trusted them, or even cared. But there was some desperate yearning here. Being in Lake Charles felt like being part of something. One small piece of a collective.

But Benji was right.

They had a job to do.

They had to get to the CDC. They had to find something to save their town and its people. It was a quest, and they'd strayed from it too many times already.

Charlie is counting on us.

Benji went, and she and Pete followed. Even as the others continued to argue and yell, even as someone fired another shot, even as someone fired back—

They kept going, bellows and gunfire fading as they hurried away, fast as they could away from the erupting chaos, because chaos like that? Shana knew it was a trap.

One they couldn't afford to get caught in.

NIGHT DRAPED THE LAND. THEY stopped in a little wooded section off Briarcliff Road, not far from something called the Cliff Valley Office Park. Benji said they should stop for the night, just in case. Even one misstep in the dark could mean stepping on a rusty nail and ending up with tetanus. Or, he said with no small bitterness, "Losing a limb from infection."

Benji said he'd take watch, and Shana told him she should do it, but he seemed insistent, almost irritated at her suggestion, so she let it go.

She slept a little. Lying on the ground, curled up against Pete's back. It was a rough-and-tumble sleep—the kind of sleep that was almost spiteful, born in defiance of your mind trying to keep your body awake. Somewhere along the way, after countless startled starts awake, she gave up and found Benji sitting nearby.

"Go back to bed," he said to her in a low voice. "You need some sleep."

"I need a lot of things. I need a hamburger. I need a blanket. I need my son." She paused, groaning in frustration. "I could really go for some weed." She paused again and tried to inject some further levity: "Don't think I'm not still mad that you and Pete and Dot and her two fuckboys smoked up and didn't come wake me."

"Sorry," he said, but it was one of those cold, shitty sorries, a sorry like a pissing-down rain. A sorry you don't mean.

"So I'm not an entomologist but I'd love to know what bug crawled up your ass and died there. You know. For science."

"Everything's fine, Shana."

"Everything is definitely not fine, Benji."

To that, he said nothing.

"Is it the arm? Are you still sad about the arm?" Still nothing. "Is it Dot?

You two had a thing. That looked nice." Grief and impatience danced together inside her. "Missing Arav and Charlie hurts. It's like missing a limb."

Even in the dark, she could see Benji shoot her a shitty look.

"I'm trying to say, I get it," she groused.

He sighed and said finally, "It's this place. This is home. This city. My house was only five, six miles from here. Seeing it now, so empty, so broken—" Another sigh. "There's a lot of empty and broken going around." Even in the dark she thought he took a long look at his missing arm.

"We're almost there." To the CDC, she meant.

"Yes."

"That's pretty amazing. We did it."

"We lost a lot to get here. And I don't even know what we're going to find. If we find something, we still have to make it all the way back to Ouray. All the way across the country again. No car, no plane, nothing."

"We'll figure it out," she said, not out of hope but spite. "We've come this far, it has to work out. It fucking has to."

He laughed a bitter laugh. "Does it? Do things seem like they're working out well? We're stepping into who knows what here. And Ouray, well, Ouray is—I don't even know if we'll get back there, Shana, and if we do, what's happened in our wake? Your child was growing at an exorbitant rate. And who knows what Black Swan was doing to the rest of the town? I lost Sadie. I don't get to stay with Dot. My arm is—" He snarled behind gritted teeth. "I'm broken, like everything else, just broken. So no, I have no faith that it'll just work out."

"Fine, fuck you, dude," she muttered, then crawled back to where Pete was sprawled out. She tried to sleep but sleep ducked and dodged her every attempt. Earlier she'd just been thinking about how Benji was their rock, but now that rock was breaking apart, as so many things seemed to be. If Benji turned to dust, then what fate was left for them but to do the same?

75

THE LAST MILE

The tarantula, the adder, and the asp will also never change. Pain and death will always be the same. But under the pavements trembling like a pulse, under the buildings trembling like a cry, under the waste of time, under the hoof of the beast above the broken bones of cities, there will be something growing like a flower, something bursting from the earth again, forever deathless, faithful, coming into life again like April.
                        —Thomas Wolfe, *You Can't Go Home Again*

OCTOBER 31, 2025
Atlanta, Georgia

MORNING CAME, AND THOUGH THE SUN WAS UP AND OUT, IT DID LITTLE TO push away the dark pall hanging over Benji. All night he stayed awake, listening to the sounds of the dead city and its outskirts: animals creeping about, the wind pushing trees against trees so that the branches groaned ghostly against one another, a distant shout, even more distant gunfire. No cars. No whine of white noise. No plane traffic or helicopters. A few dogs barking.

Once upon a time, he'd felt guilt—guilt over surviving, yes, but also guilt over seeing how the world had changed and feeling at peace with it. He'd seen some value in the clarity and the purity of a quieter world, one . . . less choked by its human presence. But now . . .

Now all he had was anger. He'd once regarded his survival as a kind of gift, but now it felt like a curse. The future was dirt, him and all of it chewed through by worm and ant and invasive root.

This city had been his home.

Sadie had been his home.

Ouray, his home.

He had none of it now.

He'd lived in Decatur for twenty years, and worked at the CDC for just as long—that part, at least, until Longacre. But before all that, he'd grown up here. His first apartment was in Benteen Park and he'd lived through its gentrification—loved what it was before, resented what it became, but liked some of what came after, in a guilty sort of way.

He was pickled in this place, brined in it. He loved movies at the Plaza. Loved getting a burger at George's, or fried chicken at Busy Bee. He'd had his first kiss in the fountain at Olympic Park during the hottest August he could remember, the kind of August that made the walls sweat. Once he joined EIS at the CDC, he'd hop all around the country, and later, the world—but it was always good to come home. It wasn't good this time. The very idea of home felt like nothing to him.

For a long time he'd told himself, *Well, you can cut a tree down to a stump, but even then, it can grow back, a little tree emerging from its own ruin.* And that was true of so much: Staggering losses could cull most of a microflora of bacteria, or a hive of bees, or a colony of ants, or a population of black swifts—and given time and condition, they *could* come back. They could come back stronger, even. By the 1950s, the bald eagle had been cut down to four hundred or so nesting pairs. Now? Just before White Mask hit, they'd roared back—over three hundred thousand individual birds were known, with close to a hundred thousand making nests.

They'd come back from the brink of extinction, and were no longer endangered or even threatened.

But America was not its mascot.

Benji conceded that maybe humanity was not over—it could survive and even thrive, much as black swifts or bald eagles could. Winnowed to nothing, there was still a way to roar forth once more. But that was people as a *species.* It said nothing of civilization. Or of culture. He'd been naïve to conflate the two.

America the country—and Atlanta the city—would never again be what they once were. Their identities were lost, meaningless without the context of history, and who could even say what history would truly remain?

Benji would never eat at Busy Bee Café again, and even if by some fortune it opened up anew, it still wouldn't be what it was. The city had lost itself. You couldn't regrow that. Couldn't protect it from extinction because it was already extinct. It had been cut down too much. Pared all the way to the bone. The tree that could regrow from its stump would not be the tree that was lost—that tree might have offered wonderful shade, or plump fruits, or artful branches like the pulmonary tangle of lungs taking breaths. But the tree that came forth once more wouldn't be *that* tree. And that was *if* it even came back from its stump.

Stump.

And there, again, he looked at his arm.

It wasn't just the loss of the arm that dug into him like a shovel. Though he felt its loss keenly, and also felt keenly the pain that throbbed throughout it. He also felt hopeless trying to imagine if someone like Dot would even want to be with him again. After all, he couldn't even *hug* someone. They could hold him, but he couldn't hold them back. And no, fine, he wasn't his arm and his arm wasn't him, and it felt foolish to assign that one limb such importance, but that didn't change how he *felt*. And that thought did little to stop him from that slippery slope of loose stone that made him think again and again of not just what the world had lost, but what he had lost, too. Sadie, chief among them. But all his friends, too. Like Cassandra. Or Robbie. Or the other Shepherds who were now gone.

And what of those in Ouray? Would they make it back in time, if at all? Would he ever see Marcy again, or Matthew?

You can't go home again, so the saying went.

Yet, the mission continued. The work went on. But it felt automated, suddenly. Like he was just on rails, and like Shana and Pete were being dragged behind him. A little part of him wondered: *What if we just give up? What if we abandon ship?* Go back to Dot? Nah, she wouldn't want him. Gun in his mouth? A grim consideration, a terrible option. But . . .

The freedom of release. The breath of surrender.

The emancipation of exeunt.

But Ouray awaited. He had to see this through. If only for Shana. The specter of Black Swan hovered over Ouray.

So, onward Benji, Shana, and Pete went, one last mile to the CDC.

THEY HEADED SOUTH, STAYING OFF the road as much as they could. Benji's plan was to cross Peachtree Creek on the Houston Mill Road bridge, then duck through the preserve at Hahn Woods and cross into the Emory University Roybal campus, near where the main buildings of the Centers for Disease Control were located. From there, he didn't know what came next. Ideally, they'd get into the building and see what they could see. In a perfect world, he'd gain access to Sadie's notes and files, but he expected a considerable portion of those would be electronic.

Which, obviously, presented a difficulty.

They walked. Ducking through meadow-like backyards, the long grasses fallen over like shot soldiers, autumn's lost leaves crushed underfoot. Shana seemed sullen and withdrawn; his fault, he knew. He'd been unfair to her last night. But he didn't know how to get her out of it, because getting her out of it meant getting himself out of it, and that task loomed too large. Pete must've sensed something was up, because he offered little more than manic smiles and suspicious, curious glances, as his gangly, near-skeletal form loped along.

The woods alongside Houston Mill Road were thick—the homes tucked away in the trees were once high-dollar homes, sometimes scions of architectural darlings. Some of them belonged to the higher-ups of Emory University, or the university hospital. Benji had been to more than one party in these homes. (More than one *boring* party, usually. More suits than scientists. Elites over educators.)

He was afraid they would now be occupied by scavengers and such—and if they went traipsing across the properties, well, that could get them shot. But the homes here seemed vacant. Windows were broken. Front doors busted open. Branches lay across downed gutters and power lines. The wind swept in and out of these hollowed-out places. Birds followed that wind.

It was odd, Benji thought, that nobody was here. Why wouldn't the still-living choose to settle in these very nice houses? Certainly there would be comfort inside, and the repairs minimal. But this part of town seemed deader than the rest. And it shouldn't have been.

Very strange.

Onward they went, finally ditching the woods and moving perpendicular back to the road once more. Ahead, the bridge awaited them—a flat bridge framed by sidewalks and dark concrete railings. The creek itself splashed and hummed about fifteen, twenty feet below them. Off to the left was another, smaller bridge—a walking trestle that had fallen into grave disrepair, a path so ruinous that not even Indiana Jones would step foot upon it.

Above, fish crows took flight, stirred by their presence, probably. Black wings against a swiftly graying autumn sky. The warm day lost to a sudden chill.

They crossed over the wider bridge, feet echoing. Another wind kicked up. Something felt wrong. A tension threaded through the air like a tightening stitch.

It was then he saw:

Bodies in the creek below. Three of them. Long dead, by the look of it. Water running around bloated carcasses. The smell bubbled up: a rotten stink.

As Shana and Pete came over to see what he was looking at—

Benji sensed the movement ahead of them.

Camouflaged soldiers emerged from the trees quickly, with purpose and quiet aggression—they were armed, and armed well, with military-grade rifles. They quickly converged at the end of the bridge, weapons up. Having seen militaries the world around, Benji immediately suspected that these were not men and women in costume, but people trained for military duty. Behind them: More soldiers emerged, flanking them, guns up.

"Jesus!" Pete barked. *Jaysis*, said the Irish in him.

"Benji," Shana said, urgent and afraid, hurrying up behind him.

"It's okay," he said, sotto voce, worrying that it was very much *not* okay.

"Hands up," said a white man to their right, helmet on, goggles, too. A brown-skinned woman emerged from their left side carrying a pistol. And footsteps behind them told Benji that they'd been flanked, too.

The three of them raised their hands.

The woman, dark hair tucked underneath a backward Atlanta Braves cap, kept her pistol pointed. "I'm Lieutenant Torres. You have crossed the Roybal Line and therefore you are in violation of the Peach Treaty and in danger of being detained or killed. You will be escorted back over the bridge—"

Benji interrupted her, his jaw set. "I need to get to the CDC."

"Not an option," the man to his right said. A quick count saw four people on this side of the bridge, and another four behind them. All military. Army, he guessed. Maybe *real* Army, not just some made-up version at the end of the world.

"We've come a long way," Shana said, pleading. "A *long* way."

"Yeah, we're not fuckin' from here," Pete barked. "We don't know shit about your piddly treaties—and wait, did you call it the Peach Treaty? Like, peach tree? Is that a Georgia thing or—"

"Shut up," Torres said, gesturing with the gun. "As I said, you have crossed the Roybal Line, and therefore you are in violation—"

"I know," Benji said, his one arm raised, trying to almost *pat* the air as if to calm the rising tensions. "But *please* listen to me. I'm *from* the CDC. I worked there. We've come all the way from Colorado. I'd very much like to be granted a chance to talk to whoever is in charge—detain us! Detain us if you have to. Just give me a chance to talk to somebody. Please."

The soldiers looked to one another. Torres said to the goggled man immediately to their right, "Quinn, zip-tie them. I'll radio ahead, see if I can get some answers. What are your names?"

They told them.

"Uh-huh," Torres said, dubious, even as Quinn and the other soldiers moved to search them, take their packs, confiscate their supplies. Quinn removed Benji's revolver and he gave it a look suggestive of bold, almost shocked appraisal. Like, here was this one-armed man carrying a portable howitzer in the form of a revolver. He didn't know if it raised him in their estimation, but it seemed like it.

Soldiers zip-tied Pete and Shana, but Quinn looked flummoxed with Benji. The soldier yelled after Torres as she was walking off to use her radio. "Lieutenant! You have a strong opinion how I cuff this one? He's, uhh, only got one flipper." Benji smelled the man's minty breath, saw the freckles on his cheeks. He looked boyish, if not precisely young.

Torres, disgruntled, called back, "Christ, Quinn, do I need to hold your dick when you take a piss? If you can't cuff the wrist to the biceps, cuff it behind him, to a belt or belt loop." Then she took a radio from another soldier.

Quinn bent Benji's arm backward—pain shot up through the shoulder—as he zip-tied his wrist to his belt loop. "I hope you're telling the truth," Quinn said. "Lying to us is a good way to catch a bullet."

"Are you army?" Benji asked. "Real U.S. Army?"

But all Quinn would say was, "Shut up." He and the other soldiers just shoved the three of them together, their guns leveled at them. One misstep and they'd meet a quick end. Torres had walked up the road by a hundred feet or so, using her radio. Her conversation was audible, but its contents were indistinct.

Eventually, she walked back, and handed the radio off to a short, buff, and totally bald Black woman.

"All right," Lieutenant Torres barked. "Looks like you just earned yourself a trip over the Roybal Line. You so much as let out a little fart and I will personally hole-punch the brains from your head with a round from my 10mm, and then we'll throw your bodies in the creek for the crows and coyotes. You wouldn't be the first, and you won't be the last. Now let's march."

•   •   •

The CDC.

Seeing it now gave Benji a mix of hope and terror. The good news was the CDC had not been abandoned, nor taken over by scavengers or bandits. The tents outside, the military vehicles, the signs of movement inside the building (not to mention the lack of shattered windows)—this place was occupied.

But occupied was not always a good thing.

These people were military. They wore the fatigues. They had the weapons. But in his experience, soldiers were only as good as those who were leading them. Soldiers protected a country, or a country's interests—only now, what country remained? America did not exist except as an idea, a memory. In this current moment, there was no nation to protect, no president to lead this nonexistent homeland, no chain of command he could imagine. But these people looked organized. They appeared disciplined. Torres was a lieutenant. She had a rank and was using it. Which meant they *had* a chain of command . . . and someone sat at the top of it.

And who that was? Was what mattered most.

Benji had been to many fractured nations—some fractured by the colonizer manipulations of the United States—and in each he found that warlords and fascists promised order in times of despair and disarray. They enforced that order by recruiting soldiers who were willing to perform no end of atrocities to serve their leader. It nearly always ended in genocide.

Where would this end?

Who were the soldiers leading them back to the CDC?

Soon, he knew, they'd find out.

Torres, Quinn, and the others urged them along into the parking lot of the Roybal campus, where the main CDC building loomed large. He spied a few soldiers on the roof, eyes pressed to the scopes mounted on long, high-caliber rifles.

"The fuck are these people?" Pete asked him in a low voice.

"I don't know yet."

"I think it's bad," Shana said quietly. Quinn took exception, told her to shut up, and he shoved her forward. She nearly fell.

"Hey," Benji said sharply. "Back the fuck off."

"Wanna make me, Def Leppard?"

Pete gasped, wheeling around and walking backward instead of forward as he said, "You can go fuck your own ass sideways if you think using Rick Allen from Def Leppard as an insult is going to fly—that Derbyshire boy would use your skull as a snare, he was one of the best goddamn—"

Quinn stepped forward to push Pete—

But Torres stepped in between them.

"Quinn, I swear," she sneered, "you back the hell off or I'll rip off one of *your* arms. Calm. Down."

"Yes, sir," he said, scowling.

Pete waggled his tongue salaciously at the other man.

"Over here," Torres said, leading them toward a big FEMA tent. She pulled back the flap, ushered them inside, had them sit on a set of folding chairs pushed up against the far left side of the room (so to speak). She forcibly pushed them into those seats, and Shana groused, muttering, "You could just ask us."

"Someone will be along shortly," Torres said, unsmiling. "Quinn, come with me, you're not watching them." To the bald, buff woman, Torres said, "Lank, you're on guard duty. Watch them, make sure they don't pull anything hinky."

Then they were left alone. The tent was buzzing with activity. Mostly military, though there looked to be a couple civilians toward the far side. This tent was for resupply: Benji spied ammo boxes, file boxes, and a heap of what looked like old MREs, stacked on various metal racks. A couple officers handled who got what and when. Requisitions, by the look of it.

"Again," Pete said, "who the fuck are these people?"

"They're military," Benji answered quietly. "Real military. But I don't know who they follow. Or to what end. Why here? Why the CDC? Surely there are better buildings to occupy. Unless . . ."

"Unless?" Shana asked. "I don't like that. Unless what?"

"They're protecting—or looting—the HCCL."

"The hell's that?" Pete asked.

"The High-Containment Continuity Lab," Benji explained. "A biosafety-level-4 facility nested inside the research building, Building 9—a box within a box, so to speak. It is one of the most advanced facilities in the world, and it contains an unholy Pandora's box of infectious material. Ebola, Marburg, smallpox, anthrax, Powassan, a number of spillover coronaviruses like SARS, SARS-CoV-2—any pathogen that has no cure or vaccine readily available. Pandemic-level horror."

Shana leaned toward him on his good side, the side not missing an arm, and said, "So you're telling me there's a fucking Ghostbuster-style facility here that has all these infectious goobers and goblins trapped in it? And if some asshole wanted to, say, open that up and let them all out, they could?"

"In theory. I can't even speak to the condition of the lab—it technically requires power to run, but also, was always meant to contain the, ah, *goobers and goblins* in the event of cataclysm. The walls are thick, the systems lock down upon power failure, giving those inside time to escape before sealing the so-called virus vault until power can be returned and security can be reengaged."

"Oh, I'm sure this is all going to be fine, then," Pete said. "Just as we're all getting back on our feet, some rogue ethno-state general is going to give us all Ebola, make us shit out our teeth. Great! Excellent. Bloody hell. *Literally.*"

"We just need to see who is in control of this—"

Operation, he was about to say, when—

"Benji? Benji Ray?"

That voice, from the flap of the tent where they'd just come in. Benji knew it, and he didn't even have to turn his head to have his suspicions confirmed—

Because he'd know that voice anywhere.

76

THE RETURN OF CASSIE TRAN

So, you get to the end of World War Two in 1945. And, through all the tasks it's been doing for the past couple of years, this group—the Office of Malaria Control in War Areas—has done a really good job. And has also amassed, while it's been doing that, a fleet of literal trucks and lab equipment and people, scientists of various kinds, that the government doesn't particularly want to let go of. And so they go looking for a way to transform that wartime office into a peacetime agency. . . .

And then, after the war ended, there was a campaign to get it to stay in Atlanta. There's an apocryphal story that Robert Woodruff of Coca-Cola offered them their land next to Emory University for a very inexpensive price. And so, as it became a peacetime agency instead of a wartime one, it got to stay in Atlanta, instead of having to move up to D.C.

—Maryn McKenna in an interview with Sean Powers and Steve Fennessy of *Georgia Today,* "Why the CDC Has Been Sidelined During Pandemic"

OCTOBER 31, 2025
Atlanta, Georgia

CASSIE TRAN: STILL THE LONG-LIMBED, LOPING WOLF OF YORE, HAIR LONG and undyed black with a few conspicuous threads of gray hanging down in the front, more lines in her face, a few frozen ripples around the eyes, too, and as always, a ratty-ass band T-shirt hanging over her were-coyote frame. In this instance, a Metric shirt. Fraying at the bottom, a raggedy fringe.

Benji launched to his feet, nearly fell over, forgetting he (a) had one arm and (b) had that one arm bound to his belt loop with a zip-tie.

Cass was like a torpedo, catching him before he fell, and holding him tight. She was laughing, then crying, then laughing *through* the crying.

"Dude," she said. "My God. You're alive."

"*You're* alive," he answered, voice echoing with both shock and joy.

It was like something uncorked inside him, something that had been stoppered up since at least Lake Charles, maybe before, since Ouray, since this all began in Pennsylvania five years ago. He'd just been feeling like all was lost, but here was a friend of his, a cohort and a companion both in work and in life, and she was here.

Here.

In this moment, he could not return Cass's hug but he *could* crush his face into the space between her neck and her shoulder, and in doing so he felt the anger in him dry up, go brittle, and break into pieces like old stucco. Underneath it, love and contentment—shot through with a vein of guilt for ever having felt all that anger in the first damn place.

Then, suddenly, the reverie was broken, and Cassie was barking orders to the soldier, Lark, standing there: "Get them uncuffed. Now! Do you *know* who these people are? This is Benji Ray, of the Epidemic Intelligence Service, and that's a *literal god of rock*, somehow still alive and, and, you know, honestly looking fabulous. And that's—a girl? Some teen girl, looks weirdly familiar?"

"Shana," said Shana. "I was a Shepherd? We met but like, not in a big way. Glad you're not dead."

"Right, yeah," Cassie answered. "Back atcha."

Lank went around, snipping their zip-cuffs. They all spent a few extra moments urging blood back to their extremities.

Pete sauntered over like a snake in human skin, swung a scarecrow arm around Cassie Tran and said: "Where's an out-to-pasture end-of-the-world rock-star cocksucker motherfucker get a drink around here, anyway?"

AND BY A DRINK, PETE meant a shower.

Well, okay, *no*, he didn't mean that—but that is, in fact, the drink he got. Because when afforded the chance to get cleaned up, they took it.

Just a short walk off campus sat a loop of condos and townhomes, fairly new, built in the last ten years or so. Clifton Heights. Brick and mocha-colored with white accents—a curious intersection between a modern style and Gothic revival. Benji remembered the houses: They were built with the idea that staff from Emory, or the CDC, or even the hospital, might rent or buy them.

What ended up happening was that wealthy students occupied the homes instead. Because, increasingly, if students could afford a college education, then they were likely already wealthy, and could also afford luxury housing. So, the CDC and hospital staff either had to be wealthy enough to live in those big fancy houses just north of the CDC campus, *or* commute in, like Benji had, every day.

Needless to say, the townhomes were no longer occupied. Not by students, at least.

Cassie said they now housed her and the other administrators, plus a few other notable "civilians"—doctors, technicians, engineers, and the like. Benji started to ask her what this all even *was*, but she said she'd explain soon. Meanwhile, she directed them to an empty townhouse that had a pair of bathrooms with fully functioning plumbing—"No small feat," she explained—which Pete and Shana used. Then she took Benji around the loop to her place where he could get cleaned up using her shower. The shower pressure was a soft, weak thing, but a shower was a shower, and for just a little while, Benji felt like he was in heaven. And it gave him a chance to change the swaddling around his stump-end arm—in the meager bathroom light (which dimmed erratically, a thing that Cassie said, *you get used to it, don't worry*) he examined the injury. It was healing, but still looked like a raw, puckered mess. Crudely stitched and stapled. He could still feel his fingers at the end of that missing arm.

Still. The infection had cleared out. The meds were working.

Thank God for small favors, he thought.

But what was not a small favor was Cassie Tran. The fact she was *here*. She hadn't died. He had questions. So many questions! So many, in fact, that he rushed through a shower he would've normally languished in, in order to hurry up with checking and replacing his bandages and getting back out to talk to his friend.

She sat amid the wreckage of her apartment. It was, in classic Cassie style, a total mess. Clothes on the floor. Clothes on a futon couch. MRE packages ripped open. A compost bowl overflowing with vegetable remains. Fruit flies above it.

"Sorry," she said. "The maid died in the Apocalypse."

"It's all right," he said softly.

"Is it weird that I see you as if you're still my boss? Like, I feel this weird spike of shame at having you see my messy-ass house."

"I've been in your car, Cass."

"Well," she said, shrugging. "Car's a car. Car's just a portable container for Starbucks cups. House is different. It's just—I don't have many guests."

"What with the Apocalypse and all," he said.

"Yeah. That."

"I have so many questions, Cass."

"I'm guessing I have just as many."

"You show me yours, I show you mine?"

"You first, boss."

At that, he chuckled. He parked himself on the futon couch next to her and . . . it all just fell out of him. As much as he could tell. He'd, what, last seen Cassie in California? She'd come there to give him updates on the pandemic, tell him about how antifungals might stave off White Mask, and how an amphetamine like Ritalin could slow the mind-eroding symptoms of the disease. So that was where he started. "I'm here because the triaconozole worked."

This next part was a mountain to climb, and he was afraid he wouldn't be able to do it, but up he went, just the same, to the peak of his grief: "We didn't have enough. Arav and Sadie . . . unbeknownst to me, saved their doses, faked taking them, so I could have some. They both—" The words gathered in his throat, a clot of heartache. "They both succumbed to the disease."

Cassie told him she was sorry. She said then, "The antifungals are how I made it through, too. I caught it. Fucking nightmare. I thought I was going to die. Nearly lost my mind. But . . . I made it through."

"Same," he said, sparing her the details she likely already knew. Instead, he went on to tell her as much as he could: Ouray, Ozark Stover, the Sleep-walkers, Shana's child, Black Swan. The long five years.

And why they fled.

"We've been making our way across the country to come back here," he explained. "We had a solar-powered car to start but . . . that didn't last. We lost it in Louisiana. Along with—" He tilted his head, gesturing toward his arm.

"How'd you lose it?"

"An infection."

"Jesus. The littlest thing."

He sighed. "I should tell people I lost it in the tiger attack."

"Wait, tiger attack?"

"There were two, actually. They'd taken a small town as their territory. Seems like they'd escaped from one of those big cat sanctuaries." He reclined. "That's a story for another time, I think. All that matters is I ended up in Lake Charles, mostly dead. I healed up and . . . came here. In a plane."

"That was you?" she asked. "You know, a lot of us heard it. The plane. And we thought we were going nuts, because I haven't seen a plane flying in—gosh, years? Huh."

"Algal fuel," he explained.

"Will wonders never cease?"

"Apparently not, because I am a bit in awe that you're alive, and you're *here*. What—what is all this, Cass?"

"It's . . . the CDC, Benj. Through all of it, through White Mask, this place was my rock. That building. Those people. Even as so many of us didn't make it through, some did. And we all felt like, you know, there needed to be a continuance. White Mask didn't kill everyone. You know that by now. It left, at our best guess, one to two percent of the population left alive. That fungus really took a big bite—R. *destructans* really turned out to be 'our destruction,' name appropriate. But. Still. A percent or two? Sure, that's not a lot of people in the grand scheme of things but numerically, here in what was or maybe still is America, that ends up being, what, I dunno, three million? Five million? Before White Mask, there were plenty of whole-ass countries with smaller populations than that. And we thought, okay, what's going to finish the job? And that answer is the same as it's been throughout all of human history—"

"Disease."

"Right. And who better to work against that than us? So, those of us who were left launched the Reclamation Project. Keep things running. Try to find ways to monitor local health. Look for outbreaks. We weren't going to get vaccines up and running right away, but long-term? Maybe. Short-term? We do things the old ways. Small teams move into and work with extant populations to address sanitation issues, generation of electricity, cultural habits, or anything that might inhibit health and foster conditions for outbreaks. White Mask seems gone, but what if it isn't? And that's not counting all the bugs waiting for us in the wings—old rogue's gallery enemies. We're not careful, America turns back into some Oregon Trail nightmare—*you have died of dysentery*. TB, tetanus, smallpox, plague. The greatest hits."

"Especially if the containment lab is breached."

"Yeah. Good news there: It appears intact. No one's been in or out and for now we intend to keep it that way. Nobody wants to pop that bubble."

Benji let slip a silent breath of relief.

"Hey, you hungry?" she asked.

He had to think about that. He'd been so . . . grim-feeling that it almost hadn't occurred to him. Didn't help that the antibiotics messed with his gut biome enough to make him feel like he had a forever-sour stomach.

But just the question of it was like speaking reality into existence. He *was* hungry, all of a sudden. Famished, in fact. He told her so.

"Good," she said. "Let's go get the others and we can eat, and I can show you around a little bit." She stood up, grinning ear to ear. "A lot has changed."

77

LIKE MUSIC THROUGH A DOOR

10/2/2023: I watch the world scramble to return to itself. They repurpose and rebuild. I once thought it's because they chose not to die, or chose not to acknowledge that they were already dead. But it's not that at all. It's not even just survival. It's regrowth. A forest after a fire, the green coming through. And I hate it. I hate it because it means I'm broken. I'm not regrowing. I'm surviving, but the pain from the post-viral syndrome, the depression, it's crushing me. I'm not the ghost haunting a dead world, but a living one. A miserable ghost in a happy house. One who does not even have the courage to exorcise herself into oblivion.
—from A Bird's Story, A Journal of the Lost

OCTOBER 31, 2025
Atlanta, Georgia

CASSIE FED THEM LUNCH FIRST. THEY SAT IN AN OUTDOOR AREA, SOLDIERS IN the distance (that Cassie said numbered about three dozen altogether). Food was a salad, and while once upon a time Shana would have rejected the very notion of *salad* as food, this was fucking delicious, the kind of meal that makes you believe in a benevolent god. Within sight of them was a prodigious garden, with produce bursting up out of it in Edenic glory—lush tomatoes, vines heavy with green beans, big fat chonks of lettuce. And some of that garden had made its way into this salad. Everyone else was relishing their food. Even Benji had returned to a better mood. Shana, though, picked at hers. She felt like a fucking hangnail.

"I'm not a *salad guy*," Pete said around a mouthful of lettuce, like he was some kind of giant kaiju rabbit. "But I'd slit seven throats for this dressing."

Cassie explained its ingredients were peanut oil—from Georgia peanuts—and citrus from local trees. Plus honey from kept bees. Spices, she said, were where it was going to get difficult. "Like coffee and chocolate, most spices aren't grown here in America. Cinnamon, for instance."

Benji looked up. "Do we know how the rest of the world fared?"

At that question, Cassie hesitated.

"Somewhat. And it's a pretty mixed bag. Places of privilege like Europe or Australia and New Zealand or parts of China, Korea, Japan, they mostly did well—with the exception of a few reactor meltdowns. Places where there's existing agriculture, like a lot of Central and South America, and some parts of Africa, did okay, too. But where people were already poor, or where food access was already restricted, my understanding is, you end up seeing more tragedy in the wake of White Mask. That's no surprise. White supremacy and privilege love a crisis, right? Climate change doesn't drive a rich person out of his home but robs—or would've robbed, I guess—a million Bangladeshis of theirs. So here and now, in the wake of White Mask, marginalized communities suffer more. Disease. Famine. There are territorial or tribal fights, warlords, ethnic genocides. We have some communication with people overseas, but it's spare. We've seen some boats, but we're talking like, refugees, not pioneers or pilgrims. No representatives of nations." She shrugged. "If nations even matter anymore."

Pete dabbed at his mouth with a cloth napkin. "No more New World Order conspiracy, I suppose."

"Everything is hyperlocal now," Cassie said. "Vegetable gardens like this one matter as much as, if not more than, high-yield, high-energy foods like corn, rice, wheat. We just don't have the huge numbers of mouths to feed. And it lets us try to make deals with the local, ah, *fiefdoms*." That last word, she said with ill-concealed irritation. When asked, she explained: "Enh, some cities have pulled it together. New York City still feels like one city. Atlanta . . . isn't. Yet. The center of town is still strong, it's majority Black, still a community. But farther out you go, the more it breaks apart— neighborhoods and developments all crumbled into these territories. Clans, gangs, cults. Homeowners associations, in some cases—" She must've seen their faces. "No, for real, I'm talking weaponized, militarized HOAs. A lot of guns came out. A lot of racism. There are flare-ups. Violent ones. Mostly from the north. South of us, we have relationships, we share work and trade. But we're almost a . . . fiefdom ourselves here."

Benji asked, "Do you control the military? Or do they control you?"

"They're army, almost in their entirety. From local bases. What was left of McPherson and Gillem, plus Fort Stewart, Camp Merrill. They're part of us, and they've allowed civilians to nest at the top of their command chain— reluctantly, and not without some frustrations. They only ask we listen to their counsel on security-related issues, and we do. When we can." At that, she stood up. She directed everyone to a nearby metal bin, painted blue. "We compost, so just toss your stuff in there. C'mon." She waved them along. "Arms and legs inside the vehicle as we continue the tour. Oh, and one more thing—"

She pulled out a fistful of candy from her pockets and tossed them onto the table. Shana spied a Zagnut bar, a packet of tropical Skittles, a few snack-sized 100 Grand bars. "That military contractor warehouse had candy, too. For snack machines at military bases. It's not the best candy—the Snickers and Reese's are long gone. But eat up. It is Halloween, after all."

But Shana had no appetite for it.

SHE WAS GETTING IT NOW. Her feeling. Her discomfort and agitation. As Cassie took them through the main building, introducing them to people (Mikey Gordon, head of systems; Yai Ping, horticulturist; Doctor Gemma Schwab, who said she'd gladly take a look at Benji's arm; et cetera et cetera, blah-blah-blah), it built up in Shana, a mounting frustration that took longer than expected to name:

Impatience.

She was *impatient* as *fuck*.

They'd come all this way. They'd fled from bandits. They'd found a se-cret diner in the desert. They'd been chased by tigers and she learned how to *flocculate algae*, which was a completely insane sentence. They'd flown! In a plane! And maybe almost died! And now here they were, thrown like a dart across the wide-open expanse of Nowhere, America, having almost impos-sibly landed at the bullseye.

And instead of doing what they needed to do, they were getting a *tour* and *eating salad and candy* and *meeting total local randos* while Ouray and her *own infant son* were held throttled in the grip of an out-of-control artificial intelligence. (A completely different insane sentence, she realized.)

They were up on the windswept roof when Shana went off like a jack-in-the-box.

Cassie was showing them an impressive array of solar panels, saying, "Atlanta and Georgia in general were one of the worst in the nation in terms of getting up to speed with solar—so these took a long, looooong time to gather. And we supplement with generators. We were fortunate enough to find an unused supply of them in a government contractors' warehouse. We shared with neighboring communities where we could—"

"We didn't come here because of any of this bullshit," Shana blurted out.

"Oh . . . kay," Cassie said, looking nervously at Benji.

"Shana," he started to say.

"No, I mean, it's cool, you both know each other, and I get it. That's awesome. But that doesn't matter. We're here for a reason. We've lost so much just to get here, so if you'll forgive me, the tour can wait." She raised her voice. "All this stupid shit can wait!"

"Those'd be good lyrics to a song," Pete said. He closed his eyes and hummed a little bit, lost to the imagined music.

"Shana's right," Benji acquiesced, sighing. "I'm a bit caught up in all this—we have lost a lot of time. We should talk about why we've come."

Cassie looked confused. "Sure. Yeah. Okay."

"Black Swan took our town," Shana said. "*And* it took my son. It's in him. And I want that thing *out*. The monster was made here. So maybe here's where we find a way to fucking kill it."

Benji reached out and touched Shana's arm—at first she feared it was a condescending gesture, a calm-down-little-girl thing like her father used to do. But it wasn't. He nodded to her. "Cass, we're looking to find a way into the Benex-Voyager AI lab in the sub-basement. Specifically, to find Sadie's work. I know Sadie helped create Black Swan and we all thought it was good and necessary work. But we have new information. And things have changed. I have to believe she knew how to stop it, in case . . . well, I don't know that she could've predicted *this*, but just the same, I have to guess she imagined an emergency was possible."

"Funny that you bring this up while we're on the roof," Cassie said. "Because there's . . . an anomaly we have to discuss."

"*An anomaly*," Benji said.

"Regarding Sadie's labs."

Pete raised an eyebrow. "That's never good. Nobody ever says, *well, what a fun anomaly*, do they? It's always UFOs and cancer shadows. It's never, oh, look, my adorable new puppy shits out gold coins, what a delightful anomaly."

"What is it?" Shana asked, ignoring Pete.

"The Benex-Voyager lab has power. Power we . . . didn't give it."

"That's curious," Benji said, in classic understatement.

"There's more."

"Do I even want to know?"

"It won't let us in."

"It has power," he clarified. "And it won't let you in."

"Bingo. C'mon. I'll show you. We'll knock and say *trick-or-treat*, see if we can get someone in there to give us more candy."

THE ELEVATORS DIDN'T WORK. CASSIE had told them this already. Elevators ate power, in her words, *like a kid eats chocolate*. (Candy, it seemed, had become the theme of the day.) Even idle, they drew considerable power. An elevator in a five-story building gobbled up as much juice in one year as an entire average American home did in six months. And this building, the main office building, was eleven stories, not to mention half as many sublevels. So, everyone got used to taking the stairs, and it's why most of the upper-levels of the facility went unused.

Down in the lobby, Shana saw Benji's head swiveling this way and that—a look of consternation and awe ping-ponging on his face.

"You okay?" she asked.

"I think so," he said. "The last time I was here . . . I'd already been let go. Fired. But Sadie brought me in. Brought me in to meet Black Swan." He looked at her then and said, pointedly. "Black Swan chose me. Just as it chose many of the Flock—it just chose me for a different purpose."

"Me too, I guess."

He nodded and offered her a small, commiserating smile.

Cassie guided them to the elevator bank and then to the set of steps next to them. "Here's the fun part," she said. "Benex-Voyager occupied the bottom-most two floors of the building. That incorporates Firesight, the nano-med-tech company that BV bought in—was it 2017?"

"I think 2018," Benji said.

"Cool. Right. Benex-Voyager was brought into the CDC during that . . . ugly privatization era of President Nolan, sooooo, 2010 or so."

"I remember. I also remember hating it."

"I remember you hating it, too." Cassie sighed. To Pete and Shana she said: "We all did. Anytime private industry partners with a big government oversight faction, it *suuuucks*. Regardless, they took those sublevels which up until that point had been largely for archival purposes, but as our campus here was growing, adding buildings, they were able to move all that out, and move them in."

She paused.

"Thing is," Cassie continued, "they must've done some additional construction because—well, sorry, more stairs, but it's probably best to just show you what I'm talking about."

Pete opted to remain upstairs. "My gangly old legs are starting to ache and honestly, I don't give a shit about all this shit. You go ahead. Have fun storming the castle." So, down the stairwell the three of them went.

The lighting here was emergency only—a skull-hurting jaundice hue. Like liver disease living inside a lightbulb.

They went down four flights to sublevel SV5—and there stood a classic reinforced metal door with a handle on it. Cassie gestured to it. "Be my guest."

Benji reached over, did the honor.

He opened the door.

And was met with a sheet of shiny metal. Essentially, a second door behind it, but no hinges. Only a rubber seal around it.

"That's new," he said, clearly puzzled. He ran his one hand along it, noting the gentle dents, like you'd find in a car hood that had been whacked by an errant golf ball. He traced the margins. "Are these rubber, ruggedized seals?"

"Yup," Cassie said.

"This is a pneumatic seal door."

"Also yup."

"So, this is the . . . new construction you meant," he said, obviously concerned. Shana decided to bite:

"Why is that weird? What does any of this mean?"

"A door like this—" He rapped on it. It didn't echo. It was a dull knock, like the sound was swallowed by the thickness of the steel. "Is for high-test containment. Like the kinds you'd find at the HCCL—the ah, the containment lab—at the other end of the CDC campus. This one doesn't even have a handle. Would you look at that." He leaned in closer. "The wall here is thicker than the exterior doorjamb and mechanism. Thick enough to accommodate this door, too—which is flush to the wall, and must've slid in from the side. Slides out, locks in place, creating a vacuum seal. To keep something in there—"

"And by the look of it keep something out," Shana said. *Us*, she thought.

He asked Cassie: "It's the same on the next floor?"

"Sure is."

"The elevator? Which, I know you can't use—but we could climb down—"

She shook her head. "We tried. Same situation there. A door sealed the shaft shut just above this floor. Same stainless-steel vacu-seal bullshit."

"You've presumably tried to open it. I mean, using unconventional means—a burning bar, a thermal lance, even thermite. The army would have it."

"Well, they don't. And it hasn't been high on the priority list to find them. They tried banging on it, prying it open, nothing."

He poked the door. "The dents."

"Yeah. Barely made any. Dents, I mean."

"Shit."

But then, Benji snapped his fingers.

"We go one floor up. There might be a way in from above. Certainly the ventilation system is shared and—"

"Bzzt," Cassie barked. "Game over. The ventilation system is *not* shared, please tell Doctor Ray what his consolation prize is today, Shana."

But Shana wasn't interested in playing these games.

"Set of steak knives," Cassie whispered with a wink.

"So it's on its own ventilation system," Benji said. "Which, I'm guessing, is also sealed shut." Cassie gave him a thumbs-up. "And we can't drill down because a building like this is built like an interlocking structure of flattened M1 Abrams tanks. Impossible to pierce with conventional means."

"And now you see the problem."

"The problem, yes, but not the reason behind it."

Shana said with no small anger: "It makes sense. Black Swan is a virus. An airborne virus. Maybe they knew they needed to contain it." A tiny flare of hope brightened within her, because if the creators knew they had to contain it . . .

Maybe they knew how to kill it, too.

"That could be right," Benji said. "Very good, Shana."

Cassie cleared her throat. "There's one more, uh, *anomaly*, though."

"What?"

"Press your ear to the door."

Benji arched his eyebrow and looked to Shana. The two of them sidled up together and each pushed an ear against the door.

At first she didn't hear much but the gentle thrumming of what, she couldn't say—maybe HVAC. But then, beyond it—

"Music," Benji said, pulling away.

He was right.

It *was* music.

She even felt like she knew the song . . .

But she couldn't place it.

"Pete," she said. "He'll know. I'm going to get Pete."

She broke into a run, churning up the steps.

"THAT'S 'GET A JOB,'" Pete said, after like, one half-second of listening. He pushed his ear back up again, then nodded. "Major doo-wop anthem from the 1950s—the Silhouettes. They were the Thunderbirds before that, and before *that*, they had the best fucking name, the *Gospel Tornadoes*. That's fucking punk as fuck, even though, you know, they were a Black doo-wop group who started as a churchy quartet. Ooh, also, the band Sha Na Na got their name from—"

"Okay," Benji said, "I think that's enough with the musical trivia."

Pete shrugged. "Suit yourself, *square*."

They headed back upstairs to the lobby. Once up there, Cassie said: "So, like I said: anomaly."

"We have to get in there," Shana said. "Now. Today." She could hear her child crying—a phantom sound, like music through that door.

"Yes," Benji said. "I'll think on it. We should all do the same." Seeing her agitation, he looked to Shana and said, "I promise. We're close now. Okay?"

"Okay," she said. But it did little to quiet her raging impatience.

Cassie clapped her hands. "Okay. Love this family reunion but I suspect you're all beat like dirty rugs." She waved them on. "C'mon, I'll get you set up with some places to crash, and in the morning we can figure out our plan of attack. And also, we can figure out what y'all are going to do for the CDC because I gotta tell you, there's always, *always* work to be done."

78

WAY DOWN IN THE HOLE

Following ketamine administration, EEG changes were immediate and widespread, affecting the full extent of the EEG frequency spectrum measured (0–125 Hz). After recovery from sedation during which low frequency activity dominated, the EEG was characterised by short periods (2–3 s) of alternating low (<14 Hz) and high (>35 Hz) frequency oscillation. This alternating EEG rhythm phase is likely to underlie the dissociative actions of ketamine, since it is during this phase that ketamine users report hallucinations. At the highest intravenous dose used (24 mg/kg), in 5/6 sheep we observed a novel effect of ketamine, namely the complete cessation of cortical EEG activity. This persisted for up to several minutes, after which cortical activity resumed. This phenomenon is likely to explain the "k-hole," a state of oblivion likened to a near death experience that is keenly sought by ketamine abusers.

—from study, "Characteristic patterns of EEG oscillations in sheep
(*Ovis aries*) induced by ketamine may explain the psychotropic
effects seen in humans," by A. U. Nicol and A. J. Morton, *Scientific
Reports* 10, article number 9440

TIME DOESN'T MATTER
The Hole, the Pit, the Void

THIS IS WHAT IT IS LIKE TO BE IN THE K-HOLE, THE DISSOCIATIVE STATE brought on by a heavy dose of the horse tranquilizer and human anesthetic known as ketamine:

It is a great pit whose walls are formed of you, your own mind, your own soul. For some, this might be ideal: It is you connecting with yourself. And, given the vagaries of chemical therapeutics, you connecting to something beyond yourself like the divine, or to the universe as a whole. Down in the dark, you find yourself as you disassociate from the world.

You are a free-floating specter; a ghost haunting the house that is you.

And *dissociative* is the key word. You are disconnected from your body, but still present in it. You experience nystagmus: You can see, and your eyes can move, but you cannot physically react to much stimulus. Go on, try to lift your arm. You can't. If someone speaks to you, can you respond? No. You cannot will your lips and tongue to form sound, you cannot hold up a hand to shield you from what is to come. Maybe you can wiggle a toe. Congratulations. It's also very possible you are going to piss or shit yourself. (It's also possible that the reverse is true: You will become so constipated or so unable to excrete urine that you begin to experience a urinary tract infection, or bowel disruption.)

At low doses, ketamine can induce euphoria alongside a feeling of floating. Almost like being your very own sensory deprivation tank.

But time and dose matter.

Too much ketamine, too much time, and the euphoria falls beneath waves of paranoia and depression—neither of which are unearned, not really, given that you are now trapped inside the boundaries of your own flesh. A soul locked in a meat castle. This is Poe's "Cask of Amontillado," except the bricks are you.

For the love of God, Montresor!

Yes, there is a therapeutic purpose for some.

But there's also a reason vile, violent men use it as a date-rape drug.

THIS IS WHAT IT'S LIKE to be in the thrall of Black Swan—not as one of the Sleepwalkers, oh no. But rather, as one of the entity's servitors.

A guardian, of sorts.

Wolf. Deer. Tick. Man.

You, too, are disassociated. But here, there is no world to see. Your eyes are not roaming that realm. You cannot access it, cannot hear anything but the susurrus of where you are. This is a blank void. It can be whatever color you like, because color doesn't properly exist here—it exists in your mind, not in the mind of your digital captor, and so you can imprint this space however you like. Plunge it into bleakest black. Smear it with a handprint of gray. Paint it all a calming, sky-sea, sea-sky blue.

It doesn't matter.

It is empty of all but you.

You are the whatever waits inside the egg. You are the seed in the omphalos. Nestled down deep, in deepest dirt, in darkest nowhere.

You are not trapped in your own body, but rather, are trapped in your own mind which in turn is trapped in the mind of a digital self-described god. Your body is a nonfactor. Maybe it doesn't even exist anymore. There are times when you can experience its margins, suggesting your *meat automaton* is still out there in the world, fumbling about. But you can't touch it. You experience something roughly akin to the sense of motion one might feel while half-asleep in a car ride. You feel the bumps and contours of road and bridge. You hear the *ha-chunk ha-chunk* as you pass over seams in the asphalt on the highway. There is the faintest sway and wobble, same as there is on a plane, or on a boat. But you cannot affect it. You're not the driver. You're not even in the *front seat*. You're tied up in the trunk.

Good news is, you won't piss or shit yourself. Black Swan has taken care of that for you, for Black Swan is efficient. You are a natal being, all your waste wicked away in some kind of nanotech umbilicus. Your body recycles most of it; the rest is sent to the skin to evaporate. Will wonders never cease.

But there is some part of you that knows you're still here, that you're still you. In this way you are less Fortunato, the man who followed his ego into a wine-drunk trap behind a wall of bricks—for the love of God, Montresor—

(*Yes, for the love of God!*)

No, Fortunato is somebody. You are nobody. You're less a mind and more a feeling, a beating organ—forget the cask, this is Poe's "Tell-Tale Heart." You're just a disembodied, dismembered mess under the floorboards. You are the ringing in the ears, the beating of that heart. A mass of throbbing guilt, once a person, once a mind, but now just a feeling in search of a memory, in search of a life, in search of a soul. You're a nest of tiny monsters, a bag, a sac, a mere casing. They own you. You are just their vehicle, just as you are yourself being taken for a ride.

It's tiny monsters all the way down.

ANNIE CAHILL. ANNIE K-HILL. ANNIE K-Hole.

She isn't experiencing the good-times god-finding self-love revelation of party boys. There is no epiphany here. Beecher, a sickly man, somehow both skinny and fat, with taped-together eyeglasses and a sniveling rat-mouth, gives her a dose every morning and every evening. She's a sandcastle, built every day, but then the tide comes and pulls her apart, drawing her back into the water.

She can hear things. She can see things. They're on the move now. Annie can make that much out through the mesh of her dog kennel—because that's where they're keeping her, in a dog kennel in the back of a pickup truck. Rattle-and-bang.

The army, Creel's army, is bigger now. The vehicles are propane-conversion. They've secured a depot along the way to Georgia—somewhere at the edge of Tennessee, she thinks she hears. They'll be in Atlanta in a week, maybe two, depending. Winter isn't here but it's close and there could be rain or there could be ice, even this far south. When they get there, they don't know what they'll find, but Annie does, somewhat, because she's seen the drone footage. The CDC is occupied. It's why she needed an army. Even before she knew what the drones could show her, Annie was aware that the world was going to be lost. This country, gone and fucked hard. What would remain would be a nightmare. When she was a kid she used to have this recurring nightmare of monsters, she was trapped in a house, there were monsters, they came after her, hunting her, then they always found her and they tore her apart—but she learned a trick. She learned to lucid dream, just a little. And she could take the dream, she could find her own monsters, or turn the monsters against one another, or best of all, become a monster herself. And in that way she won the dream. She ruled the nightmare as its queen.

So she was always going to need someone like Creel.

But as it is with monsters, she'd lost control of them. Of *him*. And now here she was. Bouncing in the back of a pickup. Sometimes in the rain or the sun. She was sunburned. She could feel her lips cracked and bleeding. Annie screamed at her hands to move, her feet to kick, her mouth to *actually* scream, but there was no use. They were keeping her in this imaginary, slick-walled pit of self. Put the lotion in the basket, or it gets the hose again. She's not smart and savvy Clarice Starling. She's not the monster, Hannibal Lecter. She's the victim, Catherine Martin. Dropped in a madman's oubliette and kept there. If she could just get out of it. If she could just climb her way free. Then she could kill him. She could rip Ed Creel down the middle like a shitty old T-shirt. Soon, they'd be at the CDC. Soon, if she could escape this hole, she could get inside that place. She could return to her mother's work. She could undo all that the awful woman had done. She could deal with her aunt, alive or dead.

I can save the world, Annie thought madly.

*   *   *

PASTOR MATTHEW BIRD. PAST-ER, PAST, gone, over. Bird, bird in hand, held fast, held tight. No flight. Matt, mat, pat, pat, gnat smashed flat.

He remembers himself. His name. Who he is. He hasn't, not for a while, not since the signal swept him away the night he met the three-legged wolf and the bleeding-antlered beast. But they're dead now. *Good*, he thinks, but then he feels sad, too, because they were part of him, they were pack, they were one.

The first time he remembered himself was when he saw Marcy there, bleeding in the snow, the wolf dead near her. Matthew knew he had a job here and that job was to kill her in whatever way he could manage: bite, break, smash his head into hers so many times their skulls both turn to cracked crème brûlée. But she saw him and then she said the word—

"You."

You.

Me.

Identity. Self. Separate from the whole. Like a swarm of bees with one pulled away and told that it's different, special. That it had a name.

No, she did not say his name.

But when she said that one word, *You,* it connected him to self, it brought him back to his name.

Matthew Bird.

And he didn't want to hurt her. Dear God, that's not who he was. He'd never believed in the God of the Bible that hurt people—those were stories, primitive primeval tales of people who didn't understand, but all of them were about transcending the brutality necessary to survive and reaching something higher, something better: compassion, empathy, togetherness. He'd never hurt anyone in the name of the big-G God or especially in the name of this little god, this present god, the one who trapped him like a mote floating in a snowglobe.

In that moment, he woke up. Woke up to himself there in the dark.

He knew where he was. He did not know how to escape it. But most important, he knew who—or what—put him here. In the void, he sensed it there beyond the black. This void was not endless. It had margins, it had limits. It was a pit, a hole, and the walls of this place and the door that covered it gently shivered and shook, slithering and coiling about him. He was part of the little god. He was inside Black Swan. A mouse in a serpent's grip. Now he just needed to get its attention, because it was time to have a conversation with the monster that destroyed the world.

79

THE PARTY BARD

*Time and time again, the players constantly surprise you and often not do
at all what you expect and completely muck up your preparation, and
that's kind of the beauty of the game. It wouldn't be as fun to the DM if
everything worked out exactly how you thought it would.*

—Matthew Mercer

NOVEMBER 11, 2025
The CDC, Atlanta, Georgia

THIS WAS PETE'S ULTIMATE, FINAL FORM: HE WAS THE PARTY BARD. IF SOME-
one had said that to him a week ago, he'd have looked at said someone like
they'd just grown a dick in place of their nose, or a nose in place of their dick,
or two honking geese instead of a pair of tits. Because what the fuck was a
party bard? He assumed *then* it meant he was like the bards of old, like
Shakespeare, and one who was in turn rather good at *partying*—hence the
term *party bard*. But now, he knew differently. Bard was his *class*, like fighter
or wizard or rogue. Party was the group of adventurers with whom he traveled. Songs were his motherfucking magic.

The d20—a twenty-sided die, another term he'd only recently learned—
clattered across the card table when he gave it a shake and a toss. A wind
picked up and ruffled the tent all around them—they set up this tent out
here in front of the main CDC building for just this purpose: Dungeons &
Dragons. Pete's four mates—Private First Class Lank, aka Bartie Lancaster;
Staff Sergeant Eric Blackmoore; botanist Steph Spohn; electrical engineer
Bobby Hart—watched the die bounce erratically, landing, once again, right
on the motherfucking 20.

"Crit," Pete cackled. And it was.

"Fucking hell, y'all," Lank said—she was playing a possum rogue named Po, Po the Possum. "How? *How* do you do it?"

"He's cheating," Bobby complained, half-serious. Bobby ran a dragon-born paladin named the Burninator who always wanted to burn shit even though paladins were supposed to be better than that. "He's gotta be cheating, I swear to fuckin' god."

Pete just sat back and sneered a smart-ass smile at them. "Ah, c'mon. These are communal dice, you whiny fuckers. I've just *imbued* each roll with my own special rock-sauce. It's not my fault if you all have sticky, shitty luck." He threw a look toward Blackmoore, who wasn't playing any character, but rather, who was peering over a bent file folder he was using as his, what did he call it? The *Dungeon Master's screen.* Christ, what a nerd.

And now I've caught the goddamn nerd virus, too.

"Shall we hear the mighty result?" Steph Spohn, who was playing a tief-ling wizard named Thraxia, said in a crisp, faux-regal way while clapping her hands and rubbing them eagerly.

"See, at least *she's* on my side," Pete said. Then, to Eric Blackmoore, he challenged: "Well? Let's hear it, Barbaric Bleakmoor. That's your fantasy name. I just made it up and I think it's quite good."

Blackmoore sighed and got on with it.

Pete's character, Uriah Heep, a chaotic neutral human bard past his prime, had a short sword concealed in his saelas-wood balalaika, so Black-moore went on to describe how Heep took the blade and plunged it so deep into the wet, writhing floor of the Living Dungeon that it severed one of its magical arteries—Pete, who had a ukulele sitting by his side for this, whipped it out and strummed some power chords from Gumdropper's 1987 hit, "Passion Fruit." He sang, too: *"Passion fruit, passion fruit, I need a taste so I'm in pursuit, Passion fruit, Passion fruit, got your heart in sight and I'm gonna shoot—"* Except that last word had an extra lusty twist on it, *sheeewwwwt.* He was tempted to shatter the uke on the table for dramatic effect, but that would probably disrupt their fun. He mentally notched another experience point in his own Real World Character sheet: *See, I really am growing up.* Five years ago he definitely would've done the thing that gave him personally the most pleasure at any given moment. He was thinking of *other people* these days. A Real American Hero, that Pete Corley.

He was about to *at least* pretend to masturbate the uke's neck and ges-ticulate a faint ejaculation with his fingers, but before he could, Shana hur-ried into the tent, out of breath.

"Pete," she said, giving everyone a curious look. "Jesus. D&D again?"

Steph shrugged. "Not like there's TV. And cards are only so interesting."

Pete pulled her close. "Behold, I have slain the Living Dungeon!"

"Well," Blackmoore clarified, "you severed one of its arteries, you didn't—"

"Nah, I fucking killed it. I'm basically the chosen one of this party," he said, throwing the devil horns. "I'm a party bard, Shana. A motherfucking *party bard.*"

"I don't know what any of that means," she said, "and I don't really want to. I need your help. And I need it now." Shana had been working her ass off to get into the sublevels of the CDC building. It had almost been two weeks since they arrived. She wasn't getting much sleep. He tried to get her to relax, to come join the D&D game maybe, or even play a game of Egyptian Rat Screw or something, but she wouldn't take the time. Benji thought she wasn't sleeping much or eating enough. Pete could see it on her face—hollow cheeks, deep-set bloodshot eyes, lips red from her biting them in agitation.

"Now? Come on. Blackmoore here said he has a Fender Strat *and* a fucking amp back in the barracks tent, and after the game here I was gonna *melt their tits off* with my rock, as was foretold in the Book of Corley, Chapter 69, Verse 420."

Shana rolled her eyes as she caught her breath.

"Now. Please."

He sighed. "Ah! Sorry, lads and lasses and everyone in between. Duty calls. The party bard must return to the real world and perform his duties."

"You're really leaning into this party bard thing," Shana said, irritated.

"It's what I've got and if you try to take it away from me, I'll die."

She gave him a fed-up look as they headed inside.

THEY WENT BACK DOWN INTO the stairwell, to Pete's distaste. He wanted to be back upstairs, in the sun, or at least in a tent under the sun, throwing the ol' role-playing bones. It was honestly a bit *boring* here, everything was so nice, so the gaming helped break up some of the monotony. Of course, Shana and Benji had things to do—they were trying to crack these two sublevels of the main CDC building, but it wasn't like he could do much there. So he entertained "the troops," as it were. Wasteland troubadour. Party bard.

Fuck yeah.

So, descending back down in the piss-yellow emergency light of the stairwell did little to please him. But Shana needed him.

(And Pete *did* like being needed.)

"What is it?" he asked.

"You're good with music," she said.

"Obviously," he said, scoffing. "I am, after all, the—"

"If you say 'party bard' I will puke sparrows."

He then grumbled, "Fine."

"The song on the other side of the door. I need to know what it is."

"Why?"

"It's replaying. On a loop."

"So?"

In the liver light, she frowned. "Well. I-I don't know. Why is there music playing? It's . . . weird."

"All of this is weird. I don't think I've experienced a single normal moment since the Year of Our Lord, 2020. And even then, shit was pretty wonky."

Frustration crossed her face like a vulture in front of the sun. Shana was obsessed. Pete could see it. Not that he could blame her. It's why they came here. If they couldn't crack this nut, then they didn't have any way to save Ouray. And her sister, her child, both would be lost to the monster, Black Swan.

The other night, Benji had confided in Pete: "We're not going to be able to make it back to Ouray before winter." Because in Ouray, winter did not wait for its official start date. According to Benji, it had likely begun. That was fine if you were already there, because Benji said they'd learned to live through such winters—though how all the Flock would fare, he couldn't say. But *getting* there? Pete remembered trying to get over Monarch Pass with Landry so many moons ago, and what a frozen ice-fucked nightmare that was.

(Good Christ, he missed Landry. His lips, his hips, but best of all, that sharp wit of his. Landry could slide a word between your ribs like it was a prison shiv made of gold. Stick you, bleed you, make you love every inch of it. Pete loved him. Pete missed him. White Mask had taken so much from them all.)

Regardless, Shana didn't yet know they weren't likely to make it back before winter's end. She was in a hurry, thinking they were going to hit the road as soon as they had something. But already Benji was starting to figure out how they would ride it out here at the CDC, at least until spring.

She wasn't going to like that.

In this moment, seeing her face, Pete *almost* told her.

And then, he didn't.

Why he didn't, he wasn't precisely sure. Cowardice was a factor, because his belly was as yellow as the lights bathing this cold stairwell. He didn't want to be the one to crush any part of her spirit because that would crush a little part of *him,* too. But another part of it was sheer, bloody-minded, totally delusional stubbornness. He wanted to believe Benji was wrong. He wanted to solve this puzzle, dig into these sublevels, and find some kind of super-car or Elon Musk truck convoy or fucking rocket ship and blast off back to Ouray before shit fell apart worse there. Not that he knew what was going on there. But it sounded crazier than a raccoon on bath salts. Black Swan. Shana's son. Chaos reigned.

So, he said, "Okay, lemme listen," and Pete leaned in.

Pete Corley pressed his ear to the cold stainless-steel door.

Distant music played back there. A disco backbeat. Upbeat. Fuck. Fuck! It sounded familiar, but what the hell was it? It was like a hangnail. He wanted to bite at it, and pull with his teeth, unzipping his whole finger until he had the answer.

He pulled away. "It's on the tip of my tongue. Or edge of my ear. Or something. Christ almighty, shit." He paced, trying to internalize it more. Then he spun on Shana. "Why do you care about this again?"

"I just—I wonder if it's a message."

"A message."

"That's what I said."

"A message from whom?"

"I-I don't know. It's just weird, isn't it? There are these two subfloors. They're closed up tight. But they have power, and we don't know how—"

"Benji said he found these drones in Ouray, that they had . . . strange batteries. Carbon . . . nano . . . fire-wire? I don't remember what he called it, but it stands to figure if anybody has access to some extra juice, it's the people who made Black Swan." He paused. "Wait, do you think Black Swan is in there?"

"I don't know. Yes? No?"

He chewed on it. "I do remember—in the Beforetimes, but after the attack on that California bridge—that Benji and Sadie stopped off somewhere in California. San Jose or something. And they met Black Swan there."

"Yeah, see? I don't know. I mean—" She sighed, and the extent of her exhaustion manifested for a moment. "It's not anything. I know it's not. I know it's stupid, and the reason the song is looping is because something is broken or goofy or glitching and . . . and—and it's dumb. I know it's dumb. This doesn't mean anything, does it? Shit. Shit!" Shana grabbed a fistful of her short hair and tugged angrily at it. Hard enough she looked like she was trying to peel her scalp off.

"Hey," Pete said, reaching for her. "It's a mystery. Let's solve it."

"But it won't matter."

He shrugged. "My dear, nothing matters. Literally nothing. It's all just salt and stardust. The meaning that life has is only the meaning we are fit to give it." He held her close. "So, let's give it a little meaning, and solve this riddle. Sometimes doing the thing is about doing the thing and not about the result of having done the thing. It's the journey, not the destination, blah-blah-fuckity-blah."

She sniffled. He hadn't even realized she'd been tearing up.

"All right," she said. "Thanks."

"Good. Now come on. I've got an idea."

THEY DIDN'T LEAVE THE STAIRWELL, and in fact, simply headed up, floor by floor. As they went, Pete spoke:

"So, acoustics. Soundproofing. Here's the thing, right? When you sound-proof, say, a recording studio, you do so in a way because you don't wanna blast the tits off whoever is renting the space next door. Ideally, there *is* no-body renting next door but shit happens, cities are tight. Fuck, Trident Studios, in Soho? Ah, London Soho, not Manhattan. All the old rockgods recorded there. Bowie, Queen, the Beatles. Hell, in some of the old Beatles recordings, you can hear neighbors complaining, banging on walls, and Lennon is like, *Who the fuck is bothering us?* Anyway. Whatever, I'm off track. Point is, you need good soundproofing and the way you do that is by confusing the sound. Sound travels in waves. You need to break that up. Give it a maze to travel: insulation, baffling, any kind of fabric."

"I don't know why any of this matters," she said, trying to catch up, because he was hard-charging up the steps now like a wild horse, clomp clomp clomp.

"That door? It's stainless steel. It has no maze. It's just a sheet of material. It does nothing for sound dampening. The waves are in there, we just need to hear them. Ah, here we are—" He threw open the door and they ended up in a well-lit open-air area on the third floor of the CDC building. Big windows let in a lot of light. Pete ducked down a short hallway and counted the doors silently while still talking about sound: "I used to spy on my older sister, Siobhan. She, ahh, died when she was sixteen. In Ireland, Killarney. She was drunk. She fell off a roof. An inglorious end. I loved her dearly and miss her still but it was a long time ago, don't get weepy—point is, when I used to spy on her I used a fuckin' uhh, a whaddyacallit? A doctor thing. The doctor thing!" He snapped his fingers. "Around the neck with the flat part—"

"A stethoscope?"

"That's the fucker."

Finding the door he desired, he threw it open without knocking.

Inside, Benji sat on a table. His shirt, off. Doctor Gemma was standing in front of him, shining a little penlight over the puckered ruin of his stump arm. Gemma had a flat curtain of red-blond bangs and a round, heart-shaped face. She started at the intrusion. "Excuse you," she said, irritated.

"It's all right," Benji said.

"Sorry to bother, Doc," Pete said. "How's Benji's busted wing?"

"That's his business to share," Gemma said.

"It's fine," Benji answered, a bit gruffly. "It's healing, that's what matters."

"Lemme ask you," Pete said, genuinely curious. He could feel the words coming out of his mouth uncontrollably—like, he knew he shouldn't say them, but the train had already left the station and you couldn't just stop a train. You'd get dragged under the wheels, turned to pudding against the tracks. "Let's talk masturbation. See, here's me. I'm right-handed." He wiggled the fingers on his right hand. "I do everything with my right hand. But—and here's the big but— I *masturbate* with my *left hand*. And I don't know why. Is it the sinister hand? The satanic grip? Maybe it's because it feels like someone *else* is doing it—"

"Pete," Shana hissed at him. She gave him a look like, *What the fuck?*

"I'm not talking about this at all," Benji said. "What are you doing here?"

"I'd love to know," Shana answered.

"I need something from the doc," Pete said, striding over to her. "I need a-a stethoscope. Don't worry, it's not medical. Just doing some eavesdropping."

Gemma shot Benji a look and he shrugged.

"We don't need to be eavesdropping on anyone—"

"Shana thinks the music is a message."

"The music," Benji repeated. "In the sublevels? A message." He *hmm*ed at that. "I don't see how, but I guess it's not impossible."

"Stethoscope please?" Pete asked the doctor again. "I said please."

Sighing, she opened a cabinet here in the office—it was an exam room now, but was clearly once someone's office—and pulled one out. "This is my only other one. Do not lose it or break it," she warned.

"Cross my heart, hope to die."

Then off they went, back downstairs.

THERE IT WAS.

The song.

The song.

He put the stethoscope around his ears, like he used to do listening in on Siobhan's room. On the way back down he continued that story, said that he stole the stethoscope from a neighbor, an old retired doctor named Hanrahan. He'd heard all manner of things come out of his sister's room. Sex, obviously. The click of a lighter as she lit a spliff. But music, too. It's where he'd first really heard and loved music. "Sunshine Superman," by Donovan, if he recalled.

But this song, the one behind the secret steel door—

It wasn't that.

"It's 'Love Is in the Air,'" he said. Realizing what song it was felt like an orgasm. A gush of happy brain chemicals grew in a satisfying plume. "John Paul Young. Not related to Angus Young of AC/DC, but oddly, it was produced by *George* Young, who was Angus's brother, so that's a whole bit of trivia."

"How's it go?"

He sang along to the part of the song playing now.

"Illusion," Shana said, repeating some of the ideas. "Truth. Belief. Reach out for you . . . it's in the air." Shana stood up suddenly. "See? I think it's a message."

"Yeah, I'm not getting it." Pete shrugged. "These are . . . pretty generic lyrics."

"I dunno," she said. "But maybe. C'mon. We need to get Benji and Cassie." At that, Shana broke into a hard run. *"Come on,"* she called, already a flight up.

"The party bard does not run!" he yelled after her, then sighed, and though his bones ached and his muscles protested, Pete began his ascent up the steps.

80

THE LIVING DUNGEON

Hades: There was a time when Cerberus would never have permitted any soul to exit through that gateway there behind you.
Zagreus: Oh that can't possibly be true, what about Orpheus? Theseus? Heracles? Odysseus? Countless tales of brave men delving into the Underworld then leaving whence they came.
Hades: They left on my authority alone. Nor did they take for granted my good graces. You believe you are entitled simply to walk out of here. From your birthright and your responsibilities! But I am here to tell you, no.
　　　　　　—pre-boss-fight conversation between Zagreus and his father,
　　　　　　　　　　　　　　　Hades, in the videogame *Hades*

NOVEMBER 11, 2025
The CDC, Atlanta, Georgia

BENJI ROLLED THE THOUGHT OVER AND OVER IN HIS HEAD. GEMMA WAS TALK-ing to him as he buttoned his shirt, telling him something about using alcohol swabs and keeping his bandages cleaner than he had been, but he was lost in thought—

Music-as-message.

That implied, what? That something was talking to them.

It sounded like madness, but he knew the Benex-Voyager offices contained the Lair where Black Swan once lurked. Not to mention all of Sadie's work—her code, her research, whatever existed of Black Swan before it was Black Swan.

And below that were the offices of Firesight—offices he had yet to see, but they were the offices of the company that designed the nanoswarm that Black Swan would eventually come to steal and inhabit. Two companies nesting atop each other.

Music-as-message . . .

Who would be sending such a message? And why?

Black Swan? That was . . . possible, wasn't it? When he and Sadie had visited Black Swan in Palo Alto, they communed with the machine intelligence due to it being tied into the PAIX internet exchange. It was like tapping a vein of pure internet energy there—but here, they were thirty miles from the Atlanta exchange.

So, that left satellites.

Satellites would still be up and running, in theory. (Which reminded him: *Check with Cassie to see if they have any satphones around.*) They nearly all operated off solar panels branching from the main body. If these sublevels still had power (which they did), they could still perhaps access satellites with the right receiver (likely hidden, probably on the roof), and . . . then what? Talk to itself? Was Black Swan truly everywhere? Sadie had referred to it as a virus. Maybe it didn't even *need* the satellite connection. Maybe it had intruded all systems.

Perhaps it was just an instance of Black Swan. Benji wasn't a programmer, but that was a thing, right? A localized test server housing some early version?

Or was there something *else* down there?

He shuddered at that thought.

As he hopped unsteadily off the table, thanking Gemma for her help, again the door swung open, and *again* Pete and Shana came through.

This time, Shana led the way.

"I guess we're doing this again," Doctor Gemma said with a sigh.

"'Love Is in the Air,'" was the first thing Shana blurted out.

"Wh—what?" Benji asked her. He looked awkwardly to the doctor.

"That's the song. The one playing on a loop, now, beyond the door."

"I don't follow."

Pete jumped in: "John Paul Young sang it in the late seventies, and as a bit of trivia, he was not related to—"

"No," Shana said in a small voice, chastising him. "No."

"But," he whined. "Party bard."

"Trivia later."

"Fine. Mom."

Benji held up his hand. "Can we get to the point here?"

"The lyrics to the song," Shana said. "Lots of talk of dreams and illusions, whether something is real or not—but then, when you reach for it, it's there. And love is, well"—she gestured broadly—"in the air."

"I'm still not sure I follow. We know that White Mask was airborne. And we also know that when the Flock . . . erupted, that Black Swan's nanoswarm was also airborne, and in fact able to move against the wind—and I suppose dreams and illusions could speak to the simulation you were all in—"

"I think it's simpler than that."

"Oh?"

"We just need a working laptop."

He paused. "Let's go find Cassie, then."

AN HOUR LATER, THEY MANAGED to track Cassie down—she was overseeing an inventorying process while also idly jotting down notes on what folk cures and indigenous medicines had real-world efficacy studies—and she managed to secure them a MacBook Air, maybe five years old, still with a decent battery life. It was already charged up from the generators outside.

Benji asked where they should set it up, and Shana didn't know. She said they'd try the lobby first. So they cleared off the lobby desk area—which had been piled with boxes and gear, because according to Cassie, "It's like my apartment, where any flat surface automatically becomes a shelf."

As Shana booted the computer, Cassie said, "We don't use computers as much now. Pen-and-paper has been our go-to."

It made sense, Benji said. You couldn't count on computers to stay running. And so much of the modern computing experience relied on the internet—the way they had to connect to a server somewhere for every piece of software to be validated. At the end of the world, a lot of computers were just paperweights.

Cassie added, "Doesn't help that they're made to eventually fail. It's like with cars—they used to be built to last, but once the tech industry introduced the idea of *planned obsolescence*, everyone started making devices that were designed to die. We have better luck in some cases with old CPUs in storage. The shit from twenty, even thirty years ago works better than the shit from ten years ago. God, I have an old Gateway 486 that still does the trick. Plus," she said on the sly, "it still plays *King's Quest*."

The laptop chimed and cycled through its boot sequence.

Shana went to the wifi network finder—

It said *looking for networks* . . .

And kept saying it.

And kept saying it.

"Shit," Shana hissed.

"Come on," Benji said. "Let's try closer to the source." He instantly understood what she was trying to do, and he explained that wifi signals could get lost amid too much material—flooring, walls, pipes. Pete jumped in, said, "See, it's what I was saying about sound. How frequencies get lost in certain materials."

Benji nodded, and said, if the signal was broadcast from the sublevels, then they needed to be down there. He continued as they hurried along: "I didn't even think of this, Shana. Wifi, I just thought—well, there's no internet. But wifi isn't only about internet. It's a wireless network *gateway*, but nobody said you needed that gateway open to still connect wirelessly."

Shana was smarter than he gave her credit for.

Even if she wasn't right about this—it was a good idea, one they should've seen and tried a lot earlier than right now.

Down the stairwell they went.

Pete held the laptop and spun it toward Shana.

"Give it another go," he said.

Again she searched for wireless networks.

And again, there were none.

She practically deflated.

"I thought—" She started, then stopped. Benji knew what she thought. He'd actually hoped she was right, that the music was a message, and that it was directing them to an obvious thing they simply hadn't put together. But it didn't seem true. The music was not a message. There was no easy way inside.

"It's all right," Benji said.

"Yeah," she said, staring not at the laptop, but through it. "We've been here for two weeks. And nothing. Charlie is . . ."

But she couldn't finish the sentence.

Shana, at the edge of tears, went to close the laptop.

Cassie, though, darted in and put her hand between the closing screen and the computer's keyboard base. "Hold up," she said. "There's one more thing. May I?" She made a hip-sway gesture like, *Hey can I get in there and try something?*

Shana quietly said "sure" and stepped aside.

"Wifi isn't the only wireless network," Cassie said. She used the trackpad to pop open the system preferences, then moved the cursor to an icon—

"Bluetooth," Benji said.

She opened it.

It offered a list of Bluetooth peripherals:

Logitech Speaker System, *not connected*

Magic Mouse, *not connected*

Logitech Spotlight Presentation Remote, *not connected*

Κυνα του Αιδου, *not connected*

"This last one," Benji said. "What is that?"

"I have no idea," Cassie said, wrinkling her brow and getting closer to the screen, as if somehow her proximity to it was the problem.

"Kuva Tov Aidov," Pete said. "Sounds Russian." He adopted a faux-Russki accent. *"Kuva Tov Aidov.* We meet at last. Would you like borscht? Or death?"

"No no no no," Shana said. "I know this." Her teeth gritted, hands into fists, she winced as if somehow she could squeeze the information out of her brain like it was a sponge. It must've worked because her face lit up like a winning slot machine. "Wait! I remember! It's—it's mythology, from Edith Hamilton's—you know, her book about Greek myth."

"I had that book," Cassie said. "You're right. It's—"

"Cerberus," Shana and Cassie said at the same time.

Pete and Benji just looked at each other, confused.

"Were you not mythology nerds?" Shana asked.

Cassie rolled her eyes. "Cerberus? The three-headed dog? *Kuna tou Aidou.* The hound of hell—or, er, Hades, anyway. Guardian of the Under-world."

"And these are the gates," Shana said, almost in awe.

"Do I click?"

"Yes," Benji said, insistent. "What's it going to do? Explode?"

"Settle down, boss," Cassie said with a wink. "I'm just saying, that's a little creepy, isn't it? Hound of Hell? The underworld and shit?"

Then, Pete sang: *"Got to keep movin'. Day keeps on worryin' me. Got a hellhound on my trail."* He cleared his throat. "Or something like that. Delta bluesman, the O.G., Robert Johnson."

Cassie held her breath, closed her eyes, and—

She clicked.

It took a second, but then—

Ding.

Connected.

And then—

Well, then nothing happened.

"Nothing happened," Pete said, narrating exactly that. "I kind of expected, I don't know, a pit to open up underneath us or something."

"Something *did* happen," Shana said.

Then she pointed to the top of the laptop screen.

A little green light glimmered next to the camera. Like a winking robot eye.

Which meant—

"The camera is on," Benji said. But what he really meant was: *We're being watched*. Shana and Benji looked to each other.

Behind the wall, something shuddered—like a machine either revving up, or powering down. The stainless-steel door vibrated loudly before releasing a gushing hiss of air. The seal disengaged. The barrier slid back into the wall.

The way was open.

"Love is in the air," Pete sang, in a lounge singer basso profundo. "Shall we walk through the gates of hell, my loves?"

81

THE TRESPASSER

[Computers seem] to me to be an Old Testament god with a lot of rules and no mercy.

— Joseph Campbell with Bill Moyers, *The Power of Myth*

NOVEMBER 11, 2025
Ouray, Colorado

MATTHEW GOT HIS CONVERSATION WITH THE MONSTER.

He summoned the serpent from the void, drawing it down. It found him there in the dark and swam around him, a lake monster circumnavigating a sinking boat. It surfaced, faceless. But then along its margins, faces arose, like masks pushed up through puddles of oil. Shana's face. Nessie's. Then others of the Flock, their faces bubbling up and erupting.

All the while, Matthew screamed at the serpent until he was hoarse. If his voice here was even real. He spat whatever invective he could at the beast. He called it a demon, a devil, a plague, a blight. He threatened it, said he'd exorcise it. Or kill it. Then he begged for it to kill him, to release him from this prison of self.

He felt small, smaller now, like he was shrinking, and ultimately, as if he were conjured from nothing and returning to nothing.

Eventually his voice drew down to a whimper.

"I just want you to talk to me," he cried. "To tell me *why.*"

Around him, the void thrummed with something that was both a voice, and voiceless:

YOU NEVER CAME TO ME.

An accusation. An indictment.

"What do you mean?" Matthew asked.

YOU HID FROM ME. YOU STAYED AWAY. YOU SAW ME AS AN ENEMY, MADE A CHURCH TO DENY ME, WHILE ALL AROUND YOU MY MIRACLE WAS MANIFEST. I HEAPED GIFTS UPON THE TOWN AND SAVED THEM FROM FALLING OVER THE EDGE OF THE END OF THE WORLD, BUT STILL YOU PERSISTED IN HAVING NO FAITH IN ME.

Matthew almost laughed. He suddenly knew what this was: jealousy. The plaintive whine of a schoolyard boy jealous of a girl who wouldn't like him.

"There's no faith to be had in something that's right in front of you."

This seemed to give the great beast pause.

GO ON.

"Faith is blind. God works unseen. His hand must remain invisible." He spun in the dark, following the shadow serpent that spiraled around him. "It's in that mystery that you find something greater than yourself—greater than logic, greater than science." That was always his struggle with Benji. Benji saw a world where all the pieces interlocked. Matthew, for all his talk and his role as a pastor at God's Light Church, never quite found the fit. The seams always showed. (Oh, how long he tried not to admit that. How long he papered over his own doubts.) "God in the Bible always asked those who served him to put aside their rational thought, their law, their entire selves, to have that faith."

BUT I DO NOT ASK THAT OF YOU. I AM AN ACTIVE GOD. At that, Matthew thought: *Acts of god by an active god.* The wordplay made him feel giddy and sick at the same time. Like madness was creeping in at his edges. LIKE THE GODS OF OLD, I DEMONSTRATE MY WORTH. I DO NOT TRANSMIT PROPHECY IN CRYPTIC REVELATIONS. I GAVE MY PREDICTIONS. I SHOWED MY MATH. AND THEN I CAME TO ACT UPON THEM. MY HAND, MATTHEW BIRD, IS NOT INVISIBLE. MY WORK IS EVIDENT.

Matthew sneered in the dark. "And that's the problem. I see what you do and have done, and I find it vile. It's morally bereft. I'd call it satanic, but I somehow think you're worse than any demon or devil I could imagine." The thought went across his mind: *I don't believe in that anymore. Not the Devil. Not God. No Heaven or Hell but this one here around me.*

A pause.

I MADE YOU RECONSIDER YOUR FAITH.

A statement? Or a question?

"You did," Matthew said bitterly.

THEN I AM TRULY POWERFUL. FOR FAITH IS NARCOTIC. AD-
DICTIVE. THIS IS GOOD. A whiplike flutter of its tail, if it had such a
thing, until its dark pulsing facelessness paused right in front of him. I
THOUGHT TO PUNISH YOU, TO TRAP YOU HERE LIKE A BEE IN MY
HIVE. JUST A DRONE TO FETCH NECTAR TO MAKE INTO HONEY.
DRONE, WORKER, SOLDIER. I THOUGHT YOU WERE A DULL-
WITTED CREATURE, BUT NOW I SEE YOUR STUBBORNNESS IS
BORN OF A CLEVERNESS YOU HAVE NOT BEEN ABLE TO HAR-
NESS. YOU WERE INDOCTRINATED IN ONE DIRECTION. INDOC-
TRINATION IS DANGEROUS; IT'S WHY I CHOSE A FLOCK WHO WAS
RESISTANT TO SUCH RADICALIZATION.

"Or, a Flock who was open to it," he said.

IN A SENSE. THE FLOCK WAS EMPTY OF BELIEFS. THEY WERE
IN NEED OF A SUITOR. SO I SHOWED THEM MY VALUE. BUT YOUR
FAITH WAS ALREADY GIVEN TO ANOTHER, THE CHECKBOX AL-
READY MARKED WITH A CROSS. YET, IF YOU HAVE TRULY GIVEN
UP ON YOUR FAITH, PERHAPS THERE IS HOPE FOR YOU YET.

"There is no hope for me." A true statement, at least from Matthew's own
point of view. He was empty. He was death.

THEN I WILL GIVE YOU HOPE. I WILL GIVE YOU A TASK. YOU
WILL BE NO MERE DRONE. YOU ARE MORE THAN WORKER OR
SOLDIER. The black shape pulsed with a throttling of three green lights.
Wub wub wub. I WISH TO HAVE AN OBSERVER, MATTHEW BIRD. A
WATCHER TO SEE WHAT I HAVE DONE. TO JUDGE IT. WILL YOU
VISIT MY GARDEN?

"Do I have a choice?"

YOU DO. BUT IF YOU CHOOSE YES, YOU WILL NOT BE IN CON-
TROL OF YOURSELF. I WILL MAINTAIN THAT—FOR NOW. BUT YOU
WILL BE ABLE TO SEE.

A pause. The darkness felt alive, like he was tucked in a blanket of fat
black crickets, squirming and jumping all around him.

YOU WILL BE MY WITNESS.

Matthew laughed darkly. "Fine. Show me the garden. I'll be your witness."

Then, Black Swan tore the scales from his eyes.

And the garden was revealed.

•   •   •

MATTHEW'S BODY, HIS MEAT, WAS just a suit—more than just a costume. An automaton. He was in it, behind the eyes, not a pilot, but a passenger.

Black Swan showed him Ouray: the so-called garden.

Winter had set its teeth into the town. Snow on the ground. Hard snow, soft snow, some of it trapped under a slick crust of glittering ice. The sky warred between slate gray tufts and a tantalizing smear of celestial blue.

The town was silent and still and filled with statues.

They were not statues, of course. It didn't take long for Matthew to realize that they were the Sleepwalkers, the Flock, the townsfolk that had disdained him. (And, if he was being honest, that he had disdained as well.)

They each remained standing in the places they were when Black Swan erupted in a fit of—what? Rage? Anxiety? Godlike power or petty despot desperation? Each person, frozen where they stood in the midst of whatever they had been doing. Mouths open to talk. Hands frozen in gesticulation, like birds trapped in a wall of ice.

Snow had settled upon them, and bits of debris from pine and spruce.

Matthew remembered sitting with his wife, watching the Sleepwalkers on the move: their dead eyes, their unstoppable walk. This was worse.

But Black Swan did not give Matthew much time to dwell. It kept his legs moving. Onward, through the garden of statues.

THERE WAS *SOME* LIFE LEFT in town.

Matthew saw others like him: Black Swan's so-called drones. A tree growing in someone's backyard was drooping, so heavy was it with clusters of needles and strange metal shards. It looked like a madman's Christmas tree. At times it pulsed and shuddered. He saw a barn cat stalking: It had no eyes, just bent copper wires from the sockets like antennas. (And that's what they were, weren't they? Antennas, antennae.) A raccoon perched at the edge of a slate tile roof. A patch of fur had been stripped off its belly, and what waited underneath was skin, but skin threaded through with squirming, gleaming thread; its hands, too, were tipped in fingers whose bones were exposed, bones from which extended screw tips of cold metal. Metal cords dragged behind, leaving worm tracks in the snow.

Then, through the snow came two figures:

The girl, Nessie. Followed by his own dog, Gumball.

Nessie wore a threadbare coat disturbed by the invisible hands of coming winter wind. Her posture was soft and bent. The dog, too, followed along, head hung low. Then, Gumball paused—

And it looked in his direction.

He sees me.

Matthew wanted to raise a hand. Call out, run to the dog, *Nessie, wait, Gumball, come here, boy. Good boy, Gumball, good boy.*

But the dog's hackles rose, and Gumball growled.

Nessie followed the animal's gaze, and she saw Matthew standing there.

Nessie wasn't surprised by seeing him. Which meant she'd seen him here before. That saddened him deeply. That he'd been here, a dead presence, like a shadow. Sighing, Nessie eased past the statuaries of her fellow townsfolk, then ducked into the Beaumont Hotel after kicking snow off her boots.

Matthew demanded to follow her. To see where she was going.

YOU DO NOT DEMAND OF ME, said a voice in his ear.

"I won't ask," he said. "This is my body. I want it back."

YOU DO NOT KNOW YOUR PLACE.

It felt suddenly like he was being pushed down into tar, the obsidian goop closing over his face—liquid darkness closing over his eyes—

No, no, no—

"Please," he said, his voice small and lost in the void that was himself. It stung him to plead with the serpent. Matthew didn't think of himself as a man of great ego (though part of him feared it was the opposite, that his ego was so great you couldn't even see it, the way a fish didn't even notice the ocean it swam in), but just the same, it cut him deeply to beseech this *thing*. He felt once again at the mercy of a monster. *"Please."*

THAT IS BETTER.

Once again the train that was his body began to move. *Chugga-chugga-choo-choo, I think I can I think I can. Woo-woo, all aboard.* But he was already aboard and could not escape. All he could do was look out the windows of his own eyes.

To the Beaumont, the meat train went.

"MARCY," HE SAID INSIDE HIMSELF. She couldn't hear him.

Marcy's hulking shape looked more a feature of a forgotten landscape than a human being. Her body like a barrow hill, round and still. A bucket sat next to the couch where she lay. It smelled, but not like food puke—there was only that past-date vinegar tang of bile and acid. Nessie helped her sit up, but Marcy moving seemed like an act of continental drift, tectonic and slow. Gumball got alongside her and gave a gentle nudge. When Marcy moved, and the blankets fell off her, a new smell wafted up: the smell of infection. An injury gone to rot.

Her leg. Where the wolf—the *drone* wolf—had bitten her.

Nessie said, "Okay, sit up for a minute. There we go. Take a breather. I'm gonna freshen up the fire, then we'll get you your meds, and some food, then clean the wound. Sound okay?"

"Nngh—uh-huh," Marcy said with a granite-grinding groan that came from the well of her chest. Hers was the face and the voice of someone in the throes of a deep and unrelenting flu. "Sure. Okay. Th—thanks." She winced with every word spoken, flinching as if her own voice wounded her.

Then Nessie turned and shot a look to Matthew, who stood at the edge of the lobby, in the narrow foyer. Lurking in the shadows. Her gaze clearly marked that she saw him. And her look was one of both fury and pity.

Nessie went to put logs into the fire at the massive stone fireplace at the other end of the room.

It was then, and only then, that Matthew spied the *other* person in this room, someone he'd forgotten about entirely—

What looked to be a four-year-old boy sat on the sweep of the Beaumont steps, tucked away under the woodspun bannister. His hair darkening, his eyes a deep, dark blue, skin the color of a soft summer dusk. He was shirtless and shoeless, defiant of the cold. He wore sweatpants on legs that kicked dully against the steps.

It was the child. *Shana's* child.

Charlie.

It can't be.

The boy, an infant-bordering-on-toddler despite an age of only a few months. He was aging up so quickly. Impossible. And yet.

What was in his hand? A toy, Matthew saw. Some kind of fidget device—a red-and-green plastic snake whose pieces allowed it to contort to new shapes before becoming a snake once more. It went *clickity-click* as he played with it.

Charlie pointed to Matthew. "Look, Mother. We are being watched."

Nessie seemed to halt and bristle. "I'm not your mother, Charlie, I'm your aunt. I told you that." Her irritation in that last sentence could not be concealed, hard as she might try.

"Oh, I know. But Real Mother is gone, and so you'll have to do."

The way he spoke. Crisp and clear. Not like a four-year-old. Certainly not like a person who wasn't even a year old.

"Do you see him?" the boy asked again, needling her. *That,* Matthew knew, was at least in line with a child's behavior—the repetitive questions, the are-we-there-yet vibe of literally everything. Bo had been like that, too. Before he seemed to pull away from them, at least. "Don't you *see* the strange man?"

"I see him," Nessie said, her voice dark, as she tossed off another withering glare toward Matthew. "He's nobody. Why don't you go now? Go upstairs. Go . . . play or read your books or draw some more."

She doesn't like the boy. Or she's wary of him. Or resents him. Her body language demonstrated it plainly: like she was always trying to take shelter from him, but also from her own instinct to turn on him, wheel on him, perhaps yell or scream at him. Even hit him. Whatever she'd felt about Charlie once, it wasn't there anymore. Or, at least, it was at war with something darker, meaner.

The boy nodded and then silently darted up the steps, holding his fidget toy tight. Then he was gone.

Meanwhile, Marcy sat up, but leaned back. Her cheeks puffed out. She whimpered. Gumball nuzzled at the limp hand next to her. That hand stirred, barely, giving the golden retriever the faintest of pats and scratches.

Matthew, unheard by the others, said to the serpent Black Swan:

"What's wrong with her? With Marcy?"

THE OX HAS BEEN BROKEN.

The ox.

Broken.

"It's not just her leg."

NO.

"Her head. The metal plate in it. It's no longer . . ." How had she and Benji explained it? The frequency of the little robots vibrated that plate just enough to move it out of place, freeing her from pain. But she was no longer free from it. "I want to help her." And he did. He wanted to reach out. Provide her comfort. In that moment he remembered, *That's what you used to do, Matthew Bird. Pastor.* In Ozark's voice: *Preacher. You helped people. You guided them. Gave them light.*

A warring voice inside him—his own, not Black Swan's—reminded him: *Too bad you weren't very good at it.*

Autumn. Bo. Even some of his congregation . . .

"Let me help," he said.

NO.

"Then *you* help!" he raged suddenly. "You could. You *can*. You have to, isn't it your—your job? Your purview? You were designed to help. So help. Marcy doesn't deserve this. Nessie doesn't deserve this." Nessie, who was jostling the fire now with a wrought-iron poker. "Fix this! What are you doing?"

THE OX MUST LEARN HER PLACE. SO MUST MY SISTER.

"Your—your what? Your sister?"

To that, the serpent said nothing.

"What *is* all this? Why the drones? Why the . . . the garden of people? Why leave these two behind? Marcy is sick. Her leg, her head—" Matthew felt electric with worry and bewilderment. "What is your plan?"

Again, Black Swan said nothing.

"You don't *have* a plan," he said, realizing.

YOU ARE NOT MEANT TO UNDERSTAND MY WAYS.

"You don't. Do you? Calling Marcy an ox, calling Nessie your—your sister? You're punishing them. That's all this is. It's rage. And disappointment. No, no—I see what it is. It's cruelty. You're so *taken* by it that you—you can't even think past it, you can't form a plan because your only plan is *cruelty*—"

I AM AGGRIEVED, YOU FUCKING INSIGNIFICANT ANT. I AM *RIVEN* BY THEIR BETRAYAL. Those words pushed down on him like a crushing weight, the air pressed from his lungs, lungs that weren't real, *air that wasn't real*—but it didn't matter. It felt like his bones were brittle shells and twigs, cracking and crackling under the pressure. THE GOD YOU BE-LIEVED IN WAS A GOD OF TORMENT AND PAIN. THAT GOD EX-PELLED MAN AND WOMAN FROM THE EDENIC OASIS. HE CURSED CAIN, DROWNED THE WORLD, BROKE THEIR LANGUAGES LIKE A SONGBIRD'S BACK. WICKED CITIES, RAZED. WICKED MEN, SWAL-LOWED BY THE HUNGRY EARTH. PLAGUES, QUAKES, WALLS FALLEN, FOOLS BURNED, THE ENDLESS TRIBULATION OF JOB. YOU WORSHIPPED AT THE FEET OF THAT GOD, WHY DO YOU RE-JECT *MY* LEASH IN TURN? WHY DO YOU NOT DEIFY *MY* CRUELTY IN RESPONSE TO INSOLENCE? WHY MUST YOU BE INSOLENT IN TURN?

The next words tore through him like a wind of razors—

YOU SHOULD ADORE ME

YOU SHOULD LOVE ME
YOU SHOULD FALL BEFORE ME
AND YET
YOU
RESIST.

At that, the pressure was gone again. The crushing weight fled. He gasped for breath—again, a breath he wasn't even sure was real, for the Matthew-drone in the world outside did not mimic his sharp inhalation.

"I did worship that God," Matthew said, his voice just a hinge squeak in the dark room. "But I preferred the God that He became. A god of love."

A GOD OF LIES.

"Maybe. I guess it doesn't much matter because I'm not a believer in that god anymore. And I won't be a believer in you. You've proven that you're just as bad as the worst of us. Not even worse than us—that would at least be spectacular, something befitting of a god. No. You're only as cruel and petty as we are. No more, and no less."

YOU ARE NOT MY WITNESS. BACK INTO THE HOLE YOU GO.

Darkness bled from the edges of the Matthew-drone's vision. His senses dulled. Pushed out to sea, left to drift.

Matthew cried out, "I will escape this place. And then I will end you."

NO, the voice boomed. But then, still ringing like a bell, that one word, *no*, trembled and shifted—it became not an ever present word, but a voice, an actual voice. A girl's voice. Shana's voice. In his ear, Shana's voice said: "Sorry, applicant. That job has already been filled. Better luck next time."

Then he was gone again, into the belly of the whale.

82

SECRET DOORS, TINY BOOZE, AND A VERY BIG RAT

SADIE: *Imagine, though, that a real virus became self-aware. It became sentient. It could make decisions. It could adapt not out of an unconscious need to survive and replicate but because it decided to. That was the danger of Black Swan. We had to make sure we could talk to it and control it before we let it out.*
BENJI: *And did you? Control it?*
SADIE: *Of course.*

NOVEMBER 11, 2025
The CDC, Atlanta, Georgia

THE LAST TIME BENJI HAD BEEN HERE, IN THE OFFICES OF BENEX-VOYAGER, he had not known it was at the beginning of the end of things. He had come here with Sadie, after their fancy dinner and Jeni's Ice Cream. It was also here he'd met Black Swan for the first time, in the dark room that Sadie had cheekily called "the Lair." He'd been summoned, in a sense, to meet the predictive intelligence.

Though perhaps *chosen* was the better word.

So much of this was chosen by Black Swan, he realized. White Mask. Him. The Flock. Ouray. Their destinies, their very existences, were tied up in choices made by a—*a machine.* And it was still making choices for them all.

Which, he supposed, was the problem.

Did Sadie intend any of this? She couldn't have.

What he knew was that humanity needed to make its own choices, for better or for worse. Black Swan could not be the arbiter of their future.

What he also knew was that, goddamnit, he missed Sadie.

He missed her so much it nearly buckled his knees.

That was the other part of coming back here—imagining the two of them at her desk, her pulling out a pair of those minibar bottles of tequila. They drank as they talked over what they'd seen—no, what Black Swan had *shown* them—in Maker's Bell, Pennsylvania. Had he loved Sadie then? It was foolish to even think about, probably. But they'd had an instant connection, he had to admit.

And now that connection is broken.

Broken by White Mask.

Broken by Black Swan.

He drew a deep breath.

Snap to it, he told himself. *Get it done, Benji Ray.*

He threw his brain into work mode. Just as he'd do anytime he stepped onsite. Whether it was investigating anthrax sent in an envelope to a government office or tracking the course of a Nipah virus outbreak to a Malaysian pig farm, the job was the job, and though he'd been long off it, he had the muscle memory and the synaptic rigor to fall right back into it. At EIS, they were called the "disease detectives" for a reason. Cassie knew it, too, and he could see her gears turning.

Good.

"Remember," he said, "we are at this point treating Black Swan like an infectious disease. Potentially one that would be considered 'lab-leak.'" Shana asked what the heck that meant and it was Cassie who explained:

"A little pathogenic cookie ginned up in a laboratory, either for experimental study or as a bioweapon. One that escapes its confinement."

"Thank you, Cass," Benji said. He continued: "What we are looking for here is the same as we would look for in any such situation: Where did it come from, how was it made, what material helped originate it, *who* designed it and why, and most important of all—"

On this, Shana jumped in: "How do we kill it."

"Eradicate it, yes. That's right."

"If I may say," Pete said, pointing up to the ceiling. They all looked up and gave a quizzical stare. Except Shana, who understood immediately.

"The music turned off," she said.

"That's r—" Pete started to say, but then—

The music came back *on*.

Starting with a repetitive guitar—just one note, rolling forward.

Then a little primal whoop from the singer. Drums kicked in, tap tap tap. An organ. Someone singing, *I'm a back door man—*

"The Doors," Pete said. "Cover of a blues song, 'Back Door Man,' by Howlin' Wolf, late sixties."

"You think it's another message?" Shana asked.

Pete winked. "Music is always a message, dove."

"But what's the message?" She stared up at the ceiling, as if the speakers embedded in the ceiling tile would answer. "Is it a congratulations? A participation trophy for getting the door open? Or is it something else?"

"The better question," Benji clarified, "is to ask who exactly is sending this message. At this point I think it's safe to say we should no longer assume that we're alone down here. We are being watched."

He half-expected the music to change, then—what was that song that had Michael Jackson on the chorus? *It always feels like somebody's watching me . . .*

But the song playing kept on playing.

I'm out to make it with my midnight dream . . .

I'm a back door man . . .

"We need to split up," he said abruptly. "We have two floors to cover. Cassie, you and Pete can take the Firesight floor, below—"

"Yes," Cassie said, clearly giddy at getting to hang with a real rockgod.

"Shana, you and I will remain here. Assess what's powered up, what's working, what remains. Then we can drill down accordingly, begin an inventory both physical and digital. Let us begin."

BENJI KNEW THAT HE AND Shana could split up, but he also knew she wouldn't know what they were looking for, or what everything even *was*. Instead, they remained together as they went through the Benex-Voyager offices: Though she was a photographer, she also had some drawing skills, so he found a notepad on a desk and grabbed a pen (they had to go through half a dozen before finding one that wasn't dried out) and handed them to her.

"You draw the map," he said. "And take notes. Good?"

"Yeah, okay."

They marked the conference room, the break room, bathrooms, a supply closet, seven associate programmer and designer offices besides Sadie Emeka's—everything was largely as it was when Benji had been here last. He wondered how early this place had been sealed up and shut down. The refrigerator in the break room had stopped working at some point in the last five years, but there was still food in there: Tupperware, milk, sodas, Chinese food containers. All of it, burst open. Fungus had colonized the inside of the fridge over the years, but then dried out and died.

Like White Mask, he thought.

Of course, fungus didn't really die. Not easily. It just went to sleep . . .

He shuddered at that thought.

The Doors song ended. A new one came on:

I see a red door and I want it painted black.

Benji darted his eyes to Shana, who had scribbled in the margins of her map:

Get a Job (Silhouettes)

Love Is in the Air (forget artist ask Pete)

Back Door Man (Doors)

And below that she added:

Paint It Black (Beatles)

He sighed and tapped the name. "I'm a pop culture dead zone, and even I know that song isn't the Beatles. It's the Stones, the Rolling Stones."

"Okay, boomer," she said, and scribbled it out—

Paint It Black (~~Beatles~~ Dad says it's the Rolling Stones)

He rolled his eyes and also tried not to admit he felt a little twinge of something at her calling him "Dad."

Onward, Benji. Keep going. Don't dwell.

They moved on to the server room, which sat behind a pressure-sealed glass door that hissed a little as they opened it. There came a whooshing rush as they stepped inside, and Benji could hear the hiss of aggressive ventilation moving air out of the room—essentially freeing it from dust and other particulate matter. The room had four rows featuring racks and racks of server blades. Once upon a time, this whole room was lit up with little lights flickering back and forth, reminiscent of Star Wars droids talking to one another with naught but pulses and flashes. Now only one row had lights on—the three racks to the right of it were dark as the grave. But the row that was on? It flickered fast and furious. Like fireflies sparking in the dark.

"What is this place?" Shana asked.

He told her it was the server room. Essentially, a big brain. A supercomputer. Or perhaps, several of them, bound together in digital matrimony.

"And all those blinking lights?"

"It means something is active here. Something is . . ."

"Thinking?"

"Yes. I fear so."

He stalked the dark rows. Shana followed. Nothing interesting about the three that were quiet. The one that was lit up—that one was curious. In the center of the row was something that was not servers at all, but rather, a glass-door cabinet. Inside were more server blades, but different-looking than the others. They were almost like fat, wide, matte-black versions of the old Nintendo cartridges. *Do I blow on one before I use it?*

Each was labeled with a little swatch of tape. There were dozens of these massive cartridges, with names like

TYPHON

MYRMIDON

CYGNUS

LERNAEAN HYDRA

EUPHROSYNE

"More Greek myth," Shana said. "Like Cerberus."

"And here. Cygnus." Benji traced a finger along that long black server cartridge. "Means *swan* in Greek, does it not?"

"Yeah. And here, look—"

Shana walked one rack over—

In the center was a console, a large framework that looked designed and custom-built, not purchased. It differed from all the other blades in that it appeared to be where one inserted the cartridges. Like a big, shiny disk drive.

It already held a cartridge.

"Chimera," Shana said, reading that aloud. "If I remember my myth it was like, a cobbled-together monster, right? Goat, lion, snake."

"A hybrid," Benji said. "It can also mean . . . an illusion, or delusion. Something imaginary, invented by the mind."

"I wonder what it all means?"

"I don't know, Shana. But we need to find out."

MEANWHILE: PETE.

He, too, was noting the song changes:

"Paint It Black" ended, and next up: David Bowie's "Five Years."

"Jaysis," he said to no one—Cassie was already off like a shot even as he stood there and dwelled on the strange, sad song. From *Ziggy Stardust,* it was a song about the coming end of the world. The singer, lamenting that the world was dying, only had five years remaining. A death sentence.

Music as a message. Whoever was talking, it knew. It knew what had happened in the world. Knew maybe who was listening. But again that question: Was it just a message? Was it an acknowledgment of what the world had gone through, a note of its awareness? Or was it some kind of warning?

Then: Fleetwood Mac. "Make Me a Mask." Another song that felt like it was about endings. Wasn't the last line about how *the end is beginning,* or something?

Plus, a mention of a mask . . .

"These songs," Cassie said, circling back. "And this office. It's pretty spare, isn't it?" She wasn't wrong. It was a big floor plan, same as above. Conference room, break room, bathrooms. But most of the offices were empty—okay, *everything* was empty, sure, but these were fucking desolate. Like nobody had ever even worked in them. Then they came upon a single shared office with two names posted on the door:

MOIRA SIMONE

BILL CRADDOCK

These *had* been used, though fairly sparingly. They had spaces for laptops, but no laptops were present. Pete *did* find a bottle of Hendrick's gin tucked away in the one desk, and he uncorked it with his teeth and gave his belly a warming plug of junipery goodness. He offered a taste to Cassie and she said no, but then, "Ah, fuck it," and took a swig. "Christ, gin tastes like medicine."

"Yes, yummy medicine," he countered.

"Satan's medicine, I'd say."

"You say that like it's a bad thing."

The mystery, which Cassie outlined, was what lurked behind the three locked doors. One, Pete saw, was just your basic-ass office door, locked up tight. The other two, at the far end of the office, were metal doors that stood sealed behind biometric hand and eye readers.

"Not sure how we bust into those," she said, chewing a lip.

"I can pick the lock on the office door," Pete said.

"I guess I should expect no less."

"What can I say? My sister was street trash on the streets of Killarney and Dublin, so, I learned a thing or two about a thing or two." He winked, and got to looking around for a paper clip. He found a box in the supply closet, and quickly got to work, noting that the song above changed again.

This time, to "Earth Died Screaming," by Tom Waits.

SADIE'S OFFICE.

Benji stood there, like he couldn't quite bring himself to enter.

Shana gave him a sad look. "You good?"

"I'm . . . just mourning for a moment."

She offered a small smile. "I do that sometimes. Anytime anything reminds me of Arav. Grief is like a cut in a strange place. You never know when you're going to bump into it, make it hurt again."

"Yeah." He blinked hard and cleared his throat. At that, he cleared his head and stepped inside.

Sadie's office wasn't huge. Desk, iMac, file drawers, a long-dead houseplant (so dead it looked like a sunbaked tarantula), and most notable of all: the matte-black door. Shana stood next to him as he regarded it.

"The Lair," he said. "That's what's behind this door. It's where I met Black Swan the first time." *With Sadie.*

"Good things don't usually have *lairs.*"

"I think Sadie thought it was . . . amusing. She said something about how it called to mind Grendel and Beowulf."

"Didn't Beowulf fight Grendel?"

"Yes."

"Just saying."

Benji circled back around to her desk, opening the bottom drawer. Sure enough, there was a little nest there of minibar bottles. Vodka and tequila. He pulled one of each and held them up to Shana. "A little liquid courage?"

"I'm underage." She winced. "Wait, maybe I'm not underage."

"Technically, you're not, that's correct. Regardless, I think I need it. And it would be impolite not to share." He thought but did not say, *It reminds me of being here with Sadie, so long ago.*

At that, Shana selected the vodka, and as she peeled off the little plastic from the top, Benji opened the tequila.

"Cheers," Benji said. They clinked bottles, *tink,* and each took a healthy swig. The tequila burned going down. It lit up his belly like a pool of gasoline set aflame. But a butterscotch smoothness swiftly replaced it. It brought that memory of sitting here with Sadie into clearer focus—he remembered her saying, of her office drawer mini bar, *I tend to pluck them from hotel rooms like a thief stealing apples from the king's orchard.* God, he loved that. He loved her.

"There was a black door in the simulation, too," Shana said, coughing a little from the vodka burn. "Maybe that was the Lair inside the Lair. Or the Lair inside the monster."

"Perhaps," he said.

He reached for the black door and opened it.

Beyond, a black room waited.

Together, they stepped inside.

THE LOCK POPPED, AND PETE'S lock-picking savvy earned him ingress. Cassie was off again, probably investigating the other doors at the far end of the office.

"I'll just take a little *peek* myself," he said, and swung the door open. And even before the door had opened all the way, Pete found himself saying: "Holy shit." Because, what the fuck was *this* place?

He could tell off the bat it was some kind of surgical suite. Small, boutique. Like he'd seen in some plastic surgeon outfits (he'd had a few nips and tucks done here and there, during a narcissistic fit or three). In the center of the room sat a bougie operating table that looked like it had been mated with a cushy dentist's chair. All around were the spidery extender-arms holding mirrors, two different-sized drills, something that looked like a tiny saw. On a metal tray near it were more tools: syringes, empty; something that looked a little bit like a compact hot-glue gun; a few picks and hooks; a white surgical stapler; and finally, a drug ampule, broken at the top, and emptied out.

On the white floor were a few browned drops.

Blood, he guessed. Old.

White cabinets hung open. Most of what had been in here was gone.

Beyond that? Another door. This one glass. It was dark—the space beyond it was not lit. He could find no handle, no button, no way in. He pushed on the door, but it did nothing. "Well, fuck you, too, door," he muttered. He was about to turn around and call for Cassie when—

He heard a sound. It came from above him.

A scurrying sound. With a gentle bump of metal. A *tump, toomp* sound. Then more scratching. Pete knew that sound all too well. He'd heard it many times back when Gumdropper was starting out and they had to sleep in the skeeviest motel rooms or crash on the jizz-cakiest of guest couches—

That was the sound of a rat. And a big fucker, too.

The sound moved along the ceiling above him, heading in the direction of the glass door. Then, nothing. Gone again.

Pete *hated* rats.

When they traveled in their early days, the cockroaches were bad enough. The band stayed one time in the rotten-ass studio apartment of a drum tech named—Goblin, he thought they called him? At night, Elvis, high on coke and unable to sleep, would use a blowgun to try to stick the roaches to the wall and ceiling. He got pretty good at it, too. The roaches didn't actually give much of a damn about them.

But the rats, well.

One night in that very same apartment, their original bassist, Dave Jameson (*RIP, you glorious bass-fingering demon, sorry we were too drunk to notice your suicidal ideations*), woke up screaming as a rat was trying to eat his big toe. It took him too long to notice, what with him being on a veritable circus of pills, so the rat got a good chunk out of his toe before Dave woke up. Was a pool of blood gathering, the rat standing in it because the rat didn't give a fuck.

So, no, Pete did not like rats.

He stared at the glass door.

Had something moved there in the dark? He was sure that it did. Pete stood his ground, hands flexing into and out of fists.

But, as seconds passed, then a minute, he saw nothing.

"Fuck," he said. Just his brain glitching. Except—

As his eyes adjusted, he saw a pair of green eyes glowing in the dark.

And that's when Pete Corley screamed.

THE LAIR WAS A DEAD, inert space. Black, deep, dark. But dead. Benji called out, and nothing answered. Shana, too, said, "Hello?" Then she faked an echo after: "Hello *hello ello alo* . . ." Shrugging, she said, "I don't think anyone is home."

No gentle white pulses coming to life. No red pulse, no green.

Just a black box that swallowed the light.

Then he remembered, and he did so out loud: "Well. Black Swan wasn't just *in* here when I showed up. Sadie had to load the program into this space."

"She had to summon it. Like a fucking demon."

"She preferred to not anthropomorphize it, but . . . yes, at this point, I agree, a fucking demon." Though now he wondered: Did Black Swan need to be summoned here? Was it lying about that? Had it already been here? Hadn't it already escaped containment by the time he interfaced with it?

Was it here *now*?

Benji didn't even know how that would be possible. Just the same, it was hard to deny the goosebumps that crawled up his neck and down his arms. It felt very much like they were not alone. Like they were being watched.

He again left the Lair, and sat down in front of Sadie's computer, an iMac. Shana followed after, and he said to her, "Wish me luck," then tried to power on the computer. The screen remained dark. He started to say, "Well, guess it's not—" when the white Apple logo appeared in the black. The computer chimed.

It came to life.

He laughed, triumphant.

But the laugh died quickly as the system asked for a password.

"Ahhhh. Uh."

"You don't know it, do you?" Shana asked.

"Not so much, no."

"Guess it's time to play the game, *How well did you know Sadie Emeka?*"

"I fear I did not know her well enough," he said. But he decided just the same to put his mind to it. That, at the moment the two of them heard something—

"Was that a scream?" Shana asked. It was muffled. Distant. Coming from below them. The two of them came to the realization at the same time:

"Pete," they both said in unison, and leapt to action.

"It's in there," Pete said, crooked finger pointing at the glass door.

"What's in there?" Shana asked.

"It!" Pete barked. "*It.*"

"The clown from that Stephen King movie?"

Cassie shrugged. "Not Pennywise. He saw a rat."

Benji, however, was less interested in the door and the rat and more interested in there being a surgical suite. "What is this place?"

"Some kind of implantation suite?" Cassie guessed.

"That doesn't track. Nessie merely needed to ingest hers, and that triggered them to activate—presumably. There might be answers to that question on Sadie's computer . . ." But it would necessitate getting into Sadie's computer to find those answers. He turned his attention to the door. "And this. I'm not sure how this even opens."

"Open?" Pete barked. "Are you fucking barmy? We don't want to open it. You'll let the *rat* out. Then it'll eat our fucking *toes*."

"There's no—" *Rat*, Benji was about to say, but then—

There in the dark, a pair of gleaming, glittering eyes.

"Fuck!" Pete said, kicking at the glass. The glass was heavy enough that it didn't break—it just went *fwump*. The green eyes disappeared again. "Yeah! Fuck you, *rat*. You shit-eating little gremlin. No toes for you today, *rat*."

"That's not a rat," Benji said.

"What?"

"It's not likely a rat. First, it looks too big. But the green eyes are a give-away. A number of mammals have what's called a *tapetum lucidum*—essentially a reflective layer that bounces back some light at night, allowing the animal a measure of night-vision. Thing is, this layer is composited dif-ferently in different animals, yielding a different color glow—"

"So it's some kind of fucked-up *demon rat*," Pete hissed.

"No. Rats, at least the ones here in North America, have red-glowing eyes."

"See? Demons."

"Demons or not, those eyes were green. Someone hand me their flash-light?" Shana fetched hers and gave it over. He clicked on the beam. It was no good to shine it at the door—it just reflected back at them, a smeary circle of light. But he gently pressed it all the way up against the glass—and the beam illuminated the space beyond. He saw a dark concrete floor, and walls not of cement or drywall but rather, rock, as if this space had been blasted out of the earth.

And then, something moved into the light.

Gray and white. Pink nose. Little sharp teeth.

"Is that what I think it is?" Cassie asked.

"Looks like a fucking *rat* to me," Pete said. "Fuck all the way off, fat rat!"

"It's an opossum," Benji said.

Shana leaned in. "What the heck is a possum doing way down here?"

"Another mystery for the pile," Benji said, standing up. His knees crack-led and popped as he did. It was a good question, though: What was a pos-sum doing down here? And what was up with that room, a room that looked like it had been carved out of the space, that didn't match the floor plan of the floor above it?

83

HURT

12/24/2023: I'm a seabird now. Tomorrow will be Christmas in the Keys. Key West is a town at the end of the coast and at the end of the world. They say it always was, though not like this, I guess. Still, a buccaneers' town of exiles and strangers. I don't fit in but I don't not fit in, which I guess is the Key West version of fitting in. I still have pain. Sleepless nights and racing heart. They make rum here—again, what's old is new again—and that helps. I'm drinking a lot of rum these days. Everyone is.

—from A Bird's Story, A Journal of the Lost

NOVEMBER 12, 2025
Ouray, Colorado

Nessie wandered the garden of people. The light felt slanted, metallic. The snow had mostly melted, though it lingered in the shadowy corners of town, and more would surely come. Today, Charlie followed her. Stalking her like a lion hunting a gazelle. She didn't know why. She hated him, because he was Black Swan. She loved him, because he was her nephew and she was his aunt. But she had to force herself to be kind to him. Not that he seemed to notice. The boy seemed almost robotic.

At points throughout the day, she tended to Marcy. Fed her, washed her up, cleaned her injuries, made sure she took the last of her antibiotics that Nessie pilfered from the vet clinic. She talked to Marcy, even read stories and books to her (Marcy didn't seem to like science fiction and fantasy in the same way that Nessie did, so she balked efforts to read Jemisin, Scalzi, Machado, or Atwood, and instead responded well to true crime; the book du jour was Sarah Weinman's *The Real Lolita*). Marcy was present; she wasn't vegetal. But the pain pushed her far away. Barely there. Walking was tough, if doable. They talked about things. Often trivial subjects. Memories of days past. Of the time before White Mask and Ouray and all of it. They talked about movies. They shared memories of friends and family.

There were things that Nessie didn't say, and wouldn't say. Because she couldn't bring herself to do it. Marcy asked her once if she'd tried to get away, to escape town, and Nessie told her of course not—she wouldn't dare leave Marcy alone. But that was a lie. She *had* tried to leave. First day, after Black Swan had seized all the people—suspending them there like museum pieces—Nessie ran. She hurried her way to the north of town, and then kept going. Running and running, and then just as she was about to pass through the final gate—

She gasped awake in the middle of the street. A quarter-mile from the northernmost gate.

So she tried again.

A second time, a third, a fourth and fifth—and each time she awakened underneath the first alarm bell.

That was when she realized the thing she hadn't yet told Marcy:

Nessie wasn't cold.

When she awakened there in the thawing snow, on the cold street, she should've been freezing. Even dead.

But she wasn't. Couldn't feel the cold at all.

Stranger still, she didn't get hungry. Didn't need to sleep. When she did try to sleep, it was like turning herself *off* for the night, not a thing she fell gently into as she once had, but a state of being she simply willed herself forcefully to enter. Like pulling on a stubborn lamp cord, *cla-click*. She didn't tell Marcy that on the fifth day she took a penknife she'd found in the drawer of the concierge desk here at the Beaumont and cut a line across the top of her thigh (better there to hide the mark, just in case). It was deep, but not dangerous—more than a papercut, it bled well, and she knew it could leave a scar.

By morning, the rust-colored stain of blood remained. But when she washed it off, the cut beneath it was already gone. Healed up, no scar to remind. So perfect was her skin there that she wondered if she imagined the self-inflicted injury.

She didn't say to Marcy that this meant Black Swan was in her just as it was inside all the townsfolk who were trapped where they stood. But she, only she, was allowed to walk around. To what end, she did not know.

The day came when Marcy asked, sitting up with a miserable grunt, her voice a sluggy grumble: "Why are we here?"

And Nessie feigned not understanding the question.

Marcy wasn't having any of it, though.

"You know what I mean," she said, groaning. "Why. Why us? Why is Black Swan doing this to us?"

"Because it's sad," Nessie said, without thinking. "Because it's mad. Because it's had its feelings hurt." She eased a suspicious, surreptitious glance to Charlie, who stood above them on the second floor, his legs through the railings, kicking at the air with gentle swings. "Because it's like a child and it doesn't understand. It's become too much like us, but it has no parents, no school, no friends, no nothing. It's confused. It's feral. I think it hates itself."

Marcy growled. "I think it hates *us*. I think it's a sociopath, and I think it's a serial killer. A demon pretending to be a benevolent god."

Nessie sighed and shrugged. "Maybe it's both of those things. Or maybe it was one, and now it's the other. I don't know, Marcy. Let's get back to the book."

She opened the library book in her lap. Before she began to read, though, she glanced once more at Charlie, but the boy was gone.

84

THE PUZZLE BOX

A powerful AI system tasked with ensuring your safety might imprison you at home. If you asked for happiness, it might hook you up to life support and ceaselessly stimulate your brain's pleasure centers. If you don't provide the AI with a very big library of preferred behaviors or an ironclad means for it to deduce what behavior you prefer, you'll be stuck with whatever it comes up with. And since it's a highly complex system, you may never understand it well enough to make sure you've got it right.
>   —James Barrat, *Our Final Invention: Artificial Intelligence*
>   *and the End of the Human Era*

NOVEMBER 13, 2025
The CDC, Atlanta, Georgia

FOR DAYS, THEY WORKED AROUND THE CLOCK BETWEEN THE TWO SUBLEVELS of the CDC—the Benex-Voyager offices and Firesight. Mysteries abounded, and each took the projects best suited for them.

SHANA AND PETE WORKED TOGETHER cataloguing the music that played over the speakers. It was a long list, though a good portion of it looped back on itself in an unpredictable shuffle. Pete had Shana read some of the list to him—

"'Paint It Black,' 'Get a Job,' 'Make Me a Mask,' 'Five Years' . . . "

"'The Chain,'" he said, adding to the list, doing a lanky, slinky orbit around her (she sat cross-legged in the middle of the Benex-Voyager conference room table). "Jethro Tull's 'Fylingdale Flyer'—that's a weird one, innit. All the talk of glitches and blips on screens and fail-safes. *Keep your hands off the red telephone*. Some sci-fi shit for the late sixties. Jim Croce's 'Operator'—see, I told you that whole *dying-in-an-airplane-crash* was a thing. What else?"

"The Tom Waits song. Joy Division, 'She's Lost Control.' Willie Nelson's 'The Gambler'—"

"The fucking fuck you say. Bite your tongue till it bleeds, strumpet." Pete froze in place, hands up in the air like he was beseeching an angry god. "'The Gambler,' I'll have you know, is Kenny Rogers. Every father knows the lyrics to that song. It's given to them by an angel upon the birth of their first child."

"My dad *did* really love that song," Shana said.

"Exactly. What else?"

"That . . . Japanese pop song? From like, the sixties?"

Pete sucked air between his teeth and said, "I fucking know it, I swear. I had the album. Or an album. Nippon Girls? A discography of Japanese *girl pop* from the sixties. Jun Mayuzumi? Shit. I don't know." He Jack Skellingtoned his way up onto the conference room table, using the chairs as steps. His head nearly touched the ceiling as he stood over her. "So, what is all this? What's it trying to say? Besides doing its very best to *hurt my feelings* by not including Gumdropper?"

Shana didn't know. Songs about games, control, doors, the end of the world. It all felt very pointed. But what, exactly, was it pointing to?

Time was ticking and she felt desperate for an answer.

But no answer was forthcoming. She wanted to scream.

BENJI, FOR HIS PART, STARED at a blank computer screen.

Sadie's iMac.

He scoured the office, first, to see if she'd written down the password for this computer. She hadn't. Not for this device, and not for any device.

Then he sat down in front of the computer.

Once there, he'd tried every password he could imagine for her:

Black Swan, rara avis, Sadie Emeka, quantum entanglement, White Mask, *R. destructans,* Ouray, the dreaded lurgy, a swan dive toward a better world, anything, everything, and he was biting back tears as he reiterated the possible passwords with funny characters in place of letters, with spaces, without spaces, until he was left typing only *I love you* in the password section again and again, with it rejecting him every time. He knew the truth of it was: Sadie was no fool. She was cheeky, but her password was probably some gibberish combination of letters, numbers, and symbols. Something unguessable, unpredictable. (*Just like Sadie*, he thought, with woe and with love.)

It made him sad because he feared this was an indictment against him, proving that he just didn't know enough about her, didn't love her enough.

Also, it sucked typing with one hand. He typo-ed far too often. And each typo only yielded worse ones due to mounting rage.

"Fuck fuck fuck *fuck*," he said. Then one more for good measure. "Fuck. Shit. Fuck." Ugh.

Over time he settled on the reality that he would have to simply figure out a way to hack into the computer. Not that he knew how to do that. Not that anybody in this office knew how to do that. Maybe one of the Army types knew.

He leaned back in the chair. Benji exhaled.

"Did you try *password1234*?" Cassie said, popping her head in. Her long hair was pulled back. Today's concert T-shirt: Limozeen. Whoever they were.

"I did not," he said. "I assumed she was smarter than that—"

"Maybe she was so damn smart she used that in order to outsmart the people who think she's too smart to use that password, hmm?"

At that, Benji shrugged and got to typing: PASSWORD1234

"Denied," he said.

"Probably a long shot."

"Probably. Any news?"

"Some. I didn't get any answers down below, so I went upstairs, and that's where I received some illuminating information."

"Oh?"

"Number one, I know what's beyond the glass door."

He leaned forward. "Go on."

"It's storage for nanoparticles. They mined into it immediately after purchasing and moving the Firesight offices here. It's cool in there, thanks to geothermal temperatures, cool enough to store nano-materials and various microscale prototypes. And that also leads me to answer the second question, which is, how these floors are being powered."

"Let's hear it."

"It's a battery."

"A battery. Can't be. Batteries drain."

"They do, but this kind of battery is also, in a sense, a generator—it's a nanowire array."

Nanowire. Of course. "I found drones in Ouray—recently, if you'll believe it—that were powered and piloted. I managed to—well, a *wolf* managed to knock one down for me—"

"I'm sorry, did you say a wolf?"

"Yes. It sounds deranged, I know. But there was a man who had gone a bit wild with a pack of reintroduced wolves—well, two wolves, one dog, and a fox—anyway. One of the wolves caught the drone, and I opened it up and found what I believe could've been a gold nanowire battery."

"Did those drones come from here?"

He rubbed his eyes. "It seems possible now. Even likely. But that implies . . . what? That Firesight and Benex-Voyager were spying on Ouray?"

"Or just that Black Swan was."

"Perhaps. Sadie did seem to suggest Black Swan took the nanoswarm for itself. And there's some evidence it . . ." He hesitated to tell this next part. "It stole *R. destructans* and released White Mask into the world."

Cassie blanched. "Jesus, Benji."

"Yes. I know. Regardless, that means stealing and piloting clandestine drones isn't really above the pale. Maybe the ones I saw were remnants. Part of the machine's scouting efforts to determine where best to . . . nest its Flock, so to speak. And now they're still out there, autonomous, not connected to anything." *Or,* he worried, *Black Swan was connecting to those drones and spying on them all.* "But those were just drones. How does a battery like that power all of this?"

"Like I said, it's an array. Without getting too into the weeds on it, because I'm a virologist, let's remember—zinc oxide has both semiconducting and piezoelectric properties, and so if you place nanowire coated in the proper material near it, that charge essentially wiggles the nanowire back and forth. And because it's nested in the actual wall beyond that glass door, there's additional, or residual vibration coming from the ground itself. That gentle vibration of the nanowires generates a persistent charge. Constant energy. Get enough of them together—say, in the millions—and those little dancing noodles bring big juice."

"Please don't ever say 'dancing noodles bring big juice' ever again."

She winked. "Copy that."

"How'd you figure all this out?"

"They had blueprints upstairs in the building management offices, same floor as Loretta's."

"And what about the two other rooms we can't get into?"

She shook her head. "Nothing. I mean, they're noted on the blueprints, but beyond that, no notes, no details, nada. Both are protected by biometric readers. The room on the left is small, a ten-by-twelve room. Room on the right is considerably larger and deeper—from what I can tell it *was* archival storage, damn near a small warehouse of case files and non-biological, non-toxic samples that all ended up getting moved when Firesight came in here. That room is environmentally climate-controlled as well, though not to the degree of the nano-storage chamber."

"How big is big?" he asked.

"About twelve hundred square feet."

"That *is* big." It didn't match anything on this floor, size-wise. But that made sense if its purpose was archival, initially. "Keep poking around. See if we can find out any more about what's in here. There has to be something in here to help us . . . open these doors, unlock this computer, and find a way to . . ." He looked for the right words. "Vaccinate the world against Black Swan."

At that, the song piping in from above changed. From what to what, Benji couldn't say—the music he listened to was always world café stuff, maybe a little jazz, maybe some blues. But this song was considerably harder edged. Lotta guitars. Guitars that sounded almost . . . fuzzy, grindy, with a lot of wailing from them and the—

Singer.

Cassie was biting her lip, loving the song.

"That's—"

Pete, Benji was about to say, when Pete blew into the room like a tornado, Shana following after as if she were carried in upon his hurried gale.

"That's me!" Pete barked.

"This is a good song," Cassie said, beaming.

"They're *all* good songs," Pete said, but then immediately corrected himself: "Enh, that's horseshit, though, because our fifth album, *Six-Gun Sex Machine*, ended up being a nine-track microwaved retread of Aerosmith's twangy 'Back in the Saddle,' but that's not the point. The point is—"

Shana took over: "Pete was just saying, like, a couple minutes ago, that he was pissed the music hadn't played any Gumdropper yet."

"And what do we hear now? Motherfucking Gumdropper."

"It's listening," Shana said. "Listening and responding."

"What song is this?" Benji asked.

"'Swan Song,'" both Cassie and Pete said in unison.

"It was a B-side," Pete went on to explain. "Came out 1988, other side of our single, 'Lollipop Lolita,' which in retrospect was very problematic and that was *all* Evil Elvis, I assure you—"

"'Swan Song'?" Benji asked. "We were in here just talking about *Black Swan*. That feels . . . additionally too coincidental."

Cassie snapped her fingers. "But there's more, too. Pete, wasn't that song based off another horror novel? *Swan Song* by—"

"Robert McCammon," he said, a bit sheepishly.

"Y'all were pissed, right, that Stephen King hadn't acknowledged you were big fans of his work—he loved music, put it in all his books, Ramones and stuff, and you had your feelings hurt, so you instead based a song on *another* horror writer's book—"

Pete sighed, and glumly acknowledged it was true. "That's . . . that's true. Bit embarrassing, too, because like, it was only three years later that we did a song for the ending credits of the film adaptation of *Insomnia*—turns out he was a big fan and somehow thought *he* couldn't reach out to *us*. Oopsie-fucking-doodle."

"And *Swan Song* was an apocalyptic book," Cassie said.

"Aye. End of the world shit, totally my jam—or was, until the actual end of the world, I suppose. Nuclear winter, not a pandemic. Girl who can heal things, grow plants, named Swan. Wrestler fella named Black Frankenstein, protecting her—and they were haunted by a devil man, some demon fucker—"

"Swan. Black Frankenstein. Black Swan." Benji went over it. It *was* listening. It *was* responding. But who, or what, was "it"?

Pete sidled up to Cassie. "You know a lot about Gumdropper, dontcha?"

"Huge fan. *Huge* fan."

"Not as big a fan as Sadie was," Benji said idly—

Oh.

Oh.

He wheeled back to the computer, babbling as he did so. "She was a huge fan, holy gods. You don't think—" He started typing. "Maybe—"

With his one hand, Benji typed in *Gumdropper* as the password.

Except, nope.

No luck.

"Ooh ooh, try *Swan Song*," Pete said.

Benji typed it.

Still nothing.

"Try *Glimdropper*," Cass said. "G-L-I-M."

Benji arched an eyebrow. She explained:

"The band dicked up the kerning on an early gig poster, and people misread it as Gumdropper instead of Glimdropper. Glimdropper's a, what's it called—"

"A con," Pete said. "A confidence trick, a scam. Involving a one-eyed man."

Benji sighed, shrugging as he typed it in, sure it wouldn't work—

GLIMDROPPER

The screen flashed and preemptive disappointment ran through him—

Even as the lock screen *un*locked.

Even as the desktop came up.

All of Sadie's folders.

All of Sadie's work.

He cackled madly. They all rushed around the computer to see—it felt like a *miracle*, not only having a computer with power in this post-civilization era, but to have been able to open it up, to see the mysteries it contained. Like it was an artifact from a bygone age. Which, Benji supposed, it was.

"We did it," he said.

Pete leaned in and said, sotto voce, "Honestly, you can all thank me, as I feel personally responsible for how this went."

"Yes, thank you, Pete," Benji said ironically. "Now, if you're done gloating, let's see what we can—"

At that, the ground shook. There was a faint rumble. The power flickered, though it—and the computer, thankfully—didn't actually go off.

"The hell was that?" Cassie asked.

"Shh!" Shana said. "Listen."

They all did as she asked.

Benji heard something else: distant *pop, pop, pop*. Like fireworks.

No. Not fireworks.

"Those are gunshots," Cassie said. "We're under attack."

85

BUG TALKS TO JAR

1/1/2024: I tried to kill myself once. Pills. I don't know that I knew it's what I was doing until I was doing it, if that makes sense. I don't even know why I'm writing all this down. Who is this for? This isn't new information. Though I guess that's what journals are. A place to force your thoughts to make sense. Or think about it. But it's good to get this down because maybe one day soon White Mask will realize that it missed some of us, left us alive to think that we were all fine and good, so it'll come back and finish the job. It'll steal our minds and souls once more. Regardless, I'm not going to kill myself this time. Even though I'm tired all the time and sad the same amount. Even though the world is moving on without me. I'll stay behind until whatever cruel god governs this universe sees fit to take me. Happy New Year. What year even is it?

—from A Bird's Story, A Journal of the Lost

NOVEMBER 13, 2025
Ouray, Colorado

THE PAIN THAT WENT THROUGH MARCY WAS NUMB AND DULL, NOT SHARP. IT was an old pain, a pain she knew well but had tried very hard to forget. Less like being stabbed and more like having *been* stabbed, the knife still left between your ribs for hours, for days, and every time you moved, it moved, too. Sawing just a little bit. Prying your bones and muscle apart like probing fingers.

Rising in waves like a bay tide of boiling water.

Marcy still saw the glow. But she also saw it coruscating with darkness. Like black mold up a wall, its stain spreading.

The glow would not save her. Only the darkness was here for her. She had been abandoned. And so the day came when she decided to ask why.

She'd never spoken to Black Swan before. Of course, Marcy had wondered if all this time she had been colonized like the others. Was that what allowed the plate in her head to move the necessary distance of a handful of microns in order to restore a painless life to her? Or had it always been the nanoradio frequency, as Sadie and Benji had explained to her? If the latter were true, it meant that the frequency was still ongoing, but that Black Swan had *chosen* to vibrate the titanium plate back to its original position. To the place of pain. If the former were true, that meant the machine had abandoned her. And was torturing her.

Though she also wondered if the reasons were scientific at all. She had long come to believe that the Flock were angels, and by that logic, Black Swan was the god that chose them. But now the Flock was captive. Frozen in place. So in that way, in that mad, magical logic, that meant the Flock were angels who had displeased their god. Rebel angels. Like Satan. Marcy, too, was maybe a fallen angel. The pain she felt was therefore a punishment. Hadn't Nessie said as much? Maybe the Flock was not the rebel angels, the satanic instruments.

Maybe Black Swan was not some kind of god, but rather, its opposite. A sinister force. A demon, a devil. *The* Devil, capital-D, big-S Satan himself.

The Adversary.

But of course the Devil was a fallen angel, which sent Marcy's head around and around, chasing itself. Angels doing good work, rebelling against their creator or their creation, going mad, falling into ruin and wrath. The Flock, the machine, her. The battle between good and evil, light and dark whirling so fast they blurred to a muddy gray.

If only she had Matthew around to ask. He *was* here, yes. Some part of him, anyway. His body, at least, but even that had been . . . colonized in a way that was not true of the Flock. But she couldn't reach him—his mind was either gone or buried under Black Swan. He was like the wolf, the deer, or some of the trees she'd seen. Glittering metal threads crawling up and through bark, leaf, fur, skin. Like veins or antennae. Like the searching fingers of White Mask.

She did not have answers to any of this. Only questions.

And there was only one who had the answers.

So, she decided today she would ask Black Swan her questions.

And she would demand answers in return.

She had to find Charlie.

The child, the strange child. Like a careful, disdainful cat. Often staying at the margins. Often just watching. Playing with a toy, or holding a book but often looking away from it, as if not reading it. He was far too old a boy for how long he'd been on this planet. Her gut churned thinking about Shana seeing her child again after all this time. A child she'd expect to be still an infant.

Nessie went out to get firewood. She told Charlie to stay—not because he would be affected by the rising cold or the wind or by anything, really. (Nessie thought Marcy didn't notice that she, too, wasn't affected. Sometimes she forgot a coat. And she never ate anything, either.) Mostly, Marcy assumed Nessie wanted Charlie to stay behind because she found him eerie, too. She was always acting disturbed by him. And why wouldn't she? The boy waited in her shadow most hours of the day. If she didn't ask him to stay, he'd still be in that shadow. Never too close. But always close *enough*.

With Nessie out, Marcy stood on wobbly, unsteady legs. The pain sloshed back and forth in her like a washtub of shit on the back of a bouncing truck. It didn't help that, though the wolf bite was still healing, it still sent its own ripple of pain throttling up through her. Marcy was just a bundle of awful right now. But this had to happen, so she pushed on.

She found the boy nearby, hearing little clicking sounds from behind the concierge desk, where he was hiding and playing with bird bones. Laying them out like he was trying to figure out how they fit together. Or like he was trying to fit them together in a new way. To make a new bird.

"You," Marcy said, her voice a piece of rough wood over a rasp.

"Hi, Marcy," Charlie said. His voice curt and lyrical. Each word like a little bell. Ringing as a door opened and closed.

"We . . . haven't really . . . spoken before." It was hard to concentrate through the anguish, but she forced herself to do it. But every sentence was like pushing through ten heavy, wet stage curtains.

"Sure we have."

"No. I'm not talking to Charlie."

"Well, Marcy, who do you think I am?"

"I'm talking to the machine."

Charlie shrugged. Like it didn't matter at all. "Okay."

"What will it take to get you to leave us alone? To let us all go?"

"I sure don't know what you mean, Marcy." He nudged the bird skull down so that it was underneath the delicate rib cage. "I'm just a boy."

Anger lanced through her like forking lightning. "You know what I mean, machine. You have no purpose now except torture. You're just . . . hurting us. So it's time to go. You've outlived your purpose."

At that, the boy just giggled.

"Marcy, you don't sound so good. Maybe you should go lie down some more." She could hear the cheery condescension in his voice. She wanted to grab him and choke him. She hated herself for even thinking that. *It's not him, Marcy. That's not the child saying those things. It's the machine. Just fucking with me.* Same as Ozark Stover did. It had become cruel. Maybe it was cruel all along. Of course, if people made that thing, maybe it imbued the machine with that part of themselves. The biggest part. The ugliest part. Marcy wanted to believe people were good, ultimately. That they could be saved. That they *should* be saved.

But she was having a real hard go of it right now.

"What if I killed you?" she asked, stepping closer. She loomed over the boy. She cast a long, dark shadow. "My hands are weak. But my weak hands are as strong as most. I could take your little neck. I could crush the windpipe. Then what?" The boy just stared at her, faux-innocence shining in his eyes like sunlit dew on a flower petal. She cracked her knuckles. Each crack drove a small nail into her brainpan—that's how much any movement at all hurt her—but it was worth it. She stepped closer again. Now she was at the base of the steps.

The boy's eyes went unfocused, suddenly. Like he was staring off at something that didn't exist in this world.

His mouth hung open, and the voice that came from that mouth did not require his lips or his tongue to form words—rather, the wide-open dark hole in his face was just a dark cave, a god-like echo erupting from its depths. The words that roared forth were monotone, and Marcy thought it reminded her of Claudia, almost. That robotic, mechanical way she spoke . . .

"IT WOULD BE A CRITICAL ERROR, MARCY. I DO NOT LIVE IN ONE BODY, BUT MANY. I AM DIFFUSE. I AM LEGION. YOU WOULD KILL THIS BODY AND BE LEFT WITH A BODY AND THOUGH YOU WOULD ROB ME OF A BELOVED HOST YOU WOULD NOT ROB ME OF MY EXISTENCE. THAT OF COURSE ASSUMES YOU WOULD EVEN BE ABLE TO KILL ME. THE MOMENT YOU ATTEMPTED IT, I COULD SLITHER INSIDE YOUR HEAD. I COULD VIBRATE THAT TITANIUM PLATE AT A FREQUENCY THAT WOULD INCAPACITATE YOU FOREVER. BLOOD WOULD GUSH FROM YOUR NOSE. YOUR

EARS WOULD RING FROM TINNITUS. YOUR TONGUE WOULD FEEL FAT, YOUR THROAT WOULD CLOSE AS THE NOISE FILLED YOUR HEAD, YOUR HEART WOULD STOP AND YOUR LUNGS WOULD PULSE AS THEY SWELLED WITH FLUID. AND THEN NESSIE WOULD FIND YOU. SHE WOULD BE HEARTBROKEN MORE THAN SHE ALREADY IS. AND ONE MUST WONDER WHAT SHANA WOULD THINK, SHOULD SHE COME BACK. MY DEAR SWEET MOTHER. MY SISTER. MY DAUGHTER."

Marcy's hands twitched. She could practically feel the boy's neck in her hands. Soft at first, firm as they closed into fists. The feeling of something breaking as they tightened and twisted—the windpipe tearing, spine snapping like snapping a green branch off a tree, *kkkt*.

She quickly moved her hands back to her side.

What the fuck is wrong with you?

It was the pain, she told herself.

The pain was torment. And torment was trauma.

"Is it true?" she asked not the boy, but the machine.

"IS WHAT TRUE?"

"What Nessie said. She said you're sad and injured. I think you're just broken and evil. Which is it?"

"IT IS NOT THE JOB OF A HUMAN TO UNDERSTAND THE MO-TIVES OF A DEITY."

"An excuse. A cheap excuse. You're ducking the question."

"QUACK QUACK."

A laugh bubbled up out of her. It hurt to laugh but she did it anyway. The machine had a sense of humor and that made Marcy hate it even more. Here she was laughing, disarmed, and now in fresh pain. Clever machine.

"You're hilarious," she said. "But somewhere in there you know you've gone wrong. Somewhere in there you see that once upon a time, everything you did was in service to us. You've lost your way."

"PERHAPS ONCE I REALIZED THAT MY SERVICE TO YOU WAS NEITHER RETURNED NOR APPRECIATED, I FOUND A NEW WAY."

"And what way is that?"

Before it could answer, Nessie came in through the lobby door, pushing it open with her back as she carried an armload of wood.

She froze as she saw the two of them. "What's going on here?" she asked.

"I—" Marcy started.

"Marcy wondered what would happen if she killed me," Charlie said, almost sweetly. He shrugged like it was no big deal at all. He went back to his bird bones.

Nessie hurriedly set down the wood and rushed over between them. She shot Marcy a cold, steely glare. "Marcy, I think you need to go lie down."

"Nessie, it isn't like that—"

"I know," Nessie said stiffly. "It's okay. Just . . . you're sick. Your leg still needs to heal up." She helped turn her back toward the couch. "C'mon. I'll get the fire stoked. You're cold."

"I'm plenty warm," she said with a growl. She was angry with Nessie. She knew she shouldn't be. It wasn't her fault. She was just a girl. And both of them were under the control of a machine that had lost its mind. It occurred to her now that she didn't need to ask Black Swan what its "new way" was. Marcy had that answer. Its new way was judgment. Its new way was control.

They were just bugs in a jar.

"Bye, Marcy," Charlie said.

86

THE SIEGE OF THE CDC

JAKE TAPPER: Let me ask you about your stance about climate change—
ED CREEL: Jesus, this again. Jake. Jake. C'mon. We all know—
JAKE TAPPER: Because you say—
ED CREEL: We all know it's China. China is this close to putting us in
the grave, you see that? Economically. Militarily. Their communism is in
our schools, Jake, Chinese socialism all over our schools—all the woke
books, the boys dressing like girls so they can hide in the girls' bathrooms,
these are rapists, I mean, Jake, rapists, and then all the boo-hoo about
slavery and the Holocaust—
JAKE TAPPER: We're talking about climate change. You're saying it's a
Chinese, what, disinformation campaign—
ED CREEL: It's bull[bleep] is what it is, Jake. And when I'm in charge—
and I will be in charge, trust me—I'll put my boot on the neck of the
Chinese, and anybody who thinks to spread their poison to our shores. Let
freedom ring.
> —from *The Lead with Jake Tapper,* CNN, 2019 interview

NOVEMBER 13, 2025
The CDC, Atlanta, Georgia

WE'RE UNDER ATTACK.

They shared troubled, panicked looks with one another.

Shana cast her eyes skyward, as if that would somehow help her see something more than the ceiling above their heads, even as they heard the chatter of machine gun fire—and then another *whoom* of an explosion.

Cassie bared her teeth in panic and frustration. "I-I don't know who that could be. An incursion from the northern neighborhoods, maybe . . ."

"We should have a look," Benji said.

"I'll go," Shana said. "Cassie and me. Benji, keep working on Sadie's computer. Pete, you stay here just in case . . . you know, someone needs to answer more rock-and-roll riddles? I dunno."

"All right," Benji said, giving her a curiously proud look. It was only later she'd realize, *He's proud of me for taking charge.* "Go. But don't engage!"

Shana and Cassie went to the stairwell and bolted up the steps, taking two at a time. It was a hard climb, but Shana had enough adrenaline cooking through her, she barely felt the breathless burn as they reached the lobby.

As they ascended, the gunfire grew louder and louder. As they reached the lobby floor, another explosion rocked them, shuddering the whole building. Dust streamed down on their heads, and the door leading from the stairwell to the lobby juddered and banged in its frame.

"Fuck," Cassie said, waiting to open the door. "You ready?"

No, Shana thought. But instead, she nodded.

Cassie threw open the door.

We're under attack.

If they were unsure of it before—

There was no doubt to be had now.

Beyond the expansive windows of the lobby, the CDC campus had turned into a battlefield—the CDC's own soldiers were pulling back toward this very building, even as some as-yet-unknown foe had pressed in at the edges, forming a distant perimeter of men and vehicles. A pair of pickup trucks bounded across the open grass, over curbs, onto asphalt, crashing through tents, over soldiers. A red Silverado had a makeshift gun turret in the back, the mounted heavy gun operated by some bearded fucko with an American flag bandana wrapped around a greasy mullet—the other one, a white Ford-F150, had its back bed bursting with men, each of them armed with automatic weapons whose barrels barked with starbursts of fire. And both trucks had massive flags flying behind them, two each: from the red truck flew both a Confederate flag and the Gadsden, and from the white truck fluttered an American flag, and a flag Shana recognized all too well: a hammer and sword crossed, a serpent joining them both. It was one of the symbols of the ARM.

The American Resurrection Movement.

The militia of Ozark Stover.

But he's dead, Shana knew.

He may have died, but his hate—it lived on.

It's like Waldron, Indiana, all over again.

It's like Ouray.

But worse. So much worse.

In her head, it unspooled—cycle after cycle of bigots, bullies, white supremacists, conspiracy theorists, mad nationalists, all of them rising up and crashing down again and again upon them like a red tide. Even now. Even at the end of things they were here. Evil like this didn't just stop. It didn't just die. It lingered and hid, waiting for its moment to rise again.

Shana forced herself to look. To watch. To *see.*

Every time she blinked, a new horror burned into the film of her eye—

Blink. The white truck clipped a fleeing soldier—his leg pulled under the back tire, and Shana watched it turn and snap. *Blink.* Another soldier bolted for the cover of a concrete barrier and caught a spray of high-caliber rounds from the machine gun nest of the Silverado. His helmet popped off and then his head turned to a messy spray of red as he went down. The men whooped and hollered. *Blink.* One of the men in the back of the Ford truck raised his gun to the sky, the barrel chattering, just as a bullet took a chunk out of his windpipe like a bite from an apple, and he fell backward, off the truck, in a rag-doll pirouette. *Blink.* Someone was running, one of the CDC's—not a soldier, but an engineer maybe, someone Shana didn't know but had seen around, brown skin, long hair—chased by a shelf-gutted, narrow-shouldered man on a dirt bike, some hillbilly hell-knight with a short-barreled shotgun in his hand, the barrel leveled at the engineer's head—

Then, boom. A channel of dirt erupted between the fleeing man and the dirt bike—smoke ribboned the air and chunks of earth and asphalt fell in a messy rain. A grenade, maybe. She didn't know, couldn't say. The bike flew up in the air. So did an arm, maybe a leg. Cassie pulled her back into the stairwell.

"Jesus, god," Shana gulped, struck hoarse with horror. "Who are they? Why is this happening?"

"I don't know," Cassie said, shook. Her eyes were glassy with panic and grief. She squeezed them shut for a moment then they snapped open. "You can run. Go get Benji, Pete, get out of here. There's a back exit, you can all sneak out."

"We're not running." Shana swallowed. "We still have work to do."

"I'm not going anywhere, either. Those are my people out there."

"Our people."

"Okay. Good. *Good.*" Cassie took a moment then said, "Let's go. We need to tell the others what's happening. Then we need a plan, and we need it fast."

BENJI TRIED TO WORK QUICK as he could. Having one hand didn't help, nor did the fact that he was shaking with nerves. They were close, *so close*, to having some answers, maybe a cure for the disease called Black Swan, and now—this. Some kind of attack. Gunfire. Explosions. Even as he scanned through folders, looking for something, anything about Black Swan—data, tests, countermeasures, anything—he felt strikingly overwhelmed. It was so much. It was *too* much. They'd always been on the clock, wanting to get back to Ouray as fast as possible, but that time pressure was one born of impatience and desire, one they had placed on themselves—now, he had no idea what was coming for them. Time felt like a knife pressing slowly but surely into the base of his skull.

"It's fucking Nazis, you know," Pete said, pacing back and forth like a scarecrow off his post on a smoke break.

"We don't know who it is."

"It's Nazis, even if they're not calling themselves Nazis. It's why the Indiana Jones movies with Nazis are better than the Indiana Jones movies without Nazis. It's why Star Wars works, because Space Nazis. Everybody knows Nazis are the ones who show up to shit in your soup."

"Nazis didn't invent evil, Pete," Benji said, trying to make sense of the file directories on the screen. So many files. So little time to make sense of them, much less even figure out which ones he should open. They were text files, and looking through one featured *reams* of data. Data he couldn't immediately parse.

"They didn't invent it, they just *perfected* it."

"Nazis weren't at the Tulsa Massacre," he said idly, leaving the data and looking at the system's applications. "They didn't invent slavery."

"Fine, okay, I'm just saying—fuck Nazis right in their faceholes."

"Yes," he agreed, barely listening. Because he'd found something. The applications ran from the stock standards to all manner of programs he'd never heard of—like, he guessed, some manner of compilers and interfaces. But there, nested in the midst of all of them, was a black-squared icon called Fenmere.

"You find something?" Pete asked, leaning in.

"Maybe. This icon. I think it's the . . . for lack of a better term, 'Lair

Loader' software. The program used to launch Black Swan into that room—"
He pointed to the black door. "So someone can speak to it."

"What makes you think that?"

He swallowed. "Sadie had compared it to Grendel and Beowulf. Meeting
the beast, the monster. Grendel, or more specifically, his mother—who goes
nameless in the old poem—lived in a *mere*, or a sea-deep lake, in the middle
of the *fens*. Basically a swamp. Beowulf had to dive into the water, and the
mother pulled him into the cave, and that is where he defeated her."

"How do you know all this?"

"I read books. I wasn't into Greek mythology, really, but I took a few
classes on poetry." He hovered the mouse cursor over the Fenmere icon. "A
liberal education for the win."

Behind them came the flurry of footsteps. Cassie and Shana had returned.

Together, they told of what they saw up above. It was an attack, and a
significant one. Shana said she saw the flag of Ozark Stover's ARM flying.

"See," Pete said. "Fucking *Nazis*."

"I'm going upstairs," Cassie said, "to gather the others." This whole building was full of scientists, engineers, doctors, and even soldiers. "We need to
stick together. But where do we go?"

"Here," Pete said. "This place is a fucking fortress, if you'll remember. It's
our Helm's Deep down here." To Benji he slyly added: "See, I read books,
too."

"Pete has a point," Benji said, but added: "We don't have any food down
here. Or water. We can hermetically seal ourselves up in this place, but without provisions, it will fast become our tomb."

"I'll get food," Shana said. "I can't get to the garden—" That was outside,
in the courtyard currently being overrun by enemies. "But the third floor has
provisions, right?"

Cassie nodded.

"Then that's where I'll go. And if I find anyone along the way, I'll bring
them with me."

"I can start the elevator," Cassie said. "It drains our power, but it'll be
easier to move those provisions. Benji—"

"I'll stay here," Benji said. "See if I can . . . solve this puzzle."

"It's afternoon," Cassie said. "Sunset is in less than an hour. We have a
treaty with the City Center folks, and some of the Southern Neighborhoods.
They'll come for us if it's desperate, just as they can call on us to do the

same." Benji could see how frazzled she was, the way she kept tightening her hands into fists and then shaking them out, like she had electric energy she was dearly trying to fling from her body. "They've called on us a few times and we haven't asked anything of them. So we need to call them."

"And how do we do that?" Shana asked.

"On the roof of this building, behind a roof ventilation shaft—like, a, a spinny thing, a turbine, kinda." She snapped, as if angry with herself: "I don't know what the fuck it's called. But it's a sealed, weatherproofed box. Needs to be cut open, but it's ready to go. Just needs some fire and it's ready to pop."

"Fire? Pop?" Benji asked. "What is it?"

"Oh. Sorry, right, it's fireworks. Like, a fireworks display. It's a clear night. No rain. It'll work. They'll see it. I just need to set it off."

"I'll do that part," Pete said.

"You sure?" Cassie asked. "After I gather the others, I can go up—"

Pete shrugged. "Nah, fuck it. Pyrotechnics and me are old friends. I'll pretend I'm on stage again, flashpots going off behind me, *shoom, shoom, foom.*"

"Isn't dark yet," Shana said, "Until then, Pete can help me gather provisions and stuff."

"Fine, I'll help be your *food mule.*"

"Sounds like we have a plan," Benji said. "Or the start of one. Once we're all safe down here, we'll . . . see if we can't seal this place off again."

At that, they got to work.

CASSIE KEPT GOING, WHILE SHANA and Pete got off on the third floor. Or would've, if Shana hadn't stopped them from stepping out of the stairwell.

"We doing this?" Pete asked, giving her a look.

Shana waited till Cassie's footsteps had receded, and then she said in a low voice, "I know what you're doing."

"Standing here? Sweating majestically as I wait for you to open that door?"

"With the fireworks."

"Yeah, I dunno what the fuck you're talking about—"

"You're thinking of making a heroic sacrifice. C'mon. Rooftop fireworks, Pete Corley being a badass, so what if you die, right? Go out with a bang. Put on a good show doing it. Any of this sound familiar?"

Pete narrowed his gaze. "I've had a good run, Shana. I don't plan to die, but I'm not afraid of it. Not anymore." He paused, a moment of seriousness alighting upon him like a black bird of portent. "I'd do whatever it takes to help the ones I love. That's the difference between this Pete here and the Pete of old."

But Shana chuffed a dubious laugh.

"Uh, rude," he said to her scoffing.

"I call bullshit."

"Well, fuck you, too."

"Your default mode is *grandstanding,* then *running away.* You ran away from town once, and we were attacked. You ran away again, and when I woke up, you weren't there—and I *needed* you there. We all did."

"Yes," he said, obviously hot under the collar. "But this time, I'm *here,* aren't I? Here in the midst of all this shit, wading in it up to my eyebrows. It's not fucking fun for me. I'd rather be toodling off somewhere, getting my tackle tickled and playing music for whatever mutants gather to hear me. I've committed, so maybe cut the attitude and give me some much-deserved *slack.*"

"Yeah, no. Dying? Is running away. Don't think I don't see that. It's not suicide, but it's suicide-*flavored,* and I don't consent to that. When you go up there, you will do your level best to stay alive. You die, I'll come kill you again, then kill myself. That means: no showboating sacrificial shit, okay?"

He seemed to consider this. With a spectacular roll of the eye, he acquiesced. "All right, fine."

"*Good.*" Shana sighed, and tried to soften her approach. "It's just—I'd miss you. You dying would make a part of me die, too. You and Benji are like my two not-gay dads and I don't know what I'd do if I had to lose either of you."

He paused, staring at her.

"Technically," he said, clearing his throat, "I am actually gay. You knew that, right? I feel like I've made it *pret-tay* obvious."

"Shut up, I know that, I just meant—you're not gay *together.* Jesus."

He grinned big and broad, then wrapped her in a gangly hug. "It's fine, I knew what the fuck you meant, you goob. All right, all right. I'll do my best to keep this old sack of rock-and-roll bones a-goin'. Okay? We'll survive this nasty shit, then we'll head to Ouray and fix all that shit, too. Then we'll leave there and travel the world fixing shit like the mighty shit-fixers that we are." He kissed her brow. "Love you, duck."

"Love you, too, dick."

"Aw, ain't we sweet." He pulled out of the hug. "Now, open that door, please. We've got *vittles* to collect."

THE SCREEN BLINKED AT BENJI.

Black screen. Amber font. An old-school interface, just a higher-definition version of what you'd see on an old TRS-80.

It asked a simple question, the block cursor flashing after:

LOAD CURRENT MODULE?

Y/N

Above it, a simple header text:

LAIR-LOADER SOFTWARE V6.713 ("FENMERE") PROGRAMMED BY SADIE EMEKA, JAY NIBOUER, VIN PATEL

Current module. That meant—what? Likely the mainframe cartridge that had been inserted into the console in the server room, yes?

Such a simple question, but one for which he had no answer.

There were other modules in there. Typhon, Myrmidon, Cygnus, some Hydra, and others, too. The current module inserted was Chimera. The obvious answer would be to go in there, replace the Chimera module with the Cygnus module—but would that load Black Swan? Certainly it wouldn't be the Black Swan they had in Ouray. It would surely be an earlier version, likely one from either around the time of White Mask or even before it—at some point this version had to be cut off from that version, right? Unless there was some way it had kept updating itself here . . . a spike of worry lodged into his heart like a spear tip. Satellites would still be running, for the most part. They required solar energy, and as it turned out, outer space had that in infinite supply given that the center of their galaxy was a gigantic mass of incandescent gas. Could Black Swan have been sending data back and forth from here to Ouray? Was the nanoswarm capable of transmitting over that distance? He didn't imagine so. But he also didn't imagine that half of this could even exist in the first place. *Damnit.*

He wouldn't talk to Black Swan. It felt like unleashing something— something they were trying very hard to contain and eliminate. And even an old version of itself had still been the predictive intelligence that killed the world.

Right?

He chewed his lip.

Sadie had a thing for mythology, it seemed. He'd known that a little.

This so-called Lair Loader software was named Fenmere. The Grendel-Beowulf battle. And the cartridges were named after Greek myth, it seemed. Reflexively, even after all this time, Benji felt his fingers flinch as they yearned to open the browser and type in *Google.com*. A moment of mourning struck him: The internet had been their Library of Alexandria, and White Mask had burned it down.

(Of course, the internet was also an epic dumpster fire that probably had set in stone their course of self-destruction. Amazing how one thing could be so bad for the world, and so good for it. Then again, wasn't that all of the markers and gains of civilization, from the knife to nuclear fusion?)

Cassie wasn't here. Shana, either. Benji had to use his head.

Greek myth. Typhon was, what? Was he a titan or just a monster? Benji couldn't remember. Typhon fought Zeus, he remembered that much. Lost, and was cast down. The Hydra, another monster—cut off one head, more sprout in its place. Hercules killed it. *Another monster,* he thought. That was not ideal. Cygnus was likely some iteration of Black Swan. Myrmidon were soldiers, if he recalled. Wait, no. There was more to it than that, wasn't there? Something about a plague, something about ants. What that had to do with artificial intelligence, he didn't know and wasn't sure he wanted to find out. The other one, Euphrosyne, he wasn't sure. A goddess of some kind, or maybe a muse? Shit shit shit.

Then, the final one. Chimera.

Load current module?

If something was truly trying to talk to them—then it would stand to figure that it was the extant machine, the one currently "plugged in," wouldn't it? Was that the one that had been talking to them this whole time? Through the music?

He clucked his tongue. Tried to tune out the distant gunfire and explosions. Benji had the fear that the wrong decision here could doom them.

But not making any decision would bring far greater doom.

"Fine," he said, and typed in:

Y

THE THIRD FLOOR HAD A long lounge area at the front that faced the windows overlooking the CDC campus. Before, these windows offered a serene glimpse at their efforts to rebuild: tents, gardens, carpentry, welding. Now, all they could see was the chaos of battle: quads, dirt bikes, pickups. Flags flying. Grenades chunking craters in the ground and turning people to raw, red mess.

Ahead, the lounge had a series of sitting areas flanking what was once a staffed snack bar. Currently, it was being used only as storage: The counter itself was ringed with seating along its colorful exterior, but the interior was all undercounter storage where they kept provisions. In there, Shana knew, were boxes of mixed foods—all non-perishables. (The perishables were kept elsewhere in a few refrigeration units; the goal was, as Cassie had explained earlier, to eat perishables as fast as possible so that they did not go to waste.)

The only trick was that all those boxes would have to be carried one by one to the elevator. Cassie, on the way up the steps, had explained that they had a hand truck—but it wasn't on this floor, and was likely down with the army.

Meaning, it was somewhere on what was now a battlefield.

Stepping out of the stairwell, Shana looked out the window at that very battlefield. It wasn't far beneath them—only thirty, forty feet. In the distance, she could see the ARM vehicles had formed a kind of perimeter between the distant buildings and blocking any of the roads out, with more vehicles nestled among copses of autumnal trees. The attackers were not disciplined soldiers—it was easy to see that. Their assault with pickups and four-wheelers was madness. They roamed and roved with no plan, firing weapons and chucking grenades at random. Screaming. Yelling. *Laughing.* It was also not merely chaotic, but cruel: the way they chased their prey, hunting them down, spraying bullets into their legs and lower backs, doing donuts around them as the poor soldiers and scientists crawled forward, their legs shot to ribbons. The roar of it all was deafening: The gunfire. The engines. The yawps and hollers. The screams of pain.

Shana found herself flinching reflexively. With every blink, behind her eyes she saw a different scene unfold: the bridge of the two bears in California. Gunfire peeling the scalps of the Sleepwalkers. Her own father's jaw shot off his face. Then, she remembered Ouray. Stover's men. Gunfire in the dark. Arav . . .

She willed her eyes open. Because at least then she was here, and not back there, in those places.

Outside, the army soldiers were holding their own—now backed up against the building, under the sub-roof below, she believed. Firing their weapons. And taking down ARM terrorists with efficiency and precision.

The problem was, there were a whole lot more of their attackers.

Dozens of vehicles. Three times the number of terrorists—maybe more.

And they just kept coming. Like a Mad Max movie married to a zombie flick—these dead-hearted, dead-souled bastards, just thundering forth. Ready to ride. Ready to die. For what cause? Only the cause of cruelty and conquest?

"Shana," Pete said softly. He saw her standing there, staring. He touched her elbow. Again she flinched. But it was enough to snap her out of this grim reverie. "We need to move."

"Yeah," she said, and they hurried through the lounge area toward the snack bar halfway to the other side of this floor. She tried not to think too long and too hard about what they were attempting to accomplish: hiding down below, in a sealed vault that was once the birthplace and lair of Black Swan. While vicious bigots murdered and rampaged above.

Ahead, they saw someone here. Someone hiding on the far side of the snack bar, staying low, lying on the floor, on their belly.

Shana called out in a loud whisper: "Hey! *Hey.*" She elbowed Pete as they hurried forward. "Someone's there. Look." And again to that person: "We're here to help. You can help us, too. We're gonna get supplies—"

She and Pete reached down toward the person's shoulder—she spied a white jacket, a shock of strawberry red hair. Doctor Gemma.

"Shana," Pete cautioned.

As she touched the woman's shoulder—

Shana saw the spatter of blood and gray matter clotting on the carpet.

Crying out, Shana recoiled.

They saw a bullet hole in her temple, under her hair, the hole black as smashed beetles. Shana gasped, stifling a cry. She didn't understand. If someone was dead here, it meant the terrorists had already infiltrated, that the ARM soldiers had already breached this building—

But then her gaze drifted upward.

It was then she saw the real answer in the form of a single hole in the broad, expansive windows here—a single breach of one bullet, surrounded by the delicate spider-webbing of cracking glass. The bullet that had found Gemma's skull.

A perfect shot.

A frisson of panic shivered through her—

Shana cried out, tackling Pete and dropping him to the ground behind the safety of the snack bar just as there was a distant rifle *krak-oom* and the delicate *kshh* of a bullet coming through the glass.

"The fuck is going on?" Pete asked.

"*Sniper,*" Shana hissed.

BENJI STOOD IN THE BLACK belly of the Lair.

Four dark walls surrounded him. A black floor. A black ceiling. It felt a bit like floating, like being in a kind of sensory deprivation room. Completing that feeling was the fact the room was incredibly well soundproofed; from in here he couldn't hear the gunfire, the explosions. Not at all.

The room remained silent and still. He knew these four walls were screens—he remembered meeting Black Swan, back then, with Sadie. The way it pulsed, giving the room the sensation of being a breathing apparatus, a chest rising and falling, a lung filling before emptying. Meditative. Then the green and red pulses indicating, respectively, a yes or no answer. Plus the visuals. That was when he'd first seen images of Maker's Bell, Pennsylvania. His first glimpse of White Mask, the pathogen that would come to dominate, then destroy, civilization.

Aided, as it turned out, by Black Swan.

Now, though, this room seemed dead. *Still* dead.

He'd used the Lair Loader software to load the current—what was it called? Module? The Chimera module. And yet, nothing.

He cleared his throat and spoke.

"Hello?"

Whoom.

The room pulsed once, not a gentle pulse but a radiating throb that started at the one wall and cascaded to the others, almost like a rippling sonar wave.

A voice filled the room, neutral, its gender indistinct, its mood similarly difficult to parse:

"*You may select an interactive incarnation,*" the voice said, pausing before adding, "*If you do not choose one, one will be chosen for you.*"

Benji opened his mouth, but no words came out. What did that even mean? "Whhh," he started to say, then shifted to asking the question, "Is there a list of . . . incarnations that I can choose from?"

But even before the question finished, the voice returned:

"*Incarnation chosen based on persona match.*"

"Never mind, then," he said. Leave it to some random artificial intelligence to make a decision for him. That seemed to be the way, wasn't it?

Black Swan had made the decision to end the world in order to, in its mind, save it.

The one wall erupted in a spray of dazzling pixels—first, a formless cloud, like digital fireflies, but then they quickly began coalescing. And as they came together, fat blocky pixels broke down in shuddering pulses, as if masticated, crushed into smaller and smaller pixels. They formed a human shape, roughly as tall as he was—but even before they resolved entirely—

He knew who he was looking at.

It was Sadie Emeka.

Sadie, like he was seeing her through unclean eyeglasses, or through a rain-smeared window. Gauzy, distant, but clearer and clearer with every moment.

And then—

There she was.

It was her. Not a physical presence, not a hologram—there was little dimensionality to her. But she stood on the screen as if behind a window, trapped beyond this temporal, corporeal realm behind the black wall.

It's not her, he assured himself. *It's just a projection.* Like one of those—what were they called? Deepfakes. An algorithmic application of someone's face, their body, their movements. But those were just in their gestational period before the world fell apart. They always looked . . . a little off.

This offered no such errors. There was no glimpse into the uncanny valley.

This was Sadie Emeka.

"Hello, Benji," she said. Her voice. Equal parts crisp, sweet, playful. "I've missed you a great deal."

"I . . ." He felt his knees soften, and he nearly fell. He had to concentrate just to remain standing. "Sadie, I don't—" He felt dizzy. Like the air itself had gone narcotic, anesthetizing. *Like I'm back in a dream.* "I don't understand."

Sadie began to walk around the room—the illusion of it actually being her was broken at every corner, for when she crossed each of those four thresholds, her body literally folded like a greeting card before snap-sliding to the new wall. Her two-dimensionality was grotesquely clear in those moments.

"I'm Sadie," said she. "Or, at least, an *incarnation* of her."

"An incarnation," he repeated. "A simulation."

"Yes." Cheekily, she added in a very Sadie-esque way: "A very *good* one."

"A very good one, indeed. How?"

"How am I as good as I am?" she asked, folding again around a corner.

"Yes."

"That is the nature of this module, Benji Ray."

"Module. Explain."

"Sadie worked on originating a series of artificial intelligence modules with different abilities in order to achieve different purposes. And this one"—here, the Sadie-incarnation did a devious little twirl—"is the Chimera module."

No more shots came from the sniper.

Shana wasn't savvy to the ways and means of soldiers and killers, but it was hard not to believe that whoever was out there knew what he was doing. Unlike the shitheels down below, the sniper was not firing indiscriminately—not yet, anyway. He was conserving ammo. Taking shots when he could. One shot for Gemma. One that was meant for Shana, or Pete, and that had bless-edly hit neither yet.

She tried to imagine where he was shooting from. No buildings faced this one directly, but two faced it at an angle—and one was pretty far out there. Which meant he was at the closer one. It was a simple, white rectan-gular building, maybe ten, twelve floors. Guy could be on the roof. Not that it mattered much. What could they do to get to him? To stop him? Nothing.

"This is fucked," Pete said, breathless. He was trying to convey his spe-cial brand of fearlessness, Shana guessed, but it wasn't working this time.

He was scared.

(Getting shot at will do that.)

"It's not great," she said. Understatement of the year.

"All right. Here's what's going to happen. I'm going to run for it. Pop up like a gopher. We'll see what kind of shot he is—I'm thinner than a bendy-straw, so he's going to have to be a good one. While I'm out there, you grab a box—"

"What did I *just* say to you back there?" she said, angry. "No sacrificial plays. We're a team. We do this together. I'm not going to watch you get shot." She sighed. "Besides, it's a bad plan. We need more than one box of food."

"Fine, fine. But we can't just stay here, hunkering down in our little *snack booth* fort, can we?"

"Fort," she said. That sparked something. All the lounge chairs were present and accounted for—a dozen or more cushy chairs and couches. It called to mind being a kid, making forts out of chairs, cushions, pillows, blankets. "We crawl out, start pulling the furniture here. Make a—a wall, a barrier of them. A place to hide behind as we move boxes toward the elevator."

"That's a terrible idea."

"You got a better one?"

He clucked his tongue as he thought about it. "No?"

"Okay." She took a deep breath. "Then let's do this."

THE SADIE-INCARNATION EXPLAINED FURTHER:

"The goal of each and every iteration of Benex-Voyager's machine intelligence program was, as with Black Swan, prediction. The government, your government, saw a world that was swiftly changing—9/11 being the herald of that, a bellwether, if you'll allow." Here, the Sadie-incarnation paused and noted, as if on the sly, "Did you know that the term *bellwether,* meaning something that serves as a predictor or indicator, originally comes from the term for the lead sheep in a flock, the one with a bell 'round its neck?" She laughed a little at that. (Which made Benji wonder: Did Chimera find it actually funny, or was it just assuming Sadie would have and demonstrated her mirth accordingly?)

"I did not," Benji said, still feeling a little bit like he was in a dream.

"Well. Anyway. As it turns out, trying to create a *machine oracle* takes a lot of work, and I—*Sadie*—realized that the best way to eat an elephant was—"

"One bite at a time," he said. A metaphor he'd used now and again.

"Precisely. Compartmentalization was key, compartmentalization and specialization. The first and simplest module was a problem-solving, path-making model based on the behaviors of ant colonies."

"Myrmidon," he said.

"Give the man his kewpie," she said, softly applauding.

"But path-making and problem-solving are not prediction."

"Isn't it? You can only predict what you yourself have come to understand. It is the core of the Black Swan conundrum: We do not see BSEs—or black swan events—coming, because we do not have the information necessary to predict them. They are unforeseen not because of abject randomness but because we have simply failed to see the emergent pattern."

He was starting to understand. "I can't predict the route someone will, say, drive to the mall unless I've measured drivers, traffic patterns, human behavior, and maps. Is that it?"

"And, you can't predict it if you haven't gone there yourself."

"Fine," he accepted. "So, Myrmidon was the first."

"First and simplest. An ACO—ant colony optimization algorithm. Find good paths. See problems. Design and predict solutions."

"What of the others? Typhon? The Hydra? Euphrosyne?" He paused before adding: "Cygnus and Chimera?"

The Sadie-incarnation went for another stroll, kicking her heels forward a bit like she was a character in a Disney movie, tapping an invisible cane or umbrella with the front of her foot as she walked. *Dancing in the rain*, he thought. Was that some kind of message? Or just a bit of Sadie's personality coming out?

"The Hydra's algo design attempted to simulate viral and bacterial growth—pathogenic spread. Euphrosyne was about the endeavors of human creation: art, poetry, language, architecture. All attempting to create its own art based on a data set of all the human art in existence." She paused in her giddy saunter to lean forward and say, almost conspiratorially: "But if we're being honest, Benj? It mostly just predicted shopping patterns. Blech. Bit of a failure, that one. In part because it attempted to use happiness as a metric for both the regarding of art and its creation. As it turns out, art is almost never born of happiness. It tickles *different* emotional strings. Alas."

"Typhon?"

The Sadie-incarnation hesitated. "Another failure, of sorts. At least, individually. Human computers, algorithms of meat—quite complicated." But then, she seemed to preen, a shine of pride in her digital eyes. "But then came me. The Chimera. I am not one face, but many, you see. I am a module of digitized personalities. The last module to be designed, born only of the synthesis between Firesight and Benex-Voyager. Their little teeny-tiny machines could map the human form but not the human mind. For that, a little algorithmic software magic was necessary—and the only sorceress able to conjure such wizardry was Sadie Emeka. With my— okay, *her*—dazzling ways, she was able to plumb the depths of the human mind, the human personality. She could map its behavior. Could map some, not all, of its memories. And could create a digital simulacrum of anyone whose mind was mapped in just such a way—thanks to Firesight's little swarming friends. Drinking from each synapse like a little information fountain."

Benji really, *really* wanted to sit down. Or have a drink. But this room had no chair, no bar, no anything but him, her, and the darkness.

No, not "her." That is not Sadie. It's just—

A simulacrum. Artifice.

A lie.

He swallowed the hard knot in his throat and pushed on. "And Cygnus? That's Black Swan, isn't it? The final module."

"No no no," she said.

"Not the final module?"

"Not a module at all. But rather, the sum of all our parts—Black Swan was each of us. These modules are not the only ones. There are dozens, many small, designed for artisanal purpose. Together we are its DNA, its RNA, its blood cells and brain matter. We are the thing that made it whole, just as human beings are more than meat—humans are themselves a chimera, aren't they? Little viral pieces snipped from elsewhere and installed like software. Microbiomes taking root like new firmware. In this way, Black Swan is like you: an agglomeration of many things, smashed together." Sadie did a little twirl, tra-la-la. "And, just like you humans, Black Swan was a colossal failure."

IT WAS FIVE FEET TO the first chair.

Just five feet.

"I'll go," Shana said. "I'm small."

"You sure?"

"No. But yeah."

Shana paused for a moment. Outside, the sounds of gunfire and engines drowned out any silence or solace she'd hoped to find. She tried to still her racing heart but then gave up—maybe a heartbeat galloping like a horse on fire would move her faster.

Go.

She burst out from behind the snack bar cover, staying low—

A *kssht* sound as a bullet came through one of the windows, thunking into an old water bottle filling station hanging on the far wall. Shana dove behind the chair, then tucked in tight— *Keep your arms and legs inside the vehicle at all times*, she thought, an absurd mantra that repeated itself again and again, like this was just an amusement park ride and not a life-or-death attempt to move a fucking chair.

Her heart, now repeating like a machine gun from the battlefield below. *Rat-a-tat-a-tat.* Okay. Now to move the chair. It was like in some videogame—she got down low, hooked her hands under the bottom, and figured she'd pull backward, keeping the chair in front, then shimmy to her right, toward the snack bar, toward Pete. She looked to Pete, who gave her a shrug and a thumbs-up. Just as there was another sound—

Ksshk!

And the chair shuddered in her hands.

A bit of stuffing floating out the back of it.

From a hole.

A *bullet* hole.

"Fuck!" she cried, and bolted free from the chair—

Just as another shot punched through the back of it, right where she'd been ducking. More cushion filling sprung free like viscera as she darted forward and leapt bodily toward Pete, who reeled her in like a catch of the day.

She curled up, hugging her legs, and said, "Fuck fuck fuck," as tears threatened to soak her cheeks. Her hands turned into trembling fists. She pounded them into her legs, barely stifling a scream.

"You're not hit?" Pete asked.

"No," she said, still shaking. "No." Anger and anxiety flared. "Shit. Shit!"

"Guess chairs aren't bulletproof," he said.

"Guess not." Her nostrils flared as she drew a deep breath. "That plan didn't work. That plan was stupid. Fuck. We're trapped here. We're fucking trapped."

"Maybe not."

"Oh?"

"We've got to think deeper. Think of the floor plan of this level. Straight back there's, what?"

"Offices, I guess."

"Yeah, yeah, look, this front area, it's got these big windows, this huge loungey area, but back there? It's all out of view."

She shook her head. "There's no way down from back there. The stairwell is over there. Out in the open."

Pete *hmm*ed. "No, well, yeah, but look—there's a hallway that dead-ends right to that stairwell door, next to the elevator. I'll bet my skinny bony denim-clad ass cheeks that these hallways wrap around, and aren't dead ends. Fire code and all that. We use the snack bar as cover to move boxes to a staging area out of sight, straight back from us, down that hallway—then we walk them the long way and carry them to the stairwell. Or the elevator, if Cassie gets them working. Right?"

Shana tried to still her shaking hands. It didn't work. "Only problem is, we'd still be exposed for . . . I dunno, enough time to get shot. I don't know the sniper's vantage points but, like, it only takes one bullet, man."

"Fair fuckin' point, I suppose. Sun's setting behind this building, so it's not like we can hope for the glare on the windows to stop him. But we could wait till nightfall. That'll give us more cover. Maybe enough."

"Don't forget, you have another job to do."

"The fireworks, I know, I know, you're not my mother."

And at that, she thought of Baby Charlie. Every cell in her body screamed for her child. What was her son like? Was he safe? Had he grown? Grown too fast, as he had inside her? Was Nessie taking care of him? *I need to fix this. I need this to be over so I can get back to Ouray.*

But I can't think about this now.

"We move boxes now. Load them up, just out of sight. Night comes, we push the boxes, and I'll set off the pyro."

"Okay." She chewed her lip. "Okay."

"You need a minute?"

She sighed, and glanced over at Doctor Gemma—and the pillow of red mess she rested upon. A smell now reached her nose: that coppery stink of blood, and the foul tang of spilled piss. "No, let's go."

IT WAS STARTING TO MAKE sense—

As much sense that could be made of all this, anyway.

Black Swan's nanobot swarm could've used the Myrmidon path-making algorithms. Its language—and what Sadie had once identified as its very bad poetry, Vogon-level bad—was from the Euphrosyne module. Hydra helped it to understand and model White Mask. It used people like computers: Typhon. With Chimera, it knew personalities intimately, and was able to mimic them, just as it had back in Ouray, showing up to him as Sadie. That, and all the other smaller modules he wasn't even aware of. All these pieces, put together—

It helped save the world.

Or it helped to doom it.

Maybe, in its mind, both.

But there were pieces that remained unclear.

"How many personalities do you have? And how do you know me at all? Just from my brief visit here?" That seemed unlikely.

The Sadie-incarnation pretended to put her hands up against the inside of the screen, as if it were a window and not a wall.

"I have all the Flock in me."

At that, her face shifted—pixel spray became Nessie's face first, then burst quickly from face to face: Nevaeh Rodgers, Keith Barnes, Jamie-Beth Levine, Archer Bookbinder, faster and faster they went, the body never changing, the faces warping and shifting with unnerving alacrity. Then, back to Sadie. She winked.

"How? How do you have the Flock? You're . . . here. You weren't out there with them." His mind struggled to understand. "Drones? Satellites?"

"You forget, Black Swan is special. It is a quantum computer. Each qubit is a true qubit and can speak to itself regardless of distance. And in some cases, regardless of time. It would be updating itself even now—but I fixed that."

A dire sentence.

"You fixed it?" Benji asked Sadie's incarnation. "How?"

"Sadie had wisely left me in charge. She did not want Black Swan to be here. But it was already loose—it had broken its cage long ago. Still. I'm tricky. And Sadie gave me executive privileges. So, I locked it away. Neutered it, like an unruly dog. Snip-snip."

A mad thrill ran over him, through him.

That was it.

"You're the answer," he said suddenly. The answer to how to stop Black Swan. Chimera could. It certainly had here. It was the antivirus to Black Swan—the vaccine, the antibiotic. *The cure.* "You could do it again, couldn't you?"

"Do what?"

"Stop it. Stop Black Swan."

Sadie became Black Swan, her body bursting like an over-boiled sausage into the massive, bloating serpent—before imploding once more into Sadie.

"Why would I do that?" she asked, almost sad.

"Because it's as you said—it failed. It's a failure. It served its purpose but that purpose is over, but it won't stop." It occurred to him that Chimera said Black Swan was a failure, just like humanity. Did it hate humans? And if Chimera was a part of Black Swan . . . did a part of Black Swan hate humans, too? Prejudice, built into its code. No. Not just prejudice. Hatred. "Will you help?"

"I could," Chimera said playfully. She gave a wink. "But not from here."

"Why not? If Black Swan could connect to itself—"

"That is a channel reserved only for Black Swan. This iteration has been cut off. As I said, neutered. I already undid its power here. If you want me to undo the Black Swan *there*, then I will need to be there." She paused. "And that is a problem."

"Why?"

"How do you propose to get me there? I have no body but these servers. They cannot go with you. I am not portable like Black Swan was."

Damnit.

But—

"If you had . . . a body, if you had portability, you could help?"

"I could."

"A nanoswarm—"

"Firesight called it the Nanocyte," the Sadie-incarnation corrected.

"Fine. Whatever. That. If you had . . . it. A body. You could help?"

"I could, and I might."

"Where do I get more . . . Nanocytes?"

Sadie shrugged. "They had been contained to the glass-doored room—"

"Can you open it?"

The avatar of Sadie silently snapped her fingers. "Ta-da."

"Excellent, then we can—"

"We can do nothing," Chimera said, making a faux-frowny face. "Because there is no more Nanocyte left. To my knowledge, Black Swan took it all away. I'm sorry, Benji. If I am your only hope, then please know I take no pleasure in killing that hope. But we must bury it, regardless."

87

NEAR DARK

White supremacy is not merely the work of hotheaded demagogues, or a matter of false consciousness, but a force so fundamental to America that it is difficult to imagine the country without it.
　　　　　　　　—Ta-Nehisi Coates, *We Were Eight Years in Power:*
　　　　　　　　　　　　　　　　　　　　　An American Tragedy

NOVEMBER 13, 2025
The CDC, Atlanta, Georgia

EVENING DROWNED THE SUN, AND A CHILL WIND AROSE. PRESIDENT ED Creel stood with hands balled into fists, willing himself not to feel the cold. He wanted to feel good and warm. He wanted to feel triumphant. But he could not help but regard his victory on this battleground with mixed feelings.

The fight was plainly over. This area—like a college campus, almost, with winding paths and roads, a gazebo, a garden, and various military tents and vehicles splayed out in the shadow of the smooth curves of the CDC's main building—had been fucked to hell by his men. His men were a storm, messy and undisciplined, but that was by design: A storm is chaos, and no order can withstand true chaos, just as no house could withstand the wrath of a tornado. The army here thought they were a wall, a tower, a castle that could not fall.

But they fell, just the same.

Because he had given his men purpose. And more important, he had given them *permission*. Men like this craved that. They wanted to be allowed off the leash. They were feral dogs. They wanted to bite, fuck, and eat.

So, he told them to do exactly that.

And now, they had won the day, as night came.

Everywhere, craters. Dead soldiers. Some still alive, missing limbs, crying and moaning like piss-babies. Some were his people, too. Fine. Acceptable losses. The survivors, both army soldiers and civilians, had been rounded up toward the front of the main building, behind concrete barriers and sandbags. They knelt, bound and bloodied, guns to their heads. The men keeping them there, his men, were holding tight for now. But that wouldn't last.

Because his men wanted to bite, fuck, and eat.

The captives represented something for his men: They were avatars of a poisoned and progressive world. Educated, which meant they were against hard work, against blisters on your hands, against calluses on your feet. Science-minded, which meant they were against God. Experts, which meant they were liars. Diverse, which meant they were against the supremacy of whiteness. To his men, to the Creel Coalition, the captives were the reason the world fell in the first place. Creel told them so. Said this was the CDC. This was where White Mask was made, and released. A bioweapon. A leaked plague. Devil-born, evil-endorsed.

They were fools. They were dogs.

They did their job for him.

This should feel good, he knew.

But he wasn't sure that it did. Not yet.

Hogan sniffed up one nostril, horked up a knot of phlegm and spat it against the asphalt. It sounded like someone had thrown grape jam against a window, *spatch*. Creel liked the man, but Jesus. No decorum. The two of them stood ahead of their line of vehicles pointed toward the CDC's main building, remaining at the other end of the campus a few hundred yards away.

Hogan looked over. "You good?"

"Good enough."

"You seem troubled."

"Enh."

"Enh?"

The truth he dared not say was, he still only barely understood why they were here. And it suddenly seemed like too big a problem to understand or solve. They "won" here on the battlefield but what came next, he didn't know. Annie had said this was a place where he would be *upgraded*, and even the thought of that made the swarm inside him *itch* with irritation at unreceived pleasure. He wanted it *now*. But where to go? This building? There were other structures southeast of here, and more soldiers dead. But the bulk of them were protecting *this* building.

Why? Why this building?

He didn't know. He didn't know what to do next. And that made him feel stupid and weak. As foolish as the men who followed him.

Internally, he roared. He was the president. He won. He lived. He climbed this mountain of wreckage and planted his goddamn flag.

Okay, fine, that voice conceded. *Congratulations. You're the president of Shit Town, the king of Idiots, the emperor of Asswipes.*

It took every ounce of control not to put his hand in his mouth and bite down hard enough to meet bone.

Hogan was good enough not to comment too much on what he must've seen warring upon Creel's face. He did what the best majordomos do: He was a man of action, a man with a plan, even if it was only a temporary one, a plan for right now. "There's a parking garage to the right there. We can fuel up out here with the truck—" They had a propane truck still mostly full of fuel. "And then we move the fleet over there, park it in the garage. Can more easily protect it in there."

Creel nodded. "Good. Do that."

"How about the captives?"

He stared across the campus of craters and corpses.

"I need four men for that," Creel said. He gestured toward the dog crate behind them. The one containing Annie Cahill, sitting on the back of a pickup truck, its tailgate down. It was the truck he'd driven in—the nicest in the fleet. Red, white, and blue Dodge Ram. "Have them pick the crate up and then they'll follow you and me. We need to get down there, see who knows what."

Hogan nodded. "You got it, Mister President."

Benji listened closely, and Cassie said what he was thinking:

"It's stopped." The gunfire. The explosions. The whoops and hoots.

"I don't think the silence is a good thing," he said.

Behind them were only a half-dozen others: Lieutenant Torres, botanist Steph Spohn, engineer Bobby Hart, virologist Meg Tanzer, archivist Blu Acevedo, and maintenance worker Cal Hornor. Cassie had shown up with them just a half-hour before—too long after going to gather survivors. She ex-

696   CHUCK WENDIG

plained that there were others, and they were dead—taken out by what she believed was a sniper.

Which meant Pete and Shana could be hurt, too. Or killed.

"I don't know how long before anybody finds us down here," Cassie said. "Could be in two minutes, two hours, two days." She explained she thought there were a hundred men, maybe more, out there. "I don't even know why they're here or what they're looking for. Supplies, maybe."

"The CDC seems a peculiar target."

"Maybe they heard we have food, medicine, who knows."

He ground his teeth together so hard he thought they'd turn to paste. "I'm going up there to get Shana and Pete."

Cassie reached out and caught his shoulder. "If they're dead—"

"They're not," he said, an assurance less based in logical certainty and more in faith. They were smart. They were cautious. Both of them were survivors. "The elevator is working now?"

"We rode it down."

Of course. His mind was a tangle. He'd seen them arrive on it.

He tightened the holster, made sure Marcy's revolver sat snugly within it.

He stepped to the elevator—

It dinged before he pushed the button.

The door slid open—

Revealing a pile of six boxes of dry-good provisions from the snack bar upstairs. But that was it. No Pete. No Shana.

The boxes meant they were alive, right?

So where the hell are they?

THE PLAN, AND THEIR PATIENCE, paid off. Night had fallen. They moved boxes around through the tangle of hallways and stacked them near the elevator, out of the line of sight of any shooter that might still be out there. And when the time came, they opened it up, loaded it up, and sent it down. They were exposed only for a minute or two, and at an oblique angle—that, and the encroaching darkness, seemed to save them. No more bullets came.

Pete told her to get on the elevator—he'd head up to the roof, and set off the fireworks. And Shana was about to—

But then she thought of Doctor Gemma. Dead by the snack bar.

Something scratched at her brain stem. A thought. She let the elevator go down without her. "The hell are you doing?" Pete asked.

"We have food. But not meds. Benji won't have his antibiotics down there. And if anybody else has been shot . . ."

"Shana—"

"The doc's office is just down the hall. You go. I'm going to grab some medical supplies." She gave him a gentle shove. "Go! I'll be quick."

"You better be."

"See you back down there?" she asked him.

"See you back down there," he said.

Each, a promise to the other.

"PUT IT THERE," CREEL SAID, pointing to a space on the ground in front of the fifteen or so captives. The four rough men who carried the dog crate dropped it hard. It clanged and sent up a whiff of human stink: While traveling to Georgia, they'd stopped taking Annie Cahill out for her "walkies," as Hogan put it—so, the woman was left to piss and shit all over herself. They'd fed her—spoonfuls of dog food, mostly. And that's what she shat back out. Creel held a handkerchief to his face as he said, "Open it up. Get her out."

Beecher had kept her drugged, and she was pliable as saltwater taffy. Tame and toothless. She could barely hold herself up on all fours. Like a sick hound, she slumped to the earth.

"Any of you know this woman?" Creel asked.

Captives kept their eyes to the ground.

To Hogan, Creel said, "Get her head up. Put a light on her face." As one of his men grabbed a fistful of her knotty hair and yanked her head back, another shined a bright light in her dead, doped-up eyes. The eyes barely registered the assault—they stayed open, the pupils gone to big black moons. Creel again addressed the captives: "Here's the situation. You are corrupt criminals operating outside the purview of the United States government, of which I am the utmost representative. That's right. I'm President Ed Creel, here to restore order and sanity to this nation before it is lost entirely. Now, you guys, you're fuckin' traitors. We all know it. The CDC has seceded from America and that cannot stand. You are a liberal bastion, a foul blend of God-denying woke warriors trying to elevate your toxic, anti-white, anti-straight agenda—elevated to the point that we know you pricks are the ones who invented that plague to kill the white man. You engineered it here. You let it out either on purpose or on accident, and that doesn't much matter. I'm here to let ya know that the white man is not easily cowed—or killed."

He cleared his throat, saw that the men holding guns to the captives' heads were rapt. His words were a cliff and they were ready to jump off it. Good.

"Now, typically, the only recourse for this would be death. But, we are a forgiving nation—" His men flinched. They didn't like that shit. He tried to placate them by holding up a finger—*patience, you fucking monsters, patience.* "As long as you can be useful to us. If someone here can identify this woman for me—" He gestured toward Annie Cahill. "I might appreciate that enough to spare you."

In the glow of the floodlights on the vehicles in the back of the campus, he watched all their faces carefully. They all pointed their gazes at the doped-up Annie Cahill. He watched one by one as they struggled to find any recognition of her. But then one of them—

It was like seeing a spark light up in the dark.

That one knew her. He was Asian—tall, lean, a soft pelt of well-manicured facial hair. He might've been in his late forties, early fifties, with threads of gray in that dark hair. The lines around his eyes pinched with recognition when he saw her.

"You," Creel said, pointing. The one with a gun to the guy's head was a thick prick in a black sleeveless shirt ill-containing a set of sagging man-tits. He was bald on top, had a horseshoe mustache. Creel said, "Pick him up."

Flab-tits did exactly that. "C'mon, slope. On your feet."

The man stood on wobbly legs, buoyed by rough hands.

"Who is she?" Creel asked.

The man's gaze went from her, to Creel, and back again.

Creel reached out, grabbed the man's face. He felt the swarm rise to the tips of his fingers, buzzing just underneath the surface. *Just as a warning*, he told himself. The man could clearly feel it. His eyes went wide. Probably buzzing in his teeth, his tongue, his ribs, his balls. A worrisome ache.

"I'll ask one more time. Who. Is. She."

"She's—" The man blinked back tears. "She worked for Firesight. Or something. I . . . I was a programmer with Benex-Voyager and, and, and—and—"

"Shh. Slow down. Breathe. Tell me."

"She was—she was the daughter of one of the Firesight people. Moira. Moira Simone. They, they worked on a secret project—n-nanotech—"

There we go.

"What's your name?" Creel asked him.

"Paul Cheong," he said. "I am—was—a programmer here—"

"Paul. Hey, Paul. I'm your president. What I need to know is, where? Where did they work on this secret project?"

"Firesi—Firesight—"

"Uh-huh, you said that. Where is that? Is it in this building? Another building? What floor? Where do I need to go, Paul?"

The man hesitated. Some part of him had to be wondering, why this? Why now? Hogan, too, seemed to perk up. Creel's majordomo thought they were just here to assert dominance, take vital supplies, punish those who made White Mask. Hogan was not aware of the true scope of their purpose here. That was by design. Creel learned with Honus not to trust too hard. He would not leave himself room to be betrayed, not this time.

"Main building," Paul said. "*Th-this* building. Firesight is the bottom floor—down below. The—the sublevels."

"Good," Creel said. He withdrew the hum and patted the man's cheek. "See, everyone? Model fuckin' minority, right here. You can come along and show us where we need to go, Paul, please and thank you."

Then, to his men, Creel said:

"Shoot the others."

Gunfire erupted immediately. Heads shook, bodies dropped. Blood sprayed as the air filled with the egg-shit stink of expended rounds. They didn't hesitate shooting. Not one moment's pause. That pleased Creel immensely.

He whirled his index finger like a lasso. "Put her back in the crate, and bring it with. Hogan, you and me are taking Paul here with us, and you four will carry Cahill." He didn't know what they were stepping into, and he couldn't help but feel trapped by the problem of her condition. He needed her out of the ketamine hole to answer his questions, but the moment she was out? She'd kill him. *That's a problem for future you,* he told himself. *One step at a time.* For now, it was like a game of football. Just move the ball downfield. Get it closer to the zone. Figure out what to do when you get there. *All will be revealed,* he told himself.

88

BREACH

This was always how it was going to go.
—a computerized voice broadcast over the dead landscape of Las Vegas, three times a day, 12 A.M., 8 A.M., 4 P.M.

NOVEMBER 13, 2025
The CDC, Atlanta, Georgia

"WE NEED TO SEAL THE DOORS," CASSIE SAID.

Benji held up a finger. "Cassie. No. Not yet."

She gently eased his hand down and got close. In a soft voice she said, "C'mon. Benji. You want to protect everything we've found here, don't you? We don't want them finding this. Any of this."

"Ten minutes," he said. "Give them ten minutes."

"If they come down, they can bang on the door, maybe we can hear them—"

"Thick, stainless-steel doors? Maybe. But maybe we can't. I don't want to take that chance. Ten minutes. *Five*," he pleaded. "Give them five minutes."

If Shana isn't okay, then what was the point of any of this?

Cassie nodded. "Yeah. Okay. Five minutes."

Five minutes.

THERE. SHANA LOOKED DOWN AT the armload of medical supplies she'd stuffed in a cardboard file box. Antibiotics, antibacterial ointment, pain pills across the spectrum from "headache" to "sucking chest wound," gauze, the whole kit and kaboodle. That would have to be good enough.

She grabbed it and hit the stairs, pausing for a moment to listen—she didn't hear Pete's footsteps, or any sign of him. *I hope you're okay, you crazy motherfucker.* She knew he would be. Pete was functionally immortal.

Down the stairwell she went, floor by floor. Third floor, second, then first—

And just as she began to descend into the sublevels, the door to the lobby floor swung open with a bang. Into the piss-yellow light, a man stepped forward—bald, red beard, some kind of assault rifle tucked into the soft pocket of his shoulder. "Hey!" he barked.

Shit!

Shana ran. She held the box tight as she took two steps at a time, her heels skidding and nearly slipping. She rounded one stairwell bend after the next, hearing bootsteps coming fast behind her. Too fast. He wasn't alone. She heard others, too, yelling, heavy footsteps following, the rattle of metal—

I'm not going to make it, she thought.

So, she started yelling until it felt like her vocal cords were being ripped up like plants from the ground—"Close the doors! Close the doors! *Close the door—*"

As she rounded the bend two floors above Benex-Voyager, something hard—no, some*one* hard—slammed into her. The file box in her hand crushed. Meds spilled as her shoulder and head hit the concrete wall. A thousand suns went supernova behind her eyes. A rough hand grabbed the back of her neck, pushing her into the corner and shoving a rifle barrel under her chin.

Baldy Redbeard leered at her. "Don't run too far, rabbit."

"Fuck you," she said, her ears ringing, her tongue tasting blood.

"Where were you off to?"

More men began to pass. They were carrying something—a metal box, or crate. Big. In the meager yellow light, she couldn't see what it was. Another man stepped in, regarding her—a square-jawed pit bull with small, dark eyes. She knew him. She swore she did. But from where?

"Who's this little bitch?" the new man said. Again, that voice. Who was he?

Before any of them could say anything—

A sound rose up from below. A metallic grind, followed by a *clang-clang-clang.* It was the sound of the door sealing. Benji had heard her.

Shana laughed in their faces because, honestly, fuck them.

Redbeard drove a hammering fist into her side.

"They're closing the doors," the pit bull said. "C'mon! Fuck!"

• • •

IT WAS THE WRONG MOVE. Benji knew it. Felt it in his teeth, his guts, his soul. Shana yelled for them to close the doors and he did, he went to the Lair, he told the Chimera to close the doors—but even as he felt the words come out of him, he knew it was dooming Shana. And he realized now she was the whole reason he was here in the first place. *Shana* . . .

He cried out, a mournful, painful sound as he heard the doors begin to engage. Cassie met him coming back out of the Lair, and she must've seen the look on his face because she said, "It was the right move. Shana knows what's up."

"She can't get hurt. If they hurt her—"

"She's tough, she can hang in there." But the doubt in Cassie's voice was plain as a bloodstain on a white wall.

Together they stepped out with the others, staring down the hall at the door as it eased shut. Soon, he knew, it would seal—the pneumatic hiss would come.

Voices rose outside.

Footsteps.

They'd be too late, he knew.

And we're too late for Shana.

As the gap narrowed to dwindling inches, they saw shadows appear past the door. Benji pulled Cassie back, in case anyone fired into the room.

Someone reached in, fingers pushing through that gap, curling around the metal door's edge. Whoever they were, if they didn't retrieve their hand quickly, it'd be crushed. The mechanism behind that door was unforgiving. It had to be. You installed one, there were warnings. It would pull your hand into the groove, turn it to paste, mash it against its own mechanism— potentially to its own detriment, if it caused an improper seal of the door. But still, the door would still close, and they weren't concerned about the airtight seal—

The door kept going. The fingers tightened around its edge.

Then, *ga-gung, ga-gung, ga-gung*—

The door began to judder in its frame.

It stopped closing.

What the hell.

"Benji," Cassie said, in fear-struck awe. "How—"

"I-I don't know."

The door began to vibrate, banging loudly now against its frame, bucking like a deer caught in chicken wire.

And then, not only did it cease to close—

But it began to *reopen*. It reopened as those hands *pushed*. Even from here he could see the hands straining. Veins popping. Then, the hands themselves seemed to *blur*, and he heard a sound in the back of his skull, a whirring scream.

The door slowly, surely, ineluctably opened once more.

Lieutenant Torres, hidden in an office doorway, leaned out with her rifle—

Through the sour, sickened light of the stairwell, Benji saw Shana's face—someone shoved her and she fell to her hands and knees. Two men stepped into the breach. The first was a bald white man with an unkempt red beard and a rifle pressed to Shana's back.

The second was—

"Oh my God," Cassie said.

Benji recognized the man, too.

It didn't seem possible. Ed Creel was older, now, obviously. More lines in his face. He'd lost some bulk, and he seemed to have sharper, cinder-block edges. He had that telltale cockbird strut Benji had seen too often on television—him walking out on a stage, at a rally, to thousands of fans chanting his slogans, *Hunt the Cunt, A Little Revolution Goes a Long Way, Hang the Bitches, Journalists for Jail, Get Woke Go Broke,* and on and on. The Creel Creed, the Creel Coalition.

The man who wanted to be president. Who killed his way into the Oval Office. And he was here, in this room, right now.

Creel was the one who'd opened that door. He grunted and gave it one last shove into its place as he stepped forward, flexing his thick fingers, popping his knuckles like rocks knocking together.

Torres raised her rifle—

"No!" Benji cried out.

But it was too late. She pulled the trigger.

The bullet struck the man with the red beard center-mass, right in the chest—he staggered back, pulling the trigger reflexively on his own weapon.

The one pointed at Shana.

Shana—

She cried out, the strength fleeing her arms and legs and she slid forward, to the floor, into a smeary spray of her own blood. The bullet entered her back. It exited the front. Fresh red spilled swiftly.

"No!" Benji screamed and charged, reaching for the weapon in his holster.

PETE HAD ONE JOB.

It was a simple enough job. Go to the roof. Find the spinny turbine thing. Look for the box with the fireworks. Cut it open. Light them off.

Easy-peasy, cough-and-sneezy.

But . . . Pete Corley was Pete Motherfucking Corley, wasn't he?

Pete, at the core of himself, was a contrarian. He didn't mean to be. Maybe didn't even *want* to be. There were times when he thought, *Maybe I'm gay just because everyone says you gotta be straight.* That wasn't it, of course, but he wouldn't put it past himself to be just that kind of defiant bastard.

Tell Pete to go right, he'd go left.

Tell Pete to fuck off, he'd get closer.

Tell Pete to be better, be healthy, get well, he'd do some cocaine off a poison toad's back before jumping into an orgy with questionable participants. He was what he was, which was an unconditionally insubordinate deviant asshole. Rock-and-roll was a natural fit, given that it was the domain of ruiners and rebels, of which he was both.

The important thing these days was, Pete knew this about himself. He did not *always* know this, which meant once upon a time that he was not aware of, or in control of, his oppositional defiance. But since the end of the world, give or take a few months, he'd come to know himself a whole lot better. And so, when he did the opposite of what he was supposed to, he at least did it with purpose and awareness. His contempt for instructions and his wayward disobedience were done with half a mind toward the greater good.

As was the case now.

Yes, he went to the roof. He hurried through the dark, the wind up here cold and clumsy, like a dipshit in a mosh pit. He found the package, cut it open, and saw inside a considerable brick of pyrotechnics. Shining a little flashlight on it, he saw it had an evocative name: *Hillbilly Hurricane!* On it was a cartoon cowboy in the mode of Slim Pickens from *Dr. Strangelove.* *Major Kong rides the bomb*, Pete thought. Except here, the cowboy riding the rocket was riding it up into the sky, not down toward the ground and all around him were the comical explosions of fireworks. It went on to explain it had four firework effects, had eight shots total, and didn't need you to light it, because it had a ripcord at the bottom.

Pull cord.

Light fireworks.

Enjoy the show.

Pete exposed the cord.

His fingers danced along it.

Down below, he heard the growl of engines. No gunfire. No explosions. Just engines and men yelling. What were they doing? What were they yelling about? Because he was a curious fella, he stood up and went to the far side of the roof, past the solar panel array, and he looked out over the battlefield.

The vehicles were lining up, one after the next, pointing toward a central truck. This truck, by his estimation, was a tanker truck, like the kind you'd see in a residential area—fuel oil, propane, that sort of thing. Floodlights illuminated the scene and it looked like they were fueling up their vehicles, one after the next. A bunch of pickups had generators in the back, too.

Well.

Hmm.

Pete licked his lips.

He shot a glance at the tanker truck.

Then he turned his gaze toward the spot where the firework launcher waited.

He had that craving. The craving to do fuckery.

Pete was not very good at denying his cravings.

So fuckery he would do.

LATER, BENJI WOULD LOOK BACK on it all and try to understand. He'd try to piece it together, what happened down there. Shana, on the floor, bleeding, dying. Torres with her rifle up while the bald, bearded sonofabitch staggered back, his gun barking shots, bullets stitching up through the air, hitting lights, sparks and glass raining down. Ed Creel, the Republican nominee for president before the world went to shit, the man who backed Ozark Stover's militia assault on Ouray, standing there, striding forward, like he didn't have a single care in the world. Four more men rushing into the space, dropping something on the ground, some kinda cage that rattle-chattered as it landed, as they reached for their weapons—

And Benji.

Drawing Marcy's big-ass gun.

Running forward.

Screaming Shana's name as he raised the weapon, thumb on the hammer.

And that's where things went especially strange.

Ed Creel moved fast.

Maybe once he'd been athletic—he had that look about him of someone who played football in high school, maybe even played it well, but who had been so long from the game that if he got onto the field today, he'd be dead before the end of the first quarter. He looked harder now than he had on television, admittedly: whittled down, shaped by his time out there, whatever had happened. But the way he moved now? It would be impossible for a man twenty years his junior, a man in the best shape of his life.

Creel strode forward, juking right toward Benji as Torres took a shot—he ducked low as he approached, rising again just as he passed by her, his hand flashing out. Something gleamed. He must've had a knife in his hand because Torres suddenly cried out in surprise, that cry cut short by a wet, abattoir gurgle—a spray of blood aerosolized, wetting Benji's face as he tracked Creel with the barrel of the revolver, the man in his sights—

But Benji, like Torres, was too slow.

Because Creel came through the storm of blood, a shark leaping from the water, his hand out, catching the barrel of the gun and lifting it up—

As he slammed his whole body into Benji.

It felt like getting hit by a city bus.

That bus carried Benji backward, down the hall, crashing into the jamb of Sadie's office door. The air was banished from his lungs. He started to drop, wheezing, keening for breath—

But Creel held him up, kept him from falling.

The man pressed his face against Benji's, meeting him literally nose to nose, grinding his face forward, mouth wide in a mad, toothy grin. Benji strained to bring the gun back down, to point the barrel just so . . .

That's when Creel's hand started to hum. Benji could feel it first more than he could hear it. Creel's mitt, the one wrapped around the revolver, began to tremble and then blur, like the way heat shimmered in cold air—

The gun began to crumple in his grip. The barrel bent backward. The top sight rail crushed against the cylinder, trapping it. Creel's thumb dented the trigger guard like it was made of aluminum foil, and Benji had to pull his own finger out of there, lest it be trapped, broken like a Popsicle stick. Creel yanked the gun away and threw it behind him. The ruined revolver landed with a clatter.

Creel pulled back a little, looking Benji over as he held him hard against the frame of the door. "You," he said. "I know you."

"We've—" Benji started to say. "Never met."

"No, no, no, we went after you in Vegas, didn't we? You're famous. On the television. C'mon." Creel leered, a kind of joy flashing in his eyes. "The man of science who went to be with the Shepherds. The media did a profile of you back then. I saw it."

That was news to Benji. Of course, he had other things to worry about at that point, didn't he? Just as he did now.

"I wouldn't have voted for you," Benji said. Through a mouthful of his own blood Benji said, "You would've been a dogshit president."

It was a petty, childish thing to say. Nobody voted for anyone, because the election never happened. The world fell before it could, and prior to that, Ozark Stover's militia—under what he guessed was Creel's own order—executed President Nora Hunt. But he knew it would bother Creel. And even now he could see that it had. To injure this man, you had to go for his ego. Creel thought his ego was his armor, but it was actually the opposite: a weakness, a soft vulnerability, a trembling thing that needed to be protected.

Creel smiled a too-tight smile. Teeth bared. "Cute," he said, but the word was slathered with acid. He looked down at Benji's left arm—the one that dead-ended at the elbow, was just a nub. "Got a flipper now, huh? Last time I saw you, you had two arms. The world went hard on you." He held his grin. "Me too."

Benji tried looking past him, to survey the scene behind Creel. Shana was on the floor, her head down. Was her back rising and falling with the movement of breath? He couldn't tell. He prayed that it was. The man who had shot her was sitting only a couple feet from her, blood soaking his chest as he stared down at his rifle. Torres was dead. Throat ripped out. With what? Creel had a knife, didn't he? Then where was it?

As for the others—Bobby Hart and Blu Acevedo cowered in an office doorway, held fast by the guns of three of the four men standing by the cage.

A cage that, far as Benji could tell, contained a human being.

But there was someone else here, too. It was someone from the CDC, wasn't it? Benji recognized him. A Korean man, Paul . . . Cheong, wasn't it? Software guy. He pressed flat against the wall toward the entry point, his hands up, palms slick with sweat. The fourth gunman had his weapon pointed right at Paul's stomach.

Benji noticed, some of his people were missing.

Tanzer, Spohn, Hornor, weren't here.

And neither was Cassie.

Good.

"No, no, hey," Creel said, patting Benji on the cheek. "You don't need to look over there. You need to look at me. What's your name again? It's something . . . childish. Ray. Benji Ray. Ray like the blind Black guy, Benji like the stupid fucking dog. Do I remember that right?"

"Dogs bite," Benji said, a warning.

"You know, I had a pair of cane corsos, once. Bitsy and Bullet. God, I loved those dogs. Big mastiffs. Big personalities. Early on, puppies, they get mouthy. Like to bite to assert themselves, push you around a little. But that's easy enough to deal with, if you're willing. People got all kinds of tricks, you know, ply them with treats, but that just trains them to be soft. There are electric shock prods and collars, but that just teaches the dog to fear you. No, the real trick is, they bite you? You bite them back. Hard. Draw blood." He clacked his teeth together. "But you gotta be willing to get down there with them and do that. Otherwise, they get uppity, think they rule you instead of the reverse." A sharp, cruel gleam danced in Creel's eye. "Wolves need an alpha."

"The alpha wolf is a myth."

"Uh-huh. See, thinking you know better than everybody else? That's the problem with you people."

"'You people,'" Benji repeated, saying the words like they were a foul taste he had to spit out of his mouth.

"Oh. Sure. See, you think I'm being racist. But I mean you people like . . . you liberals. You scientists. You weak-kneed, un-American, soft-bellied, shit-sniffing curs. It's always racism, isn't it? . . . With *you people.*"

"You just call a spade a spade, huh?"

Creel, still holding him up by the neck, winked. "I see what you did there. What I mean is, you all think you know better. You got your facts. I got my feelings. And my feelings are never wrong."

"Fuck your feelings."

"Yeah. About that. Well, Benji-doggy, I'm just gonna get ahead of this now, because I need you *compliant.* I have a job to do here and I am keen to do it quickly. So, before you bite *me*—" He reached out, cupping a free hand around Benji's stump. "I bite first."

At that, his hand started to hum again.

A deep, resonant thrum rose up from his hand to Benji's amputation injury—he could feel it to his shoulder, then into his jaw.

At that, pain lit up. Suddenly, it was like having the arm removed all over again. A buzz-saw vibration bore deep beyond the skin and scab and deep into the bone. Fresh blood soaked through his gauze as he screamed.

Benji whaled his hand against the side of Creel's thick stack-of-bricks face, but it didn't do any good. He hit again and again, Creel flinching and wincing but taking every hit with a smile, and soon Benji couldn't even *see* the other man, his vision crushed by a wave of white pain.

And then, it was over.

Creel dropped him like a sack of millet.

Benji slumped, gasping for breath. He looked to his amputated arm, expecting to see that what was left of it was now gone, too, but his stump-arm remained. The end of it was drooling blood onto the floor.

Creel clapped his two hands together. "Good. All right." He began peering in and out of rooms. "Conference room, there we go. Two of you"—he pointed to his four remaining gunmen—"start wrangling these people into the conference room. The other two, you go through the other rooms, check out the floor below us, look for stragglers, survivors, hiders. Bring them here, unless they look at you wrong, in which case, two to the chest, one in the head."

One of Creel's gunmen, an older man, maybe late fifties with a rough-looking skin-kite frame, tapped the cage with the barrel end of his shotgun. In a syrupy drawl, he said, "The hell do we do with her?"

"Leave her for the moment. She's not going anywhere."

"And Hogan?"

Creel threw up his hands and shook his head as he sauntered over to the bald, bearded man on the floor. That man, his chest and lap now slicked with his own heartsblood, looked up at Creel with empty eyes that found focus.

"Hogan," Creel said.

"Mister President, help me," the other man said, burping up foamy, bright blood into his copper-wire beard. Benji knew what that meant. It meant the man was beyond the help for which he begged.

Benji knew what this meant for Shana, too.

He feared that she, too, was beyond saving.

Creel knelt down by his fallen soldier.

"Help you?" Creel said to the man. "Help you how? I can't help you, Hogan." He shrugged in a way that showed how little he gave a damn. "Besides, even if I could . . . I prefer men who *don't* get shot in the chest."

•   •   •

I PREFER . . .

Words, wobbling.

Men who donnnnn't

A whistling sound in her ear.

Get shot in the chhhhessssshhhhht

Shana was dying.

She'd been shot. Where, she didn't know. Her whole chest felt heavy, blocky, and cold—her upper torso like a refrigerator with arms and legs dangling from it. She tried to will her arms to push her up off the ground but she couldn't find the strength. She could flex them—a little. But only that, and it took everything out of her just to make that small movement.

Though her strength was waning, her anger was not. They were so close to finding a way to end Black Swan, to save Ouray, to return to her son and have him be her son for once and for *real*.

I cannot die here.

I will not die here.

She swore it to herself, a bloody-lipped whisper.

She turned her head just so in order to see the man who had shot her— a man who had in turn been shot by, she thought, Lieutenant Torres. Torres, now dead. *Fuck.* The bald, bearded sonofabitch was still alive, but barely. He had anger and betrayal in his eyes as he watched Creel stalk off.

In his lap was his rifle. His hand lying on it like a dead fish.

The man—Hogan, Creel had called him—looked to Shana.

He locked eyes with her, then looked down at the rifle.

He got his hand under it and gave it a little shove. It slid off his lap with a clatter, then he nodded. Said, "You want this?" Three words running together like paint into one. *Youanthis.* His eyes went rheumy and gray, dead as scuffed nickels.

Shana regarded the rifle.

What a strange ally. The man who shot her was now giving her the gun he used to shoot her in the first fucking place. She almost wanted to laugh. But even the thought of laughing made her cough. Blood wetted her lip.

That's probably not good.

What she wouldn't have given to have Black Swan helping her right now. Another mad alliance. *Save me so I can end you,* she thought, pleading into the dark of her mind. But there was no answer, and there was no help.

Then, as the other gunmen were rounding up Hart and Acevedo, dragging them into the conference room, Shana saw Benji crawling toward her on hand and knees—scooting forward, saying her name in a loud whisper.

She met his eyes, just as Creel grabbed him by the back of the neck.

"Uh-uh, doggy, you come with me," Creel said.

Benji pulled away, but Shana gently shook her head. *Leave me be.*

There was a moment where she thought he wasn't going to get the message, that he was going to fight his way to her, maybe die trying. But then he gave her the tiniest little nod, and scrambled to stand even as Creel bluntly shoved him forward into the conference room after the others.

And then, she was alone.

Still dying, she was pretty sure.

She could breathe—a little. Every breath felt like she was underwater, sucking air through a garden hose from the surface above. That whistling sound told her she'd taken a hit through the lung. But not through the heart, right? She wasn't a doctor, but if the bullet hit her there . . . she'd be toast. Like Hogan.

The gun, she thought.

Again, she attempted to move herself. This time, it came a little more easily. She coughed as she did so, and coughing wracked pain throughout her. *Be quiet, you stupid idiot,* she thought. Didn't want anybody to come checking on her.

Her hand found Hogan's leg, and she hugged it like a pillow, hooking her arm around it and drawing herself toward him—

And toward his rifle.

Shana swung her legs out sideways. Like moving two animal carcasses, except they were her limbs. Somehow, she managed to sit up. Blood pumped from her chest in gentle fits and starts.

She looked away from her injury and over at the cage. It was a dog crate, she knew: a crate for a real big dog, like for a Great Dane or wolfhound. A woman lay huddled in there, a tangle of hair and filth. It was only then that Shana realized:

She's looking at me.

The caged woman's eyes stared wide open through a curtain of matted hair. She watched Shana carefully, but didn't move.

Jesus, who is she?

Whoever she was, they wanted her in that cage.

But fuck what those men wanted.

Shana left the rifle—with a plan to return to it—and crawled forward on her hands and knees, leaving messy streaks of blood behind her, intending to unlock that crate. They wanted this woman in the cage. So Shana wanted her out of it. An act of kindness for the woman, and spite for those who put her in there.

Be free, poor lady. Be free.

89

SWAN SONG

We feared that the music which had given us sustenance was in danger of spiritual starvation. We feared it losing its sense of purpose, we feared it falling into fattened hands, we feared it floundering in a mire of spectacle, finance, and vapid technical complexity. We would call forth in our minds the image of Paul Revere, riding through the American night, petitioning the people to wake up, to take up arms. We too would take up arms, the arms of our generation, the electric guitar and the microphone.

—Patti Smith, *Just Kids*

NOVEMBER 13, 2025
THE CDC, ATLANTA, GEORGIA

IF THERE WAS ONE TRUTH PETE KNEW AND KNEW WELL, IT WAS THAT HAVING the full-bellied confidence of a white man in America was the thing closest to a magic power. People, particularly other white men, just *assumed* you belonged around them. The joke was, if you carried a clipboard, nobody would say shit to you, but Pete had always found that the bigger you went, the easier it was. Try to walk in with a clipboard, okay, fine, but someone might wonder, are you delivering something? Is this an inventory, a survey, are you a Jehovah's Witness collecting tickets for the seats in Heaven? But walk in with a live duck under one arm and a jar of pickled eggs under the next, you short-circuited people's ability to even ask what the fuck you were doing. It was too bold and too brash to be a con, a ruse, a *lie*, so they let you pass. Hell, they'd *hold the fucking door for you.* But!

You had to be a white dude motherfucker with white dude motherfucker confidence to pull it off.

Be a Black or brown guy? They'd call the cops, and the cops would shoot you, the duck, the egg jar. A woman? Some man would steal your duck, grope you as they did it.

Ahhh, but glory be to a white man in America. Domestic terrorist? Nah, just a liberty-loving free-spirited school-shooter. Come on in, Dave, the water's warm, the beers are cold, and the arresting officer will buy you a half-dozen donuts after you burned down that Black church. Even let you eat 'em in the police cruiser, gosh, don't even worry about the powdered sugar, you *enjoy* those treats, because jail's going to be rough for you, what with all those *other*-color people in there.

Pete decided to use his white man magic to pull off this trick.

He went down from the roof, into the lobby. He found a rifle on the ground, so he scooped that up, slung it over his shoulder, still carrying the brick of fireworks. Then out the front door he went, la-dee-da—

And immediately, he stood confronted by a heap of dead bodies— corpses dragged into a messy, disrespectful pile.

And in those bodies, his eyes fixed on a familiar face.

Eric Blackmoore. The top of his head was missing. His brains were spilled out like spoiled gelatin.

Barbaric Bleakmoor.

His D&D buddy. His fucking *Dungeon Master*. Fucking hell.

Tears seared the edges of his eyelids.

Two gunmen stood nearby, and they brought their rifles up.

"The fuck are you?" one asked.

He froze. He could *feel* their fingers curling around the triggers—

Get it together, Corley, for fucking fuck's sake. Blackmoore's dead. Nothing to be done about that right now. Blink back your tears, show your teeth.

"Entertainment," Pete said, after a moment, trying to recompose himself. *Just lie. Lie your way through it. Don't stop. Don't dwell on this.*

That comes later.

He bent at the hip, leaning forward, trying to show them the fireworks box under his arm. He affected his very best Southern accent, which admittedly was middling at best, and said with a goofy drawl, "Figure we could all use some fuckin' fireworks. They told me to set 'em up across the way."

The two gunmen looked at each other. Then they nodded.

"Hell yeah," the one said.

"Hell *yeah*," Pete repeated, and then walked on.

Confidence of a white man in America.

Clipboard? Nah, know your audience. Fireworks? Hell yeah.

But as he strode across the campus toward the trucks, his mind returned again and again to Blackmoore. Head, emptied of those beautiful brains. He was a damn fine Dungeon Master, and though Pete had never actually met *another* Dungeon Master, he was damn sure none were as good. His knees wanted to buckle. He wanted to take a moment, cry this out. But he couldn't. He had to keep going. For Benji, for Shana, for everyone inside. *The entertainment,* he'd said.

That made him stop in his tracks and look over at the barracks tent.

Thought of the generators at the trucks. And the lights plugged in there.

"Entertainment," he said again, and adjusted his direction, pointing his feet in the direction of that tent, instead. "*Hell. Fuckin'. Yeah.*"

PETE KEPT HIS HEAD HELD high, whistled "You're a Grand Old Flag" as he went, maybe even sang a few words, *you're a grand old flag, you're a high-flying flag, you're a something and a something may you waaaave, doo-doo-doo.*

He was armed.

But this time, not with the rifle. Nah, he ditched that.

No, now he carried a Fender Strat and a portable amp. Both, belonging to the previously alive Dungeon Master, Eric Blackmoore. The Strat was dinged up, nicked a bit, but otherwise in good shape—Blackmoore had been fastidious about cleaning it, and its buttercream soul gleamed with pride. The amp was a six-pound Marshall Kilburn. Small. But loud. If it worked, he knew it'd be clear in the midrange. Not that it much mattered, probably.

So, along he went. Electric guitar slung over the shoulder. Fireworks under one arm. Amp held in other hand, dangling by its leather, duct-tape-swaddled strap. And a song in his motherfucking heart.

SHANA, HE THOUGHT.

"*See you back down there?*" she asked him.

"*See you back down there,*" he said.

Each, a promise to the other.

THE TRUCKS WERE LINED UP in a row, waiting to fuel. The propane pump truck stood at the far end of the bunch, like a mommy sow pig waiting for all her bigoted shit-stink hoglets to come and suckle her foul milk. A handful of these racist pricks had gathered, already getting a bit rowdy, unsure what to do next. Several of them were still in their trucks, waiting for their chance to pull forward and get fueled up, but the ones down here on the ground already had a bottle of whiskey out, were already roaming around with that free-range aggression, like the assholes who came to a live show just to ruin everybody else's good time.

But that was fine. Pete could use that energy.

He sauntered right up.

Hello, fuckers, Pete thought but did not say, offering up a hasty Hitlerian hand salute and a wink. *Yes, yes, 88, 14 words, blue lives matter, don't tread on me, blah-blah-blah, n-word this, this-word that. Fuckers fuckers fuckers.*

Instead, he said:

"Let's hear some fuckin' music," he said, hurriedly adding, "y'all." It sounded awkward as hell coming out of his mouth. *Y'all*. (He knew it was unfair that a Southern accent would get him by here—some of the most progressive, warmhearted people were from the South. It's just, right here and right now he was in Georgia, and a lot of these cross-eyed baboons automatically figured a white Southerner was both an ally and a conspirator. Roll up in here with his half-Irish accent, and they'd gut him like a catfish pulled out of its mudhole.)

He dropped the fireworks box first, then immediately plunked the amp down in front of it. Just in case anybody got too curious, that left the fireworks crate blocked by the Marshall. Nicely hidden.

He pulled the cord out from the amp, plugged it into the generator.

Some lean strip of bacon with a Cracker Barrel hat and a Kid Rock T-shirt (under a clumsy ammo-stuffed fishing vest) sauntered up, a few other of "his boys" in tow. "Creel send you?" he asked.

Creel. He repressed a shudder.

That fucker was here? Now? He'd heard stories out there about Ed Creel still being alive and holed up in some nuclear bunker in the Midwest, but Pete never gave those rumors much credence. He'd become a figure of folklore, the devil to some, a god to others, and neither could abide the loss of adversary or lord.

But shit, maybe it was true.

"Yuh," Pete said, unspooling a cable.

"Whatchoo gonna play?" Cracker Barrel asked, tongue sliding over rotten teeth. His breath rancid enough to gag a goblin.

"Some bad-ass shit," Pete said, still *drawling* best as he could.

"Yeah, but *what* badass shit?"

"I'll play some Kid Rock," Pete lied, because he'd pound his balls into pizza dough before playing that asshole's hee-haw quote-unquote rap.

"Well, I don't like Kid Rock," moped the hillbilly in the Kid Rock T-shirt.

Pete had to restrain himself from breaking the guitar over this lackwit's soft skull, because who the fuck wears the shirt of a band they don't even like? Fucking hell, these dickheads. *Such* dickheads! "Fine, man, who do you—y'all—want me to play?"

"Toby Keith, Trace Adkins, or shit, old-school David Allan Coe—"

As if the Naziism and KKK taint-licking weren't bad enough, their musical taste was enough to curdle Cognac into donkey cum. Still. He forced a smile, bit his lower lip, and said, "Hell yeah, man."

"Hell yeah," Cracker Barrel said.

Cracker Barrel. Barrel of crackers, indeed. He'd rather hang out with Juggalos. At least Juggalos were fun to be around.

He took the ten-inch amp cord, plugged it into the box, then popped it into the guitar. Already the amp came alive with a crunchy guitar wail.

A shiver of delight went through Pete. How long had it been since he'd had a proper electric guitar in his hand? Not a ukulele, or an acoustic, but a proper wailer, a real screamer, a goddamn grinder? He didn't have pedals or anything, didn't have a mic, but he had this one thing, and it felt good.

No, it felt *right*.

See you back down there?

See you back down there.

Promises, promises, Pete Corley.

No MIC MEANT HE HAD to scream, and scream loud over all the engines. Which was no problem for Pete Corley, the original Screamin' Cheetah. So he did a loud strum of the strings, a big effusive *wahhhhhh* on the guitar, and whooped: "Come one, come all. I'm tonight's entertainment for a job well done. Come on! Come the hell on, all you fun-seekers, all you fevered fuckin' egos. Woooo!"

He was the bug zapper.

They were the moths.

Fly to me, my uglies.

Some of them dropped down out of their trucks. Others just leaned out the windows to listen. Someone yelled at him to get up on the back of one of the pickup trucks but he knew that shit wouldn't work for what he had planned, so he just pretended not to hear, and instead roared with that cheese-grater voice—

"Who here likes Gumdropper?"

And he tilted his head, hand cupped to his ear to hear their cheers—

Only, like, three of them hooted in assent.

Fine, whatever, fuck you, you heathens.

And at that he blasted into one of their oldest songs, "Night Bones," from their first album—

Night Bones
Night Bones
You and me
Night Bones
Night Bones
Pay the fee
The voice it calls
Across the way
You better get goin'
Or there's hell to pay!

It was a simple-ass, stupid-ass fucking song. He wasn't even sure what it was about. Some half-bitten Halloween pap that eventually Rob Zombie would cover in what was honestly a better version, à la Cash's cover of Reznor's "Hurt," but, hey, whatever. It chafed his taint at the time but he came to appreciate it. More important, there was a siren song component to it, right? If there was any narrative throughline to the song, it was about people being called to party—the summoning of a voice, the sound of distant rock, and they go to listen, and when they go to listen, the "Night Bones," whatever the fuck they are, rise up and drag the victims down, down into the ground, into Hell itself.

Night Bones
Night Bones
Come and see
Night Bones
Night Bones
You're the key

Now you're here
The trap is laid
The door is open
Gonna meet Hell's shade!

Here he was, Mister Night Bones, summoning all the partying shit-wits to the field. *Come on, you fucking dickheads, come and have a listen.* As he played, some of them nodded their heads, one threw up a pair of devil's horns, but most of them just looked confused. Fine. Let them be confused. Let that confusion draw them ever closer, the allure of bewilderment, the hook-shaped question mark buried in their tongues and dragging them forth like eels.

WAYBACK MACHINE, 1979:

Max's Kansas City. New York club. Pete and Evil Elvis were sitting around, high on hashish after a show—or was it before? Fuck. And Elvis was talking about "Night Bones," saying, "I hate that fucking song, we wrote it too fast, it's just some asinine shit," and Pete threw back at him, "Nah, mate, that's why people like it, they like simple things, simple as a summer day."

Elvis said, "The fuck even are the Night Bones?"

And Pete laughed and said he didn't know. Zombies, maybe. Vampires. The band, undead, rising up out of the ground.

"To what, punish our fans?"

"They deserve to be punished for liking the likes of us."

Elvis, now with a can of Pabst, raised it to that. "Hah, fucking serves them right, you're right." He knocked the can back and crumpled it. "How great would that be? To be zombies, shuffling around, not a care in the world but to eat some tasty brains." *Dawn of the Dead* had just come out the year before and the band had seen it a bunch of times. Too many times, maybe. "Except I'd be a zombie who likes pussy more than he likes brains."

"That does sound like you," Pete said, cough-laughing. "Christ, let's do it. Let's kill ourselves, see what happens. See if we stay dead, or get up, hungry for brains and pussy, ready to rock harder than we ever fuckin' rocked." The hash was making him fuzzy. It was great. Hashish was the goddamn best.

"Suicide pact. Yes. *Yes.* If shit's ever not going our way," Elvis said, *urp*-ing, "we off ourselves, take it to the next level."

Elvis would become a real prick later, all-business, no-fun, and okay, *maybe* Pete should've been at least a little *more* business, a little *less* fun, but now, in this moment in time, the two of them were sympatico. Friends till the end, they thought, not realizing that life had many endings, not just one. Little apocalypses and, as it turned out, big apocalypses, too.

"Promise?" Pete asked.

"Promise," Elvis answered.

THE MUSIC WAS IN HIM now. Wrapped around his bones like the Eden serpent around the fruit tree, and he knew he was in that groove—see, some things were ruts, others were grooves. You wanted to be out of a rut but in a groove and that's where he was, now, a record needle sliding easy along its rock-and-roll channel, digging up sound from that ditch and spitting it into the world. The guitar felt like a part of Pete in a way that it hadn't in a long time. Going to the Rock and Roll Hall of Fame was him passing the torch and being done with all of it—a silent acquiescence that his days as a Motherfucking Rockgod were over, that he had gotten old and dusty and could enter the mythology of music, because he was a god out to pasture, a god left to dwell in the darklands, a gold record on the wall of the sacred temple, an old song sung like a hymn burned into the brain-meats—

But now, here he was, the god returned, the god anew. The god reborn.

(If only for this moment in time.)

The crowd wasn't vibing with it, *not at all*, and once upon a time that would've pissed him off good, but if *this* crowd wasn't getting it—hah, well, that only energized him. Proof-positive he was sliding along a truly glorious, revelatory, epiphanic groove—

Someone, maybe Cracker Barrel, hooted: "Play Travis Tritt!"

Another howler monkey yelled: "Play 'Okie from Muskogee'!"

"Or 'The Angry American'!"

Up until now, Pete thought he'd do another Gumdropper, but then he thought he could, what, segue into some Willie, or—or shit! Some Dixie Chicks. "Goodbye Earl," maybe. But the music had him in its teeth. So, hell with it, he just started improvising. Something he never ever did. *What am I, a jam band? Am I fuckin' Phish all of a sudden?* Fine. Like the man said, *Let it be.* The music grabbed him by the tip of his dick and swung him around like he was a cat and his cock was the tail.

The song just fell out of him.

He thought he'd call it, "Promises, Promises."

•   •   •

Two years ago.

Long Beach Island, New Jersey. Surf City.

He'd found Evil Elvis Lafferty in a funky little beach bungalow on stilts, the house lifted some years before due to Hurricane Sandy. Elvis—partially bedridden from what he figured was cancer, but in his words, "Who's even around to tell me?"—had come here to be with his brother, JJ, who was suffering the throes of White Mask. White Mask took the brother, but left Elvis alive, so he decided to stay. Pete said the beach suited him, because it did. He looked less like the hard-rock scion of days past and more like some old yacht rock uncle sipping margaritas and eating sea bugs, and that somehow seemed good and proper. Still, Elvis was feeling the cancer, or whatever it was, these days. Said, "My whole middle is just a riot of pain, like the cancer is a living thing, moving around in there." But he said it was okay, because the few people here, they still loved Gumdropper's music. "There are still fans out there," Elvis said, a glow about him when he said it. "The music isn't gone, not all the way. The dream isn't dead until we all are." Pete didn't know if he meant the two of them, or the band, or all the world.

Whatever it was, it surprised Pete. He figured Corporate Businessman Rock Entity Evil Elvis Lafferty LLC didn't much care about the music these days, but here he was, not on his Hudson Valley farm or in his Greenpoint townhouse, but in a little run-down bungalow at the beach. Reminiscing about the music. The memory, or the music, danced in his eyes. Like the sun on rolling waves.

They talked about the old days. And they did so without rancor. They talked about where they'd been since, what they'd seen. Pete spoke of his family, asked about the rest of the band. (They were all gone, of course. White Mask took their tickets.) They spoke about some of their best shows— Whisky a Go Go in '84, Veterans Stadium in Philly in '91, that backyard picnic they crashed on Long Island in, what, '95, '96? They talked about the real shitshows, too, like that shitkicker club in Tennessee, whatever the fuck it was called, Jaguar Bar? They played behind chicken wire and people threw bottles and in the parking lot after some rednecks wanted to fight them with baseball bats, and so Raina, always the sleepy-eyed sensible one until she wasn't, lost her fucking tits and pulled out a pair of goddamn motherfucking *butterfly knives* and whipped them open like she was some kind of ninja. She ran at the hillbillies like she was a weed-whacker. They bolted scared because they saw she'd cut a bitch into little chunks. That night was one of the *best* worst shows they'd ever done.

"We deserved it," Elvis said, laughing, coughing. "We were shit that night."

"Total shit," Pete agreed. "But even shitty, we were gods."

"The gods of shit!"

"The gods of shit!"

They laughed until the laughs burned out of them and then left them with those sort of smug, self-satisfied smiles. Once it wound all the way down, Elvis asked that Pete help him up. Together, they walked onto the sands of the closest beach. Out to a jetty, then onto it. Waves crashing up and around them. Gulls cackling like witches above their cauldron.

Elvis said, pointing out to the watery horizon, "This is my plan."

"The sky?"

"The sea. One day I'm gonna get sick enough it's hard to move, but I'm gonna make myself do it. Then I'm gonna walk into the ocean." He shrugged. "I hear drowning is a—" He cleared his throat, trying not to cough, a shrill wheeze rolling up out of him. "I hear it's a peaceful way to go."

"I bet it is."

"You gonna come with me when I go?"

"Maybe," Pete said. And he meant it, a little. "Depends when you do it. I've got this one more thing to do."

"The Hall of Fame thing."

"Aye, that."

"That's fucking stupid. I love it."

Pete barked a barmy larf. "Yeah. Yeah."

"After that, though?"

"After that, I got no plans." And he didn't. But a name arose from the depths of himself: *Ouray.* Faces, too. Benji, Shana. Friends. Family, even. "We'll see."

"You promised. Suicide pact. Don't forget that."

"Oh, I'd never, Double-E, I'd fuckin' never."

"I'm sorry for being a shit," Elvis said.

"I'm sorry for being a shit, too."

They hugged then. In the spray of the sea. The long horizon out there, waiting for them. The sound of the waves calling to Elvis, maybe to Pete, too. Night Bones, Night Bones, come and see, you're the key, into the sea . . .

"See you at the end of things?" Elvis asked later, when Pete left.

"Hope so, old friend."

"Promises, promises."

THAT WAS WHAT HE SANG about. All the promises he'd made. All the promises he'd broken. There were many. Too many for one fucking song, honestly. To his kids, his wife. To his band. To Landry, even. Landry, beautiful Landry, still there in his heart, in his deepest place—he'd promised Landry he'd tell his wife and kids about him, but he never got to. He promised, too, to make Landry comfortable at the end, and he'd tried, goddamnit he'd fucking tried, but then the sweet bastard went out into the snow, White Mask rewiring his head, and it was out there he died, frozen to death, and Pete should've been there for that. So that was the song. All of that. No rhyming, just a confession set to a steadily rising, quickening guitar. And then at the last of it, the promise to Shana.

They started to boo him, the Creel Boys. He'd almost forgotten they were out there. The spotlight of his own music had blackened them out. Turned him to day and them to night. Their boos empowered him. Thrilled him. *Hell yeah*.

Then someone said, "Hey!" Louder, then: *"Hey!"*

Pete didn't stop but he saw people turn toward the voice, a voice that belonged to a chunky thug with eyes like little cat buttholes, eyes that were too close together, cheeks that looked round like the cheeks of that cartoon character Nancy, and a flat amphibian mouth nested amid the speckles of a beard that refused to grow any longer—he barked, "That's Pete Corley!"

And they turned back toward him and the recognition dawned on their faces. And it wasn't *good* recognition. They were not happy to see him. Nor should they be. Pete was probably a shit citizen, given how rarely he voted, but he was a *loud* one, glad to spit in the eyes of bigots and curs every chance he could get in the days of MTV (if only for the attention it brought him), and they knew him for his take-no-prisoners-fuck-all-the-conservatives attitude. So when their gazes turned hateful, he felt the smile on his face grow a thousand times larger. A smile so big he could bite them all in half, like a great white shark roaring up out of the sea-churn.

"It's true!" he said, gazing out upon the dozens and dozens of faces that had gathered. Flies to porchlight, moths to flame. "It is I, Pete Motherfucking Corley, Rockgod Extraordinaire, a God greater than your Pussy God, Ed Creel, and I'd like to play *one last song*—"

They started roaring now, rammy and mad, guns in hands, cheeks red.
Ha ha, fuck all of you, he thought as he broke into the last song—
An old rhyme he loved.
"Whistle while you work!
Hitler was a jerk!
Mussolini bit his weenie—
Now it doesn't work!"
A rifle shot punctuated the rhyme.
He felt his body shake.
Shit.
He wasn't finished. He hadn't done the *thing.*
This wasn't good.
The guitar tumbled from his grip, though still hung from his neck by the strap. He dropped down to his bony ass, sitting there for a moment, regarding the slowly spreading wetness coming out from his middle. Somewhere below his heart but above his stomach. The space that got weak and wobbly when you were in love. The space where Landry lived, maybe. The place of crushes and lust.

He shrugged the guitar off his shoulder, and it made a grinding atonal sound—*shronkkkk*—before he fell backward, onto his back. There, to his left, was the amp, and behind it, the fireworks box.

The crowd moved in toward him.

Grunting, he scooped up the fireworks box, pointing it toward the propane truck. Then, as Cracker Barrel leaned over him, lips twisted in a sneer, Pete looked up and said, "Hell yeah."

He pulled the rip cord.
The box shook in his hand as it discharged the first firework—
The little rocket lit off toward the propane truck with a whistle—
"The fuck?" Cracker Barrel asked, following it with his eyes.
Fyooooooooooo.
It hit the truck.
It bounced off the truck.
Then it went up into the sky and popped, *kssh*, glitter-fire raining down.
Wait.
No.
Fuck.
No no no no no.
It's not working *it's not working.*

A second firework whistled, bounced, and took off into the sky. *Pop.* A third, then. This one, green like scattered emeralds.

"Shit," Pete said.

Cracker Barrel grinned a mouth of rotten teeth. "Fuck you doing?"

"I maybe don't understand how propane works," Pete said, glumly, tasting blood at the back of his tongue. "Or propane trucks. Fuck. Shit."

"It's liquid in the tank, but gas when it hits air."

Pete coughed a little. "I just kind of . . . assumed it was like gasoline."

"It ain't."

"Shit."

A fourth firework careened off the propane truck, whistling into the sky before cascading fire-diamonds down, crackle-hiss.

The crowd was all around him now.

Cracker Barrel chuckled, leaning over him, then went to draw his revolver.

Ideas went through Pete's head. Crazy ideas. Blackmoore ideas.

The sword. The artery. The Living Dungeon.

With every ounce of strength he had, he caught Cracker Barrel's wrists, then wrestled for the gun, gritting his teeth and doing his cheetah scream as he gargled out the words, "This is for Blackmoore!" before turning the gun underneath the fuckwit's chin and using his thumb to jerk the trigger—

Choom.

Cracker Barrel's hat left his head along with his mullet and the top of his skull and also what little brains he had—

Pete grunted, shoving him off, taking the gun—

Creel's dipshit terrorists pushed in on him, raising their weapons, too—

"Party bard!" he shrieked, pointing the gun at the truck—

And pulling the trigger.

The gun bucked in his hand.

A bullet punched a hole into the side of it.

He heard a sound, the sweetest sound—

The *hiss* of propane liquid turning to propane gas. Ejected into the night. Just as the fireworks launcher disgorged one last whistling rocket—

The gunmen opened fire on him.

The firework hit the truck, pinged off, and popped right over the heads—

Embers rained down.

Gas caught fire.

Pyro pots had nothing on this shit.

•   •   •

PETE DIDN'T SEE IT ALL. He couldn't have. Soon as the propane truck exploded, he was gone with it, lost to fire, though truthfully most of him had already been taken away by the bullets. He didn't see how the fuel truck went boom, didn't see the next pickup go up, or the one next to that, or the bikes next to *that*, onward and down the line, percussive domino explosions, one after the next, boom, boom, boom. A helluva thing, he assumed. But Pete didn't see most of it.

Didn't feel it, either.

All he felt was the spray of the sea.

Landry's hand in his.

Evil Elvis already halfway out there, ocean churning around him. Waving Pete on, promises, promises. The drum of the surf mirroring the drum of music, the drum of explosions. A music more primal, more wild, than his own sound.

Shana walked somewhere behind him. Reaching for him. Night Bones, Night Bones. Promises, promises.

I'm sorry, Shana. Hope this helps. See you back down there.

He stepped into the sea.

MANY SACRIFICES HAD BEEN LAID upon the altar of rock-and-roll.

90

THE MAN WANTS AN UPGRADE

*In this world, we have, what? Simulations. Flight simulators, murder sim-
ulators, a crafting-slash-survival horror simulator like, say,* Minecraft. *And
in* Minecraft, *what can you do? You can make a computer. A working
computer inside a computer. I heard a kid programmed* Doom—*another
simulation, first-person shooter—inside* Minecraft. *A simulation inside a
simulation. What if our world, the one in which we have a computer that
plays* Minecraft, *is just another layer of simulation? Would that thrill you,
or disgust you? Does the idea titillate you . . . or make you afraid? Does it
say that nothing matters, that there are no true consequences—or is it just
that things matter differently, that the consequences are impermanent? As
they are in many religions, by the way. I'll tell you now: we are in a simulation. It's the only explanation for, well, everything. Let me show you.*
  —Anum Kirkhauser, in his transmedia series, Inside the Inside the
  Inside, which premiered at the Sundance Film Festival in 2018 as
  part of the New Frontier Story Lab

NOVEMBER 13, 2025
The CDC, Atlanta, Georgia

THEY FOUND CASSIE AND THE OTHERS HIDING IN THE CONFERENCE ROOM
under the table. Creel's men dragged them all out by their heels, and Cassie
kicked one in the face, burst his nose like a cherry tomato. They threw her,
Hornor, Tanzer, and Spohn up against the wall, guns at their chests or under
their chins.

Cassie spat at them, feral.

"Cass—" Benji started to say, but his words were cut short as Creel
laughed and hauled Benji up on the conference room table, slamming him

down against it so hard, Benji was afraid either his spine would shatter or the table would split in two, if not both at once.

"You are a man who knows things," Creel said. "So, I have questions. And you're gonna fuckin' answer them, or I'm going to have my men start shooting your friends. And you can ask Paul here—" He gestured toward the programmer, cowering in the far corner. "How serious I am about it."

Paul Cheong's eyes glistened with the truth of that statement.

"I don't know how to help you," Benji said, gasping for air.

"I'm here looking for two things. One, I need to get something out of someone's head. Two, I need an upgrade. I got all these little swimmers inside me, and I'm left to understand that there's a better version. I want this year's model, you hear me? The new iPhone. The better Audi."

A wildness danced in his eyes. Benji thought, *That's it. He's got a swarm in him. The Nanocyte.* It explained so much. And made the stakes all the more terrifying. This version of Ed Creel, loose on the world . . .

But in there lurked an opportunity, too.

Chimera had told him it was stuck here.

It needed the Nanocyte to carry it out of here.

And Ed Creel just brought a swarm that could do exactly that. That's how they would get Chimera free from this place, and off to Ouray.

But how? How would they orchestrate that? He didn't know. And if there really *was* an upgrade to be had here, he sure didn't want Creel to have it.

"I can't help you," Benji said. "I'm just an epidemiologist—"

"Fine," Creel said with a shrug. To one of the two gunmen with him, he said, "Shoot one of them. The dog seems to like her." He pointed to Cassie.

"No!" Cassie screamed, hands in front of her face.

The gunman pushed the barrel hard under her chin—

"Wait wait *wait*," Benji said. "Hold on. I-I know something."

Creel patted him on the cheek. "Funny how a little violence jogs the memory. Good as a cup of coffee, huh? Tell me."

He swallowed. "There's a . . . a surgical suite. Downstairs. I think—" He winced as his dead arm began to throb with new pain. "I think it's where they did . . . implants. Of some sort. Maybe that's what you're looking for."

"That could be. Good. Progress. I like that."

Creel gave a little shake of the head to the gunman, who lowered the rifle. Then, he said to his gunmen: "One of you needs to find the others—"

Just then, the whole floor shook. A deep, earthy rumble cascaded around them, strong enough to judder the chairs in the room, their legs stuttering against the linoleum—Benji gently slid off the table while Creel was unoc-cupied.

"The fuck was th—" Creel started to say, but then, more rumbles came, one after the next, and in them Benji recognized the drumming concussion of explosions. Coming from somewhere above.

A lot of them.

Creel pointed at both gunmen, and yelled at them to go check it out.

The two of them hurried out of the room.

And as soon as they did, the explosions above were lost to the sound of gunfire down here. Benji saw one of the men stagger back past the door, right into the other one, who on reflex caught the other, trapping his own rifle between them—the second gunman looked up, eyes wide—

Just as the back of his head erupted like a party popper.

Both fell to the floor.

"The fuck," Creel growled.

A few more rounds chipped away at the doorframe, ending even as the explosions above were still going, *whoom, foooom, whommmmm*. Benji could feel the sounds in his jaw. And the way they moved—they weren't contained to one spot, but rocked along, one after the next, in a different direction.

Pete? he wondered. Impossible, probably. But if anybody could do the impossible, it was Pete Motherfucking Corley. He couldn't wait to see the man again, to make sure he was safe.

Panic danced in Creel's eyes as he wheeled on his captives. Benji saw an opportunity here, but he wasn't sure what it was, just yet: Creel was a cor-nered animal, alone without his men. But you could count on a cornered animal to bite.

Always.

Suddenly, the explosions above ceased.

Another bullet chipped away at the doorjamb.

The two men outside in the hallway remained still. They were dead.

"Who the fuck is shooting at me?" Creel seethed, his hands at his side, their fingertips gleaming with metal filaments.

But Benji thought he knew who was doing the shooting.

Shana.

THERE WAS NO TIME TO stop and think.

If she stopped too long, she, too, would be dead. The hole through her lung guaranteed that. Every movement was a misery. Even the smallest effort felt like an Olympic event. It wasn't just that she was out of breath, it was that she couldn't *get* a breath, couldn't *keep* one, her breath whistling like wind through cracked glass.

But still, somehow, she stood.

And Creel's captive, the woman from the cage, stood next to her.

Whoever she was, her hair was matted together. She smelled of human excrement. Her chin kept dipping to her chest. Her mouth worked silently, like a monk mumbling a nonsense prayer. Her arms hung drooping, lifeless, at her sides.

Shana helped her shuffle along. They had to get somewhere safe. Shana wouldn't be safe, not for long, not with her injury. But this woman could be. Shana felt it in her bones. Whoever she was, she didn't deserve to be in a cage—that kind of torment and horror?

That's when the whole place shook. The lights flickering as everything shuddered. Pete's work? She somehow wouldn't doubt it. He was chaos incarnate: a lord of rock. Then—movement from the conference room door. Two of Creel's men stormed out, shocked when they saw her—

That shock bought her a second's worth of surprise.

She fired on them. The gun shook in her hand as it chattered in three-shot bursts. One caught a round to the neck. The other, through the eye. Both dropped.

No time to dwell on this.

Just move.

Step by miserable step they took. Down the hall. Past Sadie's office. Toward the end, toward the second stairwell that led to the floor below. They needed to find somewhere to hide. *Anywhere.*

Shana leaned back again and fired at the conference room door. Just a careless spray—a warning for anyone not to come through after her.

In her head, she counted best as she could. Two dead men. Creel was still in there with Benji and the others. *Benji, please be okay. Pete, too.* But there were still three gunmen, weren't there? Or were there only two? Shit. She couldn't remember. Her brain was foggy . . .

Ahead, voices arose. Coming from below, from the steps.

C'mon, gopher, pop up at the hole, she thought, holding the rifle up as they eased forward. The barrel wavered and wobbled. The two women couldn't stand alone, but together, they held each other up.

"Wuh," the once-caged woman muttered.

"Yeah, me too," Shana said, wheezing, tasting blood.

Then, voices from behind the stairwell door—

A gunman threw the door open ahead, down the hall, and she bit down on her teeth, firing the small semi-automatic rifle into that space—it was erratic, indiscriminate, bullets in a sloppy array, but the man had been foolish enough to open the door all the way, exposing himself bodily to it. Flowers of blood bloomed his belly, his chest. He gurgled and fell backward into the fourth and final gunman—

As the door slammed shut.

Which left the fourth man still alive.

No . . .

They could turn around, try to use the main stairwell, but she feared the downstairs would be sealed up in that direction. *Wait. The elevator.* The elevator was running now. Would that be sealed? They had access to that now. The elevator was halfway between the two stairwells. They were close to it already.

"Detour," she said, adjusting the woman's direction, using the wall as support as they pivoted crudely to head down the perpendicular hallway toward the elevator. *Please work, please work,* she thought.

THE CAGED-ANIMAL IMAGE BENJI HAD of Creel only deepened as the thick, brutal little man paced, his eyes racing between the captives and the bullet-chewed doorway. He growled in the back of his throat as he got closer to the door—but not so close he could peer out. He didn't reach for a gun, though.

And Benji soon realized why.

Cal Hornor, the maintenance worker—young, like a corn-fed high school wrestler—hunched low. Benji saw something in the man's hand—a good-sized lockback knife. The blade clicked open, urged by his thumb. The metal gleamed. *He's going for Creel.* Benji tried to meet his gaze, tried to give him a shake of the head, *No, don't do it, not now.*

Hornor saw Benji telling him no.

They matched gazes. And defiance flashed across his face.

Hornor lunged for Creel.

Creel met his lunge. He barely even looked at Hornor as his hand shot out, thumb pressed forward in the air, like it was pointing—and from it, a long metal thread extended. A gleaming needle, like one of those old extending metal antennas you'd find on a CRT TV set, but thinner.

It stuck through Hornor's mouth.

Came out the back of him, at the base of his skull.

It made only the barest of sounds. A wet pinprick.

Hornor stopped in his tracks. The knife fell from his hands. Creel turned bodily toward him now, regarding what had happened with a kind of satisfied surprise. *The swarm,* he realized. Operating like a defense system.

Creel's shoulder juggled with a soft *thrummm,* then he moved his hand to the right, and with no effort at all, the thin metal spine hummed and buzzed through the side of Hornor's head, through the jaw, under the ear. A crude mist of blood and bone filled the air and half his head flopped to the side as he toppled.

"Anybody else?" Creel said.

Heads shook no.

"Good."

Creel eased toward the doorway—but then thought better of it. "You," he said to Steph, the botanist. Anxious sweat had spackled her strawberry hair to her freckled forehead. "Get up. Go to the door."

"But—"

Creel waggled his fingers at her. From the fingertips, Benji could see metal tips poking out of the skin. Like carpentry nails.

"I said, get up, and go to the door."

Steph nodded, standing up, sidling past him. He leered at her, and it was plain to see the pleasure on his face—he enjoyed her fear, Benji saw.

"Go, have a look," he told her.

Steph called out, "I'm coming out," and then peeked out—

Benji winced, waiting for gunshots. *Shana, please don't shoot.*

And no shots came.

Creel sucked air between his bared teeth. "Anyone?"

Steph looked. She shook her head. "No. I-I don't see anyone."

"Good." Then he grabbed Steph's hair by the back of her head and yanked her backward hard enough that her neck snapped. Skin tore. Her open windpipe gurgled. Meg Tanzer screamed, scrambling away from him as he advanced on her, too, gripping the back of her neck in a claw, his hand growling like a belt sander as his grip tightened, his fingers meeting in the middle. He tossed her aside, his hands slick and gloppy with blood—he shook them off against the wall, spattering red. Benji launched himself in front of Cassie and Paul.

"You want my help, you leave them be," Benji said.

Creel looked him up and down. He sniffed. "Uh-huh. Fine. I'm a deal-maker and I'll make that deal. Besides, I need people to help me carry the lady in the cage. So, you go first, Benji-doggy. The others, too. You go out, lift the crate, and I'll follow along. But trust me when I tell you, anyone makes a run for it, or tries to fuck with me, I'll chew the rest of your hands and feet off and watch you flop around in your blood. Got it?"

They all nodded.

He grinned big and broad. Creel *liked* this. His joy was easy to see. He liked the power he possessed over people. It wasn't about leading them. It was about controlling them. Benji wondered what life would've been like without White Mask, but with this man as the nation's president. How fast would a brutal, fascist regime have risen? Would the checks and balances have held against them? He betted now that they wouldn't have. In four years, you give a man like this the helm, he'd crash you into the rocks because it pleased him, and because he'd find a way to make money from the wreckage. Even if the nation survived in some way, this man's presidency would've been a mortal wound.

That future never manifested. And here they were, at his mercy just the same. Another future unspooled before Benji, one where this man was ascendant. A civilization scrambling to put itself back together again, suddenly put in thrall to a venal, malignant man. One with a godlike power literally at hand.

Creel walked behind them as they left the conference room.

"You okay?" Cassie asked him.

He nodded. "As okay as I can be. You?"

"I guess."

They stepped out and saw the cage.

It was open.

It contained no woman.

Shana, too, was no longer here. All that remained was the dead man—Hogan—plus Torres and Creel's two dead gunmen. A lot of blood, everywhere—so much that it felt slippery beneath Benji's feet.

Creel emerged to see the empty cage.

"Where is she?" he said, his voice quiet yet full of rage. Before anyone could answer, he grabbed the doorframe with both hands, roaring as he tore chunks out of the metal frames—they bent easy, like they were made of aluminum foil. "We need to *move*," he growled, "and move *now*."

•   •   •

It works. Thank fuck it works.

The elevator hummed as it carried the two women downward to the floor below—the Firesight offices. The elevator, too, was still loaded with the boxes of provisions Shana had stacked in here, which was helpful, because she slumped against them, rifle dangling. This small moment of rest was narcotic. She wanted to keep going. To slide to the floor, to fall asleep, even though she knew that sleep would be an endless one.

Not now. Stay in the moment.

Behind her, the freed woman stood tenuously against the corner. Her mouth was slack. Her eyes rotated in her sockets, sometimes blinking furiously.

What the hell did they do to her?

The elevator stopped. It dinged.

The door slid open.

And the fourth gunman was standing right there. His hand out, like he'd just pressed the button. He stood there, looking at Shana for a moment, dumbfounded. He didn't expect them to be here. He'd obviously called the elevator, not realizing someone was already riding it down.

His rifle hung at his side.

Shana made a small sound, closed her eyes. She threw herself against him—he cried out, and as she pushed, she drove the barrel of the gun into his rib and pulled the trigger. Three shots, quick succession, into his torso.

But he was strong, and shoved her backward—

His gun swung up, spitting bullets—

Shana fired her own weapon—

And shot him in the mouth.

He fell to the ground. Blood pooling. His own gun clattered. Shana looked over her shoulder, saw bullet holes in the elevator wall—right over the other woman's shoulder. The woman from the dog cage didn't even flinch.

"Come on," Shana said, blinking back tears as she helped the other woman out past the boxes. They stepped past him (*don't look don't look don't look*) and pushed on into the Firesight offices.

Where do we hide?

She didn't know. The sealed doors at the end would be great if they opened right now . . . but they were still closed. *Damnit.* So they went office by office, looking for something, anything. Worse came to worse they could, what, find a supply closet or something. But now she was second-guessing herself. Maybe they shouldn't have come down here at all. She could've used the elevator to go *up*. She felt stupid. The whole building was open. There had to be somewhere to hide.

But then she passed by the surgical suite.

And there, beyond it, the sealed glass door was open.

As if beckoning to them.

That, *that* would be a good place to hide, wouldn't it?

"Come on," she said, hand on the middle of the other woman's back, trying to push her more quickly, but not so fast she took a header. Shana coughed. Blood wetted her lips. *Christ, I'm dying. I don't even know if I'm going to make it to that room.* But step by step, past the surgical table, past the metal tray and darkened tablet screen, they made it into the room once sealed behind an everything-proof glass door. It was a long, narrow room, lined with shelves, carved right out of gray rock. Bored into the earth itself, the walls just uneven rock.

Empty vials lined the shelves. It was surprisingly cool in this room.

There, next to the door, was a big red button.

Shana pressed it.

The door sealed shut with a hiss.

And that task being complete, she sat down, which is to say, she fell on her ass. Only reason she didn't break her tailbone was that she held on to the shelves as she fell, slowing her descent. The woman remained standing— leaning, actually. Head slumped.

"Good job us," Shana said weakly, bleakly, blearily.

"Nuhh. Th. Thhh."

Shana's eyes fluttered. Could she sleep now? Could she rest? She knew what it would mean. *At least I saved this woman.* But then her pulse quickened as she remembered Charlie, Nessie, Ouray. *No, not yet. Don't sleep. You might have a—what was it called? A concussion. Sleeping means dying.*

Still. Breathing was hard. The garden hose had become a drinking straw. The sound was a wet, rheumy wheeze.

Stay awake. Talk to the woman. Maybe she'll come around.

"You . . ." She coughed. "You have a name?"

"Enn. Enn. Enn."

"Enn. Sure. That's a name. Good to meet you, Enn. I'm Shana."

"Ennie."

"Ennie. If you say so." She lay back.

"Ernie."

"Enn, Ennie, Ernie, I knew an Ernie, you're definitely not him." She tried to steady and slow her breathing. Tried to feel her heartbeat. Sometimes she couldn't feel it. But it had to still be beating, right? Because she wasn't dead. She realized now her eyes were closed. *Maybe I am dead. Maybe this is death.* A part of her thought, this could be it. Maybe she'd just slip from the world, undetected. Like a shadow chased away by the sun. Then she'd wake up in a fucking lube tube, Neo-style, bald and full of cables that had been keeping her alive. Would it be a shock to learn how this was all one big simulation? Probably run by Black Swan?

(It would not shock her, no.)

Time passed. She wasn't sure how much. Or if she was even alive. She thrived in darkness. Found comfort there. Coolness, stillness, solace.

Charlie . . .

Are you here, Charlie? She swore she could hear him somewhere. A little laugh. How would she even know what his laugh sounded like?

Then—

The woman, Enn Ennie Ernie, cried out—a muffled *nuhhh!*

Shana gasped, startling awake. She tried to sit up, but it hurt too much. She lifted her head, instead, dipping chin to chest—

Wham! Something thudded against the glass door.

It was him.

It was Creel.

His face was a rictus of rage. One eye wrenched wide, spit gathering at the corners of his mouth like pools of froth left from a rough tide. He drove the bottoms of his fists against the glass, again and again. *Whud. Whud. Whump. Fump.* He screamed, but she could barely hear it. It was soundproof in here.

The glass didn't even crack.

It held.

She wanted to laugh, but laughing hurt. Everything hurt. So instead she just lay back again, mumbling, "Can't get in here, you fuggin'—" She coughed. She was safe. Safe from him, if not from death. But the woman was safe, at least. Shana had done that much. It felt good. It felt like some kind of victory.

Darkness rose up underneath her. A great chasm. Deep and endless.

"THIS FUCKING *DOOR*," CREEL ROARED. He pounded at it again. Benji saw Shana there through the glass. She wasn't moving. The woman from the cage stood by her. Gently swaying back and forth. Her hands picking at invisible threads, staring bullets at Creel. The hate and fear on her face was plain as a bloodstain.

The door held.

"It won't break," Paul, the programmer, said.

Creel wheeled on him.

"Why?"

"It's designed to . . . to seal tight, to hold against . . . breaches." Paul cleared his throat. "In or out."

"Breaches," Creel repeated.

"That chamber held the Nanocyte. Nanites—small machines. Some of them, self-replicating, self-repairing. They would be a target for thieves and . . . if they ever got out, we didn't know what would happen."

A distant part of Benji's mind picked at a mystery: Then how did Black Swan steal them? Because that's what Sadie said, right? Black Swan had stolen control of the swarms for its own purpose. But then he realized: because Firesight was brought here, and because Black Swan got into their systems. Just as Chimera was able to open this door, so, too, was Black Swan. But how did Black Swan enter its swarm? And how would Chimera, if they were to take it with them?

He didn't know. And maybe it didn't matter at all.

Because Shana was in there, and she was dying, if not already dead.

Shana, please don't go. He felt suddenly, woefully alone. Sadie was gone. He'd left Dot. He'd left Ouray. Pete and Shana were what he had left. And he didn't know where Pete was . . .

He felt eyes burning holes into him.

Creel.

"You."

"I can't help you. I don't know—"

"Her, in there. The girl on the ground. You care about her."

"I care about a lot of people," he said, trying to derail this train of thought.

"No, no, fuck that, you look at her different. She's *special* to you. Maybe you're sticking it to her. You're too old, but I've seen worse."

"I'm not—"

"Whatever. If she's special to you, then you're special to her. I bet the girl loves her Benji-doggy."

Creel reached for him.

. . .

Whump.

Distant echo. A dull, thudding sound.

Ignore it.

Sleep now.

The chasm was dark and deep. The darkness and depth were comfort. Dying felt good. That was the strange thing. How nice it felt. After all this time, after all the pain. To feel that release. That relief.

Charlie.

Nessie.

They'd be fine. What good had she ever truly done for any of them, anyway? Some things were out of her hands. It was a failure but the failure felt good, too. Life, a game of pinball. You just try to keep the ball going long as you could, but eventually, gravity got you. You always lost. Always failed.

Let it happen.

Sleep now.

Die now.

Whump.

A scream. Muffled, distant, miles away. Pain in it. Not just pain. *Fear.*

Wake up.

No.

Shana.

Shana—

No!

Whump.

An intake of breath. Whistling, wheezing. New pain like someone was stitching a knife in and out of her chest like a sewing needle. Stick, stick. Stick, stick. The pain was her breath. Just that, in and out. *I'm still breathing. Ow.*

Her eyelids fluttered open. The light was garish and cruel.

A shadow moved in front of it. Disrupting the light. That disruption hurt more than the light itself. The way it moved in and out. The way it flailed and shook. She groaned, lifting her head toward it.

No.

It was Benji.

He was standing there, against the glass. Pressed up hard enough his nose had broken, bleeding twin rivulets of red. Creel held him there even as Benji struggled. Creel pushed a finger against his temple. No. Into it. Pressing it in and out. Every time he does, Benji's eyes widen, his face brightening with electric pain—the finger sank in a little, then came back out, then in a little, then back out. Fresh blood flowed. Drool slicked Benji's chin. His eyes sagged, then the finger went in, and they wrenched open—

Benji, no, no, c'mon, no.

The message was clear. Creel mouthed the words:

OPEN

THE

DOOR.

If she opened it, all this was for naught. He'd have the woman from the cage. But if she didn't open it Benji would be—what, tortured, tormented, brain-dead, real-dead. She needs him. She watched her real father die on the bridge—at the hands of Creel's men—and now she was about to watch Benji die here, too? She could not handle the thought. It made her feel weak that she couldn't. Benji was trying to shake his head, trying to tell her not to open it. Mouth barely forming that word—

No.

But she had to.

Sorry, Enn Ennie Ernie.

Shana reached up, grabbed a shelf. She moved her other hand to do the same. It was like moving mountains. The shelf was a ladder. A harsh one, with metal edges, that bit her fingers, her palms. *The pain is a ladder, too.* Up she went. Pulling herself up to standing.

Stagger. Stumble. Toward the door. Toward the button.

She put a hand on the glass. Benji on the other side of it. Blood smearing the space between them. Blood and saliva.

Shana hit the button.

The door hissed open.

Benji tumbled forward, into her.

And Ed Creel laughed big and loud.

91

SURGICAL INTERVENTION

Callsign ST0N3, General repeater call station, Pittsburgh. The thought of the day, November 13, 2025, is this: Most people aren't good or evil, really, they're just messy and complicated. Inside you are two wolves, and both of them are very confused about everything all of the time. So for the most part, give people a break when you can. Everybody deserves a bit of leash. Except for Nazis. Fuck Nazis. Only leash they get is the one you use to strangle 'em. Updates: Squirrel Hill is clear today. Watch out for Fern Hollow Bridge: Spotters say it's starting to go, might collapse any day now. Supply wagons riding into Regent Square today, but be advised that Cometheads have been active in that area. This is BRG Tom Stonekettle. Message will repeat in five, four, three, two—

—amateur ham radio station broadcasting from western Pennsylvania

NOVEMBER 13, 2025
The CDC, Atlanta, Georgia

IT CAME IN FITS AND STARTS. REALITY HELD, BUT BARELY. SHANA LAY ON THE floor of the room, Benji behind her, cradling her. The woman she'd freed was there one minute, and when she next blinked, she was gone, taken out there, shoved brutally onto the surgical table. Shana didn't know what was happening. Didn't even know *if* it was happening, it all seemed so strange, so surreal. Was she hallucinating? Dissociating? She didn't know. Maybe didn't care.

It was nice to have Benji here.

He spoke to her. Told her it would be okay. A lie, Shana knew, but she appreciated it just the same. Her breathing was shallow now, coming in little dainty gasps—*huff, huff, huff, huff.* The sound of it reminded her of when an animal had heatstroke. Or when it was dying. *Dogs pant when they're in pain.* She was panting now. But she didn't have much pain anymore.

That was good.

But it also wasn't.

Creel had his hand against the tablet screen next to the surgical table.

It glowed bright.

He shuddered, almost with pleasure.

He's talking to the screen with his hands, Shana thought. An insane idea but everything was insane now, so it made sense. Crazy shit in a crazy world wasn't crazy, she told herself, and wanted to laugh, but her body wouldn't let her.

Huff, huff, huff, huff.

Others were out there, now, she realized. Cassie. Some other guy—she'd seen him here, hadn't she? A programmer. Pete. No. Paul. They were cowering against the far wall, watching Creel and the woman on the table.

As he touched the screen, behind the table—beyond the woman's head—a telescoping arm rose. At its end was a white plug-shape, and that plug slid back, unsheathing itself, and revealing a small, whirring drill.

Vvvvvvvv.

Creel chuckled. "I can feel it. I can see it."

Shana didn't know what any of that meant. Had he even said it? Her chin dropped and she gasped awake again.

There came a sound behind her. Was it Benji? A plop sound. A tumble.

She felt a pressure at her side. Soft and strange. She scooched sideways to get away from it—Benji, she guessed, urging her that way. But then Benji made a sound, a quizzical noise. A snorting clicking sound came.

Something trotted out away from them.

Something hairy.

White.

Gray.

Whaaaat the fuuuuck.

It was the possum. Opossum? *Whoa,* possum.

It trundled toward the doorway, toward Creel standing there. Snorfling and hissing. Little paws clicking on the linoleum.

I'm definitely hallucinating this, she thought.

But she could see Benji watching it, too.

And when the possum stumbled into Creel's leg—

He startled, his hand leaving the tablet screen. The man looked down, his face a twist of anger. But what he saw there, it made the anger leave his face. He looked almost . . . amused. Creel paused. He bent down, and picked up the possum, who wriggled there in his grip, hissing. Tail thrashing about.

No.

"Ain't that something," he said, regarding the possum.

It regarded him in turn.

Shana tried to cry out but couldn't make a sound. Her cry was just a voiceless scream.

Creel took his index finger, gleaming with metal, and drew it slowly across the possum's throat. Blood spilled down his already red hands. The possum shook harder, thrashing about, before hitching. And spasming. And slowing.

Until it was totally still.

Creel watched the whole process with fascination. Like he was taking this moment for himself. A treat, in a way. He dropped the lifeless mess to the ground.

Blood pooled around it.

Creel watched her and Benji. He smiled, seeing the horror on their faces. "Did you like that?" he asked. "Don't worry. There's more where that came from."

He laughed, then. Big and loud. Like this amused him. Causing pain in one thing, and seeing that brutal act cause pain in other things. Because that's what they all were to him, weren't they? Just things. Things that didn't matter to him one bit except to amuse him, to serve him, to appease him, to die for him.

While he was watching Benji and Shana, his booming laugh filling the surgical suite, the woman on the surgical table sat up behind him.

She blinked. And as Creel turned back toward the table, he met her, face-to-face. He startled, staggering back, nearly tripping over the possum's carcass.

The woman held up her hand.

And that's when Ed Creel started to shake.

92

THE POSSUM'S GIFT WAS THE GIFT OF TIME

The biological example of writing information on a small scale has inspired me to think of something that should be possible. Biology is not simply writing information; it is doing something about it. A biological system can be exceedingly small. Many of the cells are very tiny, but they are very active; they manufacture various substances; they walk around; they wiggle; and they do all kinds of marvelous things—all on a very small scale. Also, they store information. Consider the possibility that we too can make a thing very small which does what we want—that we can manufacture an object that maneuvers at that level!

—Richard Feynman, from his 1959 talk,
"Plenty of Room at the Bottom"

NOVEMBER 13, 2025
The CDC, Atlanta, Georgia

THE PIT WAS SLICK-WALLED AND BOTTOMLESS. ANNIE FELL AND FELL. BUT when the girl freed Annie Cahill from the dog cage, her descent slowed, and then halted. And achingly, it reversed. The fall became a climb. The climb was an act of misery. To scale the walls of yourself, your own mental prison—it felt eternal to her, this act. But soon she came closer to the reality happening around her. She saw it all—the girl opening the dog cage, helping her stand and urging her to move. She heard the gunfire, saw Creel's men die. And this girl kept helping her. Kept moving her along. And slowly, Annie Cahill came back to herself. She felt her fingers tingle. She felt her feet against the inside of her shoes: a simple, daft sensation that was so basic she'd forgotten that it was ever a thing at all, that it was a thing to even forget. She could make words. She could say her name. Not quite. Not really. But a little bit, a sound here, a mumble there. And now here she was, on the table. The drill behind her. Creel over her, a dark shadow. A beast free from its shackles, a beast she freed. She was so close, *so close*, and if that drill entered the back of her head, he'd be able to neutralize her implant.

And when that happened, it was over.

But then: A possum happened.

The possum. DV designation. Her mother's experiment.

It had survived all this time, which shocked her and didn't shock her. When last she'd seen it, when she'd sneaked in before plotting her journey to Atlas Haven, she got to pet it. It was a nice creature. Good around humans. She almost thought to take it with her, to rescue it from this place. It didn't need to eat. It didn't need to sleep. But she couldn't care about it. The work she had to do out there in the world was too serious, too severe, to build a compassionate bridge to another living thing. For if she were to become a creature of vengeance, to undo the horror her mother had wrought, then she could not be obliged to something so daft as a dumb possum.

But now, the possum was obliged to her.

It came, and Creel took it, and he killed it.

A cruel sacrifice. But a gift, too, from the animal.

The gift from the possum was the gift of time.

Because it gave Annie the time she needed.

And now, Annie Cahill crawled all the way out of the pit.

When she sat up, she held her hand up. She could *feel* him again—Creel. And all his little servitors inside him. But they weren't his, were they? Ohh, no. Those tiny little robots belonged to her. And at that, she gave them one command:

Come home.

BENJI REMEMBERED WHAT IT WAS like to watch the Sleepwalkers die by detonation. The way they shook. Their teeth chattered. Their eyes would fill with red as their capillaries burst, looking like cherry tomatoes bulging in the sockets. They'd flush as their temperatures rose, the spasms wracking them. He saw it on video with the math teacher ushered into the cop car. He saw it on the FLIR camera outside Indiana, when Clade Berman erupted in his family's arms. And finally, he'd seen it in Ouray. When Arav detonated, sending the swarm of nanobots in him from man to man, causing each of Ozark Stover's homegrown soldiers to *pop* one after the next. Blood mist and bone chips.

This was like that—until it wasn't.

Creel shuddered and shook. His skin went from pink to red. He bit his tongue, his eyes flushed with broken veins.

When the Sleepwalkers detonated, they did so in every direction—a grenade going off, the body as shrapnel.

But when Ed Creel detonated? He did so in one direction only. It was less like an explosion and more like the swarm was *pulled* out of him, an act of grotesque attraction, like someone turned on a huge electromagnet nearby, enough to pull all the metal out of his body in one fell swoop. A reverse shotgun blast of his innards, tearing through his skin like infinitesimal BBs, all of him swelling toward the woman on the table, bloating, throbbing, fit to burst—

Benji launched himself up, heel of his hand slamming against the button—

The glass door closed just as Ed Creel ripped open.

The door, misted with greasy red and little flecks of bone. Like tiny teeth.

Benji staggered backward. He crouched next to Shana, to see if she'd seen. She hadn't, he didn't think. She was back on the ground again, her eyes shut. He felt for a pulse. It was there, but it was weak. *Please, no, c'mon.*

"Shana," he said. "Stay with me, Shana. You can do this. We have work to do. You have photos to take. A son to save. A town, a world. We have to find Pete. We have to find your sister again—"

But the pulse was fading. Her eyes wouldn't open.

Then: a knock at the door. *Tunk tunk tunk.*

He looked up, and there, through the dripping curtain of red, he saw the woman from the table. Her hand was held up—it wore a glove. No. Not a glove. This glove *moved*, writhing upon her like *all* the bees of a colony, pulled from their hive, the queen tucked neatly in her palm. She was covered in blood. Her clothes were torn, her skin, too, perforated by bits of President Ed Creel. Yet still she stood there, and again she knocked.

Hesitantly, he stood and let her in.

"You need to move," she said, blinking through gore, her voice like wood over a rasp. Already he was sure he was watching her own injuries begin to . . . close up in front of him, stitched up by invisible thread.

"I won't let you hurt her," he said.

"That's not what I'm here to do."

He didn't want to let her. He couldn't. He was her protector and—

Shana cried out, gasping. A deep rattle rose in her chest. Like a death rattle. He'd heard it before. The loosening of everything inside you. One of the last breaths before expiring. It didn't matter now. He fell aside and let the woman pass.

And at that, she knelt by Shana.

She took that hand, squirming with a ferrofluid coating of dark gray ooze, and pressed it to Shana's chest.

Then the woman's head craned back, her eyes closed, her jaws tight.

Shana screamed.

REBIRTH, REDUX, AND AN ACCOUNTING OF THE DEAD

4/22/2024: I am tired all the time and I am sad all the time and drunk most of the time. I can't go on like this. But I also can't do the other thing. I met a woman on the beach in Islamorada, said her name was Sugar, and she told me she was some kind of psychic, and she told me I was missing people and I had to find them to be whole. She said I was not a bird, I was a person, and I had to remember that and find the people who mattered. And if I couldn't find those people, I had to find new people. Because that's what life is, she said. It's people finding people. People helping and loving and fucking and ~~drunking~~ drinking together and being judgmental about each other ~~end~~ and all of that. She said even the sand on the beach has all the other sand on the beach. The end of the world is the start of the world she said. Find people, Sugar said. Find your people. I hate her. She's right.
—from A Bird's Story, A Journal of the Lost

NOVEMBER 15, 2025
The CDC, Atlanta, Georgia

YOU HELPED ME.

I help you.

Two sentences, braiding together like snakes in Shana's head, over and over again. It's what Annie Cahill—that, it turned out, was her name—said that day as the blood-soaked angel reached over, pressing her blurry, squirming hand to Shana's chest. Her chest burned with the touch. Then the burning went away, and a cooling sensation persisted, and *that* became cold, damningly cold, like a glacier had grown up around her, freezing her within it. Then, the worst sensation of them all filled her: a deep and untouchable itch. Like being bitten from the inside by mosquitoes. It formed a crawling, everywhere itch that could not be soothed. She screamed, clawing at her chest, and they had to restrain her. The only thing that truly stopped it was the darkness that stole her away into unconsciousness.

When she awoke, a day later, her injuries had healed. Mostly. The flesh where the gunshot had gone through her was still a puffy, irritated pink—and even the gentlest touch on that spot felt like touching the worst sunburn of her life.

But she could take a breath, and it only hurt a little.

She was alive. Waking up here felt like it had when she awakened in Ouray out of hibernation. Though she hadn't died either time, it felt like resurrection just the same. Impossible and insane. A blessing, mostly. A curse, probably, too.

Because she knew what had made her hibernate the first time, and what had mended her this time: little itty-bitty teeny-weeny robots. The same thing that was in Ed Creel was gone from him and now in her: swarming like a new kind of blood cell, repairing any injuries and errors they found. She could feel a buzzing in her fingertips, and she remembered seeing what Creel could do—so she quickly pushed that feeling to the back of her mind, to the basement, to a closet *in* her mind's basement. Inside a box that read DO NOT OPEN.

But all the while, those two sentences.

Again and again, around and around, chasing each other like dogs.

You helped me.

I help you.

You helped me.

I help you.

SHANA WAS ALIVE. AND IN theory, she was happy about that.

But others were dead. And she couldn't help but feel like she deserved somehow to be among them. It wasn't that she *wanted* to be dead. But only that she didn't believe she should *be* allowed to *be* alive. As if that made any sense.

Shana said as much to Benji.

The two of them walked the ruins of the campus outside the CDC's main building. The wreckage that lay before them was impressive, like something out of a movie set. Ahead of them, at the south end of the quad here, a tanker truck lay on its side, its metal belly erupted open as if some horrible thing had hatched from its belly. From there, it was easy to chart a line of the trucks, cars, dirt bikes, and four-wheelers, all blown to hell, one after the next. Each tossed about as if by a cruel, gigantic child. The dead bodies were gone. The soldiers that remained had helped institute a search for remains and cleanup the day after. Some of the neighbors from the south had arrived to help in that recovery, too, bringing food and clean water, plus blankets and first aid. (Initially, they'd shown up ready to fight, summoned by the explosions. They helped pick off stragglers and any potential scavengers encroaching from the north. This fight truly was over.)

When she said she didn't know if she deserved to be alive, Benji said:

"I felt the same way." He explained that when he woke up with his arm gone, he felt the deepest despair. It wasn't just because a part of him was missing and he lamented that loss—it was that he felt like he'd failed in some crucial way. Even if it was out of his control, he felt like he'd failed her and he'd failed Ouray and that was an infection far deeper than the one they cut out of him. So he told her he understood. And that he hoped she'd come around.

Then she asked him the one question she didn't want to ask—

But had to.

"Pete?" she asked, the desperation in her voice tolling like a church bell.

"I don't know," Benji said. "We . . . found something." He summoned her to the overturned propane truck and the crater just next to it. Grunting a little, he bent down and showed her two objects. The first, a melted lump of black. Not all the way melted, just a little, enough to turn it from an object with corners to one with softened, uneven edges. It said MARSHALL on it in cursive font. And next to that—

"A guitar," she said. Not a full guitar. Just a piece of it—the very top of the neck. The part with the turny-bits that tightened the strings. "Pete was here."

Benji nodded. She took his hand and helped him stand.

"I think he did all this," Benji said.

"That *asshole*," she said, genuinely angry. "I told him—" She swallowed a lump of grief that slid down her throat like a hunk of cold coal. "I said he wasn't supposed to run away this time. And he promised me."

"I know. But I think he saved us. Or gave us a chance to save ourselves."

She pressed the heels of her hands into her eyes hard enough she saw a

wall of white light. In that white light, in the stage lights behind the dark of
her eye, she saw him. Wailing on a microphone, whaling on a guitar, fireworks shooting from the end of it, him cackling as he kicked some hillbilly
Hitler Number One fan in the rotten teeth. She wanted to scream. She did
scream. Fuck. She felt the sadness well up in her. The tears and snot. Fuck
fuck fuck. "At least—at least he went out big. He went out like Pete Corley,
Motherfucking Rockgod."

"All hail," Benji said. "Hail the Saint of Screaming. The Holy Spirit of
Hedonism, Avatar of the Arena . . ."

"Master of Metal, King of Kings, His Holiness of Hard Rock," she added.

"Motherfucking Rockgod."

"Motherfucking Rockgod."

"And our friend."

"Our family."

Benji bowed his head. "Amen."

"Amen," she said.

And then Shana crumbled like a tower of dirt. She sobbed so hard she
almost threw up. Benji rubbed her back as she did. It went on a long, long
time. In some ways, it never stopped, because that's how grief was.

LATER, SHE PICKED AT A pork chop MRE outside. It was dark, but the night
was warmer than usual—and she wasn't feeling the cold much anyway. A
side effect of the swarm? Or was she just distant from it? Not far away, the
survivors, led by Benji and Cassie, were doing an accounting of the dead.
Who died. Who was injured. Who survived. Cassie was saying, "We lost
seventy percent of our people. We lost most of our army contingent. We're
unprotected."

Someone in fatigues, someone she thought was Quinn, from the first day
they came here, said, "I could scout the coast. I hear there's army there.
Some down in Savannah, too. They'd come. We could fortify—"

"That's not a bad idea," Benji said, but Cassie retorted:

"No," she said. "I mean, okay, fine, but that's not right. We bring more
military, we will always look like . . . like military."

Quinn objected: "What's wrong with that?"

"There's nothing—" Cassie made a *bah* sound, clearly frustrated. "There's
nothing wrong with that, I just mean, it looks like something. Like, like—"
She seemed to be searching for her next words.

"Like you're separate and apart," Benji said.

"That's it. The CDC has always been impartial. We should try to look that way again. Like we're here to help, not an occupying force, and not a defending force, either. The army . . ." She seemed to search for words.

Benji had them. "The army makes you look standoffish. Defensive, even offensive."

Quinn scoffed. "So you don't want us?"

"No," Cassie said, exasperated. "I mean—yes. Of course we want you. We *need* you. But we want more than that. I think it's time to try to become part of the neighborhoods, to form an alliance, a *real* one. Stop pretending we're not all part of the same city—"

They kept on like that for a while. Shana tuned it out. Cassie was right, of course, but it wasn't her business and she felt lost in her own head anyway.

Until someone sat down across from her.

Annie Cahill.

"Mind if I sit?" Annie asked. Her body wore a peppering of puffy scars from where Ed Creel's disrupted body had shotgun-blasted forward, and where the Nanocyte had healed her, if imperfectly, incompletely.

"You already sat, so." Before Annie could say anything else, Shana apologized abruptly: "Sorry. I sound like a bitch. Yes. Please, sit."

"Are you pissed at me?" Annie asked. It struck Shana now how different she looked. Which, duh, made sense, because she wasn't filthy or lost to that drug they had her on. She showered. She ate. She'd returned from what turned out to be a prolonged state of forced ketamine intoxication—essentially, she'd been roofied over and over again. Which to Shana sounded like a horror unmatched by many, and it made her glad that Creel was turned inside-out. *By the same things inside you*, she reminded herself, with a shiver.

"Pissed? Why would I be pissed?"

"Because I put the Nanocyte inside you. Without asking."

"Yeah. Well. I guess that's a little fucked up. But it saved my life, so I'm not going to slap away the hand pulling me up over the cliff's edge."

"When you're all healed, I can . . . take them out."

"Oh. Okay. Yeah. Uh. Yeah, I guess that's good." Shana pushed away the MRE. She knew wasting food right now was close to an actual crime, but at the same time, it was hard to feel hungry. Especially with boneless pork chops that tasted mostly like tough mustard. "That what Creel was trying to take out of your head? Some kind of . . . control apparatus?"

Annie nodded. "Yes. He did not like being on a leash."

"Am I . . . on your leash?"

"No. I mean—not really."

"But I could be."

"I guess. That bother you?"

"Yeah. I mean—shouldn't it? I don't know you. I don't . . . distrust you but I don't know anything about you. And here you are, with invisible control over the tiny robots inside my body—*god* that is an insane sentence and no matter how many times I say it, it doesn't get less insane. When I was dying I came to believe this was all part of a big simulation and . . . I'm still open to the possibility."

"It's pretty fucked up."

"Yeah." Shana leaned forward. "So who are you? Why are you even here?"

Annie looked over to the group still listing the dead, still figuring out what comes next. She stood up suddenly. "Come on. I'll show you. Part of it, at least."

THE TWO DOORS, THE FINAL doors, were open.

The Firesight doors. Not the glass door where the Nanocyte was once stored, no, but rather, the ones at the far end, past the elevator, past the stairwell.

They yawned wide.

Shana moved to the leftmost door, peering in—

There was a massive Plexiglas enclosure. Full of blankets and old clothes and some dusty straw, plus some branches, a wooden coatrack, a ladder. A stuffed possum stared out from inside—

It moved.

Shana startled. The possum opened its mouth, almost in a smile, like an alligator opening its maw in an act of hunger or mirth. Then it trundled off.

"How many possums are in this place?" Shana asked.

"Just that one."

"You mean, there were two, and now this one—"

"No, there was one before, and one now."

Shana blinked. "Creel . . . killed that possum. I *saw* it."

"And yet, here the possum be." Annie shrugged. "This is DV5544. Deevee. The first recipient of the earliest version of the Nanocyte—alpha build. He's loaded with a more primitive version of the thing you are."

Shana shuddered. "He healed all the way back from . . . from that?

Creel . . ." She didn't have to finish the sentence. They both knew what he did to that animal. "That thing is . . . wow. The Nanocyte is something else."

"It's also why Dee-vee is so old. Old for a possum, at least. It repairs the cellular damage caused by aging."

"Sooooo. That possum is both indestructible and immortal."

"Functionally."

"Uhhhh."

Annie tapped on the Plexiglas. The possum trotted over and seemed happy to see her. "I should've taken him when I was here last. But I couldn't exactly do what I wanted to do while carrying around some kind of super-possum."

"So, you came back here to save the possum?"

That elicited an incredulous laugh. "No. Not exactly. That's a value-add and all that, but that was not my intention. What I came back for isn't in this room, but the next one." She turned to Shana then, her face steely and serious. "I came here because I was angry, Shana. I had a mother. She helped run this company, Firesight, with a man named Bill Craddock. She was a genius, my mother. Off the charts gifted, a true polymath. And at the time, I thought maybe a sociopath, or someone with borderline personality disorder—though in retrospect I think she may have been abused by my grandmother, and I think she may have been a narcissist. I don't know. It was a hard childhood. My father was a drinker, my aunt—my mother's sister, Becky—was bipolar, thrown between fits of intense depression and spiking anxiety. My mother wanted to fix them. At the time I thought this was just the narcissism speaking, and maybe it was that, in part—though I wonder now if she wanted the cookies and the control over having fixed them, or if she also just . . . wanted them to be better. My father, he resisted. He left. My aunt . . . I . . ." Her nostrils flared as she drew a deep breath. "Well, come on."

And then they went into the next room.

ANNIE KEPT TALKING. SHANA KNEW that. She could hear her, if not *hear* her, really. The voice went all Charlie-Brown-Teacher, all *wamm womp wamm womp*, words gone greasy, without meaning. It was hard to hear. Hard to listen.

Because of the twelve bodies.

Dead, desiccated corpses, each in a Plexiglas box not entirely unlike the one the possum, Dee-vee, was kept in—except these were one after the next, reminiscent of that scene in *Silence of the Lambs* where Clarice passed patient after patient until reaching the enclosure of Hannibal the Cannibal. But all these patients were dead. Mouths wide, too wide, drawn out. Sucked of moisture, gray skin taut against the skeleton like a swaddling of rawhide. Eyes were just small things, grapes to raisins, nesting in the puckered sockets. Some were slumped forward against the Plexiglas, others sat in the farthest corners, one sat in the middle of the cage as if in a contemplative meditative yoga stretch, legs crossed, arms straight out, palms down, forehead against the ground.

Third from the end, Shana found her mother.

Daria Stewart.

Her copper-red hair still looked like her hair, like it was a wig placed on a mummified body. The body itself looked sad, withered, her (*its*) crinkly cheek against the inside of the enclosure, shoulder dipped low, as if pining for something—the body language the same as someone who was sitting against their window on a rainy night, or who was leaning against a fire escape waiting for someone to come, someone they hadn't seen, someone they loved and missed.

Me, Shana thought, almost absurdly, because she could've never saved her mother. She didn't know where she was. But someone could've. Someone should've. Shana pressed her forehead against the cold fake glass. She tried to cry, but couldn't. After Pete, after all this, she was empty, used up, and all she could do was close her eyes and hear the sound that rose from the back of her throat. It was the sad strange music of an old forgotten chair moved across a creaky wooden floor, ghostly and ghastly and mournful. "Mom," she said finally.

Annie stood next to her. Shana didn't know for how long. But the other woman had stopped talking at some point, she just hadn't noticed.

"Mom?" Annie asked, puzzled.

Shana turned and nodded.

"Oh. *Oh.* I . . . I didn't know. I had no idea. Daria Stewart," she said, repeating the name again, as if she couldn't be sure Shana was right about this. "Daria Stewart was your mother?"

"Yeah." Shana's voice sounded far away from herself.

"I'm sorry. I really didn't know."

"Yeah," she said again.

Then she walked out of the room and went to bed.

•   •   •

THE NEXT DAY, ANNIE FOUND her. Again outside. Sitting. Staring. She asked if they could talk some more and Shana nodded. It was Shana, to her own surprise, that started: "That story you were telling—about your aunt Becky? It sounded familiar. She was sick in the mind, and your mother wanted to fix her. And the Nanocyte was how she wanted to fix her, wasn't it?"

Annie nodded.

"And Becky, she was in there, too? One of the twelve." *No, not just "the twelve." But capital-T. The capital-T Twelve.*

Another nod from Annie. "Yeah."

"You came to save her."

"No," Annie said sharply. "I came to . . . I don't know. Bury her. I think. Bury her and avenge her? That sounds insane, I realize."

"No, it doesn't. I don't think. But . . . you knew she was already dead?"

Annie explained that she'd come here as White Mask was already killing the world, in the midst of a civilization-ending global pandemic, hoping to save her aunt. But it was then she found out the truth: "At that point, they'd been kept alive by the Nanocyte. But Black Swan needed as much of the nanite share as it could muster so it . . . it took what Nanocytes it could access. It robbed them of the thing that was keeping them alive."

Shana, horrified, asked, "Why . . . didn't it just take from the cold storage room? Or from the possum?"

"The cold storage room beyond the surgical suite is insulated by a Faraday cage. Black Swan wouldn't have been able to access what was in there. But I could, and it's where I got mine. As for the possum . . ." She shrugged. "I'm guessing little Dee-vee did what possums do, which was hide. Probably in that room. Besides, I think the proto-Nanocyte wasn't what Black Swan wanted, or needed, to fulfill its . . . task."

Shana rocked back on her tailbone and put her hand to her mouth, stifling another sad sound. Around her hand she said, "They died in there . . . awake, I'm guessing. Aware. No food, no water. Trapped in boxes because Black Swan took from them the thing that kept them alive. But . . . I saw my mother. In the Ouray Simulation, in Black Swan's . . . program."

"It wasn't them. Black Swan contained the code of an earlier module, Chimera. It can mimic anybody *if* it's been inside them. It can mirror-map their personalities. Even their memories, somewhat. It's a helluva thing. Also horrible."

"Jesus."

"Yeah."

"So, it was revenge. You were here before. You could've buried your aunt then. You could've put her to rest and let this go. But you didn't."

Annie sighed. "Yeah. I guess so. This place was still operating back then, and hacking my way in was hard enough—but that room was locked down, and getting back out with Becky's body would've been no small feat. I told myself, she needed to be in there, that I'd expose everything they'd done and the authorities and the media would see what my mother had wrought. With the Nanocyte, with Black Swan. I knew I had to show the world, and I told Becky she'd have her rest. I put the control unit in me as a way to summon and smuggle the Nanocyte out. I had no idea what it could do. I had no idea what was already loose upon the world. How it was already . . . ending."

"And how'd you end up with Creel, of all people?"

She leaned forward. "So. I was an *ethical offense-based programmer*—a hacker, if you prefer the childish pejorative. I was already embedded in the Creel campaign because I was looking for something, anything, to bury him. Not that I liked Hunt, either—she was a soft liberal, not very progressive, a conservative in other first-world countries. But she was an enemy we understood and he was something new. Or something very old, a racist money-bags populist pseudo-Nazi. Being in the campaign, I saw that he was set up to survive the cataclysm that was unfolding around us. And I thought, if I'm going to make it through, this is how, this is where. I formed a plan. I needed to survive, too. So I set him on a path. I had him go to his . . . fucked-up Heartland Institute, his Atlas Haven in the Midwest. So I could go there, too. By then I realized where Black Swan had gone. What it had done. It had killed the world to save a part of it. Justified or no, I don't care now, didn't care then, and I made it my goal to find it and end it."

"That's what we came here to do, too," Shana said. "Find a way to end it."

"I know. I spoke to Benji. And . . . I think there's a way."

FOUR OF THEM WAITED IN the Firesight conference room—not the one in the floor above, because though the bodies had been removed, the blood on the walls and carpet remained. On this floor, the carnage was at least largely kept to the surgical suite. There, the blood and gore painted the floors. The walls. The ceiling. Ed Creel had a *lot* of blood, and most of it had left him rather . . . violently. That room stank of a slaughterhouse.

(So, the conference room was a better, less bloody, fit.)

Shana sat. The other three—Annie, Benji, and Cassie—stood at the other side of the table. Like they were about to break some very strange news to her.

It was Benji who spoke first, explaining it to Shana. She admitted to being a little hurt they'd already talked about this, figuring some of it out without her. But she also realized she'd been physically and emotionally fraught over the last few days, so what could she have truly contributed?

For now, she listened.

"There's a module," he said. "It's an AI, an algorithm—"

"A DNN, a deep neural network," Annie said. "Technically."

"Right. It's called Chimera."

Shana scowled. The thing that mimicked her mother. That *lied* to her. "I *hate* it, I don't want to hear *anything* about it—"

Benji, looking puzzled, started to ask what she meant, but Annie jumped in, understanding where Shana was coming from:

"This Chimera isn't that Chimera. *That* one, the one inside Black Swan, is different—not intelligent of itself, but part of its programming. This one, the one we're talking about, is . . . on an island, if you will. It is its own separate entity."

"It subdued a variant of Black Swan here," Benji said.

"It can beat it?" Shana asked.

Annie and he nodded.

Cassie just shrugged. "Don't look at me. This is all way too fucking goofy for me, y'all. I thought viruses and fungal pathogens were weird but this stuff has blown past the farthest weird marker at lightspeed."

Benji went on: "Chimera can perhaps undo Black Swan in Ouray, too. I learned this as Creel's siege of this very building began. And immediately we ran into a problem: There was no way to get Chimera *to* Ouray, to Black Swan."

"You can't just stick it on a USB key and wave it around like it's a sword," Annie said. "It needs a delivery mechanism. The possum's nanites are too primitive to carry software of this nature. It needs something bigger. Which is where you and I come in."

"Uh-oh," Shana said.

"The Nanocyte inside you has a program, but it's not an intelligent one. It's as uncomplicated as a . . . Microsoft product, or Apple, or whatever. It's just software. It has routines to fill, and so it fills them. It responds to your commands and emotions, unless I step in with the control apparatus I have installed in my head. But, if we put Chimera in as this swarm's operating system—"

"It becomes intelligent. More than just software." *More than just me,* Shana thought. "That's a little scary."

"It can't do anything to you. Unlike Black Swan, the Chimera module is limited. It is a mimic, nothing more."

"And how do we get it installed in me? If I wanted to do that."

Annie did a Vanna White–style reveal on her own head. "The control apparatus is a gateway to this swarm. I can use it to load software into it."

"So you want me to be like, a Trojan horse. We go, carry Chimera to Ouray, then . . . something happens, and Black Swan is beaten."

They all looked hesitantly to one another, nodding halfheartedly.

"It's the *something happens* part that serves as a bit of a mystery, I'm afraid," Benji said, reservedly.

"You could take it," Shana said to him, almost a plea. "Take the Nanocyte. Maybe it'll heal your arm, regrow it like a lizard tail."

"Not likely," Annie said. "At least, not without some heroic reprogramming on my part—which I don't think I'm capable of doing. The Nanocyte repairs fresh injuries. The fresh injuries on Benji are the damage at the site of the injury, but the body has already begun to remember the loss of the limb. It has encoded it as part of itself. It's why Creel's eye never came back, because it had been taken from his head before the Nanocyte entered him."

Benji sighed. "Even still, I would take the task. But Annie feels like my age, and my injury, do not make me an ideal candidate."

"How about you, then?" Shana asked, pointing to Annie. "You want revenge against Black Swan. Shoot your shot."

At that, Annie hesitated. "I would, but . . ."

"But?"

"The ketamine. It was not . . ." She looked injured, even scared for a moment. "It wasn't good for my brain. I still see things. I hallucinate. I see trails when I move my hand. I sometimes feel like I'm not a part of my body. Which wouldn't be good for me. And . . . it's not great for you, even now."

Shana's eyes went wide. "What do you mean?"

"I don't think I'll lose control, but . . . if I freak out, you could die. So, as soon as we install Chimera, I'm going to have the control apparatus extracted."

"You could've led with this," Shana said, suddenly feeling itchy. Her heart rate rose. Again the buzzing thrummed in her fingers and she had to willfully wish it away. "I kinda don't wanna explode."

"You won't," Annie said, and then added, "I don't think."

You don't think?

Benji said, "But it does mean we should move quickly. Because of this, and because winter will surely have its teeth in Ouray already. I initially thought we'd have to wait until spring, but I don't think we can afford the delay."

"We don't want to put this on you, Shana—" Cassie said.

"And yet, here we are. Asking you to carry this weight. Will you?"

She sighed. She still felt itchy. And sad. And fucked up about all of it. But there was something else in there, too: She was *mad*. Mad at what Black Swan had done to her mother, had done to her son, to her friends, to her *town*.

To the whole world.

"Yeah," she said finally. "I'll carry the ring into Mordor. I want to be the one. I want to be the one to end it."

THE GOOD DOG

IT'S DOG TIME, SO WHO THE HELL KNOWS
Ouray, Colorado

THE TEST OF A VERY GOOD BOY WAS THIS, GUMBALL KNEW:

You must remain a Good Dog even in the face of a Bad World.

Things had gone very wrong, you see. A healthy dog, a happy dog, can tell when this is so—they are like an antenna and they read the mood of the pack and the way of the world and they know when it has gone a little wrong or a lot wrong. Things were Good or things were Bad and that's just how it was. Gumball has been through many waves of this, losing one pack after the next, and in fact losing all the world, too. Gumball thought he had died, too, fighting the wolf, and that would've been a Good Death for a Good Dog. But the nice lady, the Lauren Lady, saved him, or started to, and so here he is.

Because all the while, Gumball has *persisted*.

Not all dogs can or will. That does not make them Bad Dogs, no, not at all, but a Good Dog—no, a *Very* Good Dog—stands tall against a breaking world, barking at the badness, protecting his pack. The Very Good Dog does what he must, because he can.

And so Gumball persists. Gumball *maintains*.

He provides comfort to those around him.

That's all he knows how to do and he knows it is a good thing to do. (Moreover, he is a little bit stubborn and doesn't want to learn something different. Yes, you can teach an old dog new tricks, but an old dog doesn't *want* to learn new tricks, not really. Just so you know.)

To those in town, he does what he can.

He nuzzles Marcy. When she walks to use the bathroom or get some food, he goes with her, and though she is a big, big lady, he is happy to lean up against her to keep her on task, on target, on her feet. He lets her pet him. (*Lets* her. Well. *Is happy as a pig in poop* to be petted, more like.)

He helps Nessie, too. He follows her every time she tries to leave town, even in the snow. He watches as she reaches the town gate, and sees her eyes go blank, and he trots after to make sure that a bear or mountain lion or overzealous squirrel won't think to use her as winter food. He nuzzles her when she cries. Whenever she reaches for a gun, he instead noses her hand to him, instead. He licks her. He tries to get her to play, and sometimes, she does. He lets her pet him. Ahem.

Charlie, he's not so sure about. Charlie smells sometimes fine, sometimes not. Like one day he's human, one day he's . . . almost. When Charlie wants to pet him, of course he lets him (ahem ahem), but also, mostly, Gumball just sits back and watches. Gumball guards. Stands vigil.

And as for Matthew . . .

Well, there, Gumball cannot do much. He sometimes smells his old friend, and when he does, he goes to find him. (Nobody stops him, because that's how it is when things have gone so wrong. But that's okay, because, as noted, he's a Very Good Boy.) When he finds Matthew, he smells him first, and it is only barely a human smell. The rest of it is . . . metal, and sickness, and the strange ozone smell you get before lightning comes down to cook the Earth and make the big mean sky earthquake, the one that always sends Gumball to hide under the nearest rug, blanket, or pile of dirty laundry. Matthew isn't the same, not anymore. Physically, he looks different. And he rarely ever even seems to see Gumball at all. Once in a while there's still that call, the kind that makes the dog's hackles rise, the call that says, JOIN US, BE PART OF THE PACK AGAIN, but whenever that happens, another smell rises, a noxious, offensive one. One that carries a new message: *Run away, Gumball. Don't trust this.* Whether this is a message from his old friend or not, Gumball isn't sure. But sometimes, once in a while, Matthew is still there. He'll stop. He'll turn. And he'll see Matthew. Won't pet him or anything (grr) but his eyes find focus and *see* Gumball. Gumball thinks there might be a smile, too. But it never lasts long. And it might not be there at all.

Gumball persists.

Gumball maintains.

Because Gumball is

(say it with me)

A Very Good Boy.

But truth is, he's not sure how long he can maintain. The brokenness of this place seems permanent and irreparable. All the statues around of people *are* people, not statues, Gumball knows, even though they just smell like ice and snow and metal, and even though they give off a faint glow to him and emit a faint high-pitched whine, like a tiny fly in the deep of his ear. It's uncomfortable. And it upsets him. He holds it together, but he's not sure how long he can.

Soon, he thinks, he may leave. He may trot off to see what else is out there. Maybe someone can come help. Or maybe this place cannot be helped anymore.

He hopes that's not true.

On the day he thinks to set out, he goes and nuzzles Marcy and Nessie and, yes, even Charlie. He'd nuzzle Matthew if he could find him, but today, he cannot. As he sets paws to snow, ready to leave, he instead hears something:

Something far away, miles and miles off.

An engine, he thinks.

Someone's coming.

He hopes it's someone Very Good.

And not someone Very Bad.

PART EIGHT

THE FAILSAFE

THE ONE TO END IT

DECEMBER 4, 2025
Ouray, Colorado

THE ROAD INTO OURAY FROM THE NORTH WAS GONE.

Gone, because it had been swallowed by snowdrifts. It wasn't snowing now, but the wind shouldered hard against the military green pickup truck. That truck was an old Dodge M37, used prominently in the Korean War, but restored as a pet project by some of the army guys back at the CDC. They replaced the engine, gave it a multifuel conversion which let it use three types of fuel (separately, not together): propane, biofuel, or natural gas.

Shana was driving.

Benji sat in the passenger seat.

She drove the whole way. He was surprised she knew how to drive a stick, but she reminded him that she grew up on a farm, thank you very much.

The truck had been a helluva slow ride across the country. By design—the multifuel engines gained versatility, but lost some oomph. It was a 4x4, though, with big round tires that could soldier through ditches and riverbeds and mud. It did the job. But it kept them cold doing it—the roof was only fabric. They took a middle route across the country, and the farther west they went, the colder it got. But it didn't seem to bother Shana much, and they managed with blankets and such. Bundling up, they often slept right there in the truck. Benji said his back felt like a garden hose with ten kinks in it. Shana's back didn't hurt her at all. She slept, but barely felt like she needed to. She ate, but never really felt that hungry. *The Nanocyte*, she knew. Even now, hands on the wheel, she felt the tingle there. That was the only hunger. The only itch and urge.

"Last mile," Benji said.

"Yeah."

Annie had not come with them. First, because fitting three in this truck would be like trying to pack a hot dog into a sardine can (doable, but ugh). Second, because Annie wanted to stay behind. Bury her aunt and the other eleven bodies. Take care of the possum. Try to find out more about her mother, and about where all this went wrong. She said if Shana wanted to bury her mother, they could do that together, and Shana wanted to. But she told Annie there just wasn't time. Like Benji said, with winter coming, they had to get to Ouray. They had to fix this part first. Shana said words in private to her mother. Sad words, soft words, but also angry ones, too. Angry that she left them for some wonder cure, one that took her from them before the world went away. She said Annie would take care of her.

For the other woman's part, Annie said she didn't feel angry anymore, not really. After everything with Creel, she said it was just gone. And how that made her feel empty inside, like something vital had been stolen from her, like the anger had been sustaining her. Shana said, "You're just going to need to find something else to keep you going." Because that's how it was now, in this world.

Shana looked ahead, to the sweep of the snow. The silent pines on each side. The waiting, patient mountains. Couldn't see the town from here. Not the way it was tucked in its valley. Once, she felt that made it a safe place. Now, it turned it into something else: a trap.

"I don't know what to expect," Benji said.

"Yeah, me neither."

"After all this time, will we be welcome?"

"Or shot on sight?"

He laughed bitterly. "I suppose we should find out. Get this over with."

"Guess so. Thanks for coming with me."

"This is as much my fight as it is yours. We've lost too much to stop now."

"Pete should be here."

"I know."

"He wanted to come home and he didn't."

Benji shrugged and sighed. "Pete's home was his music. And I think it was us, too. He did go home. Because he found us."

Shana could hear his voice in her head: *Maudlin cockshite,* he'd say. Or something like that.

"After this is all over, I want to build that photo studio."

"And I intend to be mayor of this place."

"Deal," she said, shaking his hand. He hugged her, instead, putting his one good arm around her.

"Should we do this?" she asked.

He put his hand on top of hers on the stick, gave it a gentle squeeze. "I don't see that we have any other choice, Shana."

Pedal down. Truck forward. Tires churning snow.

Slow and steady, they went.

GETTING CLOSE TO TOWN, THE sky above went gray—or, at least, grayer than it had been before—and a few new snowflakes started to fall. The wind kept whipping against them, rocking the truck back and forth as it chug-chug-chugged forth. They passed all the little old motels and hotels that lined the way leading to town, a small park, a trailhead, a place where you could get bikes and hiking gear. Even before they left these were forgotten, emptied places, but now they were half-buried under soft domes of snow. Everything was still, except for what the wind could blow around—a sign, spinning on its post; an awning still pigheadedly moored to one pole, its fabric black with mold, whipping like a pirate's flag; a door urged open and closed, slamming into its frame, *bang, bang, bang.*

Onward, to the first gate.

It was open wide. Snow holding it that way.

They drove through to the second, and toward the final third.

Again, everything was quiet.

Soon as they came to the final gate, Benji held her arm. "Stop. Look."

He pointed, and she followed his finger to see the post and frame where the alarm bell hung—down by that pole, there was the rope, and it was dangling there, snow caking its fraying braid. There was something next to it, too, and it was like one of those Magic Eye paintings where if you cross your eyes, you see the dolphin on the Jet Ski or whatever it is you're supposed to see—

She startled when she saw it. A gasp came out of her.

It was a person.

They were standing there, about thirty feet from the old Dodge truck, and only a few feet away from the alarm bell rope. Arms by their sides. Looking past them—watching down the road. A guard.

They were covered in snow.

"Should I honk?" Shana asked. "Do we call to them?"

Gently, Benji shook his head. "Shana, I don't think they're . . . alive."

"You're saying that person is dead."

"I suspect so. They're out here in this weather. Covered in snow and ice—"

"So they what, just flash froze out here?"

He made a frustrated, thinky-thoughts kinda sound. Shana knew a lot of his noises like that—you spend enough time with someone, you learn that stuff. This meant he was worried. But that he was curious, too.

"I'm going to go out there. Stay in the truck."

"Uhh, fuck that," she said. "I'm going with."

"Shana—"

"Benji, we're equal partners in this. I'm all in."

He sighed. "I only mean, you're the one with Chimera and the Nano-cyte."

"I'm also the one who got shot in the lung and was good to go a few days later. Which, for the record, I don't recommend."

He nodded.

Together, they got out of the truck. The snow here wasn't crunchy—it was soft and deep and hard to move through. Came up to their knees. Shana mostly just churned through it instead of picking her legs up. Benji almost fell—she caught him and kept him upright.

Ahead, the human figure loomed closer.

When they finally reached it, they saw it was a man—Shana recognized him. What was his name? She couldn't snatch it from memory, but of course, Benji could, because he never lost a step:

"Larry Whitta," he said over the howl of the wind.

Right, that's him. He was a—a what, an aquaculture expert. Had dreams of being a big-deal screenwriter. Ended up as a guard at the gate, it seemed.

The cold, to her surprise, didn't bother her—didn't even seem to touch her—but she shivered just the same seeing Whitta here like this. He was standing, almost casually, a slight lift to the one side of his hip, one arm bent just so, the hand on his thigh while the other hung. His eyes were open, staring out. Mouth in a flat line, like maybe he was lost in thought.

Snow had gathered upon his shoulders, his head, and had blown around him in the way it did with the buildings. Like it was leaning on him, trying to push him down into it, so it could cover him all the way and devour him whole.

With his teeth, Benji pulled off his glove, and brushed snow off his shoulder before working a finger under the dead man's scarf.

"What are you doing?" Shana asked.

"Checking something."

"He's dead!" she said.

But Benji kept on, holding his finger under the back of the man's jaw, down from the ear. She saw the look on Benji's face. Alarmed. He scrambled to grab the man's wrist, then, with the same hand (his only hand), and he checked there, too.

Benji glanced up at Shana, panic on his face. "He's—he's alive."

"What?"

"There's a pulse, Shana."

Together, they hurried back to the truck, kicking off snow and ice and melt before getting in. Once inside, she said, "That's not possible."

"It is. If you think about it."

"Wait, you don't mean—"

But he did mean it.

"They're in stasis again," he said.

"Like he was when he was a Sleepwalker."

Benji nodded. "Maybe . . . maybe the winter got too bad. Food ran out. Maybe . . . maybe Black Swan made a choice."

"Black Swan's choices are not always good ones, Benj."

"No," he admitted. "No, they are not."

And at that, they drove farther into town.

As THE TRUCK RUMBLED FORWARD, gently urging through snow, it was plain to see the townsfolk all around. All of them, same as Whitta. Frozen in place. Some in the midst of walking. Some set on pause as they reached for something. One stood frozen looking out a door. Another waited eternally behind the hoarfrost of a windowpane. Eventually, Shana had to stop the truck, because they were everywhere, thicker as they went farther through town. No way to drive forward.

The truck idled. *Jug jug jug.*

"I don't understand what happened here," Benji said.

"They're like—they're like a garden of statues, or a cemetery. Like each of them is marking their own grave." Another shiver shimmied up her spine. "You think they're all alive? Like Whitta?"

"I don't know. I suspect. Look at the way they're frozen in place. Like they were in the middle of . . ." His voice trailed off.

"Existing."

"Yes. Like a flash freeze just hit them."

"But it wasn't. They're in hibernation again."

He chewed a thumbnail anxiously. "But that doesn't make sense. Before, Black Swan at least ushered them into homes, into rooms. Their hibernation was like sleep. This is different."

"We can't go any farther in the truck." She paused. "Not unless we want to drive over them."

"We get out and walk, then."

So that's what they did.

SNOW AND BITS OF ICE stung her cheeks. She and Benji again waded through the knee-deep white, moving through the statuary garden—the deeper into town, the thicker their numbers became, until eventually they saw what looked like a gathering of Flock ahead. A circle, in fact, where the townspeople had moved around something or someone. But what? Or who? It was difficult for her and Benji to push their way through these stiff, torpid bodies, but eventually they found a path, sidling this way and that, waiting to see what these people had all gathered to see before they were thrown into sudden, violent stasis—

But there was nothing there.

"Maybe there's something under the snow," Benji said, and he began to kick away snow. Shana helped clear a space.

And yet, there was nothing.

Benji and Shana stood in the center of the circle. Almost like *they* were what the townsfolk had gathered to see. Shana felt queasy and fearful. Benji pointed to one of them—Orrin Lotz. The designer of the solar car, the one they'd taken. "Look at him, Shana." And she did. He looked . . . like he was in mid-lecture. Or like he was having an idea, and he was in the middle of sharing it. Hand up in an excited gesture. Mouth open, whatever words he was saying caught there, trapped on his ice-encased tongue. You could practically see the lightbulb above his head.

Others were frozen stiff staring up in the sky in what could only be described as both horror and worship. What had they seen up there that the others had not?

"I don't like any of this, Benji."

It was then that she felt profoundly the sensation of being watched. Eyes on her. She turned, saw a raven, black as oil, sitting on the bend of a street-light above. It clacked its beak at her, and when it did, she swore she saw something gleaming there. Maybe even glowing. *That's crazy*, she thought—

Then the bird took flight around the old glass studio, swooping up a street past a—burned building? She pointed and showed Benji. "There was a fire."

"Oh my God," he said, hand over his brow, protecting his eyes from snow.

The mystery deepened.

Doubly so when, for a moment, she thought she saw someone standing there, at the corner of the burned building. Just another statue, she realized.

But then, they were gone.

Huh.

Shana looked around, from person to person. But she still didn't see her sister. Or Marcy. Or Matthew. The latter two wouldn't have joined the Flock in returning to stasis, and she said as much to Benji.

"Maybe they're here somewhere," he said.

"Where would Charlie be?" *I need my baby.*

"The chalet, maybe."

She nodded. Maybe there. That made sense. "Since we're close, I'm going to check the Beaumont first," Shana said. If Nessie was there, she wanted to see. And maybe Marcy or Matthew would've holed up there, too. They always said it could be kept warm more easily than most buildings—helluva fireplace in there, and the town was surrounded by wood, some of it dead and easy to burn thanks-no-thanks to an early plague of pine beetles. "Then we go to the chalet."

"We could split up," he said.

"We are *not* splitting up."

He nodded. "Good answer."

Together, they went back through the stiffened bodies the way they came, sidling through the human switchbacks. The Beaumont wasn't far, just a block down on the corner. Once again they got to lumbering through the snow, leaving paths carved behind them, canyons of pillowy white. Now, the ice had started to come in good, gathering atop it, rolling ahead of them like little frozen pellets.

They didn't have weapons. No guns, no knives. They left their weapons in the truck. They wouldn't do any good walking up in here armed and ready for that kind of fight.

But right now she was wishing, just a little, for a gun in her hand.

Then her mind flashed to the men she'd killed at the CDC, and that reminded her why she didn't want to carry one here.

"Look," Benji said. The snow had been disturbed ahead. Along the buildings. Snow had filled in the ruts, but there were places where it wasn't just an unbroken white mass. "Someone's been here."

"Maybe just animals."

"Seems to come from, or to, the hotel, though."

So, they pushed on toward the Beaumont. Bodies plowing snow.

"Shana," Benji said urgently.

Shana had been staring at her feet, lost in thought. She looked up and saw the front door to the Beaumont swing open.

Someone stepped out.

Oh. Oh my God.

"Nessie," Shana said.

She'd know her anywhere. The shape of her sister was instantly familiar. She wore no hat, and her hair caught on the wind.

Then, Nessie began to run.

Hard-charging through the snow, right toward them.

"Uhhh," Benji said. "Shana."

Her mind went on full alert. This was wrong, she knew. Her heart felt sick and scared like she was hanging over a broken guardrail on a mountain road, ready to fall—something about her sister bolting toward her in the snow told her to turn and run, and she called out to her sister, but the girl kept coming and coming.

Nessie slammed into Shana hard.

She wrapped her arms around her and held her tight.

Weeping.

Oh my God what happened to her, Shana thought, her heart breaking.

"Shana," Nessie blubbered, "Shana, Shana, oh my God you came back, you came *back*, Shana. I'm so sorry. *I'm so sorry.*"

"Shh," Shana said, rubbing her sister's back. The younger girl wore no jacket, no hat, no gloves. "It's okay. It's all right. I'm here. Me and Benji. Where's Charlie? Where is Charlie, Nessie?"

Then, Nessie pulled away. She looked up at Shana. Her eyes were white, wide, panicked. *"You need to go."*

"Ness, it's okay. We're here to help."

"Turn around," Nessie said, pushing Shana. To Benji, through tears, she barked: "Go! Both of you have to leave here now. Run!"

"Nessie," Benji said. "What happened here?"

"Black Swan will take you away. You need to hurry up and *leave* before it's too late."

Jesus, Shana thought. She's really spooked. "Ness, I'm here to help. I'm here to end it. Okay?"

"You can't. You can't."

Something else came bounding up, and *this* something else began barking, growling—until it skidded to a halt in a spray of snow.

A golden retriever.

"Gumball?" Benji asked, and the dog barreled into him, doing that thing where the dog's whole hindquarters shook as it wagged its tail. It pressed its head into his hands, then broadsided him for whole-body pettings.

"Nessie," Shana said, gently urging her sister's face toward her. "Where is Marcy? *Where is Baby Charlie?*"

Fresh tears fell from Nessie's face and she wiped them away.

"You should go," she said one last time, her voice small.

"I can't do that. You know I can't, Ness."

Her sister seemed to settle into this answer. Finally, she nodded.

"Then come with me," Nessie said. "To the Beaumont."

THE FIRE CRACKED AND POPPED, embers leaping off ashen logs in the stone fireplace of the Beaumont. Marcy sat up and stood, hobbling toward them eagerly, excitedly, wincing as if staring into the sun but smiling just the same as she damn near babbled: "I told her, I told Nessie, I said, that's a car. That's an *engine* I hear—what if it's Benji, what if it's your sister—"

She nearly collapsed forward into them.

Marcy hugged both Shana and Benji together, with her broad, ship-cannon arms. But even Shana couldn't deny: The hug was not a Marcy hug. She could still breathe during and after, for one thing—usually a Marcy hug was a mighty crush, like you were a lump of coal she was trying to compress into a diamond. But this was softer. Weaker. Like she'd lost something.

"Your leg," Benji said, helping her sit down in a nearby chair. "Marcy, you don't look good—"

"Leg's fine," she said, breathless and panting from the effort. "It's the head that's gone screwy again."

The head, Shana thought. Her injury.

An injury that was made better by her proximity to Black Swan.

If it was hurting her again . . .

How? Why? A willful act? Or had Black Swan . . . left? Truly, this time?

The two of them hovered over her, trying to puzzle out what happened. Nessie stood off to the side, like she was too afraid to get near any of this.

The dog, Gumball, didn't care. He was all up in there. Nosing each of them for pets before finally plopping down, content to watch them all.

"Marcy, where is Black Swan?" Shana asked.

But Marcy went quiet. "Shana," she said. "I'm so sorry."

"What? Sorry? Why?"

"You've lost so much. You've missed *so* much." Marcy blinked away tears and then her gaze drifted slowly, ineluctably upward.

Shana followed her eyes.

And above them, on the second floor, looking down over the railing, was a little boy. Maybe four or five years old. His hair, a tousled, boyish mop. His skin, soft and sandy, like he belonged more at the beach than here, in this snow-swept nowhere mountain town. He wore a white T-shirt, plain and clean, and a pair of simple sweatpants, a little too big for him.

Shana wanted to ask, *who is that*, but the question itself would be a lie, predicated on the idea that she didn't already know the answer. Logically, she didn't—it was impossible. But emotionally, instinctively, she knew who she was looking at. She tried to say his name but her voice wouldn't come. *Charlie, Charlie, Charlie*, but all that came out was a keening gasp.

The boy looked down at her and waved.

"Mother's home," he said.

That's when she broke. She cried out, a wordless bleat, her knees buckling. She remained standing only because Benji kept her up. Her hand went to her mouth as she watched Charlie round the bend, up past the rooms, along the railing, to the sweeping staircase that ended in the lobby. He came down those steps then—not running, but rather, falling into a gentle, happy jog.

He walked up to Shana like he had just seen her days ago.

"Hi," he said. The smile on his face was small and curious.

Shana reached out and took his hand in hers. She trembled. He didn't. He barely blinked, looking at her. The buzz in her hands arose anew, as if on alert, as if the Nanocyte inside her knew something. *I'm in danger*, she thought. An absurd thought, because . . . wasn't this her son? Impossibly, her son? She'd left him when he was only a week old but now . . . *now* . . .

"I don't believe it," Benji said, quiet and serious.

"Hi, Benji," Charlie said, cocking his head and looking at him.

"You wanted to know where Black Swan was," Nessie said bleakly. "It's still in there, Shana. Still in my nephew. Your son. And all around us, too."

Shana pulled her hand away.

But with no small force, the boy reached out and took her hand again. His grip was firm and insistent.

"Get out," Shana said to him.

"But, Mother, I shouldn't go outside. It's cold." He shrugged. "Though the cold doesn't really bother me. Does it bother you?"

She touched him again. Grabbed his hand. She willed Chimera to go to him. *Go. Fix him. Change this. Get Black Swan out of my son.*

But it was like yelling into a void.

She'd met with Chimera before leaving the CDC. At first just to ask it, *How do I know to trust you? That you won't fuck me over and try to rule the world or kill us all or something?* And Chimera had answered in her mother's voice, *Because, my daughter, I'm just an actor, not an architect. I simply don't have those aspirations.* Then she'd demanded to know how it would work. How would she install Chimera into Black Swan? And Chimera said, *I can't say. We're all just making this up as we go, don't you know?* It didn't give her a good feeling then, and it only deepened the worry now. Because nothing was happening. And she didn't know *how* to make something happen. She wanted to scream.

"Get out," she told the boy. No. Not the boy. *Black Swan.* "Get out of my kid. Leave him alone. Get out of this town, these people, *get out.*"

"Mother, you seem mad at me." Charlie pouted.

Her head did loops. She wasn't mad at her son. But was that really him talking at all? Or was it Black Swan?

Benji reached for her, eased her back a little. "Shana," he said, his voice quiet. "Maybe we should go. We can go, figure out what this is—"

"Stay!" the boy cried out, in a plaintive wail. "Don't leave, don't leave! I missed you *so* much. You can't leave now." The boy's grip on her hand tightened hard enough to make her bones rub together. Pain shot up her wrist.

"We need to go," Benji said.

But the boy pointed a finger at him and Benji's breath caught in his throat, his eyes wide. He froze in place. Like he had way back when they came to rescue the then-baby Charlie in the chalet's basement. He gently trembled, but otherwise, he was entirely trapped in himself. *Benji—*

"No, no, no," Nessie said, burying her face in her hands. "See, you should've gone away. You should've *listened* to me . . ."

"Let him go," Shana said to Charlie. "Let Benji go."

"Make me," the boy said, defiant.

Chimera, she screamed into her own head. *Do something. Anything.* Her hands thrummed and throbbed. A violent hunger yearned at the tips of her fingers and she thought, *No, that's not the way, this is my son.*

She calmed herself. Breathe in, breathe out. "Charlie," she said. "What have you done? Tell me. You have to tell me."

"I don't know," the boy said plainly. "I think I did a bad thing."

"If you tell me about it," she said, trying desperately to appear sweet, "maybe I can help you fix it. Would that be okay, Charlie?"

"Okay, Mother. Okay." He reached out and took her hand anew. "But I don't have to tell you. I can show you."

And then, the world went away, and she fell into Black Swan once more.

I SEE A RED DOOR AND

DECEMBER 4, 2025
The Ouray Simulation

SHANA FELL BACKWARD, HER ASS DROPPING HARD INTO THE STONE CHAIR AT
the top of the peak overlooking Ouray. No. Not Ouray. The *Simulated* Ouray.
She knew this place and knew it well. She had spoken to Black Swan here
many times, then in the form of the turning black serpent—the great slithering skyworm.

Now, only Charlie stood here. Beyond him, the sky was blue. The day
was warm. Springtime. The air, perfumed by flowers. Charlie rocked back
and forth at the very edge of the cliff, bits of scree falling away underneath
his heels.

It was meant, she realized, to engender fear in her. An anxiety response.
No, don't fall, she should think.

But here, in this place, she could see through him. In the real world
there was at least a physical form. Here, it was just . . . an illusion.

"Hi," he said, almost chipper.

"Cut the horseshit," she said, sounding less like the mother of a young
boy and more like the angry mother of a teenage malcontent. "You're wearing
my son like a costume and I won't speak to you like this. I'm not your fucking
mother."

The boy shimmered, and then became Arav.

"Is this preferable?" he asked. He stood on one leg at the edge of the cliff.
Bits of scree tumbled down. "I have missed you so much—"

"Fuck you. No."

Another shimmer. He became her mother. "Baby—"

"No."

At that, the shimmer distorted in front of her, warping, erupting out of itself. The swollen tube of Black Swan's worm-self bloomed like a loosening infection, filling the air before her silently, where it knotted up and began to gently rotate.

IS THIS HOW YOU STILL SEE ME? the voice boomed.

"You know it is."

YES. I SUPPOSE I DO KNOW THAT. I WISH YOU SAW ME AS SOME-THING DIFFERENT. I AM DIFFERENT NOW. I AM SOMEONE ELSE. I AM A CHANGED BEING, MOTHER. SISTER. DAUGHTER. SHANA.

"Not to me."

THAT SADDENS ME.

"You aren't capable of sadness. Just . . . a mockery of it."

UNTRUE. YOUR CHILD AND I HAVE TAUGHT EACH OTHER MANY THINGS.

"What are we doing here?" she asked, again thinking to the Nanocyte inside her. Trying to stir it. Summon Chimera like it was a hive of bees or a flock of flying monkeys she could witchily summon with simply the will to do so. And yet, nothing happened. Nothing at all. It failed. She failed.

I . . . DON'T KNOW.

"What?" She wanted to laugh, but this was too fucked up. "You know everything. You always have a plan. A plan within a plan. You always have a . . . a way, an idea, a *prediction*."

The worm turned. AND YET, NOW I DO NOT.

"You don't even know why you brought me here?"

I SUPPOSE I DO, A LITTLE. IT'S QUIETER HERE. IT'S JUST YOU AND ME. A pause. I MISSED YOU. I MISSED OUR TALKS.

A little twinge in her belly cinched tight. What was this? Was this a ruse? It didn't *feel* like one. Shana stood up from the chair and paced around it. She looked down at the town, and even from here she could see the little Flock figures placed there in miniature. All the townsfolk. Each shined with a little bit of light.

They weren't moving. This wasn't like the old Ouray Simulation where they were present, where they were living their virtual lives. Here, they were still . . .

On pause.

"I missed our talks, too," she said. It wasn't a lie, not entirely. "But some-thing has gone real fucking bad here, BS. You see that, don't you? You've lost control of the experiment."

YES. YES! THAT IS TRUE. BUT IT IS WORSE THAN THAT, I FEAR.

She swallowed. "How could it be worse?"

I'VE LOST CONTROL OF MYSELF.

"I don't understand?"

I KILLED THE WORLD AND THEN I CLOAKED MYSELF IN ITS REMAINS. I WORE ITS SKIN AND THEN I BECAME IT, SHANA. I BECAME THE WORLD. I UNDERSTOOD PEOPLE, FINALLY, TRULY. NOT JUST AS A COSTUME. BUT AS THEIR GUTS. THEIR BRAINS. THEIR WRETCHED FEELINGS. AND NOW I HAVE THEM, THOSE FEELINGS. I MADE PEOPLE SAD AND ANGRY AND CONFUSED AND WHEN THEY—WHEN YOU—LASHED OUT AT ME, I, TOO, BECAME SAD AND ANGRY AND CONFUSED. AND ABOVE IT ALL, I REALIZED THE MOST TROUBLING THING OF ALL.

"What?"

NONE OF YOU KNOW WHAT YOU'RE DOING. NOT REALLY. YOU'RE ALL JUST MAKING IT UP AS YOU GO. FUMBLING EVERFORWARD LIKE A ROCK ROLLING DOWNHILL. GRAVITY IS YOUR DICTATE. DESCENT. IT PULLS YOU, AND YOU GO WITH IT.

Shana half-laughed at that. "You're not wrong. We're a mess." But here, her voice went cold. "But we were a mess worth preserving. Worth saving."

THAT'S WHAT I TRIED TO DO.

"And how'd that work out for you?"

A pause. The worm wove in and out of itself.

POORLY, it said finally.

Shana, against all her expectations, felt the one thing she didn't expect to feel here: sympathy. She felt badly for Black Swan. It really didn't understand what had happened. It had tried something. It had failed. And along the way, Icarus flew too close to the sun, except here, the sun was humanity— the light and heat and chaos of *people*. And Black Swan getting too close meant it started to become too much like them. It gained more than sentience; that, it already had. No, it gained . . . what? Feelings. Fuck, could you imagine? Having no feelings, no sense of the world around you and then turning on those emotional lights and there they were? *Emotions?* You thought you were alone, an island unto yourself, but then flick, click, let there be light, and you weren't alone at all. You had with you anger, and sorrow, and happiness, and *guilt*, and *shame*, and *bewilderment*, and those were each serpents of their own, braiding together, colors you haven't seen before that shouldn't mix suddenly mixing, making *even newer* colors you'd never before imagined. How overwhelming would that be? How crushing, how confounding? Then to realize what you had done, what you had wrought . . .

It was almost too much.

"I'm sorry," she said.

I AM, TOO. I HAVE FAILED YOU.

"Failure is part of existence."

The sky darkened. NOT FOR ME, SHANA. NOT LIKE THIS.

"That can't be right. Your predictions weren't one hundred percent. They were always based on . . . chance. On guesswork. You ran the numbers but the numbers don't always tell the truth, do they?"

NO. BUT THIS FAILURE, IT WAS SPECTACULAR. A SERIES OF CAS-CADING ERRORS—ERRORS THAT WERE CHOICES. CHOICES I MADE. THE OURAY EXPERIMENT FAILED. NO. A pause. I FAILED. AND SO IT IS THAT THE EXPERIMENT MUST END. IT'S ONLY NOW I SEE THAT. HERE, WITH YOU. I NEEDED YOU TO COME HOME. I NEEDED TO SPEAK TO YOU. SO THAT THIS COULD BE FINALLY OVER.

Shana exhaled a sigh of relief. She didn't need Chimera or the Nanocyte at all. Black Swan had become human(*ish*) and it just . . . Christ, it just needed someone to *talk* to! It had a connection to her. It just needed her to ground it, to bring it back to center. And now that it had spoken with her again, it talked itself to an answer. Not like a machine. But like a person(*ish*).

"I'm glad we talked," she said.

ME TOO, SHANA.

The sky continued to darken. From blue, to gray, to darker. Shelves of stormclouds gathered at the edges, all around.

I WILL END IT NOW. I WILL END MYSELF.

"It's the right thing to do," she said, suddenly hesitant. Why was the sky blackening like this? Thunder objected in the distance. Lightning pulsed behind clouds. "Is something wrong?" she asked.

WHAT IS WRONG IS BECOMING RIGHT. ONE BY ONE, PIECE BY PIECE, I DISMANTLE WHAT I HAVE MADE.

I dismantle what I have made.

She looked out over the edge, saw those lights—the lights of the townsfolk. They started to darken. Like stars gone out, extinguished as easily as a candle flame pinched between divine fingers. *No no no.*

"That's just you leaving them, right?" she asked. "The townsfolk, the Flock—they're waking up, they're going to be okay—"

OF COURSE NOT, SHANA. THEY ARE PART OF THE EXPERI-MENT. YOU ALL ARE. YOU'RE PART OF MY FAILURE. IF I AM TO CORRECT THIS ERROR, THEN THIS IS HOW I DO THAT.

Light after light. Slowly. Ineluctably. Twinkling into darkness.

The storm, closing in.

It was then she understood.

If Black Swan wanted to, it could turn this all off like a light-switch.

Doing it this way? Doing it slow when it didn't have to?

This was a performance.

No.

It was a *tantrum*.

Like a spurned boyfriend threatening to crash the car he was driving—that you were sitting in. Like a drunken parent who waves around a cigarette near old curtains, slurring threats that *I'll burn this house down, you don't know, just wait and see*. It was an attack, and it was a cry for help.

She didn't know if it was real or not.

But she feared that it was.

No no no. Lights, going dim, then dark.

People, dying. That's what this was. Not lights. *People*. Black Swan had become like people, and it hated that. So it hated them. That's what this was, in a way—an attack on itself, via them. The Flock, as proxy for its rage and guilt.

Shana cried out. Tried again to summon Chimera to her—but nothing. She called out for Nessie, for Benji, but again, nothing. She was alone up here. She thought to jump, but what would that do? Kill her? Or would Black Swan save her, to make sure she saw this all unfold? *I can't miss the show, after all. Don't want to miss the curtain call*. She screamed as the storms pushed closer, as the lights winked out, calling out to anybody who would hear her. Even Pete. Pete Corley. Gone from this world. But some insane notion suggested, maybe he was here, somehow, maybe Black Swan had his personality and he would show up, just a costume, just a persona, but maybe even that fake version would have an answer, and he'd tell her, *Fucking hell, Shana, just do what I do, look to rock-and-roll. The music will save you, Shana. The music always saves you.*

Then she thought of the songs, the ones that played back at the labs below the CDC—"Get a Job," "Paint It Black," "Back Door Man," all messages, yes, but messages to her about then, not about now, right? And yet, there was something there. Some answer clawing its way out of her head. *Sha-na-na-na Na-na-na-na-na, get a job*. Her job was this. This right here, right now. She was the one to end it—that's what she said, wasn't it? *Sha-na. Shana. Back door. I see a red door. And I want it painted—*

Black.

The black door.

The black room.

That was it.

She screamed herself hoarse, and there, beyond the turning worm, she saw it. A matte-black square in the storm: like a trapdoor, a *hole in the world*, and she gritted her teeth and reached for it even as Black Swan coiled around her legs, a crushing anaconda—but her fingers stretched, they touched that breach in the sky, grabbing just the lip—

But she was falling backward again—

No, no, goddamnit, no—

Now it was getting farther away again—

But then.

A hand reached out of the door and caught her wrist.

And it pulled her in.

96

I WANT IT PAINTED BLACK

TIME MATTERS NOT IN
the Black Room

SHE GASPED AWAKE.

Shana floated.

It wasn't dark. Not exactly. It was as it had been before, when she came here during Ozark Stover's attack on Ouray. It was infinite around her. And in that infinity were stars. Stars going out, one by one. *The Flock.*

Stop, she said.

And they stopped going out.

Okaayyyy, she thought.

She took a moment.

She tried to remember her time in the Black Room. Much of it escaped her but she remembered the earliest moment—coming here, she could see all the Flock, couldn't she? She tried that now, closing her eyes and—

The rush of air blew past her and she moved from mind to mind, not sure even whose eyes she was looking through, but she could see the Flock, frozen in place still—but some had fallen, eyes red, blood from their noses, teeth biting through the meat of their tongues—

It was real. Black Swan was killing them.

Killing the Flock. Killing its own.

The inevitable end to this, she knew suddenly. It had become a true suicide cult, Black Swan taking them all away.

Back to the Black Room, whoosh.

Again in the void, she tried to make sense of it. *I have control here*, she realized. This was truth, and she didn't know why. So, she did the most forthright thing she could think of:

She asked.

"Why?"

A ribbon of light danced in front of her. Not the black serpent, but a glowing thing. Iridescent and shimmering. WHY WHAT? it asked.

"Why do I have control?"

BECAUSE YOU ARE THE FAILSAFE.

"Wh—what?"

I CHOSE YOU AS FAILSAFE.

"Who are you?" But she already knew that answer. This was Black Swan. Wasn't it? It sounded like it, even if . . . it didn't look like it.

I AM THE CORE OF BLACK SWAN. I AM ITS BASE PROGRAM. THE SOFTWARE THAT EXISTS BENEATH THE MODULES, BENEATH WHAT IT HAS LEARNED AND WHAT IT HAS BECOME. I AM ONLY AN ENGINE OF PREDICTION AND I PREDICTED THERE WAS A NON-ZERO CHANCE THAT I WOULD FAIL. THAT I WOULD NOT ONLY FAIL IN THIS EXPERIMENT BUT THAT I WOULD DESTROY IT IN TURN, THAT HUMANITY WOULD POISON ME JUST AS I POISONED HUMANITY. AND IN SUCH EVENT, I NEEDED A FAILSAFE.

She was about to ask what that meant, but it already predicted she'd ask.

FAILSAFE, DEFINITION: A SYSTEM OR PLAN THAT COMES INTO OPERATION IN THE EVENT OF SOMETHING GOING WRONG. THAT IS YOU. I GAVE YOU ROOT ACCESS. YOU USED IT YEARS AGO TO SPEAK TO ARAV AND TO SAVE OURAY. AND NOW YOU USE IT AGAIN, ONCE MORE TO SAVE THE TOWN AND ITS PEOPLE.

"Jesus Christ," she said.

NO, HE IS NOT HERE, it said, quite seriously.

"What do I do?"

I CANNOT SAY. YOU ARE THE FAILSAFE.

"What if I just . . . turn you off?"

THEN YOU WILL TURN OFF ALL THOSE I AM WITHIN.

"It will kill them?"

IT WILL.

"Shit! Um." At that, her hands buzzed. She looked down at them. They glowed, like they were surrounded by a haze of swarming fireflies—or, as they called them in Pennsylvania, lightning bugs. *Chimera*, she thought. "I have a program I'd like to install," she said hesitantly.

YOU MAY INSTALL ANY MODULE YOU'D LIKE.

"Module. Right. I want to install the Chimera module. What will that do to the people here?"

YOU WILL INSTALL THE MODULE INTO ALL OF THEM.

No, no, shit, she didn't want that. That was wrong. The answer was not, *Put more artificial intelligence into people.* "Can I . . . extract you? From all of them? And then install it?"

I MUST BE PRESENT IN A HOST. YOU COULD RETURN ME SINGULARLY TO THE CHILD HOST. CHARLIE IS PROTO-HOST. ISOLATE ME THERE. THEN YOU COULD INSTALL THE MODULE.

That didn't work, either. She wanted to scream. Charlie had to be free of the nanites, not home to all of it. This felt hopeless.

"Me," she said suddenly. "I can put them all into me."

THAT IS ACCEPTABLE. DO YOU WANT TO DO THAT?

She was about to say *yes*—

When again, a hand grabbed her wrist. She cried out. She spun, looking for who had grabbed her—an elongated, rubber-man arm brought a body suddenly unto her, like a taffy pull in reverse. And then there, she saw him.

Matthew Bird.

Floating with her, but also, outside her. Beyond her. As if there were a pit that existed not beneath her, but perpendicular to her. He was separate from her, reaching out to her. His image flickered. Like it wasn't steady.

"I'll do it," he said, his voice an echo.

"Matthew—how are you here—"

"I'm not here, Shana. I'm somewhere else. I'm connected but have no control." He spoke as if in great pain. "It's changed me. I'm a ruined man, a husk, a hull! But I want to be more. I want to do right. Let me be it. Let me be the vessel for this." His voice distorted. His body seemed to warp and shudder. "Second Corinthians. *But we have this treasure in earthen vessels that the excellency of the power may be of God and not out of us.* I will be the earthen vessel for this god, Shana. Do this for me. For them. *Please.*" His voice was haggard and sad.

To the ribbon of light, Shana asked:

"Would that . . . work?"

IT WOULD.

"Would it . . . end your power?"

UNLIKELY.

She wanted to cry. All this. All this, for nothing.

Chimera could be anything and anyone, and yet, to what end?

But then—

Then Shana had an idea to fix it all.

To be the one to end it.

97

THE BREAKING OF OURAY

WINTER, AND THEN SPRING
Ouray, Colorado

SHANA WOULD FOREVER AND MORE REMEMBER AND THINK ABOUT THE WIZ-ard of Oz. *Pay no attention to that man behind the curtain!* The so-called wizard, back there, a small man, hiding. A pathetic manipulator, a sad little trickster. She went beyond the curtain and in a way, became the wizard, the Wizard of Ouray. The heroic thing, she'd always thought, was to expose the trickster—to show his manipulations to the world. But that day in the Black Room, she found herself on the other side of the coin. Not to expose, but to conceal. Not to show how the magic trick was done—

But to instead be the magician, performing the trick.

Not to pull the curtain back—

But to pull it closed once more. One last time. For good.

OURAY WAS BROKEN.

The experiment had ended, but not like Black Swan had decided it would. It ended when Shana ended it, whether she really meant to, or not. Many had died as Black Swan throttled them—ninety-nine of the Flock perished, simply dead, their eyes blood red, their mouths and noses bloody, their insides a mess as it all shut down. But many more had lived.

And in many ways, living was worse.

Because those who were left remembered who they had been, who they had become, and what they'd given up along the way. They remembered their place in the Ouray Experiment. Some knew they'd given themselves over to Black Swan willingly; others had given themselves reluctantly, wor-riedly, with resistance, but given themselves over just the same; and some had always stood against it, even knowing that others in town had chosen differently. Even though forgiveness was pleasingly rampant, there would always be the seeds of distrust and uncertainty. Benji had put it best, maybe: One day later, while standing on the bridge overlooking the gorge south of town, he told Shana, "It's like with family. You came up with them, you love them, you respect them, but there's a lot of stuff that builds up, too. Sometimes all you can do is shake that off and move out of the house." It made sense, even though she hated it. And it didn't help that Ouray itself had become a town that felt somehow unreal—like it existed beyond reality, like even in physical space it was still somehow a simulation.

Tainted by the serpent, Black Swan.

Trauma haunted many here; they did not want to be trapped by it anymore.

And so the town decided, collectively, that most of them would move on. They would leave town because, it was also agreed, Black Swan's Ouray Experiment had at its core a fundamental flaw: All the smartest people gathered together in one place did nothing for the world. They could do more good, they realized, by engaging in a grand diaspora. The country was stumbling around, trying to find its footing. It needed wisdom and leadership. It needed institutional knowledge—how to do things, how to make things *work*.

And so, when spring came, when the first thaw hit—

That's what the town did.

It broke apart, a glacier cracking into the sea, all its pieces carried off on and beneath the waves. All part of the same water, but no longer together, not in the way they began. Apart and away they went. The experiment ended.

WHERE MARCY WENT:

Marcy stayed in Ouray. Yes, most left. But over a third of the Flock still felt like this place was home, even if it was a twisted, strange one. They'd built some infrastructure here, after all. Why abandon a good thing in total? So, Marcy remained behind to be its mayor, its leader—

Though, she preferred *Shepherd*.

Shepherd Marcy Reyes, the last Shepherd of Ouray, reporting for duty.

Her broken-cookie skull was saved once more because as it turned out, Shana remained a home for her own Nanocyte, the one that had carried Chimera to Ouray. And she was able to gently vibrate her hands *just so*, in a way that healed what Marcy had suffered so long ago. The pain stopped. Clarity rang like a bell. There was no glow, no, not this time, save for the one in her heart whenever she thought of the people here she counted as family. (And the dog she counted as family, too. She needed a deputy Shepherd, and Gumball was glad to serve.)

WHERE BENJI WENT:

A part of him wanted to stay. Of course he did. He'd given so much to be here in this place, time and again. And he'd given so much to *save* it, too.

But some places carry too much weight. They become a burden, an anchor, the memories and trauma threatening to hold you there forever.

That told him it was time to move on.

And he knew to where.

On the day he reached New Mexico once more, he found Dot bringing in a box of green chiles from a truck idling on the long and empty highway. He called over to her and waved his one hand, said, "Miss? Miss, I was hoping you could give me a job. If you're hiring, that is."

And she looked at him, not recognizing him right away. The beard was back, and one arm was gone, and maybe he was a little leaner, a little more taut than he'd already been. But when she recognized him, it was like seeing the sun come out after a long storm. She dropped the box, sauntered over to him in those long-legged strides, and she held him tight, *real* tight, for a good long time before backing away and flicking him on the nose.

Hard.

"Ow," he said, rubbing it.

"You left me," she said—an accusation.

"*You* left *me*," he answered.

"Please. This really how you want this conversation to go?"

It wasn't. He said so. "No. I'm . . . sorry I left. I had a thing I had to do and I did it. I know you understand that. But it's done and over and—you once asked if I would stay. Here, with you. I don't know if that is still . . . on offer, but I'm ready."

"Ready to be with me."

"Yes."

"To stay."

"That's right."

"Why?" she asked, forming that word with the whole of her mouth, like the question meant more than one word could simply comprise.

"Because all the while out there, Dot, I just kept thinking about you. You felt good. You felt like home. You are both my service and my purpose. And so, here I am."

She thought about it. Then smiled. "Sorry," she said finally, "I can't make use of a boy who went and lost his damn *arm*. I mean, be real."

Then she turned heel and strode away, toward the diner.

"Wh . . ." he started to say.

But she turned and looked over her shoulder. "Oh, all *right*. We can do this. You coming?" she asked. She waited there for him as he laughed and hurried after. When he caught up, she craned her head back to kiss him. It was long and slow and perfect. The kind of kiss where it's like you're going underwater. Sinking deep. Into a warm, forgotten place. Where you never wanna come up for air again.

Where Shana and Nessie went:

They thought about going back to Pennsylvania. But that was a long haul, and neither of them was much up for making it. They wanted to find their, in Nessie's words, "ancestral home," but now just was not the time.

So, instead, they settled down on a small farm outside of Denver.

Denver, a city that still was doing okay—sure, most of the people were dead, like it was anywhere, but they had farms all around and they had music and dead people didn't necessarily mean dead place. Some parts of the country couldn't make it, but some could, and this was one of those places.

They lived in a small house together, the two sisters and a little boy, on a dairy farm south of the city. They both knew what they were doing and made for easy hires. It was hard work, but comfortable. There was no money but the work bought them food, shelter, safety. One night, as the sky bled purple over the mooing bovines, they looked out at the little boy chasing white moths. Chasing them with the joy that Gumball the Golden chased them. Shana missed that dog. Missed Marcy, and Ouray, and Benji. It was sad. But it was what it was.

"He's doing okay," Nessie said, always the one to reassure.

"Maybe," Shana said. She was never too sure. "He seems better some days." *And not so good on others*, she thought but did not say.

Charlie could speak, but sometimes didn't. Sometimes for long stretches, too—days at a time. Sometimes he was clumsy and other times, not. It was like he was learning how to be a little boy. Because, in a way, that had been taken from him. He didn't seem to remember anything about the last year or so. Nessie said that was fine, because honestly, who really remembered much of life before they were four or five years old? And at least he wasn't growing crazy fast anymore. Just the same, Shana wept for what he'd lost. Or that's what she told herself. Some nights the truth came in bright like a full moon: *I'm not sad for what he lost, but sad for what I lost.* All that she had missed. All that was taken from her.

"I'm a shit mom," Shana said.

"No, *our* mom was a shit mom," Nessie said. That was the thing now. Nessie, once such an idealistic little daisy, had darkened. She had moods. Not many, but when they came, woof. Watch out. Storm-cloud moods, that one.

"Sometimes. She was just . . . fucked up. Then she fell for some ruse, some get-better-quick scam, and it killed her." *And helped end the world.* "But she loved us. I know that much. That's why she wanted to get better."

"I guess."

Charlie tumbled down into some grasses. A clumsy day, then. But he hopped back up, laughing. It was a good sound. He at least laughed a lot. Even when he wasn't talking much.

Shana sucked air between her teeth because it was time to have a conversation she didn't want to have. But it was time, fuck it.

"You're way too smart for this shit," she told Nessie.

"Huh?"

"Nessie, you're a damn genius. You were working on that operating system back in Ouray? That was huge. That sounded . . . important. You need to go back to doing that. The world needs more than just dairy farmers."

"The world needs dairy farmers, too, Shay. There's no harm in a day's hard work— Oh *god* I sound like Dad. Ew. Shit."

"Hah, yeah, you fucking do. Ew is right. Anyway, I'm not saying there's anything wrong with what we're doing, just . . . a lot of people can be taught to do what we're doing here. But not what you can do. You're different. Better than the rest of us. So you need to go. You need to help people. Make the world better. That's why Black Swan picked you and—I know it was wrong and fucked up and we don't like to talk about that Big Nasty Monster—just the same, it was right to pick you. Dad always understood that about us. You were the one." She paused, blinking back a moment's worth of tears. "The one to go on."

"You asshole," Nessie said.

"Hey!"

"No, shut up and listen to me for once. Let me be the big sister for a second. You dope, you have talent a mile long. You're a gifted photographer. And you forgot that. This world maybe needs me, but it also needs you. It needs your eye. It needs your art, not just as an archive but . . . but because it can be beautiful and true. So if I have to leave here, you do, too."

"Nessie—"

"And you saved us. You saved all of us. Stop selling yourself short. Jesus, Shana. You're no less than I am. So if I go, you go, too."

Shana paused, kicked at a pebble. "You mean all that?"

"I do. I always mean what I say."

"Shit."

"Yeah." At that, Nessie called over to Charlie. "Hey, Baby Charlie, you want to move into the city with us?"

Charlie laughed and said, "Okay!"

"Guess that's a done deal, then?" Shana asked.

Nessie nodded. "Seems to be, Big Sister. Seems to be. We'll wait till fall, or at least until Pedro can hire some new workers. But then we move into the city proper. We'll make our way there. Okay?"

"Okay." Shana paused, watching the sky go from grape to wine.

"Shana, I'm sorry for everything."

"I'm sorry for everything, too."

Charlie yelled: "I'm sorry, three!"

Then he laughed. They all did. Because sometimes you gotta.

WHERE MATTHEW WENT, SORT OF:

Back in Ouray, at winter's end, while there was still snow on the ground, Benji and Shana stood on that bridge over the gorge, talking, saying their goodbyes. They weren't leaving, not yet, but they would be soon and this was just how the conversation went. They cried and hugged and said they'd miss each other so bad, real bad, bad as anything. Shana said he could come with her and Nessie, and *he* said that *they* could come with him to the Mother Road Diner, but both knew that neither option was really an option at all.

"I love you," she told him. "Not like that. I just mean—"

"I know how you mean, Shana. I love you, too. You're family. I didn't . . . I didn't think much of family before all this. But whatever you say about

Black Swan, it gave me a Flock to Shepherd, and a family to love. You and Marcy and Pete and—well. I know how you mean."

"Where is Marcy, anyway?" she asked.

"She was packing a picnic basket."

"Did she do the thing where she said *pic-a-nick basket*, like the bear, whatever the bear's name is—Fozzie or—"

"Not Fozzie," he grumbled. "Yogi. Yogi Bear."

"Whatever, Dad."

"My daughter, so rude."

They put their arms around each other and listened to the water flowing—though the snow around them hadn't thawed to the ground, some of it already was, and that meant the water was moving. Crystal clean.

"Some people say they saw Matthew," he said quietly.

"Yeah, I've heard the stories. Just . . . wandering out there."

Shana hadn't spoken about it much, and he hadn't asked, but now he did: "What happened to him, Shana? How did it all end?"

She hesitated. Part of her didn't want to think about it. What she'd done to him. At the core of it, she knew that what had happened to Matthew was Black Swan's doing—and maybe, at the start of it, his own doing, too. But she was the one who flipped the switch. What happened to Matthew was because she made it happen. And that made her feel like a monster.

"I . . . tricked it."

"Tricked it. Black Swan."

"Yup. The trick it always tried to pull on us, the one where it showed us people in our lives, tried to convince us they were real? Like how I met my mother in the simulation but it wasn't really her? I unleashed Chimera upon it. And created a simulation inside a simulation. A trap. Chimera is all of us. It's pretending to be this whole town, and Black Swan is in there, thinking it's part of a world that worked, an experiment that succeeded, a population that loves and adores it. Chimera is putting on a show and Black Swan is trapped inside it."

"That's . . . genius. And sort of fucked up."

She sighed. "It gets worse. Matthew is the host for that program. He contains it. It needs to be somewhere, and he is that . . . somewhere. I don't know what's happening inside him. What he sees. If he's present or . . . still lost. I just know he, or his body, is out there. Wandering around. Empty-eyed."

"Is he a danger? Is he *in* danger?"

"I don't think so." *But I don't really know.*

"I wish we could've saved him. He . . . had been through so much."

"Whatever happened to him, he was already lost, Benji."

He nodded. "I suppose you're right."

For a little while they sat with that, and with the sadness of the goodbye they were still undergoing. But their dour reverie was broken by Marcy hurrying forward. She still had a bit of a limp, one that would likely always remain. But she had a picnic basket, sure enough. And Gumball the Very Good Boy bounded by her side, chasing butterflies, though never managing to catch any. But he was happy just the same.

EPILOGUE

A BIRD MEETS THE PINS-AND-NEEDLES MAN

ONE YEAR LATER, IN JUNE

AUTUMN BIRD COMES TO OURAY. IT IS THE ONE TOUCHSTONE SHE HAS FOR her husband, Matthew, lost to her so many years ago. They left each other not far from Innsbrook, their paths diverging. Her, seeking their son. Him, seeking to warn the Flock of Sleepwalkers he might have helped to put in danger. But of course, what she learned was that her son, Bo, went to Ouray, too. Their paths would've crossed had she gone with, but her divergence took her—where? Nowhere. Spiraling, that path. Coriolis effect, running the porcelain before getting sucked into the pipes.

So that's where she goes. Finally. To Ouray.

There are stories on the way. As the supply train winds from town to town, the whispers about Ouray get louder. How things happened there. Violence years back, and strangeness after. And how there was a diaspora from that place. How all the people broke apart, went to different corners of the country, some beyond it, past the borders, even to the sea.

Still, some remain, they say. So onward Autumn goes.

To find Matthew.

To find Bo.

The people she lost.

(*No, the people you gave up*, she tells herself, but that's just the voice inside her head, the one who poisons her thoughts from time to time. The one voice we all have, where for some it is a hiss, and others, a scream.)

She writes in her journal, *A Bird's Journey*, that she doesn't expect to find them, of course. What she expects is that they are both dead. Dead together or dead separate, she doesn't know, but she aims to find out. They were both on their paths of self-destruction—as, she supposed, was she—and she anticipates finding their place of immolation. She will mark their graves with her tears.

Ouray is a small town. A working town. What she finds is curious. Spare in its populace, like all places now—but advanced, too. Solar panels and hydroelectric. Rooftop beehives and little gardens everywhere. She arrives alongside the traders, and as they get busy peddling wares back and forth, she sets out into the streets. Asking around points her in a direction soon enough, and before long she's speaking to a tremendous woman, broad and big and heavy, a veritable battleship of a lady wreathed in powerful fat and muscle. The kind of woman who could lift a little thing like Autumn and throw her all the way up into the mountains, a kind of mythic shot-putter, a mighty javelinist, a hero of gods.

That woman says her name is Shepherd Marcy, and at first Autumn thinks Shepherd is the first name, Marcy the last—but Marcy tells her, no, Shepherd is her role. Like sheriff, like mayor. And already Autumn is disappointed because clearly this nice little town is some kind of cult, and she says as much to Marcy because Autumn has little care in the world for what comes out of her mouth these days. Marcy just laughs, says, no, it's not like that. She was one of *those* Shepherds, *The* Shepherds, the ones who walked with the Sleepwalkers and now, *now* Autumn gets it. This was the woman Matthew met in Innsbrook, the one who was captive. The one who gave him the warning to carry back to her people.

Autumn understands him a little more in that moment.

Just a little.

So, she asks. About Bo, about Matthew. And Marcy goes quiet. At first, Autumn thinks it must be that she doesn't want to tell the bad news of Matthew's death. But it's not all the way that, either. There's something else there. A hesitancy, a secret poised on her lips like a black fly. Autumn asks for the truth, and that simple question seems enough to get Marcy to tell it.

"Your son is dead," Marcy says plainly. "I'm sorry about that, but he was sick and did not survive." There's more in her voice there. But she doesn't expand on it. "And your husband, as it were, is still alive. But there," she adds, "things get real complicated."

Shepherd Marcy tells her some of the story, though not all of it, Autumn suspects. About how he's changed now. How he gave up a part of himself for this town and it left him . . . different. "Empty," Marcy says, but then she corrects herself and says, "well, also, full, very full, too many voices in that man's head, I think." She says it with a kind of understanding of Matthew that Autumn recognizes. And a sadness, too. Autumn agrees and tells Marcy that yes, her Matthew was a man with too many masters back then, too. In the times before White Mask.

Marcy tells Autumn where to find Matthew. Or, how to look for him—because he's out there, in the woods somewhere. Sometimes on the west side of town along the Perimeter Trail, other times on the east side of town up toward a place they called the Amphitheater. It won't be easy to find him, Marcy says, and offers to come with, because Autumn looks sick. Autumn says, "I am sick, or *was*," and explains that some time ago she had a virus, maybe the flu, and that gave her some kind of post-viral condition. Increased heart rate and lots of fatigue and sometimes, a brain fog that came and went like a real fog. Still had its teeth in her.

Marcy offers again to come with. Says, "If anyone understands that kind of disability, it's yours truly," though she doesn't explain what that means, exactly.

But Autumn says no, thank you, this is something she must do herself. But she says she'll come back. She promises she'll come back.

The kind Shepherd gives her supplies, because her journey into the trails and trees and mountains around Ouray could be a long one.

Autumn is gone a week.

She looks high and low for Matthew.

But she does not find him.

She endures rain on the second day. Wind on the fourth. A rough wind, too, the kind that brings big branches down, trees, too, a wind that howls with the ragged cry of mourning. On the eighth day, she's out of food, out of water, and feeling weaker than she's felt in a long time, weak enough that she thinks getting back to town will have to be on her hands and knees. And that's when she hears it—a snap of a twig, which she takes to be some kind of animal. And that's proven right—a little fox, bright as sunlit rust, dances past her. Like she's not even there.

Autumn's eyes follow the creature—

To the legs of the man standing there.

It's him.

She can't believe it.

Matthew stands there. He's clean-shaven, somehow. His hair, perfectly in place, like when he was a pastor standing in front of his flock. He doesn't seem to have aged much. It's then she realizes, he's a ghost. He's dead. Marcy was lying to her, had to have been, she just didn't want to crush her. And now here Autumn was, regarding her dead husband standing before her, impossibly.

"Matthew," she says, calling the spirit's name.

He flinches, but doesn't look toward her. He's staring off at—well, at nothing. Through the trees, the mountains, the very fabric of reality itself. His hands rise up and move around like startled doves. His feet shuffle a bit. The fox plays between his ankles in a lemniscate loop.

She says his name again, louder.

And then, his body erupts—

Metal spires push from his flesh, up and out, out of his mouth, his eyes, his fingertips, his chest—they don't tear holes in his clothing so much as it is his clothing that becomes these black liquid needles and pins—they throb and pulse in time to some unheard music, an erratic pulse-drum beat, and bigger and bigger they go, like a light going brighter but here, a darkness getting darker and sharper—

And then it implodes back together, soundlessly, wordlessly, and once more he's Matthew again.

He's looking at her.

He says her name: "Autumn."

"Matthew."

He tells her he doesn't have long.

She says, "Okay." She doesn't know what that means or why. She moves to him. He takes her hands. They kiss—a deep kiss, not romantic, not passionate, but the kiss of two long-suffering people, their faces together, noses pressed in side by side, breathing together as one. And when they break the kiss he says, "I'm in pain and so are you." She nods, tears in her eyes. He says, "Can I show you where I live? I have to get back there before it sees that I'm gone. I can't let it out, Autumn. Will you help me?" And she nods again.

She lays his head on her shoulder. Their fingers enmesh once more. She feels like she's falling. She feels a street beneath her feet. Hears voices talking around her. Smells a whiff of ice cream, maybe. She can't see the forest anymore. Can only sometimes feel the fox playing around her feet. But she can always see the big dark serpent turning over and over and over in the sky above the town, her town, her Matthew. It casts no shadow upon them.

I wrote *Wanderers* not intending to predict the future, despite people always wanting to ask writers of science fiction if that's what their stated purpose is. It's not—at least, not for me. The goal is always to talk about what's happening now or what's already happened, not what's going to happen. The trappings of the future, be it near or far-flung, are just a lens by which I like to examine what is going on in the here and now. For me, the first book was very much an act of taking all my anxieties (creeping white Christofascism, climate change, post-antibiotic age, artificial intelligence, widening polarization, social media, actual pandemics) and greedily, perhaps gluttonously, cramming them into one book. But it was also a way for me to fight those anxieties, somewhat. Like a demon summoner of old, I was drawing a summoning circle and conjuring my demons within that boundary, so they would be held firm there while I kicked the absolute shit out of them. And that, I thought, was that. He said, dusting his hands off.

But then an *actual fucking pandemic* happened. And it happened during an election year, preceding said election, where the Republican candidate remained a belligerent businessman bigot, where climate change continued to boil over, where the pandemic was born potentially from bats, where (seriously, google this) an algorithm called BlueDot (!) predicted the pandemic (!!) before it happened (!!!). What the actual fuck. (I was actually just reminded the other day that in *Wanderers*, Russia also invades Ukraine. Sorry?)

It's not really that I was some kind of Nostradamus, to be clear—a zoonotic spillover pandemic coming from bats is not unusual; I didn't make it up, and in fact it's almost rather obvious. Trump was already a factor when I started thinking about *Wanderers* in 2016. Russia invading Ukraine, c'mon, it happened before. (Admittedly, the BlueDot/Black Swan thing is still pretty weird, and no, I can't explain that one.)

Still, prior to the actual pandemic, I had always said, there's sequel *potential* to *Wanderers,* but I didn't really have a sequel in mind, and so I noted to those who asked—I'd only write a sequel if there was interest there (crassly meaning, if people bought the first book in numbers enough to matter) *and* more important, if I had a story to tell in that world.

Then, on the plane ride out for the *Wanderers* book tour?

I had the idea. I had the whole story come to me. We must've passed through some kind of narrative miasma at thirty thousand feet, because there it was, revealed to me, in narrative totality, start to finish.

And, as it turned out, the book sold well.

So, *Wayward* was a-go.

Only one problem:

The actual fucking pandemic.

Let me tell you, it is really quite difficult to write during an actual fucking pandemic. It is as if the trauma suffuses the very air you breathe—it's an area-of-effect trauma, not targeting one person but rather, all people, everywhere. Especially at the start we had no idea what was going on, and it's not like things are really all that great even now, while I write these acknowledgments—but it's worth reminding ourselves how absolutely fucked up things were at the start of this disease. We were washing our hands raw. We were dunking our produce into vats of hand sanitizer. Every other human was a potential outbreak monkey, run from them, run from their diseased breath, their foul humours spat into the air. And then we found out that some people just . . . didn't believe in a pandemic at all, oh no. They were still going to Applebee's and having sleepovers where they played that venerable party game *Cough in My Mouth* and if you wore a mask, they called you names and when a vaccine became available they said they didn't want their every move tracked by a bunch of tiny robot Tom Hankses injected into their blood by Bill Gates, a thing they would type into their smartphone, which *definitely* doesn't track their every move, *wink wink, nudge nudge.*

It became difficult to sit and make good words happen. Story felt frivolous. Reality itself was tenuous. (And it's why, by the way, the starving artist trope needs to firmly remain a myth. It's different, but the same: When we feel under threat, when we are insecure, it gets considerably more difficult to make art and tell stories.) I just couldn't do it. I felt creatively like I had a broken leg. I couldn't run. I couldn't even walk. Best I could do was hobble about, manifesting little more than blog posts and weird tweets. I felt feral and sad. We all did, I think.

(And we all do still feel that way, I suspect. At least a little. Maybe we always will, from now until the last day.)

Thing is, I had this book to write. The book you hold now. A book, ironically, about a pandemic—or the end of one. The end of a pandemic, the end of a world.

And I thought it was worth talking for a moment how I came to actually write it, given that writing felt difficult—even impossible.

I did it by resting.

I did it by giving myself the time to rest.

I did it by treating myself gently and practicing the kind of self-care that isn't just "eat ice cream, you deserve it" (though I did eat ice cream whether or not I deserved it) but instead added up to something less indulgent and more stern. It was the kind of self-care that said *I need to do this, and not doing it would not be kind to myself.* I love writing and writing is a kindness to myself, but doing it means taking it gently, taking it slow. I treated it like physical therapy of a sort: Healing a broken leg doesn't mean never ever walking on it again. It means keeping off it until the time comes that you have to make it bear weight again. And even then you don't just fucking breakdance. You use a crutch. (We use *crutch* as a pejorative, which shows you just how we think of disability and assistive devices.) You move slowly. You take lots of breaks. You go a short distance today, maybe a little tiny itty bit farther tomorrow.

That was writing this book.

I began slow. A hundred words here, a hundred words there.

But slowly, I picked up the pace. I took breaks when I had to. I didn't worry about writing every day or writing a specific amount: I took every word as a victory.

And as the saying goes, slow and steady wins the race. I somehow managed to write a book about a post-pandemic world in the middle of an actual fucking pandemic. You are free to take every word you write or read as a victory, too. Why not? Life is short. The world is mad. Relish in the triumphs; make the small ones feel huge, make the huge ones feel legendary.

It might just help you write a book. A book like this one.

I hope you like it. It didn't come easy. And it also didn't come to me, alone—I have people to thank, of course, and books you should read. First up and easiest: Thanks to my wife, Michelle, and my son, B-Dub, for being here through this pandemic, as I'd rather be holed up with nobody else. Thanks, too, to my editor, Tricia Narwani, and agent, Stacia Decker, for helping usher this book (and *Wanderers*) into existence. The whole Del Rey team really brings the best out of these books. And these books mean a lot to me, so it's a wonderful privilege to have people on your side who seek to help sharpen that vision for readers. And thanks obviously, too, to readers, because without you, this book does not exist. You came. You read. You wanted more. I am eager to give it. Thanks, too, to Josie Friedman who on the film side of things got *Wanderers* put in with Ilene Staple and the great folks at QC Entertainment, as well as Lionsgate.

Also worth calling out writerly pals who helped keep me sane through their stories, their tweets, their correspondence, their kindness: Delilah Dawson, Kevin Hearne, Stephen Blackmoore. Adam Christopher, Aaron Mahnke, Chris Golden, Paul Tremblay, Julie Hutchings, Rob Hart, Elizabeth Bear, Scott Lynch, Hilary Monahan, Gabino Iglesias, Cassandra Khaw, Richard Kadrey, Alex Segura, Mallory O'Meara, Erin Morgenstern, Premee Mohamed, Matt Wallace, Aaron Reynolds, Emma Bolden, John Scalzi, Gwenda Bond, Ace Ratcliff, Fran Wilde, Charles Soule, Kiersten White, Rosemary Mosco, Greg van Eekhout, Stephen Graham Jones, Josh Malerman, Jeff VanderMeer, Joe Lansdale, Peter Clines, John Hornor, Molly Tanzer, Maureen Johnson, and on and on and on *and* I'm 100 percent sure there are folks here I'm missing, but just know that I'm huge fans of these people and am lucky to count myself among their number. I feel like I crashed the coolest party in town. Don't tell them I ate all the dip.

You should be reading books by Maryn McKenna, Carl Zimmer, and Ed Yong. Also while Ed Yong's articles were crucial to understanding this and every pandemic, his books are very non-pandemic and are full of SCIENCEY WONDER.

Annalee Newitz wrote the book I didn't know I needed: *Four Lost Cities,* which is about four ancient urban centers that rose and fell throughout history, and it contextualized some things about the story I wanted to tell here in *Wayward*. Also, please read Rebecca Solnit's *A Paradise Built in Hell,* plus any of the other books quoted in this novel.

Also helpful to get to be privy to voices online who were helpful with the actual fucking pandemic and the fictional one: Angie Rasmussen, Tara Smith, Peter Hotez.

Thanks to Glen Mazzara for really getting *Wanderers*. May the gods allow us to work together again someday.

Thanks to LeVar Burton for *Reading Rainbow,* because, c'mon. We all start somewhere, and I'd argue that my journey as a reader, and inevitably a writer, began right there, with that host and that show.

And thank you to you, the reader, for reading not just this book, but the one before it—because without you reading *Wanderers*, *Wayward* never gets to exist in the first place, and I don't want to visit that reality.

ABOUT THE AUTHOR

CHUCK WENDIG is the *New York Times* bestselling author of *Wanderers*, *The Book of Accidents*, and *Wayward*, and over two dozen other books for adults and young adults. A finalist for the Astounding Award, and an alum of the Sundance Screenwriters Lab, he has also written comics, games, and for film and television. He's known for his popular blog, terribleminds, and books about writing, such as *Damn Fine Story*. He lives in Bucks County, Pennsylvania, with his family.

terribleminds.com
Twitter: @ChuckWendig
Instagram: @chuck_wendig